MR CAMPION'S CHRISTMAS

Also by Mike Ripley

Margery Allingham's Albert Campion

MR CAMPION'S FAREWELL *
MR CAMPION'S FOX *
MR CAMPION'S FAULT *
MR CAMPION'S ABDICATION *
MR CAMPION'S WAR *
MR CAMPION'S VISIT *
MR CAMPION'S SÉANCE *
MR CAMPION'S COVEN *
MR CAMPION'S WINGS *
MR CAMPION'S MOSAIC *
MR CAMPION'S MEMORY *

The Fitzroy Maclean Angel series

LIGHTS, CAMERA, ANGEL
ANGEL UNDERGROUND
ANGEL ON THE INSIDE
ANGEL IN THE HOUSE
ANGEL'S SHARE
ANGELS UNAWARE
Etc.

Other titles

DOUBLE TAKE
BOUDICA AND THE LOST ROMAN
THE LEGEND OF HEREWARD

Non-fiction

SURVIVING A STROKE
KISS KISS, BANG BANG

** available from Severn House*

MR CAMPION'S CHRISTMAS

Mike Ripley

SEVERN
HOUSE

First world edition published in Great Britain and the USA in 2024
by Severn House, an imprint of Canongate Books Ltd,
14 High Street, Edinburgh EH1 1TE.

Trade paperback edition first published in Great Britain and the USA in 2025
by Severn House, an imprint of Canongate Books Ltd.

severnhouse.com

British Library Cataloguing-in-Publication Data
A CIP catalogue record for this title is available from the British Library.

ISBN-13: 978-1-4483-1471-3 (cased)
ISBN-13: 978-1-4483-1702-8 (trade paper)
ISBN-13: 978-1-4483-1537-6 (e-book)

All Severn House titles are printed on acid-free paper.

MIX
Paper | Supporting responsible forestry
FSC www.fsc.org FSC® C013604

Typeset by Palimpsest Book Production Ltd.,
Falkirk, Stirlingshire, Scotland.
Printed and bound in Great Britain by CPI Group (UK) Ltd, Croydon CR0 4YY

The manufacturer's authorised representative in the EU for product safety is
Authorised Rep Compliance Ltd, 71 Lower Baggot Street, Dublin D02 P593
Ireland (arccompliance.com)

Praise for the Albert Campion series

"Clever, witty, and packed with intriguing characters, period ambiance, and unexpected twists"
Booklist on *Mr Campion's Memory*

"Excellent . . . This dead-on pastiche will satisfy newcomers and series devotees alike"
Publishers Weekly on *Mr Campion's Memory*

"The plot thickens in utterly unexpected ways"
Kirkus Reviews on *Mr Campion's Memory*

"Impressive . . . brilliant inventiveness"
Publishers Weekly Starred Review of *Mr Campion's Mosaic*

"Charming, clever, and witty . . . Another delightful mystery"
Booklist on *Mr Campion's Mosaic*

"A cunning mix of silliness and wit"
The Times on *Mr Campion's Mosaic*

"Ripley has a wonderful talent for capturing the voices, mannerisms and wit of Margery Allingham's original creations"
MINETTE WALTERS on *Mr Campion's Mosaic*

About the author

Mike Ripley is the author of more than thirty books, has written for radio and television and has reviewed almost 3,000 crime novels over the last three decades. His 'reader's history' of the heyday of British action and spy thrillers 1953–75, *Kiss Kiss, Bang Bang*, won the H.R.F. Keating Award for non-fiction in 2017.

For Margery Allingham, without whom . . .

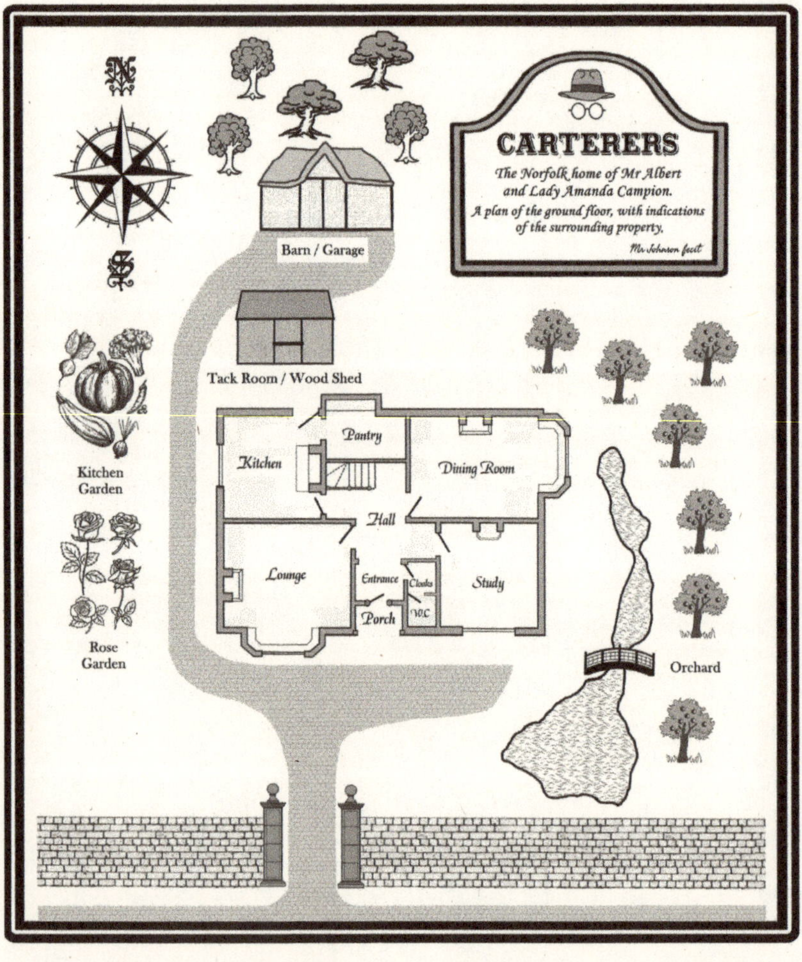

N
S
CARTERERS
The Norfolk home of Mr Albert
and Lady Amanda Campion.
A plan of the ground floor, with indications
of the surrounding property.
Mr Johnson fecit
Barn / Garage
Tack Room / Wood Shed
Kitchen Garden
Rose Garden
Pantry
Kitchen
Dining Room
Hall
Lounge
Entrance
Clocks
Study
Porch
W.C
Orchard

CONTENTS

	An Advent (of Sorts)	1
1:	Stir Up Sunday	6
2:	Let It Snow	18
3:	Charabanc	32
4:	The Tale of the Retiring Reverend	45
5:	The Tale of the Pious Postmistress	58
6:	The Tale of the Dutch Diptych	73
7:	Footprints	87
8:	Worst Meal of the Day	98
9:	Иногда	110
10:	Gunpoint	122
11:	Reporting for Duty	135
12:	Thor's Other Hammer	145
13:	The Enemy At (and Inside) the Gate	159
14:	Invoking Sinterklaas	170
15:	A Prickly Problem	181
16:	Waking Hereward	195
17:	Under Siege	209
18:	Hoplite	225
19:	Thin Ice	237
20:	Relief Column	250
21:	God and Sinners Reconciled	262
	Author's Note	273

An Advent (of Sorts)

Victoria Coach Station, London, Thursday 27 December 1962

The driver shuddered and pulled the collar of his coat tight around his throat against the chill wind as he watched his passengers slink reluctantly out of the warmth of the Waiting Room by Bay 7A, then quicken their pace when they realized the rear luggage compartment doors were open and they could deposit their bags and finally climb aboard the waiting coach.

They could do that themselves, he reckoned, as it was too cold to hang about pretending to look helpful. Staring at the posters plastered on the walls advertising Frankie Vaughan and Jimmy Edwards in *Puss in Boots* at the Palladium only increased his irritation at having to work over the Christmas period, as his wife adored Frankie Vaughan and the kids loved a good pantomime. And, he felt, it was a ridiculous run, especially given the weather forecast. Who on earth wanted to go on a pilgrimage to darkest Norfolk at any time, let alone the bleak midwinter? There would not be many of them, that was for sure, and that meant a small haul of tips – the traditional passing round of the hat at journey's end. Given their destination, perhaps he might have more luck circulating a collection plate.

The driver stomped down the length of the Burlingham Seagull coach and pulled open the passenger door, standing by the stepped entrance so that he could tally the number of bodies boarding and tick off the count against the number of tickets sold. In the circular wing mirror above his head, he could see his passengers shuffling in single column down the side of the bus, having deposited their heavy luggage. The driver's brain clicked into the mental game he always played prior to a departure: the early identification of certain types of passengers, especially those most likely to annoy him on a four-hour journey. The one who would, inevitably, be travel sick; the one who wanted to know their precise location mile-by-mile (those who brought along their own road maps were particularly despised); and the chatty one – there was always a chatty one.

The first passenger to appear in the wing mirror at his shoulder caused the driver's eyebrows to rise, though he knew he should not be surprised. As the man passed in front of him to climb aboard, the white of his clerical dog collar highlighted the sombre drab of his black suit, hat and raincoat, and the driver nodded politely and said 'Father' quietly. The priest, unsmiling and sallow-faced, returned the nod, and the driver felt sure he would have earned a blessing had his passenger's hands not been fully occupied holding not the half-expected Bible but a Thermos flask and a Tupperware box of sandwiches which the driver, from his vast experience, was confident were cheese and tomato.

The vicar would not be a problem; after all, who else had a perfect excuse to visit a holy shrine whatever the weather?

'What time do we depart Ebury?'

'Eh?'

The second passenger in the queue, now standing before him, one foot raised to step up into the coach, was a small man engulfed in what looked like an Army & Navy stores duffel coat. He had a snub nose which seemed to be recoiling from the line of a thin ginger moustache, or the large green bowtie masking his lips. He had bright piggy eyes and gobbledygook appeared to be his first language.

'Ebury, Ebury,' he said, adding to the driver's confusion. 'What time do we leave Ebury?'

'What the . . .?' The driver stopped himself, as this was, after all, a paying customer. 'What's Ebury when it's at home?' he said. Then added as an afterthought, 'Sir.'

The small man's hands fluttered as though he was holding hot coals.

'Ebury, the lost Saxon village recorded as having twenty-nine households and a manor in 1086, now long gone, subsumed by Belgravia, but Ebury was *here*, right here, where we are standing.'

'Well, we call it the borough of Westminster now,' said the driver through clenched teeth, 'and the coach will depart once all passengers are comfortably seated, so if you wouldn't mind . . .'

Now that one could be a problem, and the driver was relieved – when he consulted the wing mirror again – that the next in line was a middle-aged woman, one hand clutching the knot of the wool headscarf tied at her throat, the other slightly below it holding the upright of a plain wooden cross which hung from a thin rope chain.

He waved a hand indicating the interior of the coach and the woman stepped up silently. As she brushed past him, the driver registered the fact that she wore a heavy sheepskin jacket, a tweed skirt, brown leather gloves, thick lisle stockings and masculine, lace-up shoes. Unlike some of the flighty young girls on the holiday runs to Brighton or Yarmouth, who normally offered a flash of stocking-top whilst boarding, this female would keep herself quietly to herself. She might be a nun in *mufti*, or maybe even a genuine pilgrim.

'Hey, buddy!'

Oh no, a Yank.

Even worse; three of them. The wing mirror was full of them, all tall and impervious to the falling temperature in their fur-lined parkas.

'Does this bus go to *Why-mond-ham*, my friend?' asked the first smiling ruddy face.

'You mean Windom,' the driver said automatically.

'Excuse me?' The American flipped back the hood of his parka, revealing a blond crew-cut and an even wider smile aimed at his two companions.

'It's spelled Wymondham but the locals pronounce it Windom,' said the driver wearily, as it was a question he had answered before whenever Americans travelled into Norfolk.

'See, you guys, told you so,' grinned the young and annoyingly self-confident tourist.

'We don't go there, sir,' the driver established his authority, 'but we go through Swaffham and you can get a connection to Norwich – and then Windom – from there.'

'Oh, we don't want to go there,' grinned the passenger leading his compatriots into the bus, 'that was just to settle a bet.'

The driver shook his head slowly, and not for the first time admitted that it took all sorts, but at least these three didn't look like tearaways; in fact, he was sure they were servicemen from one of the many American bases up in East Anglia, so they should know how to behave themselves. If they were heading for the shrine at Walsingham (and what other reason was there to go there?), it stood to reason they were of a religious bent, and if they got out of hand, he had a priest on board to intimidate them.

Then his last passenger stood before him, though he automatically checked the wing mirror for any latecomers down by the luggage compartment before speaking.

'I can put that in the boot with the luggage for you, sir; it'll be perfectly safe.'

His last passenger stared at him quizzically through square, rimless glasses. He was hatless, with long, unruly white hair and a thick white beard, and gave the impression that his thin body had been squeezed into an ankle-length black leather coat buttoned to the throat. Slim white fingers gripped a worn brown leather briefcase, shiny with age, to his chest, as though it was a breastplate without whose protection he would be vulnerable to slings and probably arrows.

'Nee! Zat is not necessary!' he said, rejecting the driver's offer and tightening his grip on the case. Then added: 'Zank you very much.'

Oh Lord, a foreigner and a proper one, not American like the three lads in parkas, and definitely a strange one. Might have to keep an eye on him.

The driver followed the black leather coat up the steps and addressed the handful of passengers scattered randomly over the thirty-four-seat interior. Apart from the three young Americans, who had collared the back seats, places had been taken as if each passenger suspected the other of a contagious disease.

'All aboard? Then we'll be off.'

It was perhaps not the most inspiring send-off, but it was his usual one, and all he had to do now was hop down out of the coach, close up the luggage compartment, start the engine, turn up the heater and hit the road.

He kept his head down as he walked to the back of the coach as the wind now carried a fair proportion of sleet with it, and with a final glance towards the Waiting Room in case of stragglers, he closed the doors of the luggage hold, noting with some irritation the grinning faces of the three Americans looking down out of the back window.

Whilst he had been performing his normal ritual of meeting and greeting his passengers as they boarded his coach, he had been unaware of the shadowy figure who had appeared as if from nowhere and deposited a large canvas bag in among the suitcases before disappearing, having shown no inclination to join the legitimate passengers on their pilgrimage.

ONE
Stir Up Sunday

'Ho-bleedin'-ho! This suit hasn't half shrunk!'

'Santa! Watch your language! There are children about.'

'No, there ain't,' snapped the figure in the red suit sulkily.

'There will be when you turn up at the church hall on Christmas Eve, which you will do even if I have to sew you into your costume, which has *not* shrunk since last year. Sadly, neither have you. Now turn around and let me consider my line of attack.'

'Steady on. I'm not sure I like the sound of that,' said Santa Claus.

'Do as you're told.' Lady Amanda was brooking no nonsense. 'Now lose the jacket and let me concentrate on the trousers.'

Magersfontein Lugg, normally an irresistible force, knew when he had met an immovable object, and did as he was commanded by the lady of the house. It was, after all, a small price to have to repay the Campions for their hospitality over the Christmas period, and in truth he secretly enjoyed dishing out presents to the village children, ticking them off his nice list and threatening them with his naughty list. He did not even mind the bright red costume, set off by Wellington boots and a thick black belt, although the large false beard had begun to smell slightly over the years and the bright red fur-lined hat was actually quite a comfort to his massive orb of a bald head when it came to keeping out the chill of winter.

Lugg's position in the Campion household had long been the subject of much speculation, if not police investigation, over the years. Perhaps the description 'valued family retainer' was the safest and least likely to provoke a violent reaction from the man in question, although he would certainly amend the description to 'undervalued and unpaid family retainer'. He had, in fact, been a known associate of Mr Albert Campion since before that gentleman had surrendered his bachelor status by marrying Lady Amanda Fitton and fathering a son, Rupert. Yet to suggest that Lugg had been in any way 'in service' as a valet or – heaven forfend – a butler to Mr Campion would be inaccurate as well as potentially dangerous, although he had himself, in a moment of weakness, referred to himself as 'a gent's gent'. Mr Campion, when pressed, would simply say that their relationship had been long and fruitful and that he regarded Lugg as his left-hand man; a solid (perhaps too solid these days) ally, a trustworthy guide through the dank criminal underworld into which Mr Campion had often had to dip a toe, and a reliable source of gossip on all matters political and social with the notable exception of horse-racing tips.

On marriage, Lady Amanda had accepted with infinite good grace the fact that her husband came with a Lugg in tow, and quickly christened him 'Magers', which immediately made him less threatening, though she did rather approve of the way other people were easily intimidated by his looming bulk. Her faith had only been strengthened by his reaction to the arrival of Rupert, the junior addition to the Campion family who, from his toddling days, had taken to the fat man as other children latched on to a favourite soft toy. To see the pair of them walking together, especially descending stairs, a tiny hand in a giant's paw, conjured up an image of Christopher Robin and his bear Edward, though in this case it was always the bear safely leading the boy.

Faced with an expansive rear view of the red fake satin which struggled to contain Lugg's ample proportions, Amanda surveyed the problem with an experienced eye.

'I can sew in another "V" segment to give you a bit more breathing space, but you might have to tension your braces and promise never to take the coat off, at least not anywhere you might frighten the horses or a passing maiden aunt.'

The object of this sartorial negotiation grunted in disgust but Mr Campion, observing matters from an armchair over the rim of a glass of sherry, could not contain a chuckle.

'How fortunate I am to have a wife who is an aeronautical engineer,' he observed, 'for who else could give advice on keeping up a pair of recalcitrant trousers in terms of tensioning the braces?'

'When it comes to fitting Lugg for trousers,' Amanda said innocently, 'it always was a question of physics.'

'Or mind over matter,' added her husband.

'Ho, ho – and I says it again – ho. You can snigger all you like,' said Santa Claus, grasping the waistband of his trousers and hauling them well above ankle height, 'but I don't see any other volunteers for this particular duty.'

'No one else can make such a convincing impression in that costume, old fruit.'

'You mean no one else can stand the smell of camphor mothballs.'

'No one we know of.' Mr Campion grinned. 'Let me get you a sherry to help take the taste away.'

'That might help with the indignity.'

'Something which has rarely troubled you in the past.'

'Don't be unkind, Albert,' Amanda scolded gently, 'and you, Magers, don't pretend this is some sort of penance. You love doing it, you know you do, and the children love Father Christmas. The look on their little faces is surely worth a bit of indignity. You remember the way Rupert used to leave a pair of mince pies and a tot of rum by the fireplace every Christmas Eve?'

'And a big juicy carrot for your reindeer,' said Albert. 'Don't forget the carrot.'

'I knew he'd rumbled me,' Lugg sighed, 'the year he left a typed receipt for Santa to sign to prove I had received 'is offerings. He must've been about eight, I reckon. Smart lad. Showed promise.'

'I remember that!' Amanda squealed the way only a proud mother could. 'That year you took the carrot, left the rum, and drew a reindeer's hoof print on his receipt.'

'A marvellous piece of deflection,' added her husband. 'Santa's reindeer clearly liked carrots and were not averse to signing a legal document, whereas a Lugg masquerading as Santa would never have signed a document admitting he had broken-and-entered a property by means of the chimney, nor would he have left the rum untouched.'

Lugg attempted to look aloof. It was not one of his best poses.

'You've got the presents sorted, I suppose?' he asked Amanda, with as much dignity as he could muster whilst wearing drooping red trousers, the thumb of his left hand hooked into his braces stretched over an open shirt and vest, the pinkie of his right extended as it nursed a schooner of sherry.

'All in the sack waiting for you, wrapped as usual. Blue tags for boys, red for girls, and don't park the sack up against the radiators, otherwise the Selection Boxes will melt.'

'Does Santa get to drive to the party in a brand-new Jensen?' Lugg asked between sips of sherry.

'He does not!' declared Mr Campion. 'I hate to think what his weight plus a sack full of chocolate would do to the suspension.'

Amanda held up a calming hand.

'Don't worry, I've taken care of it. This year the parts of Donner, Blitzen, Prancer, Dancer and the rest – though not of course Rudolph' – she winked theatrically at her husband – 'will be played by one of the Alandel Land Rovers which I have commandeered for the occasion. It will, of course, be tastefully decorated with tinsel and spray snow in the absence of the real thing.'

'Oh, you never know,' said Mr Campion. 'We might be lucky and get a white Christmas.'

By Christmas Eve, though, there was no snow, and Santa had to set off to meet his overexcited audience in a green Land Rover, the logo of Alandel Aeroplanes on its bonnet covered by a wreath of holly and ivy secured by a considerable amount of electrical tape. To add to the festive spirit, cardboard cut-outs of two not-to-scale reindeer had been attached to the roof rack which was – Amanda observed dryly – hardly a good advertisement for the company's reputation for advanced aerodynamics. A large sprig of mistletoe also dangled from the driver's rear-view mirror, a refinement which Santa declared gruffly had better not give his driver any ideas.

His driver Rupert, the Campions' son, had repeatedly assured his distinguished passenger that the only idea on his mind was the hope that no one of any importance, by which he meant no one female, attractive and under thirty, should see him in his makeshift uniform as one of Santa's elves. His costume had been cobbled together on the assumption that as elves had no natural enemies at the North Pole, being best friends with all animals including hungry polar bears, they had no need of camouflage and so opted for a bright green colour palette when it came to fashion. His green corduroy trousers were a pair that had been bought by his father during a mercifully short mid-life crisis when he was tempted by golf; the green blazer had been a spur-of-the-moment purchase by his mother, who assured the would-be elf that on Rupert's slim frame you could not tell it had been cut for a woman. To complete the ensemble, he sported a long green wool scarf entwined around his throat and a matching *byecocket*, sometimes known as an 'archer's hat' or, more commonly, 'a Robin Hood hat', the medieval headgear that boasted a turn-up brim at the back and a long-pointed beak shape at the front. It was, however, less of a historic artefact and more an unused prop from an amateur dramatic production of *Babes in the Wood.*

As a red-blooded young man, home from his first exciting term at university in America, where his English accent had been an invaluable social asset, Rupert could have been expected to baulk at the idea of being recruited as one of Santa's foot soldiers, but it was impossible to refuse his mother anything, and this particular annual pageant was close to her heart. It was Amanda's personal take on an established tradition among the workforce of Alandel Aeroplanes, whereby the children of all the staff would be treated to a Christmas present from the firm, handed out alongside copious amounts of fizzy drinks, buns and ice cream. There was no doubt this was good for employee relations, and it was an event, in the suitably decorated Alandel staff canteen, which was eagerly anticipated by all.

Once in a position of seniority within the company, Amanda had introduced what she considered to be a morale-boosting improvement: the distribution of presents by Santa himself, or at least, as Mr Campion observed, his vicar on Earth, a role Magersfontein Lugg had surely been born to play. And Mr Lugg had, to the surprise of many who knew him, thrown himself enthusiastically into the role.

Rupert, though no longer an innocent and accepting child, remained a strong supporter of the Santa Claus myth, and whilst he may have had reservations about appearing in public dressed as an elfish assistant, it was only a short four-mile drive to the Alandel works and he was unlikely to encounter any of his peers. In one sense he had little choice in the matter, for he had in a careless moment of homecoming euphoria admitted to his mother that although he found his studies at Harvard Business School interesting, and likely to be profitable in terms of a future career, he had instantly fallen under the spell of student theatricals and had joined several performance groups, an activity which now consumed all his spare time and dominated his daydreams. He was thus in no position to refuse the crucial supporting role (as Amanda cunningly phrased it) of the Christmas elf and – who knew? – there might just be a West End talent agent in the audience . . .

Unlikely, but Christmas was a time for miracles.

One miracle, Mr Campion had said, was that Santa Lugg had not frightened any of the children nor given their mothers the vapours, for the Alandel party had gone off splendidly, with laughter and carol singing all round and few tears, though Rupert swore he had spotted Santa's eyes watering at the sight of excited children tearing into wrapping paper.

External duties done, the family home became the centre of operations for the rest of the festive period, though no drawbridges were raised as the Campions followed their traditional policy of offering an open house. Guests were always made welcome, especially so when expected, and doubly so if actually invited. Each year Amanda insisted on cooking the Christmas turkey, complete with the full panoply of 'trimmings', with only minimal help from the Campions' trusted housekeeper Mrs Thursby. Should a guest offer to assist in any way, her dismissal was positively imperious, declaring, 'Oh for goodness' sake, it's only a roast dinner! What's so difficult about that?'

Mr Campion and Rupert always made the offer in the certain knowledge that it would be rejected, but Lugg had long ago ceased paying lip service to good manners and had resigned himself to household tasks such as laying fires, washing up, making up beds in the guest rooms, serving drinks and decorating the Christmas tree he always provided after disappearing down the lane before dawn with a trusty axe he had found in a garden shed. No questions were ever asked about where the conifer in question had come from, and on Twelfth Night the evidence was turned into logs for the fireplace.

That Christmas, however, was a quiet one *chez* Campion, or at least it was supposed to be, and on Christmas Day itself the dining room table was, compared to previous years, rather sparsely occupied. As Lugg observed, if any passing carol singers had arrived, they could have pulled up a chair and had a turkey dinner without denting the amount of leftovers for his traditional, some would say infamous, Boxing Day curry.

Usual guests on the big day would normally have included Mr Campion's sister Valentine and her husband Alan Dell, the founder of Alandel Aeroplanes, but they had decided – quite unreasonably at the last minute in Amanda's opinion – to spend Christmas in Jamaica. Amanda's sister Mary, though, and her husband Guffy Randall, were as dependable as always and, along with their eight-year-old son Sam, promised to double the amount of Christmas cheer they would bring to the party.

Guffy was as good as his word, and his word was reinforced by the case of vintage champagne which accompanied him. Such was the good cheer generated over the extended lunch, served immediately after the Queen's televised Christmas message and well into an evening of charades and chestnuts roasting – and occasionally exploding – over an open fire, that breakfast on Boxing Day was much later than normal and notably subdued. Only Lugg appeared to have emerged impervious to the rigors of the night before, and was frankly disappointed when his offer to do 'a proper fry-up' for all and sundry was greeted with groans rather than enthusiasm. Undeterred, he donned an apron and set to with a frying pan until the fragrance and hum of sizzling bacon seeped out of the kitchen so successfully that it even woke Rupert who, as a student, was expected to be unfamiliar with mornings.

The house did come alive, albeit sluggishly, as the Randalls packed up their presents, armed themselves with a brick-sized chunk of iced Christmas cake and prepared to depart. Duty called in the form of the Boxing Day meeting of the Monewdon Hunt back home in Suffolk, where Guffy was the Master and thus required to supervise proceedings, hangover or no hangover. Lugg took a malicious delight in suggesting that a stirrup cup or two was just what Guffy needed to set him up for a bumpy ride cross-country, though he would miss Lugg's bespoke turkey curry and it was never wise to go riding on an empty stomach. Perhaps Guffy would like to take with him a Lugg 'special', an inch-thick bacon sandwich with brown sauce which was palatable both hot and cold, but the Hon. Augustus Randall's stomach disagreed and he politely declined.

Once the Randalls had been waved down the drive, the Campion household geared itself up for the traditional Boxing Day walk – or tramp, or route march, depending on who was passing an opinion – to get some fresh air into their lungs and to work off the excesses of the day before or, in Lugg's case, to generate another appetite. With overcoats buttoned up, scarves tied, hats firmly jammed on heads and walking boots clamped to feet, the household set out into the overcast and distinctly chilly countryside, as well protected from the elements as a Himalayan expedition.

The loyal Mrs Thursby, who insisted on working on Boxing Day partly because she thought it unseemly for Lady Amanda to have to clean up after, or around, house guests, and partly because she could never face two consecutive days in a small cottage with only her stone-deaf elderly father-in-law for company, was left holding the fort. Despite Amanda's protestations every year that her offer of help was appreciated but unnecessary, Mrs Thursby had been adamant and, as she had walked the three miles from the hamlet where she lived to get to the Campions', it would have been churlish to turn her away. Mr Campion realized he had made a rod for his own back by making Boxing Day the occasion when he presented Mrs Thursby with her 'Christmas box', a cash bonus for her dedicated service to Carterers.

To a man who had spent most of his life solving, or at least getting involved in, mysteries of all shapes and sizes, the name of Mr Campion's country residence remained an irritating and unsolved puzzle. When purchased, during the early years of the war, he had not given the matter much thought. There was, after all, a war on, and an isolated Norfolk farmhouse seemed an eminently safe place for his wife and baby son whilst he was serving overseas. Only later did it occur to him that Carterers was rather odd, both in diction and meaning. Was it a misspelling based on pronunciation in a broad Norfolk accent, of 'Carter's' as, perhaps, in Carter's Farm? The deeds showed no sign of a previous owner called Carter, and Mr Campion was blissfully unaware of anyone of that name.

Alternatively, did the name indicate a place where someone

stored carts, operating a pre-combustion-engine haulage business? Mr Campion doubted that as – whilst the profession of carter had existed in days gone by – he could find no reference to the trade of carter*er*, and in livery company terms, when it came to the ancient London guilds, the official body was the Worshipful Company of Carmen. On his first visit, Lugg had called the house 'The Caterers' and had insisted on referring to it thus ever since. The Campions had considered changing the name but could never keep straight faces long enough to reach agreement; Mr Campion, with an eye on retirement, suggesting 'Dunsleuthing', with Amanda insisting on 'Fitton's Folly'.

Described as a Georgian farmhouse, Carterers was no longer the focal point of a farm, although it remained surrounded by fields which had been sold off to pay, or avoid, death duties. It now stood in less than two acres of garden and orchard, rather than at the centre of a barley-growing empire, down a narrow lane which eventually joined the road running into Swaffham and then to Fakenham. The Campions' nearest neighbour was their housekeeper, Mrs Thursby and, apart from the nearby Alandel works, there were no other visible signs of civilization. Mr Campion always claimed that the only improvement possible to his rural retreat would be if the house had been located further north in the village of Little Snoring, which he had always regarded as far more refined than its neighbour Great Snoring. Lugg had grumbled that the nearest village was Cockley Cley, which was 'just as daft a name', but he would have preferred to be in any village, whatever it was called, as it would surely have a pub and he loved a good village pub. Campion had responded pointedly to this by claiming that not having a village, a church or a pub on the doorstep made it an ideal location, as it would limit the amount of time house guests from London would stay, assuming they found the house in the first place.

It was not that Albert Campion shunned or avoided company. Indeed, he was the most gregarious of men and a generous host, with a reputation for being able to mix amicably with archbishops and academics, pickpockets and policemen, dustmen and dowager duchesses. He was also a man who, when not engaged in what he described as 'adventuring on the side of the angels', and which Lugg disparaged as 'private narking', valued nothing higher than having a secure base to which he, his wife and his son could comfortably retreat.

Given the number of shady, indeed downright violent, characters Mr Campion had encountered in his career, the question of security around Carterers might have pressed more on Mr Campion's mind than it appeared, for the house was, even for Norfolk, extremely isolated. If questioned on the subject, Campion would reply flippantly that Norfolk was so flat one could easily see an enemy approaching, and besides, Carterers was defended by having a moat, or almost a moat.

The 'almost moat' curving in a crescent around the eastern side of the house had begun life as a series of badly engineered ornamental ponds, probably designed, Campion would insist, by Incapability Brown on an off-day. By either incompetence of workmanship or quirk of geology, the individual ponds had leaked into each other and now formed a banana-shaped cordon between the house and a small orchard. Two-thirds of the way along, a narrow, Monet-inspired wooden bridge provided a convenient short-cut to the orchard when plums, pears or apples were in season. After the bridge the 'almost moat' seemed to abandon defensive duties, and preferred to spread its hips and adopt a more decorative, ornamental posture. As garden ponds went, it was impressively large though, as Amanda constantly pointed out, it was not actually anywhere near the garden.

Mr Campion had always maintained that the 'third pond', as he called it, was his 'personal Giverny'; the bridge was an homage to Claude Monet, and Campion saw no reason why he should not enjoy similar views enjoyed by the painter. The third pond also added to the privacy of his favourite part of the grounds, the unkempt but extremely productive orchard, whilst Amanda preferred the rose garden she had cultivated on the other side of the house. Her husband had joked that when he really did retire and they were strapped for cash, his orchard would provide the basis of a lucrative cider-making concern, but the roses would have to be grubbed out so he could plant potatoes and turnips. Amanda had dismissed the threat by exclaiming that she did not believe Mr Campion would or ever could retire, but that she intended to plant more roses, and ones with longer, more vicious thorns, just in case.

Those who thought they knew the Campions well felt that Carterers had been bought solely to benefit Amanda's career as an aeronautical engineer with Alandel, and that Albert would never be content to vegetate out in the country cut off from the social life – and the shady underworld – of the metropolis. But as he had aged, Mr Campion had found great pleasures in fresh air rather than smog and in sitting proudly among the books in his library, which had long since outgrown his Piccadilly flat, rather than donning his 'penguin suit' and suffering the round of indistinguishable cocktail parties. And he was still able to visit London whenever he wished, by train from Swaffham or by car, as he never minded a long drive through East Anglia. Should anyone question his choice of domestic location, he would point out that East Anglia was the most easily accessible isolated spot in England, and the blinkered had only failed to realize this thanks to the region's extremely clever advertising campaign which insisted that all roads and railway lines from the capital ended in Cambridge.

Campion would often reject complaints that East Anglia was simply too flat to be interesting, often parroting Noël Coward's acidic dismissal in his play *Private Lives*, by praising the number of artists who had found that it was a place where the sky came down to meet the ground. John Constable knew that, and that was good enough for Mr Campion.

That Boxing Day morning, however, few painters – with the possible exception of Mr Turner – would have been inspired by the dark grey sky which glowered above the Campions and Lugg as they set out on their walk.

They were shivering by the time they reached the end of the driveway, marked by two granite gateposts imported from goodness knew where but no actual gate. Mr Campion believed that impressive metal gates in the boundary wall had guarded the entrance to the property until pressed into service as part of the war effort and never replaced. Only a two-foot-long six-inch-high wrought-iron sign at ground level, spelling out *Carterers* in a flamboyant blacksmith script, now identified it as the entrance to the house, though Campion took great pleasure in telling first-time visitors to 'turn in between the two standing stones' and also to assure them, despite what Lugg might say, that they were *not* gravestones.

Taking the lead, Campion and Rupert, the son matching the father's long stride, set a brisk pace across the fields to keep warm, their planned four-mile route taking them in a big circle across agricultural land blissfully devoid of any signs of human habitation, although a dozen huddled sheep eyed them suspiciously from a distant hedgerow. By Campion's reckoning they were almost at the halfway point when the wind, which had been mostly in their faces, seemed to drop.

''Ere it comes,' announced Lugg with a loud sniff.

'What does?' Rupert asked over his shoulder.

'Snow,' proclaimed the fat man with a dignified resonance.

'And you, you son-of-the-soil, can tell that simply with your highly sensitive olfactory system?' said Campion.

'That and the fact that I listened to the weather forecast on the wireless.'

As the four walkers turned for home, it began to snow.

Heavily.

TWO

Let It Snow

'Do you do requests?'

'What?'

Graham Fisk was tempted to take a hand from the steering wheel and slap the sign on the windscreen which carried the instruction PLEASE DO NOT DISTRACT THE DRIVER, but to do so would be a distraction and in the present conditions highly dangerous.

He had known from the news and the weather forecasts that a low-pressure system had gathered strength and unleashed blizzards and heavy snowfalls all across East Anglia since Boxing Day, but there had been no government instruction not to travel, and his lords and masters at the coach company had sold the tickets, so there was no question that the Walsingham run should not go ahead. Just at the moment, running might get them to Walsingham faster, as for the last twenty miles a snail wearing snowshoes could have overtaken them with ease.

The ambient temperature of the living, breathing hulk that was London had kept the city streets clear if wet, but across much of Essex, as the sleet set in, driving conditions deteriorated rapidly. Crossing into Suffolk, it was as if the Arctic weather front had decided that the county boundary was where it was going to make a stand. The snow came down like a thrown blanket and the sun disappeared, until the only visible landmarks were abandoned vehicles stuck in the deepening snowdrifts which lined the road. Progress was slow, and only possible in the tracks of heavier vehicles up ahead, but the tenuous paths they carved were quickly losing the battle against a relentless covering of swirling snow reflected in the coach's headlight beams.

Undipped headlights – and not even noon! Graham Fisk shook his head in despair and admitted to himself that he had no idea where he was. The last thing he needed was one of those tall Yanks looming over him asking bloody stupid questions.

'I said do you do requests, like request stops?'

'What?'

Fisk ground his teeth and gripped the steering wheel even tighter.

'The next stop's Swaffham, right? How long before we get there?'

'Your guess is as good as mine, squire,' said Fisk, resisting the urge to suggest that they could easily drive right through it without noticing in the current blizzard.

The figure beside him seemed determined to distract the driver further by leaning in over his shoulder and peering at the dashboard display. Graham Fisk took his eyes off the road, or what little of the road he could make out through the smears left by the creaking windscreen wipers, and risked a glance at the man pressing against him so closely that he could feel the lining of his open parka against his chin. Under the parka was the blue uniform of the US Air Force, a not uncommon sight in these parts, though the driver had never had one so literally in his face before.

'You've racked up nearly a hundred miles, so we can't be far off. Y'all agree with that?'

Fisk remembered one of the three Americans – it may have been this one – coming to the front of the bus and taking a good look at the controls just after they had set off. He had assumed the Yank, who was polite enough, was merely satisfying his native curiosity about right-hand drive vehicles, which allowed the British to drive on the 'wrong' side of the road. And then later one of them had approached him as the snow thickened and asked, 'How you doing, buddy?' He'd replied without turning his head that he would be happier if they had gritted the roads some more, or if he was driving a snowplough. Only now, with this third visit, did he realize that they had not been three wise men bearing gifts, but they had been checking the odometer in the centre of the speedometer dial, which racked up the number of miles covered since Victoria. If all three Yanks were fly-boys, maybe that was the way they navigated, by time and distance, though the conditions had wrecked any chance of sticking to a hypothetical schedule.

'I can't say for definite when we'll get to Swaffham, but we must be close. If the road stays open that is,' said Fisk, hoping the American would go back to his seat. He craved a cigarette but dared not take his hands from the wheel.

'We're seeing more and more automobiles stacking up at the side of the road. Don't you guys drive with chains on your wheels?'

'Not normally, no.' He nodded towards the windscreen. '*This* isn't normal either.'

'And no cops around to control the traffic.'

'They'll have a lot on their hands, weather like this.'

In a way it was a comfort to have someone to talk to, even if the tall, clean-cut American standing and swaying next to him would not have been his first choice. In these conditions, perhaps the priest would have been preferable. Radio reception had cracked up half an hour ago, so he could not even play the passengers music to keep them amused and their mind off the angry elements outside. He could feel the nervous tension radiating from the seats behind him, and in the central mirror he could see the passengers huddled in their coats, most looking blankly out of the windows at the churning whiteness. At least his heater still worked, that was something. Maybe that was why the nosey American was still hanging on his shoulder.

'Would you be open to a suggestion, Mr Driver?' asked the Yank.

Having waved off two invited house guests on Boxing Day morning, the Campions found themselves with two unexpected ones by Boxing Day evening.

By the time the walking party returned to Carterers, the snow was settling thick and fast and, as they entered the drive, Mr Campion announced, his voice muffled by his scarf, that he had declared a moratorium on any references to Captain Scott and his ill-fated expedition, even though all four of them had a white frosting and did indeed resemble polar explorers staggering through a blizzard. Not until they were within fifty feet were they able to make out the outlines of the house and the lights on the Christmas tree through the lounge bay window.

Entering the house resulted in an almost farcical dance routine in the hallway, as boots were stamped and overcoats and hats shaken to dislodge the snow they had accumulated, which was now pooling on the tiled floor. Rupert volunteered to get a mop whilst the others made a break for the kitchen, knowing that their faithful white Aga would be lit and, according to Lugg, there was no better way known to man for drying wet socks.

The faithful Mrs Thursby was waiting for them in the kitchen, holding a tray of steaming teacups and a plate of warm mince pies. Amanda was the first to notice that she was buttoned up in her outdoor coat and a cloche hat secured by a tartan scarf tied under the chin.

'Goodness me!' exclaimed Amanda. 'I'd quite forgotten you, Mrs T, and so sorry we've been so long. We need to get you home, don't we, Albert?'

'I'll get the car out the instance that cup of tea raises my body temperature. I do apologize for keeping you hanging around, Mrs T, but our walk turned into a bit of a trudge, reminiscent of Napoleon's retreat from Moscow, though he didn't have mince pies waiting for him. Will your father be worried? We can't ring him, can we?'

Mrs Thursby shook her head, simultaneously glaring at Lugg who was helping himself to a second mince pie. 'You know we've got no phone, not that he'd hear it if it rang till Doomsday. Deaf as a post he be. Probably didn't even notice when I left the house this morning. Normally, I'd be happy to walk back but what with the weather . . .' Her voice trailed off pathetically.

'Nonsense!' snapped Amanda. 'It's horrendous out there and getting worse. Put some shoes on, Albert, and get the car out.'

'You taking the Jensen?' said Lugg, his buttocks strategically placed against the Aga.

'Got any better ideas?'

'We've still got the use of the Alandel Land Rover. That might be safer given the general inclemency.'

Campion raised his eyebrows. 'You'd never make a weather forecaster, old fruit. Not saying things like "general inclemency" when you mean Arctic blizzard, but you do have a point. The Land Rover is certainly the safer option.'

'Of course you could take the Jensen and leave the Land Rover here so I can come and pull you out of a ditch when you skid off the road.'

'I'll drive, Mrs T,' said Rupert cheerfully. 'I've never driven in an inclemency before.'

Amanda shot a worried look at her husband, but she knew better than to try and forbid Rupert to venture out into the blizzard.

'Darling, you will be careful, won't you? The snow's coming down thick and fast out there and it's almost dark. Why don't you stay here overnight, Mrs T? We have plenty of room and one of us can run you back first thing in the morning.'

Mrs Thursby put the plate of mince pies down on the kitchen table and pulled on a pair of woollen gloves to indicate that she was not open to negotiation.

'I can't leave my old da by hisself, can I? An' if this lot get frozed overnight, the roads will be worse and driving downright duzzy.'

Campion smiled at Mrs Thursby's analysis of the situation – a weather forecast in Norfolk dialect – and could only agree that if temperatures fell in the night and the snow froze, driving anywhere would indeed be downright stupid.

'I have an idea,' he said. 'Let's invite Mr Thursby to join us. We are well stocked with victuals, we have wood for the fires and coal for the Aga, so we will neither starve nor freeze. We have jigsaws and Monopoly and, at a pinch, there's always the television.'

'Oh, he does like his television does Da,' said Mrs Thursby thoughtfully.

'Has it on really loud, does he?' asked Lugg, despite a warning frown from Amanda.

'Oh no, he don't turn the sound on, leastwise not when I'm home. There'd be no point. He just looks at the pictures. Says he's lurning to lip-read.'

'So you watch your lip, old fruit,' Campion warned. 'No foul language, even in a whisper. I don't want you upsetting the old gentleman when you call to collect him.'

'Me? I've taken me boots off.'

'Well put them on again and go with Rupert. Even a Land Rover can use some extra ballast in these conditions; and take a couple of shovels in case you need to dig yourself out.'

Mrs Thursby pulled her gloves tighter and then double-checked the knot on her scarf.

'If you're sure it's not an imposition, then I'd better come along. Da won't open the door to strangers.'

'Good idea,' said Amanda, eyeing Lugg suspiciously. 'We don't want to give him a sudden shock.'

'He'll get enough of one when we roll up with those reindeers on the roof rack,' muttered Lugg. 'Still, it is Christmas.'

And with a flash of his hand, he snaffled two more mince pies and thrust them into his jacket pocket as he padded off to find his boots.

'We're heading for Marham,' said the Yank, pronouncing it Mah-*ham*, as an American would. 'You know where it is?'

Graham Fisk responded through grinding teeth. 'The RAF base? Yeah, I know where it's supposed to be, but you could walk by the front gates and not see it in all this. Anyway, it's not on our route.'

The young American strained closer to the windscreen to peer through the semicircles of glass which the wipers were straining to keep clear of splattered snow. In front of the coach, the few yards of road visible where the headlights managed to penetrate the blizzard was a blanket of white. There were no tyre tracks in front of the coach, and for some time they had not been passed by a vehicle travelling south in the opposite direction.

'There sure ain't much traffic about,' said the American.

'I wonder why. Such a nice day for a drive in the country,' said Fisk, wondering if it was true that Americans did not understand sarcasm. It seemed to make little impact on this one.

'Me and my guys were supposed to be picked up in Swaffham, which we reckon must be up ahead, but it don't look like much is moving and the odds are we get stuck in a drift or slide off the road into a ditch before we get there.'

'Tell me something I don't know.'

'I'm just assessing the situation, Mr Driver, that's all. If we carry on along this road, we risk getting stuck. It's already dark and this bus will become a refrigerator if we have to spend the night in it. Some of your passengers back there ain't exactly spring chickens, you know, and I'm guessing you don't have a supply of blankets and hot soup on board.'

Fisk clutched the steering wheel even tighter as the coach

moved distinctly sideways over a patch of ice. In his mind he ran through the possibilities before him as, in effect, the captain of this particular ship. The coach, which had not managed more than fifteen mph for over two hours, was unlikely to make Walsingham before the pubs closed, assuming they had even opened that evening. Only the three American servicemen were booked as far as Swaffham, which meant he would be stuck with the others and could, literally, be stuck with them in a snowdrift at least until dawn, when he at least might be able to get his bearings. If he pressed on, and the coach did get stuck, he realized that the three Yanks were the only passengers young enough and fit enough to dig it out, and they would have disembarked.

'You have something in mind?'

'Like I said, me and my buddies have been doing some calculations – we've all been up this road before – and in a mile or maybe two as far as we can guess, there's a turning to the left which is a back road straight to Marham. Well, as straight as you get round here.'

'I ain't a taxi service. We only call at scheduled stops.'

'But what if we can't make the next scheduled stop? It sure don't look healthy up ahead.'

'What makes you think a back alley through the villages will be any easier?'

'Likely it won't be, but it's only a coupla miles—'

'A couple of miles in *this* is more than a couple.'

'But the closer to the base, the clearer the roads. The RAF have bulldozers and snowploughs there to keep the runways clear, and they'll be using them to clear the approach roads.'

'You know that for a fact, Yank?'

'No, but it's a good bet, and Marham has heat and food and shelter. If we make it to Swaffham in one piece and can't go any further, what're you gonna do with your passengers, just sit it out? Have you even got enough gas to keep the heater running?'

Fisk glanced down at the dial of the petrol gauge. 'We're getting low,' he said grimly, masking his surprise and angry that he had not considered the fuel situation, 'and there'll be no garages open in weather like this. Nothing'll be open.'

'Except the base, and they've got all the comforts of home and plenty of fuel.'

The driver, eyes glued on the road and the swirling white and grey vortex surrounding the coach, heard another voice shouting from the back seat, but did not break his concentration, not even to look in his rear-view mirror.

'Staff Sergeant!'

'Yo!' the American breathing down Fisk's neck answered.

'Best guess: Marham turning in one mile, maybe less.'

The American leaned in again, over the driver's shoulder.

'Odometer mileage checks that out. Thanks, Pete. Well, Mr Driver, you gonna take the turning?'

'If you fly-boys can find it for me, I'll take it, but just remember, if we end up in a hedgerow, you three will be the ones pushing us out.'

'Hey, come on, Mr Driver, have a little faith.'

'My name's Fisk. Graham Fisk.'

'Mighty pleased to make your acquaintance, Mr Fisk. I'm Staff Sergeant Ed Kosloffski and my two guys are Pete and Oscar. We're here to help bring this bus down in a safe landing. We could even spell you at the wheel. You look like you need a break.'

'You mean share the driving?'

'I surely do. Oscar's our best driver, but don't tell him I said that, and he's even driven over here before, on the wrong side of the road, or the left as you Brits call it.' The sergeant leaned forward and followed the driver's fixed gaze through the windscreen, but no matter how much he screwed his eyes, visibility was no more than five yards to where the headlight beams collided with a dancing wall of falling snow. 'Not that I could say for sure which side of the road we're on at the moment. Good thing there's nothing coming the other way.'

Fisk was tempted, even though he knew it was against company rules, because his eyes hurt, he had a pounding headache, and his hands were cramped from gripping the steering wheel, which he had not dared to let go of in order to light a desperately needed cigarette.

'You're not insured,' he said.

'I'm sure the US Air Force is and you can always say we commandeered the bus in order to guide it to the base. Believe me, that will put us in more trouble than you, but your passengers will be safe and warm.'

'You sure your chap Oscar can handle this old bus?'

The sergeant grinned down at Fisk. 'Hell, Oscar's flown an F-101 Voodoo.'

'I don't know what that is.'

'It's a plane with more oomph than this crate. Trust me, he can handle it; I've even seen him drive stick shift.' He turned to the interior of the coach. 'Oscar, get up here! Let's give this guy a break. Now Graham, bring this bus to a nice smooth stop and let Oscar take the wheel.'

For the first time since the blizzard had hit, Graham Fisk relaxed at least some of his tensed muscles as he gently pressed the foot brake. The night was a white curtain ahead of him, snow was piling up on both sides of the road, he was hours behind his schedule, and he was now turning his vehicle and the passengers in his trust over to a pair of foreigners and deliberately going off his planned route. Still, it was a relief to have someone giving him orders, taking a weighty responsibility from his shoulders; shoulders which he rolled forwards and backwards to uncramp as the Burlingham Seagull slipped gingerly to a halt, its tyres crunching fresh snow. He applied the handbrake but kept the engine and windscreen wipers running and stood up, flexing his stiff fingers and stretching his compressed spine.

A second blue-uniformed figure appeared next to the one Fisk was beginning to think of as a guardian angel, the one who had been called a staff sergeant and who seemed to be in charge.

'This is Oscar,' he was saying, 'and he's going to spell you.'

Fisk looked his replacement up and down; mostly up, as the tall, thin American towered over him, a concerned expression on his frighteningly youthful face. Whether it was concern over the usurping of the driver's command, or at the prospect of steering a right-hand-drive vehicle in Arctic conditions, Fisk could not tell, but he was happy and relieved to change places.

The sergeant, meanwhile, was zipping up the parka he wore over his uniform, flipping up the fur-lined hood and then pulling thick leather gloves from the pockets.

'You've come prepared,' said Fisk, fumbling a pack of cigarettes from his own coat.

The American grinned. 'I'm from Texas and I've been in England before.'

'The winters aren't normally this bad.'

'Winter? I came prepared for your summer.'

It was three hours before Rupert and Lugg returned to Carterers, one of them being taken up entirely with getting Lloyd Thursby from his cottage and into the Land Rover.

The snow had drifted to a depth of two feet against the front door of the cottage, and Mrs Thursby insisted that it be dug away as she would not have it falling into the house when the door opened. As Lugg saw it, this could only be a Pyrrhic victory against the elements, as snowflakes as big as cotton balls continued to fall, making him and Rupert look like snowmen working on a chain gang under the gimlet gaze of Mrs Thursby, who remained seated in stately fashion in the Land Rover.

Through a gap in the curtains came the flickering light of a television, the only indication that the place was inhabited, for no matter how many times Lugg accidentally on purpose rapped on the front door with the blade of his shovel, there came no response from within. Eventually the snowdrift had been parted, like the Red Sea, sufficiently to meet with Mrs Thursby's approval, and as she descended from the Land Rover and glided to the front door, Lugg had the distinct impression that the falling snow missed her completely, almost as if the snowflakes were frightened of landing on her best coat with its fake fur collar.

She held a key like a gun in her gloved hand and poked it into the keyhole.

'I locks him in,' she explained in answer to Lugg's quizzical look, 'in case he goes wandering.'

'Terrible weather for wandering about,' Lugg agreed earnestly. 'Even Captain Scott and Titus Oates wouldn't chance it on a night like this.'

Rupert flicked a shovel-full of snow over Lugg's boots and shook his head, dislodging white flakes from the flat cap he had borrowed from his father.

'Not a good example, Magers,' he said but Lugg, to whom the young man shaking his head looked like a figure trapped in a snow globe, ignored him, stamped his feet and followed Mrs Thursby inside.

The first thought of both Lugg and Rupert was: how old was

Lloyd Thursby? With the careless arrogance of youth, Rupert's first guess was at least a hundred. Lugg, having the more charitable view of someone almost a pensioner himself, estimated late seventies, early eighties.

Whatever his age, Mr Thursby (senior) was enthroned in an armchair with a blanket over his knees, an arm's length away from a roaring coal fire, watching the flickering pictures on the television screen of a set encased in enough polished wood to make a small coffin. To his left, within easy reach, was a coal scuttle and shovel, so he could keep the fire stoked, and to his right was a small brass-topped circular table conveniently placed for him to reach out and refresh the glass he held from the bottles of Bullard's brown ale balanced there. Lugg's expert eye noticed the necks of two other bottles peeping out from under his chair, along with an abandoned plate decorated with crumbs and the fatty rind from a slice of ham.

To Lugg, Lloyd Thursby appeared well set-up for retirement, and a lucky man to have a daughter-in-law prepared to look after him, as Mrs Thursby had done for nearly twenty years since the death of Mr Thursby (junior) in an agricultural accident involving a combine harvester, the sort of accident which shocked city folk but was accepted stoically out in the countryside.

With his eyes fixed on the screen, where the latest domestic drama on *Coronation Street* was being silently played out, the old man did not notice the arrival of his visitors, despite the blast of icy air they came in on and the resultant hiss and puffs of smoke from the fire. Only when Mrs Thursby planted herself in front of the television, turned off the set and bent over so that her face was in his direct line of sight did Thursby acknowledge the presence of others in the room with a single, incomprehensible cry of 'Rawhide!'

'Now come on, Da, get up and get a few things together,' said the woman, speaking loud and slow. 'We've been invited to stay with the Campions until this storm blows over.'

'*Rawhide*!' shouted Mr Thursby, pointing the glass he held at the television.

'We can watch it at Carterers,' said Mrs Thursby, opening her mouth wide and moving her lips in slow motion. Without a reduction in volume she turned on her two assistants. 'It's his favourite programme is *Rawhide*. He reckons he can lip-read his hero, Rowdy Yates. He's always said if we had a dog, he'd call it Clint Eastwood.'

'What's she on about?' Lugg hissed at Rupert out of the corner of his mouth.

'Cowboys. Old Mr T is a fan of cowboy shows. I've seen it in America. Not sure Ma and Pa are fans.'

'They might have to be if it keeps him quiet.'

'Quiet? I hardly think so.'

Lugg shook his head, scattering melting snow on to the carpet. 'If 'e can lip-read, we can turn the sound down and supply 'im with enough brown ale so he don't notice. Now let's get him up and out.'

Getting Lloyd Thursby up from his chair and out into the storm was achieved surprisingly quickly, as the old man was clearly disciplined when it came to obeying orders from his daughter-in-law; orders issued at a level of decibels most parade-ground sergeant majors would envy. Whilst Lloyd disappeared upstairs to pack a bag ('Just a clean shirt, your pyjamas and your razor – you're not going on holiday!'), Mrs Thursby instructed Lugg to damp down the fire whilst she 'gathered a few unmentionables', at which Rupert blushed and averted his eyes. When she reappeared she held a large handbag and a heavy shopping bag, which she handed to Lugg, saying, 'There's a tin of mince pies, a ham hock and the best part of a fruit cake in there. Our contribution to the larder up at the house.'

Lugg nodded his approval. 'Iron rations, eh? Might just keep us going on the drive back.'

Conditions outside had worsened, and by the time they reached Carterers Lloyd's favourite programme was long finished. Not that he seemed to mind – he was fast asleep as Lugg carried him like a baby from the Land Rover and into the warmth.

Although no one knew it, Lloyd Thursby was only to be the first unexpected guest at Carterers that Christmas.

Rather him than me, thought Graham Fisk as he huddled, shivering, deep into his coat, his hand cupped around a cigarette. However cold he was now seated away from the heater near the driver's seat, however cramped his spine and however much his head throbbed and his eyes ached from the strain of the day's driving, he was better off inside the bus rather than outside like that crazy Yank.

The one who said he was a sergeant had offered to go out into the snowstorm and guide the bus by frantic hand signals to the one called Oscar, who was wrestling with the driving. Without the sergeant scouting ahead, they would have missed the back-road turning to Marham, although it was a dangerous role, as to be seen by the driver the sergeant had to stay within the beams of the coach's headlights. Should he slip and fall over, he could easily go under the wheels, but the two Americans seemed to have faith in each other and some form of telepathy which kept the coach on a steady course down, as far as Fisk could tell, the middle of the minor road.

At least he assumed it was the middle of the road. Through the snow-spattered side windows it was impossible to tell whether they were actually on a road at all, and the fear in the passengers' faces showed they shared the same opinion.

Fisk had stood in the aisle between the seats and addressed them, saying they were unlikely to make any of their scheduled destinations that night and so were diverting to RAF Marham, where food, shelter and heating would make life more comfortable. They were in the capable hands of the American Air Force who would guide them into a safe landing, he added in an attempt to lighten the mood. It was met with a stony silence, and Fisk sank into the nearest empty seat, grateful that he had not asked the priest to say a prayer for them after all. He looked at his watch and noted that it was seven p.m., realized he was hungry but could do nothing about it, and decided to follow his own advice and put his faith in the American Air Force. Freed of responsibility, he nodded off to sleep, unaware that his few passengers were all regarding the back of his head with a mixture of horror and contempt.

He was jolted awake, his forehead bashing against the back of the seat in front and his teeth clashing painfully together, as the coach came to a sudden and violent halt amidst a chorus of gasps and curses from the passengers.

The coach was leaning over to the left at an unnatural but not dangerous angle and the engine was no longer throbbing. Even as Fisk staggered to his feet and prepared to clamber to the front, the door opened and a snow-covered staff sergeant hauled himself in.

'Good news and bad news folks,' he announced, flipping back the hood of his parka. 'We've hit a brick wall, or something just as solid as a brick wall, and I don't think we're going any further. Good news is there's shelter nearby, a place with lights on, and if we have to spend the night, it gets my vote over staying in here and freezing our nuts off.'

'Where are we?' asked Fisk.

'No idea, but we're here and we're staying here.'

As the passengers, clutching their coats around shivering bodies, disembarked into knee-deep snow, none took any notice of the mangled piece of metal which had been churned by the front nearside wheel of the bus.

It was a strip of wrought iron which, if straightened, would have spelled out the word 'Carterers'.

THREE
Charabanc

Amanda had been worried about the length of time it had taken to collect Mrs Thursby's father-in-law, imagining all manner of scenarios where Rupert, or rather the Land Rover with him at the wheel, had ended up nose-down in a snowdrift, or alternatively he was lost and snow-blind, struggling through the blizzard carrying an injured Mrs Thursby in his arms and slowly freezing to death. Her anxiety had manifested itself after the first hour, with an inability to sit or stand still for more than two minutes, and from then on frequent trips to the window in the front room which under normal conditions would give a clear view down the drive to the gateway, the only sound from that darkened room being the unrhythmic tapping of her fingernails on the glass and the hiss of logs burning in the fireplace. After the second hour, she was, by her own admission, becoming tetchy, and Mr Campion, who was also becoming increasingly anxious, trod warily in her presence.

To distract himself he volunteered, in the absence of Lugg's legendary Boxing Day turkey curry, to make dinner, but in a kitchen which still had the air of a battlefield and which, at the best of times, was a foreign country to him, Mr Campion's inspiration deserted him. Part of the problem lay in the very geography of the kitchen, at the rear of the house, as it offered no view over the drive, and so he was kept on tenterhooks, reacting to the sudden exclamations of Amanda on look-out duty whenever she thought she had detected the return of the expedition to rescue Mr Thursby. They had both, without discussion, agreed that it was not an evening to watch television, and Campion resisted the urge to turn on the radio in the kitchen in case he missed the joyous cry of pent-up welcome as Amanda greeted the returning expedition.

He considered ferrying a series of hot drinks into the front lounge, but when he delivered the second cup of tea to find the first cold and untouched, he discontinued the service. Knowing that an offer of alcohol 'to help relax her' would be swiftly spurned, he resisted the temptation to pour himself a stiff whisky for, in solidarity with his wife, he could not relax until Rupert was safely home.

To keep himself busy he made sandwiches of white turkey meat, stuffing and Cumberland sauce, cut them into fingers and arranged them on a plate. He plucked one of Mrs Thursby's flowery aprons from the hook on the kitchen door and put it on, then he carried the plate, like a pretentious waiter, one-handed above his head to Amanda's lonely outpost.

''Ere we are, deary – comforts for the troops. I bring supplies to the forward observation post!' he announced, wafting the plate balanced on his fingertips in front of her.

Amanda was neither impressed nor amused. 'I'm not in the mood, Albert. I am seriously worried. They've been gone hours, so do not be frivolous.'

'But my darling, I am the spirit-lifter, the mood-lightener pursuivant. That is my job, my purpose in life.'

'Well, take the day off.' Amanda folded her arms and stared out into the white night. 'If they don't show in the next half-hour, I'm going looking for them.'

'You most certainly will not! If anyone is going to make a futile gesture by walking out into the storm, it ought to be Lugg, and he's already out there. You know Lugg, he's not going to let a little thing like ten-foot snowdrifts or sub-zero temperatures keep him from all the beer he's got stashed in the tack room, not to mention he hasn't cooked his annual leftover turkey curry yet, for which, I suppose, we should be grateful, but it will only be a respite. We will just have to suffer it tomorrow.'

'If he gets back,' Amanda said quietly.

'Of course he will. The old boy will have laid a trail of mince pie crumbs so he can find his way back here, but just in case, I've turned on every light in the place so we're lit up like a homing beacon. I think we should also put the Christmas tree lights on in here.'

'We'd need a searchlight to cut through this. Visibility is virtually nil. I wouldn't attempt a landing in this.'

Mr Campion allowed himself a smile of domestic pride. 'There speaks the aeronautical engineer of the family, but we're not expecting an aeroplane, just a Land Rover with reindeer on the roof.'

He moved to stand at the side of his wife, put the plate of sandwiches down on a side table and used his arm to encompass her, the two of them concentrating on the almost non-existent view through the snow-splattered bay window. The wind outside had dropped and the window frame no longer creaked and groaned, leaving the room deathly quiet. The steady fall of large snowflakes outside filled the panes, reminding Mr Campion of the fuzz of a television screen when there was nothing more to broadcast.

He felt Amanda's shoulder blades stiffen.

'Is that them? There, those lights turning into the drive.'

Mr Campion had long deferred to Amanda when it came to any test of long-sightedness, and in all honesty he could make out nothing more than a white blur, but he leaned forward and pulled his spectacles an inch from his nose, closer to the window.

'You could be right, darling,' he said cautiously, but then his tone changed as he caught, or thought he did, a flash of a headlight beam. 'It could very well be them, or some rather late carol singers. Should we turn the lights off and hide, just in case?'

A sharp female elbow jabbed into Campion's ribs. 'Don't be an ass, Albert. Go and put some kettles on.'

'Tea or coffee to warm the innards of the weary travellers?'

'The kettles are to fill hot-water bottles. As for the inner man, or woman, get the brandy out.'

With the efficiency of an experienced quartermaster general setting up a permanent base camp, Amanda organized the incoming members of the Thursby Expedition, as Albert insisted on calling it, so that boots and wet clothing could be removed and left in what the Campions called the 'tack room' even though it had never known the presence of a horse or any associated 'tack'. Like many an outbuilding on a working farm, it had been built from pieces of other buildings and situated as close to the farmhouse as possible, on the logical assumption that after trudging across wide fields in all weathers, a farmer coming home for the night does not want to have to trudge far to get the coal in. Now used mainly to store logs and firewood for kindling, Lugg was convinced it had once housed a cider press, otherwise what was the point of that orchard on the other side of the house? There being absolutely no evidence, either commercial or archaeological, for such a claim did not dent his conviction, although he dropped many a hint that if there had not been one in the past, there was no reason why there could not be one in the future. In the meantime, he had put it to good use, with several ham hocks hanging from the roof beams, along with the odd rabbit and pheasant when in season, though mainly as his personal beer cellar, with a healthy stack of wooden crates marked as property of Bullard's or Morgan's breweries.

Once their outer layers had been removed, both rescuers and the rescued were issued with hot-water bottles, placed in front of a roaring fire and had a restorative drink thrust into their shivering hands. Even the normally abstemious Mrs Thursby partook of a glass of mulled wine – three, in fact – while Amanda prepared food for them all, although she took a dim view when Lugg offered her the tin containing Mrs Thursby's fruit cake from which an oxbow-lake-shaped segment had been removed by, she suspected, Lugg's thumbs.

'Iron rations on the trip back,' he said sheepishly.

Rupert, massaging his eyelids with the tips of his fingers, admitted that the drive through the snow had been exhausting, and spent the remainder of the evening avoiding the fussing of an over-protective mother, opting to go straight to bed once he had been fed and his feet had thawed out.

Mrs Thursby appeared to be the least affected by the journey and, as soon as she was warm enough to remove her coat, was rolling up her sleeves and preparing to attack whatever kitchen duties needed performing. She was dissuaded by the strictness in Amanda's voice, which told her to leave everything until the morning, to which Lugg added, ''Cos nobody'll be going anywhere.'

The fat man's prediction turned out to be completely accurate. The next day, that Thursday, dawned with a stunning bright whiteness that only nature, rather than the advertising agencies who sold soap powder, could conjure.

The residents of Carterers peeped out from behind thick curtains or through frosted windows, and unanimously decided that it was a day for hunkering down, though hibernation was out of the question as both Amanda and Mrs Thursby began to find and allocate domestic tasks. While the two women naturally took charge of cooking, menu planning and taking inventory of all the food in the house, everyone else was allocated chores and duties and no one was to be exempt. Albert and Rupert were designated to undertake a trek to the garage which, although only a few yards from the rear of the house, now involved wading through knee-deep snow in order to salvage several oil lamps which might be needed in case of a power cut. As a similar precaution, Lugg was ordered to place candles, of which the Campions always kept a healthy reserve, in strategic points around the house, and to make sure everyone had access to a box of matches. Whilst he was at it, Lugg offered, he would do a stock check of 'beverages and refreshments' and, what was more, do it 'at no extra charge'.

Surprisingly, Lloyd Thursby took to his specified jobs with enthusiasm, having been put in charge of cleaning the grates and laying fires in all the fireplaces of the house. He proved to be an energetic chopper of firewood and had suggested, in a voice so loud no one dared argue, that the ashes from the fires be saved in a bucket in the tack room to be used to grit an icy road or driveway if a car's tyres could not gain traction.

'That was good thinking on Mr Thursby's part,' Campion confided to Amanda as they dried crockery in the kitchen. 'From the impression Mrs T gave, I thought the old boy had gone doolally years ago, but give him something to do and he's quite sprightly for his age. I was a bit worried when he arrived last night as he didn't seem to know where he was.'

'Can you blame him? He'd just been kidnapped by Lugg and driven through a blizzard in Santa's Land Rover.'

'Fair point, but he was mumbling quite incoherently for a while. Something about missing his raw hide, whatever that means.'

'*Rawhide*.' Amanda's face bloomed as she grinned. 'It's his favourite thing on television apparently. It's a Western starring a rather dishy actor called Clint Eastwood.'

'It sounds as though you are a fan.'

'Of the programme, not particularly, but I do like him. He's rugged, strong and very . . . masculine. Just my type.'

Mr Campion smiled innocently. 'Remind you of anyone, does he?'

Amanda glanced sideways, surveying her beaming husband, the flowery apron he was wearing and the tea towel – proclaiming it was a souvenir of the commune of Pisa – he was wielding. 'No, not remotely.'

No one ventured outside further than the tack room or the garage – a large and exceedingly ugly wooden-framed building, big enough to house a combine harvester, which it probably once had – and the view from the front of the house was a pristine, virginal white blanket thanks to the continuing snowfall overnight. For a few grey hours that morning the snow held off, but in the early afternoon the clouds turned battleship grey again and released another broadside, throwing snow and sleet against the windows until the frames rattled.

Throughout the day, Mr Campion had kept a radio tuned to the Light Programme, claiming that he never missed *Housewives' Choice*, but in reality was listening intently to news bulletins and weather forecasts. The blizzard that had swept over Lincolnshire and Norfolk on Boxing Day and paused for breath during the night had now, quite literally, got its second wind, and by the afternoon was pushing its way into Suffolk and points south, prompting official warnings for drivers (basically don't unless you really have to) and travellers hoping to catch a train in East Anglia (good luck with that).

Towards evening the storm intensified, and the radio cracked and crackled as the reception faltered. Out of curiosity and perhaps the reassurance that there was an outside world still there beyond the snow, Mr Campion turned on the television to find no reception at all on either channel.

'Dad will be disappointed,' said Mrs Thursby, suppressing a giggle. 'He's been out in that shed of yours all day, an' he's chopped enough wood to see you through to next Christmas. He likes to pop his boots off and put his feet up in front of the telly, even the kids' programmes.'

When he did come in from his wood-chopping duties, Lloyd

Thursby sank into an armchair and promptly fell asleep, which Mr Campion at first put down to the toll of a hard day's work on a man of his age, until he became aware of the rather malty fumes coming from fluttering lips as Lloyd began to snore gently.

'I hope he hasn't overstrained himself,' Amanda had said as she tucked a blanket over his knees. 'Mrs T has been nipping out to the tack room every hour to see how he was doing. She seemed to think it was funny, him doing household chores. Couldn't stop sniggering about it.'

'She has seemed in a suspiciously good mood all afternoon,' Mr Campion had said, 'considering the circumstances.'

It was only as the besieged residents of Carterers gathered in the kitchen, by far the warmest room, where they would have their evening meal, did things become clear.

'I'm afraid the bad news is there's no television,' said Campion, 'so it looks like an evening of board games.'

'That's not the bad news,' said Lugg. 'I've done a stock check' – he paused for dramatic effect – 'an' we've completely run out of milk stout.'

The fat man turned a fierce and burning eye on both Thursbys. Lloyd looked down at his stockinged feet; his daughter-in-law simply giggled.

With so many willing hands to call on, or be dragooned into action, the remains of their makeshift dinner were cleared away and the kitchen scrubbed and cleaned to a standard which would have satisfied a *Country Life* photographer. The three Campions and their three house guests then returned to the front living room, where a large fire had been burning all day and, with curtains closed and the tree ablaze with coloured lights, could almost justify the adjective 'snug'.

From his personal study – library, office, sanctum, or den, depending on his mood – Mr Campion retrieved a selection of board and card games which, he hoped, would amuse and entertain, the alternative being a performance of his world-famous magic act.

'Save the conjuring tricks for when the power lines go down and the electricity goes off,' said Lugg with a sigh of resignation.

'So you can't see how the magic is done.' Campion nodded in agreement.

'No, so we can doze off without you noticing.'

'I will ignore that.' Campion hefted the armful of boxes he was carrying. 'There are cards for bridge or whist or' – he glared at Lugg – 'pontoon, and I have Monopoly, draughts, Lotto or Scrabble.'

'How about Cluedo?' asked Rupert innocently.

Amanda quickly intervened as peacemaker. 'You know very well your father will not allow that ridiculous game into this house. What was that?'

Amanda's heart-shaped face turned away from her son and towards the long curtains drawn over the bay window.

'That noise, that loud *thump* . . . outside . . . out there. Didn't anyone else hear it?'

It appeared that no one had, though inexplicably they all looked at Lloyd Thursby, the least likely person to be able to confirm a distant sound, who was busy picking at loose threads in the blanket over his legs.

'I didn't imagine it,' protested Amanda. 'It was a sort of dull thudding noise.'

'A big lump of snow sliding off the roof perhaps,' suggested Mr Campion. 'Probably from around the chimney. The fire's been going all day and it could have dislodged a small avalanche.'

Rupert moved to the window and pulled open the curtains just wide enough to put his head in the gap and peer out, the icy cold glass chilling his face.

'Can't see an avalanche or a rogue iceberg, or anything for that matter. It's still snowing if anyone's interested. Must be two or three feet deep where it's drifted.'

'Deep, crisp and probably even,' said Mr Campion, opening out a Queen Anne games table and laying out the Monopoly board on its green baize surface. 'And tomorrow, if the sun comes out, we really must take some photographs for next year's Christmas card. Now who wants to be what?' He rattled the Monopoly box. 'Rupert usually insists on being the racing car and Amanda lets me have the top hat as it gives me the illusion of being a property tycoon.'

Rupert began to shuffle the Chance cards. 'And who gets to be banker?'

'Anyone but Lugg.'

Rupert smiled at the joke his father made every time the board game was produced. 'In America,' he said, 'the character on the box – the cartoon mascot with the moustache and top hat holding the bag of cash – is known as Rich Uncle Pennybags.'

'We are so pleased to hear that your university education in America is proving useful,' said Campion as he sorted the Monopoly money by value. 'Let us roll the dice – highest score gets to be banker. Should we warn our guests that there are well-established family tactics in this game?'

'Tactics?' Amanda picked up the pewter piece in the shape of an iron between two delicate fingers, as if weighing its suitability as a weapon.

'You, my dear, always aim for Mayfair or Park Lane, preferably both, and I would not deny you the pleasure of them. Lugg on the other hand, always makes a beeline for Regent Street.'

'Why Regent Street?'

'Because if he lands on Regent Street, he's avoided the Go To Jail square.'

'Cheek!' muttered Lugg. 'Let's get on with it and maybe we'll get a winner before the thaw sets in.'

In fact, none of the paper currency had been spent, few dice had been rolled, no property had been bought and no one had gone to jail when the game was interrupted by a frantic knocking on the front door. With the exception of Lloyd Thursby, who was energetically rattling the china eggcup which the Campions used as a dice-shaker, the Monopoly players looked up from the board and then at each other.

'I'll go,' said Lugg, heaving himself upright. Then he patted Mrs Thursby on the shoulder. 'Keep an eye on my piece – I'm the boot as usual. Make sure it don't suddenly start going backwards.'

'If it is a rescue party, tell them we are safe and comfortable, thank you very much, and we are sure there are others in more pressing need. If it's the Salvation Army, do not offer them a drink but do buy a newspaper or two.'

Lugg grunted as the knocking persisted and ambled out into the hall, closing the door behind him to conserve the heat.

'Double six!' exclaimed Lloyd Thursby. 'Is that good? What do I get for that?'

He spoke so loudly it was impossible to hear anything from the hall but a muffled stamping noise and an indistinct voice which was certainly not Lugg's, then the door opened and the icy draught which entered was accompanied by a moon of face which certainly was Lugg's.

'Keep yer eyes on the silver. We've got visitors. A flamin' charabanc full of 'em.'

As the refugees from the storm trooped into his home, a goodly amount of snow falling from their shoes, coats and hats as they stepped in single file, Mr Campion assessed both the quantity and quality of Carterers' latest visitors.

In the light of Lugg identifying them as 'a charabanc full', he immediately conjured a vision of a coachload of distraught holidaymakers clutching sticks of rock and wearing kiss-me-quick hats on their way to Cromer or Great Yarmouth, who had suddenly realized they were miles off course. But this was not the right time of year for holiday day-trippers, nor the right weather unless they had skis and were in another country, as Norfolk, though mercifully free of avalanches, was not noted for its mountain slopes. Nor was it the time for idle and whimsical speculation, as there were blankets to fetch, chairs to be arranged near fires, hot-water bottles to fill and hot toddies to dispense. As the visitors were marshalled by Amanda (with Mrs Thursby as her sergeant major), wet coats and ruined shoes were removed and reviving drinks dispensed, Campion had only the briefest of opportunities to analyse and categorize them as they trooped single file into the front lounge.

The first figure he noted was the woman, and quickly realized she was the only female among the incomers, which certainly ruled out the possibility that this was any sort of family outing, as she appeared detached, and clearly so, from any of the men. Campion guessed she was of a similar age to himself, but when he wished her welcome, her expression was like glass. She made no sound, merely nodded, and for a moment Campion thought she might suddenly clutch at the wooden crucifix hanging from her neck chain.

Of the men who followed, hurrying to get near the fire, he had time to make even hastier judgements as he slotted them into his brain's filing cabinet. There was the priest; that one was easy, the dog collar giving it away. He was followed by a short, red-faced figure with a ginger moustache, which twitched in time to his audibly chattering teeth; he bustled in, heading directly for the fireplace, almost elbowing the priest out of his path, and reminded Campion of a self-important professor hurrying to give a lecture which his students could not possibly live without hearing. Yet it was the third male who looked more the stereotype of the absent-minded professor, possibly a professor of the sciences rather than the arts, though philosophy was an outside bet. Campion was distracted by the fact that the thick white beard the man sported and his long, unruly hair actually had snowflakes embedded, perhaps even a small icicle or two. From the way he clasped a brown leather briefcase to his chest as though his life depended upon it, Campion pigeonholed him as something of an eccentric, and from the way he responded to Campion's overly cheerful 'welcome one, welcome all' with a polite 'Gut evening' and a curt bow, clearly a foreign one.

The next in line looked the most shell-shocked of the arrivals, as he shuffled forward stiff-limbed and wide-eyed with, ridiculously, the wet remains of a cigarette stuck to his bottom lip. The sound of Campion's voice seemed to surprise and then wake him.

'Come through, come through. My name is Campion and that's my wife Amanda who pulled you in from the storm.'

'Fisk, Graham Fisk, an' I'm the driver.'

'You must be a brave man to drive anywhere in this,' said Campion, placing a hand on Fisk's shoulder and steering him nearer the fire. 'Did you really come in a charabanc?'

Fisk seemed at first to be confused by the word. 'A coach, yes, but it wasn't full. Only seven passengers, and I'd've stayed in London and got them their money back if I'd known it was going to be this bad.'

'Where were you headed?'

'Walsingham, with stops in Swaffham and Fakenham.'

'Aren't you somewhat off your route?'

'The passengers took over.'

'There was a mutiny on board?' said Campion with mock horror.

'No, nothing like that. These lads' – he flapped a shaking right hand over his left shoulder – 'them Yanks, they're stationed at Marham and they reckoned we could find shelter there, but we never made it.'

'I would have been amazed if you had. We've been snowed in here since yesterday evening.'

'It wasn't the snow that stopped us,' said Fisk blankly, 'it was that bloody great gatepost at the end of your driveway.'

Mr Campion could not stop himself from apologizing for a static piece of granite which had somehow come alive and caused an accident. 'Oh dear, I am so sorry. Was anyone hurt?'

'Just shaken up a bit, but the coach will probably need a tow in the morning.'

'I'm not sure if this weather intends to clear overnight, but you are all welcome to camp out here. We have food, drink and firewood. Did you just not see the gateposts? Under normal conditions they're jolly hard to miss – a bit like Stonehenge.'

Fisk averted his eyes and they flicked everywhere but at his host. He spoke so quietly Campion strained to hear him. 'It wasn't me driving, it was one of the Yanks – the three airmen. They reckoned I needed a break. I'm sure the insurance'll cover any damage.'

'Don't worry about that for a single second, old chap. Go on through, get warm and have a rest. I doubt your charabanc could have done much damage to the megaliths guarding our driveway. For the integrity of your vehicle I could not speak, but there is nothing anyone can do about that tonight.'

Campion gave Fisk a reassuring pat on the soaking sleeve of his coat and turned his attention to the rest of the arrivals, who were accompanied by flurries of snow on an icy draught from the open front door.

'The queue seems to be thinning out, thank goodness. Come in, come in. You must be one of our American allies.'

'Does it show?' Staff Sergeant Kosloffski had not unzipped his parka to reveal his uniform, and seemed determined to remain cocooned in its fur lining.

'Process of elimination after forewarning by the coach driver,' said Campion, 'plus you are head and shoulders taller than most natives of the old world, so you must be of the new. Welcome to my house. My name is Campion.'

'Ed Kosloffski, US Air Force,' said the American, pulling off a glove and offering a handshake, 'but my friends call me Sometimes.'

Campion did an elaborate music hall double-take as they shook.

'Am I going to regret asking why they call you that? We are innocent country folk here and easily shocked.'

'Oh, it's clean enough. Whenever I was asked my name and I said Kosloffski, there would always be a wise guy who said, "Can you spell that?" and I'd always say, "Sometimes." I got sort of stuck with it.'

Campion chuckled his approval. 'I can think of far worse nicknames to be lumbered with. At school I was called Old Gig-Lamps.'

'I'm sorry, I don't follow.'

Campion tapped his spectacles. 'My glasses reminded people of the big round lamps on the front of horse-drawn carriages, but that must make me sound absolutely ancient to a young fly-boy like yourself. You'll just have to take my word for it, but there were such things before there were cars and aeroplanes. And that makes me sound even older, so just ignore me and come in and have a drink – and, naturally, your comrade-in-arms.'

Kosloffski turned to the parka-clad figure shivering behind him.

'This is Senior Airman Oscar Rivero. Don't play him at poker or trust him with your daughter.'

'Poker is completely beyond me,' admitted Campion, 'and I don't have a daughter, only a son, who is actually studying in America so he may have picked up the basics. I will, however, pass on the warning. Didn't your coach driver tell me there were three of you?'

'There sure are. Pete Quinn will be along momentarily. We left him securing the bus.'

It was not until sometime later that Mr Campion asked himself why the bus needed 'securing'.

FOUR

The Tale of the Retiring Reverend

The kitchen – the engine room of the house – was busier than on Christmas Eve, providing for the influx of refugees from the storm. Amanda, combining the role of chief engineer and ship's captain, issued a flurry of orders on the preparation of food and the regular supply of hot drinks. Lugg and Rupert were dispatched to scour the house for spare blankets, eiderdowns, and anything that would serve as a mattress for the guests who would be spending the night on the floor, though she had not yet thought through the exact sleeping arrangements. In truth she was putting off making such a decision as it may involve someone sharing a room with Lloyd Thursby, which she had no particular wish to impose on cold, hungry and tired travellers who had surely suffered enough that day. To be fair to the old gentleman, though, Lloyd had taken the influx of eight more orphans of the storm remarkably calmly, seemed happy to keep the fires stoked, and positively enthusiastic when it came to helping to distribute the Campions' liquid hospitality.

Mrs Thursby was put on bread-making duty and set to with a will, sleeves rolled up and hands moving through a cloud of flour as she pummelled enough dough for three large loaves. Amanda began to strip the Christmas turkey carcass of meat, wielding a carving knife with terrifying speed and skill, piling the bones into a large stainless-steel stockpot as the basis for a soup, on the assumption that once the scent of baking bread began to permeate the house it would stimulate the appetites of their guests.

It was as he was peeling onions and potatoes under her close supervision at the kitchen table that Albert and Amanda managed to have a *sotto voce* discussion about those guests.

'We really ought to find out a bit more about our temporary house guests whilst they are under our roof,' suggested Campion.

'Out of duty as their host, or simple nosiness?'

'A little bit of both. I cannot deny I am curious about them. Unexpected visitors at Christmas time are usually shepherds or wise men from the east bearing gifts.'

'If they were on their way to the shrines at Walsingham, there's a religious element to their journey which sort of fits with the season.'

'They could be pilgrims, you think?'

Amanda pouted her lips and dismissively blew a rogue hair out of her eyeline. 'My priority is feeding them, not interrogating them,' she said out of the corner of her mouth, 'but by all means give them the third degree under the guise of being a concerned host. It will amuse you if not them, and is bound to be more entertaining than Monopoly. You know Lugg becomes unbearable if he draws the Get Out of Jail Free card. Get him to quiz the pilgrims; that should make sure they don't outstay their welcome. Better still . . .' she lowered her voice to a whisper, '. . . get old Lloyd to chat them up, tell them grim realities of country life.'

Campion recoiled in mock horror but kept his voice low. 'Please, darling! We don't want to drive them back out into the blizzard, but you have given me the germ of an idea. We could almost treat it like a board game. We each engage with one or more of the pilgrims, get them to tell the story behind their interrupted journey and then we compare notes. Whoever discovers the most unusual tale wins.'

'That sounds slightly sinister, Albert, a bit like snooping.'

'Nonsense. We are concerned hosts showing a polite interest in our guests, and it's either that or Monopoly . . . or charades.'

'Anything but charades.' Amanda sighed. 'I suppose I get the rather prim elderly spinster because she's female.'

'Actually, I thought you might tackle the American Air Force. You have more common ground with those three wise men than anyone else. I thought Lugg should tackle our female visitor and Fisk, the driver. Rupert can chat up the reverend vicar, who looks as if he could give a good sermon, and I'll take the two loose cannons, no pun intended: the foreign gentleman who looks like a mad scientist and the one who bustles around like a clockwork doll playing the part of the absent-minded professor.'

'Just let me get them fed before we start,' conceded Amanda, 'and ask Lloyd if he wouldn't mind circulating with a few bottles to keep their glasses topped up.'

'I don't think I need to ask him.' Mr Campion winced as Mrs Thursby planted a bomb of bread dough from a great height on to the kitchen table and began to pummel it with some force.

'Keep an eye on Dad if he's anywhere near an open bottle,' she warned, showing that her hearing was more acute than the Campions had estimated. 'Mind you, it's coming up to his bedtime so he won't be much trouble for long.'

The Campions exchanged raised eyebrows and Amanda mouthed the question: *What time is it?*

'It's only seven thirty,' said Campion quietly. 'Let's give ourselves two hours to listen to the tales of our pilgrims, then compare notes.'

'Pilgrims?'

'Well, if they were heading to Walsingham, I think we can justifiably call them pilgrims. In a way it's a shame we are not on the road to Canterbury.'

Rupert Campion, should anyone ask such a thing of him, would always say that he hoped he took more after his mother than his father. If pressed, he would explain that for all his father's exploits, many of which had made the pages of the popular press and more the pages of the *Police Gazette*, it was his mother's determination, application and intelligence in succeeding in a profession thought unsuitable not just for a woman of her class, but any woman, which impressed him. Not that he had any interest in, or aptitude for, aeronautical engineering. In fact, his aversion to all things mathematical and general inability to make mechanical objects obey his commands were clearly traits inherited from his father.

Both parents, though taken somewhat by surprise, had supported his decision to study at an American university, Amanda perhaps the keener as she knew that Harvard was about to admit women to its famous business school, whilst Albert quipped that perhaps Rupert had chosen the wrong Cambridge and the light-hearted suggestion that he should study something more frivolous.

Rupert had yet to inform his parents that during his first Fall term (something his father insisted on calling Michaelmas) at university he had spent far more time infiltrating the amateur dramatic scene on campus and the semi-professional one in Boston than he had listening to lectures. He had proved a willing and receptive host for the acting bug thanks to the attention lavished upon him by every young female of his age (and a few older) who gushed excitedly over his English accent, whether he was trying to engage them in conversation or simply asking for directions or for advice on which was the nickel and which the dime. It was impossible for a nineteen-year-old young man, liberated by three thousand miles of ocean from familial responsibilities and supervision, to ignore such an onslaught of feminine approval, much of it aimed at recruiting him to suitably aristocratic roles on the amateur stage.

Naturally flattered, Rupert agreed – nervously at first – to tread the boards whenever a production called for the brief appearance of a stiff-backed butler or when a tousle-headed gay young thing had to come bounding through the French windows seeking a tennis partner. His accent, deportment and ability not to trip over the furniture, plus his natural reluctance to hog any limelight going, stood him in good stead with his fellow thespians; the males found him unthreatening, the females thought him sweet if not downright dishy.

At first he had reservations about his father's suggested 'game' involving Carterers' unexpected guests, thinking it rather intrusive if not downright rude. There again, the Campions had given food and shelter to eight complete strangers and surely they had a right to know something about those staying under their roof. And quite why he had drawn the priest in his father's allocation of human chess pieces, he was not sure, but at the back of his mind was the prospect that at some point in the future he might be called upon to play a vicar on stage, and chatting to one on a pilgrimage to the holy shrine of Our Lady at Walsingham might well be useful research.

His target, or victim – he was not sure which – was doing exactly what might be expected of him, circulating around the Campions' lounge, now a staging area for the shivering refugees, checking that his fellow travellers were as well as could be expected in the circumstances. Ministering to his congregation – was that the phrase? Rupert dismissed the thought. The reverend gentleman was simply showing Christian concern and, if there was any ministering to be done, surely it was down to him out of sheer politeness as the son of the house in which they had taken refuge.

'Can I get you anything, Father? It is Father, isn't it?'

The priest turned away from the fireplace where he had been comforting the white-haired foreigner Campion had called the mad scientist, who was hunched in a chair clutching his briefcase to his chest, as if drawing warmth from that rather than the fire. As he did so, the priest's overcoat fell open to reveal the standard black clerical uniform of dark suit, grey shirt and white dog collar, with only a thin brown cardigan added as an extra layer against the cold weather.

'To some of my parishioners I was Father, to others Vicar – as Anglo-Catholics we are fairly flexible. I believe that was behind your enquiry.'

'Can I get you anything, Father?' Rupert said quickly to cover his embarrassment. 'You must be freezing. I'm Rupert Campion, by the way; this is my parents' house.'

'For which we are all very grateful. I almost said it was a godsend – should I have? My name is Breck, by the way, Elis Breck.'

Rupert had inherited some of his father's skill in identifying regional accents, though this one was hardly difficult. 'I thought I detected a Welsh lilt in your voice. You are a long way from your parish.'

The priest smiled gently. 'It's a long time since I called anyone "boyo" and my parish was in Buckinghamshire, though I am no longer of it. And if you are still offering, a neat whisky would certainly aid my central heating.'

Rupert signalled as politely as he could without appearing to be summoning a waiter, and Lloyd Thursby snaked his way across the room holding a tray of bottles and glasses, keeping the tray and his own balance through sustained concentration as revealed by the tip of his tongue protruding from clenched lips.

He dispensed a large measure of Mr Campion's second-best single malt with appropriate reverence, having noted the priest's dog collar, bowed his head at the profuse thanks offered in return and then withdrew to find another deserving customer.

'A family retainer?' asked the Reverend Breck.

'No, *he* isn't,' said Rupert, 'just a neighbour. We thought he might get isolated by the storm so we brought him into the fold. His daughter-in-law is my mother's housekeeper, and his too, I suppose.'

'It was good of your parents to open their house as a refuge.'

'I don't think they thought twice about it, though we were not expecting arrivals by the coachload. Christmas time is pretty much open house here and they always host a party on New Year's Eve, complete with fireworks at midnight. You can see them for miles.'

'I suppose you can, Norfolk being so very flat, as Mr Coward wrote.'

'My father always misquotes the next line from that play as "There's no need to be unpleasant, Amanda" because my mother is called Amanda. Shall we sit?' He indicated an unoccupied sofa; unoccupied as most seats had been pulled into a semicircle around the fireplace. 'Unless you'd prefer to be near the fire.'

'This will do fine. I don't feel the cold like most, in fact I welcome it, and if you see me shivering, it's not a chill, it's a recurrent bout of malaria.'

'So you have spent time in the tropics?' Rupert's ears pricked up. Could this be a winning pilgrim's tale in the family's ad hoc party game? 'As a missionary?'

The priest studied his glass of whisky as he raised it to his mouth. 'No, not as a missionary, it was with the army, as a chaplain, during the war, in India and then Burma. Burma was the worst.'

'The Forgotten Army.'

'Yes, that was us, and ironically it is us who are still trying to forget.'

'Is that why you are making a pilgrimage to Walsingham?' Rupert probed.

The priest sipped more whisky and leaned back into the sofa, relaxing.

'Are you after my job, young man?'

'Excuse me?'

'I'm the one who is supposed to hear confessions. Don't look so surprised. Anglo-Catholic congregations still believe in the power of confession, though we don't make as much of a song and dance of it as our friends in Rome. There were even confessional boxes in my church until relatively recently.'

'You have left your church?'

'My parish, but never my church. I am retiring to Walsingham – and this is the point where you should say that I look nowhere near old enough to have to retire, and I would be duly flattered, but there are some forms of tiredness – of exhaustion – which don't always show in lines on the face.'

'So you are relocating rather than on a pilgrimage?' Rupert wondered if that might not count in the family's game, and immediately felt guilty for the thought as the Reverend Breck seemed a decent enough chap.

'I have made pilgrimages to Walsingham in the past, every year with a Mothers' Union outing. My late wife used to joke that I was their best customer for bottles of holy water. We had enough Walsingham Water to wash in, she used to say.'

Rupert felt another pang of guilt.

'After she passed, there was little to keep me in my parish, and I had made good friends among the community at Walsingham, so it seemed the ideal place to find peace and tranquillity in retirement. You must know it; it must be close, but in this weather . . .'

'I think you've fallen a good twenty-five miles short, I'm afraid.'

'Oh dear, still, the shrine of Our Lady has been there for over nine hundred years; it will be there when the snow melts. Have you visited it?'

'As a tourist rather than a pilgrim,' said Rupert sheepishly. 'My father swears by the Honeysuckle Ale sold in the Oxford Stores in the village there. I'm sorry, that sounded disrespectful.'

Father Breck raised his glass, either in a gesture of absolution or requesting a refill, Rupert was not sure.

'You really should go there,' he said after catching the eye of Lloyd Thursby, who was still floating around the room with his tray. 'It is a holy place in every sense, even for those without religious conviction. There is a sanctity about it which is good for the soul, though you would expect me to say that. A young man like you probably does not think his soul needs refreshing.'

'It is not something I have given much thought to.'

'Perhaps you should. I know I find it a great comfort, but then I am old and carry burdens I wish were lighter. You are young and can have few troubles. Girls, perhaps? Or your studies? I'm assuming you are at university somewhere.'

'In America actually, just finished my first term.'

'How interesting. You were there during the missile crisis in October? That must have been very frightening.'

'It was rather tense, I admit, with bomb shelters and air-raid sirens, but I had to keep a stiff upper lip.'

'Why did you think you needed to do that?'

'Funnily enough, because of my accent. Being British, everyone assumed I had gone through the London Blitz, which of course I had not, not having been born then, but I was expected to ooze steadfastness and resilience and not show fear.'

Rupert did not add, just as he had not told his parents, that his solid, very Britishness had proved a very successful attribute when dating skittish young American females who had a uniquely amorous interpretation of the phrase 'four-minute warning'.

'It is a noble thing to keep one's head when all around start to panic.'

'Oh, I don't know about noble. Isn't that what vicars do every day?'

The vicar smiled graciously, taking the compliment. 'It is expected of us, though it is not always easy.'

'Your presence must have been comforting for your fellow passengers on the coach. It must have been an awful journey.'

The smile twisted into a dismissive smirk. 'Should I have led them in prayer or organized some hymn singing? I did not have to, although I think one or two silent prayers were said when we hit your gatepost. Everyone was very calm considering the conditions, and frankly rather relieved when our American cousins took charge. By then we had all realized that our journeys had been badly interrupted. In my case, of course, it matters not a jot. As long as I get to Walsingham at some point, it is only my own retirement being delayed.'

He raised and emptied his glass in a minor toast to Rupert.

'But enough of me. Tell me about yourself, young man. I assume you're worried about your own travel arrangements.'

When Rupert stared at him in confusion, he added: 'You'll be anxious about getting back to your studies in America, won't you?'

'Oh yes, of course, but I'm sure London Airport will be kept clear and I don't fly until January the third.'

'That's only next week, so perhaps we should pray for a warm front. Tell me, what do you intend to do when you've finished your studies? What are you studying, by the way?'

'Economics, economic history, business law, accountancy, that sort of thing; all terribly dull.'

If Rupert was expecting the gentle, sympathetic and rather patronizing disagreement he usually got from adults, he was disappointed and somewhat shocked by the reaction of a man of the cloth.

'Good Lord, that does sound as dull as ditchwater! Do you really have ambitions to be a bean counter? A healthy young chap like you? Surely not.'

'Well, no . . . I . . .'

'And you the son of Albert Campion? Not only dull, but positively boring and so utterly *safe*.'

'You know my father?' said Rupert as the priest shook his head in despair.

'Not until he welcomed us in out of the snow and helped me off with my coat, but of course I've read about him over the years and all my friends in Walsingham regard him as one of Norfolk's favourite sons, at least since Nelson.'

'Please do not tell him that!' Rupert pleaded. 'And as for following in the footsteps of my dear father, I wouldn't know where to begin, and to be perfectly honest I doubt he could tell you where his footsteps led him or why he trod them in the first place, whatever they say in the newspapers.'

He kept his voice low, conscious of the fact that his father was across the room, having drawn up a chair so he could sit knee-to-knee and converse with the white-haired foreign gentleman who gave the impression that his briefcase was welded to his chest.

Appreciating the need for discretion, Breck also spoke quietly. 'It was what the newspapers did not print that intrigued me. When the name Campion featured, it was either in a story about what we might call "high society" or it was in connection with a court case or a police investigation. Yet there was never any indication of Mr Campion having any official position or commission. He seems to be some sort of shadow agent – an agent for law, justice and all things good, but always operating slightly in the wings. One might almost think he was some sort of spy; perhaps he still is.'

'Don't tell him that, either; he would have a seizure from laughing, but I admit he does seem to have had a colourful career. It would be a difficult act to follow, or even attempt to. I mean, where would the dutiful son start, assuming the proud father actually wanted to be emulated? I might add that Pa has never tried to push me down any particular career path.'

'I am sure he hasn't. He seems far too sensible to try and do that, but equally I am sure he would want you to have an exciting life. A start in the military, perhaps, or the police or the law, journalism at a pinch; somewhere where you could make your mark.'

Rupert took a breath and leaned in. 'Could I tell you something in complete confidence?'

'Of course, but on the basis that I am a guest in your home and bound by the rules of politeness rather than as, I take it, a more formal confession?'

'Oh, I don't think we're talking *sin* here.' Rupert grinned. 'It's just that I don't quite know how to break it to the family that I am seriously thinking of becoming an actor.'

Rupert had mentally rehearsed the possible reaction of both his father and mother to such an announcement, but could not in his wildest imaginings have anticipated the reaction of the stranger to whom he was confessing. The man, after all, was a priest, for goodness' sake.

'An *actor*?' The reverend gentleman almost spat the word. 'What on God's good earth put that idea in your head? I'm betting it was a female, for which I suppose allowances must be made given your age, but *really* . . . a more worthless, futile, ego-salving profession I cannot think of.'

'You don't think much of actors, then?' Rupert tried to keep the surprise out of his voice. He had never considered acting to be sinful, but perhaps the priest knew better.

'I think they're scum.'

'Come off it, Father, that's a bit harsh, isn't it?' Rupert tried to keep it light, although he feared he may have uncovered a streak of the Savonarola in the clergyman.

'You are quite right to berate me, young man. I should not generalize, not all actors are scum, but the one I am personally acquainted with certainly is.'

'One of your parishioners? If I am allowed to ask.'

The priest stared at the few drops of whisky left in his glass as he swirled them around, almost as if trying to hypnotize himself.

'Not one of my former flock, I am happy to say, but a man I knew in the war and fortunately have not seen since, at least not in the flesh, for if I had I doubt I would have been able to control myself.' His eyes flicked up and back to Rupert's face. 'I have shocked you. I am sorry.'

'You clearly hold strong opinions on the subject. How did this actor offend you?' Even as he spoke, Rupert was thinking that if the vicar's umbrage – though it seemed much stronger than mere umbrage – was the result of this 'actor' simply giving a poor performance in the chorus of *Oklahoma!* or even being a bad Hamlet, then the vicar was either mentally unstable or a frustrated theatre critic. Perhaps both; it would not be unknown. But no, this was something deeper, more serious.

'Are you now the confessor and I the supplicant?' asked the priest, though there was no twinkle in his rather sad eyes.

'Please . . . it is not really any of my business.'

'No, I have been rude and for that I offer an apology and an explanation for my outburst.'

'There really is no need.'

'My conscience instructs me otherwise and I have to obey it or I will be in trouble with my commanding officer.' He raised a forefinger from the hand still holding his glass, pointing upwards. 'Don't worry, it will not be a long confession and *He's* heard it all before.'

Without waiting for permission from above, the priest told his tale, as Rupert was to think of it; for receiving a confession from a priest must surely be way beyond the rules of the game his father had invented, if indeed there was a rulebook.

'In the war, while serving with the Fourteenth Army in Burma, I came across a man who was the very essence of cowardice. I do not mean someone who flinched under fire or was frightened when ordered into action – any sane person would experience fear fighting out there where the jungle was often more of a deadly enemy than the Japanese. I am talking of the sort of cowardice which deliberately puts others in harm's way, which he did on numerous occasions *and knew full well what he was doing.*

'A man more self-centred, more selfish of his own safety, I have never encountered. One of the Roman writers – Sallust, I think – said that a coward was more at risk in a battle than a brave man, but not this man. He made sure that brave men always went before him and took all the risk, and when the fighting got hot and close, which it often did, he was nowhere to be seen. If his absence was ever questioned, he had a ready excuse: a signal to answer, a wounded man to help, the need to find a better position, having to check the ammunition reserves. His excuses were legion and, if questioned, given with an arrogant confidence and a completely straight face. The man had not a scintilla of shame in his person. He was a disgrace.'

'I take it he was an officer,' Rupert said quietly.

'A captain, though goodness knows how, and it was a miracle one of his own men didn't put a bullet in his back.'

'Could you not report him somehow?'

'I tried, but I did not persist enough. I was not a front-line soldier, so of course I could not fully appreciate the military, the tactical decisions of an officer in the field.'

'So you were given the brush-off?'

'Yes, but very politely; I was a man of the cloth, after all.'

'But you've never forgotten, or forgiven, this captain?'

'I never thought it my place to forgive him and I thought I had managed to forget him, but he did not allow me to. You see that odious man had been an *actor* before the war and as soon as the war was over he established himself as a film star. In fact, he's become something of a stalwart in British films, especially war films. He has played the caring general who values his men above glory, the stoic captain of a torpedoed merchant ship, a commando, a fighter pilot and the commander of a submarine.

He has stormed beaches, roamed across deserts and even led missions behind Japanese lines, always noble, always brave, the exact opposite of his actual military experience. The total coward always playing the noble hero; he has even won awards for his performances and been presented to the Queen.

'Every time I see one of his films I think of the men who died to keep him safe in the jungle and I am consumed with anger. That is my sin, pure wrath at the very sight of the man. From that I seek respite, if not forgiveness, in Walsingham.'

For the want of anything more perceptive, Rupert said, 'I think I understand why you don't like actors,' but was saved from any further embarrassment by a touch on the shoulder from his mother.

She had emerged from Campion's study, where she had been talking with the three American airmen, and had stopped level with Rupert, though the real object of her visit was engaged in animated conversation with the white-bearded foreign gentleman over by the Christmas tree which, had it not been bedecked with baubles and fairy lights, gave the impression that it wanted to embrace the pair in its branches.

'Albert! Could I have a word – in the kitchen, please?'

As she spoke, Amanda squeezed Rupert's shoulder in an invitation to join them, which he did after a polite 'Excuse me' to Reverend Breck.

Lugg appeared with the stealth of a ghost who required no invitation but one determined to call the meeting to order. 'What's up, then? Found out summat juicy?'

'The telephone's dead,' said Amanda solemnly. 'The snow must have brought the line down. We really are completely cut off.'

FIVE

The Tale of the Pious Postmistress

Well aware that Lloyd Thursby and his unstoppable daughter-in-law were floating in and out of the kitchen victualling the unexpected guests, Mr Campion was studiously calm at the news and concentrated on nibbling the crust of a mince pie without shedding pastry crumbs down his shirt front.

'Such things happen in these conditions, my dear; I wouldn't worry too much about it. After all, who were we going to call? The AA are unlikely to send out one of their motorcyclists in this, even for you who always returns those polite salutes the riders make when they see the badge. Similarly, police, fire brigade and ambulance will all be terribly busy if not snowbound. Have I missed anyone? I suppose we could try the coastguard at a pinch.'

'I was chatting to those nice American boys who were trying to get to Marham,' said Amanda, 'and thought I'd do the decent thing and let the base know where they were sheltering from the storm. I wouldn't want their commanding officers to think they'd deserted or anything.'

Lugg had been innocently counting the number of mince pies cooling on a metal rack hot off Mrs Thursby's production line and, when he was satisfied with the total, felt he ought to contribute to the unscheduled family conference.

'I thought Marham was an RAF base. What're Yanks doing there?'

Campion and Amanda exchanged looks before Campion answered.

'The American Air Force has been all over East Anglia since the war. They were, I believe, on our side, and Marham hosted some of their big bombers, B17s and B29s; what they called Flying Fortresses and Super Fortresses, I think. Is that right, dear? You're the expert.'

Amanda nodded. 'They flew on the famous Operation Ruby from there, trying out experimental giant concrete-busting bombs on submarine pens in Heligoland and North Germany. Without much success as I recall.'

'That's as may be,' said Lugg with what he thought was perfect logic, 'but that was during the war, wasn't it?'

'Actually it wasn't,' said Campion. 'It was 1946, almost a year into peacetime.'

A startled Rupert, already distracted by the priest's tale of wartime anger, was sure he had misheard. 'We were bombing Germany a year after the war *ended*? That can't be right.'

'It wasn't an act of war, son,' Campion said benignly, 'it was, ironically, part of the reconstruction programme. You see, those U-boat pens built by the Nazis were so well constructed that civilian engineers and contractors trying to develop the ports simply could not budge them, so the air force offered to help. It also gave them an opportunity to try out some new toys. I'm not sure it worked very well, though, as some of those submarine bases are still intact even now.'

'And the Yanks are still here,' grumbled Lugg, 'playing with their toys.'

'Three of them are here, literally,' said Amanda. 'Here in this house, I mean, so we'd better work out where everyone is going to sleep.'

What had attracted Campion to Carterers and persuaded him to buy it, apart from its isolated and therefore relatively safe situation, were two physical attributes of the house's interior. Firstly, the fact that all the rooms on the ground floor, including the kitchen and what was to be sequestered as his study-cum-library, had unusually high ceilings, which made him think, rather dreamily, that they could accommodate a really large Christmas tree, just the sort of consideration which would occur to a new father establishing a family home. The second feature which attracted him was the fact that it had seven bedrooms which, in a fit of whimsical enthusiasm (Amanda called it 'idiocy'), he declared meant a different bedroom every night of the week.

Now, as the four of them stood around a kitchen table groaning with trays of mince pies and loaf tins throbbing with Mrs Thursby's rising bread dough, they looked like four generals considering strategy over a battleground map. Only one of them, however, was giving the orders when it came to troop dispositions.

'If Rupert and Lugg don't mind bunking together and Lloyd is happy sleeping in an armchair in the lounge . . .'

'Oh, 'e won't mind at all,' Mrs Thursby chipped in from the sink where she was elbow-deep in washing up. 'Lloyd's a regular for kipping in front of the fire on a winter's night.'

'Good, then he can be in charge of keeping the fires going all night to stop our guests from freezing.' Amanda splayed the fingers of her left hand and began to tick off her orders for the coming night. 'We have spare blankets, pillows, sleeping bags and two ex-army camp beds, so all those will have to be located and allocated. What I suggest is that our female guest gets one of the bedrooms.'

'I don't mind sharing,' offered Mrs Thursby, who fortunately did not hear Lugg whisper, 'She might.'

'No need, Mrs T, you can stay where you are. We can manage. I think the Americans should camp downstairs around the Christmas tree.'

'Like Christmas presents waiting to be unwrapped?' asked Mr Campion. 'This isn't some strange fantasy of yours, Amanda?'

'Don't be ridiculous. They won't mind roughing it, they're servicemen. That leaves us with three bedrooms and four sleepers. That shouldn't be a problem. Any suggestions?'

'From my limited interaction with them,' said Campion, 'I can only speak for the Dutch gentleman, whose name is De Vries, by the way. I think he'd feel more secure in a room to himself. What's the score on the vicar, Rupert?'

'Seems reasonably sane, and surely wouldn't complain about sharing a room out of Christian kindness, as long as it's not with an actor.'

'What an interesting qualification.' Campion raised an eyebrow in his son's direction. 'It sounds as if Rupert has heard a pilgrim's tale—'

'Your silly parlour game will have to wait, Albert.' Amanda was not to be distracted from her role as quartermaster general. 'If the vicar doesn't mind doubling up with that silly little man who simply cannot stop talking, then your Dutchman can have a bedroom to himself, and I suggest we put the coach driver by himself in the room Lloyd had. He looks shattered.'

'You're absolutely right, my dear,' agreed Campion, 'he's almost dead on his feet.'

'Now Rupert, come upstairs with me to sort out as many dry socks and pullovers as we can find and get extra supplies for the downstairs bathroom. Mrs T, once you've got the bread in the oven, can you put the old clotheshorse in front of the Aga so our guests can dry their wet things and you two' – for lack of a swagger stick, she pointed a finger at Campion and Lugg – 'bring in more logs and coal from the tack room and keep our guests calm if not happy. Have you considered doing anything about the bus or coach which is probably blocking our drive out there?'

'I did consider it, darling, and almost immediately dismissed the idea of struggling through the blizzard – a blizzard still raging, by the sound of it – to assess the damage to vehicle and my treasured gateposts. There is absolutely nothing we can do until daylight and then probably very little. Unless we had a spare red lamp or two to put out there to warn other drivers, I don't think there is anything useful we could do. Fortunately, there will not be many other drivers out there tonight.'

Amanda accepted her husband's logic. 'Probably best to batten down the hatches and stay inside. Rupert, let's go and raid your father's sock drawer and thin out his collection of old jumpers, whilst he keeps our guests entertained by handing out the chocolates and candy canes on the Christmas tree.'

Mr Campion positively beamed. 'My turn to be Santa! Just the ticket, if I'm not pinching Lugg's job, that is.'

The fat man shrugged his shoulders as if adjusting a fully laden milkmaid's yoke. ''Long as it stops you doin' yer magic tricks.'

'Anything but that,' agreed Amanda. 'Those poor travellers have suffered enough.'

Elbowed out of the way by Mrs Thursby, as all men loitering in a working kitchen should be, so that she could concentrate on bread production, Campion tested Lugg on his encounter with the sole female orphaned by the storm.

'I saw you snuggling up to our lonely lady sitting by the fire. I was tempted to sashay over there with a sprig of mistletoe.'

Lugg's expression suggested that the season of goodwill to all men, or at least ones who made such salacious suggestions, was well and truly over.

'She's a very nice spinster lady, I'll have you know,' he said haughtily, 'and on our brief acquaintance, I reckon she wouldn't hurt a fly and probably call a policeman if a goose needed saying boo to.'

'You sound to have got on like the proverbial house on fire, so what's her story? To be honest, I didn't catch her name if she offered it, but I did spot the crucifix around her neck, so I'm guessing she's a genuine pilgrim trying to get to Walsingham.'

'That's just about the gist of it,' Lugg admitted. 'She didn't have much of a story to tell.'

'I'm sure you could make something up, something juicy.'

But Lugg, for once, could not be tempted into too much embellishment, and simply laid out what facts he had been freely given with only minimal speculation.

The lady in question, he guessed, was on the plus side of forty-five, though of course he had not been crass enough to ask. When he had introduced himself as Magersfontein Lugg, she had smiled and said that was an interesting name, though it did rather date him, which was undeniable. She had responded with an icy handshake – her gloves were drying by the fire – which meant Lugg could observe that she wore no rings and thus mentally put a 'miss' in front of the name she offered, Florence Pounder.

Miss Pounder volunteered the information that she was the postmistress of a small village in Devon and had used the opportunity of the Christmas break, now that all the cards and parcels had been delivered, to take some much overdue leave and make a pilgrimage to Walsingham as her Christmas present to herself. It would be the first time she had ventured out of Devon since the war and it had been something she had been promising herself for many years, though she had not counted on the journey being quite so eventful.

When she seemed reluctant, or too shy, to offer anything more personal, Lugg had asked her if she had bonded in any way with her fellow passengers. Possibly because there were no other females on the charabanc, which might have laid her open to charges of jealousy or bitchiness, she was very open and forthcoming in her assessment of her fellow pilgrims, even though she knew none of their names and had exchanged no more than a polite nod with any of them.

Apart from the back of his neck, she had not paid the driver much attention, apart from saying the occasional silent prayer that he kept the coach on the road as they ploughed through the snow, until he had relinquished the steering wheel to the young American and announced that they were going to try for Marham. It was then fairly clear that the driver was a nervous wreck, a classic case of battle fatigue, and it was a relief to have a younger, keener pair of eyes in the cockpit in those conditions. She was sure the others shared her view and certainly no one objected to the takeover by the US Air Force. In fact, they had probably forgotten the Americans were on board as they had occupied the back seat, but until the takeover had kept themselves to themselves, talking quietly and not interacting with the other passengers which, come to think of it, was not at all like Americans abroad as they were usually very friendly and often rather loud.

She had had high hopes that the priest might prove an interesting travelling companion and that they might be on the same spiritual journey, but he showed no interest in mixing with his fellow passengers, sat by himself and kept his face to the window though he could not have seen anything. Perhaps the sight of the snow blurring the window like a television set when transmissions finish hypnotized him, or perhaps he was praying. It was odd that he did not try to comfort those on board as the journey became obviously more hazardous and they became more nervous.

The pilgrim who seemed oblivious to the weather was the strange little man who said his name was Professor something-or-other, and initially Miss Pounder had politely responded to his attempts to strike up a conversation. Long before the storm hit, in fact possibly before they were clear of Victoria Coach Station, she had realized that the 'professor', if he really was one, was not after a sociable chat, rather he was seeking an audience. Whatever his subject was – and it seemed to be a heady brew of history, archaeology, genealogy, palaeography, folklore, mythology, and several other 'ologies' that she may have missed – he followed it zealously. He was obsessed with the legend of Hereward the Wake; or perhaps that was his name. He spoke so quickly that words sprayed from him like random jets of water from a leaky garden hose, never giving his actual thoughts time to catch up. Fortunately, the professor's speed of delivery was such that he never gave the person he was addressing even the slimmest chance to formulate a reply, and so Miss Pounder adopted the successful tactic of nodding in a caring but noncommittal way until her orator had run out of breath, at which point she took a prayer book from her handbag and buried her nose in it. The hint was eventually taken, though it was a good five minutes before the professor admitted defeat, opened a book of his own – literally, he pointed out that he had written it – and fell into a sulky silence.

The enigmatic foreigner, Miss Pounder thought, was probably a Dutchman. A German would have been more polite, a Pole more friendly and a Frenchman obviously French. He reminded her of the eccentric, absent-minded but brilliant scientist figure often found in low-budget science-fiction films, but perhaps that was being unfair as she had had no direct communication with him at all. For his part, he seemed content to keep himself very much to himself and she could not remember him talking to anyone at all. He had appeared unconcerned when the coach deviated from its normal route, not even when it came to a sudden and rather dramatic stop. The only thing which seemed to concern him was that vintage, soft-leather briefcase which he clutched tightly to his chest as if his life depended upon it.

'A very observant lady,' said Mr Campion when Lugg had concluded his report.

'Dunno about that. I'm no wiser about her than I was this time yesterday when I'd never heard of her.'

'I'm not sure I am, but she's certainly no fool. She pegged De Vries for a Dutchman without exchanging a word with him, and she refused to suffer the verbose and stupefyingly boring professor chappie, who really is called Hereward as it turns out. She also made some good observations about the American contingent, as to them being unnaturally quiet.'

'You mean like the dog that didn't bark in the night?'

'Something like that, and I'm impressed with the reference. Your Miss Pounder also got the poor Mr Fisk spot on. She did say "battle fatigue", didn't she? I think that summed him up, though after the day he'd had, you can hardly blame him. It was a curious choice of phrase, though. Makes me wonder where a spinster postmistress from Devon encountered it.'

Lugg's forehead crumpled into a frown. 'You've got a picture of her as some sort of Miss Marple, haven't you? The little old lady who sits quietly doing her knitting but keeps her ears flapping to pick up all the gossip until she can finger the villain.'

'My, my, another literary reference,' Campion laughed, 'but the only villain worth naming at the moment is the snow piling up outside. Come to think of it, if Miss Pounder didn't spot *you* as the villainous type, then she's not much of a Miss Marple.'

Lugg blew a rude noise through compressed lips. 'She's a decent enough sort; we should leave her be. I reckon she has hidden depths.'

'Based on what?'

'When you told me to chat her up, she was wet and shivering and I thought I'd break the ice with a warm drink, so I took her a mug of hot Bovril.'

'Not the normal *aperitivo* in most boy-meets-girl scenarios,' Campion observed drily. 'How did she take it?'

'Just my point – how she takes it. Once she saw what it was, she asked if we had any vodka! Said hot Bovril and vodka was the only drink for weather like this. Now where did a spinster postmistress from Devon learn that?'

As Amanda and Rupert dispensed dry clothing, sleeping bags and blankets and allocated sleeping accommodation to their grateful visitors, Lloyd Thursby continued to circulate, if somewhat unsteadily, with a tray of warming beverages, and Lugg ventured out to the tack room, allowing in a gust of snowflakes as he did so, to return with both arms stacked with logs for the fire, which produced a curse from Mrs Thursby on the subject of letting the cold in whilst she was baking.

Although keen to get ahead in the game he had invented by securing the most interesting pilgrim's tale, Mr Campion could not help himself from drifting back into the kitchen on a regular basis, attracted by the deeply comforting scent of baking bread. He had always felt it was a wholesome smell which, if it could be bottled, would be used by estate agents to spray around the kitchens of particularly difficult-to-sell properties just before prospective purchasers arrived for a viewing. Never mind the damp and dry rot, the resident ghosts from all the murders which have taken place here and the rats which only come out at night, just inhale that warm smell of homeliness.

'Working the room' as Americans would have put it, he had noted Rupert and the priest deep in quiet, head-to head conversation; a confessional which might end in a blessing from one side or the other? For the sake of the game, he certainly hoped so. He was less sure that Amanda was learning the innermost secrets of the handsome Americans who were now their temporary lodgers, although they seemed very interested in her. She seemed to be giving them a lecture on the history of the house and, by extension – by pointing to the various paintings and framed photographs on the wall – on the area and its history and connections to various air forces and things aeronautical. They were naturally fascinated by the numerous pictures documenting Amanda's achievements with Alandel Aeroplanes, and if they were surprised or shocked that a female could achieve so much in a very male environment, they had the good manners not to show it.

He had never had any qualms about turning Lugg loose on the lonely postmistress, whom he now knew to be Miss Pounder, although he had initially catalogued her as a librarian or possibly a teacher in some village infants' school. He had long ago recognized the fat man's ability to get along with members of the opposite sex of all ages and most classes, unless they attempted to talk down to him or were magistrates; being both was naturally the most dangerous of combinations.

For his own part, Campion had breezed over to introduce himself to the white-bearded foreign gentleman who had never, since crossing the snowy threshold of Carterers, allowed the briefcase he clutched to slip from his chest. He held it there as if it contained a hot-water bottle, which perhaps it did, and on a night like this, Campion could hardly blame him.

Aside from exchanging names – his being Fred, just Fred, not

Frederick, de Vries – Campion learned that the man came from a place called Harlingen in the Netherlands and was travelling to Walsingham because he had 'an interest in the shrine there' but that seemed the sum of personal information freely available. He was an odd figure, Campion decided, and not just because he was nursing a battered and very wet briefcase. His steel-rimmed glasses and full-length black leather coat could well have come from a theatrical costumier who supplied extras playing Gestapo officers in a standard British war film. But facially, Fred de Vries was nobody's image of a Gestapo man, unless he was auditioning for the role of a Gestapo man's kindly Bavarian clockmaker uncle.

The white hair and luxuriant beard made him look older than he probably was, but Campion knew he was of an age where he was in danger of assuming everyone he met was younger than himself. De Vries certainly was, though he could tell by how much because the beard and long hair were an effective disguise which, after a shave and a haircut (and possibly the use of hair dye), could be abandoned and a dapper young man would appear.

Whatever his age, the Dutchman had little to say for himself, which Campion thought unusual. Surely the foreign visitor had every right to complain about the British weather and the way the whole country stuttered to a complete stop at the first fall of a snowflake; in the case of the coach he was travelling on, a sudden and rather violent stop. Perhaps he was being ultra civil or simply stoic, but forthcoming he was certainly not.

The same could not be said of Mr Campion's other 'target' that evening.

'Henderson. Hereward. Professor.' The little man enunciated each word as if talking into a Dictaphone as he offered a handshake, his piggy eyes gleaming and his short ginger moustache bristling.

Campion bit back the urge to ask 'Professor of what?' as he was sure the man was quivering to tell him.

'Campion, Albert,' he said politely. 'My wife and I are happy to provide refuge for you storm-tossed pilgrims.'

'Oh, I am not a pilgrim. Well, not in a religious sense, though I am on a pilgrimage in search of knowledge. It is a lifelong quest rather than a single act of devotion.'

In his long and varied career, Mr Campion had found himself at many a cocktail party or official reception where the most dangerous thing a person could say was 'You must tell me all about it', and this seemed exactly that sort of perilous occasion. Unfortunately the professor, if such he was, gave his host no time to take evasive action.

'As you will no doubt have guessed, my area of research concentrates on one of the region's great local heroes.'

'Lord Nelson?' Campion offered, wary of being dragged into the man's orbit.

'No, no, worthy figure though he was. My name should have given it away, for I did not introduce myself as Horatio Henderson.'

For a split second, Mr Campion was tempted to tease the man by claiming he knew of no famous Hendersons other than Arthur, the Labour politician and peace campaigner from the 1930s, but that might only prompt another lecture in addition to the one he felt sure he was about to receive.

'Hereward? You mean Hereward the Wake?'

'The very same.' The man nodded, reminding Campion of a pugnacious bank manager whose explanation of the words 'no more funds' to a particularly stupid account holder had finally sunk home.

'Hardly a local hero, I would have said. The legend puts him over Ely way and in the Fens.' Even as he spoke, Mr Campion's eyes swept around the room until he located his wife holding the attention of all three American airmen. He could not tell what she was saying, but he was certain it would not be about the adventures of an Anglo-Saxon warrior's futile resistance against William the Conqueror nine hundred years ago.

'Hereward hailed from Bourne in Lincolnshire and certainly his most famous exploit was the siege of Ely in 1071, but it was not his only claim to fame, or should I say infamy? There is much little-known material in the *Liber Eliensis* chronicle written by the monks of Ely and Crowland. Have you read it?'

'I'm afraid not.'

'Well, it's not translated, so you would have to brush up on your Latin, but it gave me enough clues and leads to follow to map Hereward's rather colourful career. Did you know he was a bank robber?'

'I didn't even know they had banks back then,' said Campion, now imagining the professor as a medieval miser hoarding groats and pennies. 'Oh dear, is that my wife signalling me?'

If Amanda had been, it would have been by the slightest of movements of her eyebrows, but fortunately Hereward's namesake had not noticed.

'Of course there were no banks in the eleventh century, but there were monasteries and religious house aplenty, which was where the wealthy deposited their wealth for safekeeping, usually in the form of silver plate and jewels. Which made them prime targets for brigands and raiders.'

'You mean like Vikings?' Campion said vaguely, stretching his neck in the direction of his wife, hoping to catch her eye.

'Interesting that you should say that.'

'Was it? Oh dear.'

'Not only interesting, but rather astute of you.'

'I am so sorry—'

'No need to apologize for making such a crucial observation, dear sir.'

'I meant I am sorry, but I feel I really must go and rescue my wife from those handsome young colonials.'

In Campion's world, the professor would have reacted in one of two ways. He could have either nodded politely and deferred to his host's marital obligations with good grace, or clammed up and sulked furiously for being unseated from his hobby horse.

Hereward Henderson adopted a third course. He simply continued talking and followed his host across the room like an affectionate gun dog.

'You see, Hereward came from good Viking stock, so you might say that raiding and pillaging were in his blood, therefore it was quite logical for him to make a beeline for a place like Walsingham.'

'Amanda . . .' Campion whispered loudly, trying to attract his wife's attention without success. She was deep in conversation with the staff sergeant, the other two airmen completing a semi-circular wall of protection round her.

'I am hoping to find evidence to support my theory . . .' Henderson droned on.

'That Hereward made a pilgrimage to the shrine at Walsingham?'

Campion threw the remark over his shoulder as a bone to the irritating man dogging him as he came up to Amanda's impromptu seminar group. But it was not his arrival which caused the nearest American to turn sharply and glare at them, but Henderson's reply, delivered with a mocking laugh.

'Highly unlikely! Hereward's natural inclination would be to appeal to the Norse god Thor!'

The nearest American swung around as if stung.

'What the hell . . .?'

The angry expression on the younger man's face succeeded where Mr Campion had failed in damming the professor's flow.

'The professor here was telling me of his research into history, ancient history,' Campion said, feeling there was a need to calm troubled waters, though he was not sure why. 'I'm sure you'd find it fascinating.'

'Hey, we're keen to learn. Sorry if Oscar here sounded rude just now, but we Americans don't have as much history as you guys.' The staff sergeant also seemed keen to smooth things over, and added, 'And Oscar's had a hard shift driving that bus.'

'And driving it into my treasured gateposts, I understand,' Campion said with a smile.

The airman called Oscar looked Campion in the eyes. 'Wouldn't have happened if you guys drove on the right side of the road.'

'That's exactly what I say every time I knock an onion-seller off his bike when motoring through France. Now, I really must drag my wife away from you as we have urgent domestic business to consider in the kitchen.' He deliberately ignored Amanda's 'We do?' expression. 'I am sure Professor Henderson here will keep you amused.'

'Well, if you gentlemen . . .' was all Campion heard as he had linked an arm through Amanda's and was waltzing her towards the kitchen, but he had no doubt that Henderson would have plenty to say.

'Is that little man really going to amuse them?' Amanda whispered out of the side of her mouth.

'Amuse, yes; entertain, no,' said Campion once they were in the kitchen, breathing in the warm smell of bread as Mrs Thursby decanted loaf after loaf from the Aga. 'I fear I may have drawn the short straw in my choice of pilgrim for our little parlour game.'

'The game you invented in a moment of madness? Serves you right.'

'It probably does. The one I thought looked like the absent-minded professor turns out to be a tight-lipped Dutchman who is giving absolutely nothing away, and the one who looks like a Rotary Club treasurer claims to be a professor and won't stop talking.'

'Professor of what?'

'I didn't like to ask in case it punctured his illusion.'

'Then it looks as if I am the hot favourite in our pilgrim game. What was the prize, by the way?'

'We play simply for the honour of it, rather like when we play Scotland at football. What is so interesting about your Americans?'

Amanda moved casually until she was hovering over a hot loaf resting on a circular trivet. When she was sure Mrs Thursby was not looking, she picked up the loaf, turned it over, and with a fist knocked twice on its flat bottom. Impressed, she quickly replaced it and turned back to her husband.

'Distance, that's my advantage. Chaucer might have had a pilgrim from Bath, but I've got three from much more exotic places. The sergeant comes from Texas, one of his men is from Santa Fé and the other from New York. Now, you have to admit, that's pretty impressive when it comes to distance travelled to get to little old Walsingham.'

'But they were not going to Walsingham, were they?'

'Well, they were on the pilgrim charabanc and they know all about Walsingham and its history. Apparently it was our American allies who held a mass in the priory grounds in May 1945 to celebrate the end of the war, the first Catholic mass since the Reformation.'

'Nothing lasts any more,' Campion said with an exaggerated sigh, 'but that is quite an interesting entry in our little game.'

They were disturbed by the sound of a throat being discreetly but pointedly cleared. Fred de Vries, the Dutchman still clutching his briefcase high on his chest, almost as if trying to cover it with his beard, stood in the kitchen doorway.

'Excuse me, Mr and Mrs Campion,' he said formally, 'do you have a safe in your home?'

'Only a fireproof document box really.'

Long experience with Lugg had taught Campion to be cautious when discussing safes with strangers.

'Then do you, perhaps, possess a firearm?'

Campion and Amanda exchanged glances, which Campion hoped expressed the notion that he now had an advantage when it came to pilgrims' tales.

SIX
The Tale of the Dutch Diptych

If Mr Campion was wary about disclosing the location of the small fireproof safe he did indeed possess to a complete stranger, he was definitely and firmly set against discussing any firearms he may or may not own with anyone short of a magistrate with a fistful of warrants.

'That was a curious request, Mr De Vries. Do you have something which needs securing, or is your person in need of defending and, if so, from whom?' Campion asked his visitor, having guided him into his study, closed the door and taken up a commanding position behind his writing desk. De Vries had no option but to stand sheepishly in front of the desk, adopting the role of the nervous schoolboy called to the headmaster's office; precisely the scenario Mr Campion was going for.

'I realize that what I ask is an imposition, and as an unwanted guest in your home I am in no position to ask it, but ask I must.'

'Unexpected guests, not unwanted,' said Campion politely. 'We are happy to be a sheltered port in this particular storm, but have you, perhaps, brought an additional storm with you?'

When the Dutchman did not offer an answer, even though his white bushy beard quivered as if he was about to, Mr Campion pointed an accusatory finger at the leather briefcase still firmly clamped to his visitor's chest.

'I am guessing that what is exercising you is in that case, the case which has not left your grasp since you crossed our threshold. What is in there, Mr De Vries?'

'You are not going to believe me.'

'Oh, I'm very gullible, Mr De Vries. Just ask my wife.'

Fred de Vries began his tale with two apologies. First, for his English – which was totally unnecessary as it was impeccable – and secondly in case he appeared to be lecturing his host on segments of English history with which he would clearly be very familiar. Mr Campion had the good grace to acknowledge the Dutchman's needless concern on that score whilst wondering if there was a Dutch equivalent of the old adage that grandmothers should not be taught to suck eggs. Even so, he was slightly surprised that his chosen pilgrim had a tale which spanned quite so much history.

He was aware that the origin of the holy shrine at Walsingham lay in a vision experienced by the then lady of the manor, Richeldis de Faverches, in or around 1061, at least according to a ballad recorded in a book printed some four hundred years later. Lady Richeldis's vision was of the house in Nazareth where the Virgin Mary was visited by the angel Gabriel, there to make a rather important announcement. Filled with religious fervour, the lady of the manor (Campion vaguely remembered that she was a widow, which explains why the lord of the manor had little say in the matter) ordered the building of a replica house to the exact measurements, conveniently provided by an angelic surveyor, as the one in Nazareth, or at least in her vision. The house soon became a chapel of worship, attracted some early pilgrims and was adopted by Augustinian canons who established a priory there. With papal approval and the backing of the church, Lady Richeldis's holy house became one of the most-visited shrines in medieval England.

At some point in the thirteenth century, a fine wooden statue of 'Our Lady of Walsingham' – Mary and the baby Jesus – was placed next to the altar in the chapel, attracting the veneration of even more pilgrims and not just from God-fearing Englishmen and -women. The Dutch (naturally) philosopher and theologian Erasmus described the shrine as 'dimly lit by tapers and scintillating with jewels' and even Henry VIII walked a 'holy mile' barefoot (Mr Campion did not know this) to visit it.

The king's barefoot pilgrimage might have done wonders for his soul at the time, but it did not prevent him, a few years later, from breaking with Rome, dissolving all the monasteries and sequestering their assets, which included the statue of Our Lady of Walsingham. The destruction of the original shrine, and the absence of pilgrims for more than three hundred years, is well recorded, and legend has it that the king's commissioners took the oak statue of Our Lady to the home of Thomas Cromwell, where it was burned in his garden in Lambeth on 14 July 1538.

Mr Campion sensed there was a 'but' on the way, and he was not wrong.

It was, however, just possible that devout local Catholics had spirited away the statue before Cromwell's bailiffs descended on Walsingham. Such a thing had happened elsewhere, in Ipswich for example, where a similar statue, almost certainly following the fashion set by Walsingham, known as Our Lady of Ipswich, was rescued in the nick of time by a band of good Catholic sailors and smuggled to Italy where, although now known as Our Lady of Grace, it is still revered in the basilica of Nettuno, south of Rome. (And just round the corner along the coast from Anzio, though Mr Campion refrained from offering this information in case it disrupted the Dutchman's tale, for another qualification was clearly on its way.)

There was also an ongoing debate about the provenance of a rather battered wooden statue of the Holy Lady and Child, which had been discovered in the dusty bowels of the Victoria & Albert Museum, misfiled as having come from Langham near Colchester in Essex rather than the parish of Langham in Norfolk, only a few miles from Walsingham where it could, conceivably, have been hidden from King Henry's army of looters.

Fortunately, we have some idea of what the statue looked like (Mr Campion was unsure whether he should acknowledge this blessing), as its image was reproduced on the official medieval seal of Walsingham Priory, which survives on several documents. Sadly, the noble Erasmus had described it as 'a little image remarkable neither for its size, material or workmanship', but still, its fate is undecided.

Mr Campion judged it the appropriate moment to prove he had been listening.

'The mystery being was the statue of the Madonna and Child destroyed by Protestants in 1538 or rescued by Catholics and hidden away since?'

'There is no mystery about it,' said De Vries.

'Don't tell me, you have it about your person!' Campion exclaimed. 'Hence your request for armed security. But surely not in that briefcase you seem so attached to. It would have to be a very small statue, as I can see no unsightly bulge.'

The Dutchman did not answer immediately and, after moving the briefcase until it was safely tucked into his left armpit, he removed his rimless spectacles and breathed on the lenses as a prelude to polishing them. Mr Campion knew the tactic well enough as he often employed it himself in order to buy himself 'thinking time' when challenged with a delicate, or indelicate, question. What he had not expected, though he was terribly impressed by it, was the way De Vries used his long white beard, or at least the flowing bottom half, as a cleaning cloth. It was a good trick which made the Dutchman look even more like a rather jolly but very eccentric Cambridge don and, for a moment, a very brief moment, Campion thought it could be something which might amuse Amanda, but then it would involve all the irritation, quite literally, of growing a beard.

Once his spectacles were back in place, De Vries transferred the briefcase to the nursing position against his chest, hugging it more tightly than any baby should be cuddled.

'Of course I do not have the statue – no one does any more. What I have is proof of its fate, and that is what needs protecting.'

'Proof that Thomas Cromwell threw it on a bonfire more than four hundred years ago? If it was carved from seasoned oak, it would probably have burned for a long time, but burn it would. Are you saying you salvaged a few charred bits of it?'

'You are misunderstanding my meaning, deliberately so I think,' De Vries said sternly, the jolly professor having been replaced by a strict policeman. 'I carry proof of the burning of the Walsingham Madonna, illustrative proof.'

'A photograph?' Campion immediately bit his tongue. 'I apologize, that was uncalled for, not to mention ridiculous.'

De Vries seemed neither humiliated nor offended.

'Not a photograph, of course, but the next best thing: a painting by an eyewitness, the famous painter Jacob Suycker.'

'Who?'

'Clearly not as famous as I thought.' De Vries really had got the sardonic policeman off pat. 'He came from my hometown of Harlingen, where we are very proud of him, and more people would know of him had not most of his paintings been destroyed in the great fire of Haarlem in 1576.'

Mr Campion adopted what he hoped was a suitably sympathetic expression but, if the Dutchman appreciated it, he did not let it interrupt his flow.

'Haarlem suffered many great fires in its history, and that one destroyed a third of the city: houses, churches, warehouses and many, many works of art, including much of the work of Jacob Suycker. He was a painter in an age of great painters and he worked for a time in England. As a good Catholic, he despaired at your king's Reformation and the vandalism and theft which came with it and, as it happens, was in London in 1538 and saw the statue of Our Lady of Walsingham brought there.'

Campion allowed his face to light up as if he was enjoying a revelation of his own. 'And your Dutch master did what he did best and painted it!'

'Better than that! Jacob Suycker painted its destruction!'

'How is that better?'

'Because it confirms once and for all the fate of the statue. Suycker was there, in Lambeth, when the Madonna was burned, and he painted an eyewitness account of the martyrdom of a venerated icon, as he saw it. I told you he was a good Catholic.'

'Don't tell me you have a four-hundred-year-old painting rolled up in that briefcase of yours?'

De Vries gave a snort of derision, his white whiskers fluffing out angrily.

'That would be ridiculous, *Meneer* Campion, but I do have something equally valuable.' He patted his briefcase gently. 'Something which needs protecting.'

Campion was torn between wishing his visitor would get on with it and genuine curiosity.

'I was not completely honest with you earlier,' he said. 'I do have a safe, though not a big one, which could offer some sort of sanctuary for your . . . image? Would that be an accurate description?'

He did not add that the safe in question was no more two inches away from his left leg, hidden behind a false cupboard door in the knee-hole of his desk. Mr De Vries was, after all, still a stranger under his roof, and a strange one with a strange tale at that.

At last the Dutchman relaxed his stranglehold on his briefcase and made to open it. He produced, very carefully, and as delicately as if handling a newly hatched chicken, a rectangular parcel bound in what appeared to be a red silk scarf. Once that wrapping had been removed, again gingerly without any conjuror's flourish, Campion could see the object was made of wood and measured about eighteen inches by six. Or rather, two pieces of wood joined down one long side by a leather hinge, giving it the form of a book with wooden covers.

De Vries laid the object on the desktop in front of Campion. He gently prised apart the two slices of wood until they lay flat and, using only his fingertips, turned it so that Campion did not have to view it upside down. It was a book with no pages.

'A diptych, my goodness! And it looks as if it has been through the wars.'

The diptych – two hinged painted panels of smoothed oak or occasionally poplar, which could be folded together making them safely portable – was an ancient method of displaying religious art and had been popular for private devotions. In times of religious turmoil, their size made them relatively easy to conceal, at least more so than the larger triptychs with three panels, or the incredibly elaborate polyptychs, which had adorned the altars of many a church in Italy since the days when Giotto first picked up a brush. Campion doubted that the example De Vries was protecting was quite that old, but it was old and had suffered the ravages of, if not time, then certainly something.

It was, in effect, half a diptych, as the left-hand panel had been scored and burned as though the painting that had been there had been violently erased, only microscopic blobs of paint surviving on the edges of the frame. Miraculously, perhaps the most appropriate word, the panel on the right side had survived with barely a trace of damage. It was an oil painting in need of specialist cleaning, but still clearly depicting in impressive miniature detail a scene where figures in cloaks and caps of Tudor fashion surrounded a blazing bonfire. They appeared to be enthusiastically pitching things into the fire, and Campion's initial thoughts turned from childhood memories of Guy Fawkes Night to newsreel footage of the Nazi burning of books in the Bebelplatz in Berlin in 1933, though he knew that both references were anachronistic. After all, De Vries had dated the scene quite specifically and, sure enough, as Campion leaned over the desk and peered down, there in the centre of the flames was the figure of the Madonna and Child, seated on a chair or throne as if it had been placed centre stage. Despite being in the heart of the bonfire, the red flames which licked up and around it seemed – again, miraculously? – unable to consume or even damage the icon.

This was no devotional altarpiece, as the thin-legged, black-cloaked figures depicted around the fire were partaking of an unholy act. If he strained his eyes and imagination, Campion felt sure that in the black smoke drifting up from the bonfire he could discern the outline of a wraith or a demon rearing up in triumph over the fate of the Madonna and Child.

'What happened to the left-hand panel?' he asked.

'We do not know for sure,' answered De Vries, 'but it probably suffered in the Haarlem fire which destroyed much of Suycker's work. We do know from his letters and account books, which did survive, that he painted several religious scenes in oils on wood whilst he was in London in 1538. The diptych form would be popular because they could be easily concealed, and most of Suycker's customers were, of course, Catholics who felt threatened and did not want to advertise their faith.'

'And you think this painting is, in effect, an eyewitness depiction of the destruction of the original Our Lady of Walsingham statue?'

'I am convinced of it.' The Dutchman tugged his beard in one firm movement, similar to pulling a bell-rope, almost as if signalling that a point had been made and there was no room for doubt. 'It is vital that I present it to the guardians of the shrine at Walsingham, and therefore it, and I, need your protection.'

Campion was not sure that the various associations of priests, lay clergy, monks and nuns who tended the shrine would be happy with the term 'guardians', as he felt that had sinister implications of a dedicated militaristic unit guarding something secret, whereas there had hardly been anything secret about the place for the better part of nine centuries.

'I am sure Walsingham will welcome such an important historic artefact,' he said, 'and I will do everything I can to get you there in one piece – or should that be two pieces in the case of a diptych? – so you can present it in person.'

'I am anxious to obtain confirmation from them that the scene depicted is as I suspect. Their verification would add immeasurably to its value.'

'In the eyes of the Walsingham faithful, such a gift would surely be priceless,' Campion observed, reverentially he hoped.

His guest, however, appeared shocked. He straightened his back and stretched his neck, and if his white beard had crackled with static electricity or given off sparks, Campion would not have been surprised.

'You are mistaken if you assume I am donating the Suycker diptych to Walsingham,' said De Vries, as if he had been accused of shoplifting an unbelievably trivial item.

'So you are not on a religious pilgrimage to Walsingham?'

'Of course not. I am an art dealer.'

The house was eventually settling down, though it was not going quietly into that long, cold night. There was the constant tread of stockinged feet ascending and descending the stairs, as the unexpected guests were shown their allocated bedrooms, towels fetched from the airing cupboard and spare blankets rescued from pine boxes and battered steamer trunks. Amanda established a rota for both upstairs and downstairs bathroom usage, and hoped fervently that there would be enough hot water to go round.

When those assigned bedrooms had drifted upstairs clutching hot-water bottles or alcoholic night caps (Florence Pounder, much to Lugg's approval, had persuaded him to provide her with a Bovril and vodka 'to keep her warm'), and the three Americans had set up camp in the lounge, the Campions and Lugg convened in the dining room, standing at the mahogany console with marble top, on which were a tantalus with three decanters and assorted bottles. It was, needless to say, Lugg's favourite room in Carterers, and his favourite piece of furniture.

'They all seem to have gone quietly,' said Mr Campion, pouring measures of whisky, 'so I think we deserve a nightcap.'

'I'm tempted to take a full bottle up to that poor vicar chap with 'im havin' to bunk with that chatterbox,' grunted the fat man. 'Don't he ever draw breath?'

'Ah yes, our friend Hereward Henderson; he is rather preachy, isn't he?'

'I thought it rather cruel of you to dump him on those poor young Americans,' Amanda chided him between delicate sips. 'They didn't have a clue what he was talking about. One of them asked me who the heck Hereward was and why he worshipped Thor. I think they were confused by the fact that it was this Hereward talking about that Hereward of the eleventh century.'

'Can you blame them, dear? The poor man is rather confused. I gather he thinks that Hereward—'

'As in Hereward the Wake?' Rupert asked. 'We did him at school. Didn't *The Water Babies* chap write a book about him?'

'Charles Kingsley did indeed, but people only remember his Victorian fairy tale about a boy chimney sweep going for an unscheduled swimming lesson. Perhaps *our* Hereward should read it, though I've no idea how good it is as history, but I do know, because he told me at interminable length, that he is clutching at straws hoping to fit the facts to his theory.'

'How so?'

'Well, from the little I gathered – and I do admit to switching off quite early on – he regards his namesake as a bit of a Robin Hood character who made a career robbing abbeys and priories, though whether he gave the proceeds to the poor is moot. Bank robbers are not usually noted for their charity. Anyway, he has this notion that Hereward – the real one, assuming he existed of course – might have tried pulling a job at the priory at Walsingham. The problem is I think he's got his dates wrong. The priory was not established during Hereward's time.'

'So your pilgrim is a crackpot; an' I thought mine was a dead loss.' Lugg sighed.

Mr Campion did his best to look surprised. 'Oh yes, our little parlour game. I had almost forgotten about that.'

'No, you hadn't,' said Amanda, 'and if Hereward isn't your pilgrim of choice, I bet your first reserve is. You had two to choose from.'

'You had three.'

'They hardly count, as none of them are really pilgrims, just young men following orders, and they weren't even heading for Walsingham. It was purely a fluke of the weather brought them to our door, not a pilgrimage. Lugg's spinster postmistress and Rupert's vicar seem to fit the bill as conventional pilgrims and therefore unexceptional, and the bus driver was just doing his job. The Hereward-obsessed professor you seem to have dismissed, so that leaves the rather odd Dutch person you were closeted with in your study. I suspect you got a winning story there because, from the smug look on your face, you found him *interesting*. Am I wrong?'

Mr Campion beamed at his wife. 'Almost never, darling, and in this instance absolutely dead right. Mr De Vries does come with an interesting tale.'

Lugg couldn't resist a balloon in need of puncturing. 'Well let's 'ave it then. Yer dyin' to spill the beans, we can tell.'

Firmly resisting the urge to overact – he did, after all, have a captive audience – Mr Campion told his tale, or rather Fred de Vries's tale of half a diptych, the fate of the original Our Lady of Walsingham statue and a Dutch master no one had ever heard of. In the telling he expressed considerable sympathy for the painter Jacob Suycker who had been a devout Catholic in a country embracing Protestantism and burning, in his eyes, a sacred symbol of his faith. Ironically, it was fire which later destroyed much of Suycker's work, and what survived was mostly forgotten for more than three centuries. It was only because they shared a hometown that Fred de Vries pursued an interest in Suycker and his work, having identified the painter's accounts book in an auction house conducting the sale of a cache of old documents rescued from the ruins of an Antwerp museum bombed during the war. That De Vries had subsequently tracked down the Suycker diptych (and, he had claimed, two non-religious pictures by the painter), was a tribute to his detective skills and persistence in rescuing the reputation of a forgotten artist.

Ever practical, Amanda asked, 'And he's taking this diptych to Walsingham why? To give it provenance?'

'No, he has all the provenance he needs back in Holland and he is confident that any scientific test will prove that he has dated it correctly.'

'So he is simply returning it to what one might say is its spiritual home?'

'Well, yes, he is, but only temporarily. I think he is hoping that those who are devoted to the shrine will confirm it shows the destruction of their original statue.'

'And thus add to its value?'

'I would certainly think so,' agreed Mr Campion.

'It's valuable?' Rupert said, open-mouthed.

'Very, I would imagine. Even without the Walsingham connection, it is a genuine sixteenth-century painting, both historically and artistically interesting.'

'So that's why he wanted to know if you had a safe and a gun?' Lugg, even more practical than Amanda, could not resist asking, and when Mr Campion nodded, he added, 'You didn't tell 'im, did yer?'

'I allowed him the use of my safe for the night; I had to, otherwise I do not think he would have gone to bed. I did not offer to provide a firearm.'

'You still keep the shotgun in that cupboard upstairs?'

Campion caught the frowning glance aimed at him by his wife. 'Safely out of sight and always unloaded. The ammunition is in the tack room, probably lost behind all those crates of brown ale you've got stashed there.'

'So yer'll not be posting an armed guard tonight, then?'

'Certainly not. I think our Dutch friend is paranoid that he is going to be robbed and murdered or murdered and then robbed. Mind you, his journey here was pretty horrendous, all things considered, and he must be exhausted – they all must be. Hopefully they'll sleep like logs and things will sort themselves out in the morning.'

'So that's your pilgrim's tale, is it?' Amanda pursed her lips. 'I suppose you think you've won the game.'

'You cannot deny that Mr De Vries spun an interesting yarn, so I am happy to claim the victory honours.'

'Would have been better,' growled Lugg, 'if the Dutch feller suspected that one of the other passengers was out to rob him. I mean, who else could? Nobody in this house had heard of him or that painter chappie until just now, and nobody, but nobody, is going to come in from outside in this weather, even if they knew he was here.'

'As a matter of fact, he did have a couple of suspects, though they were so ridiculous I discounted them immediately as figments of his overtired imagination.'

'Who, f'r'instance?'

'Rupert's pilgrim vicar, for one.'

'That's insane,' said Rupert. 'Father Breck is retiring to Walsingham for the good of his soul, not to steal antique art.'

'So you told us earlier, and in your report the good vicar came across as a kindly, reflective piece of humanity, albeit with some wartime demons. Indeed, I too feel great sympathy for him having to share a bedroom with Hereward the Horrible Historian, and if he really is retiring to be part of the religious community at Walsingham, then all he would have to do is wait for De Vries to bring the diptych to him. He would have no need to steal it en route, assuming he knew about it in the first place. I'm sure my Dutch art dealer was simply imagining things, just as he was when he said he distrusted Mr Fisk, the driver, for taking the coach off its normal itinerary. He found that highly suspicious.'

'Bus drivers are usually suspicious,' postulated Lugg gravely, seemingly oblivious to the three pairs of incredulous eyes that turned on him. 'Well, I've always found them so,' he added without explanation. 'Not that Fisk will give anyone any trouble. 'E was shattered when I put him to bed, 'ad to damn-near carry him up the stairs. He'll sleep well tonight.'

Mr Campion waved his whisky glass in front of Lugg's moon of a face. 'You didn't ply him with one of your trademark boozy nightcaps, did you?'

'Might have done,' said Lugg with a shrug of his shoulders. 'And here's another heading for the land of nod.'

Only Lugg had noticed the dining room door being quietly opened by Lloyd Thursby, who entered the room in complete silence apart from the musical tinkling made by the bottles and empty glasses on the tray he was carrying. He moved with the careful tread of a drunk driver attempting to walk a straight line under police supervision, and with his eyes down, concentrating on his tray, was oblivious to the presence of the four people seated at the dining table.

His destination was clearly the drinks console, and he was halfway there when Amanda, fearing for the safety of her good crystalware, took pity on him.

'Be a darling, Mr Thursby,' she shouted, aware of the man's deafness, 'and take those to the kitchen, would you?'

Startled, Thursby's tray began to shudder, but he tightened his grip and looked in astonishment at the four faces staring back at him. He cleared his throat and asked, 'Is Perce there?' in a voice loud enough to be heard outside.

Rupert leaned into his mother and whispered, 'Who's Perce?' but Amanda ignored him.

'Yes, she's there, doing the washing up. We couldn't stop her – she insisted,' she said loudly enough for it to register, and Mr Thursby turned very slowly and carefully on his heels and padded out into the hallway, even managing to close the dining room door after him, though he did so with the delicacy of a soldier defusing an unexploded bomb.

'Perce is Mrs Thursby?' Rupert persisted.

'Persephone,' said Amanda quietly, and Rupert issued a long low whistle.

'Who knew? Hey, there could be a winning pilgrim's tale behind that name.'

'Not allowed,' ruled Mr Campion. 'Mrs Thursby is not one of our pilgrims, so her tale would not count. I still think my Dutchman has the edge, but let's mull on it overnight and celebrate my victory over breakfast.'

As they wended their way to the stairs, Amanda opened the kitchen door and looked in.

'Everything all right, Mrs T?'

'Just about finished here,' came the answer. 'I've told Lloyd to stop grumbling and settle down for the night with those Yank boys.'

'What's he grumbling about?'

'Them Americans. Says they're talking in some foreign lingo.'

Lugg sidled up to Mr Campion and spoke out of the side of his mouth. 'The old coot's stone deaf, surprised he can hear anything.'

'Perhaps he can't lip-read American,' Campion replied, and politely stood by to allow his wife and son to precede him up the stairs.

Lugg followed at his shoulder and continued to speak in hushed tones so only Campion could hear.

'When your Dutchman asked about weapons, did you tell him about the shotgun?'

'Yes, but only to reassure him. I wasn't going to lend it to him.'

'And you didn't mention any *other* firearms?'

'Good Lord, no,' hissed Campion.

SEVEN
Footprints

When asked, which was rarely, if he was a light sleeper, Mr Campion would maintain that he had the instincts and agility of a startled cat and was ready to spring, wide awake, into action at the slightest hint of anything untoward. He was supremely confident that he could react to such disturbers of his peace as a surprise attack by Apaches, a creaking floorboard, a poisonous snake slithering down a convenient bell-rope or the pop of a champagne cork over a mile away. He had been known to boast that a ripe apple, falling from one of the trees in the orchard, or the splash of a duck landing gracefully in the moat which curved around Carterers, could wake him from the deepest of sleeps, but only if his dreams were less than blissful.

That Friday morning he came awake slowly and reluctantly only after a persistent hissing noise, slowly increasing in volume, penetrated the eiderdown pulled over his head to deflect it. His mind still fogged with sleep, he considered and dismissed the possibilities of a gas leak (there was no gas fire in the bedroom), an angry wasp drunk on fermenting apples (entirely the wrong season) and a lone rogue mosquito (far too cold). And the hissing did have a certain urgent human quality, almost a 'Psst! Psst' exhortation, which is exactly what it was.

As Campion's head emerged from under the covers and he reached for his glasses on the bedside table, he made out the tall, thin strip of light coming from the open bedroom door and the bulky shadow blocking half of it which could only belong to Lugg.

'Psst! Psst! Oi, sleepy head, you awake?'

'He is now,' said Amanda from the other half of the bed.

With as much stealth as he could muster, and with as little disruption to the bedcovers as possible, he slid out of bed and tiptoed across the room towards the slit of light by the door frame, scooping up a wool dressing gown from a chair along the way. Pulling it on, he was tying the belt as he reached the door and flicked the tassel ends at where he guessed Lugg's face must be through the gap.

'I hope this is not your idea of re-enacting the Pyramus and Thisbe story,' he whispered.

'Yer what?'

From the bed, Campion heard Amanda giggle.

'The two lovers forced to communicate through a crack in a wall – oh never mind. Let me come out and you can tell me face-to-ugly-mug.'

Somewhat to his surprise, he saw that Lugg, apart from shoes, was fully dressed for the outdoors, wearing at least two pullovers, a scarf, gloves, and with trouser bottoms tucked into socks.

'Going for a morning stroll? It is morning, isn't it?' He glanced towards the window, opaquely patterned with a lacing of ice, at the end of the landing. 'Still looks dark out there.'

'It's just after six, but it ain't snowing at the moment.'

'And are either of those two facts worth disturbing my beauty sleep?'

'If my kip's disrupted, then I don't see why yours shouldn't be. I was dragged out of bed by my ear like a naughty schoolboy. Very h'undignified it was, I can tell you. Lucky I was decent. Mind you, young Rupert slept like a baby through it all. Could 'ave scarred him for life, seeing someone he looks up to treated like that.'

Campion flexed his toes against the cold floorboards. 'It all sounds intriguing, but would you mind getting to the point? My breath is frosting in front of my face and my extremities are feeling rather brittle.'

''Ow d'yer think I felt? Could've given me a nasty turn, a shock like that. I'd no idea she was so forward or so flamin' strong.'

'*She?* Now I really am intrigued. Pray tell all.'

In deference to Amanda, Lugg kept his voice low and told his tale quickly, though at one point Mr Campion was sure he heard a snort of laughter from the other side of the bedroom door.

Lugg had been rudely awakened by the nails of a thumb and forefinger squeezing the fleshy lobe of his left ear, and the squeezing was followed by an insistent tugging which his giant orb of a head had to obey. Once his eyelids had reluctantly opened, the shock really set in as he made out, backlit by the landing light, the figure of Miss Florence Pounder; a fully clothed Florence Pounder, mind you.

With a vice-like grip on his ear and strength which both impressed and amazed Lugg, Miss Pounder pulled her victim's head free of the blankets and instructed his body to follow in its wake and sit up. Keeping her voice at a whisper so as not to disturb Rupert snoring softly in the adjacent bed, she apologized for waking the big man, but after all, he was a big strong man and she was but a weak and feeble woman (and for once the reference was not lost on Lugg) and she had been herself rudely awakened by the sound of someone trying to get into the house via the back door in the kitchen.

Lugg's initial reaction was one of 'So what?', thinking it was probably the milkman or the postman, before realizing that in their wintry isolation it was unlikely that any deliveries to Carterers could be expected that morning. An intruder, perhaps another blown-off-course traveller was a possibility, of course, but however distressed, any self-respecting pilgrim would surely have knocked on the front door before asking for sanctuary. Which left the possibility of an unofficial incomer, perhaps one with nefarious intent. Even though not fully awake, Lugg considered the matter professionally and thought it unlikely that any burglar worth his salt would have made enough noise to wake someone asleep upstairs, and in any case would soon be brought up short when finding three strapping young, uniformed men camping in the living room, though getting past a snoozing Lloyd Thursby would not be a problem. He even allowed himself a grin at the thought that getting past a fully awake but very deaf Lloyd Thursby would not be too much trouble.

'Yer sure you 'eard someone coming back *in*, not goin' *out*?' he had asked Miss Pounder, who seemed remarkably calm and not obviously in need of a big, strong man to investigate.

'I distinctly heard the back door open and close, then a noise which I would suggest was somebody bumping into the kitchen table in the dark,' she had said. 'I was wide awake. I have always woken up around five thirty, even in strange beds in strange houses. And why would anyone go outside in weather like this?'

Lugg was about to suggest – delicately – that it might involve a call of nature, but thought the better of it and asked her if she had heard any subsequent noises, treads on the stairs perhaps, to which she had shaken her head.

'And I listened carefully,' she had asserted. 'I got out of bed and even opened the bedroom door a crack, but nobody came upstairs and I was not going to investigate further without a weapon, so I came and got you.'

Lugg was unsure quite how to take that. The nervous ramblings of a delicate spinster far from home in a house full of strangers or the cool calculations of a confident woman? Either way he felt rather flattered, though at pains not to let it show in front of Mr Campion.

He had made Miss Pounder return to her bedroom, showed her how to wedge the back of a chair under the door handle – a technique she had said she was familiar with – and told her not to open it until she got the all-clear from him personally. He had then raised Mr Campion from his slumbers on the basis that this was his house and he therefore deserved to be disturbed.

'Have you heard anything yourself?' Campion asked.

'Not a peep, an' I crept halfway down the stairs quiet as a church mouse wearing slippers and kept my earholes open. Nuffin'.'

Campion did not doubt his old companion, whom he knew really could move as silently as a ghost when he wanted to, despite his bulk. Plus, as a matter of professional pride, Lugg had long ago familiarized himself with every squeaking door hinge and creaking floorboard in Carterers.

'Is there something here worth investigating other than Miss Pounder's insomnia?'

'I reckon so,' said Lugg. 'She doesn't strike me as the sort who hears things going bump in the night if there's nothing bumping.'

'Fair enough; let us proceed below as if we are sneaking into the kitchen in search of a late midnight snack or a very early breakfast.'

'Not a bad idea.'

'As it is my house, there is little need for actual sneaking, which is just as well as there's one heck of a draught here and my feet are freezing, so let's hop to it.'

With Campion leading, they went downstairs and paused in the hallway at the door to the lounge which now served as a dormitory for the American airmen and Lloyd Thursby, whom Campion suspected was responsible for the sonorous rumble of snoring, surely loud enough to cover any noise made by a burglar.

Lugg seemed to agree. 'Good job the old boy's deaf,' he observed as they moved to the kitchen. 'Only hope them Yanks are.'

'They're young and in uniform; they'll be used to roughing it.'

Mr Campion flung open the kitchen door, strode in and turned the light on as if he owned the place, which of course he did. He and Lugg were confronted by a scene of simple domesticity, if the detritus of catering for eight unexpected guests arriving in a snowstorm could be described as simple. Everything seemed to be in its place, or at least where Amanda and Mrs Thursby had left it.

'If we 'ad a burglar, he wasn't peckish,' said Lugg, indicating the tray of geometrically arranged mince pies Mrs Thursby had baked 'just in case' before she went to bed. As if moving chess pieces, he carefully picked out two which did not disturb the pattern unduly and began munching.

'Can I get you the brandy butter and a pot of tea perhaps?' hissed Campion. 'Or can we get on? The back door is unlocked, but that doesn't mean anything much. You had better check outside though.'

'Me? It's your house.'

'I am hardly dressed for an Arctic expedition.' He wafted a hand down his thin frame and pulled the cord of his dressing gown tighter. 'Whereas you are fully suited and booted against the elements. Well, almost. Where are your boots?'

'In the tack room with everybody else's.'

'Then head down and out into the storm. Do it for Captain Scott!'

'That didn't end well, did it?' said Lugg. But without waiting for an answer added, 'What am I looking for?'

'Footprints of course. If we have been visited in the night, there will be prints in the snow, unless we are dealing with an elfin spirit or a ghost. It's not snowing so heavily now, but tracks will get covered up so out you go. Grab your boots and circle the house. There are torches in the tack room if you need one. Try not to run into the Abominable Snowman while you're out there. I'll go and get dressed in case I have to pull you out of a snowdrift.'

Lugg pulled his scarf up over his mouth to hide a scowl, and with a grunt lumbered out of the kitchen door accompanied by a faint flurry of snowflakes, which glistened as they melted on the tiled floor, making Campion shiver.

He hurried, almost pranced out of the kitchen on cold feet, and stealthily climbed the stairs, pausing occasionally to listen carefully, but apart from old Lloyd's snoring, the house was deathly quiet. On the landing, as he tiptoed towards his bedroom, he felt a distinct draught as he had when conferring with Lugg earlier.

He reassured himself that he was not imagining it. There was a stream of cold air coming from somewhere, even allowing for the age of the house and ill-fitting or warped door and window frames. It was almost as if someone had left a window open – something not even the most health-conscious Spartan would do on a night like this. It was certainly not coming from his bedroom; although Amanda was an advocate of fresh air, she did not allow icy draughts. That left the other bedroom at the front of Carterers, which also looked out over the driveway, that had been allocated to Graham Fisk, the driver of the stranded coach, who had looked the most exhausted of the travellers and the one most likely to sleep the soundest.

Campion extended a bare foot to the bottom of the bedroom door and his toes confirmed Fisk's room as the source of a distinctly chilly gust. If Fisk had opened a window on a night like this, he was either a fresh-air fiend or related to a polar bear, and Campion had no qualms about disturbing either, so he knocked once and entered.

The room was unlit but not dark, as what moonlight there was, reflected from the white layers of snow outside, filtered in through the open, uncurtained sash window along with an icing of snow on the sill. The bed had been slept in, the blankets flung back as if the occupant had only recently abandoned it, but the sheets were cold to Campion's touch and of the sleeper there was no sign.

His breath condensed before him as he crossed the room to

pull down on the open sash, though not before poking his head out of the window and looking down. Directly beneath him, the snow which had drifted against the house had been disturbed and a subsequent light dusting of the latest fall had not yet covered the signs almost certainly of someone lowering themselves, or jumping, from the bedroom. The drift was deep enough to make sure that a landing, albeit wet and cold, would be soft, and footprints leading at an angle to the driveway showed that the jumper had survived. Interestingly, the footprints joined another set heading directly to Carterers' monumental gateposts.

Campion shook snowflakes from his hair as he twisted his head to confirm that the second set of tracks had come from the back of the house and was rewarded by the sight of Lugg rounding the corner, the beam of his torch following the prints immediately in front of him.

Campion gave a soft, low whistle and Lugg immediately brought his torch up to illuminate the bespectacled, pyjama-ed figure leaning out and gesticulating like an animated gargoyle.

'Strewth!' was his reaction, before the gargoyle signalled him to be quiet and to stay where he was, then disappeared inside and closed the window.

It was a thoroughly chilled gargoyle who hopped from one frozen foot to the other as he got dressed, determined not to disturb his wife.

'What's going on?' asked Amanda, showing the minimum amount of her face necessary from under the eiderdown.

'Nothing untoward,' said Mr Campion, struggling into a second pullover, 'just Lugg sleepwalking to the drinks cabinet and it's still two hours short of breakfast. I didn't wake you, did I?'

'No,' said his wife as she submerged again.

Protected by several layers of clothing and his thickest socks, Campion made his way downstairs, the house silent about him, apart from old Lloyd's muted snoring, and into the kitchen.

Lugg had not waited outside at the front of the house as instructed, but was standing outside the kitchen near the open door to the tack room, holding a pair of Wellington boots in one meaty hand.

'You have that bloodhound look about you, old fruit. What have you sniffed out?'

'I might have noticed something you should have picked up on,' the fat man said airily, rolling his eyes. 'If we 'ad an h'interloper in the house, they would have tracked in a bit of snow on their boots or at least left wet footprints, but the kitchen floor's as dry as a bone. Unless that is, said intruder took 'is boots off in the tack room.'

He held up the Wellingtons as if they were Exhibit A. They were shiny and wet and the ridges of the rubber tread on the soles and heels were packed tight with frozen slush.

'Do those boots coincide with the footprints outside?'

'Both coming *and* going, but more interesting . . .' Lugg paused for dramatic effect, '. . . these boots is yours.'

Mr Campion hoped he looked suitably outraged. 'Borrowing a man's Wellingtons without asking is beyond the pale. Where were they headed?'

'Down the driveway – not that you can actually see the driveway – but in the general direction of the gateposts. You'll have noticed that the driver chappie, Fisk, was defenestrated.'

'I think he jumped rather than was thrown.'

'Whatever he did, he landed nice and soft and set off following your bootprints. He wore shoes – I saw him drying them in front of the fire earlier on. His prints go down the drive but don't come back, unlike your wandering Wellies.'

'Then let me grab a coat and reclaim my boots and I will make them retrace their steps.'

Wearing a duffel coat with the hood up and with Lugg having pulled on a balaclava to protect his domed head, Campion could not imagine two more suspicious figures wandering the snowy grounds of Carterers. Had he been in the house looking out and seen them, he would have rung the police.

They followed the meandering trail of footprints, through snow knee-deep in places, by the light of Lugg's torch. Snow was still falling, but lightly, and by wiping his spectacles with a gloved forefinger, Campion was able to appreciate the silent snow-covered trees in the orchard and the icicles dangling from the curved wooden bridge over the three ponds which formed a partial moat around the house. It was a scene, he felt, worthy of a Japanese woodblock print.

The interconnecting ponds forming the moat were frozen and covered in a white blanket, and Campion imagined that – given the number of guests in the house – he could recreate a Victorian skating scene to be photographed and used as the design for next year's Christmas card. He dismissed the fantasy to concentrate on trudging forward and snapped back to reality as Lugg's torch illuminated the megalithic gateposts and the spectral outline of the pilgrims' coach resting against the right-hand stone blocking almost half the gateway.

'Judging by the mishmash of prints, I would hazard that two sets of feet came down here but only one set went back to the house, and they didn't even bother to do the old Red Indian trick from the comics of walking backwards in your previous prints.'

'Probably thought they'd be covered by more snow,' said Lugg over his shoulder, 'if he worried about such things.'

'That's what disturbs me somewhat. Whoever appropriated my Wellingtons seemed very keen to get back to the house.'

'Maybe he got what he wanted out of the charabanc.'

'Or perhaps he left something in the coach he wanted to get away from,' said Campion. Then in response to Lugg turning his head and glaring at him, 'Two pairs of feet going in, one set coming out . . .'

The fat man shrugged his shoulders, disturbing snowflakes which gave his head the appearance of a snow globe just shaken. 'Best we have a look then.'

'You're the one with the torch,' said Mr Campion. 'After you.'

It was impossible to see inside the coach as the outside of the windows were splattered with snow and the insides crazy-paved with ice, though Lugg carefully shone his torch into each window in turn, perhaps in the hope of disturbing a malevolent shadow. There was no movement from inside the bus, which remained as enigmatically silent as an abandoned refrigerator, which was almost precisely what it had become.

Lugg grasped the passenger door handle and pushed until the door folded in with surprisingly little resistance, then pointed his torch up and into the interior.

'Well, there's dedication for you,' he grunted.

'What is?'

'Our missing coach driver is so dedicated to his job, he's in the driving seat raring to go, 'cept 'e ain't going nowhere. Did I say dedicated? Should have just said dead.'

Mr Campion knew he had neither the skill nor the stomach to conduct a detailed medical examination of the body, but as they stood over Graham Fisk in the light of Lugg's torch, two things were clear to him. Firstly that the driver was dead, most likely from a broken neck, and that he had been squashed, post-mortem, into the driving position. He speculated that the scene could have been arranged so that if discovered by passers-by in daylight, given that rigor and the freezing temperatures would have taken their toll, it would look as if poor Fisk had died in a bizarre – though understandable given the conditions – road accident.

The fly in that particular ointment was that there were plenty of witnesses, hopefully sleeping soundly in Carterers, who knew that Graham Fisk had survived the coach's collision with the gatepost and had been tucked up in bed until . . .

'I reckon he saw somebody rooting around his precious bus,' said Lugg, following Campion's train of thought. 'From his window, you could just about make out somebody with a torch snooping around here if the snow let up for a minute or two. You could have too, from your bedroom, if you'd bothered to look. He didn't like the idea of somebody robbing his charabanc, so he came charging down here and got his come-uppance. It could have been you if you didn't like your kip so much.'

'As usual you are less than comforting, my old misanthrope, but I think you've hit on the right scenario. Fisk saw something from the house, perhaps the person who borrowed my Wellingtons, heading for the coach and followed to confront them. There was some form of struggle and it ended badly for him, but that leaves the question: what was the intruder doing? The coach wasn't going anywhere and there seems little of value in here.'

Campion took the hand in which Lugg held the torch and turned it so the beam no longer played on Graham Fisk's deathly white face but shone down the length of the empty bus.

'They'll have put all the luggage in the boot,' said Lugg with enthusiasm, 'and didn't you say that foreigner was carrying a valuable painting or such like?'

'Mr De Vries. It was a diptych and it certainly could be valuable, but he carried it with him at all times and it is now in the safe in my study. But we should go and look in the boot.'

'And leave him here?' Lugg flicked the torch back on to the dead driver.

'What else can we do? This is a crime scene now and we have to wait until the police can get here.'

'And when is that likely?'

'The sooner the better.'

They climbed down from the coach and Lugg pulled the door closed, sealing Fisk in his chilly metal coffin. As most of the nearside of the vehicle was tight up against the boundary wall, they had to go around the front, averting their eyes from the driver's seat, and trudge down the far side, now a slab of pure white crystal. At the rear of the bus, Lugg's torch illuminated churned-up snow which indicated signs of a struggle, and he and Campion exchanged knowing glances without words, then he pulled up the boot door.

'Oh dear,' said Campion, after Lugg had slowly shone the torch over the stacked luggage. 'I was hoping for a clue.'

'Oh dear what, Sherlock?'

Campion pointed a gloved finger at each piece of baggage in turn. 'Look, there are three kit bags, clearly the property of our American servicemen. Then there's a small pink suitcase that I suspect belongs to your Miss Pounder, a brown one with a KLM sticker which suggests it belongs to Mr De Vries, and a valise and haversack which belong to the Reverend Breck and to the annoying Professor Henderson respectively. No great feat of deduction, old chap – they have luggage labels with their names and addresses attached to them. The conclusion is obvious.'

'It is?'

'Nothing seems to be missing, unless . . .'

'Go on, you know you want to.' Even under the balaclava, Mr Campion could tell Lugg was leering, but he was not to be denied.

'Unless there was something on board the coach which Graham Fisk was not aware of. Something worth killing him for seeing.'

EIGHT

Worst Meal of the Day

'You just left him there?'

Mr Campion had known Amanda would take the news with a mixture of disbelief and anger, and had hoped that by breaking it to her as she was concentrating on getting dressed might divert some of that anger away from himself. On that count, he was predictably very wrong.

'How could you just leave the poor man out there?'

Amanda did not allow the indignity of having to struggle into a tight, round-neck Bri-Nylon sweater to interrupt the flow of her invective, and the fact that she was keeping her voice down in order not to disturb the rest of the house somehow made her scorn even more wounding.

Perched on the edge of their bed with his fingers linked over his knees, Campion spoke quietly and calmly. 'There seemed no advantage in bringing him into the house. It would only cause panic among our guests, and in any case, the charabanc is technically a crime scene to be turned over to the police at the earliest opportunity.'

Amanda's head emerged like a bobbing cork from the neck of the sweater and she ran her fingers through her hair before tackling the black ski pants she had laid out on the bed.

'I still think it's awfully cruel. You are sure it could not have been an accident?'

'Sadly, I am positive he was killed, and rather depressingly, I think I know how.'

'Was it gruesome?' Amanda asked tentatively.

'Well, I think it was quick. It looked to me as if he'd received a vicious but well-placed karate blow to the neck. I'm afraid I saw something similar during the war. Several commandos I knew were frighteningly proficient at it.'

'So we have a murderer under our roof?' Amanda added a

thick, cable-knit woollen cardigan to her ensemble, going for insulation rather than following fashion.

'That is a distinct possibility.'

'Then I think breakfast might be rather awkward, don't you?'

Mr Campion had always doubted the truth of the old adage that breakfast was the most important meal of the day. Perhaps it was a uniquely English belief, for the Italians tended to eat small pieces of cake and the French made do with a croissant and perhaps some *confiture*. The Germans at least had a stab at a meal, scoffing a selection of salami, hams and cheeses, though they did terrible things to boiled eggs, and Americans liked their bacon so crisp they could use the slices as a knife to cut their rubbery scrambled eggs and also insisted on 'hash browns' and 'grits', whatever they were.

Friday morning's breakfast at Carterers, always destined to be chaotic, offered somewhat restricted menu choices, though all those partaking agreed that Mrs Thursby had done a splendid job coping with the stream of demands for tea, toast and porridge, which continued for two hours or more as the unexpected house guests awoke, formed themselves into orderly queues for bathrooms and then congregated in the kitchen and dining room where they sought nourishment and the chance to swap gloomy stories about the terrible state of the weather and groan at the news reports of no change in the situation coming out of the radio.

Mrs Thursby had crept downstairs shortly after seven o'clock to find Amanda up and dressed for the outdoors like Mr Campion and Lugg. She was busy conducting a stocktake in the kitchen and larder, while Campion and Lugg carried coal, logs and kindling from the tack room to restart fires and stoke the Aga. The consensus was that while supplies of fuel seemed adequate until a thaw set in (hopefully before Easter, Mr Campion had observed unhelpfully), on the culinary front eggs would have to be rationed, and they would likely run out of milk by the end of the day as deliveries were out of the question, and so the larder's supply of tins of condensed and evaporated milk would have to be pressed into service.

There was, thankfully, enough bacon to allow Lloyd Thursby

his daily bacon sandwich without which, according to his daughter-in-law, 'he'd be in a right sulk all day'.

Yet even clutching a bacon sandwich almost two inches thick, Mrs Thursby having gone into mass production on the bread-making front, and having appropriated Lugg's favourite spot in front of the Aga, Lloyd looked far from happy.

'What's the old boy griping about, Perce?' Lugg asked with a twinkle in his eye, but Mrs Thursby, busy stirring a cauldron of porridge, either missed or ignored the overfamiliar use of her Christian name.

'He's going on about those Yanks again, says they've been yapping in some foreign lingo. Hardly got a wink of sleep, he says.'

'How would he know? He's as deaf as an adder,' said Lugg loudly, not two feet from Lloyd. 'Is it what they call selective deafness, like when you never hear a publican calling "Time, gentlemen, please"?'

'Oh, he's deaf all right. You can say what you like about him as long as he don't see your lips move.'

Lugg did not accept the offer, but thought that the young Americans Lloyd was bunking with were the ones most likely to have a few choice comments, having had their sleep disturbed by his ground-trembling snoring.

The three airmen looked remarkably spruce despite their ordeal. They had washed and shaved – Lugg gazing in envy at the first battery-powered shaver he had ever seen – and seemed happy to breakfast on porridge with honey as long as there was coffee on offer rather than tea, which Amanda provided knowing that Mrs Thursby would bridle at the suggestion.

'I thank you kindly, Lady Amanda,' said the staff sergeant with a polite bow, 'and if there is anything my men can do to help out round the house, just give the order.'

The airman called Rivero nudged the one called Quinn with his elbow. 'There goes Sometimes, volunteering us for chores again.'

'I'm sure there's wood to chop and snow to shovel.' Amanda smiled graciously. 'Eat your breakfast and then Lugg will put you to work. It doesn't look as if anyone is going anywhere today.'

'Still snowing, is it?'

'Not as bad as yesterday but it's still coming down, I'm afraid.'

'Hey, Sarge, can we make a snowman?' Rivero suggested with childlike enthusiasm.

'You'll have to forgive Oscar,' said Kosloffski. 'He's from Santa Fé and they don't see much snow there. But joking aside, we really should make an attempt to get to Marham. Do you have a vehicle we could borrow?'

Amanda shook her head. 'Neither my husband's nor our son's cars could get anywhere in these conditions. I fear we may have to wait to be rescued.'

'Then we'd better keep warm while we wait.' The staff sergeant gave a broad smile, showing perfectly white, perfectly American teeth. 'Me and guys will chop you a cord of wood to keep the home fires burning.'

'I have no idea how much a cord is, but please feel free. You'll find axes and saws in the tack room, which is what we call that shed just outside the back door. You will be careful, won't you? We don't want any accidents. Oh, and no smoking in there, it's where my husband hides the fireworks for our New Year's Eve party, though whether that will happen this year is a moot point given the conditions.'

The American smiled again. 'Don't worry, we'll be careful, and we aim to be out of your hair long before the new year.'

'I do hope so,' Amanda said lightly, 'but of course I mean that in the nicest possible way.'

Hereward Henderson and a rather weary, hangdog Reverend Breck reported for breakfast together. All logic told Mr Campion that Henderson must have stopped talking at some point during the night, but the expression on the priest's face suggested that sleep had not come soon enough. They were followed into the kitchen by a yawning Rupert who, much to his mother's dismay, had not yet summoned up the strength to run a comb through his hair, favouring what she called a 'rat's nest coiffure'.

'Good morning, gentlemen,' Campion greeted them from his position of authority in charge of a large teapot and a steaming kettle, 'tea or coffee? As we still have electricity, I can offer both, plus toast and homemade jam.'

'Tea, please,' said Elis Breck. Then he added in a whisper, 'Unless you have something stronger.'

Mr Campion poured him a large mugful and indicated a bowl of sugar and a can of condensed milk with two triangular holes punched in the top.

'We're having to ration the milk, I'm afraid. It would be churlish to expect the milkman, or the postman, or the boy with the newspapers for that matter, to get through to us today. Would it be sacrilegious to ask you to pray for clearer skies?'

'That would be more the remit of Professor Henderson's Norse god,' said the priest, his lip curled.

'Not Thor again?'

'Not this time. I take it you've had the lecture as well.' Campion nodded gloomily. 'Well, it seems this inclement weather is the responsibility of Thor's stepson, a deity called Ulla or something.'

The Reverend Breck's face fell as he realized he had spoken too loudly and been overheard.

'Actually it's "Ullr" pronounced Oool-er. Tea, please,' announced Henderson, holding out a hand and squeezing between Campion and the priest. 'He was the stepson of Thor and the god of snow and is regarded as the patron saint of skiers, if, begging the vicar's pardon, pagans have saints, that is.'

'Well, we seem to have got on the wrong side of him.' Campion attempted to intervene. 'I certainly don't remember praying to what's-'is-name for yet more snow. Couldn't his stepfather have a word with him and tell him not to be so enthusiastic? Would not your Hereward have done the same?'

'Perhaps in private,' said his namesake thoughtfully, as if it was a seriously academic question. 'Nominally, he would have been a Christian, though his ancestors were certainly Vikings and old habits would have died hard. Plus,' he raised a forefinger to emphasize his point, 'in Hereward's time, in the mid-eleventh century, there were significant Viking incursions into England, including here in Norfolk.'

'And famously at Stamford Bridge up in Yorkshire in 1066,' said Mr Campion, noting the disparaging look on the Reverend Breck's face, an expression which clearly indicated that it was unwise to follow the professor down that particular rabbit hole.

'Ah, 1066, a significant year in so many ways and a notable one for Hereward and the Battle of Hastings.'

'Dare one ask why?' ventured Campion over the sound of a deep sigh from the priest.

'Because Hereward wasn't there! Whilst the flower of Anglo-Saxon nobility was being slaughtered by our Norman conquerors, Hereward, who is often held up as the symbol of Anglo-Saxon resistance, was nowhere to be seen.'

'I take it you've checked the Bayeux Tapestry?'

'Every inch.' Mr Campion's gentle sarcasm was lost on the smaller man. 'Twice in fact, but then Hereward only came to notoriety after 1066 when his penchant for going a-Viking irritated the Norman King William. He robbed numerous abbeys and chapels, was declared outlaw, and ended up besieged on the Isle of Ely in the Fens, and it really was an island back then.'

'I know about the siege,' said Campion. 'It was quite a spirited defence, but I do not recall how it ended for Hereward. Did he escape?'

'It is my contention that he did and that he continued his outlaw activities here in what we now call Norfolk, picking on the smaller religious houses.'

'Is there any way of proving that?'

'It is thought that much of the loot Hereward acquired was shipped to Denmark on Viking ships operating out of King's Lynn, although it was just called Lynne in those days. Some of it was even returned to England years later by Danish Christians.'

'I think that counts as a victory over the pagans,' said Reverend Breck in between slurps of tea.

'Definitely,' Campion agreed. 'One–nil, Christians versus Thor.'

It seemed that neither sarcasm nor ridicule could staunch Professor Henderson's flow, but it did divert him slightly.

'Interesting thing about Thor,' he began without noticing the silent groans of his audience, 'is that he was Thor in old Norse and Old English and in old Friesian, but in old Saxon he became Thunar and in High German he was Donar, the god of thunder.'

'As in *Donner und Blitzen*, the reindeers pulling Santa's sleigh?' Rupert chipped in.

'Along with Rudolph the red-nosed one?' Breck added, feeling they were on safer, or at least less boring, ground now, but oblivious to Rupert's suddenly startled expression.

'Well, yes and no. Donner and Blitzen featured in the poem "The Night Before Christmas", which was written sometime in the nineteenth century, but Rudolph with his nose so bright was only added in 1939 for the song 'Rudolph the Red-Nose Reindeer', and what is really fascinating is that the chap who wrote the song was originally going to call him Reginald.'

The professor fixed Campion with an inane grin and a malicious gleam in his eye. 'Things might have been so different if he'd gone with Reginald, rather than Rudolph, don't you think, Mr Campion?'

Mr Campion did not return his smile.

Florence Pounder and Fred de Vries descended the stairs together, though their demeanour was upright and correct, making it quite clear that they had met on the staircase by pure coincidence and that nothing untoward could or should be implied in their leaving their respective bedrooms simultaneously should anyone be observing them. The only person who did notice them was Lugg, who ambushed them in the hall before they could mingle with the breakfast throng.

'Did you get back to sleep after I left you, miss?' he asked politely, noting the Dutchman's eyebrows shooting up in surprise.

Florence Pounder smiled sweetly and remained unflustered. 'Thank you, Mr Lugg, I did manage to doze off for a couple of hours after our little disturbance.'

'Disturbance?' De Vries abandoned any semblance of neutrality and interposed himself in the conversation.

'I thought I heard an intruder in the night. Silly me.' Miss Pounder batted her eyelids and wafted a hand in front of her face as though warding off a swoon. Even Lugg thought it a poor attempt as a damsel-in-distress act, though the foreigner seemed eager to be convinced.

'But my *lieve dame*,' he said before immediately correcting himself to English, 'that is not silly, that is serious.' He turned his head nervously, his eyes seeking the door to Campion's study. 'I must speak with Mr Campion.'

'Keep your hair on,' Lugg threatened, 'it wasn't anything worth losing sleep over. It wasn't somebody breaking in, it was someone going out that Miss Pounder heard.'

Miss Pounder did not appear convinced. 'Going out? In weather like this? Who?'

'Your coach driver,' said Lugg, his face impassive. 'He's gone for help.'

'In the middle of the night? What was he thinking?'

'I couldn't speak as to his state of mind, but maybe he felt responsible for wrecking the charabanc and he's searching for a telephone box to ring head office. Don't worry about him; the snow's not coming down so thick now—'

'But it is still snowing. The poor man, out there in a blizzard; he could freeze to death.'

'I don't think there's much chance of that,' said Lugg, showing his best poker face and quite happy to continue and even embellish the lie. 'We couldn't talk him out of it. He insisted on going for help, said he felt it was his responsibility.'

Miss Pounder, though clearly distraught, seemed to accept Lugg's version of events, but De Vries narrowed his eyes and made as if to poke the fat man in his vast chest with a forefinger but fortunately thought the better of it.

'Are you sure he has gone for help?' he said severely.

Lugg relaxed and put his head on one side. 'That's a curious thing to say. Why else would he go out there? To make a snowman?'

The Dutchman was not mollified. 'I must see Mr Campion. Immediately.'

Mr Campion had been keeping an eye on the triumvirate in the hallway as he ferried plates and cups between kitchen and dining room, confident that Lugg was sticking to the story they had concocted on the trudge back from the coach, which now acted as an icy coffin for Graham Fisk. While Miss Pounder seemed to accept Lugg's explanation – and it had been important to 'head her off at the pass' before she publicly demanded to know why their driver was missing breakfast – but clearly the Dutchman also had his concerns.

As Miss Pounder politely but firmly pushed her way into the crowded kitchen, carefully avoiding Hereward Henderson who was now haranguing a hapless Rupert, De Vries stood his ground and glared down the hall at Mr Campion. A flurry of raised eyebrows, facial twitches and violent jerks of the head by Lugg indicated that there was a problem needing his urgent attention.

Taking a deep breath, Mr Campion assumed his responsibilities as head of the household and, having a good idea what was worrying the art dealer, he took him by the elbow and guided him into his study. Relieved of his burden, Lugg pursed his lips to blow a silent whistle and set off in search of a bacon sandwich.

Even with the lightest of grips on his guest's arm, and through several layers of clothing, Campion could feel De Vries quivering, but whether with anxiety or anger he could not tell. When Campion had closed the door behind them and he spoke, there was a tremor in his voice and a recurring trace of that elusive Dutch accent.

'Tell me true, *Meneer* Campion, *zeese* disturbances in the night. Were they burglars?'

'No, Mr De Vries, I can assure you we were not burgled,' said Campion with a straight face.

'But people came and went, did they not?' The Dutchman leaned forward on the balls of his feet, his hands fidgeting over his chest as though still clutching at the briefcase he had carried over the threshold like some holy relic.

'Your coach driver, Fisk, decided to go for help.' Campion kept his voice neutral.

'Did he take anything with him?'

'You mean your diptych, don't you? No, he did not, of that I can assure you, but I can see that you will not believe me without proof.'

'I do not call you a liar . . .'

Perhaps you should, thought Campion.

'. . . but I would like to see it is still safe.'

Mr Campion moved behind his desk and bent to unlock the small safe with its brass key, pulling out the Dutchman's slim leather case and handing it over.

'Safe in the safe, as you see.'

De Vries, making no apology for mistrusting his host, opened the case and unwrapped and examined the contents. Not until he had securely re-packed his precious rectangle of painted wood and handed back the case did he break the uncomfortable silence. 'I needed to be sure, once I heard of the burglars.'

'My dear sir, there were no burglars. Your picture was exactly where we left it and it will stay there until you leave.' He glanced out of the window to the snow-covered orchard and the wooden bridge across his personal moat. 'That may not be today, though. Even if it's letting up, it's still coming down, so to speak.'

'That does not reassure me.'

'What would?'

'When I asked if you had any weapons in the house, you said there was a shotgun.'

'Which we keep safely out of sight and temptation's way.' Mr Campion was loathe to admit that his twelve-bore, in its distressed leather slip case, might well be out of sight, but resting in the back of the Campions' bedroom wardrobe was hardly the most secure of locations.

'I would be happier if the weapon was more . . . more . . . public, in order to deter thieves.'

Mr Campion folded his arms across his puffed-out chest and stood his ground.

'Mr De Vries, I have no intention of lending you my shotgun, nor of standing armed guard over your property because you suspect you may be robbed by a fellow traveller. What sort of a signal would that send to them? They may be unexpected and uninvited guests, yourself included, but they are guests in my house, not yours. I am not aware that any of them have shown the slightest interest in you or the Suycker Diptych, and you were only suspicious, perhaps a little paranoid, about one person, your driver, who is no longer in the house.'

De Vries narrowed his eyes. 'What if he returns with accomplices?'

'I think that highly unlikely,' said Mr Campion.

As the Dutchman left the office in dissatisfied silence, Amanda and Rupert appeared in the doorway.

'My goodness, it's like a doctor's surgery this morning. Come in, come in. Next patient, please.'

Although his voice was nothing less than jovial, Mr Campion

fiddled with his spectacles as though they no longer fitted properly, and it was a sign which his wife recognized.

'You've been telling lies, haven't you, Albert.' It was not a question.

'Only white ones, darling, in order to sooth the savage beast that is our resident Dutch art dealer. How are the rest of our guests?'

'Just as odd as that Dutchman, but at least they are distracted by breakfast for the moment. They all seem to have resigned themselves to being stuck here at least for another day, perhaps two, and several have suggested an expedition to the coach to rescue their luggage to get some fresh clothes. I do have to report that we are running out of spare pullovers.'

Campion exchanged a hurried glance with his wife before answering in front of Rupert. 'That might keep them happy. Lugg and I will venture forth and act as porters – or should that be sherpas?'

'I'll come with you,' Rupert offered. 'We could take the sledge Lugg made me when I was a kid, it's in the garage doing nothing, which seems a shame with all this snow.'

'That's a good idea, but you must stay here,' Campion said firmly with Amanda nodding in agreement.

'What for?'

'To keep up morale, help your mother and Mrs Thursby and to keep your ears open for any juicy titbits our guests might scatter. Remember, this particular Christmas will be the basis of many an after-dinner story in years to come.'

'Not if that dotty professor is involved with his old Norse gods stuff. Mind you, one of those Americans pricked their ears up every time he mentioned Thor.'

'I noticed that too,' said Mr Campion, 'though slightly more worrying was Henderson's naughty little dig about the name Rudolph, and I don't mean the reindeer with the scarlet hooter.'

'He says he's a historian, so maybe he researched the area before he came up here and was just showing off.' Rupert paused for thought. 'Not that he could have known he would end up here.'

'Using a family name I have not used for more than forty years.'

'I always wondered,' Rupert grinned, 'when I was little, why we never sang "Rudolph the Red-Nose Reindeer" in this house.'

'Talking of names,' said Amanda, clearly in earnest, 'that American sergeant, Sergeant Sometimes or whatever he's called, addressed me as Lady Amanda this morning and I don't remember ever mentioning the title in his presence. And another thing which Rupert can help with – Sometimes said that one of his men wanted to build a snowman because he came from Santa Fé and had never seen snow. Does that sound right to you?'

'It sounds a bit odd,' Rupert answered. 'I have American friends who go skiing in the mountains there and I always thought that snow was a basic requirement for skiing.'

'Odd indeed,' said Mr Campion quietly.

NINE
Иногда

Campion and Lugg retrieved their boots from the tack room and, after moving several beer crates, picked up two shovels, which would normally be reserved for gardening duties but would now be put to clearing the snow that had drifted up against what had been a barn in a previous life but now served as the family garage. Once they had cleared enough for the wooden doors to be pulled open by two feet, Campion slid inside and found the light switch to illuminate the interior. Lugg jerked the door six inches wider so he could squeeze through the gap and join him.

The barn provided ample garage space for two vehicles, but three were a tight squeeze. Mr Campion's red Jensen, being the most valuable, was protected by an all-covering tarpaulin, and next to it Rupert's Riley Elf seemed to stand cold and abandoned, but both were dominated by the Alandel Land Rover, still decorated with cut-out cardboard reindeer.

Beyond the cars, hanging from hooks in the back wall was Rupert's childhood sledge. It was an impressively sturdy affair, about five foot long with curved iron runners which had been forged by the last surviving blacksmith in Southwark to owe Lugg a favour, the slatted wooden frame cut from seasoned oak, proudly planed and polished by Lugg himself. Being solidly built with little if any regard for aerodynamics, it was incredibly heavy and it took the pair of them to lift it down from its hooks. As a means of transportation for a young boy hoping to skid swiftly down a snowy slope, the wind whistling through his hair, it had always been impractical as, until he was a teenager, Rupert did not have the strength to pull the thing up a snowy slope unaided, and by then his interests had shifted to impressing girls in ways other than sledging. And so it had remained in suspension on the garage wall, along with spare bicycle tyres and the random coils of rope and wire which naturally gravitate to fill such spaces.

With some contortions and much heavy breathing, they manoeuvred the sledge outside, laid it on the snow, and Campion tugged on the rope attached to the curves of the runners to satisfy himself that the thing was still snow-worthy.

'It's a bit of a juggernaut, but it will have to do,' he decided.

'That,' said Lugg pompously, 'is the Rolls-Royce of toboggans.'

'Except they forgot to put an engine in it.' He held out the rope. 'So you'll have to do. Come on – mush!'

They stomped around the side of the house, sticking, they hoped, to the driveway rather than disturb the blanket of snow covering the dormant flower and kitchen gardens which were Amanda's pride and joy. It was only when they were clear of the house, following their own tracks left that morning, that Lugg, towing the sledge, spoke, but only after looking over his shoulder back at Carterers where Miss Pounder was outlined in the living room window, observing them.

'That Miss Pounder is a sharp cookie, you know. No one would cash a dodgy postal order in her post office.'

'You've taken quite a shine to her,' said Campion, masking his smile with his scarf.

'She might come across as a bit of a country mouse, but she keeps her eyes open – and her ears. She's noticed how the Dutch feller's accent seems to come and go when it suits him.'

'Yes, I'd noticed that too. Probably just a nervous tic; the man is very worried about his painting. Wanted an armed guard put on it.'

'You told him you had the shotgun?'

'I did, but made no effort to lend it to him.'

Lugg glanced around to make sure they were in splendid, freezing isolation. 'You didn't tell him about the *other* weapon, did you? The one you've got squirrelled away?'

'Of course not. Not even Amanda knows about that one.'

'Gathering winter fuel?'

'I beg your pardon?'

Amanda had joined Miss Pounder at the frosty living room

window. In the distance, in between flurries of snowflakes, they watched two figures, heads bowed, trudging down the invisible driveway, the second, larger, figure pulling a sledge behind him.

'Good King Wenceslas, as in the Christmas carol. In this case, *two* men came in sight, gathering winter fuel. It reminded me of an illustration in one of Rupert's Sunday School books when he was little. There was a really quite patronizing note to the illustration, explaining that winters in Czechoslovakia were much harsher than here so peasants had to forage for wood from the forest. Hah! They clearly hadn't seen this lot coming.'

Florence Pounder continued to stare silently at the whiteness outside.

'Wenceslas was Czech, or Bohemian, or something,' Amanda added limply.

'I know,' said Miss Pounder dreamily. 'Prague is a beautiful city.'

'I've heard so. You've been there? I thought Lugg told me you had told him that you had lived in Devon since the war.'

'That is true,' said Florence Pounder, but ventured nothing further.

'Well, those two are not gathering fuel,' resumed Amanda. 'Hopefully our strapping young Americans are doing that. Albert is collecting the luggage from the coach and I'm sure you'll feel better for a bath and a change of clothes. I think we can manage enough hot water. The television's still off and the phone line seems to be down, though.'

'That does not worry me,' said Miss Pounder. 'There is no one I need to telephone.'

Too many people were getting under Mrs Thursby's feet in the crowded kitchen, and while she had no compunction when it came to pushing, shoving or even punching her father-in-law out of the way, deference to her employers suggested a gentler, more diplomatic approach to their visitors. Normally, house guests at Carterers were of the 'good sort' and anything but common – even that Mr Lugg knew how to behave in company. But she did not know how to handle the motley crew which the snowstorm had deposited on the house. The vicar should be the least problem, because vicars were not supposed to make waves. The same could not be said for that chatterbox professor chap who just would not, or could not, shut up, and insisted on talking about ancient history that nobody knew or cared about. Even the vicar couldn't stand it any longer, and had asked Rupert if he could go into Mr Campion's study to find something to read from all the dusty old books he kept there. Rupert, being a polite lad, had said of course it was permissible, and the vicar had shown a clean pair of heels, with that funny foreigner, similarly not keen to stay in the kitchen and get stuck with the windbag professor, was soon off chasing the vicar into the study.

'What are you doing here, Pastor?'

'Looking for something to read,' said Elis Breck without turning round from the bookshelf he was perusing. 'It's Mr De Vries, isn't it?'

'Anything in particular?'

'A good detective story, Caesar's *Gallic Wars*, something on astronomy, or perhaps how the Fens were drained – that was mostly by Dutchmen, I believe – but basically anything which isn't about Anglo-Saxons and Hereward the all-too wide-awake as far as our verbose little professor is concerned. Mr Campion's library shows fairly eclectic tastes, so there should be something to tempt me.'

'Does he have anything on religious art history?'

If the priest thought it a question addressed to him because of his vocation, he took it in his stride. 'Haven't spotted anything in that area yet, but I haven't really been looking. I'm after something to take my mind off our current situation. And here it is.' He pulled a book from the shelf. '*Birds of the West Indies* – just the thing, should one be trapped on a desert island.'

'But we are not on a desert island,' said De Vries.

'No, but we are trapped, aren't we?'

The Reverend Breck sat down in the chair behind Campion's desk, opened the ornithological guide and began to read.

De Vries shifted uneasily from foot to foot then began to slide a finger along the bookshelves until he too selected a volume – Alan Moorehead's *The White Nile* – and took the chair on the other side of the desk.

The two men settled down to read in the uncomfortable silence of a monastery library.

*   *   *

'It is my contention,' Professor Henderson was saying, 'that Hereward met his end in conditions very similar to those we are experiencing today. It was winter and Hereward was once again on the run. He had been a declared outlaw most of his life and had returned to the life *silvaticus*, that's someone who lives in the woods.'

'Like Robin Hood in Sherwood Forest?' asked Rupert, attempting to be both politely interested while vainly trying to unseat Henderson from his hobby horse.

'A common comparison, but Hereward did not have a band of Merry Men, only one loyal follower, who legend says was called Martin Lightfoot, and they were being pursued – hunted – by twenty-four Norman knights.'

'Like a posse in a Western?'

'I suppose so.' Henderson paused as if filing the image away for future use. 'It did not end well, of course. The Normans caught them in a peasant's hut in a snowstorm and set fire to it. Ironic, really, as Hereward had something of a reputation as a fire-starter. He would ignite marsh gases in the Fens against the Normans when they besieged Ely; it was one of his favourite weapons of what today we would probably call guerrilla warfare.'

'Fascinating,' breathed Rupert, suddenly emboldened by the sight, over Henderson's bald head, of Florence Pounder entering the kitchen.

His heart sank as Miss Pounder swerved by the both of them with the silky skills of Stanley Matthews and headed directly for Mrs Thursby.

'Is there anything I can do to help?' she asked the housekeeper who, once again, was elbow-deep in a large mixing bowl pummelling together a congealing lump of sausage meat and shredded onions.

'Not here, deary,' said Mrs Thursby, screwing her eyes against the sting of the onions. 'I'm just knocking up some more sausage rolls to feed the five thousand. Mr Campion will be back with your luggage soon and you can get a change of clothes. You'll feel better for that.'

Miss Pounder was not sure how to take that, but felt you had to give the benefit of the doubt to a woman who had sausage meat oozing between her fingers and onion tears dribbling from her eyes.

She lowered her voice and asked, 'Would you happen to know if anyone has a spare cigarette?'

It was not that she particularly wanted or needed a cigarette, in fact she very rarely smoked these days and never in public, but she had seen that awful bore Henderson register her presence and perhaps a cigarette might keep him away, rather like a persistent mosquito.

'Nobody in this house smokes any more,' confided Mrs Thursby, as if it was a state secret, 'and I don't let Lloyd light up his pipe even in our house. Those Yank boys out in the tack room might have cigarettes – that's what they're famous for, isn't it? Dishing out cigarettes, chocolate bars and nylons.'

'That was certainly their reputation once. I'll go and ask,' said Miss Pounder, surprised that memories died hard in Norfolk.

As her shoes, along with all the footwear of the stranded travellers, were still drying out, Miss Pounder accepted Mrs Thursby's instruction to help herself to a pair of thick woollen socks warming on the Aga, which would get her across the icy flagstones to the tack room where she would find a selection of Wellingtons. The socks came with the advice not to 'catch your death' and the strict instruction not to 'let the cold in' when she opened the back door.

Miss Pounder sat on a kitchen chair and pulled on the socks over her still-damp lisle stockings, flexing her toes and luxuriating in their warmth. She had slept in her clothes, grateful for the insulating properties of her tweed skirt and the sheepskin coat which she was secretly proud still fitted her all those years after it had first seen active service. If anything, she was almost uncomfortably warm sitting there in the kitchen. Perhaps Mrs Thursby had the right idea: keep busy and stay in the warmest room. At least that way, in her sensible dress and pinafore, she looked normal and at home, unlike the other intruders who resembled a gang of refugees from some unspecified natural disaster. Perhaps, when her suitcase was brought in, she would make an effort and smarten herself up, though she knew she could not match the elegant appearance of Mrs Campion, to whom clothes, make-up and carefully managed coiffures seemed to come naturally, despite the anarchy which had descended on her home.

Steeling herself to face the elements, she fastened her coat, tied a tartan headscarf tightly under her chin, pulled on her gloves and padded over to the kitchen door, remembering the instruction not to let the warmth out or the cold in. Prepared to be blasted by a blizzard, she was surprised to find herself in a snow-globe winter, where there was no wind and thick flakes of snow floated gently from a milky sky. For a moment she was tempted to stick out her tongue and catch one, but already she could feel the chill swirl around her legs, reflected from the flagstones which someone had thoughtfully swept or shovelled clear so that only a light dusting of white remained.

The tack room's partly open door was only five yards away and the light inside was on, but the snow deadened any sounds from within. Florence put her head down and with long, ungainly strides staggered towards it.

To her surprise the shed was empty of people, though rammed to the rafters with what she presumed were the essential addenda to life in a country house which had not quite forgotten it had once been a working farm. Rusty implements, rakes, pitchforks, scythes and long, two-handled saws rested against the walls as if in an abandoned armoury, and just inside the door was a line of Wellington boots, adding to the impression that any resident soldiery had deserted in a hurry.

With one hand against a wall to keep her balance, Miss Pounder selected a pair of boots and slid her feet, now encased in wet socks, inside. As she did so she noted that the interior of the shed was filled by beer crates, a large metal trunk and logs, which had been stacked with regimental precision. Except the log pile had been disturbed, with logs removed but not in an orderly top-down way, almost as if someone had been burrowing into the stack. Given that there was a crate reserved for kindling and sawdust, splinters and two hand-axes on the floor, it seemed likely that somebody had been busy chopping firewood.

It was only as she stamped her feet firmly into the rubber boots, wincing slightly at the squelching sound produced, that she wondered where the woodcutters had gone. That was a mystery easily solved by opening the shed door just wide enough to put her head out and, screwing up her eyes against the snow, looking not back at the house but to the timber-framed barn and the tell-tale sets of footprints leading there.

Being unfamiliar with the rear of the house, she had no idea whether she was walking across a driveway or a courtyard, or even trampling over a dormant kitchen garden. The footprints in the snow were her only point of reference, and she was mildly shocked, on looking back, to discover that she could see the outline of the tack room, but Carterers itself had disappeared behind a shimmering white curtain.

She plodded towards the barn, which she guessed must be the Campions' garage, each icy intake of breath quenching the need for a cigarette, which did not surprise her as she had never been a serious smoker, at least not since the war, but it had been good to get out of the house whatever the weather, as she found confinement, however comfortable, unsettling.

One of the large double doors of the barn was ajar, and that was exactly where the trail of footprints led. As she trod in those prints in snow almost a foot deep, she imagined the scenario where the American airmen, being young and male, had soon got bored chopping kindling and had been unable to resist the opportunity to snoop and discover what kind of a car the Campions drove, no doubt hoping to find it was a vintage Bentley. Had not Sergeant 'Sometimes' addressed Mrs Campion as 'Lady Amanda' and so presumed that Mr Campion was a Lord? Surely then, the garage must contain at least one Bentley . . .

Yet the first thing she saw when she peered through the gap in the door was the silhouette of a pair of reindeer antlers at head height. It took a long moment for her to comprehend that the antlers were not attached to a real reindeer but were cardboard regalia adorning the roof of a Land Rover. By the time she had come to terms with what was clearly meant to be the modern version of Santa's sleigh, she was distracted by the sound coming from further within the garage. It was clear that this was a garage, for apart from the Land Rover, behind which she found herself, there were two cars, one considerably bigger and more expensive than the other.

The noise, sudden and strange as it was, made her cower behind the rear of the Land Rover though she could not exactly say why. It was a melange of sounds, a high-pitched swooping and whooping noise coupled with an electric crackle and a bass line trying to recreate the buzzing of an angry wasp trapped under a glass. It reminded Florence Pounder of a badly tuned shortwave radio, which was exactly what it was.

Through the windows of the Land Rover she spied the three Americans standing over the front of the expensive red car, its protective tarpaulin cover thrown back, studying an open suitcase from which a cable snaked under the open bonnet. One of the Americans had one cup of a pair of headphones clamped to one ear, and the attached microphone in front of his mouth, whilst he twiddled a variety of knobs, each rotation producing an ethereal whine.

Suddenly the static noises stopped and he spoke into the microphone to acknowledge the signal in a language which was not English, nor even American.

Florence loosened her headscarf, pulled it away from her ears and pressed herself into the flanks of the Land Rover. She held her breath and was confident that she heard what the airman said correctly as he offered the headset to Staff Sergeant Kosloffski.

'Иногда.'

'*E-nug-da*.'

Sometimes.

'He's still 'ere,' muttered Lugg, coming round the rear of the coach.

'The driver? Where else would he be? You didn't really expect him to have gone for a brisk walk to get his circulation going again?'

'Suppose not, be too late for that. Funny, but nobody seems to have missed him much.'

'Let our pilgrims go on thinking the noble Mr Fisk has gone for help,' said Campion, peering into the open luggage compartment. 'That's the British way of thinking when there's any sort of catastrophe. The driver, the pilot, the mountain guide, even the scout troop leader are all expected to assume responsibility for the rescue of those in their charge whatever personal danger it might involve.'

'In 'is case, quite a lot of personal danger.'

'So it would seem. I wonder what brought him down here in the first place?'

'Stands to reason,' said Lugg confidently. 'He saw somebody rootling around his coach in the middle of the night, or saw a flashing torch where there shouldn't be one, so he leapt into action and went to investigate.'

'By jumping out of a bedroom window into a snowstorm.'

'Good job he was fully dressed then,' Lugg sniffed, 'and that he'd had a few stiffeners before bedtime.'

'He had?'

'Old Lloyd saw to that. He was dishing out your brandy like there was no tomorrow, which for 'im there wasn't. Sorry, that was uncalled for.'

'Decent of you to notice,' said Mr Campion. 'Could whoever he saw have been after something in the luggage?'

'I don't think they were after a spare set of spark plugs and there's nothing on the coach itself, so the luggage was the only thing worth taking, but nothing seems to be missing.'

'That we know of. When the wayward pilgrims sought shelter last night – goodness, was it only last night? – one of the airmen lagged behind the others. That nice staff sergeant said he'd been delayed "securing the bus" and that struck me as odd at the time. What could possibly have needed securing?'

'The luggage, like I said. There's nothing else on the coach worth pinching, so anything valuable would be in here.'

'Our Dutch friend had something valuable, and he brought it with him into the house, hardly let it out of his sight. Nobody else brought anything with them, so perhaps it was something they did not want to be seen with . . .'

'So left it here to collect later – early this morning, when he got spotted by our driver chum who wasn't havin' anyone taking liberties with 'is charabanc. He should have stayed in bed.'

'Fine advice, my friend, but far too late for poor Mr Fisk,' said Campion sombrely, 'but there's little we can do for him here. Let us get these bags up to the house and see who claims what. Pull your sledge over here, Santa, and start loading.'

When Rupert's childhood sledge was loaded, precariously, with all the baggage from the boot of the coach, Lugg took up the reins and began to pull. The weight it now carried, plus the softness of the falling snow, made the sledge's progress painfully slow, even with Campion at the rear pushing on the pile of cases.

'Strewth,' groaned Lugg, pulling the looped reins of the sledge over his shoulders and around his chest to complete the image of him being in harness. 'This thing weighed a ton empty, now it must be two.'

'If you stop moaning, I'll paint "Rosebud" on it and chuck it on a bonfire when we get back,' offered Mr Campion, suspecting that Lugg did not appreciate the reference.

They trekked on in silence and were halfway home – at least the outline of Carterers was now visible between flurries – when Lugg pulled up so suddenly that the momentum from Campion pushing at the rear took the front edge of the sledge into his calves. Campion himself received a rather undignified face full of American kit bag.

'What now?' he snapped, straightening his spectacles with damp, gloved fingers.

'Damsel in distress by the looks of it,' said Lugg.

It was a damsel, though Florence Pounder may not have liked the label, and she did seem to be in distress. She was running, or as best as one could run in outsize Wellington boots through deep snow, flapping her elbows like an injured bird. From her left hand streamed her headscarf, her right hand clutching at something at her neck. Twenty yards from the sledge she dropped to her knees and waved her scarf as if in a gesture of surrender.

Abandoning the sledge, Campion and Lugg staggered towards her, taking large, awkward steps which in other circumstances would have been quite comical.

When they were almost within touching distance, Miss Pounder began to talk to them or, more accurately, at them, and she appeared to be speaking in tongues.

'*E-nug-da, e-nug-da. Rooskie.*'

'Are you hurt, Miss Pounder?' asked Campion, concerned that the woman was still clutching at her neck, but then he realized that her hand was holding a wooden crucifix, twisting its neck chain around her gloved fingers.

'The Americans – they're Russians,' she said, defiantly, as if daring them to contradict her.

'Now steady on, miss.' Lugg was gentleness personified as he offered a hand to help her stand. 'Take a breath and tell us—'

'I saw them and I heard them. They were in your garage, that barn thing with the cars. They had a radio and I think they were running it from the battery of the red one. They were speaking in Russian and the sergeant was called *Enugda*, which is Russian for "Sometimes".'

'Where did they get the radio?' Campion asked.

'They had a big bag, like a cricket bag, but I've no idea where it came from.'

'We might have,' said Lugg under his frosting breath.

'Could you hear what was being said on the radio?'

Whilst Lugg was impressed with how serenely Campion appeared to be taking all this, Miss Pounder's eyes were growing wider and her grabbing at her crucifix more frantic.

'I could not hear what they were receiving, but my guess would be instructions. What I did hear was them discussing things together *in Russian* and I saw what else they had in that bag; they had guns.'

'Shooters?' exclaimed Lugg involuntarily.

'Pistols . . . automatic pistols. They were checking them and loading them as they talked about their main target.'

'Target?' This time it was Campion who prompted her.

'They were talking about Lady Amanda.' For the first time, Florence's eyes watered and snowflakes were not responsible.

'Amanda is a target?'

'Yes, no, I don't think so.'

'Breathe,' advised Lugg again.

'Amanda may be some sort of target, but they were saying how they first had to take care of her bodyguard.'

Mr Campion straightened up so quickly that snow fell from the peak of his flat farmer's cap.

'Then I must go and protect my wife immediately.'

'Oh no,' said Miss Pounder, turning her wide-eyed gaze away from Campion and staring at Lugg, 'they weren't talking about *you*.'

TEN
Gunpoint

'That's a Colt .45, innit?'

'Good call, old guy. This one was made by Remington-Rand, but it gets the job done just the same.'

If anything, those who witnessed, open-mouthed in shock, Kosloffski's entrance into the kitchen, were more startled by Lloyd Thursby's full-volume question than the reality of the American waving a large automatic pistol at them.

Mrs Thursby's eyes widened and her expression suggested she had something stuck in her throat, but her hands never paused in their pounding of sausage meat in the bowl in front of her. Hereward Henderson gave an involuntary squeak and had the good grace to look embarrassed about it. Old Lloyd, after his initial interest in firearms, went silent. Which left Amanda to regain her composure and attempt to restore order.

'Just what the hell do you think you are doing, Sergeant? Put that thing away, you're frightening us.'

'Sole purpose of the exercise, Lady Amanda,' said Kosloffski with an infuriatingly charming grin on his face. 'Now please just behave while we round everybody up.'

The two airmen, Rivero and Quinn, materialized behind him and they too brandished pistols.

'Where's the priest – and the Dutchman?'

Kosloffski took a step forward, his gun pointed directly at Amanda's face.

'They're in the study,' said Henderson, almost immediately slapping a hand across his mouth as if an obscenity had slipped out.

'Oscar,' said Kosloffski, and Rivero pushed by him, heading for the hallway. 'Pete, check upstairs. Find the son and the woman.'

'Sergeant Kosloffski! You have not answered my question. Just what do you think you are doing?'

Amanda stood ramrod-straight; her voice had a steel which had been known to impress, even silence, military ranks far higher than sergeant.

'We are doing a simple head count, Lady Amanda,' said Kosloffski with disarming reasonableness, 'and once everyone is taken care of, it is our intention to quit the house.'

'What do you mean by taken care of?' snapped Amanda.

'Neutralized might be a better word, but rest assured we mean no harm to anyone.'

Amanda glared at the American and spoke through gritted teeth. 'Should that be no harm to anyone *else*?'

Kosloffski's smile faded but did not totally disappear. 'That was a case of wrong place, wrong time. Now we are in control and you will cooperate.'

'I doubt that very much, whatever it is you are planning.'

'Oh, I think you will. In fact, I'm pretty sure of it.'

Rupert was emerging from the bedroom he was temporarily sharing with Lugg with an armful of pullovers and rugby shirts from his schooldays which he had hoped his mother might have donated to a local charity by now, when he was confronted by one of the American airmen who had just mounted the stairs.

'Oh, hello,' he said cheerfully, 'looking for something? It's Pete, isn't it? Pete from New York.'

'Good memory,' said Pete from New York, his face impassive, his hands deep in the pockets of his air force parka. 'I was looking for you. Your mother sent me. She wants you to get your dad's shotgun.'

'Who is she threatening to shoot this time?'

Rupert's response fell on stony ground, adding to all the preconceptions his new friends at Harvard had about New Yorkers.

'No one I know,' said Quinn after considering the question seriously. 'She wants to fire a couple shots outside into the air so anyone nearby will figure out we're in here.'

'Good idea,' Rupert agreed, sticking to his policy of always agreeing with his mother. 'Any search parties out there would be alerted because they probably can't see the house from the road. On the other hand, we might even attract more wayward pilgrims.'

Quinn stood to one side and jerked his head, indicating that Rupert should lead the way downstairs.

'So shall we go get it?'

'Don't have to go far,' Rupert said helpfully, 'it's up here in my parents' bedroom.'

He noticed that Quinn had raised an eyebrow in surprise, which in turn surprised him. From what he had heard in his brief time across the Atlantic, Americans were prone to keep firearms in virtually every room in a house, especially, according to one of his married tutors, the bedroom.

Quinn followed Rupert in silence as he led the way into Carterers' master bedroom, but his eyes flashed as he took in the décor. The overall style could be described as 'comfortably rustic', with its brass bed frame, a teak, kidney-shaped dressing table, oak wardrobes and, perhaps incongruously, a varnished three-legged milking stool by the window which acted as a plant stand, the plant in question being a vicious-looking, long-spined cactus growing in a glazed Victorian chamber pot.

Rupert saw him scan the framed paintings hanging from the picture rail which ran around the room. He passed quickly over a couple of East Anglian landscapes, which Rupert thought might be quite valuable, a colour print of a medieval map of Florence, a fittingly regal portrait of Mr Campion's grandmother, a set of three etchings of the sail lofts and boatyards of Maldon in Essex, and a rather splendid portrait of his mother in all her youthful vivacity which Amanda refused to put on show downstairs, claiming its natural home was in the attic. This eclectic display of art seemed not to interest the American, apart from one exhibit, a large technical drawing of a de Havilland Mosquito fighter-bomber, and the faded lettering in one corner declaring that it was Top Secret that suggested it might well be a wartime original.

'Here it is,' said Rupert, having opened his father's wardrobe using the key which lived permanently in the lock, and pushed aside hangers full of shirts and his father's bespoke tailoring. He produced a vintage leather gun case and handed it to Quinn, who hefted it then slung the strap over his shoulder.

'Ammunition?' was all he said.

'No idea. Pa keeps it somewhere else. Says it's safer that way.'

'OK,' said Quinn, 'let's go downstairs.'

It seemed more of a command than a suggestion, but Rupert picked up his collection of spare pullovers and followed obediently.

If the Reverend Breck and Fred de Vries had heard raised voices or any sort of commotion coming from the kitchen, it had not disturbed them, for they were both engrossed in their chosen reading material when Oscar Rivero entered Mr Campion's study.

The American stood in the doorway, his right hand behind his back, and after a good twenty seconds the two bookworms seated either side of Campion's desk glanced up to acknowledge his presence.

'Would you two gentlemen kindly join us in the lounge?'

Neither looked enthusiastic at the prospect; Breck fearing another lecture from Professor Hereward, De Vries reluctant to leave his post as a self-appointed guard over the valuable item in the office safe.

Rivero did not wait long for an answer. He brought his arm from behind his back and flourished the large automatic pistol he was holding.

'I asked nicely,' he said, 'but it wasn't really a request.'

'Are you sure of what you heard?' asked Mr Campion, hoping that an air of perceived calmness would comfort Miss Pounder.

'When they said "bodyguard", they were definitely referring to Mr Lugg. The "big one" they called him, the one as big as a bear.'

'They'd have said pussy cat if they'd meant you,' said Lugg, grinning through frosting breath.

Mr Campion ignored him. 'And all this was in Russian?'

Miss Pounder nodded vigorously.

'Do you speak Russian?'

'Obviously. I'm a little out of practice, but I can get by.'

'And you thought they said Amanda was their target?'

'Not exactly. They were talking as if Amanda was going to help them to their target, which is why they needed to get her bodyguard out of the way, but perhaps I didn't hear clearly. I think I was in a mild state of shock and terrified they might see me.'

'Did they give nothing away?'

'Don't badger the poor miss,' growled Lugg. 'She's doing her best.'

'She's doing splendidly,' said Campion, 'and it was a stroke of brave genius to come and warn us. They didn't see you, did they?'

'No, I'm pretty sure they didn't.' She gave a nervous laugh. 'I have often said that women of my age become invisible to men, and for once I was grateful for that.'

'I am sure that is untrue, but if they failed to notice you, that gives us two advantages.'

'It does?'

'Certainly. Firstly, they do not know we know they are up to no good, and secondly, they do not know we have a Russian speaker on our side.'

'Just a minute . . .' Lugg started, but Miss Pounder was on the same wavelength and ahead of him.

'You mean to go back into the house, don't you?'

'But of course; it's my house.'

'But they have guns and I feel they know how to use them.'

'All the more reason. My wife and our son are in there and I intend to join them. Plus, it is very cold out here and a long and difficult walk to anywhere which might offer sanctuary or help.'

'What about our driver, Mr Fisk? Did he not go for help?'

'I'm afraid he did not get very far and will not be returning.'

Miss Pounder shook snowflakes from her scarf and retied it over her hair. 'I think I understand. Which means they are dangerous.'

'Quite.'

'Yet we wander back in as if we know nothing?'

'Exactly. I' – Campion glanced at Lugg – 'we – have no option. Our nearest and most dearest are at risk in there, but we have no claim on you. If you wish to make a run for it, though I would beg you to think carefully given the conditions out here in the wild, I cannot stop you.'

Miss Pounder flapped her sheepskin-coated arms over her chest as if generating heat. 'I have no penguin blood in me, so am unsuited to this weather. I think I'll take my chances in a nice warm kitchen.'

'Mrs T will have a fresh batch of sausage rolls ready by now,' said Lugg. 'Can't beat her sausage rolls. You'll love 'em.'

'I'm sure I will,' said Florence Pounder, 'even at gunpoint.'

'It could be dangerous and we are completely in the dark as to what the Americans—'

'Russians,' Lugg interrupted, and Miss Pounder nodded enthusiastically, dislodging snow from her headscarf.

'Whatever they are,' Campion continued, 'we have no idea what they are after. Surely their arrival on our doorstep was a matter of pure chance . . . the weather, the bus crashing into our gatepost . . .'

'The Dutchman,' said Lugg.

Mr Campion conceded the point. 'It could indeed be that they are after Mr De Vries's diptych.'

'That's an old painting,' Lugg advised Miss Pounder.

She gently replied, 'I know. But how do they expect to get away with it? Physically, I mean. Why steal something when there's no obvious escape route given the inclement weather?'

Lugg snorted loudly at the word 'inclement'.

'Unless, of course, they have yet to put their plan into action. Miss Pounder, when you saw them with their guns, they were in the barn, were they not?'

'Yes.'

'Not the house, so they may not have shown their weapons in the house, at least not yet. And you are sure they did not see you observing them?'

'They would have come after me to stop me warning you if they had.'

'Yes, they probably would.' Mr Campion was quietly impressed with the woman's stoicism. 'But if they have not revealed their hand, we might have another slight advantage in that they don't know we know they are armed.'

'That's a bit thin, isn't it?' Lugg was not impressed.

'I am having trouble, old fruit, in listing all the advantages we have on our side. We cannot abandon Amanda and Rupert and our unexpected guests while we go seeking help, even if we could get anywhere to find any in these conditions. Nor can we telephone for assistance, which makes me think that the phone line may have been cut rather than brought down by the snow. Therefore I suggest that our best plan is to return to the house with this sleigh full of presents, having met Miss Pounder here as she was out for her morning constitutional exercise and, being British, was not going to let a spot of bad weather disrupt her routine.'

'And then?'

'We play it by ear, old chum, as we always have. Sorry, but that's the best I can come up with. I think my brain, along with my toes, is in danger of frostbite. We must remain calm and give no indication that we suspect anything untoward is going on. That could be a strain on you, Miss Pounder. You must keep what you saw to yourself and not say a word to anyone. Above all, because it could come in useful, keep the fact that you speak Russian absolutely top secret.'

'I can do that,' said Miss Pounder.

The first inclination Rupert had that something was seriously wrong in the household was when, near the bottom of the stairs, he saw the Reverend Breck coming out of his father's study heading for the living room, followed by De Vries, who was shuffling with spasmodic jerks due to the grip the American Rivero had on his coat collar. The Dutchman was clearly moving under protest, but not struggling too hard because of the pistol Rivero had pressed into the small of his back.

Rupert froze and felt the pressure of the other American, Quinn, behind him.

'Just keep moving, buddy.'

He did not have to turn around to know that it was a gun with which Quinn was tapping him on the shoulder.

They trooped into the living room where Rupert made a beeline to the side of Lady Amanda, who was standing, hands on hips, in front of the fire.

'What's going on, Mother?'

'I wish I knew, darling. It seems that our American friends, whom we brought into our home to shelter them from the storm, are dissatisfied with our hospitality and being rather boorish about it. I have indicated that they are welcome to leave and find better accommodations as soon as they can, if not sooner.'

Rupert knew from family legend, if not historical fact, that both his father and mother had confronted armed adversaries over the course of their relationship though, as far as he was aware, never before in their own home. He had the distinct impression that his mother, confronted with an armed uprising, was struggling to contain the outrage and anger she clearly felt behind a defensive wall of good manners and calm control, fixing the intruders with a defiantly icy glare.

The aura of strength which Amanda exuded certainly appealed to the unarmed population of the room, who all moved to stand by her as Rupert had: Mrs Thursby obsessively wiping her hands on a tea towel, her father-in-law looking generally bemused but fascinated by the scenario of gunmen in the flesh rather than on the small screen, the priest clutching the bird-watching book he had been reading over his heart as if it was the family Bible, and Hereward Henderson looking more confused than usual, though aware enough of the situation to know that this was not the time for one of his lectures. Only De Vries displayed obvious agitation, his face a swirl of tics and twitches as he wrung his hands together as if trying to rid them of marauding ants.

'Now if y'all will settle down and be quiet,' Kosloffski ordered, levelling his pistol directly at Rupert, although none of his victims was moving unduly and all maintained a sullen silence, 'then I'll tell you what's going to happen.'

If anything, it was Kosloffski, flanked by his two armed compatriots, who appeared the most unsettled. His eyes flicked over the faces of the seven people lined up before him, giving away only the slightest hint, no more than a suggestion, that perhaps he was not totally in control of a situation all logic said he must be.

'Where's the other woman?'

Amanda flinched as if struck, silently cursing herself for not noticing that the mousey religious woman who seemed to have taken a shine to Lugg was not present, but she instantly regained her impassive composure. It was Mrs Thursby who broke the uncomfortable silence.

'Went outside, so she did.' And when everyone, prisoners and captors alike with the exception of her father-in-law, looked at her as if to say 'in this weather?', she added, 'Said she needed some fresh air, didn't like being cooped up.'

'She can't have got far,' said Rivero to his sergeant. 'I can get her, easy.'

'Not until we've neutralized the bodyguard,' hissed Kosloffski, 'then we'll haul her in.'

Amanda now struggled to remain emotionless, though she was well aware of Rupert squirming with confusion next to her. The situation had transitioned remarkably quickly from unexpected to alarming to frightening to the bizarre. Bodyguard? What bodyguard? *Whose* bodyguard?

'There's no need to worry,' announced Hereward Henderson, who had positioned himself at the end of the line of hostages and was the nearest to the window, its view of the driveway hampered by the curtain of tumbling snowflakes. 'Here she comes, with Mr Campion and that large fellow, and they're bringing our luggage.'

Amanda made a silent vow to slap Hereward Henderson for being annoying, just as soon as she had punched Sergeant Kosloffski for threatening her son.

The one called Quinn strode over to the window, but at an angle so that he could not be seen from outside.

'It's them all right,' he said, 'heading straight for us.'

'OK, folks, everybody down!' ordered Kosloffski, emphasizing his commands with sharp waves of his pistol. 'Down on your knees – now!'

With varying degrees of speed and grace, the prisoners sank on to their knees, most eyes on the Reverend Breck as if expecting him to lead by example. Only Lloyd Thursby appeared reluctant to comply, as though he was taking his time to fully grasp the instruction, but then his face lit up and he loudly announced, 'Hit the dirt! *That's* what they say in the cowboy films!'

'Be that as it may,' snarled Mrs Thursby, grabbing him by the arm and pulling him down, 'the carpet's cleaner.'

'They're heading down the side of the house, going round back,' reported Quinn from his vantage point by the window. 'Looks like they're gonna fall right into our arms.'

'Where else they going to go? You stay here and keep our happy household covered – and don't hurt anyone, you got it?' When Quinn nodded, Kosloffski turned to the other gunman. 'Oscar, you come with me and form the reception committee.'

'So how do we play this?' asked Lugg as he pulled the sledge down the side – the blindside – of the house.

'Quietly, diplomatically, delicately, but with style and panache,' replied Mr Campion.

'Y'aven't got a clue, have you?'

'Not a one. However, I suggest we pretend we know nothing – I have found that always works. We play it by ear, as they say. We do not admit to seeing anything suspicious on the bus; we were only there to collect the luggage. We met Miss Pounder on our return and advised her that it was not the weather or the season for a stroll in the gardens. Miss Pounder, of course, saw nothing untoward before leaving the house and most certainly does not speak or understand Russian. Are we agreed?'

His compatriots nodded. The trio turned the corner of the house and, heads down, trudged towards the tack room and the kitchen door, all three of them staring at the barn, its doors now firmly closed, as they passed though resisting the urge to investigate.

They were stamping the snow off their boots and preparing to unload the sledge when the kitchen door was opened and Staff Sergeant Kosloffski stood there smiling and pointing a gun at them.

Mr Campion, when briefing Lugg and Florence Pounder, had considered adding the proviso that they should remember to look surprised at whatever was waiting for them at Carterers. The sight of Kosloffski's pistol, and the one held by Rivero, ensured that the surprise on their faces was entirely genuine, although Mr Campion's was tinged with curiosity, and possibly a little hubris, as to why both automatics were inflexibly levelled at Lugg. Surely it could not be simply the fact that he offered the bigger target.

'Do come in from the cold,' said Kosloffski with the air of a solicitous commissionaire, 'and leave the luggage; we'll take care of that.'

'May I ask, as this is my house,' Campion began politely enough, 'just what the devil do you think you are doing waving guns around? And where is my wife? If you have harmed her in any way, I promise that you will regret it.'

Kosloffski's smile did not waver. 'Relax. Lady Amanda is with the rest of your guests and is perfectly safe and sound. Now take off your boots – you won't be needing them again – and come through and join the others.' He jerked his head in Lugg's direction. 'But him first. Oscar, pat him down.'

Rivero waved his pistol, instructing Lugg to come into the kitchen, and the big man padded forward, at one point with Rivero's gun in the small of his back and Kosloffski's aimed at his ample stomach.

'Hands flat on the table, legs spread.' Rivero punctuated his commands by pointlessly stabbing the muzzle of his gun into Lugg's well-padded – under several layers of clothing – back. 'Legs apart.'

It may have been an undignified position for a man of his age, but given his proportions it meant that Lugg's stomach rested comfortably on the edge of the kitchen table and Campion was almost sure that he was eyeing the plate of cooling sausage rolls which Mrs Thursby had placed frustratingly just out of reach.

Rivero used his hand and the flat of his pistol to slap, pat and feel his way down his victim's arms and flanks, under the armpits and down both legs.

'I should have warned you, he's ticklish,' said Mr Campion.

'He's clean,' said Rivero, giving Lugg a whack on the shoulder with his pistol as if congratulating him, a blow which Lugg shrugged off with indifference.

'Front room,' ordered Kosloffski, 'and keep both eyes on him.' He waved his gun, indicating that Campion and Miss Pounder should follow.

'Are we not to be subject to a body search?' quipped Campion. 'How disappointing.'

Once again the Kosloffski smile beamed out and Campion thought that although the man might well be a Russian, his dental work was flagrantly American. 'We do not regard you as dangerous.'

'I think I find that insulting.'

'Well, you ain't a threat to us.' The smile faded. 'Not as long as we have your wife and son.'

Mr Campion bit his lower lip and allowed Miss Pounder to precede him as they followed Rivero and his prisoner to the lounge where the population of Carterers were kneeling in a line as though awaiting Holy Communion.

Amanda greeted his arrival with damp eyes and open arms. 'Albert! Thank God. What is going on? Who are these people and what do they want?'

Campion linked an arm through hers as he kneeled down at her side and did a rapid survey of their fellow captives, nodding reassuringly to each in turn. Lloyd Thursby grinned inanely and raised his eyebrows, as if saying that these proceedings were indeed a rum do, though he flinched as his daughter-in-law flicked her tea towel at him. Hereward Henderson looked simply bemused, but at least he was silent; De Vries was twitchy, his gaze rarely straying from the door to Campion's study across the hallway; Rupert pulled Miss Pounder down next to him and she, now parted from Lugg, seemed grateful for his company. Only Elis Breck dared to speak.

'I am sorry if we have somehow brought this upon you, Mr Campion. I assure you it was not by design or intent.'

'I wish I knew what has brought this upon us, Reverend. We offered sanctuary from the storm for stranded pilgrims and we seem to have invited pirates into our home.'

'We are not pirates!' Kosloffski commanded their attention, his compatriots to either side of him, all with their pistols levelled. 'We are not here to steal from you.'

Campion was sure he heard De Vries exhaling loudly.

'We have a mission to complete which will require you to remain here for twenty-four hours, not that you were going anywhere. I'm not saying it will be comfortable, but if you all behave, we will be out of your hair by this time tomorrow.'

'Why us?' demanded Campion. 'Why here?'

'This house was always part of the plan,' answered Kosloffski, 'but our timing was thrown by the snowstorm.'

'Dare I suggest that your charabanc crashing into one of my impressive gateposts was not quite the accident you would have everyone believe? And our telephone line is not so much down, but has been cut, hasn't it?'

'You're smart,' said the American.

'Clearly not smart enough.'

ELEVEN
Reporting For Duty

Further instructions would be forthcoming, Kosloffski had announced, once the situation had been secured, and once again Mr Campion had the feeling that 'being secure' was not something which would apply to the line of hostages, kneeling like quiet penitents in a line on the lounge carpet, backs to the fire.

While Kosloffski and Rivero covered them, Quinn disappeared to the kitchen and the back door banged. He was gone for no more than two uncomfortably silent minutes, then the door slammed again and Quinn reappeared carrying a large canvas holdall, placing it gently at his sergeant's feet after unzipping it.

Mr Campion leaned forward, as though about to receive the communion wafer, until he could peer into the bag and make out a variety of metal cylinders, a camera case and a collapsible tripod. As he leaned back imperceptibly on his haunches, he glanced at Miss Pounder who was sheltering behind the mountainous bulk of Lugg, who had quietly edged near her. She too had peered into the bag and now exchanged a knowing look of confirmation with Campion.

Kosloffski crouched down and delved into the bag with his free hand, rummaging then drawing out items as if he was in charge of the bran tub at a village fête. The prisoners – for now they clearly were prisoners – watched in shocked silence as Kosloffski removed three spare magazines for their pistols, handing one each to his subordinates and pocketing the third.

He looked into the bag, sorted through its contents and spoke to himself rapidly in Russian, as if conducting some sort of inventory. Campion felt a gentle nudge from his wife's elbow signalling that she had noticed the language the sergeant had slipped into. Kosloffski then produced something shiny, something jangling, which prompted him to bark out a one-word order, this time in English: 'Chairs!'

The command confused Campion further even as he realized that the jangling steel bracelets Kosloffski was holding were not handcuffs, as he had first thought, but manacles, which had much longer chains. When Rivero appeared with two dining room chairs and placed them back-to-back in the middle of the room, he began to see the possibilities, which caused his stomach to churn and his mouth to go dry, but nevertheless he made as if to get to his feet.

'Not you!' Kosloffski's gun was levelled at Campion's face. 'You're not going anywhere, Mr Campion.' The dead eye of the gun barrel moved to hover over Lugg. 'You, big man, get up and take a chair.'

As Campion sank back on to his haunches, Lugg puffed his bulbous cheeks, exhaled and shook his head in despair as he made heavy weather of standing up, producing an impressive array of grunts and wheezes along the way, but if he was looking for sympathy, it was in vain. The unblinking eye of Kosloffski's pistol ushered him to the right-hand chair, which faced the Christmas tree, whose twinkling baubles just added a mocking irony to the season of goodwill. Once seated, Lugg's pudgy ankles were unceremoniously manacled, the chain of his restraints looped over his chair's stretcher and the legs of the second chair, then his hands, on a shorter leash, were cuffed behind the chair back. Lugg's immobilization was done with such efficiency that Campion suspected the exercise had been well rehearsed.

Kosloffski's gun swung to point at Rupert. 'Now you get to share the best seat in the house.'

'No!' yelled Amanda, bucking against her husband's arm as it tried to restrain her. 'Not him! Take me!'

Fending off his mother's clawing fingers, Rupert rose to his feet and allowed Kosloffski's automatic to guide him to the chair where he sat, back-to-back with Lugg, as his ankles were similarly manacled and his hands cuffed, though with the added touch that the chain of his handcuffs was looped through the one restraining Lugg's wrists. Thus the two of them, the big one and the slender one, were bound to both their chairs and each other like mismatched bookends.

'Are we just going to sit here and take this?' Amanda hissed to Mr Campion. She shook her head in frustration and shouted at Kosloffski, 'Why am I whispering? This is my house, damn you!'

'You are right on the money there, Lady Amanda.' The American's tone was so patronizing that Campion was sure his wife's perfectly manicured nails would target his eyes with precision if he came within range. 'And if all goes to plan, we'll be out of your hair by this time tomorrow.'

'May one be given a hint of your plan?' asked Campion politely, his left hand restraining Amanda's right arm.

'We are good soldiers,' Kosloffski smiled, 'and we will be reporting for duty. But first, a little housekeeping. Oscar, see to it.'

Rivero pocketed his gun and strode to the line of kneeling hostages, who all turned their heads as he walked by until he reached the last figure in the line.

With no attempt at gentleness, he grabbed the collar of Hereward Henderson's jacket, hauled him to his feet and pulled him, howling, from the room.

Campion recognized the technique when it came to dealing with prisoners who outnumber captors: disarm, corral, immobilize, explain nothing then increase the level of uncertainty by singling out, for no obvious reason, one prisoner for special treatment.

Rivero, pushing Henderson before him, disappeared into Campion's study across the hall, and closed the door behind him with a violent flick of a heel. The eyes and ears of all the kneeling prisoners, plus those of Lugg and Rupert, chained in their bizarre courting chair, were fixed on the study door, anticipating at best a scream, at worst a shot.

Amanda was the first to break the spell. 'What are you doing to the professor?' she demanded. 'How dare you mistreat him? What right have you to mistreat any of us?'

'We have to ask your professor some questions. It shouldn't take long, but we have to be sure.' Kosloffski's smile seemed to be a permanent fixture, even when he was waving a gun at you. 'Like I said, a piece of housekeeping and when that's done, we're out of here.'

'And just where do you think you are going?'

Even as she said it, Amanda knew it had come out in the tone of an infants' schoolteacher scolding a recalcitrant child in her best 'George, don't do that' voice. The American did not appear remotely rebuked.

'Oh, you'll find out, Lady Amanda. You're coming with us.'

Mr Campion felt his wife's upper body go rigid next to him, and she seemed oblivious to the fact that he had taken her hand in a reassuring grasp.

'And just how do you expect to go anywhere in this weather?' he asked, drawing Kosloffski's gaze and the barrel of his pistol on to him.

'We'll be taking the Alandel Land Rover we found in your barn. That should handle the terrain. I would have preferred the flashy red coupé – is that yours? – but that just won't fit our purpose. The Land Rover is just perfect; a lucky break for us. All we need are the keys.'

Still smiling, Kosloffski turned his gun until it was levelled an inch from Rupert's forehead. Mr Campion felt proud that his son did not flinch or struggle against his restraints, and somewhat relieved that it was not Lugg, who with his back to the action was blissfully unaware of the threat, in that particular seat.

'They're in my coat pocket,' said Amanda quickly. 'It's in our bedroom.'

'Go get them. Pete, go with her, and don't bother looking for the shotgun, Lady Amanda – we've already confiscated that.'

'Didn't find no ammo though,' said Quinn.

'If they ain't got the gun, that won't do them much good.' Kosloffski moved along the line of supplicants until he towered over Fred De Vries, though the Dutchman refused to acknowledge his presence, his eyes fixed on the door to Campion's study until he was spoken to. 'And I overheard our friend here asking Mr Campion if there were any other firearms in the house. Seems he thought he was in need of protection.'

The sergeant turned on his heels and swung his pistol back on to Campion. 'There aren't, are there – any more guns here?'

Mr Campion looked up and blinked rapidly behind his glasses. 'An Englishman's home is supposed to be his castle, but we have been rather lax recently in taking steps to defend it. We didn't really see the need, until now.'

'You want me to make him give a straight answer?' said Quinn through a curled lip.

'I don't think that will be necessary,' replied Kosloffski, without taking his eye from Campion. 'Mr Campion is a sensible man and is not going to give us any trouble as long as we have his wife and son. Now go upstairs with the lady of the house and get those keys and let her get into some warm clothing.' He glanced out of the window. 'It's cold out there.'

Campion was secretly relieved that Amanda had been escorted upstairs and was not present when Rivero emerged from his study, virtually dragging a distressed Hereward Henderson by the collar back into the lounge and depositing him, on his knees, between Lugg's chair and the Christmas tree.

His appearance affected all of them, for blood had leaked from his nose and lower lip, staining the front of his shirt. There was a bruise developing over his left cheekbone and his bowtie was askew, resting on the side of his neck like a green vampire bat. The sight of him made Lugg growl and strain forward against his chains, while Rupert twisted his neck and head to see what was making everyone gasp. The Reverend Breck looked shell-shocked, Miss Pounder gave a cross between a sigh and a sharp intake of breath, and Mrs Thursby began to whimper while her father-in-law merely grinned inanely. Only De Vries seemed impervious to the plight of the abused professor, preferring to stare beyond him to the open door of the study across the hall while wringing his hands as though trying to dry a sopping wet towel.

'For God's sake, what have you done to him?' Campion pulled out a neatly folded white handkerchief from an inside pocket and began to get to his feet.

'Down, boy!' Kosloffski jabbed his gun at Mr Campion, who hesitated, then caught the look of fear in Rupert's eyes, and sank back to his knees. Lugg, unable to see what was happening, grunted loudly and rocked his chair violently from side to side with such force that the baubles on the Christmas tree tinkled.

Rivero approached Kosloffski and spoke rapidly in Russian. Campion looked at Miss Pounder and surreptitiously pulled at the lobe of his left ear.

When Rivero finished his report, Kosloffski nodded his approval then returned to giving orders, aiming specifically at the Thursbys.

'You, lady, get back in the kitchen and prepare some food for us. We'll need rations for three to take with us, plus a couple of Thermos flasks of coffee – black, no milk, but don't spare the sugar. And you, old guy' – he raised his voice and spoke slowly into Lloyd's face – 'bring more wood in from that shed. Then start collecting all the boots and everybody's shoes and throw them out of the back door. Go with them, Oscar, and make sure all the sharp knives and axes are put out of temptation's way. Now, what's keeping Pete?'

The Thursbys got to their feet and Lloyd took his daughter-in-law's arm to guide her, although Mrs Thursby's expression of disgust suggested she knew perfectly well where the kitchen was. Rivero followed and Kosloffski backed out of the lounge and into the hall.

De Vries twitched and tensed like a sprinter on the starting blocks, and Campion thought he might be contemplating a dash to the study.

'Relax,' he whispered, 'they're not after your precious diptych.'

'Well, that's put my mind at rest,' said Lugg out of the side of his mouth, his eyes fixed innocently on the tinsel angel on top of the Christmas tree.

Rupert turned his head towards his father. 'Then what are they after?'

Campion shrugged his shoulders and shook his head, but felt Florence Pounder edging sideways on her knees closer to him. She had her head bowed and was fumbling the crucifix hanging from her neck. When she spoke, Campion had to strain to hear her.

'They were asking the little professor what he knew about the Norse god Thor, which was quite a lot, it seems, but not what they wanted to hear. Or perhaps it was, as they seemed happy with that result. I don't understand.'

'Neither do I,' said Mr Campion, 'but I think my wife might.'

'Catch!'

The airman known as Peter Quinn did not move and neither did his gun hand, allowing the small bunch of keys to bounce off his chest and land at his feet on the bedroom carpet. Without taking his eyes, or his pistol, off Amanda, he crouched until he could scoop them up with his free hand. 'Now get dressed for the great outdoors,' was all he said.

'Where are we going?'

'You'll see soon enough. Now put a spurt on.'

Amanda already had her wardrobe doors open, having taken out her favourite blue duffel coat and laid it on the bed, removing a pair of fur-lined gloves and the keys to the Land Rover from its pockets. Idly she ran her fingers along the line of dresses and tops on hangers which presented themselves for inspection.

'Casual or business? Or will we be dressing for dinner?'

'Don't be so smart, lady. Just get into your warmest duds.'

Taking as much time as she could without provoking her captor, Amanda selected a thick white, high-neck woollen sweater – which her husband said made her look like a U-boat *Kapitän* – and a pair of heavy tweed plus fours which she insisted were called her 'shooting breeks' and were made for life on the Highland moors rather than the golf course, though she patronized neither. She threw them on the bed and from the drawer in the base of the wardrobe selected a pair of long red socks, telling herself that this was not the occasion, or the weather, to worry about the fashionable aspects (there were none) of her makeshift ensemble.

Quinn watched her every movement closely, though Amanda studiously ignored his presence until she unbuttoned her cardigan, removed it and put one hand behind her neck to grasp the zipper of her dress. At that point, she locked eyes with the American.

'I can manage this next bit by myself, thank you very much.'

The staring contest lasted for half a minute, but Amanda had outstared wing commanders and generals and a mere airman was no competition.

'I'll step out, but you hurry up. The door stays open.'

He stepped back on to the landing and Amanda moved behind the open bedroom door for privacy.

'Everything OK up there?' Kosloffski shouted from below.

'Fine,' Quinn replied. 'I got the keys.'

'And our special lady?'

'She's getting dressed for the trip.'

'You got eyes on her?'

'She ain't going anywhere.'

'You'd better be sure 'bout that, Pete.'

To Quinn's relief, Amanda flitted briefly into view through the bedroom doorway. She was smoothing down the folds of the white sweater which, clearly two sizes too large for her slender frame, came down over her hips and the waistband of the plus fours. Then, in clear sight of the American, she sat on the edge of the bed and began to pull on the thick red socks.

Airman Quinn, if he noticed at all, might have thought it an English eccentricity that ladies of Amanda's quality wore thick leather gloves in order to put their socks on.

Mr Campion was so relieved at his wife's return downstairs that he buried the fatuous thought that he had never known her get changed so quickly.

Seeing the beaten and bloodied Hereward Henderson slumped on his haunches between the Christmas tree and the restrained bulk of Lugg, who was glowering a mixture of sympathy and fury, Amanda's first thought was to move to his aid. She was prevented by Kosloffski, who placed himself and his pistol between them.

'He's fine, just a little shook up. Now tell your husband that while you're away he's responsible for keeping everybody in this house *in* the house. Nobody leaves, understand? That way, everyone stays warm and cosy.'

'Whatever you're up to,' said Mr Campion, slowly getting to his feet, 'take me, not my wife.'

'That's not gonna happen and just to be sure, these two' – he waved his pistol over the heads of Rupert and Lugg – 'stay tied up and Pete here will stick around to make sure they stay that way. Any trouble and your boy will be the first to get it, are we clear?'

Mr Campion could only admire, yet again, his wife's bravery, and also her restraint.

'Your behaviour to date convinces me to take your threats seriously, Sergeant. Just remember, we don't like bullies in this country.'

'Sticks and stones may break my bones, but words will never hurt me,' Kosloffski chanted in a childish, singsong voice.

'I know a few that would,' said Lugg grimly, at which Campion could not contain a smile.

Amanda stepped closer to her husband, close enough to place her gloved hands on his shoulders. 'Everything will be all right, Albert, as long as you behave sensibly.'

'Don't I always?'

'Very rarely, actually.'

Mr Campion looked down into his wife's almond eyes and rested his cheek on her gloved hand. 'Good idea,' he murmured, nuzzling the leather. 'Keep yourself warm.'

'Best way, when dealing with a prickly problem,' whispered Amanda, caressing Campion's cheek with her gloved fingers.

'I hope they allow you some boots,' he said, 'as they seem to have confiscated ours. Those red socks, of course, are rather stylish and they could help locate you should you end up face-down in a snowdrift. It's piling up out there.'

'And that's quite enough smooching,' commanded Kosloffski. 'We need to move if we're to get back before dark. Now listen up.'

He took a step back so that he could be seen by all in the room except Lugg, who glared furiously at a shiny tinfoil star dangling from the closest branch of the Christmas tree.

'While we're gone, Pete here will be in charge. You will remain in the house; there's nowhere to go anyway and the prospect of any visitors is remote, so there ain't nobody riding to your rescue. All you have to do is be good. You'll stay warm and they may get the TV back on this afternoon if you're lucky. Our generous hosts have made sure you won't starve and there are books to read in Campion's study.'

At the mention of the study, De Vries began to twitch and shake and the Reverend Breck, kneeling next to him, put an arm around him to restrain the convulsions.

'If you give Pete any trouble, and I mean *any* trouble, Pete will shoot Campion Junior here.'

He tapped Rupert lightly on the head with his pistol, but stared at Mr Campion as he did so. 'And then I guess he'd have to shoot the big guy here, because he's paid for taking a bullet for his boss.'

'*Eh???*' the word exploded from Lugg's mouth and he bucked and heaved in his chair in an attempt to turn and face his tormentor.

'Settle down, Magers,' said Amanda gently, asserting control. 'This is my house and I expect to find it and all its inhabitants in one piece on my return. I apologize for the inconvenience and the discomfort but, as you can see, the situation is out of my control.' She turned calmly to face Kosloffski. 'I take it I will be returning, Sergeant?'

'You sure will, Lady Amanda. Now we really have to go. Oscar will find you some boots.'

'I would still like to know where you are taking me.'

'It's more a case of you taking us. You'll need your security pass.'

'My what?'

'Your high-level civilian security clearance for RAF Marham. It's in your purse in the kitchen. I checked.'

'Marham?' As she said it, Campion could see her shoulders stiffen and her gloved hands ball into fists.

'I told you,' Kosloffski said sweetly, 'we're reporting for duty.'

Amanda turned back to her husband and leaned in to kiss his cheek. 'Behave yourself, Albert, and keep everyone calm.' Then as she delivered the kiss, she whispered, 'Thor.'

TWELVE
Thor's Other Hammer

It had often been said that Lady Amanda Fitton (as was) had made aeronautical engineering a peculiar choice of career, especially on the sole criteria of being a girl who liked tinkering with mechanical things. It was not that being female and a fondness for aviation were incompatible, for the globe-hopping *aviatrix* was a regular feature on the newsreels and usually greeted on each landing with the adoration normally reserved for Hollywood starlets. There was also an established coterie of society ladies who had the means to own their own aeroplanes and thought nothing of nipping over to Le Touquet for lunch. The young Amanda had neither the means nor the inclination to join a flying luncheon club and was far more interested in the oily mechanics and aerodynamics of their small private planes rather than the cocktail lounge gossip of their owners. The war, and the formation of the Women's Auxiliary Air Force, made her chosen profession respectable, if not entirely understood by her peeresses. Females may not have been allowed to be part of the front line 'Few' in the Battle of Britain, but their role in ferrying fighters and bombers from factories to operational squadrons was a vital one, even if naturally undervalued – if not blithely ignored – by the male majority in RAF blue.

There were a few women, far fewer than the legendary Few, who worked behind the scenes and whose weapons were drawing boards and slide rules, designing new and improving existing aircraft. Amanda was one of them, and her work in Alandel Aeroplanes had attracted the attention of minds more interested in military than civilian applications of her talents. Her wartime work thus involved her signing the Official Secrets Act and in peacetime its provisions were, if anything, more strictly observed, as a hot war became a cold one and a former ally turned into a potential enemy. The evolution of jet engines and rockets with nuclear warheads hardly simplified matters. As much of Alandel's, and Amanda's, work involved close cooperation with the Royal Air Force and, inevitably this being East Anglia, the USAF, she was well aware of the existence of Thor.

Not, of course, the Germanic god of thunder with his magical and very deadly hammer *Mjölnir*, which returned to Thor's hand whenever it had vanquished a foe. The Thor with which Amanda was familiar was far from mythical and considerably more dangerous than a hammer, however lustily thrown, though it did produce thunder of a sort.

The Thor in question was an American IRBM, though only a minority of the population could swear to those initials being shorthand for Intermediate Range Ballistic Missile, and those who did know preferred to deny they did or simply changed the subject. Since the Cuban Missile Crisis of that autumn, the topic was one only raised with trepidation, as few were reassured by the deployment on British soil of a rocket which could deliver a 1.44 megaton nuclear warhead over an 'intermediate range' of up to two thousand miles, which even the dullest student of geography would have realized was convenient for Moscow. Politically this was explained as a boon, graciously granted by an ally, to national security, but many thought it a provocative act which put Britain in the front line of the Cold War, though the cynics would say that Britain, with its own stock of nuclear weapons, was already on the front line and digging trenches. To bolster their argument, they would point out that a compliant Britain had been the only NATO country willing to accept this gift, either from the Norse gods or the Americans.

As a mother and a resident of East Anglia, which had basically been a static American aircraft carrier since 1942, Amanda had her own views on such a national strategy. Professionally, as a civilian engineer who worked closely, often secretly, with all three branches of the armed services, she had no direct involvement in the disposition or – God forbid – the actual operation of Thor missiles, but it had been impossible to avoid their arrival and dispersal around various RAF bases she frequented. Their launch sites, being above ground, were impossible to miss: two-hundred-foot-long concrete pads in the shape of a Latin cross surrounded by revetment blast walls and serviced by underground conduits and pipelines supplying liquid oxygen and kerosene to fuel the sixty-five-foot rocket which arrived on its own trailer before being hoisted upright.

To prepare a Thor for launch took an estimated fifteen minutes, with the help of a small township of technicians and engineers, and Amanda had never had the desire to attend a test firing, knowing where one shot in anger may land in a further fifteen minutes.

Moving in the circles she did, despite the urgings of the Official Secrets Act, Amanda had been well aware that during the Kennedy–Khrushchev confrontation over Soviet missiles deployed on Castro's Cuba two months previously, there were perhaps sixty Thor missiles on British soil, and it did not take a genius to guess where they were aimed. That was why when, after hearing Hereward Henderson's jibber-jabber about Vikings and Germanic gods and then the surprise of Kosloffski speak in Russian, her suspicious mind began to forge a connection with the Thor system of nuclear weaponry.

The revelation that she was being taken to RAF Marham clinched it.

The only thing was, there were no Thor missiles stationed at Marham.

'Have you always been Russians?'

Even as she said it, Amanda thought her question sounded nonsensical, but then, she could be excused for not thinking straight.

From the moment they had bundled her into the Alandel Land Rover at gunpoint and driven out of the barn, Rivero having ripped off and discarded the cut-out reindeers, her brain had been in turmoil. Had she really just left her husband and son captive as hostages against her cooperation with an armed gang which had invaded her home and killed once already? Was she now expected to accompany them to an active RAF base, where admittedly she was well known and, she felt, respected and – what? – smuggle them in? To do what? Sabotage? Hardly an appealing prospect for a law-abiding citizen. Her attempts to think straight were further hindered by the blinding white landscape which rushed towards her through the windscreen of the vehicle. It was no longer actually snowing, and a weak sun had stabbed a few exploratory rays through the dark grey clouds, not crisp enough to create the perfect Christmas card vista but strong enough to reflect from the white blanket which covered everything.

Amanda silently cursed herself for not bringing a pair of sunglasses with her (and immediately felt guilty for worrying over such trivialities), especially as the two Americans had donned wire-framed Aviators. But then, they were not Americans, were they?

'Today we are American Air Force men who have been stranded by the winter weather. A true Russian would never admit to being defeated by snow.'

Although he was seated behind her, Amanda was certain that Kosloffski was smiling his most charming smile. She could not see him, but just knowing he was there with the large automatic in his lap was somehow more frightening than a face-to-face confrontation.

With Rivero driving, the Land Rover had crunched around the side of Carterers, using the footprints and sledge tracks left by Mr Campion and Lugg as a rough navigational aid as the outline of the gravel driveway was invisible. Amanda breathed a sigh of relief that they had avoided driving over her personal pride and joy, the flower and kitchen garden, and immediately bit her tongue to remind herself to concentrate on more serious matters.

Once on to the main drive, Rivero lined the vehicle up on a straight run to the gateposts, visible now the lace curtain of falling snow had been temporarily pulled aside to reveal the two grey monoliths and, nuzzled against the right-hand stone, the white frosted shape of the front end of the charabanc. The arrival of the coach had been the starting pistol for the disruption of the Campions' Christmas holiday, but now, Amanda knew, it served as a temperature-controlled mortuary for the body of Graham Fisk.

It was a grim thought, and she averted her eyes to the left, to the white, strangely magical, display of the orchard on the other side of Albert's ridiculous 'almost moat' and the curved bridge of which he was so fond. She considered glancing back to the house where, perhaps, Albert was watching in despair as his wife was being kidnapped, but refused to give Kosloffski the satisfaction of seeing any display of weakness on her part. Whatever was going to happen, she was determined not to show any trace of feminine fragility, unless it aided her determination to turn the tables on her family's tormentors. In that, she was confident that an opportunity would arise, though it had yet to present itself to her, as long as Albert protected Rupert – which he would – and the larger imponderable, managed to control Lugg and prevent him reaching boiling point.

At the gateway, the Land Rover inched forward through the gap between the left-hand gatepost and the front of the coach, which seemed to protrude across the gateway as a frozen extension to the right-hand stone post. It was a tight squeeze, and though the coach's windscreen was totally coated in snow, Amanda's imagination conjured the sight of a ghostly Graham Fisk sitting upright behind the steering wheel.

As Rivero carefully turned left to enter the lane, the Land Rover hit a patch of ice and began to slide sideways towards the garden wall. For a frightening few seconds, Amanda thought that, being on the passenger side, she would be squashed up against it. But the Land Rover did what Land Rovers did best: got a grip and ploughed on despite the conditions, almost relishing them, and Amanda had to admit that Rivero was a more than competent driver, turning into the skid rather than out of it.

Free of the gateway and with the stranded charabanc behind them, the lane lay before them, a straight tunnel of virgin snow between hedgerows which looked as if they had been coated in cotton wool.

'We'd better get our stories straight,' said Kosloffski from the back seat.

Amanda refused to turn her head and acknowledge him, but her eyes locked with the reflective lenses of his Aviators in the driving mirror.

'I am merely a British citizen being held against her will by a bunch of armed terrorists. That's my story.'

'Yeah, well, that ain't gonna get us very far.' Kosloffski's pistol appeared at the side of Amanda's head and the muzzle tapped her gently on the cheek. 'We'd better rehearse your part in this little expedition.'

'So I have a role in your sordid scheme?'

'Oh yes, Lady Amanda, you always did.'

Without Amanda, the house felt empty, as it always did even in normal circumstances. Under the current abnormal conditions it was, physically, far from empty, but there was a void which needed filling, and Campion realized he must take on that role. The question was how to play it. Blustering and demanding as an innocent subjected to the vilest of crimes would probably have little impact on a professional with military training, who was less than half his age and considerably fitter, not to mention armed. And so he resorted to his favourite persona, that of the genial idiot who bumbled through unafraid of danger because he simply did not recognize it. It was an act which had served him well before a variety of audiences in the past.

He had taken a moment to assess the audience he now had to impress or perhaps distract. Rupert and Lugg did not count; they knew his act and were immobilized. The priest, Breck, would go along with most anything as long as it was non-violent and aimed at a peaceful resolution to their situation. Or at least he assumed that, though he had misjudged the odd vicar before now. The Thursbys, who had rejoined the supplicants in the lounge after their duties in the kitchen, could be relied on to follow his lead even if they did not understand where he was taking them. De Vries would be compliant if nothing threatened his precious diptych, and Hereward Henderson could be easily distracted by being asked to talk about his research, or indeed anything. Miss Pounder did not need to be fooled and could turn out to be a useful ally. The great unknown was the American Quinn, whom Campion was ninety per cent sure had been responsible for the death of the coach driver.

As he had remained on his feet, Mr Campion surveyed the room doing his best impersonation of a befuddled owl and reluctantly adopted the role of master of ceremonies, keeping his fingers crossed that Quinn would not interpret his action as rabble-rousing or a declaration of rebellion.

'Ladies and gentlemen,' he began formally, keeping one wary eye on Quinn's gun hand, 'we find ourselves thrown together in unusual circumstances. We have been stranded and isolated against our will but we must make the most of our situation. As all our sensible footwear seems to have been confiscated, I will not suggest that we go outside and build a snowman, despite the near perfect conditions. We could, I suppose, gather round the Christmas tree and sing carols, or even improvise some form of religious service if the Reverend Breck could be persuaded to lead us.' The look on the priest's face suggested he was not keen. '*Or* we can accept our situation in a peaceful and civilized manner and await the resolution of our predicament.'

'You mean sit around in silence, like schoolboys in detention?'

It seemed that idea did not appeal to the Reverend Breck either.

'Not quite,' Campion persevered, 'though we are in a sort of detention. I thought we could have a decent chat, relax a bit. Certain subjects will be off the table, of course, but we would not be sitting in awkward silence. Above all, we will be *sitting*. We have perfectly good chairs' – he glanced at Rupert and Lugg – 'only two of which seem to be occupied, and I see absolutely no reason why guests in my home should have to remain on their knees. The days when that was obligatory during an audience with my ancestors have long gone.'

'And don't he miss 'em,' grumbled Lugg loud enough for all to hear.

'I would like, therefore, for everyone to get up off their knees and find a comfortable seat.' Campion removed his spectacles, examined them for non-existent dust particles and replaced them. 'I do not believe Mr Quinn there will shoot us all for the transgression. At least not yet.'

Quinn had positioned himself with his back to the wall by the open door leading into the hall and a view of Campion's study, which De Vries continued to gaze on as if it was the promised land. He held his pistol in his right hand, his arm folded across his chest. It was a pose Campion had seen adopted for nineteenth-century daguerreotype or photographic portraits of solemn American Civil War soldiers, or notorious Wild West outlaws, and his expression suggested he was comparing the number of people in the room to the number of bullets in the automatic's magazine. Campion tried to do the same mental calculation, factoring in the spare magazine he knew Quinn had in his coat pocket, but abandoned the exercise as both futile and frightening.

He raised an eyebrow requesting permission.

'I'll allow it,' said Quinn slowly, 'but you stay far away from the boy and the bodyguard. You go near them, you even look at them twice, and I start blasting.'

'Blasting is absolutely the last thing we want,' said Campion. 'There are some valuable family heirlooms in this room.' He wondered, conceitedly, if Rupert and Lugg appreciated his description of them before making an 'all rise' gesture to his fellow prisoners.

'Please, everyone, get up and make yourselves as comfortable as you can. And for the sake of my family, do nothing to upset our jailer.'

Gallantly, Campion helped Miss Pounder to her feet, while Mrs Thursby gallantly helped her father-in-law to his, gently chiding him 'to get those knees creaking' and ignoring his growls of exasperation. Reverend Breck took charge of the battered and bruised Hereward Henderson.

They all took seats as far from Rupert and Lugg as possible and tried to relax – or at least pretend to relax.

It was Rupert who decided it was safe to speak. 'Are you quite all right, Professor?'

Henderson waved a limp hand as Breck helped him into an armchair and the tip of his tongue explored his bloodstained moustache as he spoke. 'It's nothing serious, dear boy. I've survived far worse scuffles as a result of academic disputes.'

Mr Campion smiled at that, then realized the little man was probably not joking, and gently pulled Florence Pounder down next to him on the sofa nearest the fire. He unfurled a large white handkerchief and made to dab at the woman's eyes as if drying tears. She looked at him in bewilderment and made to push his hand away.

'Bear with me,' Campion whispered, 'and tell me what they said when they brought in that canvas holdall.'

Miss Pounder was not slow to catch on and tilted her face so that her mouth was masked by the handkerchief. 'The one in charge, Sometimes, was checking off their equipment, their guns, ammunition, cameras and films and something else, something I had trouble with but seemed quite important. He called it a diagram – I suppose schematic diagram would be the best translation. It was rolled up in a cardboard tube like a painting or a school photograph.'

'Did they mention explosives?'

'No, not explosives,' she said calmly, 'but they had flares. The sergeant was anxious about them, he said they were important for their *vykhod*.'

'And what's that?'

'Their exit, or it could mean escape.'

'That's most useful, Miss Pounder, but please keep it to yourself.' Campion folded away his handkerchief but kept his voice low. 'Where did you learn Russian? I suspect it was not in a Dorset post office.'

She put her hands in her lap and bowed her head so Campion had to strain to catch her answer. 'No, it wasn't. It was in another life entirely.'

Campion was not sure that the Reverend Breck realized he was conspiring with Florence Pounder, but was very grateful for the diversion the priest provided as he comforted Hereward Henderson.

Pulling up a chair so he could sit next to him, Breck spoke loudly enough to make sure that Quinn was listening, while positioning himself so he blocked Henderson's view of their armed guard.

'Why was that thug so brutal with you? What were they after?'

'I honestly don't know, Vicar. The one who beat me kept demanding to know what I knew about Thor, but he did not like the answers I gave.' Henderson sniffed loudly. 'I tried to explain that it was not my area of expertise and I was in the area simply researching my namesake and, I admit, my passion. In the end I think he got tired of punching me and believed me only because he was short of time. He actually said he – they – were on a tight schedule, but for what I have no idea.'

'We are all in the dark, Mr Henderson,' said Breck. 'All we know is that we are being held here against our will by a combination of the weather and these terrorists.'

'Are they terrorists?' Henderson asked innocently, as if he had only just become aware of the situation. 'Or crooks, or spies, or kidnappers? Has Lady Amanda really gone with them?'

'She wasn't given much of a choice.'

'Odd though,' Henderson frowned, 'that they took Lady Amanda. I would have thought that Campion would have been the more valuable hostage given his family connec—'

'Think of it as a siege, Professor,' interrupted Campion forcefully, 'ignoring the fact that one of our besiegers is actually in here with us. Your famous namesake had considerable experience of surviving a siege, I believe.'

'Ah yes, the siege of Ely,' said Henderson, unable to resist the bait and quickly warming to his subject. 'The great defiance by the last Saxon resistance fighter against the Norman invaders.'

'I thought that was supposed to be Robin Hood, wasn't it?' Mr Campion's throwaway remark dented neither Henderson's conviction nor enthusiasm for his subject, but it drew a silent groan from the tethered Rupert, who knew he could not escape another lecture.

'If Robin Hood ever existed, that is.' Despite his injuries, Henderson chortled at the very thought. 'Hereward certainly did, and one might even suggest that he was a prototype Robin Hood. He was certainly declared an outlaw and attracted a band of merry men, or at least some loyal followers. Did he steal from the rich? Oh yes – his gang of outlaws thought nothing of robbing abbeys and monastic houses, but did he give to the poor? Doubtful.'

Mr Campion had noticed that Quinn was listening closely to Henderson's sermon and hoped that the gunman would eventually glaze over and let his guard drop, given the reaction of those who had already experienced Henderson's high-pitched monotone delivery. If nothing else, it was a useful distraction, and Campion encouraged it.

'So Ely Cathedral, that great battleship of the Fens, was a prime target for him?'

'Not the cathedral as we know it; building work on that impressive structure didn't begin until forty years after the siege, but there was certainly a religious house there and some of the monks possibly fought with Hereward. The Isle of Ely was a natural place to retreat to for anyone seeking safety or sanctuary and had been for years. It was actually an island back then, approachable only by water or one or two causeways through the marshy fens, which made it relatively easy to defend.'

'So it became the outlaws' hideout, to avoid the Norman posse?'

Breck's question was clearly thought rather trivial by the professor, though Campion enjoyed it and knew that Lloyd Thursby would have, if only he had been in a position to lip-read, instead of bending over the fireplace prodding the burning logs with a poker.

'As it happens,' Henderson continued, 'Hereward and his men, including some raiding Danes, had robbed an abbey in Peterborough in a quite outrageous attack, so you might say they were on the run when they came to Ely. King William had a garrison of troops in Cambridge Castle and sent them in hot pursuit, but by wrecking the causeways and setting fire to the marsh gases produced by the fens, Hereward kept them at bay and inflicted many casualties, so the Normans settled in for a siege in order to starve out the defenders. Then they resorted to witchcraft.'

Any lecturer, or children's entertainer, worth their salt would have paused for dramatic effect there, but Henderson continued as if reading the less interesting pages of the telephone directory.

'Those were deeply religious times and people were also deeply superstitious, so the Normans recruited a well-known witch in Cambridge and brought her to the front line of the siege. There they built a tower for her to perch on so she could look out over the marshes and hurl curses at the defenders – eye of newt, tongue of frog, all that sort of stuff. But of course it didn't work.'

'I'm glad to hear that,' Breck admitted.

'Come nightfall, Hereward and a few men sneaked out commando-style and set fire to the witch's tower, burned her alive. But it did not affect the outcome of the siege. Eventually the Normans found a way through the fens to Ely and Hereward was on the run again.'

'Let me guess,' said Campion, 'the defenders were betrayed by someone who showed the Normans a safe passage over the fens.'

'Quite right.' Henderson perked up at the interruption. 'How did you know?'

'I didn't, I just guessed. It's the traditional way in history, isn't it? Think of the Spartans at Thermopylae: they copped it when the Persians were shown a secret pass so they could outflank them. And then the Varian Disaster in the Teutoburg Forest, when the Roman legions of General Varus were led into an ambush by Arminius, one of his own German auxiliary commanders and himself a Roman citizen. Just shows, sometimes you can't trust anyone, not even your own comrades.'

Campion thought he might have over-egged the pudding by including 'sometimes' and 'comrades' but Quinn, who had been observing this rather obscure debate, had taken the lure.

'You getting at something?' he drawled, using his pistol as an accusing finger.

'Merely engaging in academic badinage to pass the weary hours of confinement.'

'You, friend, have a smart mouth.'

Mr Campion nodded his head in agreement. 'So I have been told.'

Had any other vehicle overtaken the Land Rover as it stood with its engine idling at the side of the lane, a highly unlikely event given the conditions, a passing motorist could have been forgiven for thinking its occupants had chosen an odd time and peculiar place for a picnic. They had kept the engine running, and presumably the heater, and were tucking into doorstep sandwiches and circulating a steaming Thermos flask. The windows were fogging up nicely and the staff of Alandel Aeroplanes, as its livery suggested they were, may have chosen the worst possible weather in which to venture out for lunch, but they seemed to be making the best of it.

Kosloffski had the greaseproof paper parcel of turkey sandwiches Mrs Thursby had prepared open on the seat next to him, and was dispensing coffee from the Thermos into the white plastic cups which came in the cap.

'What's this red jelly?' Kosloffski asked her. 'It's not cranberry, is it?'

'It's Cumberland sauce. Redcurrants, oranges and port wine and clearly wasted on you.'

'No, it ain't, I like it.'

'Well, don't get used to it.'

She had refused a sandwich but accepted black coffee from the Thermos and toyed with the idea of hurling the contents of the plastic cup into the faces of her kidnappers. She did not put the thought into action. The rapidly cooling coffee had not been very hot to begin with and the amount doled out positively meagre. If she tried to blind Kosloffski in the back, Rivero could and probably would punch her unconscious. If she aimed at Rivero, Kosloffski would shoot her between bites of his sandwich.

'You won't get away with it,' she told them defiantly, despite not being sure what 'it' was. 'You won't even get on to the base.'

'Oh yes, we will. Our credentials are perfectly in order. Better than that, they're genuine. The only problem might be you, but you have your security pass, your face is known around the base and we are arriving in an Alandel vehicle which will be recognized with no questions asked. I admit that was a lucky break for us; far less exhausting than walking there through all this snow.'

'Do you really think no one will question us wandering about a front-line RAF base?'

'I'm sure they will. Like I said, you're a face there. They've got framed pictures up in the officers' mess of your Queen's visit in 1956, and there's little old you smiling at the camera. You weren't smiling on the one they took when Khrushchev visited though, were you?'

'Perhaps I didn't approve of that visit as much,' Amanda said, unsmiling. 'You seem very well informed.'

'We are. We know exactly where Alandel has its workshop, which will be empty due to the Christmas holiday, and the security patrols which will be minimal thanks to the weather closing in and shutting most flying operations down. Most of the personnel will be on leave anyhow.'

'So the rumours are true.'

'What rumours?'

'That you Russians have a network of base watchers here to spy for them.'

'As you Brits would say, I am not going to dignify that with an answer. Now we must get moving again, so we'd better get our stories straight, as we will be very much your guests when we're on the base.'

Amanda turned in her seat and gave the sergeant the haughty look she normally reserved for members of parliamentary committees when they visited Alandel and asked her 'and what does your husband do?'

'You expect me to help you?'

'If you value your husband and your son, yes.'

'I have no intention of being coopted into the KGB!'

'We are not KGB,' scoffed Rivero. 'We are officers in the GRU.'

'Soviet Military Intelligence,' Kosloffski explained.

'Then the GRU is not very intelligent after all if it's Thor missiles you're after. There aren't any at Marham.'

In the driving mirror, Kosloffski's smile turned into a sneer as he spoke. 'Not yet.'

THIRTEEN

The Enemy At (and Inside) the Gate

The picnic in the Land Rover ended in a bizarre game of musical chairs, minus the music, as Amanda was told she would be driving the rest of the way to RAF Marham. It must have been the most suspicious game ever played as Kosloffski got out of the back seat and covered Amanda with his pistol as she tramped through the snow and across the headlight beams, exchanging places with Rivero. If she had seriously considered making a run for it, and there was nowhere really to run to, she was well aware that she was always in sight and in range of one of her captors. In front of her was the white valley of the snowy lane, with deeper snowdrifts against the hedgerows to either side, which would mark her navy blue duffel coat as an easy target, with absolutely no help, or witnesses, for miles.

She kept her gloved hands deep in her coat's pockets, feeling a comforting solid weight in the right-hand one, until she was in the driving seat and gripping the wheel. Kosloffski climbed into the passenger seat and Rivero to his place in the back. Engaging first gear, Amanda edged the Land Rover forward at walking speed to gauge the grip of the tyres on the virgin snow ahead, concentrating on what she guessed was the middle of the lane. If they met another vehicle coming the other way, it would be, well, interesting, as neither driver would be keen to give way and pull into the drifts which might well conceal a drainage ditch.

That Amanda should drive was a key part of their plan. When they reached the gates at Marham, should they be questioned, hers was a familiar face and she had the credentials to show she was a permitted civilian visitor. The Alandel Land Rover would also be readily recognized, as Alandel Aeroplanes had a small office on the base, though 'office' might be too grandiose a term for a partitioned-off corner of one of the workshop hangars.

Their cover story – Kosloffski called it their 'legend' – was that he and Rivero were radar technicians on secondment to Alandel for six months as of the first of January. They had flown to England early on Pan-Am to take up Lady Amanda's kind offer to stay at her home and join in the family's New Year's Eve party, although the weather had put a damper on those plans, not least because the telephone lines seemed to be down. When the snow had stopped falling, or at least paused for breath, Lady Amanda had insisted on driving them to Marham so they could check in with the American duty officer before they were declared absent without leave, and to get a glimpse of the Alandel facility there.

'Do you really intend reporting to the duty officer?' Amanda had asked.

'Of course not, but if we're challenged our papers will hold up long enough for us to do what we have to.'

Concentrating on keeping the Land Rover on a straight course, Amanda resisted the temptation to look Sergeant Sometimes in the eye. 'And that would be sabotage, would it?'

'I'd call it payback.' Kosloffski grinned.

'For what?'

'Cuba.'

The nearer they got to the base, the easier the going became, as the snow still held off and a few other brave drivers had already ploughed an icy path for them, though they did not encounter another vehicle. The thought had crossed Amanda's mind that she might stage an accident with an oncoming car – a gentle collision, easily explained under the current conditions – which would bring other human beings as witnesses into the equation; someone, anyone, she could appeal to for help. Yet the countryside remained stubbornly, beautifully, crisp, clean and devoid of human activity. Perhaps there would be a guard on the gates at Marham who would frisk her and *that* would surely raise an alarm, but then military guards were not policemen who searched suspects. They demanded to know who went there and allowed friends to pass and occasionally took potshots at foes.

Her first sight of the base proper was of the flagpole from which hung a stiff and clearly frozen flag, blue with a small Union Jack and the RAF roundel. It should have signified a safe haven but instead simply added to Amanda's mood of abandonment as the base appeared deserted without a friendly face in sight. On previous visits, the Administration Building had been a wasp-nest of comings and goings, there was a distant hum of machinery and the louder growls of engines being warmed up or run down, not to mention the ear-splitting roar of jet aircraft taking off and landing. There had even been, on occasion, music, as auditions were regularly carried out for the RAF regimental band, and Amanda, whose reputation as an aircraft designer preceded her, had always been greeted cheerfully and courteously by the older pilots.

Now all the buildings, coated in snow like a tray of iced buns, seemed deserted, the only sounds of activity being a pair of bulldozers jousting to clear snow from a snowy runway. Personnel on duty would be in the duty room and the control tower; those off-duty would, sensibly, be indoors keeping warm, and those with families making the most of a disjointed white Christmas.

'Head straight for the Alandel shack,' Kosloffski ordered.

Amanda bridled at the term 'shack' but was grateful that RAF snowploughs had cleared the internal roads of the base. Ironically, she could now accelerate just when she did not want to. On the journey there, she had driven as fast as she could in order to find other human contact. Now she slowed down in the hope that the Land Rover would be noticed and a curious military policeman might come to her aid.

They were not challenged or even noticed, and she knew there would be no one within the Alandel office to rescue her, having generously insisted the staff take the whole of Christmas week as holiday. She had informed the base hierarchy and hoped that by parking the Alandel Land Rover outside the sliding door of the hangar which housed their allocated square footage, someone might comment on its presence and investigate further.

There were two plaques on the door, or rather a sign saying Alandel Aeroplanes: No Unauthorised Entry and the official station badge of RAF Marham showing a muscular bull and the motto 'Deter', which possibly dated from the establishment of the base in 1916 when its main role was to deter Zeppelins.

'Unlock the door, please.' Amanda could feel the bulk of Kosloffski's body behind her as she tramped through undisturbed snow to the hangar. 'The key is on the ring with the Land Rover's.'

'You are remarkably well-informed,' she said, wondering if she could throw the key she held into a drift of snow to delay matters.

'And just in case, I have a spare. You do some interesting research here at Alandel, but it's not as secret as you'd like to think.'

'So it appears,' Amanda said calmly, but her gloved hands were not shaking with the cold as she clicked open the large padlock and pulled back the hasp, sliding open the door with some difficulty and crackling of ice.

Anger gave her added strength; anger at having been satisfied with such minimal security precautions, but then the Alandel outpost was in the middle of a functioning air-force base with enough firepower at its disposal to deter any conventional enemy. The only way the location could be more secure was if it hosted Thor missiles, a thought which brought her crashing back to the reality of her present situation.

The two Americans followed her inside, Rivero carrying a canvas bag taken from the back of the Land Rover and sliding the door closed as Amanda flicked the master light switch.

It was a draughtsman's office rather than a workshop, in area less than a quarter of the hangar it nested in. On the other side of the partition walls might be engines, perhaps even whole aeroplanes, or electronic equipment or weapons systems in various states of disassembly. Surely a more tempting target for a spy or a saboteur than the drawing boards, models, graphs and slide rules which Alandel offered.

'This will do perfectly,' said Kosloffski, his eyes fixing on the wall behind the long plain desk – Amanda's desk – on which, in addition to a draughtsman's drawing easel, were two telephones and one of the new Bell Punch desktop calculators known as an Anita, although most of the Alandel crew referred to it as 'the boss's fancy typewriter' and those who knew were privately horrified that she had paid over £350 for it.

Kosloffski was admiring not the desk but what was on the wall: a large-scale plan of the layout of RAF Marham.

'Pin it up there, next to the map,' he told Rivero, 'and set up the camera for a wide shot.'

'Camera?' Amanda said automatically.

'We're taking some pictures.' Kosloffski's smile was at its full charming wattage. 'You might want to run a comb through your hair.'

Photographs? What sort of sabotage was that? It could be espionage, but there must be far bigger secrets on an air-force base worth photographing than an empty Alandel office. Alandel did have secret projects, of course, though the most sensitive plans and drawings were safely locked away at the company headquarters, but would the Soviets think them worth this raid by the goons of the GRU?

And it was a *raid*, Amanda realized. The essence of espionage, either military or industrial, was that it was done secretly, preferably so that no one ever knew it had been done. If the object was subtlety, an armed gang hijacking a coachload of pilgrims then holding the household of a prominent local figure (Amanda thought that was not too immodest) to ransom whilst infiltrating an RAF station was hardly the way to go under the radar. It was an operation almost designed to attract publicity, and there would be no way to keep the event quiet – there were far too many witnesses. Unless, of course, they had orders not to leave any witnesses, but that was unthinkable.

They may be Russian agents in American uniforms – surely a capital offence in itself – but even the most cocksure of assassins do not normally insist on taking photographs of their victims.

'You are not being serious! You want me to pose for a photograph?'

A photograph of something was certainly on the cards, as Rivero had unpacked an expensive-looking thirty-five-millimetre camera and was fitting it to a shiny extendable metal tripod.

'You don't have to pose like Monroe would, just be present. You'll be there to give scale and perspective.' Kosloffski was caring charm personified, the perfect wedding photographer calming the mother of the bride. 'Truth is you'll probably be out of focus, but we'll know it's you. Now take your coat off and sit behind your desk.'

Amanda complied without complaint as she did not want Sergeant Sometimes offering to help and discovering the unexplained weight in the duffel coat pocket. Laying the coat carefully on the floor behind her desk – out of sight but still within reach – she stood behind her office chair, took off her gloves and without thinking ran the fingers of both hands through her hair, fluffing the natural curls.

'We ain't ready for your close-up quite yet.'

Rivero was fiddling with the lens of the camera, now suspended at chest height on its tripod as Kosloffski rummaged in the canvas bag and pulled out a cardboard tube. He prised off the circular top and tipped out the contents, as if he was helping himself to an expensive cigar. Out popped a long spool of what Amanda recognized as technical drawing paper and, as he unfurled it, Rivero produced a large roll of adhesive masking tape.

It was only after Kosloffski had smoothed out the sheet and taped it to the wall so that it just overlapped the map of the base did Amanda realize what it was, for despite the word CLASSIFIED rubber-stamped in one corner, she had seen such a diagram before.

But only long afterwards did the realization hit her that she had been so mesmerized as the plan was being stuck on the wall that she'd failed to realize it was the only time since they had left Carterers that neither of the Americans was holding a gun on her. The one chance she had to bolt for the door, or even snatch up her coat, was lost as her brain took in what she was looking at.

It was an annotated drawing showing in precise detail the launch site of an Intermediate Range Ballistic Missile, specifically a Douglas SM75 Thor. The layout was in a crucifix shape, the same as a basic aeroplane outline as seen from directly above. In the nose section, as it were, was the actual missile; in reality sixty-five feet long, waiting to be hauled upright into the firing position. Behind it, the fuselage was represented by a runway along which the Thor trundled on its trailer, out of the prefabricated building which housed it, which could be taken as the tailfin of the aircraft. Its wings were lines of pipes leading to fuel storage tanks, compressed gas cylinders and a large liquid oxygen tank. Around it, drawn to scale, were dotted the trucks and trailers containing pumps, air-conditioning units and electronic control sets needed to service the launch.

'It's a Thor launch site,' she said as Kosloffski stood back to admire his handiwork.

'Got it in one.'

'And the juxtaposition with the map of the base makes it look as if it's here at Marham.'

'Or *coming* here.'

Amanda was temporarily distracted by three rapid clicks as Rivero began to take photographs. 'I don't understand.'

'I think you do.' The sergeant was all charm again. 'Two months ago the Cuban crisis was provoked by aerial photographs of missile sites on the island. It ended in great embarrassment for the Soviet Union.'

'A red face in the Kremlin is a small price to pay for almost starting a nuclear war and scaring the world half to death.'

Kosloffski's smile remained but was veering towards a sneer. 'Thus speaks the capitalist who works for the military aggressors here and in the US.'

Amanda gripped the arms of her chair and struggled to keep her temper, despite the continuous provocation of the clicking of Quinn's camera as he pressed the shutter and thumbed the film advance lever.

'I make no apologies for believing in a free economy or for working with my country's allies, and I am not the aggressor here. I am the one held at gunpoint.'

'Film change,' said Quinn, breaking the ensuing uneasy silence.

With deft, rapid movements, he opened the back of the camera and removed the thirty-five-millimetre film, slotting it into the small metal canister from which he had taken a new roll. The canister he threw over the desk to Kosloffski, who caught it one-handed and pocketed it. Quinn then reloaded the camera, wound on the spool and, after checking the lens settings, began snapping again.

'Why do I have to be in your damned pictures?' Amanda demanded.

'You won't be in all of them.' Quinn unscrewed the camera from its tripod and began to move around the desk to get close-ups of the launch-site plan and the map of the base. 'You'll probably get cropped out of most, but some will be useful for verification purposes.'

'Verification?' Amanda almost choked on the word.

'When they go public,' said Kosloffski reasonably, 'and everyone sees that the British are secretly allowing the Americans to site even more missiles within range of Moscow. So who is now the aggressor? England will become Russia's Cuba. It will be difficult for your government to deny, especially when it appears that a respected member of the aristocracy seems to be in on the secret when your Members of Parliament are in ignorance. Do you think your so-called free press could resist such a story?'

'Sadly, I do not, though few will believe it, especially not the bit about me being an aristocrat. If that's your attempt to ferment a class war in this country, you are sadly misguided. Britain is not a natural home for Bolshevism.'

'Because it is content to be America's lapdog. Now its empire has gone, it remains a small, inconsequential offshore island, useful only as a strategic forward base for missiles. Like I said, you are Russia's Cuba, and this time it will be America who turns tail and runs.'

'That's what you meant by payback.' It was not a question.

Amanda resisted the temptation to punch Kosloffski's perfect teeth down his throat when he said, 'Neat, don't ya think?'

'We're done here,' said Rivero, unloading the camera and pocketing the spool of film. It did not escape Amanda's attention that they had divided the spools of film between them to double the chances of one set of pictures making it home to Moscow.

Kosloffski pulled down the launch-site diagram, rolled it and threaded it back into its cardboard tube while Rivero packed away the tripod and camera.

'You think you're just going to walk out of here?'

'Why not? We walked in here easily enough and anyway we're not walking; you're driving us.'

Before a fuming Amanda could come up with a suitably cutting response, Kosloffski began to bend down to pick her coat up from the floor where she had hoped it had been forgotten. She virtually flung herself out of her chair, muttering 'I can manage' to get to it before he did. 'You'll never get away with this,' she said defiantly as she threaded her arms into the coat.

'Oh, I think we will. You want to get home to your family and make sure they are safe. You'll take us.'

'I meant your phoney photographs. They won't convince anyone that Thor missiles are coming to this base.'

'To yet *another* forward base for the aggressive Americans? Does the great British public know how many Thor sites they have already?'

'The public might think they offer protection against Russian aggression,' said Amanda, knowing that it sounded weak.

'By making them a clear and obvious target? Don't you find it odd and just a little bit scary that no other NATO country will give the Thor missiles house room?'

'We stick with our allies.'

'Only one of them, it seems. I believe Britain is trying to get closer to Europe by joining the EEC. How do you think these pictures will go down in Paris or Bonn, where they know it isn't wise to prod the Russian bear?'

Dammit, the man had a point she had not considered. 'I will tell everyone it was all fake!'

Kosloffski's smile at her outburst was positively vulpine.

'The RAF will deny there are Thors here and journalists will be able to come and see for themselves. The Americans will deny there were ever any plans to site them here.'

'Will they? Will anyone believe them? Won't it look like they are spoiling for a fight, so long as it takes place in somebody else's country? They're getting quite a reputation for that in Vietnam.'

'You have a very low opinion of your country.' As she spoke she knew it came out in the same tone a teacher would use to insist she wasn't angry at a pupil, merely disappointed.

'America is not my country,' scoffed the sergeant with a slow shake of his head. 'I have had to suffer its corruption and its degeneracy for ten years, but this mission means I can go home.'

'Leaving no witnesses.'

'Not at all. There have to be witnesses, especially you.'

'Me?'

'Sure. You're the star of the show. You have a title, you are the leading woman in your field, which is very much a man's field, and you will attract publicity on both sides of the Atlantic. Not all of it will be good publicity. There will be plenty of generals and admirals and air vice-marshals who will scream about a civilian being allowed near a Thor missile site.'

'But there are no Thor missiles here!' Amanda's voice squeaked in frustration.

'Then why do you have the plan of a launch site – a classified document, and genuine by the way – on the wall of your office? The camera does not lie.'

'It can be made to, and I'll tell everyone exactly how you faked the pictures.'

Kosloffski looked at her pityingly. It was the cruellest thing he could have done. 'That will be even more embarrassing for you, explaining how you escorted two enemy agents on to an RAF base and allowed them the use of your office. No one will be able to deny that this is your office at Marham and that is actually you in some of the pictures.'

'I am here under duress. Three armed men broke into my home and held my family hostage. There are witnesses to that.'

'As I recall, we were invited into your house, but no matter. We will be long gone and I have a feeling the US Air Force will deny they ever had airmen called Kosloffski, Rivero or Quinn and certainly never posted them to England. We flew Pan-Am, as civilians, under different names – and you'll love this: there was an article in the in-flight magazine about how American tourists should visit the shrine at Walsingham. That could connect us to joining the pilgrims on the bus as far as Swaffham, where a contact was supposed to have a vehicle waiting for us, but the snow screwed everything so we had to improvise.'

'And invade my house instead.'

'Oh, we were always going to do that. We needed you to give our operation the royal stamp of approval, so to speak.'

'You'll never get away with it,' snorted Amanda.

Kosloffski flipped up the hood of his parka and nodded to Rivero who hefted the canvas bag. 'We will succeed in one objective, even if the pictures are disputed.'

'Really?'

'Sure we will. You've just colluded in a major breach of security, and as soon as this gets airtime – and it will, no matter how hard your people try to sit on it – do you think the Americans will trust you Brits ever again? Face it, you've got a lousy track record when it comes to keeping secrets. The last coupla years have not done your reputation for security any favours and this ain't gonna boost it.'

Amanda bit her tongue and grimly, but silently, agreed with him.

In the few steps she took to cross the Alandel office, Amanda considered her options for escape. Once outside she could run and seek help, which was surely available *somewhere* in a military enclave, and not the place where her guardians were likely to start a gunfight. There again, she did not rate her chances in a foot race through ice and snow against two much younger and physically fitter males. Plus, if successful, she would have left her family in a hostage situation without any idea of how to extract them.

Rivero slid open the hangar door and they stepped out into a wall of crisp, cold air. Amanda pulled on her gloves and pushed her hands into the pockets of her duffel coat, taking only a little comfort from the solid object under her right hand.

She felt Kosloffski's body press against her and his breath on the side of her face. 'Play it cool or someone gets hurt.'

It was not an idle threat.

Her brain snapped back into action as she took in the scene which Kosloffski had already assessed.

Parked directly in front of the Alandel Land Rover was a blue Standard Ensign staff car. Its windows and bonnet had been cleared of snow to reveal the RAF roundel near the offside headlight, but a crust of four inches of frozen snow remained, like icing, on the roof.

A uniformed man was climbing out of the driver's door, and as he straightened up he lodged a peaked hat on his balding head. The hat, like the car, was topped with a white band, indicating that the wearer was a 'Snowdrop', the informal name for a member of the Royal Air Force Police.

'Hello there, Lady Amanda,' said the Snowdrop. 'Everything all right?'

FOURTEEN
Invoking Sinterklaas

'So how do we amuse ourselves? I would suggest charades but our best player is unfortunately chained to a chair and thus his movements are somewhat restricted.' Mr Campion turned to confide in Miss Pounder. 'His interpretation of King Kong batting away the biplanes atop the Empire State Building is an absolute treat, and though quite easy to guess is a wonderful distraction.'

Miss Pounder's smile was rapidly replaced by a frown of concern as she registered the low growl coming from Lugg as his sedentary bulk quivered with such rage that the energy generated spread down to his stamping feet like a toddler's tantrum, but with such force that the adjacent Christmas tree shook violently.

'No telly,' said Lloyd Thursby emphatically.

'I'm afraid not. That could have been a useful distraction.' Campion locked eyes with Rupert across the room as he spoke. 'The television is always a comforting diversion on a dark winter's evening.'

Rupert's brow furrowed then he blinked rapidly, which Campion hoped was Morse Code for 'message received'.

'I could always do us some lunch,' chirped Mrs Thursby, clearly happier to be thinking of kitchen duty rather than gunmen or grumpy fathers-in-law.

'What a splendid idea, Mrs T!' Campion slapped his knees with enthusiasm. 'If my wife can be abducted and given a packed lunch for the journey, I think those who remain deserve a little sustenance.'

'Too right,' echoed Lugg, the ornaments dangling on the Christmas tree turning and tinkling in support.

'If, that is,' Campion looked at Quinn, 'our guard allows it.'

'Don't see why not, but only the old lady,' said Quinn, waving his pistol at Mrs Thursby.

'Colt .45,' said Lloyd Thursby as if in admiration. 'Six bullets.'

'We ain't in a cowboy film, old timer. This is an automatic and carries eight. Do the math.'

Lloyd's mouth opened and closed silently as he carefully scanned the room, but Campion was well aware that with Mrs Thursby in the kitchen there would be eight targets in the room, two of them incapable of movement, and that Quinn had at least one spare magazine in his pocket.

'I could help,' volunteered Miss Pounder.

'No, you stay put. Just the old gal.'

Campion wondered if – by some instinct – Quinn was wary of, or at least distrusted, Florence Pounder; and for reasons he could not quite put his finger on, Campion thought that the American might have good reason.

'Good on you, Mrs T. I'm sure you'll do us proud with a few cold cuts.' Campion's encouragement did little to prevent her giving Quinn a lethal glare for the 'old gal' remark.

'Better make it something I can take through a straw, Perce,' bellowed Lugg, rattling his chains to make his point. 'Some of us can't 'andle cutlery even if we was allowed.'

'Perce?' Miss Pounder said the name under her breath, almost to herself.

'Persephone,' Campion said out of the corner of his mouth, to which she made a silent 'O' with hers.

The housekeeper named after the queen of the Greek underworld walked out of the room in regally haughty fashion, ignoring Quinn and his weapon and pointing herself towards the kitchen. The American dragged his chair into the hallway and took up position between the open doors of the dining room and Campion's study. That way, he could supervise his main nest of prisoners and be able to keep an eye out should Mrs Thursby emerge from the kitchen armed with a rolling pin and the attitude of a whirling dervish.

Mr Campion assessed their guard's new position and his sightlines through the doorway. He estimated that the position of the sofa on which he and Miss Pounder sat meant that he was clearly in Quinn's sights – literally – whereas, if she sat back, only the woman's legs and feet would be visible, the rest of her masked – if not fully shielded – by the door jamb. It might prove an advantage somehow, depending on Quinn's alertness, which was something he decided to test.

He sprang to his feet in as sprightly a fashion as a sixty-two-year-old man could spring up from a soft, far too comfortable settee, and noted immediately that Quinn's gun hand, resting on his knee, reacted accordingly. Campion took a long, loping stride towards the fireplace, which made him an even better target, and bent to stoke the fire with a chunk of gnarled oak from the log basket. He felt Quinn's eyes, and those of everyone in the room, on him as he prodded the log with a poker until he was satisfied with its position and flames were licking around it, then he carefully laid the poker down in front of the dog irons and made a point of letting Quinn see that his hands were empty.

'What a pity we don't have any chestnuts to roast,' he said as he straightened up.

'Perce put 'em all in the stuffing for the turkey,' offered Lugg, twisting his frame to what, if anything, was happening behind him.

'Well, it was delicious.' Campion winked at Rupert. 'I'm sorry, old fruit, I had quite forgotten you were with us.'

Rupert smiled nervously as Lugg's massive frame quivered furiously, shaking the chairs they were both shackled to as Campion concentrated on Quinn's reaction.

Their gaoler did not seem alarmed by Campion's sudden movements, nor by the rumblings coming from Lugg. There was no reason he should be, Campion reasoned. He had a clear field of fire and his most valuable hostage, Rupert, was severely restrained along with Lugg, whom the intruders clearly perceived as the most dangerous person in the household. Mr Campion could have taken the fact that he was dismissed as a threat as something of a snub, but he had always thought of being underestimated as one of his major attributes.

He stepped into the middle of the room and played to his core strength, giving a passable imitation of a bemused scout master trying to raise the spirits of a troop whose campsite has been washed out by a torrential rainstorm.

'So while we wait for Mrs Thursby to do us proud,' he began, 'perhaps we can get to know each other a little better as we have had very little time to socialize so far. I admit the present circumstances are perhaps not best suited for idle gossip, but as there is little else to do, let us enjoy a round robin of introductions. As the host, albeit under strained circumstances, let me begin.'

Campion flared his arms and brought both hands down to point at Rupert, as if he were a stage magician introducing a beautiful assistant.

'This is my son and heir to not very much, Rupert, who is a student aiming to resume his studies at university in America at the earliest opportunity. He is currently attached – anchored, one might say – to Mr Lugg, a loyal family retainer who, despite appearances, would rarely say boo to the most aggressive goose.'

Campion twirled theatrically, his stockinged feet sliding across the carpet, to indicate the Reverend Breck.

'And we are fortunate to have a man of the cloth with us for our Christmas celebrations, though we might have wished it to be in more auspicious circumstances. It's Elis, isn't it? Elis Breck? And please do not look so worried; I am not expecting you to conduct a service.'

'Nor give a sermon,' said Breck, looking pointedly at Hereward Henderson. 'I will happily leave that to others, but of course if anyone wishes to talk in private, assuming I am allowed, I will of course accommodate them.'

'Thank you, Vicar.'

'Please do not call me that, Mr Campion. I am no longer the vicar of any parish. The last service I conducted was Midnight Mass on Christmas Eve and I am now looking forward to retirement. Please call me Elis.'

'Do I detect a Welsh heritage?'

'Welsh mother, Scots father. Best of all worlds.'

'Yet you have chosen the noble county of Norfolk to retire to.'

'Walsingham offers me the spiritual peace I have sought for some time.'

'Getting away from all those annoying parishioners, I suppose,' said Campion with a twinkle in his eye. 'Weddings, funerals, the Mothers' Union, endless whist drives and village fêtes where you have to judge the Bonny Baby competition correctly or risk a diplomatic incident, not to mention making sure the lead isn't pinched from the church roof. It all sounds far too stressful for me. I know I could never cope and I am sure you deserve a good long rest. What prompted the sudden decision?'

Campion knew that had Amanda been present she would have scolded him for being rude, or at least insensitive, in order to keep up appearances, though she would have guessed he had an ulterior motive; testing the patience of their guard.

The Reverend Breck's blank expression did not register offence, though neither did it encourage further exploration of the subject.

'It was not a sudden decision; it was one I came to some time ago and I do not require a good long rest, merely time to pray for forgiveness. Walsingham offers the ideal environment, where I would be in a holy place surrounded by a supportive community.'

Rupert flashed a despairing look and shook his head in a warning his father chose to ignore.

'Forgiveness, Elis? Which particular sin have you taken on if that's not an indelicate question?'

The priest might not have looked uncomfortable at Campion's tone but Miss Pounder certainly did, squirming deep into the cushions of the sofa, while Lloyd Thursby leaned forward in his chair to hear, or lip-read, every word he could.

'The sin of anger, of bearing a grudge for many years. It is an indelicate sin, but your question is not, because I know I am guilty of it.'

'I believe you told my son that it dated back to your wartime service.'

Now Rupert glared angrily at his father, as if he had broken the seal of the confessional.

'I did and I take no pleasure in the fact that my anger has festered for so many years. Perhaps, through prayer and meditation, I can finally lay it to rest and be forgiven.'

'It concerned, I believe, a fellow officer you judged to be a coward and who is now a popular actor.'

'He *was* a coward and I did nothing to stop him putting men's lives at risk. I have lived with that for nigh on twenty years, watching him play the noble hero on the silver screen. And please do not preach to *me* about this being the season of goodwill to all. When I saw that *that man* would be on television on

Boxing Day in one of his most heroic roles, it was the last straw.'

'No telly here,' said Lloyd Thursby, showing he had been paying attention.

The old man's intervention broke the spell woven by what had appeared to be Campion's deliberate taunting of the priest. Rupert was visibly relieved though still puzzled by his father's inquisition, Miss Pounder tried valiantly to suppress a giggle and Hereward Henderson's face was frozen in that expression of shock and distaste long perfected by the English middle-class male and usually reserved for dropped catches in a cricket match or women drivers. Only De Vries seemed unaware of the tension in the room as he remained completely focused on the open door to Campion's study, beyond where Quinn had established his guard post.

And Quinn himself had seemed totally uninterested in the entire exchange, viewing his prisoners with a detached air, his eyes flicking occasionally in the direction of the kitchen from which the clatter of crockery and the clanging of pans signalled Mrs Thursby's progress with lunch.

Campion was about to follow a different tack, his Plan B, when Hereward Henderson decided to fill the silence.

'Heroism is very subjective,' he began pompously, 'and there is often a very thin line between the hero and the villain. Indeed, in the early medieval period, there were numerous heroic villains who lived on in folklore for centuries . . .'

'A very good point, Professor,' Campion said hammily, as if he was a barrister acknowledging a point of law, and no one looked more surprised than Henderson himself. 'It has always been difficult to distinguish the heroes and the villains, as I have discovered to my cost in the past twenty-four hours.'

There was a loud, dismissive grunt from Lugg, which set several Christmas tree ornaments tinkling, and which Mr Campion blissfully ignored as he resumed his oration.

'You see, everything in my upbringing conditioned me to trust and respect anyone in uniform unless, of course, they were actually shooting at me. Naturally, when three men appeared at my door wearing the uniforms of a close ally, who did not, at least initially, show any signs of shooting at me, my immediate reaction was to welcome them out of the storm and into my home. I did not automatically regard them as heroes, of course, but neither did I suspect them to be villains. I should say, before Professor Henderson corrects me, that I use the word in its modern sense, though he is probably more familiar with the term *villein*, the feudal tenant farmer who was subject to the local lord of the manor.'

Staring open-mouthed at Mr Campion, Henderson did not seem remotely interested in debating his host's terminology.

'What I was guilty of,' Campion continued, 'was suspecting someone else of being a villain; you, Mr De Vries, who demanded to know if I possessed firearms or a safe in which to secure an antique painting which you claim to be your property . . .'

Now Campion had the Dutchman's undivided attention, along with a glare of anger and some muttered curses, which fortunately no one could understand.

'I remain unconvinced of the provenance of your painting. Your nervousness about its security and the fact you have admitted to being an art dealer suggest to me that you are more interested in its cash value than its worth as a historical document or as a religious artefact.'

'How dare you!'

'I dare because this is my house and you have wormed your way into it with a cock-and-bull story about seeking some sort of holy approval from Walsingham for what is for you a purely commercial transaction.'

Out of the corner of his eye, Mr Campion noted that Quinn was paying attention to his rather histrionic performance, which pleased him, whereas Rupert's downcast look of embarrassment did not.

'You are betraying a confidence!' De Vries snapped angrily, and although he remained seated, he was concentrating on Campion rather than Campion's study.

'I have no compunction in keeping confidences if I believe them to be purely in the pursuit of greed.'

'Greed?'

'You say you are an art dealer. What do you estimate the Suycker diptych to be worth? I would have thought any piece of art which has survived from 1538 would have considerable monetary let alone religious value.'

'Religious value?' The Reverend Breck's head snapped up.

'Mr De Vries,' Campion began re-establishing his prosecuting barrister persona, 'is in possession of a painting which he claims depicts the burning of the original statue of Our Lady of Walsingham during the Reformation. As a sixteenth-century piece of art alone, I would imagine it to be worth many thousands of pounds. If it can be authenticated, and I believe such things can be accurately dated these days, it is a valuable historical document. To a major museum or a religious house, it would be invaluable as an attraction, perhaps even a destination for pilgrims. Can you imagine a bidding war between the Vatican and the Church of England? We could be talking a million dollars.'

De Vries's face had reddened as he contained his anger. More to Campion's satisfaction was the fact that Quinn was leaning forward in his chair, listening intently. He had feared that his switch of currencies from pounds to dollars had been too crass, but it never paid to be subtle when tempting greed.

'How did he come by such a thing?' Breck asked Campion, as if De Vries was not there.

'A very good question, Vicar. A gift from Santa Claus perhaps – or should that be Sinterklaas as he is known in Holland. I believe he visits earlier there than he does in this country, around the fifth of December, and throws presents for children down the chimney. Traditionally they were sweets or mandarin oranges but perhaps Sinterklaas was feeling particularly generous this year.'

'This is madness. Why are you saying these things?' the Dutchman wailed.

'Yes, Pop,' Rupert chimed in, 'what are you trying to prove?'

'I was merely ruminating, my boy, on the traditions of Christmas. During the war, RAF bomber crews who were flying missions in December were told a little Dutch rhyme which, translated, basically urged them to "drop bombs on the Germans but sweets over Holland". It was so that the children would think they had come from Sinterklaas. He was supposed to carry a big red book, a ledger, listing everyone who had been good or naughty that year. Mr De Vries must have been very good to have received such a valuable present.'

De Vries was positively fuming now, his lips twitching as he struggled to speak. It reminded Campion of something he had once been told, that there were four times as many swear words in Dutch as there were in English, and De Vries seemed to be selecting quite a few of them.

'I am not answerable to you. You have betrayed my confidences.'

'And you could well have abused my hospitality by bringing a stolen religious icon into my home and suggesting that your fellow passengers were planning to steal it.'

For the first time, Hereward Henderson looked genuinely shocked. 'He can't have meant me!'

'I'm afraid he probably did,' Campion lied smoothly. 'As an academic and historian with an interest in Walsingham and all things medieval, you are just the sort of person to gossip publicly about such a treasure.'

'But the sixteenth century is not my period,' the little man said weakly. 'It's far too modern.'

'Be that as it may, our art dealer friend was very anxious that none of you saw the diptych and he wanted it hidden from sight in my office safe as soon as he got here.'

'He was very secretive on the coach. Couldn't tempt him into conversation at all.'

From his limited contact with Hereward Henderson, Mr Campion could not bring himself to blame anyone for failing to engage with the awful bore. Since his arrival at Carterers, only Lloyd Thursby had shown any enthusiasm when it came to chatting to the professor – if indeed he was one.

'Anyone carrying such a valuable item incognito on a public excursion charabanc is surely suspicious. It smacks to me of smuggling rather than the careful importation of a genuine antiquity showing an important event in English history.'

Campion's latest accusation resulted in an unhealthy silence, and all eyes fell on him apart from Lugg's; he was still pointed firmly at the Christmas tree, though his shoulders heaved with silent laughter.

'Is it possible to see this historic treasure?' Henderson asked quietly, almost secretively.

Campion adopted what he considered to be a suitably pompous pose. 'It is certainly possible, but whether it is permissible is another matter entirely.'

'The Suycker is private property – my property,' hissed the Dutchman.

'Are we absolutely one hundred per cent sure of that? In any case, my hands are tied.'

'So are mine,' muttered Lugg.

'I meant metaphorically,' said Campion, now the schoolmaster rather than barrister. 'I no longer have the freedom to act in my own house.'

'I would kinda like to see it.'

Campion turned on his heels to look at Quinn as though surprised as to where the voice had come from. 'It's in the safe in my study, just behind you.'

'No! Do not touch it!' De Vries sprang to his feet and shouted his instruction at the American, whose only reaction was to wave his pistol at the Dutchman's midriff.

'Sit down, buddy. This gives the orders round here and it lets me see what I want.'

'He's got the drop on ye,' contributed Lloyd Thursby loudly and unhelpfully.

'If you insist,' conceded Campion, 'I will gladly show you, but I will need the key to the safe. It's upstairs in my bedroom on the dressing table. That's up the stairs, turn right and last door on the left, if you wouldn't mind.'

Now the pistol transferred to Mr Campion as Quinn shook his head slowly. 'Oh no, I ain't falling for that. I go upstairs and you crash out of here.'

'I hardly think that likely. You have locked the doors and confiscated our shoes and, in any case, where would we go? How far do you think we would get?'

'I'm taking no chances.' Quinn stood and, after straining his head and making sure that Mrs Thursby was still busy in the kitchen, he came into the lounge, orchestrating his hostages by conducting with his pistol. 'Everyone but you' – he jabbed the gun at Campion – 'back down on your knees.'

The Reverend Breck led by example, and when De Vries remained on his feet, shaking with either anger or fear or possibly a combination of the two, the priest reached out, grabbed him by the arm and pulled him downwards.

'Stuff and bloody nonsense,' wheezed Lloyd Thursby as he

hauled himself from his seat, and there was a groan of agreement from Lugg, who was still straining to see what was going on behind him.

He ceased squirming as he felt Quinn approach and stand at Rupert's side.

The American placed his left hand on Rupert's shoulder and rested the butt of the automatic on the back of his palm, pressing the muzzle firmly into Rupert's cheek, making him squeal in pain.

'You go get the key,' Quinn told Campion, 'and don't take too long about it.'

FIFTEEN
A Prickly Problem

'It's Warrant Officer Neel, isn't it?'

'Yes, ma'am. Didn't expect to see you on the base today. Thought all you Alandel boffins were off on your Christmas holidays.'

Amanda assessed the situation quickly. The Snowdrop was unarmed, perhaps had a wife and children, and she was sure that Kosloffski would have no compunction in shooting him dead and making a dash for it in the Land Rover. There seemed no one else around to stop him. She would remain their prisoner, and her family, isolated and several miles away, would still be hostages. Unless she reached into her coat pocket and took matters into her own hands, hoping to beat both Americans to the draw. Discretion, she decided, was the better part of valour, and if her enemies were to be dealt with violently, it was better done when all of them could be in the firing line.

'All my chaps are snuggled up at home sleeping off their Christmas pudding.' She said brightly, 'If they've any sense, that is. We're here totally unofficially' – she felt Kosloffski tense at her side – 'as tourists, would you believe. These gentlemen are USAF and will be stationed here in the new year. They arrived early and fell foul of the winter wonderland that is our current weather, so we offered them shelter in our home. Frankly, Mr Neel, we needed to get out of the house after being cooped up, so when the snow let up slightly, I suggested a visit to the office here to break the monotony, though I hadn't counted on the roads being so bad. This is Master Sergeant Kosloffski and Airman Rivero. You'll be seeing them around.'

Kosloffski straightened to attention and for a moment she thought he might salute the Snowdrop who, as a non-commissioned officer, would find such a move unusual, even for an American. But whatever Kosloffski was, he was a professional, and had chosen a non-confrontational strategy. After all, he had got what he wanted on the base. Now he had to get it back to his masters.

'Do you want to see our deployment orders, Mr Neel?'

'That won't be necessary,' said Warrant Officer Neel, 'not if you're in the care of Lady Amanda and she vouches for you. If you want my advice, you'll head off home pronto. The snow'll be coming down again within the hour and it won't be long before it's dark.'

'You're tracking the storm here, I presume? The base seems deserted.' Amanda kept her voice steady, determined not to betray her nervousness.

'Nothing much else to do,' said Neel amiably. 'No flying in this muck, so everybody not on leave is kicking their heels and trying to keep warm. Mind you, there's a fair few over in the Ops Room watching the radar screens, probably 'cos the telly's on the blink.'

'Same with us. Have they picked up anything interesting?'

'For want of anything better, they're tracking one of them Telltales that was spotted by a coastal patrol day before the snow hit. He seems to be trying to get inshore to ride it out and he's north of The Wash at the moment. Got to hope he's not in trouble as there's none would fancy going out in this unless they had to.'

Amanda's pulse quickened. 'Any distress call?'

'No, not a peep.'

'But we did get eyes on it?'

'Two days ago, when it was well outside territorial waters.'

'Was it identified?'

'Specifically? I wouldn't know, but it was definitely an AGI pretending to be a trawler, like all them Telltales do. Wasn't making much of an effort by all accounts as it was carrying a Hoplite on its deck.'

'Good to know you chaps are tracking it, Mr Neel. Now we'd better take your advice and get ourselves back to my house.' She stressed the 'my house', hoping that it would be remembered when Warrant Officer Neel reported, or at least gossiped about, her presence that afternoon.

'You get these boys in front of a fire with a mug of cocoa as soon as you can, Lady Amanda, but you be careful on them roads, it's dangerous out there.'

How right you are, Mr Neel, she thought as she started the Land Rover and pulled away, giving a regal wave to the warrant officer as he snapped to attention and threw a perfect salute in farewell.

At the gate, a sentry shrouded in a greatcoat appeared out of the guard post and gave the Alandel vehicle a perfunctory nod as a salute would have required him taking his hands out of his pockets. Amanda took some small comfort in the fact that the sentry would at least make a note of their time of departure as well as Warrant Officer Neel knowing their destination. It wasn't much of a trail of crumbs but someone might decide to follow it.

It was little comfort to her to hear Kosloffski, in the passenger seat, exhale loudly as they passed out of the gate. It was the first indication of nerves shown by the American, or perhaps the Russian as she should now think of him.

'You handled that very well,' he said, his conversational tone at odds with the fact that he was holding his pistol on his lap and it was pointed at Amanda's midriff, 'especially the news of the trawler.'

'You followed that?'

'All of it, once I worked out what a Telltales was.'

Amanda was not surprised. The nickname 'Telltales' was probably a British invention to describe the increasing number of Russian 'fishing trawlers' which dotted the seas between Britain and Greenland, their prime purpose being not to catch fish but to spy on NATO naval exercises, listen in on radio traffic and try and plot the positions of the alliance's submarines. Officially, the 600-ton 'trawlers' were known as AGIs, or Auxiliary General Intelligence ships, and the one being tracked on Marham's radar system was clearly a state-of-the-art model if it carried a Hoplite – NATO code for the Russian Mil Mi-2 helicopter – on its deck.

Kosloffski would surely know what the NATO nomenclature Hoplite meant.

And now Amanda knew how the Russians meant to go home.

Campion padded up the staircase in his stockinged feet, instinctively listening out for the fourth step which usually creaked loudly under the slightest pressure. It was a stupidly trivial, irrelevant thing to worry about, but it took his buzzing brain away from the image of Rupert's terrified face and the cold metal gun pressed against it.

On the landing, he went directly to the master bedroom, assuming that everyone downstairs in the eerily quiet lounge was straining to hear his footfalls, and opened and rattled the bedroom door to reassure the listeners that he had not deviated from his destination. As the bedroom was directly over Campion's study rather than the lounge, he knew he could not be heard and was effectively on 'silent running', but he thought it best not to dawdle as Quinn was unlikely to be a man of infinite patience.

He went immediately to the window, in front of which stood the most incongruous piece of furniture in the room, if not the house. The three-legged milking stool, surely too big for milking even a generously endowed cow in comfort, was at least fifty years old, while the chamber pot which perched on it had a floral print design and was thirty years older. Few Victorians, however, would have imagined the use to which the Campions had put it, as a home for a fat, eight-inch tall and very spikey snowball cactus. Despite its seasonally appropriate name, the plant contrasted sharply with the white snowscape view through the icy window out over Campion's frozen 'almost moat' ponds, the curved bridge from which long icicles dangled and the trees in the orchard which looked like a regiment of bone-white skeletal scarecrows.

That the plant had survived thus far said much for its hardiness and the night temperatures it experienced in its desert homeland, plus the fact that it was planted in the bare minimum of soil and compost as it was to all intents and purposes a Trojan cactus.

Cursing softly that he had left his gloves drying in the kitchen, Campion pulled the sleeves of his sweater down over his hands and grasped the plant, spines and all, as if handling a precious vase. It came out of the chamber pot easily – too easily – and only then did he notice the crumbs of black soil on the seat of the stool and on the carpet it stood on.

He should have registered immediately, had he been thinking logically, that the cactus had been disturbed and sat lower in its pot than it should. It had been lifted out and what it had hidden in the bottom of that Victorian heirloom had been removed.

Mr Campion caught his breath and steadied his shaking hands, which were dislodging soil from the plant's roots as if the cactus was taking revenge for being so roughly handled.

What the cactus had guarded was a 1934 model .25 Beretta pistol with the stamp RM around an anchor on the butt, showing it to have once been the property of the Regia Marina, the Italian Navy. Campion had acquired it as a souvenir at the end of the war, in circumstances he was still hesitant to talk about, and had kept it oiled and in working order with annual test firings (under police supervision) in an army drill hall in Norwich. He always kept it complete with a full magazine of fresh cartridges, wrapped in muslin, and the house plant was only the latest in a line of ingenious hiding places.

Only one other person on Earth made a sport of discovering those secret locations.

Campion stood there, holding the cactus up to the window like a communion chalice, as still as the skeletal white trees in the orchard beyond. His plan of action, and it had never been much of a detailed plan, had fallen at the first hurdle. Perhaps it was for the best as Quinn did not look the type to give up without a fight, and a shooting match inside the house could have resulted in collateral damage to innocent bystanders, two of whom were incapable of getting out of the way of a random bullet.

If he could not liberate his family and his guests, both the invited and the unexpected, could he do it from the outside?

He dropped the cactus unceremoniously back into its pot where it sat sulking at an awkward angle like a short, fat, spikey bell tower in Pisa, and examined the palms of his hands, not for wounds from the plant's spines but for inspiration on how to protect them from a far more dangerous adversary.

Knowing that Quinn's patience was likely to be limited, any Plan B would have to be developed on the hoof and Campion began to move rapidly. He scooped up the key to the safe in his office from the kidney-shaped dressing table where he always left it overnight, pocketed it, and after two long strides was opening the doors of his wardrobe. From the drawers under the hanging clothes he extracted three pairs of his thickest woollen socks and then took a sweater and a crisp white dress shirt from their hangers and flung them on the bed. He quickly removed the pullover he was wearing and put on the one he had selected, then replaced the original. If his torso looked unusually bulky, he could explain it away by simply saying he was feeling the cold. Then, with some difficulty, he pulled on two pairs of socks over the ones he was wearing and hoped no one would notice that his feet had suddenly swollen. The third pair he stuffed into a trouser pocket and dropped the dress shirt on the floor by the bedroom door as he started downstairs.

Quinn was exactly where Campion had last seen him and the muzzle of his pistol was still embedded in Rupert's cheek. Rupert's eyes were watering and his nose was starting to run.

Henderson, Breck and Miss Pounder were seated on the sofa, transfixed by the tense scene in front of them, while Lloyd Thursby was leaning so far forward in his chair that he seemed tempted to reach out and adjust the volume on the television set he imagined was broadcasting the drama.

'Here we are,' Campion announced, brandishing the safe key. 'Shall I release the treasure?'

Quinn moved his gun from son to father. 'Not so fast, I need to be there. You wouldn't have a gun in that safe, would you?'

Mr Campion did his best to look outraged. 'A pistol in the safe? That's a bit of a cliché from the Westerns, isn't it? That's when the innocent Wells Fargo clerk gets shot by the bank robbers.'

Campion fought to control a smile when the lip-reading Lloyd Thursby began to nod enthusiastically in agreement.

'I assure you,' he said loudly to be sure that Lugg heard, 'there are no more weapons in this house.'

'Then let's go to it. Just you. Everyone else stay where you are.'

Campion, with Quinn's gun now pressed into the small of his back, led the way into the study. With both doors open, the prisoners in the lounge strained necks and heads to see what Campion would produce from the safe. All, that is, except De Vries, who had slumped forward, head in hands, concentrating on his stockinged feet.

The days when Mr Campion might have spun around and with two or three well-placed blows disabled or at least disarmed the American were long gone; a depressing realization at the best of times, but particularly frustrating when his family were in danger. Not that the younger, stronger Quinn expected violent resistance – he had seen little evidence of it so far – and Campion was convinced that his only chance to rescue the situation was to do the unexpected. For that he would need diversion and darkness. Until then he would do what it was often said he did best, and be harmless.

With Quinn towering over him, he knelt and unlocked the safe in the cubbyhole of his desk, leaning back to allow Quinn to see that no machine guns or crossbows were concealed therein. Then he carefully removed the rectangle of red silk, placed it on the desk and gently unwrapped the diptych, opening it so that both panels were visible.

'Is that it? Don't look like much; kinda small for a painting. You sure it's valuable?'

'Unless it is a very clever fake,' said Campion, 'it could be over four hundred years old, which automatically makes it valuable. Think about it. This could have been painted sixty or seventy years before those other pilgrims landed on Plymouth Rock, if you believe your country's origin myth. But then, America isn't really your country, is it?'

'I've warned you about that mouth of yours,' snarled Quinn. 'Stick to the picture. What's it called?'

'I have no idea if it has a formal title, but I am told it depicts the burning of the original statue of Our Lady of Walsingham in London, possibly in the garden of the house of Thomas Cromwell, in 1538, perhaps even an eyewitness account by the painter. Those were turbulent times in British history; they usually were when religion was involved, and its value, historically and religiously, would be considerable.'

'You saying that someone like the Pope, say, would pay top dollar for this thing?'

'I wouldn't say that he personally would, but the Vatican might be interested and certainly many big museums would be. But why ask me when you have an art dealer, a historian and a priest in the next room?'

Mrs Thursby had staggered in from the kitchen carrying a large wooden tray loaded with plates, pyramids of sandwiches, a log cabin of cocktail sausages, condiments, pickle and sauces, only to find her efforts not only unappreciated but almost totally ignored. Only her father-in-law showed any interest in her provision of lunch for the masses, lightening her load by taking a sandwich in each hand, which would have earned him an admonishing slap had she not been carrying the tray.

Apart from the involuntarily static Rupert and Lugg, everyone was crowded over the low table usually reserved for drinks or board games, on which Mr Campion had placed the diptych on a cushion of the folded red scarf. Even De Vries had abandoned his scowl and was providing an accompanying commentary on Jacob Suycker, one of the unsung masters of religious paintings in the period of the Reformation.

'So is it real?' Quinn asked the onlookers.

Hereward Henderson was, naturally, the first to volunteer an opinion. 'Diptychs are very real. The most famous is the Wilton Diptych, painted for Richard II around 1395, I think. It was in the Royal Collection for centuries, and is now in the National Gallery. Amazing it survived, especially during the Puritan campaign against icons.'

'And what's that worth?'

'Goodness knows what it would fetch if it ever came up for sale. I would say it was priceless.'

'What does the priest say?'

Quinn might have taken a passing interest in late medieval art but not so much that he had let his guard down, and when he invited Breck to speak it was at gunpoint.

'From what I can see, that looks like an accurate representation of the Walsingham statue as we think it looked, and if this actually shows its destruction, it is, of course, a valuable historical document. As to its value? I could not say in terms of money, but as a treasure of the Catholic Church in this country, it would be prized highly.'

'All this talk is pointless, you fools!' exploded De Vries, as Campion had hoped he would. 'The diptych is mine.'

The Dutchman made to fold the diptych and gather up it and the red silk scarf, but his grasping hands were batted away by Quinn's swinging pistol. De Vries recoiled with a squeal of pain, folding his hands into his chest.

Mr Campion, ostensibly pulling Miss Pounder out of the line of fire, took her gently by the arm and stepped back towards the fireplace, pulling her close.

'Get a message to Lugg for me, would you?' he said quietly.

Miss Pounder looked at him wide-eyed, then nodded once quickly.

Campion turned away to face the fire, and on the pretence of taking another log from the basket and poking it carefully into position, continued in a whisper.

'Tell him I need a diversion, as violent as possible, when it starts to get dark. The password will be Platelayers' Arms. Got that? I would be very grateful.'

He sensed Miss Pounder move away and smiled into the fire when he heard her announce 'You are very welcome' for his benefit and then, for the rest of the room, said, 'Mrs Thursby, we could all do with a bite to eat.'

The quiet spinster from Dorset had hidden talents not only as a linguist but as an actress, and Campion was smugly content that he had chosen her as an ally. As she moved to relieve Mrs Thursby of her tray, Campion innocently ran a hand along the oak mantelpiece until his fingers located the box of matches always kept there for fire-lighting purposes. Smoothly he scooped up the box and pushed it into his trouser pocket alongside the spare pair of socks.

'So what's this thing *worth*?' Quinn was demanding irritably.

'It is impossible to estimate,' said Henderson in a tone which suggested he could be pressed to have a go. 'Only this month there was talk of the *Mona Lisa* being insured for one hundred million dollars prior to its tour of America, but the Louvre in Paris preferred to spend the cost of the insurance premium on additional security. This, of course, is not a Da Vinci, and one has to consider its religious significance as well as its artistic merit.'

'There was a religious study by Da Vinci sold earlier this year,' said the Reverend Breck almost dreamily. 'A cartoon in charcoal of the Virgin and Child with Saint Anne. The Royal Academy put a value of eight hundred thousand on it and there was a public appeal to which I subscribed, but it didn't raise enough.

In the end the government coughed up three hundred and fifty thousand to meet the target and bought it for the National Gallery. All the experts said it would have made more than eight hundred thousand had it gone to auction or private sale.'

Quinn emitted a long, low whistle. 'Eight hundred grand? Dollars or pounds?'

'Pounds, of course,' said Breck.

Mr Campion cleared his throat and nonchalantly asked, 'What's that in roubles?'

Luncheon at Carterers that day was an uneasy refuelling rather than a meal. Mrs Thursby had done wonders but received no more thanks than the prison trustee who had been forced into serving the porridge to a line of convicts. Sandwiches were devoured in silence, Mr Campion, unusually, eating four in rapid succession. Had Lugg been in a position to observe his appetite, he would no doubt have made some remark about 'keeping his strength up' which, in fact, was exactly what Campion was doing.

Only De Vries abstained from the communal feeding frenzy, sitting by himself, his lips moving but no sound emerging as he stared fixedly at Quinn. The gunman had retreated to his chair, which he had moved into the doorway of the lounge now his prisoners were corralled there, and had balanced the Suycker diptych on his knees. To De Vries's horror, he was using the red silk scarf covering the painting as a plate for a pile of sandwiches.

The Reverend Breck automatically assumed the charitable role of feeding the restrained Rupert, holding a sandwich at mouth-appropriate level, for which Mr Campion was grateful, and even more so when Miss Pounder did the same service for Lugg. Replenishing her stock at least twice, the woman held each sandwich dangerously close to Lugg's gyrating jaws with little regard for the safety of her fingertips. Clearly she was a female of iron nerve, and at one point she leaned over the fat man to brush imagined crumbs from his chest. When she raised her head she checked whether Quinn was observing her and then winked once in Campion's direction. Message delivered.

For dessert, Mrs Thursby passed around a plate containing

squares of a dark fruit cake, each topped with a slice of cheese, which gave rise to a lecture by Hereward Henderson on which sort of cheese, English of course, was best suited for this delicacy. After some deliberation, mostly with himself, he decided on Wensleydale, and no one had the energy or inclination to argue with him.

Campion was grateful for the distraction and the slight lightening of the mood. The question of the value of the Suycker diptych seemed to be no longer a matter of debate, though its ownership had clearly passed from the Dutchman to the gunman.

'Your comrades are coming back, aren't they?' Campion had sidled up close to Quinn's guard post.

'Don't you worry about that.'

'But I do worry, because my wife is with them and it's starting to get dark outside. The roads are treacherous enough in daylight in conditions like this, not to mention they could have fallen foul of the Royal Air Force or the police.'

The only sign of nerves Quinn showed was to glance at his wristwatch. 'They'll be back, but you're right, it is getting dark. Put the lights on.'

Campion reached for the light switch next to the door frame, pausing to look out of the window to judge the fading afternoon light. Already the room was filling with shadows from the fire and he knew that full dark would come quickly outside.

'Can we switch on the lights on the Christmas tree?'

The suggestion was greeted with a distant grunt from Lugg.

'The plug is down there by the skirting board. We could pull on the curtains to avoid attracting passers-by.'

'Sure.' Quinn waved the gun as Campion illuminated the room. 'But you stay where I can see you. Hey lady, yes, you.'

Miss Pounder stood in response.

'You do the tree and the curtains.'

As Miss Pounder gently made her way around the two captives to get to the tree, taking Quinn's attention, Mr Campion leaned casually against the doorway no more than two feet away from Quinn's pistol.

'Rupert always insisted on the tree lights being left on all night just in case Santa Claus had forgotten to leave a present and needed to find his way back here. I always told him to stay put and stay quiet and everything would be fine in the morning.'

Campion's homily was greeted with a look of utter bewilderment on his son's face, but all other eyes in the room were on Florence Pounder as she made great play of pulling the heavy curtains with far more violence than was necessary.

'Of course, our little *Tannenbaum* pales into insignificance compared to the massive tree they used to put up at the Platelayers' Arms in the good old days.'

Miss Pounder suddenly dropped out of sight, masked by Rupert and Lugg and the Christmas tree, as she stooped to find the plug and socket for the lights.

Quinn instinctively got to his feet and took a step into the room, tucking the diptych under his left arm and raising the pistol in his right hand.

There was no obvious suggestion of anything untoward, but Quinn was being careful. Campion hoped he had every reason to be.

There was a loud click as an electric switch was flicked, followed by a flash. The tree lights sputtered and then went out, but the collective gasp from those in the room was more in reaction to the blood-curdling scream from Miss Pounder and the fact that Lugg seemed to burst from his chains like an artillery shell and the Christmas tree began to topple.

The exact choreography of what then happened will probably never be known. Miss Pounder, having decided to unexpectedly join in the diversion Mr Campion had requested, had short-circuited the coloured tree lights with the aid of a straightened hairpin and reacted as if electrocuted. At the same moment, almost as if they had rehearsed a magic act, Lugg erupted from his chair, having somehow smashed the chair legs with his still-manacled feet.

Lugg lurched forward into the falling tree which had been helped on its way by Miss Pounder. He would have caught it in a bear-hug, or at least rugby-tackled it, had it not been for the fact that his hands were still manacled behind his back and connected to Rupert's chains. Thus a seemingly immovable object propelled himself forward, dragging with him a reluctant but eminently moveable Rupert complete with the chair he was attached to.

The resultant crashing, splintering of wood, persistent screams (Miss Pounder throwing herself into her role) and startled shouts from Rupert, plus the tree ornaments which flew off and burst like shrapnel, produced gasps of shock from all witnesses, including Quinn.

'What the . . .?' Quinn started, striding towards the melee by the window.

It was the moment Campion had been waiting for; the guard had left his post.

Like a phantom – or so he hoped – he slipped by Quinn's chair and with two loping strides was on the staircase. He resisted the temptation to look back into the lounge and took the stairs two at a time, delighted that his triple-socked feet made no sound.

On the landing he did not pause as he scooped up the white dress shirt he had chosen because it was of a generous oversized cut and usually reserved for formal, eight-course dinners. Now it was to serve another purpose and he pulled it on over his pullovers, fumbling at the buttons as he strode into the bedroom previously occupied by the late Graham Fisk, where the sash window was still open by two inches and snowflakes were fluttering in.

He cocked an ear for any sound of alarm or pursuit from downstairs, but all he heard were dull thuds and muffled shouting, from which he took heart as he slid the window up to give him room to climb out.

Straddling the ledge, he took the other pair of socks from his pocket and pulled them over his hands. As gloves they were a poor substitute but as mittens they would do at a pinch. Then he looked down at the drop facing him.

The coach driver had left the house that way and survived the plunge, only to have his neck broken later by one of his passengers, though all traces of his landing had been obliterated by fresh snow. Fisk had been younger and fitter than Campion, who could only hope for a similar soft landing.

There was only a dim light below from the lounge as the curtains were drawn and the returning snow limited visibility, which Campion was almost thankful for. He took off his spectacles and stuffed them down the neck of his outer pullover, his breath frosting in front of his face as he lowered his legs and released his hold on the windowsill.

It was as he was falling through the ice-cold air that he heard the shot.

SIXTEEN
Waking Hereward

'So how long have you been American?' asked Amanda. 'You never gave me a straight answer.'

'There is no straight answer,' said Kosloffski, struggling with the wheel of the Land Rover.

He had insisted on driving, although he was clearly not as proficient as Rivero. Perhaps it was the unfamiliar left-hand drive, or the manual gear change or the icy conditions and poor visibility, or possibly all of the above, but he was definitely a nervous driver. Amanda, in the passenger seat next to him, had braced herself in the hope that he would drive off the road into a ditch, which might give her the opportunity to escape. Even though the snow limited visibility, she began to recognize the outline of fields and hedges and knew they were nearing Carterers. If she could get away there was a chance, albeit a slim one, that she could evade them on foot across country and get back to the house before them.

But then what? There was still the third Russian, as she now thought of them, to contend with, and laying siege to Carterers by herself seemed impractical. She had one secret weapon, literally – the Beretta hidden deep in her duffel coat pocket, which if she screwed up her courage she could pull and at least shoot Sergeant Sometimes before Rivero in the back seat could shoot her. She might get a shot off at Rivero, she might not. The Land Rover might career off the road and kill them all, or leave them trapped, preserved in a freezer until help or a thaw arrived, although neither seemed imminent.

In an odd way she was grateful that Kosloffski broke her morbid train of thought. 'All you need to know is that we are all legally American citizens, at least for the next twenty-four hours.'

'Will that help your propaganda when you release those staged photographs – the fact that Americans took them?'

Kosloffski seemed to consider the idea carefully. 'It could be an angle – American airmen disgusted with their supreme commander's aggression in bringing more Thor missiles to England in secret, but exactly how the intelligence is used is up to our superiors in Moscow.'

Amanda did not try to keep the cynicism out of her voice. 'It would be a steamier story for the world's press to have Americans betraying their allies rather than this coming to light as a result of an action by a Russian hit squad.'

'Hit squad? Pah! My good lady, you have seen too many gangster films. We are soldiers of the Soviet Union, not hit men.'

'I am not your good lady.' Amanda spoke through tight lips. 'I am your captive. I and my family are being held hostage by kidnappers and murderers.'

'Murderers?' He thought for a moment. 'Oh, you mean the coach driver. That was not planned, just an accident of war. We have not harmed your family.'

'Not yet, but do you expect me to believe you will leave us alive as witnesses?'

'You should because that is exactly what we intend to do. You were always part of the plan.'

Amanda became aware that her teeth were chattering – but due to anger rather than the temperature – as Kosloffski continued.

'Bringing a coachload of passengers to your door was not in the plan, that was improvisation brought on by the weather, but we were always coming for you – you especially. You were our way into Marham and you were our model, a sort of pin-up girl.'

'What?'

'Our pictures might be dismissed as fakes, as mock-ups.'

'Which they are.'

'But with you in them, the famous female aero engineer, as well as part of the British establishment, people will say they must be true; for surely the good Lady Amanda would not pose before a fake plan in order to embarrass her American allies. The press – the international press – will have a field day. You will not have an easy time of it, I'm afraid.'

'I will tell the truth: I was a prisoner and my family were held hostage.'

'By a gang of American traitors or Russian patriots who

appeared in a blizzard and then disappeared without trace and whose existence will be denied by your secret service.'

'Don't be ridiculous. Even if you manage to get away, you were seen at the base.'

'By the Snowdrop who knew you – and you vouched for us, saying we were your guests. That won't look good, will it? And what makes you think your secret service and your RAF will ever admit they let three Russian agents walk into and out of a high security base?'

Amanda sensed that Kosloffski wanted to rub salt into the wound.

'Face it, Lady Amanda, whether you like it or not, you have provided us with what the advertising men on Madison Avenue call celebrity endorsement.'

Amanda reached instinctively into her coat pocket, but reason and the continued deterioration of the weather stayed her hand.

The snow flurries increased as darkness fell. The Land Rover's headlights were proving useless except as a warning to any oncoming vehicle. Fortunately there was no other traffic on the narrow country road, and not a sign that there had ever been any on the even narrower lane which led to Carterers. Even their own tyre tracks from two hours before had been obliterated.

Amanda strained her eyes, seeking familiarity in the landscape through the metronomic swipe of the windscreen wipers fighting a losing battle with the snow, large flakes dodging the wiper blades and spattering like bullet fragments on the windshield.

Suddenly, high and to the right, her eye caught the yellow twinkle of a star making its presence felt through the curtain of falling snow. And there it was again, and again; and then there were three or four tiny stars, red ones, which clustered and then disappeared as suddenly as they had sparked. Christmas, traditionally, was a time when important stars were said to appear in the sky, beckoning wise men to follow them, but stars were not usually yellow and red; nor did they flicker and die so quickly, or surely most astronomers would be unemployed.

'What the hell is that?' Rivero blurted out from the back seat.

Amanda said nothing, but she had a good idea what she had seen and was sure she knew where it had come from.

* * *

Mr Campion registered the gunshot as he was in mid-air and the fact that the sound had come through the lounge window he was currently plummeting past. Then, unable to keep his balance as he landed, he was rolling through knee-deep snow, struggling for breath as the impact and the glacial night air made twin assaults on his lungs.

He pulled off one of his sock mittens with his teeth and retrieved his glasses from inside his layers of pullover. With his spectacles back in place, he took stock of his situation. All his limbs seemed to be intact and his triple-socked feet, although caked with snow, responded to his commands albeit reluctantly. His white dress shirt would provide a modicum of winter camouflage; an idea inspired by memories of cinema newsreels of long ago showing the valiant resistance of the Finns to the Russian invasion of 1940. Now he had a Russian invasion of his own to deal with, and without weapons.

Much as he felt the urge to press his ear to the window to try and make sense of the muffled shouts, thumps and bumps coming from within, he knew his absence would soon be noticed and it would not take Quinn long to work out how he had escaped. Having got out of the house, the last thing he should really be thinking about was going back inside; he must concentrate on getting Quinn to come outside, but not until he was ready to confront him.

He pushed through the snow which had blown against the front of the house, crouching as he passed the front door and the pool of light spilling out from the study window. Gambling that the ructions in the lounge were keeping the occupants of the house well and truly occupied, Campion moved out on to the driveway where the snow was less deep, and ran as best he could beyond the rectangle of orange light, heading for the curved wooden bridge over his frozen 'almost moat'.

His shoeless feet, when they made contact with the ice-covered bridge, were almost his undoing. With the grace of a drunken mime artist attempting to perform the dying swan, he scaled the short incline with the help of the handrails. Coming down the slope on the orchard side was easier by adopting the schoolboy technique of sliding on a frozen playground, and he was inordinately pleased with himself for staying upright.

The trees in the orchard with their bare frosted branches offered virtually no cover, but Campion thought it unlikely that he could be spotted from the house, other than from the window in the master bedroom, and even then he would present a wraith-like figure through the falling snow, no more than a tiny figure in an overshaken snow globe.

Nonetheless he stooped as he ran the length of the eastern side of the house, although running was hardly an accurate description for his stumbling gait, and he fell face-first into the snow on several occasions. Wiping snowflakes from his glasses with a damp sock mitten and cursing his now wet and very cold feet, he paused when he could make out the dark outline of the corner of the house. There were no lights on in the dining room, and it seemed safe enough to approach, though he knew he was on the far side of his 'almost moat', albeit one of the narrowest parts. The problem was that a covering of snow concealed the frozen surface of the long, thin pond, and although it should have frozen hard enough to take Campion's weight, he stepped out gingerly and was rewarded by a creaking sound rather than a splintering followed by a plunge into icy water.

Three soggy strides and he was across; two more and he was hugging the flinty corner of Carterers. From there he could, in theory, see the length of the house down to the tack room and the old barn, now the garage, but he could not make out any detail through the swirling whiteness, other than a faint cone of light coming from the kitchen window. At least that gave him a point of reference to aim for.

He was almost at the kitchen window before he was able to clearly make out the shape of the tack room shed which he had selected as his prime target. He could no longer feel his toes, his layers of socks were crunchy blocks of ice and his makeshift mittens were frozen shovels as stiff as plywood. He put both hands into his armpits to try to warm them, but found himself shivering uncontrollably. His dress shirt might be useful winter camouflage but it was providing poor insulation.

He risked a look into the empty kitchen and resisted the urge to smash his way in and embrace the Aga then, flapping his arms to restore circulation, he made a dash for the tack room.

Once inside and with the door firmly closed behind him, he

risked turning on the single bulb light. It was unlikely to be seen from the house in the current conditions and vital for him to find what he was looking for. Without a light he would have stumbled into Lugg's cache of beer crates and empty bottles, twisted an ankle negotiating the stacks of logs or skewered himself on the blade of one of the rusty gardening tools lying in wait for the unwary.

He had to move half a dozen logs carefully stacked in one corner of the main pile. It was a makeshift hidey-hole which only he and Lugg knew about and it hid a small metal cash box, though it had been a while since it contained loose change. Now it housed a dozen or so shotgun cartridges, kept a safe distance from the weapon in the house as ordered by Amanda during Rupert's childhood. Mr Campion now had ammunition but no way of delivering it.

He shook his head as if to warm his numbed brain, and his eyes lit upon the metal box of fireworks which had been purchased for the Campions' traditional New Year's Eve dinner party display. Mr Campion had selected them personally, being a long-standing customer of Standard Fireworks of Huddersfield and being, in Amanda's words, 'basically a big kid', he had insisted on mostly rockets.

He selected six of the most impressive, their sticks more than two feet long and then, with numb fingers, rummaged in a wooden crate containing gardening ephemera including old seed packets, small plant pots, a rusty pair of secateurs and a ball of green gardening twine. Using the firework box lid as a table, he cut lengths of twine and tied a shotgun shell to the stick of each rocket, just below the blue touchpaper. When his armoury was complete, he selected two empty pint beer bottles from a crate, promising himself to refund Lugg his lost deposit.

He packed everything into a hessian sack which had once contained malted barley, and swung it gently over his left shoulder, knowing he would not fool anyone into believing he was Santa Claus. As he left the shed, he picked up a garden spade which he hefted like a javelin and laid it across his right shoulder.

Should anyone catch a glimpse of his silhouette through the storm, he would appear more as an Elizabethan gravedigger than the Spirit of Christmas.

With his long legs attempting the gait of a high-stepping dressage horse, he retraced his indented footprints in the snow along the side of the house until he was back at the north-east corner. He identified the spot where he had crossed the frozen 'almost moat' and had gently stepped out, listening intently for a warning creak from the ice, when he found himself caught in the oblong of light coming from the dining room where the lights had suddenly been switched on.

Animal instinct told him to freeze in his tracks but a more rational part of his brain reminded him that an immobile rabbit caught in headlights was doing nothing to slow or deter the advance of those headlights. Hefting his sack and the garden spade, he plunged forward, the crack of breaking ice underfoot as loud as the gunshot he feared might follow.

Then he was in the orchard, among the bare, white trees which offered little protection but were at least outside the zone of light beaming from the house. He flung himself down behind the nearest trunk, shovelling snow into piles around him to break up any outline he might present to an eagle-eyed sniper, thankful for the continued falling of chunky white snowflakes which probably did more to hide him than his own frantic efforts.

He risked raising his head and peering round the tree trunk, wishing it was a fat oak in full leaf rather than a skeletal dormant apple, and tried to make out what was going on in the dining room. Something certainly was, given the flurry of activity, though Mr Campion, dabbing snowflakes from his spectacles, could get only the blurriest of images.

There were two figures in the dining room, and he was pretty sure they were the two Thursbys, who appeared, incongruously, to be laying the dining table. Except they were not laying the table, they were clearing it – and suddenly the room was filled with jostling, gesticulating figures dragging and heaving something large and ungainly towards the table.

His eyes watering with cold and frustration, Campion desperately tried to make sense of the fuzzy tableau being played out a few yards away behind the window glass and a blizzard of snowflakes. He identified the Reverend Breck and the smaller Hereward Henderson as they struggled to lift their bulky cargo on to the table. Then he clearly saw the Dutchman De Vries manhandling what could only be a pair of legs, and realized that a body was being laid out on the table, and a body of such proportions – in silhouette it resembled a Pacific atoll – that it could only be Lugg's.

His view was suddenly obscured as Florence Pounder filled the window frame, outstretched her arms and closed the curtains. Although he could not be sure, Campion felt that the expression on her face was one of pure horror.

Ignoring the cold creeping into his bones and fuelled by an anger at what he had witnessed, Campion grabbed his sack and his spade and ran as best he could back through the orchard towards the curved bridge. He had no clear plan and was tormented by the thought that he was running away from an old friend clearly in need of his help, but the bridge offered a semblance of cover, perhaps the location of an ambush. If he could lure Quinn out of the house, he could lie in wait under the bridge over the frozen moat like a vengeful troll, and vengeful he intended to be, given that his oldest friend had been hurt and his only son was still a prisoner.

At the orchard end of the bridge he quickly dug a hole in the snow big enough in which to stand the two beer bottles about six inches apart, packing the gap between them with loose snow. He gave their necks a twist and a wiggle to make sure they were secure, then he threaded the stick of one of Standard Fireworks' finest rockets into the nearest bottle, taking care to make sure his added explosive element was securely tied on but not likely to go off until it was high up in the air or at least well away from him.

With the aid of his front teeth he pulled his sock mittens from his numb fingers and fumbled for the box of matches in his trouser pocket. This was the scene in the thriller film where the hero finds that his matches – dramatically, one after the other – refuse to ignite, but for once luck was with him. His first match struck and with cupped hands he applied it to the blue touchpaper, mentally repeating the mantra to retire immediately, which he did by stumbling clear, slipping and falling flat on his back.

From that supine position, cold but not uncomfortable in the soft snow, Campion felt the heat on his face as the rocket ignited, and though he had instinctively closed his eyes, he was sure he could see the tongue of blue and orange flame through his eyelids. The whoosh as the rocket leapt from its bottle was deafening, and then Campion, lying on his back, saw the night sky above him burst with a satisfying double explosion into a cluster of brightly coloured stars over the roof of the house.

As he sat up, Campion became aware of a pitter-patter sound which he was at a loss to explain, until he realized that mingled with the falling snowflakes were pellets of shot from the cartridge he had tied to the rocket falling to earth and bouncing off the wooden bridge. His home-made mortar seemed to have worked, he had survived being hoist by his own petard, and now was the time to maintain the pressure and give them both barrels.

He selected two more rockets and reloaded his weapon, taking a childish delight in the way wisps of smoke curled out of the bottle he had used first and the memories evoked by the damp, sulphurous gunpowder scent lingering in the air.

This time he crouched over the fuses, prepared to roll sideways out of the way as he lit another match. There was no more than a microsecond between the two rockets igniting, and this time Campion kept his eyes open to follow their trajectory as they burst almost simultaneously over the roof of Carterers. The residents must surely have heard the double bangs, even if they had not noticed the night sky light up. The windows must have rattled and the falling shot from the cartridges would have played a tattoo on the roof tiles, yet the front of the house remain stubbornly lifeless.

As he prepared two more missiles, the thought occurred that even through the snowstorm his display of pyrotechnics would be seen beyond the immediate vicinity and might, just might, attract help, but from where he did not know. Was he really making a serious effort to rescue the situation, or was he merely following the frantic efforts of the desperate junior officer charged with firing off the distress rockets from the listing deck of the *Titanic*?

It had never been much of a plan but it was all he had, and what he had witnessed through the dining room window meant he did not have the luxury of time to reassess his strategy. He adjusted the angle of his two launch bottles, aiming the rockets lower, closer to the house – perhaps close enough to shatter an upstairs window – and struck a match. He did not have time to retreat to whatever was the recommended safe distance; both fuses ignited immediately and covered him in a cloud of choking smoke as the rockets whooshed up into the night sky.

The results were, however, satisfying, as both rockets and the shells they carried exploded at roof level. Even before the doubled bang had faded and red and blue stars were still falling to the ground, Campion was reaching for the last rocket in his sack when the front door of the house opened and light flooded the snowy driveway.

Instinctively, Campion dropped to his knees and edged under the wooden bridge, confident that his outline was not sufficiently clear enough to be a target. He was mildly surprised to find he could feel the slippery ice of the frozen moat under feet he thought would never feel anything again, as he wrapped his arms around one of the supports and pulled himself upright.

There were two figures in the doorway, backlit by the lights in the hall. One was Rupert, his movements restricted by the manacles on his ankles and his hands at his back. Behind him stood the taller Quinn, his pistol levelled at the side of Rupert's head.

'Stop messing about, Pa!' Rupert's voice was tremulous, quaking with more than just the cold. 'People are rattled enough as it is in here. Tensions inside are running rather high.'

Crouched beneath the bridge, Campion struggled to remain silent. Trolls should not easily give away their positions, though he was sure the average troll of legend did not have teeth which chattered so loudly.

'Give it up and come inside, Pa. You're just making a spectacle of yourself, though that always was your strong point, wasn't it?'

Mr Campion gripped the wooden beam on the bridge as much as his dead fingers encased in wet socks could grip. Rupert was going off-script, sending him a message; he would never have accused his father of making a spectacle of himself – quite the reverse, in fact, as he regarded his father's knack of gentle self-deprecation as one of his most endearing characteristics, even if his mother did not always agree.

'Why must you always do the opposite of what everyone expects?'

There it was. Rupert was telling him do the opposite, wasn't he?

'Lugg's hurt and you can only help him if you give up and come inside.'

So: don't stop causing a nuisance; stay outside; and Lugg was hurt but not dead. At least that was what Mr Campion's sluggish brain was telling him. It might be good advice, it might not, but Campion could not think of another course of action without putting Rupert at risk.

If he could lure Quinn out of the doorway and towards the bridge, Rupert, even in shackles, might be able to make a break for it. He was young and fit and hopefully innocent enough to think he was invincible when it came to flying bullets, although with luck they would all be aimed at the senior Campion.

'Are you out there, Pa?' Rupert was shouting into the snowflakes, turning his head to the left then right, as was Quinn, which Campion, from his icy troll-nest, took to mean they had no idea where he was. He decided it was time to enlighten them.

With Rupert's plaintive question ringing in his ears, Campion crawled back to his foxhole and his armoury, such as it was. Sliding through the snow on his stomach, he located the garden spade and carefully pushed it behind him on to the ice of the moat, then he took his last rocket from his sack and loaded it into one of his bottle launchers, padding snow around it to ensure a vertical angle. Turning his back on the house to shield his striking match, he lit the blue touchpaper and this time did retire immediately, scuttling back under the bridge and grabbing hold of his favourite supporting timber as the rocket whooshed into the air.

The firework and the shotgun shell exploded simultaneously high above the frontage of the house. Rupert and Quinn could not help but follow the track of the rocket as all children on Bonfire Night instinctively did with a chorus of 'Oohs' and 'Ahhs', though these two spectators flinched at the double bang and the shower of shotgun pellets which rattled off windowpanes and then fell around them.

Quinn's reaction shocked the watching Campion in his hidey-hole. The American, frightened or angered by the firework exploding above his head, pushed Rupert in the small of the back and, as he staggered out into the storm, swung his pistol like a club at the back of his head. Rupert sprawled face-down in the snow and Campion scrabbled frantically for the spade, his one remaining weapon, which had slid just out of reach on the ice.

Campion released his hold on the bridge support and tried to find purchase on the ice, standing in a crouch and holding the spade like an axe, briefly imagining himself as a Norman warrior on the front line, besieging Hereward and his Viking allies in Ely a millennium ago. Or perhaps he was a Saxon defending the last bridge or secret pathway across the frozen Fens. Either way the analogy was ridiculous: he was an old man with a garden spade, shivering violently, struggling to stay almost upright, faced with a professional military man with a gun, and he had no idea how to get near enough to his enemy to tackle him.

That problem was partly solved by the enemy himself as Quinn, having felled Rupert, stepped out of the doorway, arm extended, and began firing indiscriminately in the direction of the bridge and the orchard.

Campion flinched at the crack of the shots and attempted to make himself smaller, though all logic told him that Quinn was shooting wildly, aiming at the take-off point of that last rocket. He was sure that through the whirling snow, the darkness and the shadows of the bridge, Quinn could not see him, though he could see Quinn, thanks to the light from the house.

Campion could even hear him cursing and venting his anger above the cracks of the gunshots as he strode nearer, one of which sent a chunk of wood from the handrail whirling by Campion's head, then spinning away across the ice like a curling stone.

If Quinn actually chose to cross the bridge, Campion reckoned he had a chance, a slim chance, to cross the ice under the bridge and come up behind him.

He heard the American say, 'Come on, show yourself, you son of a bitch!' and realized how close his enemy now was, only two or three yards from his end of the bridge. He could see the flash of another shot from his pistol, the sound ringing in his ears, and then realized he could see Quinn in considerable detail as suddenly there was more light illuminating the frontage of Carterers.

Struggling against the cold, with his concern for Rupert, and all too conscious that Quinn's shots were, almost certainly more by accident than design, coming very close to home, Campion had totally missed the fact that the additional illumination was being provided by the bouncing headlights of a vehicle skidding up the driveway.

He risked sticking his head out from under the left side of the bridge, the side away from the trigger-happy Quinn, to get a better view, though it was far from a clear one. With snow still falling and the wavering headlights, the scene again resembled one on a poor television set suffering massive interference.

Campion recognized the vehicle as the Alandel Land Rover and realized he had done so before Quinn seemed to have noticed its presence, for he was still advancing on the bridge and still shooting.

The Land Rover swirled to a halt, sliding in a half-circle, its headlights now spotlighting both the prone Rupert and the standing Quinn.

'Stand down, soldier!' came the shout from the driver's door as Quinn loosed off two more shots. 'I said cease firing!'

Then Campion felt sure he heard the plaintive cry of 'Rupert!' and figures emerged from the Land Rover, one of them Amanda, who rushed over to Rupert's body.

'Stop it, Pete, you're just blasting snow! That's an order.'

Kosloffski and Rivero both had their pistols drawn but held them at their sides, and when Quinn finally registered the sergeant's commands, he lowered his gun and turned back towards the house.

'What the hell were you shooting at?' Kosloffski demanded.

'Campion. He made a break for it.'

'Did you get him?'

Quinn shook his head. 'No, he must be long gone.'

'Let's hope you're right. We don't want any more complications now we've got what we wanted. Now help Lady Amanda get her son inside and Pete, play nice. She's one of our assets.'

'So the job's done?'

'All you have to do is get us home.'

Campion watched in angry silence, burying his mouth in the necks of his pullovers in case his frosting breath gave him away, as Rivero switched off the lights and the engine of the Land Rover. His eyes adjusted to the reduced light and he focused on Amanda as she nursed Rupert up on to his knees, clearly protesting that he was all right and that his mother shouldn't fuss.

Campion imagined Amanda reprimanding their son by pointing out she was his mother and it was her sworn duty to fuss, but instead he saw that her face was turned towards Quinn and it was a face of pure fury. As she helped Rupert to his feet, her hand went to the right-hand pocket of her duffel coat and Campion had a stomach-churning premonition.

'Don't, darling, please don't,' he whispered almost as a prayer to himself.

As if by telepathy, Amanda heeded his plea and withdrew her hand in order to throw an arm around Rupert. Fending off any help from Quinn, she helped Rupert across the threshold and into the hall.

The three Americans followed and the door slammed shut, leaving Mr Campion out in the cold.

SEVENTEEN
Under Siege

Rupert knew that 'the Platelayers' Arms' was some sort of coded message; he had heard Florence Pounder whisper it to his fellow captive, Lugg, when she had fed him one of Mrs Thursby's sandwiches. He knew it must be a message from his father, as that particular East End hostelry was an established haunt of Mr Campion, Lugg, and a colourful array of their friends, both the dubious ones and members of the Metropolitan Police. It was not the sort of place likely to be on the social circuit of a postmistress with religious leanings from rural Dorset, therefore Miss Pounder could only be acting as an innocent messenger.

He was not surprised that when his father mentioned the Platelayers' Arms it triggered such a violent reaction from Lugg, as he had always appreciated there was some sort of telepathy between the two of them and neither would be happy to docilely accept the current situation. He guessed that the code word was the starting gun for Lugg to provide a diversion, and certainly his father had been acting even more eccentrically than usual, though eccentricity was only to be expected in the present rather eccentric circumstances.

Rupert had watched, trying not to be seen watching, as Mr Campion had casually wandered across the room until he was so close to Quinn that he could have reached out and touched the pistol he was nursing. Rupert sincerely hoped his father was not going to do anything so foolish as to grab for the gun or tackle the man. He knew that his father, albeit slim, healthy and active for his age, would be no match for an unarmed Quinn in a fight, and Quinn was very definitely armed. Only a Lugg, dropping on him from a great height, would be favourite to be victorious in a rough house. Surely the senior Campion was not thinking of attacking Quinn alone, for it would be a solo effort.

Rupert and Lugg were restrained, literally, in their movements, Lloyd Thursby and his daughter-in-law were hardly combatant material, and Hereward Henderson and the Reverend Breck seemed unlikely allies if violence was called for. Only the Dutchman De Vries, whose eyes had never left Quinn since he had appropriated his precious diptych, seemed fired up enough to take physical action if the opportunity arrived.

He gave no serious thought to Florence Pounder as a useful ally – something he later felt ashamed of – until he realized that she was actively and enthusiastically participating in the diversion triggered by the phrase 'Platelayers' Arms'.

As he had his back to most of the action, Rupert was never able to describe the choreography of the diversion with any precision, as the room seemed to explode into chaos, which in fact was the sole purpose of the exercise. He was jerked backwards in his chair by Lugg jerking forwards, and conscious of the crack of splintering wood as Lugg broke partially free of his bonds and began his bull-in-a-China-shop act.

Out of the corner of one startled eye, he saw Miss Pounder drop to her knees, and at first he thought it was because she had been knocked off her feet by Lugg's explosive imitation of a jet fighter ejection seat. Only much later did he realize that she had made a deliberate dive towards the skirting board and the power point into which the Christmas tree lights were plugged. At the time, in that moment of maximum confusion and disorientation, all he could think was that Lugg must have been poked with some form of cattle prod or, bizarrely, a trident.

Lugg was certainly bellowing like an angry animal – perhaps a water buffalo – as he launched himself head-first into the Christmas tree, which toppled just as the lights flashed and fused. Rupert's chair went over and he found himself winded, on his side, and being dragged into the branches of the tree, wincing as pine needles scraped his face and Christmas ornaments cascaded around him. He felt his arm being grabbed as someone – the Reverend Breck? – tried to haul him upright, then a boot flashed in front of his face and connected with what he assumed were Lugg's ribs, which produced a howl of genuine pain from the big man and a string of obscenities from Quinn the kicker.

In a brief hiatus in the chaos, as Lugg attempted to push the tree using his shoulder and head into Quinn's face, and Quinn began to lash out with his pistol, Rupert found himself still chained to his chair, lying on his side amidst a frantic forest of legs and broken branches. Purely by chance he had been manoeuvred into a position which put him in direct eyeline with the doorway where Quinn had been sitting on guard and his father had been casually loitering. Quinn was still in the room, towering above him, fending off a pine tree and several yards of tinsel, propelled by a roaring Lugg, but of his father there was no sign. If the diversion had been intended to cover a disappearing magic trick, it had succeeded, for Mr Campion had indeed disappeared.

To make sure he was not seeing things, Rupert turned his head rapidly but failed to spot his father in the melee, which now seemed to involve everyone apart from the Thursbys, who were sitting on the sofa as if pinned to it, both slack-jawed and stunned by the brawl taking place in front of them.

Quinn was shouting, Lugg was bellowing and Rupert yelped as someone trod on his chest. Hereward Henderson howled in pain as Quinn's swinging pistol caught him on the nose, and there were some very unclerical sentiments expressed by the Reverend Breck as he tried to restore order.

And then Quinn's gun went off, so close to Rupert's ear that his head rang and he could no longer hear anything of the ruckus in the room. He was only aware that something warm and wet and red had splashed over his face.

'You've shot him!' was the first thing Rupert registered when his hearing returned. The phrase was uttered in such a high pitch that he assumed the voice belonged to Florence Pounder, but it had actually been Hereward Henderson, who was clutching his nose and leaning over him. Yet he was not the object of the professor's concern; that was the spreadeagled form of Lugg who, despite the manacles restraining his arms and legs, was thrashing about like a beached whale determined to crush the Christmas tree flat under his weight.

'We have to get those chains off him, unless you want him to die.'

Lying on his back on the floor, his view restricted by a stampede of legs and stockinged feet, Rupert heard the Reverend Breck attempt to bring order to the proceedings.

'Back off, Priest! All of you, back off.' Quinn was in no mood to take suggestions from anyone and waved his pistol even more violently.

'He's bleeding badly,' said Breck defiantly. 'We need to get him off the floor and seen to.'

'Are you a doctor?' sneered the gunman.

'I know some first aid,' volunteered Miss Pounder, 'but we have to get him up and apply a tourniquet. For a start, those manacles need to come off.'

'No, they don't.'

'Oh, don't be ridiculous,' Miss Pounder snapped back. 'You've shot the poor man in the leg; he's not going anywhere.'

'Get him into the saloon and give him a whisky,' offered Lloyd Thursby, clearly having made his own interpretation of the dramatic scene in front of him.

'Shut up, Dad.' Mrs Thursby punched her father-in-law on the arm. 'This isn't one of your cowboy films.'

There was a huge, heaving groan from the body in the wreckage of the Christmas tree.

'Listen to the old boy,' said Lugg, grimacing in pain, 'he might be talking sense.'

Reluctantly, and with considerable bad grace, Quinn waved everyone back, away from the incapacitated Lugg and Rupert, and then casually – to a gasp of horror from De Vries – tossed the wrapped diptych he was still holding on to a chair in order to fish the key to the manacles from his pocket. He went down on one knee in the wreckage of pine tree and broken furniture, keeping his gun pointed at the small crowd of spectators as he worked the locks. Then he took a step back away from the groaning Lugg and pointed the pistol straight down into Rupert's face.

'Any funny business and the kid gets it, right?' His audience nodded in silent agreement. 'Now get him up.'

'Dining room,' said Mrs Thursby suddenly. 'We could put him on the table.'

Her suggestion met with murmurs of approval, almost as if Mrs Thursby was an acknowledged authority on laying out bodies, which as far as most of them knew, she might be.

'Do it,' said Quinn, stepping back to allow Breck and

Henderson to lift Lugg by the arms, leaving a sour-faced De Vries to struggle with his legs. As the stretcher party moved off, they did so to the constant crunch of fallen tree ornaments underfoot and, from his carpet-level-eye view, Rupert was mesmerized by a long length of sparkly silver tinsel which Henderson's left shoe was trailing.

And then Miss Pounder was leaning over him, her face all seriousness and concern, asking if he was all right and reaching her arms out to help him up.

'Leave him,' snapped Quinn, 'he can stay where he is. You see if you can rustle up some bandages or towels.'

Miss Pounder gave Rupert a weak smile and a brief shrug of the shoulders and followed the cortège carrying – or rather staggering – under the weight of the wounded fat man.

They had made it into the hall, chided by constant complaints of 'Take it easy, will you?' from their far-from-cooperative patient, but froze when Quinn let out an angry shout.

'Hold everything! Where the hell is Campion?'

As Florence Pounder made to draw the curtains over the icy dining room windows, she thought she should try and reassure poor Rupert that his father had escaped the house, though she was far from clear on exactly how, and was probably miles away by now, seeking help.

She had no idea that Mr Campion was studying her from out in the snowy orchard, less than twenty yards away.

They've got me on the slab at last, thought Lugg, as far too many inquisitive hands pawed at him and then, to his horror, realized that the lower half of one leg of his trousers was being ripped away. He was pacified when he felt an arm behind his neck raise his head in order to press a tumbler of whisky to his lips, and then immediately dismayed to hear someone say, 'I'm not sure that's a good idea, he could be in shock.' He wanted to make an acid retort about how people – who were probably vicars – should mind their own business, but to have done so would have meant taking his mouth away from the proffered glass.

'It looks like a flesh wound. The bullet went right through without hitting a bone or, thank goodness, an artery.'

Lugg heard the news from a disembodied but distinctly female voice which he found oddly reassuring. It must have come from the spinster postmistress lady, the only one of this bunch of pilgrims who seemed to know what they were doing. He also became aware that the slab they had laid him out on was the Campions' dining room table, which would not go down well with the lady of the house, but then he remembered that Amanda was not in the house and, given the angry howl from Quinn, neither was Mr Campion. Realizing that his distraction had worked he relaxed, despite the hands holding him down and the sudden painful stinging in his thigh as his wound was doused with some sort of antiseptic – hopefully not Mr Campion's best single malt. He realized that – even unwounded – there was little he could do to affect the fates of Amanda and Albert, but he still felt an instinctive responsibility towards young Rupert.

Wincing as a tourniquet or bandage was tightened around his leg, he made out through half-closed and watering eyes the face of Miss Pounder leaning over him.

'How's the lad?' he said in a whisper.

The woman leaned in closer to give Lugg something to concentrate on as her hands worked furiously to tighten his bandages.

'He's scared, like the rest of us, but he's in one piece. The little rumpus you started seems to have worked. Our American friend is tearing round the house trying to find Mr Campion. How did he get out?'

'Upstairs window, same as the coach driver chap did first thing this morning.'

She lowered her voice further when she asked, 'Did the driver get away?'

Lugg closed his eyes slowly and turned his head to one side rather than answer. 'You shouldn't have got involved,' he said quietly. 'It could have been you lying here. Mind you, that was a nice trick with the hairpin and the electrics; where did you learn that one?'

Her eyes widened, as if remembering something she was not ready to admit.

'I was trying to fuse the house lights, not just the twinkly ones on the Christmas tree, which I think is only good for kindling now.'

'Don't you worry about that,' said Lugg, trying to lever his upper body from the horizontal in order to view the damage to his leg. 'You keep yourself safe and stay out of the way when the fun starts.'

Miss Pounder bent over Lugg's giant head to whisper in his ear. 'You're expecting trouble?'

'Where Albert's concerned, expecting the unexpected is usually the best bet. He's what the bookies call a long-shot favourite when it comes to stirring things up. When 'e does, you watch yourself. Keep an eye on young Rupert if you can, 'cos I can't, but above all watch yerself and don't trust this bunch of Herberts as far as you can throw them.'

Miss Pounder tightened the bandage around Lugg's wound and used a damp towel provided by Mrs Thursby to wipe the blood from his naked leg and then mop up the pool which had formed on the shiny tabletop. The basic first-aid kit Mrs Thursby had produced had been designed mainly to combat minor cuts and scaldings in the kitchen, but had come with an unopened roll of bandage of uncertain age which proved invaluable. When Miss Pounder had enquired as to whether there were any pain-killers in the house, Mrs Thursby had said only aspirins as far as she knew. At this point, clearly having read the lips of the two women, Lloyd Thursby produced a bottle of brandy and the decanter of Mr Campion's finest whisky, and offered them as if expecting Paris to make a judgement call. Lloyd winced at the disapproving look he received from Miss Pounder, but grinned with pleasure when Lugg nodded enthusiastically.

There was a general consensus that Lugg should remain where he was, on the dining room table. The Reverend Breck opined that he should not put any weight on his wounded leg; Mrs Thursby, practical as ever, agreed, saying he had bled on the carpets quite enough already, and Hereward Henderson showed a touching compassion by bringing cushions and a blanket for the injured hero.

She had been so involved in treating Lugg that Miss Pounder had almost forgotten Quinn, apart from registering his angry footsteps as he rushed from room to room, upstairs and down, in a frantic search for the missing Mr Campion. That he was jittery – or spooked as the Americans would say – was clear, and it was just possible he might let his guard down. There again, nerves might make him even more trigger happy, but she sensed that this might be a chance for the hostages to escape, though the first problem was: escape to where?

The second challenge was who *could* escape. Lugg was clearly *hors de combat* and far too big and bulky to be carried; Rupert was incapacitated by manacles; the Thursbys, although their local knowledge might be useful, were too old to go on a cross-country run in the dark during a blizzard; Breck, the vicar, looked the sort who could keep his head under fire, something she did not think could be said about the little professor. And then there was the Dutchman. Where was De Vries?

Even as she asked herself the question, she suspected she knew the answer: he would be near his precious diptych – he had hardly taken his eyes off it since Quinn had appropriated it, and there had been genuine horror on his face when Lugg's personal demolition of the Christmas tree had made the gunman casually toss it to one side.

Sure enough, she found De Vries in the lounge, which resembled a bombsite with one casualty, Rupert, chained to an overturned chair. Calmly ignoring the desolation and the plight of Rupert, De Vries sat in an armchair by the fire, holding the wrapped painting in his lap.

'Oh, for goodness' sake,' Miss Pounder admonished him. 'Don't just sit there, help get the poor boy upright.'

Reluctantly, and clutching the package to his chest, De Vries helped Miss Pounder right the chair to which Rupert was attached.

'How's Lugg?' Rupert asked as soon as he was vertical.

'Took a bullet through the leg and lost a fair bit of blood, but he'll live.'

'What was it all in aid of?'

Miss Pounder checked over her shoulder to spot Quinn stalking the hallway, muttering to himself but fortunately out of earshot.

'It was a diversion,' she said quickly, 'so that your father could escape and get help.'

'Did he make it?'

'Well, he got out of the house. That's why our American friend is spitting feathers, making him more dangerous than ever, but by now your father should be miles away from here.'

At that precise moment something exploded above their heads, above the house in fact, followed by a deeper thump which made the windows rattle.

'I think he chose to hang around,' said Rupert.

By opening a chink in the curtains and observing the colourful pyrotechnic stars mingling with falling snowflakes, Miss Pounder was assured that the explosions were not actually artillery rounds targeting the house.

'Fireworks,' she said after the next round of detonations. 'Somebody's shooting off fireworks at us.'

The commotion had brought everyone to the lounge, with the exception of Lloyd Thursby, who had either not heard anything untoward or had decided to keep both Lugg and Mr Campion's whisky company.

'Campion, that son of a bitch . . .' muttered Quinn.

'My goodness!' Hereward Henderson sounded genuinely shocked at the outburst, but also mildly excited. 'Are we under siege?'

The Reverend Breck made no attempt to soften a weary groan of, 'Oh no, not again.'

'In the siege of Ely in 1071, Hereward – Hereward the Wake that is' – he blushed with false modesty before carrying on undaunted – 'used fire as a weapon against the Normans.'

'And how did that turn out for him?' asked Breck.

'In the long run, not well,' admitted Henderson.

'And weren't the Normans the ones outside doing the besieging?' Rupert chimed in, if only to remind them of his presence now he was upright.

'Er . . . yes, so perhaps that wasn't an accurate comparison to our situation.' He flinched and ducked his head as another missile exploded outside, shaking the window glass. 'Still, we must be providing a spectacle for anyone watching.'

'You're damn right,' snarled Quinn, waving his pistol in Henderson's face, which caused the professor to flinch and duck once again. 'Now get down, all of you. On your knees, hands on heads.'

There was no doubting the American's tone, a mixture of violence tinged with fear, and a dangerously rattled man with a loaded gun is best swifty obeyed. The three men and both women sank to their knees and adopted the stance of prisoners of war on a battlefield, leaving Rupert forcibly enthroned on his chair in the position of a king receiving a party of submissive courtiers.

As another rocket exploded outside the house, causing all those inside to wince, Quinn stuffed his pistol into the pocket of his parka and fumbled to unlock the manacles securing Rupert to his throne.

'Get up, kid,' Quinn shouted as the next blast seemed to shake the house. 'You're coming with me. I'm gonna end this.'

He hauled Rupert to his feet which, free of manacles, seemed to have a life of their own and, with his hands still restrained behind his back, did not help his sense of balance. Quinn was able to propel him as if guiding a newborn foal into the hall and towards the front door, holding him with his face pressed into the wall with one hand as he unlocked the door and pulled it open.

Only then did he produce his pistol again, holding it to the back of Rupert's head before pushing his prisoner out into the night.

From the dining room, the kneeling pilgrims felt the icy draught from the open door and heard the whoosh of the fire at their backs. They watched the unfolding scene in horror as Rupert and Quinn were briefly enveloped in a flurry of snowflakes before Rupert suddenly disappeared from their restricted view.

'We should do something,' said Miss Pounder.

'This could be our chance,' said Breck.

When Quinn began shooting, the penitent pilgrims cowered at each report and winced as another rocket bomb exploded, bathing the gunman in a red and orange glow as if he was standing on the rim of an active volcano. He stepped into that glow, out of the house and out of sight, the open door allowing more snow to drift along the hallway, bringing with it, faintly, Quinn's angry shouts.

'Is this where we make a desperate break for freedom?' Henderson said as if reading from a boys' comic.

'Kitchen,' said Breck. 'We go out the back door.'

''S locked,' a frightened Mrs Thursby nodded towards the hall, 'and 'im out there has the key.'

'A window. We can smash a window,' suggested Breck, which

seemed to horrify Mrs Thursby more than the prospect of tackling an armed man.

'Forget it,' said Miss Pounder, 'we're not going anywhere. Listen. There's a vehicle coming.'

'Help has arrived!' Henderson said gleefully.

Miss Pounder had heard the snarl of an engine before the others and recognized it as the returning Alandel Land Rover.

'Don't count on it.'

'Just what the hell has been going on here?'

Despite having been abducted, finding her only son lying unconscious in the snow outside her house, shivering with cold and shedding a layer of snow from her duffel coat, as well as being surrounded by three armed men, Lady Amanda appeared to have lost none of her natural composure. Indeed, it was not so much that she had come in with the blizzard, it was as if she was the storm itself.

As she stepped into the dining room, she took in the scene of prisoners with hands on heads kneeling among the debris of a felled Christmas tree, scattered decorations, broken furniture and a string of coloured lights lying like a dead python.

'He shot Mr Lugg!' squealed Mrs Thursby.

Amanda, showing no fear, turned on Quinn, who was casually inserting a fresh magazine into his automatic.

'You shot an old man who was chained up as your prisoner?'

Quinn met her gaze whilst working the slide of his pistol, making an ominous double click sound.

'Lady, you give us trouble and I'll shoot you.'

It was Kosloffski, as he shook off his snow-covered parka, who defused the situation with a stream of Russian, to which Quinn reacted by straightening to attention.

'He's in the dining room,' said Rupert weakly, still recovering from Quinn's blow and having to be supported by Rivero.

Amanda made to take Rupert's arm, but Kosloffski moved between them.

'You can go. He stays here with the others.'

He then began to rattle off orders in Russian to his compatriots.

She helped Rupert to sit on the lounge sofa, watched silently by the kneeling prisoners, and after making him as comfortable as possible with cushions behind his back, she kissed him on the cheek and whispered in his ear.

'Stay brave, darling; this should be over soon. I must see how Lugg is.'

She hurried to the dining room, pushing through the three airmen as though they were inconsiderate commuters clogging up the Central Line, and gave a sharp intake of breath at the sight of Lugg decorating the tabletop. She just knew that Albert would have made some inane observation about the only things missing from the scene before her being a gigantic silver salver and an apple for his mouth.

It was unnerving to see such a defenceless Lugg. The very definition of the phrase larger than life, this was a pale, helpless, fading Lugg she could not remember ever seeing before. What was worse was that Lloyd Thursby, having pulled up a chair so that he could apply a tumbler of ochre liquid to Lugg's lips, had a beatific and rosy glow to his countenance, which made him look a good ten years younger than his patient.

In a show of false modesty, Lugg attempted to cover his wound with shards of his torn trouser leg, but Amanda's hand reached out and stopped his.

'How did you manage to get yourself shot, you old devil?'

Lugg turned his head so that Lloyd Thursby could not follow what they were saying.

''Elping His Nibs make his escape. Didn't know 'e was planning a firework display.'

'I guessed that was Albert, but I don't think anyone else saw his distress flares. The snow's coming down pretty thick again out there.'

'Maybe he wasn't signalling for help,' Lugg said smugly, though it was a smugness mixed with a twinge of pain. 'Maybe he was trying to get that Yank outside; didn't want to risk starting a gunfight indoors, though that's what happened in the end. Thank Gawd it was me what caught the bullet. Is the lad OK?'

'Rupert's a bit shaky. That thug clouted him, but we arrived in the nick of time to stop anything worse.'

Lugg raised a single plump forefinger in warning and Amanda

sensed a presence behind her. From the doorway, Kosloffski and Quinn were watching them. Amanda ignored them and said loudly, 'Don't worry, old chap, we'll soon have you back on your feet and running around.'

'Will I be able to play like Jimmy Greaves?' said Lugg, with pursed lips and closed eyes.

'Of course you will.' Amanda sighed, knowing what was to follow.

'That'd be flamin' fantastic, considering I couldn't before being shot.'

Amanda smiled and patted the back of the fat man's hand until he said, 'They've gone into the kitchen. What's their plan?'

'I don't know; they've switched to Russian but they seem to be on the move now they've got what they wanted.'

'And what's that?'

'Some photographs we can't really let them get away with.'

The fat man's body shuddered in frustration. 'Not a lot we can do in here.'

Amanda's right hand strayed to the pocket of her duffel coat. 'We might be able to lower the odds.'

'Don't be daft. Albert had the right idea – get them out of the house. If he's still out there, as long as he's not a snowman, he'll think of something as long as he knows you and Rupert are out of the line of fire.'

'We have to get a message to him somehow. You can't go, Rupert can't go and they won't let me out of their sight because I'm afraid I'm part of their plan.'

'Get Florence in here,' said Lugg.

'Who?'

Amanda was not to be denied. She stomped into the kitchen where Kosloffski and Quinn were repacking their equipment into the large canvas bag that had been smuggled in the charabanc.

'Lugg's wound needs its dressing changed; he could bleed out. I need the woman who knows first aid.'

Kosloffski shrugged his shoulders, stepped into the hall and shouted. 'Oscar! Send out the woman – not the housekeeper, the other one.'

Ignoring Amanda, he spoke to Quinn in Russian as he took

three metal cylinders from the bag and laid them on the kitchen table. Each had a spike on the bottom and a ring-pull device, like that on a hand grenade, on the top.

'How's your bodyguard doing?' Kosloffski asked, looming over Amanda.

'He's not . . . Oh, never mind. He's lost a lot of blood but he'll live.'

Sergeant Sometimes met her eyes and said, 'You're welcome,' but Amanda had no idea whether he was apologizing or being sarcastically cruel.

She had no time to dwell on it as Kosloffski turned his back on her and returned to Quinn and the kitchen table just as Florence Pounder appeared from the lounge looking excited, her cheeks flushed and her grey eyes wide.

'Do you need me, Lady Amanda?'

'Lugg's bandages need attention. I think he needs a tighter tourniquet.' Amanda spoke loudly so that Kosloffski and Quinn could hear her as she took Miss Pounder by the elbow and guided her into the dining room, where Lugg greeted her with a sickly grin and a raised thumb from the hand resting on his mountainous stomach.

Amanda dropped her voice and leaned in so close to the head of the other woman that she could detect the scent of Devon Violets perfume behind her ear.

'I do need you, Miss Pounder. It's Florence, isn't it?'

The woman nodded.

'Good, I'm Amanda, and I understand that my scatterbrained husband is outside laying siege to the house. I need to get a message to him before he does something really stupid and gets himself hurt or freezes to death.'

'But they're pulling out,' whispered Miss Pounder. 'The Americans. They're packing up ready to leave. It won't be long before they're gone. I heard them planning it, just after they brought you back.'

'They were speaking Russian.' Amanda almost bit her bottom lip for stating the obvious.

'I know. I presume they are Russian spies.'

Amanda concealed her surprise at Miss Pounder's extremely calm assessment of the situation.

'Did you understand what they were saying?'

'As far as I could tell they had got what they came for and were getting ready to leave. They used the expression "going home" several times and the one who shot Mr Lugg was told to make the arrangements.'

'Arrangements?'

'They have a radio out in your barn. Quinn has to radio for their transport to come and get them. I got the impression it would not be long before something arrived, though I don't know how they expect to make a quick getaway with the roads snowed up.'

'They're not going by road,' Amanda said urgently. 'They've got a helicopter coming for them, flying off a Russian trawler out in the Wash.'

'In this weather?'

'They're playing for high stakes, so it's worth the risk. They'll use their radio to guide in the chopper and they've got flares to mark a landing site. I've just seen them in the kitchen. We have to warn my husband, but they are unlikely to let me out of their sight, I'm afraid.'

'So you want me to go out there?'

'Is it too much to ask?'

Of course it was. Amanda was asking an older woman and complete stranger to put herself in danger without knowing – for Amanda could not tell her – what exactly was at stake. Miss Pounder did not blink.

'Not at all,' she said coolly. 'When Quinn goes out to the radio, I could slip out of the back door if you can keep the sergeant occupied with some sort of diversion. They won't notice I'm gone. I'm used to going unnoticed.'

'As soon as Quinn goes out to the barn, I'll get Kosloffski in here. The rest is up to you.'

'Don't worry, I'll find Mr Campion. I have a feeling he's not too far away.'

'Tell him we can't let them leave; you understand? They have photographs which could do this country great damage and they must not be allowed to leave with them.'

'How is he supposed to stop them?' asked those cold grey eyes.

'I don't know, but he'll think of something,' said Amanda, a tremor in her voice. 'He must. You'll need something for your feet.'

'Slippers,' croaked Lugg.

'Better than nothing,' said Amanda, brightening. 'Lugg keeps his slippers in the warming drawer of the Aga. And you'll need a coat, so take mine. If anyone asks, say you're drying it in front of the Aga.'

Amanda handed over her gloves and began to unbutton her duffel coat, then reached into the pocket and produced the Beretta she had been hoarding.

'Do you know how to use one of these?'

'Probably better than you do,' said Miss Pounder without a flicker of emotion.

EIGHTEEN
Hoplite

Mr Campion was cold. He could never remember being so cold, or so appreciative of the phrase chilled to the bone – so chilled his fingers felt like icicles and his feet were frozen blocks which had no feeling at all. Only once before had he come close to such a deathly elemental chill and that, ironically given his current circumstances, had been in Russia, although many years ago when he was younger, much younger; not much more than a boy in a uniform, a nice, warm uniform. Back then he had the energy of youth, the energy to keep warm by doing jumping jacks or running on the spot, and the intelligence to know that to curl up and fall asleep in the snow was the most dangerous thing he could do. Although the cold had permeated his very being and he was exhausted, the thought of digging a foxhole in the snow and giving up never occurred to him as an option. Amanda and Rupert had been swallowed back into the house that was now their prison, and Campion had been able to do nothing to prevent that. With no outside help coming to their aid that he was aware of, and doubtful that his firework display had been seen much further afield, it was up to him to rescue them – and Lugg – before it was too late. He had no weapon other than a garden spade and no plan of any sort.

The one thing which made him crawl from under the curved bridge and stand up straight, amidst a gentle tinkling sound as the thin skim of ice which had formed on his dress shirt crackled and cracked, was the thought that whatever had happened at Marham, Amanda was in one piece and, with Rupert in the house, would fight like a lioness to protect her cub.

By now she would have realized that he was outside, an ally in waiting, albeit out of touch, unarmed and freezing to death. All logic would describe him as a pretty useless ally.

But Amanda would think of something.

* * *

'You don't take your eyes off her and you don't damage her. Got it?' Kosloffski was pointing at Amanda and talking to Quinn. 'She's valuable as long as she's in one piece.'

'I assure you I am not prepared to be a silent witness to your little scheme.' Amanda was defiant.

'Excellent!' Kosloffski flashed a white-toothed grin. 'We don't want you to be silent – we want as much publicity, as much uproar, as possible.'

'As much embarrassment as possible.'

'You English would think it that way, but, yeah, that would do very nicely.'

Miss Pounder held up a bloodstained tea towel as if it was a ritual offering. 'I could do with some hot water and clean cloths.'

Kosloffski, barely registering her presence, looked beyond the fuming Amanda at Miss Pounder's patient, who was squirming convincingly.

'Sure, help yourself,' he said casually, then turned to Quinn and they spoke in Russian as they headed back into the kitchen.

'He's going to move the Land Rover to the garage,' Miss Pounder whispered to Amanda, 'then the other one has to go and work the radio.'

'Then we haven't much time.'

'I'll try and get near the back door. This might be our chance if you can distract them.'

'I'll think of something.'

They heard Kosloffski remind Quinn to keep an eye on Amanda and then, as he strode down the hall towards the front door, he told Rivero to stay on guard in the lounge but to stand by, ready to pull out.

Amanda and Miss Pounder held their breath as they heard him unlock the front door, as though the click of the tumblers in the lock would somehow release them as well the door, and they felt the invading gust of icy air. Only when the door slammed shut did they exhale.

'Wait until he returns,' murmured Amanda. 'You don't want to get out only to run smack into him.'

Miss Pounder nodded and slipped into the kitchen. When

Quinn saw it was her and not Lady Amanda, he ignored her and resumed sorting his equipment.

Mr Campion was stamping his feet, trying to restore some feeling in them, when he saw the front door open. Automatically he went into a crouch but was confident that the curved bridge and the falling snow were concealment enough. Standing tall he could well be mistaken for one of the frosted trees in the orchard behind him.

He watched as Kosloffski marched to the Alandel Land Rover without a glance in his direction, climbed in the driver's side and started the engine. With a grating of gears the Land Rover performed a U-turn, spraying snow from all four wheels, and Campion ducked as the headlight beams swept over him but then was gone down the west side – the 'blind' side – of the house towards the barn which was used as a garage.

Campion waited until he was sure the engine had died before stepping carefully on to the bridge, using the spade as a staff or walking stick to keep himself upright as his feet seemed determined to slide away from him. He could not work out whether it was due to the planks of the bridge, which were covered in ice, or because his stockinged feet had turned into small, personal ice rinks. Either way, his slippery progress up and over the bridge felt as if he was traversing an Alpine glacier. Coming down the slope of the bridge with ungainly speed, he hobbled across the frontage of Carterers, thinking that he would not look out of place in one of those giant nineteenth-century oil paintings of Napoleon's retreat from Moscow in 1812, along with the frozen remains of his Grande Armée. The irony was not lost on him that here he was, freezing and badly shod a hundred and fifty years later, trying to prevent someone *getting* to Moscow.

He edged up to the window of the lounge, distracted by the scent of wood smoke from the chimney driven downwards by the falling snow, which brought to mind thoughts of being snug, relaxed and above all, warm. Consequently, he was unable to resist pressing his nose to the glass where the curtain had not been closed properly after gently rubbing a spy-hole in the film of snow and ice.

He was still rational enough not to expect to find himself a spectator (courtesy of the Ghost of Christmas Past) at Mr Fezziwig's office party, but he was not prepared for the scene of war-torn desolation which greeted him. From his restricted view, only possible because there was no Christmas tree blocking it as there should have been, he could make out three of the pilgrims, plus Mrs Thursby, kneeling with their hands on their heads amidst a carpet of debris. Clearly they were prisoners and therefore there must be a guard somewhere out of his line of sight. On the edge of the view his peephole allowed, he could make out the back of the chair to which Rupert was secured, and the fact that his head was moving suggested he was conversing with his fellow prisoners and was, therefore, alive and well, if not comfortable. At least he looked *warm* in there – they all did – and Mr Campion felt guilty for envying them.

Turning the corner, his spade clutched in both hands in what he thought Hereward Henderson might recognize approvingly as 'the battle-axe' position, he edged down the western side of the house, walking in the tyre tracks left by the Land Rover. He strained his ears to catch any sound not muffled by the snow, and when he heard the rattle of what he recognized as the kitchen door opening then closing, he stopped dead and glanced around frantically, looking for a hiding place in either Amanda's cherished rose garden or her equally prized kitchen garden. In their present state of hibernation, neither would offer decent opportunities for concealment other than if he threw himself face-down and pretended to be part of a snow-covered compost heap.

When he heard nothing but silence, he wiped snowflakes from his spectacles, judged that they were not coming down quite so thick and fast, and pressed on, ready to meet whoever had left the house head-on if need be, keeping low to slink by the kitchen window and peering cautiously around the corner.

He could make out footprints leading to and from the tack room and the barn beyond, and the border of light around the door indicated that someone was in there with the vehicles.

Tightening his jaw to stop his teeth chattering, he reasoned that with the element of surprise he might be able to reduce the odds against him from three to two, and there was the possibility that he might get access to a vehicle, ideally one with a powerful heater.

His dulled thought processes made no further progress as he

became aware that within a few feet of him the kitchen door was opening again, this time very quietly.

'We're going to need all your am-dram skills in a minute.'

'Me what?'

'She means amateur dramatics, don't she.'

Both Amanda and Lugg looked at Lloyd Thursby in astonishment, as if they had only just noticed his presence in the room and had been unaware that he had pulled his chair closer to the table on which Lugg was displayed, so close that if he dropped his head it would be hidden behind the hillock that was Lugg's stomach.

If the old boy was determined to lip-read his way into the conversion, Amanda reasoned, he might as well be included, and so looked directly at him as she spoke clearly but quietly.

'When the sergeant comes in, we have to keep him here for a few minutes, so I need you two boys to cause a diversion, keep him interested. Could you start a violent argument perhaps?' She glanced down at Lugg. 'Why am I asking *you* that?'

'You want us to have a fight?' Lloyd Thursby asked enthusiastically.

'That would do nicely.'

'Hang on a minute,' hissed Lugg, his eyes rolling. 'I'm severely incapacitated, if you hadn't failed to notice.'

Amanda poked his shoulder with a stiff finger. 'You could start a fight at your own funeral – and you probably will.'

'A saloon bar brawl,' said Lloyd, his eyes shining, focused on an imaginary television screen showing one of his favourite cowboy films.

'Not quite so violent, but noisy, and you can use some of those Norfolk cuss words Persephone says you're so fond of. And you' – her finger jabbed at Lugg again – 'just be yourself.'

Amanda fussed around Lugg's makeshift hospital bed, listening carefully for the sound of the kitchen door opening and closing. She heard Kosloffski return and give an order in Russian, which Quinn acknowledged, and then felt the cold draught of the back door opening again. She counted silently up to ten before nodding to both men.

'OK, boys, nice and loud. Do your worst.'

* * *

'Give it here, you old scrounger!'

'Now hold you hard.'

'That's the guv'nor's good stuff, only to be dispensed to the lower orders in cases of medical emergency – like now.'

'Stop crocking – you ain't hurt bad.'

As amateur dramatic productions went, it was hardly inspiring, but it was loud, both performers giving their all, even if the action required little in the way of stage direction as it was limited to one elderly fat man flat on his back, struggling with the even older, very deaf gentleman leaning over him. The object of their dispute was the cut-glass decanter of amber liquid which Lloyd Thursby was reluctant to release unless prised from his cold dead hand, and perhaps not even then.

'Behave, you two!' Amanda put an extra shrill into her voice.

'He's guzzling the lot!'

'Stop talking squit, you fat bugger!'

And then the inevitable happened and the decanter, whether pulled or pushed, flew out of Lloyd's hands, over Lugg's stomach and smashed against the wall with a loud crash. Without their prize, the two combatants continued to flap their hands at each other like demented toddlers.

The little drama enacted before her would, under other circumstances, have induced a fit of giggles in Amanda, but she limited herself to a glow of satisfaction knowing that their little distraction had worked, for Kosloffski came storming into the dining room, taking in the debris of the broken decanter on the carpet and the alcoholic fumes rising from them.

'What the hell is going on in here?'

'A minor dispute over the quality of the house whisky and two old men behaving very badly.'

'There you go.' The American grinned. 'The classic British need to say sorry for bad manners.'

'I was not apologizing,' Amanda rebuked him, her face grim but her attention really focused beyond him into the kitchen from which Miss Pounder had suddenly disappeared.

Mr Campion's first thought, which cheered him immensely, to the extent that he was sure he felt a semblance of warmth kindling in his chest, was that the woman sneaking, definitely sneaking, from the house was Amanda. It was Amanda's navy duffel coat with the hood up, but it was not Amanda wearing it, though it was clearly a small, female shape.

Even though his brain felt as if it was locked in the cold room of a butcher's shop in another county, the cogs turned just enough for him to work out, given that there were only two other females in the house, he had a good chance of identifying the escapee.

'Missss P-p-p-ounder?' he said through chattering teeth.

The figure stopped in its tracks – tracks being made by large, plaid woollen footwear.

'Are those Lugg's slip-p-p-ers?'

Miss Pounder shook her head as if to clear it of such nonsense. 'No time to waste, Mr Campion.' She was suddenly close up against him, pressing a gloved finger – Amanda's gloves, he noted – against his lips. 'We must move away.'

'How did you know I was here?' Campion asked her as he indicated she should follow him around the side of the house.

'I didn't, but I could have heard you shivering a mile off. Lady Amanda thought you'd be near. Now listen—'

'Is she safe?'

'For the moment. They seem quite keen to see she doesn't come to any harm.'

'Did they get what they wanted at Marham?'

'I think so.' Miss Pounder was now pushing Campion in the small of his back to hurry him along. 'But you have to listen—'

'And how's Lugg? I heard a shot . . . earlier.'

Miss Pounder already held the suspicion that Mr Campion was prone to vagueness, or at least the appearance of vacuity when it suited him, but now she felt he was close to losing his mind and she needed him to concentrate. She pulled him into the side of the house, against a portion of the wall where the fire in the lounge had warmed enough to leave it clear of snow, and held him there with one hand on his chest.

'Mr Lugg is fine. He's been shot in the leg and lost blood, but he's alive.'

'Mag-ers-font-ein,' said Mr Campion feebly.

'*What?*' The hand on his chest increased its pressure.

'Lugg's name is Magersfontein. Ridiculous, I know, but there it is.'

'*Listen!* Lugg's alive, and your wife and son are safe for the moment. The Russians are getting ready to leave by helicopter. Amanda said to tell you they had a Hoplite. Do you know what that means?'

'A hoplite was a citizen-soldier of Ancient Greece who fought with a big shield and a long spear, about twice the size of this,' he held up the garden spade and grinned foolishly, 'and with a pointy end of course.'

Miss Pounder thought about slapping his silly face, but realized that it was so cold he would not feel anything.

'Helicopter. Lady Amanda said it was a type of helicopter coming from a Russian trawler out at sea somewhere. She said you'd think of a way to stop it leaving.'

'Hoplite . . . helicopter.' Campion spoke his slow thoughts aloud. 'Amanda would not have confused them. It is her area of expertise.'

The eyes behind the frosted spectacles sparked as if suddenly connected to the mains, and he grabbed Miss Pounder's wrist with his free hand, as if to pass the electricity through to her.

'It's not a type of helicopter. Hoplite is NATO code for a new Russian helicopter. From a trawler, she said? I've never heard of that before, but some of their trawlers, which are spy ships really, are pretty big and could launch one if it came close to the coast.' He looked up, noticing that the snowfall seemed to be thinning out. 'But surely not in this weather.'

'Quinn is in your garage on the radio to them right now and they'll home in on his signal. Then he's got flares to put out to mark a landing site, somewhere out in front of the house, I guess.'

'That would be mine too. They'd have to avoid the orchard and they could use my megalithic gateposts and the charabanc as a landmark if they can see them. They don't intend to take Amanda with them, do they?'

'I don't think so. Kosloffski seemed to relish the idea that she would be put in a difficult position here at home after they got their booty back to Moscow.'

'Any idea what booty they got at Marham?'

'Not really, but they had camera equipment with them. Whatever it is, Lady Amanda stressed that they must not get away with it. She said you must prevent them and you'd think of something.'

Campion had released his grip on Miss Pounder's wrist and was silently pressing his shoulders back into the wall in an attempt to control his shivering. The woman thought for a moment that he was slipping away again and needed another shock to his system. She grabbed at the white dress shirt which clung, sodden and frozen to his thin frame, but failed to get a firm hold.

Her action, clearly showing her frustration, was reinforced by an angry outburst. 'For God's sake, man, there isn't time to feel sorry for yourself. Now think! How do we stop this helicopter from landing?'

Mr Campion breathed out slowly, his breath a frosty cloud between them. 'Oh, I don't think we can,' he said calmly, 'but we might be able to stop them taking off again. Can you run in those slippers?'

'In this?' she waved a hand, indicating the snow as if Campion had not noticed it. 'Not very fast, I would think.'

'Oh, you really must try and be very quick,' said Mr Campion severely. 'You might be running for your life.'

'Contact made. It's on its way; twelve, fifteen minutes.' Quinn had returned from the garage and, to Amanda's disdain, was stamping snow from his boots on the dining room floor until he noticed he was also crushing broken glass, and then the aroma of spilt whisky reached him. 'What happened here?'

'The proletariat fighting over the property of their masters,' said Kosloffski. 'Nothing to worry about. You'd better get back outside and set the landing flares.'

Quinn turned, but towards the lounge rather than the kitchen.

'Where you going?'

'If we're out of here, I need to get something.'

'The Dutchman's painting,' croaked Lugg, whose attempts to give the sergeant the evil eye had finally paid off, ''e fancies it as his nest-egg, I reckon. Pensions not up to much in Russia?'

'Leave it,' said Kosloffski without looking at Quinn. 'We are not thieves. Go out the back and do your job.'

'Hah!' Amanda's voice overflowed with scorn. 'The honest

spy? You're not fooling anyone. What would one more crime be to you?'

The sergeant glared at her. 'You – and your class – can't be expected to understand. We are soldiers.'

'Who have murdered, kidnapped, taken hostages and blatantly committed espionage. Are we to believe you are going to leave us alive when you go?'

'Why not? You yourself are much more use to our cause alive, squirming in the glare of publicity and the others, the civilians—'

'The innocent bystanders.'

'—if you say so. They will talk about what happened here and your security service will be kept busy trying to keep them quiet. We will count that as a bonus.'

'So you'll just fly away and leave us here?'

'Where are you going to go? We have disabled all the vehicles and you have no telephone. My advice is that you stay put and keep warm until help – and the wonderful British press – arrives.'

Mr Campion and Miss Pounder huddled together at the corner of the house, only a few feet away from the lounge's bay window. If anyone had pulled the curtains aside, they would have thought a pair of guilty lovers were lurking in the shadows.

Campion had politely refused Miss Pounder's offer of Amanda's duffel coat and she had ridiculed his gentlemanly principles and insisted on pressing herself, keeping within the bounds of decency, against him to share her warmth.

It had almost stopped snowing, as if the wintry blizzard had lost heart. An eerie silence had fallen and for the first time Campion could make out the dark shapes of the gateposts down the drive. Neither fact seemed to energize him. Indeed, he appeared more and more lethargic, which Miss Pounder took as a warning sign that he was finally succumbing to the cold. When she heard the back door open and close, she reached up and pinched both his cheeks with gloved fingers.

'That'll be him coming now. Ready?'

Mr Campion shook his head to clear it and flapped his elbows like a penguin's wings to get his circulation going. 'Are you?'

Miss Pounder nodded.

'Don't forget to duck,' said Mr Campion.

She hurried along the side of the house, retracing the steps of her escape, but was not halfway along when a figure turned the far corner, saw her and stopped dead with an oath. 'Jesus!'

Miss Pounder realized that Quinn had automatically thought she was Amanda because of the duffel coat; an Amanda he must have seen inside the house only moments before. Grateful that Quinn had his hands full, clutching something close to his chest rather than brandishing his pistol, she said, '*Dobry vecher, tovarich*,' then turned and ran back the way she had come, as quickly as she could through the snow, with every step feeling as if she was wading through a sea of mud and Quinn fast behind her.

As she approached the corner of the house, she remembered Mr Campion's instruction and ducked into a low, crouching run, convinced that Quinn would tackle her at any moment. In the farcical stance of someone doing a bad impression of Groucho Marx's 'duck walk', the figure of Mr Campion was nothing more than a shadowy blur to her as she stumbled by him. Later, she had to admit that she was glad her view had been restricted.

Mr Campion swung the garden spade at what he guessed was head-height. It was a swing which any half-decent cricketer would have been ashamed of, but a baseball player might have got away with. More by luck than fine judgement, the flat back of the spade's blade connected fully with Quinn's face, or Quinn's momentum took him face-first into the spade. Either way, both the sickening sound and the end result were satisfying for Campion and devastating for the American. He collapsed in a spray of blood, which formed a dark stain on the snow around him, spilling the three metal tubes he had been carrying.

'The flares,' said Campion, shaking violently with both shock and cold. 'Could you pick them up for me, please?'

Miss Pounder scuttled to Quinn's inert body and collected the tubes, handing them to Campion, who had thrown the spade away in disgust.

'Is he dead?' Campion asked weakly.

'No, just damaged. Damaged a lot actually,' the woman answered whilst rolling Quinn over as she removed his parka. 'You need his coat.'

'I'm beyond that,' said Campion stubbornly, 'and he might freeze to death.'

'You're the icicle here, now take it and put it on. If the others see you, they'll think it's him putting out the flares.'

'Flares?'

'For the helicopter. That was the plan, wasn't it?'

'Yes, the plan.' Campion was drifting into vagueness again. 'You'd better hide. Under the Monet bridge is a good place. I made it my troll cave.'

'I can take care of myself.'

'I am discovering that. Still, take care. We don't have much time.'

Miss Pounder helped Campion into Quinn's parka and zipped it to the chin, then paused and pulled back the hood of her duffel coat, her head on one side, eyes alert, ears pricked.

'Listen!' Before Campion's dulled brain registered them, Miss Pounder had detected the whirring, slow *thump-chug-thump* of an approaching helicopter. 'We don't have any time at all,' she said.

NINETEEN
Thin Ice

The Hoplite, technically a twin-engine Mil Mi-2 three rotor-blade helicopter and the latest product of Mikhail Mil's Helicopter Plant in Moscow (much admired professionally by Lady Amanda), approached Carterers from the north-west and it was Amanda who heard it first.

'The pilot will come in over the garage,' she told Lugg, 'and circle the house, then land on the driveway. If he makes it in these conditions in one piece, he deserves a medal.'

'Nivver mind a medal,' growled Lugg, attempting to sit up. 'I 'ope 'e breaks 'is bleedin' neck.'

'Lie back and try not to move,' she said, pushing down on the fat man's shoulders. 'There's nothing you can do about it.'

As she leaned over him, Lugg lowered his voice. 'Do you think the lass has found His Nibs?'

Amanda could not help but smile. 'Lass? Miss Pounder? She's older than me. Does old Magers have a bit of a crush on her?'

Lugg's reply may have been read by Lloyd Thursby, who was observing the exchange closely, but Amanda's delicate ears were spared by the increasingly loud throb of the approaching helicopter. As it flew low over the house, the windowpanes rattled loudly, almost as if an assistant stage manager in the wings was shaking a thin metal sheet to simulate a thunderstorm.

'Our ride's here!' Kosloffski announced over the noise. 'Oscar, get your gear together.'

He was zipping up his parka and holding the canvas bag of equipment, his gun out of sight, confident that it would not be needed any more.

'Wait!' Amanda followed him into the hall, relieved that Miss Pounder's absence had gone unnoticed. 'What about my son?'

'He's fine, isn't he?'

'He's still chained up,' Amanda said in the voice of a reproving schoolmistress.

Kosloffski shrugged away responsibility. 'Quinn's got the key; he's out front.' His eyes narrowed as he remembered something. 'Your husband's outside somewhere as well. You wouldn't have any idea where, would you?'

Amanda set her jaw full square. 'Sitting in front of a roaring fire drinking our neighbour's best brandy as he telephones every policeman in the county.'

'Don't try and kid a kidder, as they say in America.' He gave her a sly smile. 'We know you haven't got any neighbours – that's why you made such a good target.' To add disdain to indignity, he stood to attention and executed a perfect salute. '*Dos vidanyia*, Lady Amanda.'

Amanda clenched her teeth, partly in frustration and partly against the blast of cold air swirling down the hall from the front door which Rivero was holding open. The noise of the approaching helicopter's engines was now growing very loud.

From her position, crouched down by the orchard end of the curved bridge, Miss Pounder watched Campion weaving and stumbling through the snow as he attempted to set the landing flares. As she had never seen the front grounds of Carterers in daylight and without the camouflage of snow, she had no idea how Campion planned to position them, but he seemed to know what he was doing, clearly pacing out as best he could the distance between them.

He had placed the first directly in line with the window of his study at, presumably, a safe distance from the house. The second, which slightly worried Miss Pounder, he placed no more than thirty feet from the middle of the bridge and then he set off, treading carefully, in a diagonal line towards the entrance to the driveway, those monumental gateposts and the wreck of the charabanc, which was now visible in outline as the snow had finally decided to stop falling.

Campion was now taking longer, more deliberate strides, as if pacing out a specific distance, and when roughly equidistant from the bridge and the gateposts he placed the third flare, making it the apex of a triangle, or perhaps that first flare was the apex.

Miss Pounder could not tell. What she could tell, even though he was now a hundred yards away from her vantage point, was that Campion was at the end of his tether and close to collapse.

At least the flares were easy to operate once planted firmly in the ground, or in this case snow, and ignited by removing a ring-pull pin, a mechanism similar to that found on a British hand grenade. Campion's frozen fingers had pulled the pins as he positioned them, and he exhaled a frosty sigh of relief as each one ignited.

The first two, forming a baseline parallel to the front of the house, quickly glowed red like a firework and then began to emit bright red smoke, clearly visible from the air against the white landscape of the triangle he was creating. By the time he pulled the pin on the third at the apex of his triangular signal, the frontage of Carterers was silhouetted through a spreading red mist. It was almost a painting of hell, but thankfully not yet at the stage Bosch would have imagined it.

As his third flare fizzed into bright swirling life, Campion felt his legs give way under him. At least he assumed those were still his legs and not frozen appendages operated by a third party with a remote control. He felt very, very tired, and the distance back to the bridge, which he was sure he remembered telling someone was a safe place to hide, seemed much too far on frozen legs which he was sure did not belong to him.

He knew there was a good reason why he needed to get somewhere safe, but it was difficult to think straight with the thundering noise of engines above him and that powerful downdraught of air that was whipping up the most recent snow into minor tornadoes, which danced in and out of the red flare smoke.

Ah yes, there was something he had to remember, and it involved a helicopter.

'What the hell is Pete doing?'

Kosloffski was standing at the front door, looking down the driveway to the gateposts, where a hunched figure was staggering as if drunk through the pink mist from the flares. Beyond and above the figure loomed the face of a giant metal insect, its wings rotating with a loud percussive rhythm.

'That's not Pete!' Rivero, standing next to him, had to shout above the *whoop-whoop* thump of the helicopter. He was pointing frantically to his right where something – someone – was crawling on elbows and stomach through the snow under the bay window of the lounge. Where there should have been a white face there was only a mask of blood, and no discernible sound was coming from where the mouth was opening and closing in vain.

Amanda had made her way down the hall, finding herself drawn to the sound of the approaching helicopter and unnoticed by Kosloffski and Rivero in the open doorway. She was startled to see them gesticulating, clearly in a panic over something. And then both of them disappeared from her view.

Framed by the open door, Amanda could see the dark shape of the helicopter descending slowly over the stone gateposts and drifting towards the house, aiming for the triangle of flares on the driveway. It was perhaps fifty feet from the ground when the pilot switched on a landing spotlight situated in the belly of the machine and Amanda gasped in horror.

Illuminated by the helicopter light, she could see a bedraggled human figure up against the left-hand gatepost, flattened, seemingly pinned, against the giant stone, unwilling or unable to move. Although the figure was small and her sight line distorted by the red flares, the smoke, the snow and the fearsome flying machine heading directly towards her, she was absolutely sure she knew who it was.

Who else but Albert Campion would attempt to tackle an enemy helicopter and three armed men – four if one counted the pilot – single-handed?

'Mom! What's happening?'

Rupert's anguished cry distracted her from the surreal scene outside and she plunged into the lounge where another astonishing prospect greeted her.

Her son was still chained to his chair, but both the chair and Rupert lay on their sides. The Reverend Breck and Hereward Henderson stood over him offering concerned looks, while the Dutchman De Vries was on his knees fumbling suspiciously at Rupert's ankles.

Before she could formulate an enquiry of suitable motherly concern, there was a loud *click* and De Vries looked up triumphantly. He was holding the short length of twisted wire with which he had just picked the lock of the manacles holding Rupert's legs. Breck and Henderson helped Rupert to his feet and he smiled at his mother as De Vries set to work on the handcuffs holding his hands behind his back.

'I was coming to rescue you, but it appears I am surplus to requirements. It seems, Mr De Vries, that special skills are required in the art world,' she said with obvious relief. 'Do you always travel with a set of lockpicks?'

As his efforts produced a second, satisfying click, De Vries gave her a polite nod then held up the bent wire. 'It's from one of your Christmas tree decorations, Lady Amanda, and I apologize if it was a favourite or a valuable one.'

'He just crushed it! Crushed it underfoot! One of your favourite silver baubles.' Mrs Thursby seemed oblivious to the general wreckage of the Christmas tree and its trimmings, and clearly needed something to do, Amanda thought, otherwise she would be itching to get the Hoover out and start tidying.

'I wouldn't worry about that, Mrs T.' Amanda raised her voice to be heard over the pounding of the helicopter engines. 'Would you go and see to Lugg, please? I left Lloyd in charge of him.'

That was all the incentive she needed and, wiping her hands on her apron, she bustled off, anxious to administer to one elderly gentleman and no doubt rebuke the other.

Rupert wrapped his now-free arms around his mother, and when his mouth was buried in her hair asked, 'Where's Pop? What's going on?'

Even though she could feel Rupert's breath on her ear, Amanda could only just catch his words over the pounding of the helicopter's engines, and as Breck was pulling back the curtains, the sound intensified.

'He's outside somewhere.' She raised her voice so she could be heard. 'Gentlemen! You will have noticed there is a helicopter landing outside to collect our unwelcome guests, though it would be better if they did not leave.'

'Too late to worry about that,' shouted Breck, his hands pressed against the juddering window glass. 'They're making a run for it, or at least two of them are. One's in no fit state.'

Amanda and Rupert joined him at the bay window. The helicopter was now only a few feet from the ground. Kosloffski and

Rivero were floundering through the snow which lay over the driveway towards it, handicapped by having to carry between them their canvas bag of equipment and the inert body of Quinn, as well as crouching to avoid the sweep of the helicopter's rotor blades.

They were struggling through the spray of snow whipped up by the downdraught and being frantically encouraged by hand signals from the pilot, who had turned on an interior light and could now be seen behind the split Perspex windscreens above the machine's bulbous nose.

It was a matter of seconds before the helicopter touched down and Kosloffski reached the side door.

'Why is he landing on the third pond?' shouted Rupert into his mother's face.

'Because he can't see it's a pond, he's just landing where the flares tell him it's safe,' Amanda roared back.

'Is it safe?'

'I hope not.'

From the small cloakroom in the hall, Amanda grabbed a blue peacoat from a hook and pulled it on as she walked to the doorway. It was an ancient garment which Mr Campion only wore to demonstrate that it still fitted perfectly, thirty-five years after he had purchased it; a family parlour trick which would have greatly irritated a less phlegmatic wife.

Clutching the collars of the coat to her throat, she stepped outside and set her face against the blast of sound and cold air generated by the helicopter which was coming in to land. Amanda knew that the pilot would opt for a no-hover landing, as to hover would merely stir up a snowstorm, blinding him and the passengers he was picking up. It was the same principle as if landing in a desert. To avoid creating a minor sandstorm, the pilot would bring the helicopter straight down, having observed the pilot's mantra of the two 'w's' – see your way in and check you have a way out.

The helicopter touched down, the engines were throttled back and the rotors slowed, spinning lazily though still quite deadly to anyone approaching who forgot to duck. Kosloffski and Rivero were well aware of those three slowly twirling blades and were virtually on their knees, struggling through the snow as they half-carried, half-dragged the inert Quinn, hindered by the canvas bag, which contained the equipment and spoils of their mission. The pilot saw their plight and was out of his seat and sliding open the side door to offer a helping hand to his passengers.

He would know, Amanda reasoned, that he had landed illegally in enemy territory and would want to spend as little time on the ground as possible. Except he wasn't on the ground, certainly not solid ground, and did not seem aware that the helicopter's fixed triangular landing gear was resting on the ice covering the surface of Mr Campion's pride and joy.

Amanda felt a surge of pride at the thought that her husband's plan to lure the helicopter there had worked, tinged with no little satisfaction that some harm had come to Quinn along the way. But although the helicopter had landed, the ice had not broken beneath its weight.

As the passengers scrambled or were pulled on board, it did; or so Amanda thought, but the large *crack* she heard had come from her left.

Miss Pounder, wearing Amanda's duffel coat with the hood up, giving her the outline of a medieval monk, was standing in the middle of the curved bridge, holding a very large pistol in two hands and calmly, and accurately, shooting at the helicopter.

Mr Campion, his shoulders pressed into the stone gatepost, watched from the bottom of the driveway with the depressing certainty that he was incapable of influencing events any further. He had done his best, hadn't he? The helicopter pilot had taken the bait he had laid, but the trap had not sprung shut. The only glimmer of optimism was that through his snow-spattered spectacles he could see that Amanda was not among the passengers piling on board.

Which was a great relief, as at that point the right wheel of the undercarriage sank through the ice and the entire helicopter lurched over and began to sink.

He was sure he heard the sound of repeated snaps as the ice gave way and he saw the tail rotor rise up as the cockpit sank, giving the impression of a scorpion's tail stinging its own body.

He knew he ought to move – go and offer whatever pathetic amount of help he could – but his legs would not obey him. Slowly he sank down until he was sitting at the base of the gatepost, pulled his knees to his chest and passed out.

It was not clear, and never would be, whether it was the extra weight of three passengers, the moving around of the pilot, or the effect of Miss Pounder's bullets which finally sent the helicopter through the ice. As it rolled over on to its right side, the edge of one of the rotor blades hit solid ground at the edge of the pond, the impact sending a juddering shock wave through the entire fuselage as more ice broke around it, swallowing the front landing wheel.

Thanks to the interior light, it was possible to see the frantic efforts of those inside as they were thrown across the cabin by the lurching of the machine whilst trying to avoid the bullets Miss Pounder was sending through the windscreen.

And then, with frightening speed, the front end of the helicopter sank, the tail rotor came up and water swirled in through the still-open side door.

'Bloody hell!' said Rupert, appearing at his mother's side, immediately transfixed by the sight of a disappearing helicopter and the prospect of a quadruple drowning. 'Are we going to help them get out?'

'I'm thinking about it,' said Amanda severely before relenting. 'Get coats and boots for the men and tell old Lloyd to bring the wooden ladder we use in the orchard. I'm going to find your father.'

Another shot rang out followed by a metallic *clang* as it ricocheted off the frame of the helicopter.

'Christ!' Rupert had ducked automatically at the sound, but raised his head to identify the source. 'That's not him on the bridge shooting, is it? Jesus, it's the postmistress woman Lugg's taken a shine to.'

Amanda turned her most maternal look of disapproval ('I'm not angry, just disappointed') on her son.

'Yes, it's Miss Pounder, and Rupert, please don't blaspheme – we have a vicar in the house.'

* * *

Afterwards, when all witness statements had been taken (and subsequently 'mis-filed'), the bravery of three women featured strongly in the legend that grew around the siege of Carterers. Mrs Thursby's calmness in extremely trying circumstances and her ability to produce food and hot beverages at a moment's notice, not to mention the ability to keep her father-in-law in check, were commented on by all present. Florence Pounder was much admired for her resourcefulness and her skill with firearms, but perhaps the incident viewed with the most respect, even awe, was the way Lady Amanda marched down the snowy driveway to aid her husband. That a concerned wife should hurry to her husband's side was not surprising, but it was the way she strode past the helicopter, now half submerged and filling rapidly with icy water, without so much as a second glance, totally ignoring the grunts and cries from the passengers struggling inside.

'Albert?' she said softly, then again more forcefully, as she gently brushed snow from his white hair, then placed her hands on his cheeks.

At the sound of her voice and the faint amount of warmth transferred, she saw his eyes flicker behind those large round spectacles.

'Did we win?' he asked, looking up into her heart-shaped face, his voice little more than a squeak, the sound an old and battered child's toy might make.

'Not yet,' said Amanda, taking off the peacoat, 'but we're not losing. Now get up and get moving before you turn into an ice sculpture. Can you walk?'

Accepting a helping hand, Campion rose painfully to his feet and pulled on the coat, then threw an arm over Amanda's shoulders.

'I think I can manage a hobble, but a trot is out of the question. As always, I will have to lean on you.'

They trudged back towards the house, Amanda trying to quicken the pace to get Mr Campion's blood flowing again, and they reached the drowning helicopter just as the rescue party led by Rupert did so, though they had all been beaten by Miss Pounder. She stood at the edge of the third pond, pointing her pistol at the half-submerged door of the helicopter through which Kosloffski was trying to scramble, the lower half of his body in the icy water which was filling the cabin. The cockpit had already disappeared under the surface and the rest of the machine, which Amanda knew weighed more than two tons, was slowly following.

'Get inside, Pop, and get yourself warmed up,' ordered Rupert as he embraced his father. 'We've got everything under control here.'

Breck, Henderson and De Vries were already laying the wooden ladder that Lloyd Thursby had brought with him flat on the snow, and were inching it out over the ice towards the helicopter.

'You will relieve them of their guns before you offer them sanctuary, won't you?'

'I think Miss Pounder has that covered,' said Amanda. 'That was good shooting. I was worried that pistol wouldn't work.'

Miss Pounder turned with a smile and pulled Campion's Beretta from the pocket of Amanda's coat with her left hand, whilst hefting the much larger automatic in her right.

'I confiscated this one from Quinn when I relieved him of his coat. I thought I might need more stopping power.' She casually waved the Beretta. 'This is very much a ladies' gun.'

'It's mine, actually,' said Mr Campion, 'but I bow to your superior knowledge, and at some point I would love to know where you acquired that knowledge.'

Miss Pounder looked at him blankly, slipped the Beretta back into her pocket and turned back to guard duty without answering. Instead, she shouted an order in Russian to the sinking helicopter, which was gradually disappearing before their very eyes.

'Get along, Pop,' said Rupert. 'Get inside and in front of the fire.'

Amanda, an arm around his torso, made sure that he complied, then Rupert remembered something.

'Pop, how deep is that pond?'

Mr Campion glanced towards the wrecked helicopter, then allowed his wife to lead him away. 'I have no idea, but I think we'll soon find out.'

Kosloffski, struggling to hold Quinn's battered face above the rising water line, was in no mood to find out. Contorting his upper body, he threw his pistol towards Miss Pounder. It landed on the ice at the edge of the pond and skidded neatly to a halt near her feet. Reaching behind him, Kosloffski took Rivero's gun, held it up to show Miss Pounder and threw it also. Rupert dived by her to retrieve them.

'Wait!' she ordered. 'There should be another one.'

Rupert stared at her in puzzlement; surely she was holding the other one?

'The pilot,' she said patiently, 'will have a side-arm.'

She shouted in Russian again, and after more struggles and thrashing inside the cockpit, a third automatic flew through the air, landing safely in the snow near Rupert, who picked it up carefully by the barrel and handed it to Miss Pounder.

'A Russian Tokarev,' she said as she took it and weighed it against the one she was holding. 'I might have guessed. It will come in useful as I think this gun's empty. Now let's get the water babies on to dry land.' She glanced around at the snowscape in which they stood. 'Well, dry*er* land.'

They edged the ladder over the snow, and then over the dark tide of water spilling over unbroken ice after being displaced by the sinking helicopter. When it was within arm's length of the waterlogged cabin, Breck and Henderson set their feet on the bottom rungs to counter-balance the weight of the escapers, whilst De Vries and Lloyd Thursby took up positions on either side of the ladder to help the escapers – or perhaps prevent them from doing any more escaping. They did this quite naturally, without instructions or discussion, as if rescue missions over snow and ice were regular occurrences.

Miss Pounder, fully occupied in her role of arresting officer/ prison guard and (if required) sniper, realized that Rupert, quivering as much with excitement as with the cold, needed to be useful.

'Would you go into the house, Mr Campion,' Rupert did a double-take until he realized she was talking to him, 'and collect those handcuffs used to restrain Mr Lugg and yourself? They might come in handy. I think you'll find the keys in the coat your father is wearing.'

Rupert found his father enthroned among the wreckage of the lounge, in an armchair pulled so close to a stoked-up fire that he could have roasted marshmallows with the shortest of toasting forks. Two large logs and a cushion had been pressed into service as a footstool to allow his naked feet the chance to thaw out, and several pairs of socks lay abandoned on the hearth, steaming away merrily. Apart from his feet, a soundly asleep Mr Campion was fully covered in an eiderdown and several blankets, with a tartan scarf covering his ears, tied under his chin.

Amidst the scattered tinsel and the overwhelming scent of pine sap, plus the Christmas cards interspersed with sprigs of holly and mistletoe which had somehow remained undisturbed on the mantelpiece, the scene reminded Rupert of a mad Dickensian tableau illustrated by Cruikshank or, given the position of his well-rugged father, seated with legs extended and the scarf around his head as a sort of bonnet, he could have been posing as Whistler's mother in a bath chair.

'Is this where the walking wounded report, then?'

Rupert turned to find himself confronted by another nineteenth-century illustration, this time a character study from *Treasure Island*. Lugg may not have had a parrot on his shoulder, but otherwise he was giving a half-decent impersonation of Long John Silver. Only half because he was not actually missing a leg, but from the bloodstained tea towels and torn trousers, one had clearly been damaged. To help his balance and support his not inconsiderable bulk, he had adopted Cap'n Silver's crutch, or rather an upturned sweeping brush, the bristles nestling in his armpit, which made a suitably eerie *tap-tap* noise as he approached in order to loom over the unconscious Campion and give, though it had not been asked for, his considered medical diagnosis.

'Well, his feet 'aven't turned black or dropped off yet, so that's a good sign,' he pronounced solemnly. 'A bowl of warm water'd be better for his tootsies though, otherwise they'll roast like chestnuts and 'im in the land of nod won't feel a thing.'

'Mom is fetching a bowl and some dry clothes. Can you keep an eye on him? I have to go back outside.'

Rupert rooted around the debris of the Christmas tree with the toe of his boot until he found the handcuffs on long lengths of chain which had been used as manacles. As he picked them up, Lugg raised a quizzical eyebrow.

'Keep the fire stoked, would you? And tell Mrs Thursby to start brewing a couple of gallons of tea and one of hot soup if she's able.'

'Expecting more guests, are we?'

'Miss Pounder's been busy taking prisoners.'

Lugg smiled. 'Good girl.'

TWENTY

Relief Column

Mr Campion was not allowed to sleep for long. Before Carterers became a prison again (though with a different set of inmates), he was carried upstairs by the Reverend Breck at the head-and-shoulders end and Rupert in charge of the legs, hindered rather than helped by Lugg in peg-leg pirate-captain mode, supervising the ascent from below.

'Steady as she goes, left 'and down a bit. Mind 'is 'ead on the banister, it's 'is weakest spot.'

In their bedroom, Amanda had assembled a pile of towels and two complete sets of dry, warm clothing, making it clear that she intended Campion to wear both. Mr Campion did not object and in fact quite enjoyed the rough towelling of his arms and legs as circulation was restored to frozen limbs.

'You know, darling,' he said, grateful that his teeth were no longer chattering, 'when the vicar was carrying me up here, I opened my eyes and looked up at his dog collar and I was sure he was there to administer the last rites.'

'Nonsense!' Amanda towelled more vigorously. 'Anyway, I don't think he, or you for that matter, are in that particular branch of the church.'

'He seems like a good man. He would probably have made an exception.'

'He might have to be even more flexible with two of our godless communist invaders.'

'Oh dear. The one called Quinn?'

Amanda nodded and then Campion lost sight of her as she pulled a vest over his head.

'What did you hit him with?'

'The flat of a garden spade; it was the only thing to hand. Is he badly hurt?'

'If he survives what we are now calling hypothermia – he got well-chilled without a coat before being dunked in ice-cold water – then he will need a good plastic surgeon to repair his face.'

'Oh dear,' Campion said again as Amanda helped him into a blue denim work shirt she had bought him in America but he had never worn, claiming it would make him look like a rodeo rider. 'I feel awfully responsible – in fact I am responsible for clouting him and, I suppose, his immersion in the pond, but taking his coat, that was Miss Pounder's idea.'

'And a very good one it was,' said Amanda sharply, 'because you might not have lasted as long as you did without it. Thank goodness she had her head screwed on and was there to help you in your madcap plan.'

'She certainly proved a useful ally out there, but you said that *two* of our unwelcome visitors might be in need of the last rites.'

'The helicopter pilot took a bullet in the chest. If he doesn't get to a hospital, it could be the end of him, and that was quite definitely Miss Pounder's responsibility.'

'A most resourceful lady. I wonder where she learned—'

'We've all wondered that.'

Once dressed, Mr Campion insisted on going downstairs. He was not exactly dressed for dinner, a mustard-yellow V-neck cardigan hiding most of his 'rodeo' shirt and clashing loudly with green corduroy trousers, but it must be dinner time and he really ought to go and inspect the troops.

'Lugg is on duty, so the troops are being properly supervised, but you are right about dinner.' She looked at her wristwatch. 'Good Lord, it's only seven thirty. It's been a very long day and people must be starving. I know I am.'

Campion sat on the edge of the bed and gently squeezed his feet, now in thick, dry wool socks, into a battered but wonderfully flexible pair of tennis shoes. They did little to enhance his sartorial elegance but he was beyond caring.

'I must go and check on Lugg; see how he is. That should have been the first thing I did.'

'Don't be silly, you were in no state to do anything when we got you inside,' Amanda chided gently. 'You flaked out as soon as we sat you in front of the fire. Lugg actually came to check on you. Said you looked like an old lady in a bath chair on the front at Frinton, and how things had gone nice and peaceful now you were asleep.'

'Charming. I have a vague memory of somebody lumbering about on a crutch. Was that him?'

'Yes, he's up and about after a fashion, but he does need to see a doctor as soon as we can get to one. Also, the helicopter pilot.'

'That could be problematic,' said Campion ruefully. 'How bad are the wounds?'

'Lugg's is a flesh wound – and no cracks please about there being plenty of flesh to aim at – but the pilot is in a bad way. Professor Henderson is caring for him.'

'Hereward? You surprise me.'

'He says he was inspired by the way Miss Pounder treated Lugg's wound and thought he ought to do his bit. What is surprising is that he seems to know what he's doing, not that there's much he can do, but he's taken charge and turned the dining room into *Emergency Ward 10*.'

'And the rest of them?'

'They're all mucking in, even De Vries who, Rupert says, proved a dab-hand at picking the locks on his handcuffs to release him.'

'You surprise me again. I take it his precious diptych is safe.'

'He doesn't let it out of his sight, but apart from that, he's genuinely helping to put things straight. The lounge looks as if a bomb's gone off in there.'

Campion peered at his wife over the tops of his spectacles. 'Did any bombs go off on your excursion to Marham?'

'Thankfully no. That wasn't the object of the exercise, but our Soviet friends did take some very incriminating photographs, which hopefully are in their helicopter deep in your favourite garden pond.'

'And where are our Soviet friends?'

'Quinn and the pilot are in Hereward's Hospital, as we now call the dining room. Kosloffski and Rivero are chained up in your study under the eagle eye of Miss Pounder, who has taken charge of all the weaponry, although she turned her nose up at your Beretta.'

'Yes, I recall her making that quite clear.'

'We had to raid your wardrobe for dry clothes for the Russians, which is why your fashion choices are somewhat limited, and just about every blanket and towel in the house has been pressed into service. Mrs T is in charge of the kitchen production line, producing a makeshift dinner, and Lloyd is trying not to get under anyone's feet.'

Campion reached out and took his wife's hand. 'I'm sorry to have ruined your Christmas holiday, darling.'

'Don't be ridiculous. House guests who outstay their welcome, drink and eat us out of house and home and then start violent arguments? Sounds like a traditional Christmas to me.'

'Well, hopefully we'll have a quiet New Year.'

'I don't think we have much say in the matter.' Amanda sighed. 'It has stopped snowing for the moment, but the roads are going to be bad for a while so I don't think anyone will fancy driving here for our New Year's Eve bash, and no one can get through to us on the telephone either. Not that we would have anything left to feed them with, and our stock of drink has been decimated.'

'And I've let off our best fireworks,' Campion admitted glumly.

'In a good cause, darling, and I appreciated them – what I saw of them – but the baseline of our situation is that we are stuck here unless help comes from the outside world, so we just have to make the best of it. If you really feel up to it, come downstairs and help keep up morale. You're quite good at that.'

Campion seemed genuinely hesitant. 'I feel terrible about poor old Lugg,' he said softly. 'It was my fault he got shot. I told him to create a diversion so I could escape.'

'You're just being mawkish. You would have done the same for him.'

'Let's not be foolish, darling, but I do feel responsible for the old boy, though he is fairly stoical and he's not likely to hold it against me, is he?'

'Now who's being foolish? Of course he will. Elephants never forget, so put on your most disarming smile, comb your hair and come and address the troops. You are the head of the household, well nominally anyway, and you have to cheer them up despite the fact that we are cut off from civilization, might run out of food and have two men with gunshot wounds plus two desperate enemy agents in our midst.'

'What a very merry Christmas we're all having.' Campion stood up unsteadily, watching his feet closely as though he did not trust them. 'Come on, then, let us go forth and spread goodwill and cheer to all men. Well, most of them.'

Mr Campion and Lady Amanda descended the staircase arm-in-arm; she offering emotional backing, he requiring physical support. It was a poor recreation of a scene from an epic movie, more the walkdown by the lead players at the end of a low-budget pantomime. Their audience was, however, appreciative and were in danger of breaking into applause at their appearance.

Breck, De Vries, Miss Pounder, Rupert and Mrs Thursby (armed with a tray of freshly baked currant scones) had gathered in the hall as soon as they heard the Campions leave their bedroom.

'I think you are their hero,' whispered Amanda.

'Let us not disabuse them until my ego is fully inflated,' Campion replied out of the corner of his mouth.

No one actually attempted to slap Campion on the back – he looked too frail to withstand violence, however affectionate – but as they crowded round him, De Vries insisted on shaking his hand.

'I understand now, what you were doing earlier when you told the American about the Walsingham diptych. It was to confuse and distract him before your escape, which was very brave.'

Campion nodded a grateful acknowledgement but wished that the Dutchman did not have such a crushing grip. 'I must apologize,' he said, trying not to wince, 'for slandering you in the process. I do hope the icon is safe.'

'It is now, and the would-be thief has been suitably punished. Would it be un-Christian of me to thank you for that?'

'You'd better ask the Reverend Breck here about such matters, or wait until you get to Walsingham and seek advice from a higher authority. On a more secular level, in the police investigation which is bound to follow, I take full responsibility for the injuries to Mr Quinn, or whatever his real name is, and to the helicopter pilot.'

At that moment, Miss Pounder's eyes flashed and locked with Campion's and she took a breath as if to speak, but Amanda forestalled her.

'How are our prisoners, Miss Pounder? I thought you were on guard duty.'

Miss Pounder, recovering her composure, nodded towards Campion's study. 'They have been given dry clothes and are suitably restrained. They are being watched closely by Mr Thursby, who seems to have appointed himself my deputy.'

'Deputy as in a cowboy film?' Campion asked.

'I'm afraid so.'

'This I must see.'

Campion stood at the doorway of his study and could not help but smile at the scene which greeted him.

Kosloffski and Rivero, their hands manacled behind their backs, sat on the floor back-to-back. They were dressed in a spectacular mixture of clothing (which Amanda later described as an explosion at a jumble sale) and had both been gagged with Rugby School scarves. They looked cold, wet and miserable, and their mood was unlikely to be lightened by the taunting of Lloyd Thursby, who was perched on the edge of Campion's desk holding a .45 calibre pistol in each hand. As he waved them in the faces of their previous owners, he quoted lines from his favourite Westerns, urging them to go for their guns, get out of town or meet him at the OK Corral at high noon, or whatever time was convenient.

Campion struggled to contain a smile. 'Isn't this rather dangerous?' he asked Miss Pounder quietly.

'Those guns are not loaded.' She patted the waistband of her skirt under her long cardigan. 'This one is.'

'But the prisoners don't know that.' Campion nodded his approval.

'Neither does Mr Thursby.'

Amanda pulled him towards the lounge and Campion shuffled after her with some reluctance. The object of his trepidation lay full length on the sofa, which had been strategically placed to get the maximum warmth from the fire. The pose reminded Campion of a Renaissance Sleeping Venus, but fortunately this figure was fully clothed, was clutching the handle of a sweeping brush and was wide awake.

'Strewth!' said Lugg. 'Get dressed in the dark, did we?'

'I've gone smart-casual,' replied Campion, 'though perhaps I got the proportions wrong and erred on the side of couldn't-care-less. How's the leg? Still attached?'

'One of 'em is, the other is giving me gyp. Looks like you'll have to strap me to Rupert's old sledge and pull me to the nearest hospital.'

Campion feigned horror. 'What a ghastly thought – me in the traces and you shouting "Mush" and cracking a whip over my head. Given the state I'm in, I doubt we would get very far before the wolves took us.'

'Then there's the chap you bashed and the one shot in the chest by—'

'That was probably me,' Campion cut him off.

Lugg nodded in agreement. 'I saw you do it if anyone asks.'

'I knew I could rely on you, old fruit. Meanwhile, the problem is, who is going to ask? We can't get out, certainly not before daylight, and we have no telephone so we can only pray for some Good Samaritans to come and help us.'

'Better get that vicar on the case, then.'

As if he had been poised waiting for his cue, the Reverend Breck entered the lounge, pulling on his overcoat. 'Mr Campion, there are lights down at the bottom of the drive; headlights from a vehicle, down by the crashed coach. I think it's a car that's stopped to investigate. I'll go down there and see if they can help us.'

'So you've found us a Good Samaritan, Vicar?'

'I hope so. That helicopter pilot won't last the night unless he gets medical assistance, though I must say that Professor Henderson is doing sterling work tending his wounds. The man has hidden depths and deserves a medal.'

'He's not the only one,' said Campion. 'And if you don't mind charging down to the lane and hijacking that passing vehicle, it would be much appreciated. Take Rupert with you. He knows the line of the drive and I don't want anyone else falling through the ice into the moat.'

'Moat?'

'A little fantasy of mine, which the family always ridicules. We have water guarding one side of the house, so I call it my "almost moat", and today it served its purpose by thwarting an invader.'

'Interesting,' said Breck, not quite sure how to react. 'I'll grab your son and we'll go marauding.'

As soon as he was out of earshot, Lugg exhaled loudly. 'This power-of-prayer business; works fast, don't it.'

'If you have the right contacts,' admitted Mr Campion.

Although the much younger man, Rupert had trouble keeping up with the Reverend Breck as they charged down the drive, their breath frosting in clouds as if they were smoking a crafty cigarette on a sports day cross-country run. While Breck kept his eyes on the lights shining on the charabanc, which now looked as if it had been grafted on to the granite gatepost, Rupert could not resist gazing at the helicopter, which appeared to have found the bottom of the pond. It had sunk at an angle, nose down and on its right side. What remained above the surface were the rotor blades, or at least two and a half of them, tilted at an acute angle, the top half of the cabin and the tail boom and rotor. A sheen of frost was already forming over much of the fuselage, as were icicles from the rotors' blades. By morning, thought Rupert, it could be an ice sculpture or the most bizarre Christmas decoration ever.

The lights down at the gateway seemed to be moving, reflecting off the snow-covered front of the pilgrims' coach and flashing into the grounds of Carterers as if probing for a safe passage of entry. From Rupert's viewpoint, there was enough room, just, for a vehicle to enter the drive between the left-hand gatepost and the coach jammed up against the right-hand sentinel. The Alandel Land Rover, with his mother as a reluctant passenger, had managed to leave and return, so surely another vehicle should be able to manage it, especially if it was a car which had successfully braved the back roads and lanes thus far.

He was unable to identify the type of car outside the gateway, although the deep throb of its idling engine suggested it was something considerably bigger than his own Riley Elf, and the beams of its headlights, reflecting off a white canvas of snow, were quite blinding. So too was the additional beam which swept over the coach and then into the driveway as if someone was waving a powerful torch.

'Good Lord!' exclaimed the Reverend Breck, skidding to a

halt on an icy crust of snow and reaching out an arm to restrain Rupert.

'What is it?'

'Rescue, I hope,' said Breck, a hand shielding his eyes.

Following his example, Rupert screwed up his eyes and followed Breck's gaze. His first thought was that at worst he was hallucinating, at best he was tucked up in bed and dreaming.

The vehicle in the lane was now nudging its way between the gatepost and the wrecked coach, the headlights and its third more flexible beam all spotlighting Rupert and Breck as if they were a top-of-the-bill double act at the Palladium.

Once his eyes had focused, Rupert took in the squat, dark, brutalist outline of the vehicle and menacing snout of the cannon in the turret mounted on it.

'That's not a car,' he said in wonderment, 'it's a tank!'

There was a further surprise for him when the wandering beam, shone from a spotlight on a swivel on the turret, flicked away out of his face and he was able to make out the silhouette of a man operating it. The man smacked a hand on the side of the turret and the vehicle halted its progress, which was just as well as the two civilians were firmly in its intended path, spoke into the microphone slung around his neck, then addressed the onlookers in a voice straight off the parade ground.

'It's young Rupert Campion, isn't it? Good, we must be in the right place.'

Rupert, who had never been confronted by a tank anywhere, let alone in the garden of his home, and who could not tear his eyes from the dark circle of the howitzer or whatever it was which seemed to be pointed directly at him, said the first nervous thing which came into his head.

'You have me at a disadvantage, sir.'

Even as he spoke, his voice betraying him as a girlish falsetto, he was aware of the Reverend Breck turning on him with a very un-Christian gaze and hissing, 'Is that the best you can do?'

'Warrant Officer Neel here,' boomed the voice from the turret, 'from RAF Marham. I've seen you there at the Alandel facility with your mother, Lady Amanda. She training you up as her apprentice, is she?'

'Not really,' said Rupert, his voice now back under control.

'She will be glad to see you. How did you know we needed rescuing?'

'Rescuing? Are there people still on that bus?' He swung his spotlight on to the windscreen of the coach.

'There's no one on the bus, Mr Neel,' the Reverend Breck intervened as though declaiming from the pulpit, 'but swing the light over to your right, to about two o'clock.'

The figure in the tank turret complied, clearly recognizing an authority in the voice which suggested that the pulpit and the parade ground were in the same neighbourhood if not the same parish.

The spotlight beam swept over the heads of Rupert and Breck, pushed a quivering finger of light into the trees at the bottom of the orchard, then swung back on its arc as though doing a surprised double-take, to settle on the third pond.

'Bloody hell!'

Warrant Officer Neel, in a distinguished career with the Royal Air Force police, had seen many strange things, which for a variety of reasons had to remain confidential even if not officially classed as secret. The wintry scene which now greeted him, the dark night made bright by the snow, was one he would not forget but instantly knew he would never be allowed to talk about.

'We've found it,' he said into his neck microphone. 'You'd better get here sharpish, sir.'

He looked down at the two figures standing in the headlights.

'Climb aboard and we'll give you a lift up to the house. We've no spare seats inside, so you'll have to ride topside, but you can hang on to the seventy-five.'

Rupert and Breck approached the metal monster, which wasn't actually quite as big a monster as Rupert had expected as he looked for a foothold.

'What's a seventy-five?' he asked Breck.

'The calibre of the gun; it's a seventy-five-millimetre cannon. Put your arms around the barrel and hang on.'

Scrabbling for purchase on the slippery metal, Rupert wrapped his arms around the cold gun barrel, as did Breck. They stood close together, elbows touching. Somewhere beneath their feet, the driver gunned the engine and the machine began to advance up the drive.

'Stay to the left, away from the pond,' yelled Rupert over the throaty noise of the engine.

The driver seemed aware of the instruction, though it was unclear whether Warrant Officer Neel had heard as he was staring open-mouthed as he played his spotlight on the watery grave of the helicopter.

'I can't wait to see Pop's face,' Rupert said into Breck's ear, 'when I turn up riding a tank.'

'It's not a tank,' said Breck, turning his head, 'it's an Alvis Saladin armoured car. Tanks have caterpillar tracks; this has wheels, six of them. Still, it's quite an impressive way to make an entrance, though a sledge and a team of reindeer would have been more seasonal. Had you noticed that we're being followed?'

Concentrating on hanging on to the bouncy armoured car (which he still thought of as a tank), Rupert had not noticed that a pair of Land Rovers were following in convoy, having negotiated the gateway and driving in the tracks left by the wheels of the Saladin to aid their traction. Both vehicles slowed notably as they passed the third pond and its newest resident.

The noise of three approaching engines brought a welcoming committee to the front door of Carterers, comprising the Campions, De Vries and Miss Pounder. Old Lloyd had been left on guard duty, Hereward Henderson remained on medical duties and Mrs Thursby, at the prospect of more visitors, was naturally busying herself in the kitchen boiling kettles and doing a head count of clean cups.

'Look what we found!' Rupert cried gleefully, jumping down from the Saladin as it pulled up.

'Warrant Officer Neel, my favourite Snowdrop,' said Amanda as the man in the turret joined Rupert and stood to ramrod attention, 'how clever of you to know we needed help.'

'We were tracking that Hoplite,' Neel said, as if making his report. 'It came off the trawler I told you about at Marham this afternoon. Couldn't believe it was coming here, but there didn't seem anywhere else it could be going, so we took a chance and headed out, keeping in contact with the radar boys by radio, until they lost contact, that is.'

'That showed great initiative, Mr Neel,' said Campion, resisting the urge to salute a warrant officer, which would have been inappropriate.

'Only following orders, sir.'

'Really? Whose?'

'Gentleman from Security. He arrived at Marham not long after you left, Lady Amanda, because of that Russian trawler. Once they launched their whirly-bird, he got really interested and insisted on coming with us.'

Neel turned and indicated the first Land Rover which had followed the Saladin. It had slid to a halt and was disgorging men in military greatcoats, clearly following the instructions of a figure wearing a long, non-regulation fur coat and a Russian-style fur hat.

'Elsie!' exclaimed Mr Campion.

'Albert!' replied the figure in the fur hat. 'You appear to have a particularly unique specimen of water lily growing in your garden pond.'

'It has a metallic perfume which isn't to everyone's taste. It is very good to see you, Elsie.'

Mr Campion was one of the few people who dared, or was permitted, to call L.C. Corkran by the epithet Elsie, although to be fair, Lugg also dared, even though he was not allowed. Mr Corkran had been Campion's erstwhile boss in the security services during the war and, if truth were ever told, on several occasions subsequently. Now he held a position of such importance in the secret world that if one had to ask what it was, one did not need to know.

'Amanda, I had a feeling you might need some moral support,' said Corkran, his fur hat bobbing in a polite bow.

'An ambulance, a doctor and some strong men with guns would be more appreciated,' she replied, 'but your arrival – even five minutes after the nick of time – is most welcome. Do come inside.'

'Of course.' Corkran took a step forward then stopped and stared at the welcoming committee. 'Hello, Florence. What are you doing here?'

'Hello, Brigadier,' said Miss Pounder.

TWENTY-ONE
God and Sinners Reconciled

The extreme cold snap, which had seen the Upper Thames and the sea at Dunkirk across the Channel freeze, as well as paralysing most of East Anglia, lasted into 1963. The thaw that eventually saw off the Big Freeze began on the first Wednesday of Lent, prompting the Campions to revive the idea of their cancelled New Year's Eve house party, aiming for the Easter bank holiday weekend in April and converting it into an elaborate Easter egg hunt with, Mr Campion insisted, a firework display. He also requested that formal invitations must include the restriction that no guest should arrive by helicopter, a suggestion which was quietly but ruthlessly overruled by Amanda.

It would have been, she argued, a self-indulgent 'in' joke which the majority of guests would not understand. Of the friends, family and acquaintances to be invited, only Lugg, the Thursbys and L. C. Corkran were aware that a new model Russian helicopter had ever landed in the grounds of Carterers. She insisted that it was to be a party for their friends, not a reunion of their 'Christmas pilgrims' and a reminder of a day she would rather forget.

Before the old year had been counted down and out by the White Heather Club (the BBC's compulsory annual celebration of Scottishness), all traces of the helicopter had been removed from the Campions' property. Mr L. C. Corkran and Warrant Officer Neel had seen to that.

Mr Campion was never sure exactly how many men had been in the armoured relief column (as Lugg referred to it) which had arrived to lift the siege of Carterers, or whether they were regular RAF personnel, 'Snowdrop' policemen, or officers of the security services. They seemed to know exactly what was required of them and went about their business with a quiet efficiency and only a minimum of direction from Corkran and Neel, who had assumed joint command of the rescue operation, deferring where necessary to Lady Amanda and, of course, Mrs Thursby. The latter was included in the chain of command because, as is well known, every British military action requires a reliable supply of hot tea.

The first priority had been to get medical treatment for the three injured men. As two of them were at best illegal aliens, and one of them likely a murderer, it was decided to transport them to the base hospital at Marham, where Warrant Officer Neel's men would be responsible for their security. Lugg they would treat as a VIP private patient, which pleased the fat man immensely, although he was disappointed when he was told, quite categorically, that he would not be taken there in the Saladin for the simple reason that he would not fit.

Another, more sober, role was allocated to the armoured car. As the charabanc was very much a crime scene complete with a dead body, it was vital that the police had access to it, yet the weather meant that police resources were thinly stretched, and road traffic conditions difficult if not impossible, the same considerations applying to ambulances and hearses. It was decided, with Mr Corkran taking responsibility, that the coach and its driver, the late Graham Fisk, should also be taken to Marham, towed by the Saladin.

Warrant Officer Neel, on learning there was a corpse on board the coach, insisted that he steered it himself once towing chains had attached it to the Saladin, rather than put any of his men through the ghoulish experience of chauffeuring a dead body. It was a practical solution in many ways. It would clear the gateway and the lane for the other vehicles which Corkran had ordered by radio to be sent from Marham, and it would also keep intact the crime scene for police examination, though Mr Corkran was uncharacteristically vague when it came to the question of exactly when the police would be called.

The injured Russians were packed into one Land Rover under guard, and Lugg stretched out in the back of the other on a makeshift bed of folded eiderdowns in a pose which resembled that of a Middle Eastern *pasha* surveying his servants, or his harem. Both vehicles were dispatched back to Marham.

Only then did Campion privately brief Corkran on what had happened at Carterers, while Amanda did the same for the events at Marham that afternoon. Mr Campion assumed that Corkran the spymaster would want to interrogate Kosloffski and Rivero immediately, but he had forgotten how methodical his old boss could be when assessing new information and making practical decisions in a crisis – or in this case, in the aftermath of one.

'You had no telephone service after these so-called pilgrims arrived,' he had said, 'which suggests to me that they cut the line out there in the lane. One of my lads will shimmy up the telegraph pole and fix that and I'll get somebody to repair the vehicles our chums disabled. Next item of business: the photographs these fellows took. Are the films still in the cameras? If they are in the helicopter, they can stay there for the moment, but we'd better do a thorough search of their clothing in case they removed the films. Then there's the question of firearms, which we ought to secure.'

'Miss Pounder is in charge of weaponry,' Campion had offered.

'She would be,' Corkran had replied, at which Campion and Amanda exchanged quizzical looks, though 'Elsie' tantalizingly refused to elaborate. 'And I'll need to speak to your other temporary residents. Could you put up with them for another night? I doubt if we could find a hotel to take them at this time of night; assuming, that is, that we could get them there, and assuming you have hotels out here in the wilds of Norfolk. I should be able to get them out of your hair tomorrow.'

'I will ignore your disparaging of this fine county, Elsie,' Amanda had scolded him, 'and of course we will put up the pilgrims. Now you've whipped Lugg off to hospital, there's probably enough food to go round and, as our New Year's Eve party is unlikely to happen, we may even be able to offer you a drink.'

Corkran had accepted enthusiastically as, unlike conventional policemen, and RAF policemen, he was not constrained by regulations covering drinking on duty.

'Pity about your party. I was looking forward to seeing Guffy Randall again.' He had toasted his hosts. 'Guffy and Lugg made a good team at charades; well, good for a laugh anyway. As a matter of fact, I was on my way here, in a roundabout sort of way, when this business blew up. I was due a spot of leave and was in Cambridge for Christmas. I aimed to wander over here to see in the new year at the traditional Campion bash when I was informed we had a Russian spy trawler moving into the Wash and coming too close to the coast for comfort, especially in this weather. So I thought I'd pop over to Marham where they were tracking it. As it turns out, I arrived too late to catch you red-handed cooperating with Soviet spies.'

Corkran had looked sternly at Amanda as he spoke, but not too sternly, and Amanda was not to be cowed.

'You would also have been too late here to catch them if Albert had not scuppered their escape.'

Campion had waved a hand casually but magnanimously. 'You are very welcome, Elsie, but my valuable assistance comes at a price. As that thing sticking out of my beautiful pond is a positive eyesore, I have a hankering to blow it up, and so I would like to borrow that Saladin you appropriated and take a few potshots with its impressive cannon.'

But it was Amanda, not Corkran, who had turned on Campion to disabuse him of the idea.

'You will do no such thing! That's one of Mikhail Mil's latest designs and we should take this opportunity to examine it closely, even if Albert has bent it a bit. It ought to be lifted and taken to Alandel's workshop at Marham.'

Although there were no witnesses to the actual event – at least none who would ever admit to having seen or heard anything – that was exactly what happened.

As promised, one of Corkran's men had repaired the telephone line, which was immediately commandeered by Corkran himself, issuing orders, requesting favours, and disturbing several high-ranking officers until almost midnight. By then Amanda and Mrs Thursby had sorted out the feeding and sleeping arrangements, allocating the late Graham Fisk's bedroom to Mr Corkran.

Two of Corkran's men were assigned to guard the two prisoners overnight. Only when they had removed their overcoats did Campion realize they were civilians rather than military, as they wore casual clothes not uniforms, one even sporting a bright red knitted sweater with a green Christmas tree motif, suggesting that he had been called to duty from the bosom of his family, or possibly an aged aunt still attempting to master the garter stitch.

Both of the young men – Corkran's newest intake not long out of university, Campion guessed – seemed to know their jobs, looked tough enough to be able to handle themselves, and were polite enough to ask Amanda if they should remove their shoes before treading snow into the house. They insisted they would be comfortable taking turns to sleep between spells of guard duty in the lounge in front of the fire.

Before the house retired for the night, Campion asked Corkran if he intended to interrogate Kosloffski and Rivero, but Mr Corkran shook his head, saying he would let them shiver overnight before sweating them the next day at Marham in the presence of some very interested American security officials, to whom he had promised their heads.

The next day, a Saturday, did not so much dawn as splutter into life as the sky remained grey and pregnant with more snow. A new convoy of RAF Land Rovers and a three-ton truck arrived just as Mrs Thursby had somehow magically produced breakfast for everybody. She emitted a small howl of despair that there were more mouths to feed, but was quickly mollified when she discovered that this relief force had come armed with a tray of eggs, flour, milk (powdered), sugar, butter, two Christmas puddings (surplus to requirements in the officers' mess) and a bottle of Watson's Trawler Rum ('special request from the fat bloke in the sickbay').

A pair of Snowdrops armed with Sterling sub-machine guns took over responsibility for the prisoners from Corkran's young apprentices and bundled them unceremoniously into the back of the truck. Only Amanda came out of the house to see them off, locking eyes with Kosloffski and saying, 'You shouldn't have threatened my family,' before turning her back.

The four pilgrims collected their things and made to leave in two Land Rovers. Campion took up position in the hallway to shake their hands and wish them well. He kept his farewells light and pleasant, knowing that at Marham they would be given a severe lecture by Mr Corkran and told that they had to sign the Official Secrets Act.

'Best of luck with your research, Professor. I look forward to your *magnum opus* on your namesake Hereward, and I believe that wounded pilot is still with us thanks to your medical care.'

The smaller man pursed his lips, making his ginger moustache bristle like a woolly boy caterpillar.

'Too kind, Mr Campion, too kind, but I must confess I am not an actual professor of anything. That is a nickname given to me by fellow students in my Workers' Educational Association evening class, so I am used to responding to it. As for my medical expertise, such as it is, that was acquired during the war, driving an ambulance during the Blitz. It was the one way a conscientious objector could do their bit.'

De Vries almost clicked his heels and bowed as he shook hands with Campion, who wished him luck now that the Walsingham diptych was back on track for Walsingham.

'It had a lucky escape,' said the Dutchman, 'but I am glad it is going home.'

'Home? I expected to see it in a Sotheby's catalogue.'

'Perhaps you will, perhaps not,' was the enigmatic reply.

To the Reverend Breck, he said, 'We normally enjoy a very quiet Christmas here, Vicar.'

'It has been eventful,' conceded Breck, 'and your family has been very brave. In Walsingham I will pray for you all.'

'By all means do,' said Campion, 'but then try and forget us and the events here. You will be encouraged to do so officially. You have to pretend you were never here.'

'I understand, but I still think goodbye is too final. I prefer "till we meet again".'

'Then let it be until we meet again, but if you can't find me in heaven, you'll know where to look.'

Breck's eyes widened at that, then he smiled and moved on, leaving Campion facing Florence Pounder.

'Before you go, Miss Pounder, I simply have to ask—'

'You do not *have* to ask, Mr Campion. I wish you wouldn't, and Brigadier Corkran certainly would not allow me to answer.'

'My dear lady,' Campion lifted her hand and kissed it lightly, 'that explains everything.'

When the pilgrims had departed, Campion put on a coat, gloves, Wellington boots and his second-best fedora, wrapped a scarf around his neck and ventured out to the curved bridge, where Corkran, in fur coat and hat, was surveying the scene with a burly figure whose hands were deep in the pockets of an RAF overcoat.

'This is Flight Sergeant Briggs.'

'One of your chaps?' Campion asked.

'On occasion, but he's here as the best engineer at Marham.'

'The best who was on duty,' said Briggs, resigned, 'with access to some heavy lifting gear.'

Campion threw up his hands in mock horror. 'Don't tell me you're planning to steal my lovely new garden sculpture?'

'We can do that easy with a crane and a flat-back. Lifting it is not the problem.'

'What is?'

'Those bloody gateposts down the drive. Did you nick them from Stonehenge? It'll be a nightmare getting our machines in here. They'll have to go.'

'Don't you dare!' exclaimed Mr Campion.

His fears were unfounded, and when the mobile crane and flat-back lorry arrived at Carterers, they both negotiated the gateway safely, though with an ear-splitting screech of metal on granite as they scraped into the driveway.

The Thursbys insisted on staying until the remains of the helicopter were lifted and transported away, on the grounds that the two frogmen who had to go into the pond to attach chains to the wreckage would need an almost constant supply of hot chocolate to keep their spirits up. Thus fortified, Mr Corkran's work party completed their task on the Sunday and the remains of the helicopter were spirited away.

The heavy traffic to and from Marham had cleared the lane of snow but on the next day, the last day of 1962, the wind brought more blizzards and freezing temperatures across the whole of southern England. The Campions were extremely grateful for the fresh snowfalls.

From the curved bridge over the once-more frozen pond, the pair looked out over the sea of white which, albeit temporarily, disguised the damage done to their driveway and garden by heavy RAF rescue vehicles and the odd armoured car.

'Do you think we have an insurance claim?' mused Mr Campion.

* * *

For the 'Great Easter Sunday Egg Hunt' at Carterers, Mr L. C. Corkran was invited earlier than the other guests – a full day earlier, with the incentive that he would enjoy a good dinner and a comfortable bed, giving the Campions a chance to 'catch up on things'. Arriving on Easter Saturday would also give him an advantage in the actual egg hunt, as he would be able to observe where Lugg and Lloyd Thursby were concealing the chocolate prizes around the grounds.

It was just the four of them for dinner. Mrs Thursby, having helped out in the kitchen, had been driven home along with her father-in-law, who was anxious not to miss the new episode of *Wagon Train* on the television. Rupert, having made it back to his studies in America with some difficulty, had decided to stay there and experience something called 'Spring Break', which he had explained was an American institution whereby students retreated to the quiet countryside, or perhaps a sleepy seaside town, to spend time in contemplation and study revision. It was an explanation which neither of his parents believed for a minute.

Mr Campion thought it only polite to make sure that 'Elsie' was well-fed with a roast leg of lamb (naturally) and all the trimmings before interrogating him. Lugg had the task of making sure his glass was never less than half full of a Burgundy *grand cru*, appreciating that it was best, when interrogating a professional interrogator, to have him as relaxed as possible.

'We have kept our heads down these past three months,' Campion began, 'not that we've had too much choice in the matter. The whole country seems to have been paralysed by the weather. Our Christmas blizzard was just the start, and it brought a different sort of blizzard with it.'

'That was a terrible segue, Albert.' Corkran grinned.

'I haven't segued into anything yet. Give me time. I could have drawn similarities with Chaucer's Tabard Inn housing an assortment of pilgrims, or suggested that we were visited, appropriately for the time of year, by three strangers – I won't call them kings – bearing gifts. Except their gifts were not pleasant ones and, technically, they came from the west. But I think "blizzard" is a good description of what actually happened to us on that day in December and remarkably it was only one day. Quite a lot happened in those twenty-four hours, but in the end the day went well? I think so, or at least I will say it did in my memoirs.'

'You will do no such thing!' ordered Amanda. 'Elsie – and Alandel – have managed to keep a lid on things so far and I think the lid should stay firmly on.'

'You are probably right, dear,' said Campion, swirling the remains of wine in his glass, anticipating Lugg's skilled, serpentine reach for the bottle. 'Official Secrets and all that, but it's a pity. I had a chapter all planned out with a scene at the dining room table where there was an empty chair and a single crutch leaning against it, or rather a kitchen broom.'

Lugg moved the Burgundy pointedly out of Campion's reach.

'Then in the next chapter I could add that Lugg DID NOT DIE and put it in capitals just like Dickens did in his *Christmas Carol*.'

The fat man snorted with such velocity that the table shook. 'It's no thanks to you I still has use of my pins,' Lugg growled. 'You and your diversions and stupid code words.'

'But you got the message.'

'Too right I did; you mouthing off about the Christmas tree at the Platelayers' Arms when everybody knows the Platelayers' 'as never run to anything so gaudy. Down there you might get a sprig of holly on Christmas Eve if you're lucky, though not necessarily where you wanted it.'

Lugg's arm, seemingly under its own volition, moved the bottle across the table back in Campion's direction.

'Seriously, though, if it hadn't been for that Miss Pounder and her ministrations, I could have lost me leg, the doctors said.'

'Ah yes, the resourceful Miss Pounder. She was something of a revelation, wasn't she.'

It was not a question, but Campion stared at Corkran as though he expected an answer. When Mr Corkran put his glass to his mouth and did not reply, Campion tried another tack.

'Of course, our little group of pilgrims were all interesting, in their own ways. I take it you're keeping tabs on them, Brigadier?'

'Discreetly,' Corkran said at last. 'They all had to sign the Official Secrets Act at Marham before they went on their merry way. The Reverend Breck is over in Walsingham, retired there, in fact. De Vries went back to Holland and the last I heard about his precious painting was that he was in negotiations with the

British Museum. That chap Henderson seems to spend his time in libraries, probably to keep warm. None of them have tried to sell their stories to the newspapers and they all seem to have kept quiet about their little adventure.'

'And Miss Pounder?' Campion asked, noting Lugg's ears pricking up.

'Ah, yes, Florence.' Corkran savoured the moment along with his wine. 'Florence first signed the Official Secrets Act back in 1943. She never talks about what she did before she retired to her Dorset post office, nor should she.'

'And you are not going to tell us because if you did you'd have to kill us.'

'Something like that.' Corkran smiled.

'And the others who were involved?'

Corkran became serious. 'The three fake Americans were shipped back to the USA where they will face charges of espionage and, quite possibly, the hangman. The helicopter pilot we kept separate and returned him, when he was fit enough, to the Russians via their embassy. The story we agreed – that's me and a certain embassy official – was that his helicopter had been lost at sea and the pilot rescued by our coastguard.'

'Did he not notice he'd been shot in the chest?'

'He was prepared to overlook that fact in return for repatriation.'

'And the coach driver, Fisk?'

'That was a sad affair; he had a family. I'm not proud of it, but we covered that up quite well, all things considered. The driver's death was put down as a road accident during those blizzard conditions and the police went along with that. Goodness knows they had enough on their hands at the time. We had a word with the coach company and we invented an extra personal accident insurance policy which paid out to Mrs Fisk. It was the best we could do.'

'I would have liked them to hang for killing the driver,' Amanda said with a cold certainty.

'Does it matter *where* they hang?' said Mr Corkran. 'They are still being put through the mill by our friends in the CIA and I hope we'll get two things out of them about their little invasion of Carterers.'

'Such as where they acquired their guns and flares and equipment,' said Campion.

'Exactly. As far as we can ascertain, they arrived in London and headed straight to Victoria Coach Station, so we're thinking that someone already here had set that up for them and smuggled their gear on to the coach there.'

'And they did seem to know an awful lot about us, or rather Amanda, before they turned up on our doorstep.'

'Yes, they did.' Corkran's eyes flashed to Amanda, then back to Campion. 'You've guessed, haven't you?'

'That there might be a spy, or should that be a mole, inside Alandel?' Campion answered as his wife remained silent with a face of stone.

'I think it is something we should consider as we go forward. Alandel is involved in some sensitive defence work these days.'

'I am sure Amanda will put the matter in hand.'

'I already have,' said Amanda.

Campion poured wine and demanded Lugg put a spring in his step and fetch another bottle of the 'good stuff', which he did with an outrageously theatrical limp.

'All that can wait until after Easter and our great egg hunt tomorrow. Some of our guests will have children with them, so it will probably turn quite feral. I think it only fair to give you, as our most distinguished guest, a bit of an advantage, so here's a tip: head straight for the curved bridge and go over it. The first two apple trees are positively festooned with chocolate eggs. Then, after the party, there will be fireworks!'

Campion sat back in his chair, as though waiting for applause.

'When you're around, Albert, there are always fireworks,' said Mr Corkran.

AUTHOR'S NOTE

I have to thank Fred de Vries and Peter Quinn for permission to take their names in vain. To have such characters named after them seems poor recompense for their loyal support over the years, for which I thank them.

One other name worth an apology is that of Oscar P. Rivero, an American soldier who lost a dog tag near Witham, Essex during World War II, only a few miles from the home of Margery Allingham. It was found (by me) during an archaeological dig in 2002. Apart from the fact that he had been drafted into the US Army in 1943, had a tetanus shot in 1944, was blood group A and a Catholic, I know nothing about him.

The character of the Reverend Breck is based on the village priest of my childhood, who really had served in the Fourteenth Army during the war and did retire to Walsingham. Out of sympathy for his experience with the cowardly officer who later became a film star, in our house the television was quickly switched off when certain British films came on.

Once again, I am in debt to Roger Johnson, not only for his map-making skills, but also his in-depth knowledge of the canon of Albert Campion stories by Margery Allingham. There has always been some debate among Campionologists (a word I have invented, which has nothing to do with bell-ringing) about exactly where the Campion family home was located. Placing it in Norfolk is my responsibility and mine alone.

I have taken enormous liberties with RAF Marham, where security was surely better than I have suggested here, and for details of Thor missiles I have pillaged, almost certainly inaccurately, the paper presented by Wing Commander Colin Cummings at the RAF Historical Society's seminar on *The RAF and Nuclear Weapons 1960–1998*, held at the RAF Museum,

Hendon on 11 April 2001, and reported in *The Journal of the Royal Air Force Historical Society*, number 26.

The UK's 'lousy track record' on security matters (chapter thirteen) was a fair assessment in late 1962, following the exposure of the Portland spy ring and the unmasking of double agent George Blake in 1961, plus the trial of 'honey-trapped' Admiralty clerk John Vassall in October 1962 (the 'Profumo Affair' and the defection to Russia of Kim Philby were to follow in 1963), which was the month that saw the cinema release of the first James Bond film and the publication of Len Deighton's mould-breaking novel *The Ipcress File.*

Miss Pounder's familiarity with firearms and her disparaging of a .25 Beretta for lacking 'stopping power' (chapter nineteen) suggests that she might have read Ian Fleming's *Dr No*, published in 1958.

Undoubtedly Britain's reputation for being a safe pair of hands on security matters was in tatters and may have affected wider political relationships. Strange as it may seem today, Britain was once rather keen to be a part of Europe, and in 1962 was negotiating to become a member of the European Economic Community. The plan was vetoed by General De Gaulle with a resounding '*Non*' in 1963.

Walsingham was, and is, a place of pilgrimage. My mother would organize annual coach trips for the local Mothers' Union to visit the shrine from our West Yorkshire village and over the years amassed quite a collection of bottles of Walsingham holy water.

The Pan-Am trans-Atlantic in-flight magazine, *Clipper*, of July 1962 carried a feature on Walsingham, quoting Erasmus's description of the shrine as 'dimly lit by tapers and scintillating with jewels'.

Margery Allingham, who created Albert Campion in 1929, died in 1966 leaving the novel *Cargo of Eagles* unfinished. It was completed by her husband Pip Youngman Carter, who went on to write two further Campion novels and had started a third when he died in 1969. I completed that novel as *Mr Campion's Farewell* in 2014, and *Mr Campion's Christmas* will be my twelfth and last.

Albert Campion, born in 1900, was one of the few fictional

characters to age with the century and in my stories I have tried to imagine a 'Golden Age' detective still active and avoiding retirement in the Swinging Sixties. Thus my novels have been set in the period 1962 to 1972.

It has been great fun, and a privilege as a lifelong Allingham fan, to write them.

Mike Ripley

Also by T.C. LoTempio

Tiffany Austin Food Blogger Mysteries

EAT, DRINK AND DROP DEAD *
A CRUST TO DIE FOR *

Nick and Nora Mysteries

MEOW IF IT'S MURDER
CLAWS FOR ALARM
CRIME AND CATNIP
HISS H FOR HOMICIDE
MURDER FAUX PAWS
A PURR BEFORE DYING
BELL, BOOK AND CORPSES

Cat Rescue Mysteries

PURR M FOR MURDER
DEATH BY A WHISKER

Urban Tails Pet Shop Mysteries

THE TIME FOR MURDER IS MEOW
KILLERS OF A FEATHER
DEATH STEALS THE SPOTLIGHT
CATS, CARATS AND KILLERS

* *available from Severn House*

MURDER ON THE BOOKS

MURDER ON THE BOOKS

T.C. LoTempio

SEVERN HOUSE

First world edition published in Great Britain and the USA in 2025
by Severn House, an imprint of Canongate Books Ltd,
14 High Street, Edinburgh EH1 1TE.

Paperback edition first published in Great Britain and the USA in 2026
by Severn House, an imprint of Canongate Books Ltd.

severnhouse.com

Cover and jacket design by Piers Tilbury

British Library Cataloguing-in-Publication Data
A CIP catalogue record for this title is available from the British Library.

ISBN-13: 978-1-4483-1526-0 (cased)
ISBN-13: 978-1-4483-1832-2 (paper)
ISBN-13: 978-1-4483-1527-7 (e-book)

All Severn House titles are printed on acid-free paper.

FSC
www.fsc.org
MIX
Paper | Supporting responsible forestry
FSC® C013604

Typeset by Palimpsest Book Production Ltd.,
Falkirk, Stirlingshire, Scotland.
Printed and bound in Great Britain by
CPI Group (UK) Ltd, Croydon CR0 4YY

The manufacturer's authorised representative in the EU for product safety is Authorised Rep Compliance Ltd, 71 Lower Baggot Street, Dublin D02 P593 Ireland (arccompliance.com)

Praise for T.C. LoTempio

"Featuring a plucky, likable heroine, plenty of suspense [and] unexpected twists"
Booklist on *A Crust to Die For*

"Captivating characters and plenty of intrigue . . . Delightful"
Publishers Weekly on *Eat, Drink and Drop Dead*

"This light-hearted series debut has oodles of charm, mouth-watering descriptions of southern cuisine, and a sassy, savvy heroine"
Booklist on *Eat, Drink and Drop Dead*

"It's sure to satisfy fans of Lucy Burdette's 'Key West Food Critic' mysteries"
Library Journal on *Eat, Drink and Drop Dead*

"Easy enough to appeal to a variety of cozy palates"
Kirkus Reviews on *Eat, Drink and Drop Dead*

"An exciting mystery . . . I was hooked from start to finish!"
Laura Childs, *New York Times* bestselling author of the Tea Shop mysteries, on *Eat, Drink and Drop Dead*

"Entertaining . . . Cozy fans will be satisfied"
Publishers Weekly on *The Time for Murder is Meow*

"What more could a cozy mystery reader want?"
Publishers Weekly on *Death by a Whisker*

About the author

T.C. LoTempio is the award-winning, nationally bestselling author of the Nick and Nora Mysteries, the Urban Tails Pet Shop Mysteries, the Cat Rescue Mysteries, the Tiffany Austin Food Blogger Mysteries and the brand-new Cozy Bookshop Mysteries. Born in New York City, she now resides in Phoenix, Arizona with her two cats, Maxx and Rocco. Rocco prides himself on being the inspiration for her Nick and Nora series.

www.tclotempio.net

For Rocco and Maxx – always my inspiration.

Acknowledgments

Many thanks to my agent, Josh Getzler, and his more than able assistant Jon Cobb! Also thanks to Rachel Slatter, Tina Pietron, and the team at Severn House for taking a chance on Charley and company!

As always, I thank all the loyal fans and readers who support this and all of my series. We wouldn't be published without you! And I mean that from the bottom of my heart.

PROLOGUE

From his position on the corner, he watched the woman move through the store, wiping down counters, sweeping, mopping. Her movements were slight, like a dancer's. He felt something stir deep within him.

His throat tightened as he recalled the last time he'd seen her, and what she'd been doing. She'd betrayed him, in the worst way possible.

Now she had to pay.

The hour was late. Tentatively, he descended from the curb on to the empty street. He moved swiftly to the other side on to the wide, clean sidewalk. Above him, a streetlamp flickered, and then went out.

He paused, his breathing ragged. He leaned against the street-lamp. He closed his eyes and thought, in, out. In, out. Slow, deliberate breaths. Finally, his breathing returned to normal. He straightened, headed for the door of the shop. He raised his hand and let his knuckles rap against the door. One knock, then two. He stepped back, folded his arms across his chest and waited.

After a moment he heard slow, measured steps pause behind the door. She opened it a crack and peered out. Surprise registered on her face when she saw him. 'Hey,' she said. Her voice was soft, breathy, like a summer breeze. 'What a nice surprise. I didn't think I'd see you for a while.' Her smile turned coquettish, and her lips turned up in a sly smile. 'I knew you couldn't stay mad at me.'

For a moment he hesitated. She sounded genuinely glad to see him. Had he misjudged her? For a moment he weakened but then resolve washed over him. *She has it coming*, he reminded himself. *She's brought it on herself.*

She stepped back, opened the door wide. 'Come on in. I was just puttering around, making some little touches. The painter finished yesterday, and now I've got to order some furniture. But I'm sure you don't want to hear about *that*,' she added, closing one eye in a broad wink. 'How about I brew some tea. I've got chamomile.'

He nodded and forced a smile. At his side, his fist clenched, and then unclenched.

She motioned for him to follow her. She moved toward the counter and said over her shoulder, 'I'm really glad you stopped by. I got a shipment in today, and I found a few books you might be interested in. Patterson, Cussler, and the latest C.J. Barrett. All your favorites.' She turned to give him a wink over her shoulder. 'I'm giving you first pick. These'll sell like hotcakes.'

With a smile, she disappeared into the back room. He moved around behind the counter; thrust his hand into his jacket pocket. His hand closed around the Swiss Army knife that rested there.

She emerged, two steaming cups in hand. 'Here you go. This will hit the— what on earth?'

Her eyes widened as she caught sight of the knife. He raised the blade high above her, and saw her lower lip start to tremble. She backed away and as she did so, the cups clattered to the floor, sending hot tea and shards of china in all directions. 'What are you doing?' she cried, her voice barely above a whisper. 'Have you gone crazy? Put that down!'

Her hand reached into the pocket of the vest she wore, fumbling for her phone, no doubt. He moved swiftly. His other hand shot out, grabbed her forearm, and twisted it cruelly. She gave a sharp cry and pulled her hand from her pocket. Another twist and her phone dropped from her hand. He moved forward, snatched the phone up, then pinned her against the wall.

'Please,' she whimpered. 'Let's talk about this.'

He shook his head and held the knife aloft. 'The time for talking is over,' he said. 'You have to pay for what you did to me.'

Her jaw dropped. Her eyes popped. 'What are you talking about? What did I do to you?'

He took a step closer. 'I think you know.'

'Didn't we have this discussion? I told you, you're wrong.' Her eyes darted around, looking for an avenue of escape.

There was none.

A feeling of peace and contentment settled over him and he

saw her lip open in a silent scream as he brought the blade down, into her soft white skin, again, and again, and again . . .

The knife dropped from his hand, and he leaned against the wall, spent. He straightened and stood there, looking down at the bloodied body, the shattered teacups. He bent, picked up the knife, and slid it back into his jacket pocket.

Then he walked over to the far corner, grabbed the broom that stood there, and proceeded to clean up the mess.

saw her lip open in a silent scream as he plunged the blade down into her soft white skin again and again and again.

The knife dropped from his hand and he looked around the small room. He was [illegible] and understood [illegible]. Looking down at the bloodied body, he shuddered [illegible]. He bent, picked up the knife and slid it back into his inner pocket.

Then he walked over to the [illegible] and proceeded to clean up the mess.

ONE

'So, let me understand this. For all intents and purposes, C.J. Barrett is going to just vanish off the face of the earth, but Charlotte James is alive and well and living in, oh God – Hooterville?'

I tapped one polished red nail against the steering wheel of my rented SUV. Max's use of my given first name was never a good sign. He'd always called me by my nickname, Charley, for as long as I'd known him. I raised my hand and tapped the Bluetooth speaker in my ear. 'I wouldn't say C.J. is vanishing. Think of it as a brief retirement. And I'm not living in Hooterville. Austin doesn't resemble the town on *Petticoat Junction* at all.'

'It was *Green Acres*.'

'Huh?' I swerved to avoid hitting a rabbit who'd popped up unexpectedly in the road before me. 'Sorry, what did you say?'

'I said, Hooterville was the name of the town in *Green Acres*.' Max's tone had turned sulky, as it always did when he didn't get his own way. If he weren't such a good literary agent, he and I might have parted ways years ago. As it stood now, I owed my successful career as thriller writer C.J. Barrett to him. I'd been fresh out of college, journalism degree in hand, when I'd written my first Steve Sheppard novel. I'd sent out query letters and the first fifty pages to over one hundred agents, and it hadn't been long before the rejection letters started piling in. I was about to give up and concentrate on my job as research assistant for a popular New York magazine when I got an email from one of the top agents on my list, Max Molenaro: *Loving your book. Please send the rest.*

Max had liked the feisty, CIA agent from the get-go and he'd signed me as a client a week after I sent him the completed manuscript. He worked tirelessly with publishers and he'd gotten me my first book contract. More than that, he'd hand-held me through every inch of the daunting process of publishing a first novel. Yes, Max had always been there for me. I certainly couldn't blame him now for feeling that I was deserting him, because in a manner of speaking, I was.

But it couldn't be helped. The malady every professional writer fears had struck me, harder than I'd ever thought possible. Yes, I'm talking about writer's block. After twelve years and fifteen books, eight of which had made the *New York Times* bestseller list, I was burned out. I didn't have another original plot left in me. Every time I turned on my computer and called up Word, I found myself just sitting at my desk, staring at a blank white screen.

I knew that I couldn't go on like this. It was time for C.J. Barrett to take a break, and for Charley James to . . . to do what, exactly? I had no idea.

I cleared my throat. 'Sorry, Max. You're wrong. It was *Petticoat Junction*. I'm positive of it,' I replied. 'I've seen every episode on TV Land.'

'Sorry, you're the one who's wrong. It's *Green Acres*,' Max said stubbornly. 'I've seen every episode of it too, and I can still hear Eva Gabor telling Eddie Albert, "What are we going to do out here in Hooterville?" in that Hungarian accent of hers. New York was where she wanted to be, and it's where you should be too, Charley. It's where all the action is, and you like action. Just what do you envision yourself doing out in the sticks? Milking cows? Churning butter?'

I huffed an auburn curl out of my eyes as I navigated the SUV around another sharp curve. Max had been born and bred in New York City. To him, anywhere with twenty square feet of solid grass qualified as the 'sticks.' 'I'm sorry to disappoint you, Max, but Austin isn't a hick town. It's only fifteen miles from Philadelphia and we have electricity there and everything. And to be perfectly honest, I haven't seen a cow yet.'

'Very funny.' Max paused, and I visualized him shaking his head, rubbing his eyes beneath his wire-rimmed glasses. 'Have I mentioned Parker Press is willing to up your advance for the next Steve Sheppard novel? We're talking a lot of zeroes here, Charley. A lot.'

I exhaled a deep breath, wishing that I could just drive and enjoy the blooming fall foliage and leaves turning color instead of arguing with Max. 'Yes, you mentioned that,' I said. 'And I believe at that time I told you that money had nothing to do with my decision.'

'Oh, I'm sorry, I forgot for a moment you're independently wealthy.'

I bit back a groan. For a moment I was tempted to pull over to the side of the road so I could beat my head against the steering wheel. 'Max . . .'

'Look, if you're tired of writing the Sheppard series, you could start over. A new series with a new protagonist, maybe make him a younger guy? Or even a woman. A new career, maybe. Your hero or heroine doesn't have to be CIA. They could be FBI or better yet, how about MI6?'

I bit the inside of my cheek and counted slowly to ten. 'You're not hearing me, Max. I'm not tired of Steve Sheppard. How could I be? We've been together twelve years, fifteen books. I've had the longest relationship of my life with him – aside from my dentist, and you. What I'm tired of is writing in general.'

'*What*?!' Now Max sounded outraged. 'You're kidding, right? How can you be tired of writing? It's what you do – it's all you do.'

'Precisely my point. It's because it's all I ever do that I'm burned out. Listen to me carefully, Max. Right now I'm not going to write any novel, Steve Sheppard or otherwise. I can't. Try to understand, I've got no more original ideas. I'm tired of staring at a blank computer screen day after day. I need a change of scenery, something to recharge my batteries. I need a break where I'm not sleeping, eating, and breathing plot points that just don't work anymore.'

Dead silence. I hoped that Max was digesting everything I'd just said. Then he spoke, dashing all my hopes. 'OK, so you want a break. Does it have to be so drastic? Why not just take a vacation. Go to Italy or the Caribbean. But to hole yourself up in Hoot—'

I cut him off before he could finish. 'If you say Hooterville again I will hang up on you and never answer any of your calls again. I mean it, Max.'

'OK, OK,' he grumbled. There was a brief silence and for a minute I thought we might have gotten disconnected. Then he said, 'Just how long of a break are we talking about here?'

'I don't know, Max. As long as it takes. It could be a few weeks, a few months.' I paused before delivering the final blow. 'It might even take a year.'

'A year!' I could hear the tinge of panic in his voice. 'It might as well be a lifetime.'

'Relax, Max. Nothing's cast in stone . . . yet.'

'Yeah, well I don't think you've fully thought this little idea of yours out, Charley.' Max's tone had taken on a smug undercurrent, one I'd heard before. It was his cat-ate-the-canary tone, the one he used when closing a difficult deal. 'How are you going to live? You've got to have a way to support yourself, don't you?'

Fortunately, I'd never been much of a spender, and thanks to my ex-boyfriend, a financial counselor, I'd invested the money I'd made from my novels so that I had enough discretionary funds to live comfortably, if not lavishly, for at least eighteen months, maybe more. 'I'll get by,' I told Max. 'If need be, I'll get a job.'

'You'll . . . get . . . a . . . job?' He enunciated each word slowly, as if he were speaking to a three-year-old. 'A job?'

'Yes, a job,' I snapped. 'You know, when you perform a service in exchange for money.'

'Ha, ha. I know what a job is. I'm not sure you do.'

'What's that supposed to mean?' I bristled. His smug tone irritated me. I could just see him making air quotes around the word job.

'Thanks to me, you've been writing ever since you graduated college. It's all you know, except for the eight months you worked at *New York Today* magazine. You haven't just had a job, you've had a career. Big difference.'

'I realize that,' I said stiffly. 'And FYI, I know the difference. I worked part-time jobs while I went to college. I waitressed at a local diner my freshman year, and then in my sophomore year I got a job clerking at a local bookstore.'

'A waitress or a sales clerk?' He let out a snort. 'You'll be bored in a week. Maybe sooner. You've got a quick mind, Charley. You need to be challenged.'

'Maybe so. But right now writing isn't challenging me. It's suffocating me.' In a gentler tone I added, 'My mind's made up, Max. Nothing you can say will change it, believe me.'

More silence and then, 'Fine. I guess all that's left to say is . . . good luck, Charley. You're gonna need it. A lot of it.' He paused. 'And it was *Green Acres*. Look it up.'

He hung up abruptly, and I released the breath I'd been holding. Max was hurt and I couldn't blame him, but at the same time I was also pretty sure I hadn't heard the last from him. Max was even more stubborn than I was. He had made two good points, though. One, I was going to have to find some type of work, and two . . . I was going to need a lot of luck. As for *Green Acres*, well, the jury was still out on that one.

Two hours later I was all checked in at the Austin Inn and walking through the door of the local café. The Jumpin' Beans seemed indeed to be jumping as I pushed through the front door. I paused in the doorway and inhaled deeply, entranced already by the smell of freshly brewed coffee. The room was fairly large, and I noticed that almost every table was filled with people enjoying a cup of joe. The walls were painted a light pink, the same shade as the exterior of the building. A glass case to the left of the counter displayed a small selection of donuts, and a blackboard on the wall right behind it featured a number of breakfast and lunch dishes, along with a few specials. I debated ordering the waffle and egg platter, since all I'd had to eat before I left Manhattan had been a bagel, and a stale one at that.

I got on the end of the line and let my gaze wander over the booths by the large plate-glass window that overlooked the street, then toward the tables in the back of the shop. I frowned. Where was Zane? Was it possible I'd actually gotten to our meeting place first?

'Charley! Over here!'

A purple-clad arm shot up from a table all the way in the rear of the store near the kitchen door and I spotted my friend. She waved madly with her arm while bouncing up and down in her seat. I suppressed a chuckle. That was Zane Adams all right, and she was as she'd always been ever since fifth grade, a whirling dervish of energy and enthusiasm. I waved back to let her know I'd seen her and then eyed the line of coffee carafes behind the counter. I was half tempted to reach over, grab one, and hightail it over to the table, but I figured if I did that, the woman behind the counter would be on me like a duck on a June bug. Best to wait my turn. The line moved forward quickly, and after a brief mental debate I placed my order for a mocha latte and a bear claw.

The woman, whose name tag read Phyllis, moved swiftly behind the counter, and a few minutes later she pushed a brown plastic tray in front of me which held my order. 'Six ninety-five,' she said. She looked me up and down as I fumbled in my bag for the money. 'You're new in town,' she said. 'I know pretty much everyone around here.' She took the bill I handed her. 'Phyllis Wooster.'

'Nice to meet you. I'm Charley James.' At her sharp look I added, 'It's a nickname. For Charlotte.'

Phyllis smiled as she handed me my change. 'Charlotte's cuter. You ought to stick to that. So what brings you to our little town? Are you visiting a friend, or a relative?'

'Neither.' I stuffed a dollar into the tip jar, then picked up the brown tray which held my latte and pastry. 'I'm not really new in town. I grew up here, and now I'm moving back. Maybe you remember my parents? They lived here all their lives, only moved a year ago. Paul and Maureen James.'

Her eyes lit with recognition. 'Oh, sure, I remember them. Paul James owned the hardware store, right? And he did some glassblowing on the side. Very talented. I have a few of his pieces. And your mother worked for City Sewing. She was handy with a needle. I think I still have a few of her embroidered towels. After your daddy sold the business they moved to Florida, right?'

'Arizona. They got tired of the cold winters and wanted somewhere warm that wasn't too humid.'

'Can't blame them. Winters can be brutal here. So, how come you didn't go out west, move near them?'

I chuckled. 'I thought about it, but I'm a four-season gal. Call me crazy, but I actually like the winter weather. And turtlenecks, and down coats.'

She grinned at me. 'Remember that when the snow is four feet high and your driveway is blocked in.' She leaned across the counter and said in a low tone, 'Listen, honey. You've been away awhile, so if you need any info on any of the locals, you just stop by and ask me. I'll give you the real skinny.' She closed one eye in a wink. 'Count on it.'

'I may just do that, thanks.' I cast a quick glance over my shoulder and saw the line now stretched almost to the door. 'I'd better get going.'

Still smiling at her, I tried to edge around a chair that was blocking the aisle and accidentally kicked another customer's expensive-looking leather messenger bag. A dark-haired man glared up at me from his seat. 'Hey, watch it,' he said. He reached down and snatched up the briefcase, clutched it to his chest. He shot me another dark look. 'Clumsy,' he muttered under his breath as he shoved the briefcase under his chair. He didn't deign to give me another look, instead turning his attention to the ten-inch tablet that lay on the table.

'Sorry,' I muttered. The man shifted his position so that his back faced me and continued shoveling food into his mouth, eyes glued to the tablet screen. He'd ordered the waffle egg platter and I had to admit it looked good, especially since it was covered with my favorite: hollandaise sauce. I felt my mouth watering. Maybe I should have ordered that. The man must have sensed me ogling his platter, because his head jerked up in my direction and his lips curved downward. Eyes the color of a storm-tossed sea bored into mine. 'Can I help you?' he asked.

Surprised, I took a step backward. 'No. It's just . . . I'm so sorry I stepped on your bag. It was an accident.'

'Sure,' he muttered, and turned his attention back to his tablet. I took a minute to study him. He didn't appear to be much older than me, and he really wasn't bad-looking either. His thick dark hair framed a face with a strong chin with a slight dent in it. His complexion was tan, his cheekbones high, and he filled out the cream-colored shirt and denim jacket he wore nicely. The only thing that kept him from being drop-dead handsome was the slight bump on his nose, as if it might have been broken at one time. And, of course, there was the perpetual frown and the stick up his butt which didn't help either.

'Your breakfast looks yummy,' I heard myself say. When he stared at me blankly, I pointed to his plate. 'That. It looks delicious,' I amended, just in case he had no idea what yummy might mean.

'Oh.' He glanced at the half-eaten food, then shrugged. 'It was adequate,' he said.

I stared at him. 'Adequate?' I repeated, not certain I'd heard correctly. How could something that smelled so good just be adequate?

His shaggy brows arched. 'Passable. As breakfast food goes, it's tolerable.' With that clarification, he turned his attention back to his tablet and I stood there awkwardly for a minute, unsure if I should say anything else.

'Charley!' Zane, her tone edged with impatience, half rose from her seat and made a wild, waving gesture at me. I turned away from the man and moved on. After skirting a group of teenagers in denim jackets and distressed jeans, I finally reached Zane's table. My friend looked up at me with a grin, and I couldn't help but think how true that old adage was about opposites attracting. Zane and I were as different in both looks and personality as you could get. I'd always been more serious, laid back, with a wild mane of untamed auburn curls, grass-green eyes, and creamy, freckled skin that belied my English–Irish heritage. Zane on the other hand, had always leaned toward being impulsive, and with her clear mocha skin, large brown eyes, and cap of short, springy black curls, could easily have become a top model. Now she slanted a glance toward the man's table. 'What's up with Mr Charm over there? Someone should tell him to drop the scowl, or his face might freeze that way.'

'I accidentally kicked his briefcase,' I said, easing into the chair opposite my friend. 'I tried to compliment his breakfast, and nearly got my head bitten off.'

Zane took a bite of her blueberry muffin and set it back on her plate. 'It sounds to me as if he's got a case of no personality.'

'Oh, he's got personality,' I answered. I slid another glance the stranger's way. 'He's got a rotten one, which is a shame, because he's actually rather good-looking, scowl and all.'

Zane brushed some crumbs from her blouse and shot me a slow smile. 'The fact that you can notice that about a man so soon after your breakup is a very good sign,' she said.

I picked up my latte, took a sip, and set the mug down again. 'I don't want to think about Henry,' I said. 'As a matter of fact,

I don't want to dwell on my old life. Not when I've got a brand new one stretching out in front of me.'

Zane shook her curly head. 'I've got to hand it to you, Charley. You've got a lot of guts, to pull up stakes like that and start all over. Giving up a successful writing career to move back to the old hometown. I wish I had your kind of courage.'

I curled my fingers around the mug. 'I'm glad you think I'm courageous. Max thinks I'm pretty stupid.'

'Your agent?' Zane waved her hand. 'Typical man. He just doesn't understand. Plus, he's probably thinking about all those commissions he'll be losing now that C.J. Barrett is retired.'

'Semi-retired,' I corrected. 'I'm not giving up writing, I just need a break.' I gave a quick glance around the café. 'Remember, I'm just Charley James from now on. I don't want anyone knowing I'm also C.J. Barrett. I'm just on a temporary break to get my mojo back. I don't need people quizzing me about Steve Sheppard or speculating about what I might be doing here.'

'You mean like scoping out possible characters for your next novel? If that's the case, you're in luck. There are plenty of characters right here in Austin.' I shot her a stern look, and she grinned and put a finger against her lips, then made a motion of zipping them. 'Don't worry, mum's the word,' she said. 'I'm just glad you plan to keep on writing, eventually. I love those books!'

'Thanks for those kind words, friend.' I leaned back in the chair and stretched my legs out to the side. 'So, tell me, what's the latest on that business you plan on opening?'

Zane leaned back in her seat too. Her fingers toyed with the edge of her napkin. 'Yeah. About that . . . not so good.'

I frowned. 'What happened? Don't tell me you changed your mind and decided to stay on at the bakery?' Zane was an excellent baker. She'd graduated San Francisco Cooking School, and after working at several upscale bakeries in California had returned home to care for her sick father. When he'd passed last year she'd decided to stay in Austin and got a job as head baker at Frederick's Bakery in Clarkville, a few towns over. The last time we'd spoken, though, she'd been all excited about the possibility of opening her own bakery-slash-café right here in Austin.

Zane shook her head. 'Oh no. I still want to open my own business, especially since Mr Frederick is still planning to retire next year. God knows who would get his business. His son has zero interest in it. That's the main reason I decided it was time to strike out on my own, but it seems my plans have hit a rather unfortunate snag.'

I took a sip of my latte. It was delicious. 'What sort of snag?'

Zane picked up a spoon, tapped it against her coffee cup. 'It seems that Sheila – the girl I was supposed to go partners with, Sheila Crowder – well, she took a powder.' The bitterness in her tone was unmistakable. 'She left me a note stuffed in my mailbox yesterday, saying that something unexpected in her life came up and she had to leave town. She was sorry for any inconvenience her leaving so suddenly might cause me.' Zane let out a bitter laugh. 'Inconvenience? Was she kidding? She up and takes off six weeks before we're set to open, and she's sorry.'

I didn't know much about Sheila, other than she and Zane had met a year ago when Sheila had moved to Austin and they'd hit it off immediately. Knowing how picky Zane could be about relationships, I'd figured that Sheila must have been pretty special. Now I reached across the table and grabbed Zane's hand. 'Oh, Zane. I am so sorry. I know how you must be hurting.'

'Yeah, well, I guess that'll teach me to open up so quickly to a virtual stranger. Funny thing, though – Sheila and I, we clicked right away. We had so much in common – or so I thought.' She blew out a sigh. 'Guess I'm not such a hot judge of character after all.'

'I wouldn't say that,' I replied. 'We're all entitled to a mistake in judgment occasionally. Lord knows I've made enough of them.'

'Making them with men doesn't count,' said Zane. 'Everyone knows what complex creatures they are.'

'No argument there. So what are you going to do about the store?'

She leaned across the table, cupped her chin in her palm. 'Dunno. The landlord – Otto Krebs – was thrilled to rent it to us, and I've got a feeling it won't be easy to get out of the lease. At least, not without paying a stiff penalty, which I really can't afford right now.' She gave her head a brisk shake. 'I tell you,

I'm sick of it. We already had the rooms painted and were supposed to set up a meeting with the electrician for the light installations this week, start getting ready for a grand opening for the first week in October but now . . .' Her voice trailed off, ended in a long sigh. 'That's not happening.'

I reached across the table, grabbed her hand and gave it a squeeze. 'What a shame.'

'Sure is.' She slanted me a glance. 'You would have loved it, Charley. She was going to call it Mainly Mysteries. She was going to specialize in mysteries and thrillers. Oh, it seemed perfect,' Zane said with a sigh. 'There's no bookstore in this town. The only thing that passes for one is the rack near the counter at the Emporium, and those are mostly outdated paperbacks. Edna Scribner says mysteries are always the first books checked out at the library. And . . .' Zane lowered her voice as she added, 'I happen to know Sheila had a whole case of C.J. Barrett books delivered. Number one right up to your latest.'

'She did?' I couldn't hide a pleased smile.

'Yeah. Too bad they won't get sold now. I bet they would have gone like that!' Zane snapped her fingers in the air. 'I suppose I should return her stock, but I haven't the faintest idea how to go about it.' She shot me a hopeful look. 'Do you know, Charley? Could you help me with it?' She leaned over and waved her hand in front of my eyes. 'Hello. Earth to Charley. Did you hear me?'

'Huh, oh, yes. I heard you. I was just thinking.' I leaned forward. 'What about trying to find someone else who might want to partner with you, maybe take over the bookstore?'

'Hm. Well, I don't know about that,' said Zane. 'I mean, a business partnership is like a marriage. After this experience it would have to be someone I really, really trusted, and that leaves out the majority of people.'

I leaned forward and turned my index finger inward toward my chest. 'What about me? You really, really trust me, don't you?'

Zane's jaw dropped. 'You! You'd want to do something like this?'

'Why not? It's not as if I'm not familiar with the concept.

Lord knows I've been in a ton of bookstores over the past twelve years. I've gotten friendly with a lot of booksellers. I know how the business works. Plus, let's not forget my years clerking at Blackmoore Books when I was in college. I've ordered many books in my day. Sent 'em back, too.' I let out a soft chuckle. 'And Max was right about one thing: I'm going to need a job, a source of income. My savings are pretty substantial, thanks to Henry, but I don't want to drain them.'

Zane's eyes sparkled. 'Oh, Charley! That would be marvelous! The best part is, you wouldn't have to put out a dime initially. Sheila was a pretty frugal person. She told me she cut back on a lot so she could pay off her stock and rent for the first three months.'

I paused. 'What if Sheila should come back? She could, you know.'

Zane's lips tightened. 'Then she's out of luck. Anyway, it didn't seem from her note that she'd be returning, at least not any time soon. She said she was officially giving up her half, and that's good enough for me. We never did get around to drawing up a formal partnership agreement, so she wouldn't have a leg to stand on. She's not coming back,' Zane said with an air of finality. She tapped at her midsection. 'I feel it in my gut.'

'OK, then,' I said. 'How about we do this? I'll run the bookstore on trial for six months. If it's successful at the end of that time, then you and I can have a formal partnership agreement drawn up.'

'Sounds perfect,' Zane said. Her face split in a wide grin. 'It does seem like fate, doesn't it? You giving up your career at this particular time and coming back here, just when I need you the most. Now, you're sure you want to do this?'

I met her gaze. 'Yes, Zane. I really, really do.'

'Well, then, let's you and I go have a look at the store!' Zane hopped up from her chair and grabbed her jacket. She kept hopping as she shrugged her arms into it, then tugged at my arm impatiently. 'Come on!'

'OK, OK.' I started to laugh. I couldn't help it. Zane's enthusiasm was contagious. 'I'm coming.'

As I rose I stole a glance over at the man whose bag I'd kicked. His head was down and he was still looking at his tablet. As I started to push in my chair, he raised his head and for a brief minute, our eyes locked. I felt a little chill run down my spine before he tore his gaze away from mine and went back to his tablet.

I bowed my head and studiously avoided his table as I followed Zane out of the coffee shop.

TWO

Ten minutes later, I found myself standing in front of a worn-looking brick storefront. Zane fished around in her voluminous tote bag and finally produced a ring of keys. 'There are some built-in glass cases and shelves already in your half,' she said as she fumbled with the lock. 'I hope you like dove gray. That's what Sheila painted the interior.' Zane poked at the key again. 'Sorry, this could take a while. The lock to the bookstore is a bit tricky,' she added apologetically. 'The back door is too, and the service entrance in the basement. They need new locks, I just haven't gotten around to it yet.'

'Let me try.' I moved forward and took the key from Zane's hand. I slid it in the lock and turned. The key didn't move. 'I see what you mean,' I said. I pulled the doorknob toward me and then turned the key. The lock clunked and released.

'Wow,' Zane cried. 'How'd you do that?'

'A trick my dad taught me,' I said. 'I've used it in my books a few times.' I shoved the door forward and stepped over the threshold.

'The light switch should be on this wall – here it is,' Zane announced. She flipped the switch and the room was filled with harsh fluorescent light from the lighting fixture overhead. I took a quick look around. Sheila had been busy. The store had indeed been freshly painted, the hardwood floor polished. Several glass cases were scattered through the store, and there were several rows of tall, deep shelves, perfect for storing books.

I glanced around. 'You said that Sheila ordered books? Where are they?'

'I helped her carry some boxes down to the basement, and I think she mentioned she had some boxes in the back room,' replied Zane. She pointed to two doors at the far end of the store. 'The one on the left leads to the basement, and the one on the right opens into the bakery. I'm not sure where the back room is here.'

I walked over to the far wall and raised the window shade. Bright sunshine immediately radiated through the floor-to-ceiling windows, making dust motes fly around like airplanes. The room was actually pretty cheerful. 'Nice view of the main street,' I observed. 'The location is actually pretty prime.' I walked over to one of the painted walls, ran my palm along it. 'Nice paint job,' I commented. I tipped my head to study the ceiling, then pointed upward. 'Sheila missed the ceiling. It could use a coat of fresh paint. That lighting fixture will have to be replaced with something softer, too. Maybe some schoolhouse globes on bronze rods?' I pointed to some wires jutting out from the end of the fixture. 'Those will probably have to be replaced. Do you know if she ordered any furniture?'

Zane's lips puckered. 'Not sure. She didn't say.'

I waved my arm at a wide space situated in-between two rows of shelving. 'This area would be perfect for a small reading nook. A large, comfy chair with an ottoman – two maybe – and small tables with lamps. Books can be stacked on the tables. Do you know if she ordered any children's books?'

'Some Nancy Drew and Hardy Boys, I think. I saw those familiar yellow and blue spines in one of the boxes we took downstairs.'

'Hm. I could expand on that, put a children's mystery section over here,' I gestured with my hand. I gazed around the room, trying to imagine it fully furnished and full of inventory. 'The checkout area could go there.' I pointed toward an attractive antique counter that stood near a curtained portion of the back wall. 'And maybe two chairs and a table over on the other side of that archway for another reading nook. Not too many nooks, though,' I added quickly. 'I want people to buy the books, not treat this as a lending library.'

'Maybe you could put a small table in the window,' suggested Zane. 'Pile it with books. Maybe even have a basket overturned beside it with books tumbling out of it.'

'That's a good idea.' I tapped at my chin. 'We'll need a sign,' I said. 'Nothing too fancy.'

'Sheila was supposed to have taken care of that,' remarked Zane. 'Now I wonder if she ever got around to it. I'd better call Jon Landry over at Custom Signs and find out.'

The fluorescent light above us winked. 'You mentioned an electrician?' I asked. 'I want to be sure there's no short in the electric system here.'

'There's a good local one.' Zane's eyes twinkled as she added, 'Jeff Connors. Remember him?'

I felt color rise to my cheeks. 'So he went into the family business. Is he as good-looking now as he was in high school?'

'Better.' Zane's eyes danced with mischief. 'Better looking than when he took you to the junior prom, too. Even Sheila said he was a hunk.'

I swallowed, tamping down the memory of me in my pink silk full-skirted evening gown and Jeff in his white tux, corsage in hand. 'Then by all means, let's call him.'

Zane chuckled. 'I'll put in a call to him this afternoon, and to Glenn Chesney too. He's a locksmith, and he's very good – and reasonable with pricing.'

'Fine.' I walked over to the curtained area just to the left of the antique counter and parted the curtain, peered inside. 'I think I've found the storage area. Complete with hot plate, too.'

'I should have known she'd have a hot plate tucked away somewhere. Sheila always did like to have a cup of tea at the ready,' Zane said. 'She used to carry a box of tea in her tote. She never liked to be without it.' She walked over and we both entered the small room. There were several brown packing boxes stacked in one corner, one on top of the other, and a small table on which rested a hot plate, three cups, and a box of herbal tea. I glanced at the box. Chamomile. My favorite. I picked it up and looked inside. The box was pretty full. There were only two bags of tea missing. I set the box back on the table. 'Curious,' I said.

Zane had opened one of the boxes and turned to me, a book in each hand. 'I think we've found some of her inventory,' she remarked, then frowned. 'What's curious?'

'That box of tea. It's practically full. I just think it's odd for someone who carried tea around in her purse to leave an almost full box of tea in a place she wasn't planning on returning to.'

Zane shook her head. 'That's the mystery writer in you coming out,' she remarked. 'Her note said something came up unexpectedly. She was probably in so much of a hurry she never gave a thought about the tea.'

'Maybe,' I murmured. I gestured toward the books Zane held. 'What have you got there?'

She waved the books under my nose. 'The latest James Patterson, and Clive Cussler. Don't worry, I'm sure yours are here somewhere.'

'I'm not worried.' I ran my finger along the hot plate, paused as I noticed a piece of paper sticking out from under it. I reached over and pulled it out. I looked at the paper then turned to Zane. 'Who's Mara?'

Zane frowned. 'I have no idea. Why?'

'This paper. It says *Call Mara*. No phone number.'

Still holding the books, Zane walked over and peered at the paper over my shoulder. 'That's Sheila's handwriting,' she said. 'I guess she knew someone named Mara. The name's not familiar to me.'

I turned the paper over. 'It looks like she wrote something else on here, but then erased it,' I said. I squinted at it. 'Did a pretty good job of it, too.'

I started to put the paper back, then paused and slid it into my pants pocket instead. I looked over at Zane, who had gone back to the box and was rummaging through it. 'How's your half of this enterprise coming along?'

Zane beamed and pushed the books she'd removed off to the side. 'I thought you'd never ask. Come, I'll show you.'

We exited the storeroom and went over to the door that led into the bakery. I saw at once that Zane had put a great deal of work into the shop, more so than Sheila had. Light radiated through the floor-to-ceiling windows, illuminating the fresh paint job on the walls. Zane had painted the walls a soft yellow, and they seemed to virtually glow. She'd furnished the interior with half a dozen oak glass-topped tables and matching oak chairs. There was a large glass case in the center of the room that looked as if it could easily hold a large quantity of pastry, and the faux-marble counter stretched the length of the wall. Zane had placed several stools there for counter service as well as table service.

'I want to have a bud vase with a single carnation on each table,' said Zane. 'I haven't yet decided if I'll have tablecloths or not.'

I shook my head. 'I wouldn't. The glass tabletops are so nice, why cover them?'

'Yeah, I got a real good price on them. There's a secondhand store over in Posey and the owner found them for me. Say, I bet he could get you some chairs and tables for the bookstore real cheap, too.'

'I'll have to check him out,' I said. 'But first things first. I need an electrician and a locksmith before I worry about décor.'

'I'll get right on that, especially if we want to keep that October opening date.' She grasped both my hands. 'We can do this, right? We're going to do this.'

'Yes, we are – what on earth was that?'

We both paused as a loud yowl reached our ears. 'It sounds like someone in pain,' I remarked.

'It came from the back alley.' Zane had turned on her heel and was halfway toward the back door. I followed. We pushed through out into a small, narrow alleyway. A large dumpster sat at the end, across from the service entrance door. Seated on top of it was a large black cat. As we stared at the cat, he opened his mouth and let out another loud yowl.

'Well, we've found the source of the noise,' I remarked. I moved closer to the dumpster and peered up at the cat. The cat stared right back at me. 'He doesn't appear to be in pain, or ill.'

'Yowling for attention, most likely. I remember Otto mentioning there was a stray cat that hung around back here,' Zane murmured. She cast a doubtful look at the cat. 'He didn't say it was a black cat, though. Aren't they bad luck?'

'Not always,' I said. 'In lots of places black cats are regarded as symbols of good luck. They've just gotten a bad rep over the years. Black cats were actually considered sacred in Celtic mythology. Anyway he's not totally black.' I pointed at the animal. 'He's got a spot of white on his nose, and I think I see some under his chin.'

The cat rose from his position on the dumpster, stretched, and then hopped down gracefully. He sauntered over to us and positioned himself between us, then sat back on his haunches, head cocked to one side.

'He looks like he's studying us,' whispered Zane.

'Maybe he is,' I whispered back. 'After all, we are infringing on his territory.'

The cat straightened, walked over to me, and wound his furry body around my ankles. He looked up at me, golden eyes meeting green, and meowed.

Zane giggled. 'I think he likes you.'

I bent down and stroked the cat on his head. He let out a loud purr. 'Believe it or not, I always wanted to get a cat or a dog, but Henry wouldn't hear of it. He said Manhattan was no place for a pet.'

'Well, Henry's not here now,' said Zane. She peered at me. 'You've got that look in your eyes, Charley. You want to adopt him, don't you?'

My fingers lingered over the cat's soft fur. 'I'd like to. But I haven't gotten a place of my own yet, and I don't think pets are allowed at the Austin Inn.'

'They aren't, but . . .' Zane paused, her cheeks starting to flush a delicate shade of pink. That always happened when she was embarrassed. 'I meant to make this offer sooner, but what with everything that's been happening . . . heck, Charley.' She kicked at the ground with the toe of her boot. 'You don't have to stay at the inn. That could turn out to be pretty expensive, especially if you don't find an apartment right away. Why not stay with me?'

I stared at her. 'Are you sure?'

'Yep. I'm in that big house all by myself, and there are two extra bedrooms. You can have your pick. It's no trouble. Besides, I'd relish the company.' She looked over at the cat. 'He can come too. He can earn his keep by catching some mice. I've trapped three so far this month.'

The cat raised his paw, displaying razor-sharp claws. 'I think he understands you,' I remarked. 'He looks like he'd be a good mouser. He might come in handy keeping mice away from our store, too. And what self-respecting bookstore doesn't have a cat for a mascot?'

Zane's lips twitched. 'Are you trying to convince me or you?'

'Both,' I laughed. I looked at the cat. 'He needs a name. We can't call him cat. If he's to be the mascot of a mystery bookstore then he deserves a name worthy of such.'

'How about Steve, after your character Steve Sheppard,' suggested Zane.

I threw up both hands. 'Heaven forbid. I said a worthy name.' I bent down and gave the cat another pat on the head. 'How about the father of the detective story? Edgar Allan Poe?'

The cat sat back on his haunches, let out a sharp meow.

'I think he likes that,' said Zane. 'But that's a mouthful. Why not just call him Edgar?'

The cat narrowed his eyes and let out another loud hiss.

I bent over him and whispered, 'I agree. You're not an Edgar. You're more of a . . . a Poe.'

The cat seemed to preen at that. He leaned into me, and his pink tongue darted out, licked the back of my hand.

I laughed. 'OK, then, Poe it is. Come on . . . I've got to make a stop at the pet store and get you some things, and then cancel my reservation at the Austin Inn.'

Zane turned to lead the way back inside. 'I'll go over to the locksmith and get a house key made for you. I'll make an appointment to get the store locks fixed too.'

I rubbed my hands together. 'Things are starting to really take shape, now.' I grinned at Zane. 'Say, Zane – ever watch *Green Acres*?'

The manager of the Austin Inn didn't give me too much trouble when I informed him that I needed to cancel my week-long reservation. They were hosting a wedding on Saturday and apparently some members of the wedding party wanted to arrive early, so my vacating the suite was a plus for them. My realtor sounded a bit relieved when I told her that there wasn't a big rush to find an apartment. She had a house and two condo deals she was working on, and I had the feeling she would rather concentrate on what paid her the higher commission right now, which was just fine with me.

I put Poe in the back seat of the SUV and headed over to the Pet Palace over on Main Street, where I picked up the necessities: litter box, cat food, and a few toys. I also purchased a cat bed with a soft Sherpa lining. Then I drove over to Zane's house, a two-story brick colonial located a short walk from the center of town and our storefront. Zane jumped up from the porch swing when I pulled into the driveway. Poe and I exited the SUV, and she leaned over the railing, waving a key in the air.

'Got a locksmith appointment for tomorrow morning at nine. And Jeff Connors will be by at nine thirty,' she added with a wide grin.

'Excellent,' I said, ignoring the fluttering in my chest at the mention of Jeff's name. 'I guess we should get to the store early, maybe quarter of?'

'You mean you'd better get there,' said Zane. 'I'm still a working gal. My last day at the bakery isn't for another three weeks. I've got to be there bright-eyed and bushy-tailed by five a.m.'

'Then I'd better get my alarm clock all set up,' I said with a laugh.

Zane helped me bring in my suitcase and the boxes that held my computer and work materials. We went up to the second floor, and she tapped on the first door on the left. 'I thought this might work for your room. It's bigger than the other one,' she announced as she swung the door open.

I was pleasantly surprised. Although not as opulent as the suite I'd have had at the Austin Inn, the room was large and airy and painted a delicate shade of pink. The bed was full size with what looked like a comfy mattress. A large chest of drawers and a large closet occupied one corner, and in another there sat a desk large enough to accommodate my laptop and writing materials, should I choose to use them. A small end table was on one side of the bed, and there was another stand positioned in front of the bed on which sat a thirty-two-inch flat-screen TV.

'See,' Zane said with a sweep of her arm. 'All the comforts of home.'

I went over and tested out the mattress. It was comfortable, not too firm but not too soft. I nodded toward the TV. 'Cable?'

'But of course. Only the best for my guests.' Zane looked over at Poe. The cat had wandered around the room, sniffing here and there. Now he lofted himself up on to the bed beside me and rubbed his portly body against my arm. 'I imagine he'll sleep in here with you?'

'Yes. I even bought him his own bed.'

Poe lifted his head and began to purr.

'Agreeable, isn't he,' chuckled Zane. She bent over and gave Poe a scratch behind one ear. 'I'm looking forward to seeing you catch your first mouse, my friend.'

At the word mouse Poe's ears flicked forward, and he made a little rumbling noise deep in his throat.

'I think he's looking forward to that as well,' I remarked.

Zane laughed. 'I'll leave you two to get settled in. Unfortunately it's got to be an early night for me, so how does pizza for dinner sound?'

'Fabulous,' I said and Poe gave a sharp meow.

Zane left and I rose from the bed. I went and picked up my suitcase, set it in front of the bed, and snapped it open. Poe stretched out on the far end of the bed and lay, paws tucked under him, watching me as I unpacked. After I'd filled half the drawers in the chest and hung up my clothes in the good-sized closet, I opened one of the boxes and pulled out my clock radio. I set it down on the end table, then pulled out my phone, called up Wikipedia. A few minutes later I shot a quick text off to Max. We were both right. Hooterville was the setting for both *Petticoat Junction* and *Green Acres*.

Poe had ambled over to me and now looked at me quizzically. I ruffled his fur. 'Long story,' I said. After a minute, I added a line that I knew would surely get under Max's skin: *Petticoat Junction* came first.

I set the phone down and grinned at the cat. 'I've got to get my little pleasures in where I can,' I said.

Poe lifted one paw, began to wash his face.

'I wish you could talk,' I said to the cat. 'I bet you'd have plenty to say about Sheila, and why she left.'

The cat's eyes narrowed. Then he let out a sharp meow.

I nodded. 'Yes, I'm quite sure there's more to the story. I'm not buying this whole had-to-leave-abruptly scenario. Something just doesn't smell right.'

Poe laid his head on top of his paws, blinked his eyes.

'Then again, I could be making too much out of it. Writer's imagination and all that. But somehow I don't think so.' I let out a sigh. 'Oh well, it's really none of my concern. It's just that it's a puzzle, you see. And I love to solve puzzles. That's why I became a mystery writer, you know.'

Poe blinked at me again, then rose to a sitting position. He lifted his paw, pointed at the clock.

'Good idea,' I said. 'I'll set the alarm for six and have breakfast at Jumpin' Beans. Phyllis Wooster said if I had any questions about the locals she'd fill me in, right? So let's see what, if anything, she's got to say about Sheila Crowder.'

THREE

I was awakened from my sound sleep by a rough tongue caressing my skin. I winked one eye open and found Poe sprawled across my chest. I winked the other eye open and eyed my alarm clock, then sat up so abruptly I startled the cat, who slid to the end of the coverlet. The clock read almost seven thirty. I was certain I'd set it before I tumbled into bed, but the alarm had failed to go off. I'd have to check that out later. I threw back the covers, slid my feet into my slippers, and reached for my robe. 'This will be the quickest shower ever,' I called over my shoulder as I headed for the bathroom. 'Be ready to go in fifteen minutes.'

Poe let out a yowl, then burrowed back under the covers.

Twenty minutes later Poe and I were off. Fortunately I managed to find a parking space in front of Jumpin' Beans, which gave me just under an hour to not only eat a quick breakfast, but pick Phyllis's brain. I wasn't sure of the coffee shop's policy toward animals, so I left Poe in the back seat with a few treats and a catnip mouse to keep him company. He gave me a baleful stare when I wiggled my fingers at him and then turned to enter the shop, but I figured he'd get over it.

There were only a few people seated in the café when I entered. Phyllis was indeed behind the counter, and thankfully there was no line. I walked right up to the counter and gave her a wide smile. 'Hi there. Remember me?'

Phyllis tapped her finger against her chin, eyes twinkling. 'Let me see now . . . oh, yes. You're Charlotte, the girl who prefers to be called Charley. What can I get for you this morning?'

'I'll take a large coffee, milk and sugar, and one of those waffle and egg specials,' I said. 'And if you've got the time, maybe a little information too?'

Phyllis's eyebrow rose and I was certain I saw her eyes gleam when I said the word 'information.' I was pretty sure that to Phyllis, information equated to gossip. 'Why don't you have a seat right there and I'll be with you in a few minutes.' She pointed to a table set in the back corner, near a door I was pretty sure led to the kitchen. I nodded and went over to the table.

I'd only been seated a few minutes when Phyllis appeared, carrying a large mug of steaming coffee which she set in front of me. Then she pulled out the chair directly across from mine and eased into it.

'Unfortunately I haven't got much time,' she said. 'In about ten minutes my regulars will start pouring in. So, what sort of information are you looking for? Recommendations on good restaurants? The best place to grocery shop? What stores have the best sales?'

I took a sip of the coffee, which was just as strong and delicious as it had been yesterday. I leaned back in the chair. 'I imagine you heard about my friend Zane Adams opening a bakery?'

'I did. I was looking forward to it too. We could use a decent bakery around here, and I would have definitely ordered from her.' She sighed. 'I guess that's out now, since her partner took a hike.'

'So you've heard about that?'

Phyllis chuckled. 'News gets around fast in a small town.'

'I can see that.' I took another sip of the coffee and thought again how frightfully good it was. 'Did you know Zane's ex-partner?'

'Sheila Crowder?' Phyllis's nose wrinkled. 'As good as anyone, I suppose. She came in here for breakfast two, three times a week. And by breakfast I mean three cups of coffee. I didn't have much interaction with her. She wasn't the overly chatty sort, from what I could see.' She shot me a sly grin. 'At least, not with women.'

'So she had a boyfriend?'

Phyllis hesitated, then said, 'I'm not certain there was one special fellow. She liked to flirt. But I guess it was understandable. She was a pretty woman. She had one of those smiles, you know, like that actress, Julia Roberts.'

I pulled the slip of paper from my pocket and laid it on the table. 'I found this in the store yesterday. Do you know anyone named Mara?'

Phyllis's brows drew together, cutting a deep V in the center of her forehead. 'I know Marilyn Cutter. She likes to be called Mara, like you like to be called Charley. Works over at the Clip N Curl.'

'I'm assuming that's a beauty parlor?'

'You guessed it.' Phyllis leaned in closer to me and said, 'Getting back to Sheila – it doesn't surprise me that girl took off in a hurry. The last few times she was in here she seemed nervous about something. I tried asking her what was wrong, and she basically told me to mind my own business. But it seemed to me like she was trying to avoid someone.'

'Avoid someone? Like who?'

Phyllis shrugged. 'Who knows? Maybe she had a fight with a guy, or something. It was pretty evident she didn't want to talk about it, at least not with me.'

My finger tapped idly at the paper on the table. People sometimes confided in their hairdressers. If this Mara had been Sheila's, might she have confided something to her? I let my mystery writer's imagination take over. Maybe she was being pursued by an abusive ex. Or maybe it was something else? I thought again about that box of tea . . .

I started as I realized Phyllis had been speaking to me. 'I'm sorry,' I apologized. 'What did you say?'

'I was wondering. You said you moved back here. Where were you living?'

I should have figured it was only a matter of time before a first-class gossip like Phyllis started trolling for information. I took another quick sip of coffee. Well, quid pro quo, right? If I wanted information, I had to be prepared to give out some. 'New York.'

Her eyebrows rose. 'City? And you left there for here?' Her tone indicated she considered such a thing to be plumb crazy. 'So what did you do in the big city?'

I shifted in my chair. 'I . . . ah . . . worked at a magazine as a research assistant.' I reached up, touched the tip of my nose. Good, it hadn't grown after that little white lie. And I had worked at *New York Today*, only it was fifteen years ago and for only eight months before I'd gotten my first book contract.

'Research assistant?' Phyllis gave a little yelp. 'That sounds as if it might bore you to death.'

'You're right, it was boring at times. So I decided to chuck it and take a risk.' I paused. 'Actually, yesterday I took a big one. I decided to take Sheila's part of the store and open up the bookstore.'

Phyllis's eyes popped. 'You did! Well, that is quite a risk these days, opening up your own business.' She gave a self-conscious laugh. 'I should know.'

'True, but I've always loved books and reading. And as you know, Zane was in a bit of a bind. She didn't think her landlord would let her out of the lease.'

Phyllis clucked her tongue. 'Old man Krebs probably wouldn't have. In his defense, though, he's been trying to rent that property ever since Mamie Fitch left town. That was the woman who rented that property before your friend. She and her sister had a crystal shop and a tea room. They did OK, but then the sister took ill, so that was the end of that. And renting a double storefront is no easy feat around here.' She smoothed out her apron. 'When do you girls plan to open your stores?'

'We're shooting for the first week in October.'

'Good timing. Maybe I'll pay you a visit. I have a lot of relatives who are voracious readers. Actually, a bookstore is just what this town needs. The library's way too small, and the good books are always gone.' She grinned. 'As for the bakery, tell your friend I'll be happy to place the first order. The one I'm using now just changed bakers, and just between us, their goods aren't that great.' She shook her head. 'Hard to imagine they can ruin a plain donut but . . . they can.'

'I'll definitely tell her.' I paused and then asked, 'You wouldn't happen to know if the former tenant had a pet? A cat, perhaps?'

Phyllis shook her head. 'Not that I know of. Why?'

'We found one in the alley behind the store yesterday.'

Phyllis stared at me, then let out a chuckle. 'Oh, I've seen him. A big black cat with a white spot on his nose, right? He's been hanging out behind the stores for a few weeks now. A stray, most likely. Some of the shopkeepers, including myself, put out some food for him. The mouse population seems to have decreased a bit since he's been around.'

'He seemed friendly, so I thought I'd adopt him. A bookstore can always use a cat for a mascot.'

'True.' A little bell dinged from the back room and Phyllis pushed her chair back. 'Your breakfast is ready. I'll be back in a few.'

She rose and disappeared into the back room. I sat, sipping my coffee. I reached up and patted my shoulder-length auburn hair. I could use a trim. I'd just have to stop by the Clip N Curl later, see if Mara was free. She might not be willing to talk about a former client, but then again, she might.

Let it go, a little voice in my head said. You're making mountains out of molehills. Sheila's departure is probably very innocent, and nothing sinister at all. She'd never defined in her note just what the 'something unexpected' had been. It might not be something bad after all. Perhaps a family member had taken ill.

Phyllis returned and set my breakfast waffles and eggs in front of me. I sniffed the air appreciatively. 'That smells wonderful.'

'Thanks. My own recipe.' She glanced up as the front door opened and a crowd of people filtered through. 'Sorry I don't have any more time to chat right now. My regulars are here.'

'No worries. I'll come in again.'

'Anytime, Charlotte. Anytime.' She pulled her pad out of her pocket and placed the check beside me. 'You can just leave it on the table when you want to leave.'

Phyllis hurried back behind the counter and for the next twenty minutes I concentrated solely on my delicious breakfast. At eight forty-five I scooped up the last of my egg and scraped my chair back. The locksmith was supposed to arrive at nine and I wanted to get there a little early. I left a ten-dollar bill on the table and threaded my way through to the front of the store. I paused to waggle my fingers in farewell at Phyllis, who flashed me a quick smile in return. I smiled back and as a result wasn't watching where I was going, until I felt myself come in contact with something hard and firm. I looked up and found myself meeting the gaze of the irritable stranger from the previous day. I swayed, and he reached out both arms, laid them on my shoulders to steady me.

'You really never watch where you're walking, do you?' he said, a trace of irritation in his tone.

'You remember me? I'm flattered,' I said, not bothering to hide the sarcasm in my tone.

'Hard not to remember you when you keep butting into me or my things,' he muttered. He removed his hands from my shoulders and pushed past me on to the line without another word. I was tempted to say something, but a glance at the clock on the wall told me that I had places to be, things to do.

Confronting Mr Irritable would just have to wait for another time.

FOUR

As I walked swiftly up the street, I made a mental note to ask Phyllis about him the next time I stopped in for coffee. Might he be one of her regulars? If so, maybe she could tell me why he was so unpleasant. Did it come naturally, or had something happened to put that stick sideways up his butt?

And why did I care?

As I approached the store, I saw a figure come around the side of the building and peer in the window of my half. The figure straightened and turned, and I saw that it was a man. He was big boned and powerfully built. His dark hair was tousled, and the lower portion of his face was obscured by a thick, dark beard. He had on pressed jeans and a neat denim jacket and seemed to be well put-together. The only thing that appeared out of place was the pink iPhone case peeping out of the jacket pocket. Squaring my shoulders, I walked up behind him, placed a hand on my hip and said loudly, 'Hello. Can I help you?'

He started and whirled around, his dark gaze boring into mine. 'H–hello,' he stammered. 'I'm sorry, I was just curious. I heard a bookstore was opening here?'

'It is,' I answered. 'I'm the manager.'

One shaggy eyebrow rose. 'Oh.' He jerked his thumb toward the window. 'When are you planning on opening? It looks pretty bare in there.'

'Beginning of October,' I said shortly. 'There will be signs up and an announcement in the local paper. We're planning on a grand opening the first week.'

He frowned and peered inside the shop again. 'That's not far away. Think you'll have the place all fixed up by then?'

'My partner and I are planning on it,' I answered. I nodded toward the second entrance. 'She's opening up a bakery next door.'

'Baked goods and books. Who could ask for anything more?' He reached up to pat at the phone in his pocket. 'Well, I'll check back for sure. Have a nice day now.'

He turned and hurried off. I stood for a moment looking after him. Something about his manner struck me as odd, but then again, it could just be my imagination going into overdrive. I remembered peering into the windows of many bookstores when I was younger, eager for them to open so I could add to my collection of whatever writer had struck my fancy at the moment. I opened the door and put the stranger out of my mind. After all, I had other things to worry about.

Glenn Chesney arrived promptly at nine, and by nine twenty-five had changed the locks on both storefronts as well as the back door and cellar entrances. I thanked him profusely as I accepted the keys and handed over my charge card. Poe, glad to not be confined, watched from his supine position on the counter. As Glenn left, Jeff Connors sauntered in.

He's still drop dead gorgeous, was my first thought upon seeing him. He strode into the shop with an easy-hipped swagger, dark blonde hair rumpled and just a hint of stubble along his square jaw. I felt my heart start to go into overdrive as he approached me with an easy smile. 'Hey, Charley,' he said. 'It's good to see you. Zane said you looked the same, and she didn't lie.'

I cleared my throat. 'Thanks. She didn't lie about you either. You look the same too.' *Devastatingly handsome. Be still my heart.*

His answer was a flash of perfectly white teeth. 'You're too kind. So, what have you been up to the past – what has it been now? – sixteen years since graduation?'

'About that. Well, I've been working in Manhattan.'

His eyes popped. 'The big city? Wow! And you came back here? Why?'

I sighed inwardly. Was everyone going to ask me that? 'I just decided I needed a change of scenery.'

'Well, opening a bookstore certainly qualifies, I guess,' Jeff said with a laugh. 'I can't even imagine living in the big city.'

I waved my hand. 'You'd do fine, I'm sure. It's not as bad as you might think.' I smiled and added, 'You followed in your father's footsteps, I see.'

He frowned. 'Not entirely. I left town for a while, too. Tried dabbling in a few different ventures, but nothing seemed to pan out, so home I came. My father was glad to welcome me back with open arms. So you and Zaney decided to give your own businesses a whirl, eh?' He glanced around. 'Sure looks different than when that old biddy and her sister had their shops here. Everything was so dank and dark.' Poe chose that moment to crawl out from behind the counter and Jeff gave a start, then looked at me. 'You have a cat. A black one.'

I nodded. 'We sort of adopted each other,' I said. 'I found him in the back alley.'

'I thought he looked familiar,' said Jeff. 'Oh, yeah – he's the stray who hangs around the dumpsters back of these shops.' He started to move toward the cat, but Poe sat upright and regarded him with blazing eyes. A hiss rumbled, deep in his throat. Jeff took a step backward. 'Guess he remembers me, and not in a good way. I've chased him away a couple of times,' he confessed.

I looked at the cat. 'Poe, behave. Jeff's OK. He's an old friend of mine. He took me to my high school prom.'

Poe cocked his head and let out a sharp meow, as if he disagreed. Then he jumped off the counter and stalked over to the far corner. He turned around twice, then lay down, head on paws, gazing balefully at the two of us.

I shook my finger at the cat. 'Where are your manners?'

Jeff shot me an apologetic smile. 'Guess he's nursing a grudge. I guess I can't blame him too much.'

Poe blinked, hissed softly, and then turned his back to us.

Jeff angled me a glance. 'So you remember the prom, huh? That was some night.'

'It sure was,' I said. There was a long, awkward pause and then I pointed to the overhead fixture and the wires jutting out from either end. 'I guess we should get down to business. I'd like to replace that fixture with some old-fashioned globes, but I need to make sure the wiring is safe first.'

'Sure, I can check that,' said Jeff. 'I'll just go out to my truck and get my ladder. It shouldn't take too long. I parked in the driveway next to the bakery half.'

As he turned to leave, I laid a hand on his arm. 'You didn't by any chance see anyone hanging around outside when you came, did you? A dark-haired man in faded denim jeans and jacket?'

He shook his head. 'Nope, I didn't see a soul. Why?'

'He was peering in the window when I came.'

Jeff barked out a laugh. 'So? He was probably just curious when you were going to open.'

'That's what he said, but I don't know.' I shrugged. 'He just gave me a funny feeling, is all.'

Jeff cocked his head to one side. 'You haven't changed, Charley. You're still the same girl you were in high school, making mysteries out of commonplace events.' He let out a chuckle. 'You know, lots of us thought you'd end up being a detective, or maybe a mystery writer.'

I started at Jeff's last comment. 'Really?' I said, making my tone light. 'Well I ended up as a junior researcher for a New York magazine.' At his blank look I added, 'A researcher is a sort of a fact checker.'

'A fact checker, huh?' He rubbed at the stubble on his chin. 'Well, I guess that's a detective of sorts, right?'

'In a way.'

Our eyes locked for a few moments. I tore my gaze away first and cleared my throat. 'I guess you should get busy checking those wires,' I said. 'I'm sure you've got other stops to make today.'

His head bobbed up and down. 'Yep. Got a full schedule. I'll get my ladder and be right back.'

Jeff exited out the door. Once he'd gone, Poe rose from his supine position, stretched, then ambled back toward me.

I knelt beside the cat. 'You're still in hot water,' I whispered. 'You could at least try to be civil.'

Poe let out a soft meow, then butted his head against my hand.

I straightened and gazed around the room, trying to visualize how it would look once I'd had it all fixed and furnished. That reminded me that there was more inventory to look over. Zane had said that Sheila had put some of the boxes in the basement. I figured that while Jeff was looking over the lighting, now might be as good a time as any to see if I could locate them. Before I could start downstairs to the cellar, though, Jeff came through the door, carrying a tall ladder. He set it up underneath the fixture and climbed quickly up the steps, started to fiddle with the light. I didn't see the need to disturb him, so I opened the door that led to the basement and beheld a flight of stone steps leading downward. Poe decided to accompany me, but we'd only gone down two steps when the lights flickered and went out. 'Great,' I muttered. I turned and yelled up the steps, 'Jeff? Is everything all right? Did something happen with that fixture?'

'I don't think so,' Jeff called back. 'It's more likely a fuse blew. Where are you?'

'On the stairway leading to the basement,' I answered. 'I'm sorry, but I have no idea where the fuse box is.'

'I think it's in that curtained area,' he said. 'It'll just take a minute to fix. Stay where you are. You don't want to take a tumble down those steps. They're pretty steep.'

I hesitated, unsure of what to do. I felt in my pocket for my phone, found it, and turned on the flashlight app. The beam cut a wide swath of light, illuminating the basement floor. I looked at the cat. 'Well, what do you say? We can see where we're going, so we might as well continue.'

Poe meowed in assent, so we continued on down to the bottom. I flashed the light around in a wide arc, illuminating a far corner of the room. I saw a door that was most likely the service entrance, and a large chest shoved under an eave in a far corner, and about two feet away from that three large boxes stacked one on top of the other.

I looked at Poe. 'I think we've hit pay dirt,' I said.

Poe's eyes slitted, and he made a rumbling noise, deep in his throat.

I made my way forward, pausing in front of the chest. It was quite large, and rectangular in shape. An oblong curved lid rested atop it. I recognized the wood as oak. The chest appeared to be well made, with the look of a piece fashioned by a master craftsman. Intricately carved rosettes decorated its lid and sides. *It would be perfect in front of a bed*, I thought, *an excellent storage place for blankets and pillows*. Had it been Sheila's? If so, I couldn't imagine why she might have gone off and left this magnificent piece.

I made my way over to the boxes. I noticed that the flap on the top one was open. I pulled it back and reached inside. I pulled out two books that looked very familiar to me. *All the Dead Bodies* and *Coroner's Court*. The first two Steve Sheppard novels. I flipped to the back cover, where there was a very brief biography of C.J. Barrett. As was the case with all of my books, the requisite author photo was absent.

'Look Poe. My C.J. Barrett novels,' I whispered. I held them up, but Poe was nowhere to be found. 'Poe,' I called. 'Where did you go?'

No answering meow. Great. A second later, I heard frantic scratching sounds. 'Poe,' I called again. 'What the heck are you doing?' I tucked the books under my arm and shone the light around the room. I spied the cat on top of the chest in the corner. He was pawing frantically at its top. 'Poe,' I called again. 'Get down from there.'

His answer was to paw even more frantically at the lid.

I started toward him but my foot caught in a crack in the cement floor and I pitched forward, arms flailing out in front of me. My phone and the books went flying, skittering across the concrete. I hurled forward and banged full tilt into the chest just as the basement was plunged into darkness. Poe let out a loud yowl and jumped off the top of the chest just as it tilted forward. I twisted my body just in time to avoid having it land right on top of me.

At that moment the lights went back on. Jeff's head appeared at the top of the stairs. 'Everything all right down there?' he called anxiously. 'I heard a loud bang.'

'I'm fine,' I shouted back. 'I just tripped and crashed into this chest—' I stopped speaking as the words died in my throat.

The chest had fallen over, and the lid had popped open. Dangling over the side of the chest was a human arm.

FIVE

For what seemed like an eternity I stood rooted to the spot, staring at the arm. I'd written scenes like this on more times than I could count, but it was one thing to do it in the safety of one's den, on one's computer.

It was quite another to actually find one in the flesh, so to speak.

I willed my leaden legs to move and walked closer to the chest, Poe at my side, and was immediately hit by a sickly sweet odor I'd described many times in my books. I thought about turning away but frankly curiosity got the better of me. I reached up, pinched my nose and bent over for a better look. The body was that of a woman. She lay sprawled in the chest's center, her knees drawn up, her neck cocked at an awkward angle. Sightless eyes stared straight ahead, and her mouth was shaped in an almost perfect O. Frosted blonde hair skimmed her chin, and I noticed a faint blue tinge to her skin. I leaned a bit farther over, saw splotches of red splattered against her white blouse. There were several deep gashes in the material. She'd been here awhile, at least twelve hours, and she was definitely dead, like I'd had a doubt. And I was willing to bet she hadn't died of natural causes either.

I heard a thumping sound behind me and a few seconds later Jeff appeared at my elbow. 'I see you're still stubborn,' he said. 'How come you didn't wait on the stairs till I fixed . . .' His gaze fell upon the chest and his cheeks paled. 'Oh my God,' he whispered. He pointed at the arm. 'Is that . . . is that . . .'

'A dead body. Yep, it is,' I said. I backed away from the chest. 'She's been down here for at least twelve hours, maybe more.'

Jeff stared at me. 'You sound so certain. How on earth could you possibly know that?'

I shrugged. 'I don't know for certain. But I've done— I mean, I read a lot of mysteries.' I'd caught myself in time. I'd been about to say, 'I've done a lot of research,' which would have undoubtedly invited questions I had no desire to answer. I looked over at Jeff, who was staring at the floor as if he'd never seen one before. 'Think you could take a quick look?' I asked. 'See if you might recognize her?'

'What?' His head snapped up and I thought I saw something, some emotion, flicker in his eyes. He cast a tentative look at the chest.

'Do you think you might take a look, see if you recognize her.'

'It–it's a woman? O–OK.' He moved slowly over to the chest, peered inside, then quickly stepped back and stood, hands shoved in his pockets.

'Well,' I said impatiently. 'Do you recognize her?'

He passed a hand over his eyes. 'Do I recognize her?' he repeated my question back to me. 'I–I'm pretty sure it's Sheila.'

The knot in my stomach tightened, even though that was the answer I'd been expecting. 'Sheila Crowder?'

He nodded. 'Uh-huh. I think.' He moved a bit closer to the chest and reached out a hand toward the body. I stepped forward and grabbed his arm. 'No, Jeff, don't touch anything,' I warned. 'This will be a crime scene now. We have to leave everything exactly as it is and call the police immediately.'

He shot me a blank stare, then gestured toward the chest. 'It doesn't seem right, to leave her lying there like . . . like that.'

'No, but trust me, it will be far worse if we touch it. Police take a dim view of that.' I tugged at his arm. 'Go upstairs and call 911 on your cell. I have to find my phone. It fell out of my hand when I tripped.'

He hesitated, then turned and practically ran up the stairs. I myself found it hard to turn away from the chest and its macabre contents, but turn away I did. I looked toward the opposite end of the cellar where I'd seen the phone slide. Poe scampered ahead of me and a few minutes later let out a sharp meow. I hurried over and found him beside the water heater, my phone tucked between his paws.

'Good boy. This makes up for your earlier behavior.' I picked up the phone and looked at it. The screen was intact, no cracks. I turned it on and breathed a silent prayer of thanks when it still appeared to be working. I slid it into my pants pocket and looked around for Poe. I saw the cat over in the corner, playing with what looked like a square of paper. 'What have you got now?' I said. I walked over to the cat, who sat back on his haunches as I approached, one paw possessively on the paper. I bent over and picked it up. It was a torn piece of lilac stationary. There was no writing on it, but there was a name embossed across the top. Sheila Blackwell.

'Charley,' Jeff called. 'You OK?'

I stuffed the paper into my pocket. 'Yes. We're coming.' I hurried back up the stairs, Poe right behind me. I emerged back into the store just in time to hear Jeff say, 'We'll be here.' He turned to me. 'Dispatcher said police are on the way,' he said. 'They're usually pretty prompt, and I guess in a case like this . . .' He spread his hands and didn't finish the sentence. He didn't have to. After a few moments, he remarked, 'I wonder what happened to her?'

I arched a brow. 'Judging from the red spots and tears all over her blouse, I'd say someone stabbed her and then stuffed her in that chest.'

'So you mean she was murdered? Golly.' Jeff reached up to scratch behind one ear. 'I guess it's a good thing you found her. Imagine if you hadn't, and she started to decompose.' He wrinkled his nose. 'That would have definitely put a kink in your store opening.'

I refrained from mentioning that the grisly discovery would no doubt put a kink in the planned opening anyway. I fingered my phone in my pocket. I needed to call Zane, inform her what had happened, but I figured I might as well wait for the police before doing so.

I didn't have to wait long. A few minutes later there was a sharp rap on the door. 'Open up,' came a commanding voice. 'Police.' I hurried over to the door and opened it. A female officer stood on the steps, and as she swung her gaze to me I felt a sudden flash of recognition kick in. I was certain I knew this woman, and not in a good way. A moment later she confirmed my worst fears.

'I'm Officer Barbara Donaldson,' she said in a crisp voice. 'Someone here reported finding a body?'

Oh, I hadn't been wrong. I knew that voice only too well. This was Barbara Jeanne Donaldson. Save for a few extra pounds, she looked exactly as she had in high school. Zane and I had called her Barbie then, because she'd always reminded us of a perfect little Barbie doll – blonde hair never out of place, fashion model figure, always on the arm of some football jock. I'd always pegged her to go into some glamorous profession like acting or modeling, but police work, heck no! Her gaze flicked over me, and I could swear I saw a flash of recognition in her eyes as well. That, however, lasted barely a moment and then her gaze went flat again. If I'd been describing it in one of my books, I'd have said she had cop's eyes. 'Someone here find a body?' she asked again.

I stepped forward and raised my hand. 'I did. I went down to the basement to check on some stock and my cat started pawing at a trunk down there.'

Barbie's gaze flicked to Poe, curled up at my feet. 'This would be the cat?'

'Yes, Poe.' I reached down to give the cat a reassuring pat on the head and got a loud, rumbling purr in return. I straightened and continued, 'The lights went out, and I tripped and crashed into it. The chest fell over, and the lid popped open, and . . . the arm fell out.' I paused, out of breath.

Barbie (I couldn't bring myself to call her Officer Donaldson) reached into her pocket, whipped out a notebook and a pen. She jotted down a few notes, then looked at me. 'Can you show me the way to the basement?' she asked.

I nodded. 'Of course.' With Poe at my heels, I took her over to the door, pointed down the flight of steps. 'It's down there.' Barbie started down the steps. I began to follow her, but she whirled around and held up her hand. 'Please remain here,' she said. Without waiting for me to answer, she turned on her heel and descended the steps.

Jeff came up behind me. 'Who'd have ever imagined that the prom queen would end up on the Austin police force?' He whispered in my ear.

I turned my neck to look at him. 'Not me, that's for sure,' I confessed. 'Barbara Jeanne being a police officer is a little like taking a spill through the rabbit hole and ending up in Wonderland.' I eyed him. 'You knew she was a police officer, didn't you? Why didn't you warn me?'

He chuckled. 'I wasn't sure she'd be the one to show up. I should have figured it, though. Rumor has it she's bucking for a promotion to detective. Guess she saw this as her chance to make an impression on the captain.'

Barbara Jeanne a homicide detective? That was a scenario worthy of Stephen King. 'Who's the regular homicide detective?' I asked. 'Does the Austin PD even have one?'

'Yeah, they did. Rodney Bratt, but he retired last month. The chief and the mayor have been taking their time finding a replacement. They don't think it's too necessary. We don't have many murders in Austin. Gee, I can't remember when the last one was.'

'That would be three years ago, when some guy shot his wife 'cause he found her in bed with the gardener. It was a pretty simple open-and-shut case – especially since he broke down in tears and confessed when the police came.'

We turned and saw Barbara Jeanne behind us. She had a tablet in her hand and was typing on it. She fixed us with a penetrating gaze. 'I don't suppose either one of you can identify the body?'

I hesitated, my fingers closing around the paper in my pocket, and then I shook my head. 'I've only just been back in town a few days,' I said. 'I've never seen her before.'

Barbara Jeanne glanced at Jeff. 'How about you, *Jeffrey*?' she barked out. 'Any idea as to who she might be?'

I looked up sharply at her rapid change in tone. It seemed Barbara Jeanne remembered Jeff. If I recalled, she'd had a huge crush on him as well. Judging from the way she said his full name, though, that was long over.

He rubbed absently at his forehead. 'I'm not one hundred percent sure, but . . . she looks like Sheila Crowder.'

'Sheila Crowder? That name doesn't ring any bells?' Barbie said.

I fingered the paper again as I put in, 'I don't think she was in town long. My business partner would know for sure. She and Sheila were supposed to go into business here together.'

Barbie shot me a narrow-eyed gaze. 'Does your business partner have a name?'

'Zane Adams.'

Once again, I thought I caught a spark of recognition in her blue eyes, but it was gone in a flash. 'I'll need to have her make a positive ID,' she said, her tone brusque.

'Of course,' I murmured. I gave Barbie the name of the bakery where Zane was working. 'So, what happens next?' I asked, even though I was pretty sure I knew the answer.

Barbie shut her tablet and slid it into her jacket pocket. 'We'll need a full forensics examination,' she said briskly. 'I've put in a call to the county coroner. So for the time being, I'm afraid this part of the storefront is off limits as a crime scene.'

'So we're free to leave?' Jeff asked. He glanced at his watch and added, 'I've got another appointment in a half hour.'

Barbie gave him a hard look. 'Better cancel it,' she said. 'I'm sure Detective Grant will want to speak to both of you, get your statements.'

Jeff and I exchanged a glance and then Jeff asked, 'Detective Grant? Who's that?'

Barbie eased one hip against the glass counter. 'As you know, *Jeffrey*, Austin doesn't have a homicide detective on the force right now. The mayor hasn't felt sufficient need to replace Rodney. When I saw that body downstairs, I immediately put in a call to Detective Grant. He's one of the senior homicide detectives on the Philadelphia force, and as luck would have it, he's in the area this week attending a series of lectures at Swarthmore. He should be here shortly.'

'Swarthmore, huh?' I was familiar with the college, which was about four miles away from Austin. 'What sort of lectures is he attending?'

'It's got something to do with their criminal justice program,' Barbie replied. 'Sorry, I don't know specifics.' The look she shot me plainly said, *nosy, aren't you*?

Seeing the expression on Barbie's face, Jeff stepped forward. 'She didn't mean anything by that. Charley's always liked mysteries,' he offered.

Barbie swung her gaze back to me. 'Yeah, I remember,' she said softly.

My eyes widened. So she did remember me! I was about to call her out on it when I heard the front door open and an authoritative voice call out, 'Officer Donaldson. You called for my assistance?'

Barbie's head shot up, and I swear I'd never seen a person's expression change so quickly. Her scowl vanished, replaced by a smile worthy of Scarlett O'Hara as she moved forward. 'Why yes I did, Detective Grant,' she said. Her voice was almost a purr. 'Thank you for answering my summons so promptly.'

I was tempted to stick two fingers down my throat at the sickeningly sweet tone in her voice. I turned toward the doorway, curious to see this man who'd obviously captured Barbara Jeanne's fancy and my breath caught in my throat as recognition set in.

Standing there was none other than the unpleasant man I'd encountered in the coffee shop.

SIX

For a minute I couldn't speak, and then I found my voice. 'Oh my gosh. You!' I croaked out. 'You're Detective Grant?'

His eyes darkened. 'I am,' he said.

I took a minute to study the man again. My impression was that he probably spent a great deal of his time at the gym. The navy blazer he wore over pressed jeans seemed molded to his angular frame. He stood, legs planted apart, his hands on his hips, and looked down at me from his well over six-foot height. I'm no shrinking violet, coming in at five eight in my stockinged feet, but I felt a little like a shrimp under his penetrating gaze. He stepped forward and held out his hand. 'Allow me to formally introduce myself. Ian Grant, Philadelphia Homicide. And you are?'

I squared my shoulders and lifted my chin. 'Charlotte James.' I took his hand, and he held it just a fraction too long for my taste before he released it and said, 'Charlotte, eh? Now there's a name one never hears much these days.'

'She always hated it,' piped up Jeff. 'We all called her Charley in high school.' I turned my head and shot him a black look. He looked back at me, puzzled. 'What? Everyone did.'

Much to my annoyance, I noted the corners of Grant's lips turn slightly upward. 'I'd prefer Charlotte, myself,' he remarked. 'Charley is a boy's name and you . . .' His gaze swept over me rather appreciatively, I thought. 'Are definitely not a boy.'

I felt heat sear my cheeks. 'Thanks. I think,' I mumbled. I slid a sideways glance over at Barbie. Her brows were knit in a deep frown, and the corners of her lips turned down. Apparently she hadn't appreciated Grant's remark. To cover my embarrassment I lifted my chin and said quickly, 'Ms James will do just fine, thanks.'

Grant regarded me silently for a moment, then nodded. 'All right. *Ms James*.' He glanced over at Jeff. 'And you are?'

Jeff swallowed. I noticed he paled a bit under Grant's intense gaze. 'Jeff – Jeffrey Connors. Of Connors Electrical. I was here looking at the wiring.'

'I see,' said Grant. He reached into the pocket of his blazer and pulled out a small black notebook and pen. He opened the notebook, flipped to a page, and held the pen poised over it. 'Which one of you discovered the body?'

I raised my hand. 'That would be me.'

He looked over at me, raised one eyebrow. 'Now why does that not surprise me?'

Barbie moved forward to stand next to Grant. She touched his arm. 'Ian? Do the two of you know each other?'

'Not really.' The two of us said it at the same time. I couldn't help but notice Barbie's use of the detective's first name, or the way she looked at him. There was definitely more than a professional interest there – at least on Barbie's part.

Grant, however, looked as if he could care less. Apparently he was immune to Barbie's many charms. Score one point for him.

I cleared my throat. 'We've, ah, bumped into each other on a few occasions,' I said.

His lips twigged upward again. 'Bumped being the operative word,' he said.

Grant turned away, motioned to Barbie. The two of them retreated to a far corner and I could see Barbie talking to the detective earnestly, most likely filling him in on what had happened. After a few moments Grant walked back over to where Jeff and I stood. 'Now that introductions have been made, I'll need to take statements.' He fixed his stormy gaze on me. 'I'll need to interview each of you separately. Is there somewhere private where we can talk?'

I motioned toward the curtained area. 'There's that storage area over there.'

Grant nodded. 'Fine.' He jerked his thumb at Jeff. 'You first.'

Jeff shot me a quick look, then shuffled off toward the storage area. Barbie stepped forward and said, in an almost eager tone, 'Do you want me to interview Ms James, Detective?'

'No thank you, Officer. I'll handle it.' Grant turned to me. 'Please remain here with Officer Donaldson, Ms James. I'll be with you shortly.' Then he glanced back at Barbie. 'I believe you know what to do, Officer?'

Barbie seemed to get the unspoken message. 'Yes, Detective Grant,' she said meekly. 'I'll take care of it.'

'Good.'

Grant vanished into the curtained area and Barbie gave me a hard look. 'Stand over there where I can see you,' she directed. I leaned against the glass counter, and Barbie moved off a bit into the corner and whipped out her cell phone. She stood with her face slightly averted from me, and I wondered if she was contacting Zane.

For my part, I was suddenly starting to become a bit nervous. I fidgeted against the counter, uncomfortably aware that I was next to be questioned in what was undoubtedly to become an official murder investigation. While I'd put many of my characters through this process many times, it was a first for me, and one I found myself not liking very much.

About fifteen minutes later Grant and Jeff emerged from the curtained alcove. Jeff appeared a bit pale but otherwise none the worse for wear. Grant walked over to speak to Barbie, and Jeff sidled up to me. 'How was it?' I whispered.

'Not as bad as I thought,' Jeff said, and I could tell from the tone of his voice he was relieved. 'He just asked me what I was doing here, what time I got here, and to describe what happened. So I told him I was working on the light fixture and the fuse blew, and I went to fix it and then I heard a crash downstairs and after that . . .' his shoulders lifted in a shrug. 'He told me he might have more questions for me later, but right now I'm free to go.' He reached out and squeezed my hand. 'Good luck.'

'Thanks.'

He started to turn away, then paused. 'Charley? My next appointment shouldn't take long. Want to meet up for some lunch, say, around one, one thirty? Grant should be done with you by then. We can catch up.'

Ordinarily I'd have jumped at the chance to have lunch with Jeff, but now . . . I shook my head. 'Not today,' I said. 'How about a raincheck, though? After all, you'll still have to come back at some point to replace these fixtures.'

He brightened a bit. 'Sure thing.' He gave me a wave, and

then hurried out the door. Poe watched him go, then stretched out at my feet and let out a soft meow. I got the feeling he was glad to see Jeff depart.

I knelt down and gave Poe a chuck underneath his chin. 'Don't nurse a grudge, Poe. Jeff's an OK guy.'

Poe opened his mouth in a large, unlovely cat yawn. I couldn't tell if I'd gotten through to him or not.

'Your turn, Ms James.'

I started at the sound of Grant's voice. I rose, and Poe started to as well. I leaned over and whispered to the cat, 'Stay here, Poe. I won't be long.'

Poe stared at me for a moment, then blinked, lay back down and turned over on his side.

Grant looked at me. 'Talking to the cat, I see? Does he answer you?'

'In his own way,' I retorted. Grant turned on his heel and I followed him back into the curtained area. There was a small wooden desk in one corner, and one uncomfortable-looking wooden chair. Grant eased one hip against the desk, motioned for me to take the chair. I plunked down, wincing as my bottom came in contact with the hard wood.

'Take me through your movements today, please,' he said.

I crossed my arms over my chest. 'Well, first I got up— wait, no that's not correct. My cat woke me up, and a good thing too, because I forgot to set the alarm. I showered and dressed and—'

Grant held up his hand, and from the expression on his face I was certain he was fighting the urge to roll his eyes. 'I'm sorry. Perhaps I should have been more specific. Take me through your movements *here* today. Starting with why you went into the basement.'

'Fine,' I said. I explained about going to look for the books in the basement, the lights going out, Poe clawing at the chest and my subsequent tumble and fall into it, revealing the contents. Grant listened, his expression impassive, not revealing anything of what he was thinking. When I finished he was silent for a few moments, and then he said, 'Mr Connors identified the body as that of a Sheila Crowder?'

I nodded. 'He said he wasn't entirely certain, but it looked like her.'

'So the deceased wasn't familiar to you?'

I shook my head. 'No, I never saw her before. As I told Officer Donaldson, I only just relocated here a few days ago.' I paused and then figured he'd find out anyway, so I added, 'but my friend Zane had told me all about her.'

He arched one shaggy eyebrow. 'Zane?'

'Yes, Zane Adams. She and Sheila were supposed to go into business together, but Sheila had to bow out unexpectedly. So I offered to take over this half of the storefront.'

'I see.' He scribbled a few moments longer, then raised his head and said, 'We'll need to get in touch with Ms Adams and have her make a positive identification of the body.'

I grimaced. 'I already gave her contact information to Bar— to Officer Donaldson.' I paused and then remarked, 'From the gashes in her blouse and the blood spatter, I'd say cause of death was loss of blood from multiple stab wounds. If I had to make a guess, I'd say it appeared to be a crime of passion.'

Grant's bushy eyebrows took on Spockian proportions. 'You seem rather knowledgeable on the subject,' he remarked. 'Don't tell me you've worked in a coroner's office.'

I felt my cheeks grow warm again. 'No, but I do read a lot of mysteries,' I said.

His eyes narrowed. 'Oh, well. That explains it. You'll forgive me, though, if I wait for our coroner's official report.' The tone of his voice was derisive, mocking even. 'I imagine you have a theory on why the body was stuffed in the trunk too?'

'Since you asked, I do. If it were a crime of passion, the killer wouldn't have thought the details out. Maybe they didn't know what to do with the body, or maybe they didn't have time.' I paused and when Grant remained silent I added, 'I think it was probably someone she knew, though.'

'And why do you think that?'

'Because I didn't see any evidence of forced entry on any of the doors. I also had the locks changed, and the locksmith didn't notice anything amiss either. So I'm thinking that she must have known her assailant. Possibly it was someone familiar with the store.' I paused. 'It also explains the tea.'

Grant shot me a blank stare. 'The tea?'

'Yes. Zane said that Sheila was a passionate tea drinker and always carried tea around with her. Yet I found a practically full box in the storeroom, with only two bags missing. It didn't hit me right. Someone that passionate about tea, particularly someone who was considered frugal, wouldn't leave behind that full box.'

Grant stared at me and I had the feeling he was trying very hard not to roll his eyes. 'Very interesting,' he said at last. 'This is real life, though, not a mystery novel, or an episode of *Murder, She Wrote*.' His gaze swept over me, head to toe. 'And you're a bit young to be taking on the mantle of Jessica Fletcher.'

Another left-handed compliment? I arched a brow, but before I could think up a suitable retort there was a *tap-tap* on the wall and then the curtain parted. Barbie thrust her head in. 'Detective Grant, the coroner's team is here.'

'Thank you, Officer.' He swung his gaze back to me. 'I think that'll be all, Ms James. At least for now.' He put up a hand. 'Another thing. I'm afraid this half of the building will be off-limits for a while until we release the crime scene.'

'I expected that,' I said, as a vision of the yellow caution tape barring the doors flitted through my brain. 'Have you any idea how long that might take? There's a lot to do here if we're to be ready for our grand opening.'

'And when would that be?'

'We're shooting for the first week in October.'

'Hm, that's not much time. I really can't say at this moment,' Grant replied. His brows drew together and something flashed in those deep gray eyes. Sympathy? Annoyance? It was hard to tell. Finally he said, 'I'll do my best to speed things along.'

'Thank you,' I murmured, wondering if he really meant it or if he was just trying to placate me. I leaned toward the latter.

I followed Grant back into the main store. Poe saw me, rose and stretched, and when I approached him wound his furry body around my ankles, purring all the while. Two men stood off to one side, talking to Barbie. They straightened at the sight of Grant, who walked over to them. They spoke in low tones for a few moments, and I watched them curiously. Grant glanced up, saw me watching. He said something to the men who turned and started for the basement stairs. Grant walked over to me and his gaze took in both me and Poe. 'I guess I wasn't clear. You and your cat are free to go. If I need anything else, I'll be in touch.'

His brusque tone irritated me. I placed a hand on my hip and said, 'You'll let me know when I can come back into the store, start getting it ready?'

He looked at me for a moment, then waved his hand dismissively. 'We'll be in touch.'

With that, he turned and followed the other two men down the stairs. I noticed that Barbie didn't accompany them but remained upstairs in the far corner, flipping through her notebook. She glanced up, saw me, and shoved the notebook back into her jacket pocket. Then she strode over to where I stood and planted herself, legs apart, in front of me. 'Detective Grant said you're free to leave,' she said.

I avoided her gaze. 'I heard him,' I mumbled. I gestured toward the counter. 'I need to get my tote bag.'

I walked over to the counter and retrieved it, conscious of Barbie's gaze on me the entire time. As I turned toward the front door she suddenly appeared at my side. She cocked her head and said, 'So, Charley James. What ill wind blew you back into town?'

I shifted my tote on my shoulder. 'So you do remember me,' I said.

One corner of her lip turned down. 'Like I could ever forget you, or Zane. You always did have an insatiable curiosity regarding things that were none of your business. Zane too, but you were far worse.' Barbie placed a hand on one hip. 'I know you all thought I was an airhead in high school, but I've changed a lot since then.'

I shrugged. 'I guess we all have.'

She gave me a hard look, then leaned in closer and said, 'I'm a good cop, Charley. I know how to do my job. And Ian – Detective Grant – is an excellent homicide detective. We'll get to the bottom of this, don't worry.'

I pretended I didn't notice her casual use of the detective's first name. 'OK, Barbie,' I said. 'I'll keep that in mind.'

She leaned toward me. 'Oh, and by the way, when I'm on duty – it's Officer Donaldson.'

So she wanted to flex her power muscle, huh? Fine. 'OK, *Officer Donaldson*,' I remarked.

I brushed past her and headed out the door, Poe beside me. I noticed a small crowd had gathered – to be expected, I supposed. A tall man detached himself from the crowd and hurried over to me. 'What's going on, miss?' He asked. 'What happened that brought the police here?'

Before I could say anything Barbie was at my side. 'Move it along, Derek,' she said brusquely. 'Everything's under control here.'

Derek, however, would not be deterred. 'I thought I saw Ian Grant go inside,' he persisted. 'I know he's a homicide detective. Was someone murdered in there?'

'Detective Grant is merely here as a consultant,' Barbie said smoothly before I could answer. 'As to what happened, we're not entirely certain of the circumstances. We'll make an official statement shortly. In the meantime, we'd all appreciate your discretion.' She looked past Derek at the rapidly gathering crowd. 'Nothing to see here now,' she yelled. 'It's all under control. Move along, please.'

The crowd slowly started to disperse. Derek moved off to one side, pulled out his cell phone, started to speak rapidly into it.

'Derek Proust. Reporter for the *Austin Bugle*,' Barbie said, so close to my ear that I jumped. 'We'll take care of him.' She fixed me with a stare. 'And you – don't go blabbing any details of what you found here today. The department will release a formal statement.'

'No worries on that score,' I muttered.

I started to move away, but Barbie stepped in front of me and stood, her hands on her hips. 'Oh, and Charley? One last thing, just in case Detective Grant neglected to mention it: Don't leave town.'

'I wouldn't dream of it.'

Barbie turned and marched back into the store. Once the door had slammed behind her, Poe's lips peeled back, and he let out a loud hiss.

'You can say that again,' I told him. 'Touchy, touchy.'

SEVEN

I decided my next move should be to go to the bakery where Zane worked and inform her what had happened. I wasn't certain if Barbie had contacted her already, but if not I wanted to give her a heads-up. Poe and I got in the SUV, and I punched the address of Frederick's Bakery into my satnav. Not too long after I pulled up in front of a small white building located in the center of Clarkville. I shut off the motor and looked at Poe. 'You can stay in the front seat,' I told the cat. 'I shouldn't be long.'

Poe blinked, let out a sharp meow, and his head swiveled in the direction of the window. His pink tongue darted out, swiped across his lip.

I reached over to pat his head. 'OK, I'll see if they've got something in there a kitty might like.'

Poe blinked again, and his pink tongue darted out, licked at his upper lip. Then he stretched out on the seat and put his head on his paws.

The smell of fresh baked pies, namely apple and pumpkin, assailed my nostrils the moment I stepped through the door. I'd sent Zane a text before I started out, informing her that I was coming to the bakery and needed to speak with her, but so far hadn't gotten a reply. I paused and took a quick look around. The place was packed, and the line at the counter was pretty long. A large glass case to the right of the counter displayed an array of mouthwatering pastries. I was willing to bet Zane had baked most, if not all, of them. As I debated whether or not to get on the line, a girl exited a door at the rear of the shop, balancing a large platter on which rested several packages of cookies. She walked over to a display to the left of the counter and started unloading her wares. I sauntered over and tapped her on the shoulder. 'Excuse me?'

The girl whirled around. She looked very young, not more than seventeen or eighteen, with a peaches-and-cream complexion and wide hazel eyes. 'Yes?'

'I'm looking for Zane Adams,' I said. 'My name is Charley James. It's rather important that I speak with her.'

Her eyes lit up, and she gave me an appraising glance. 'Oh, you're her friend from New York. She speaks of you a lot. I'm Masie Hanson.' She held out her hand, and I took it. 'She told me that you're going to take Sheila's place and open the bookstore,' she said when I released her hand. 'That's so great of you. I know Zane was real upset when Sheila just up and took off like that.' She let out a sigh. 'She's so lucky to be getting out of here. I wish it were me.'

'Yes, well, I really hate to be a bother, but there's an important matter I must speak to Zane about. Could you tell her I'm here?'

Masie shot me a smile. 'Sure thing.'

She turned on her heel and vanished back through the door. About five minutes later Zane emerged. Wisps of black curls crept out from under her hairnet, and the red apron she wore was spattered with flour. 'Hey,' she said. 'I got your text but I haven't had a moment to myself. We got a rush order for three dozen pies for McCauley Printing for an office event tomorrow and it's been like a nuthouse back there.' She blew out a breath. 'I really wish he'd let Masie help with the baking, instead of making her stock shelves. The girl's really good.'

I held up my hand. 'Can you take a break? I've really got to talk to you, and it can't wait.'

Zane's eyes narrowed. 'This wouldn't have anything to do with a text I got from Barbara Jeanne, would it? She wanted to know if I were available to talk. I didn't have a chance to answer her, either.'

I had an idea that wouldn't deter Barbie. I was glad, though, that she hadn't relayed the news about the grisly discovery in her text. I cleared my throat. 'I believe our two matters could quite possibly be related,' I said.

Zane let out a sigh. 'I knew it. What's wrong? Did someone try to break into the shop?'

I folded my arms across my chest. 'First I have a bone to pick with you. Why didn't you tell me Barbie is a police officer?' I asked.

My friend shot me a sheepish grin. 'It didn't exactly come up in conversation, now, did it? Besides, at times I can hardly believe it myself. Who would ever have thought our prom queen would end up on the Austin police force?'

Pretty much the same observation Jeff had made. 'Not me, that's for sure.' I tugged at Zane's arm. 'Enough about her, we need to talk. Is there somewhere private we can go?'

Zane's eyes widened. 'Whenever someone says we need to talk, it's never good. Wait here.' She disappeared into the back room, emerging a few minutes later with both the hairnet and apron ditched. She motioned for me to follow her, and we went out the side door into a narrow alley. Zane walked a bit away from the building, then paused and turned to me. 'I've only got ten minutes,' she said. 'So what's happened? Why does Barbie want to talk to me?'

There wasn't time to ease into the subject, so I just came out with it. I slipped my arm around Zane's shoulders and said, 'There's no easy way to say this, so I'll just come out with it. I went into the basement looking for those boxes of books you mentioned, but what I found was a dead body.' I paused. 'Sheila's.'

Zane's face paled and she swayed. For a minute I thought she might faint, and I reached out, grasped her around the shoulders. She leaned against me for a few moments, then pushed away. Brushing a hand over her eyes, she murmured, 'I'm all right. It's just that— are you sure, Charley? You never met Sheila. How do you know it was her?'

'Jeff was there, and he thought it was her. Barbie wants you to make a positive identification.'

'She wants me to identify . . . oh gosh!' Zane swayed again, but straightened just as I reached for her. She waved my hand away. 'I'm OK. It's just . . . where did you say you found her, exactly?'

'Poe was clawing at the top of a chest under the eaves. The fuse blew and it was dark and I tripped and fell into it. Sheila's body was inside. From what I saw she appeared to have been stabbed multiple times.'

Zane clutched at her stomach. 'Oh my gosh. I think I'm gonna be sick.'

'Bend over,' I directed. 'Put your head between your knees.'

Zane squatted, did as I directed. A few seconds later she lifted her head. 'Feel better?' I asked.

'Not about Sheila,' said Zane. 'When I think of all the terrible things I thought about her, leaving me like that, blowing me off with a note, and all the while she was in the basement . . .' Her shoulders hunched in a shudder. 'I don't know how I'm ever going to be able to look at that body and identify it without breaking down.'

'It won't be easy,' I agreed. 'Can you think of anyone who might have done this to her?'

Zane pressed her hand to the side of her head. 'Not offhand. Sheila didn't have many friends.'

'What about an ex? Did she ever mention one?'

'Not that I recall,' she said. 'Although I have to admit my thinking at the moment is a bit muddled.' Zane bit down hard on her lower lip. 'So what happens now? With our store, I mean? Will we still be able to open?' She gave a loud sigh. 'Oh, listen to me. Am I a bad person for worrying about that, when poor Sheila is dead?'

'Not at all. Detective Grant said he'd notify us as soon as we could go back into the store.'

Zane's brow furrowed. 'Detective Grant?'

'Yeah. Remember the guy from Jumpin' Beans the other day? The one who had a fit when I bumped into his briefcase?' At Zane's nod I went on, 'He's a homicide detective – Ian Grant. Apparently he's on loan here from Philly.'

'A homicide detective, huh? Guess we should have known that from his sparkling personality.'

'He's made quite an impression on Barbie. You should have seen the way she was sucking up to him.'

Zane barked out a dry laugh. 'That doesn't surprise me. He's a man, right?'

The door opened just then and Masie stuck her head out. 'Zane? There's a police officer here that wants to talk to you.'

Zane groaned and looked at me, and I patted her arm. 'It'll be OK. Remember, act surprised.'

'That won't be hard,' she mumbled. 'Wish me luck. I have a feeling I'm gonna need it.'

Zane went back inside to face the music, so to speak, and I made my way back to the SUV. Poe was napping on the front seat, but he woke up as soon as I started the motor. He looked at my hands as I slid behind the wheel.

'Sorry, boy,' I said. 'I forgot to check about a treat for you.'

The cat let out a soft growl.

'But don't worry,' I said, 'I'm going to cook dinner tonight, so I'll make sure you get something extra special. Cooking's therapeutic, right? It's just what I need right now, believe me.'

Poe moved closer to me, and his pink tongue darted out to lick my wrist before he flopped over on his side. Apparently I was forgiven, at least for the moment.

I took the highway back to Austin, stopping at the superstore along the way for all the fixin's to make my specialty for dinner: one-pot garlic Parmesan pasta. As my mother would say, it was quick and easy. As for the garlic part, well, neither Zane nor I would be kissing anyone soon. That thought brought an image of Ian Grant sharply into focus. I shook my head to clear it. Where had that come from? If I were going to kiss anyone Jeff would be a more logical choice. But still, the vision of Ian Grant's handsome face and his thick, full kissable lips kept popping up.

Focus, Charley. Focus.

My thoughts turned back to the poor, unfortunate Sheila. Once word got out about her body being found in the basement, it could adversely affect our potential businesses. In New York they would be lining up to visit a bookstore where a dead body had been found, but Austin wasn't New York. Right now, though, there were no suspects, which wasn't a good thing. I had no doubt the person the police would be zeroing in on would be Zane. After all, she had the most to lose by Sheila's backing out. What I needed right now was more information about Sheila; namely, people with whom she'd had dealings with. The fact she'd been so close-mouthed about her past suggested there was something there that might bear looking into. I found myself wondering what my character, Steve Sheppard, might do in this situation. Most likely he'd contact one of the many teams of experts he had at his beck and call as a top CIA agent to dig into her past. Unfortunately, I had no such team at my disposal.

I turned off the highway on to the main drag of Austin, and decided to drive past the storefront. Sure enough, the yellow crime scene tape was spread across my half of the storefront. There was no crowd of people gawking, and Derek Proust was nowhere to be seen. I sighed. I hoped that Barbie was right in her assertion that she and Ian would solve the crime swiftly. There wasn't much time to waste if we were to open on schedule. After dinner, Zane and I were going to have to do some brainstorming.

I was just about to make the left turn to Zane's house when a flash of movement caught my eye. A figure emerged from the bushes surrounding the side of the store, turned and started to walk swiftly up the street. I strained to get a good look, but whoever it was cut across the square and down the hill, vanishing from view.

I frowned. At this distance it was hard to be certain, but from the brief glimpse I'd had it looked like the same height and build as the man I'd caught looking in the shop window. If so, what was he doing back here?

I froze as another thought occurred to me. Could it have been Sheila's killer, returning to dispose of her body? If so, then he'd have realized it was no longer necessary. I gave myself a little shake. *Get a grip, Charley*, I told myself. *You're making mountains out of molehills, seeing shadows where there are none.*

Ignoring the sudden chill that nickered down my spine, I turned the SUV in the direction of home.

EIGHT

I pulled into the driveway of Zane's house and parked. I got out, hefted the grocery bags into my arms, and walked over to the side entrance, Poe right at my heels. It took a bit of maneuvering but I finally got my key out of my jacket pocket and let us into the kitchen. Once inside I dropped both bags on the kitchen table, then took off my jacket and hung it on the peg by the door. Poe squatted beside the island and watched as I rummaged through the cabinets, finally emerging with two chipped bowls. They would be perfect for Poe, since I'd forgotten to pick a set up at the pet store. I held it up and dangled it over the cat's head. 'See. No more paper plates. And I'll get you a proper set soon, I promise.'

Poe let out a soft purr. I filled one bowl with water and set it over by the far wall. Poe walked over, hunkered in front of the bowl, and a few seconds later was happily lapping up the water. More hunting through the cupboards produced a large can of tuna. I spooned a generous amount into the other bowl and set it down in front of the cat. He immediately moved over to it, and a few minutes later I heard the sounds of contented slurping.

With Poe taken care of, it was time to concentrate on tonight's meal, one-pot Parmesan pasta. I emptied the bags of the ingredients and laid them out on the counter: butter, milk, garlic cloves, chicken broth, fettuccine, salt, black pepper, fresh ground parsley, and fresh ground Parmesan cheese. I got out the chopping board and a sharp knife and dumped the garlic cloves on the board. As I chopped I let my thoughts wander back to Sheila. If I were penning this as a mystery, Sheila's death would either be the result of an attack by a serial killer or a crime of passion. I was pretty certain the serial killer possibility could be ruled out. That left crime of passion. Those were usually committed by jealous spouses or wounded lovers. Had Sheila been running from one? Had she changed her name hoping to avoid detection? Once again, I wished I could have Steve Sheppard's experts at my command. The crime would be solved just like that. But this was real life, not fiction. Not so easy in real life.

I glanced over at Poe and noted that the cat had cleaned out the tuna and was now stretched out in front of the bowls, licking his front paw. I picked up the empty bowl and smiled at the cat. 'You are definitely a member of the CPC. That's Clean Plate Club.'

Poe continued grooming. Apparently that didn't impress him.

I set the bowl in the sink and ran water in it. 'We have to find out more about Sheila,' I said to him. 'That's the key to solving her murder and restoring our storefronts to normalcy.'

Poe stopped grooming and let out a soft meow of assent.

I finished chopping the garlic and set the finished product in a small bowl on the counter beside the rest. I sniffed at the air, enjoying the scent. The entire recipe took less than twenty minutes, so I had plenty of time to start it before Zane arrived. I went to my room and got my laptop. I sat down at the table and typed 'Clip N Curl' in the search bar. I was in luck – they were open late tonight. I dialed the number and a woman's staccato voice answered, 'Clip N Curl. Josie speaking.'

'I'd like to make an appointment for a trim,' I said. 'Tonight, if possible.'

'Okey-dokey.' I heard the sound of pages rustling and then, 'Glenda's got an opening in fifteen minutes. If that's too soon, Georgia has one in an hour.'

I paused. 'How about Mara? Is she free anytime today?'

'Mara, huh?' More paper rustling and then the staccato voice was back. 'Mara only works till five tonight,' she said. 'And she's booked right up to four forty-five.'

'I only want a trim,' I said quickly. 'It shouldn't take longer than fifteen minutes. I'll gladly pay her extra if it goes past five.'

'Wait one second.' I was put on hold. I presumed the woman had gone to check with Mara. At least the music was palatable – The Four Seasons. I was tapping my foot to 'Walk Like a Man' when the receptionist came back on the line. 'Mara said OK, but you'd better be on time.'

'I will, thanks.' I gave my name and phone number and disconnected. If Sheila was as close-mouthed as Phyllis had suggested,

Mara might not know much more than Zane. Still, it was worth a shot.

I went on the Austin Chamber of Commerce website and typed in the name Sheila had wanted to call her store: Mainly Mysteries. Nothing. I couldn't check Zane's bakery because she'd never told me the name. The website said they opened at nine the next day, and I made a mental note to stop there. After some mental debate, I typed 'Sheila Crowder' into the search engine. Fifty-seven thousand entries popped up. Apparently Sheila Crowder was a popular name. I clicked on the tab marked 'Images' and when the page popped up scrolled down slowly. Midway I saw a photo that resembled the body in the trunk, except the hair was a dark brown. I clicked on the photo and it opened up. I saw writing in the upper right-hand corner, and I sucked in a breath when I saw the name Sheila Blackwell there. There was a link to click for address, phone number, and public record info. As I debated whether or not to click on the info or bookmark the page and wait for Zane, a loud knock sounded at the side door.

I glanced up sharply. 'Zane? Is that you?' I called out. I lowered the lid on my laptop and pushed back my chair. Poe jumped down from his post on the chair beside me, hurried over to the door and let out a loud meow. I paused, suddenly wary. 'Zane?' I called out again. 'Did you forget your key?'

'Sorry,' came a masculine voice from the other side of the door. 'I'm not Zane. It's Detective Grant.'

I stopped in my tracks, my heart beating wildly in my chest. What on earth did he want? Well, I supposed there was only one way to find out. I walked over and opened the door. Grant had been looking out over the backyard, but now he turned and fixed those stormy gray eyes on me. I leaned against the doorjamb. 'Wh–what are you doing here?' I asked. 'How did you know where to find me?'

He tapped a finger against his forehead. 'Duh! I am a detective, you know. I hate to bother you, but I just had a few more questions.' When I remained silent he added, 'I can ask them out here, or . . .'

I swung the door wide. 'Please. Come in,' I said, albeit a bit reluctantly. He followed me into the kitchen. I went over to the table and casually closed my laptop. Poe, now seated in front of the refrigerator, looked at the detective curiously, then ambled over, sniffed at his shoes. He let out a soft purr, and Grant reached down to scratch him behind one ear. 'Nice cat,' he said. 'I didn't get a good look at him before. He's quite handsome.'

Poe rubbed against Grant's ankles. Obviously Poe was a sucker for flattery and a good scratch behind the ear. I eased a hip against the counter. 'You said you have questions?'

He nodded and pulled his notebook and pen from his pocket. 'Yes, just a few follow-ups.' He inclined his head toward the table. 'Mind if I sit?'

'Suit yourself.'

He settled himself into the chair I'd just vacated. 'I'm surprised you use a notebook,' I heard myself say. 'I would have thought you'd use your tablet for making notes, like Officer Donaldson.'

'I do use my tablet on occasion, but I do prefer this method. Call me old-fashioned, I guess.' He held the pen poised over the notebook and his head dipped toward the chair previously occupied by Poe. 'OK, Ms James. Tell me again just how you found the body.'

I launched into the story again. Grant scribbled in his notebook, his face expressionless. When I finished, he raised his gaze to meet mine. 'Did you touch anything?'

'Well, the chest of course. I crashed right into it. Prior to that I touched the boxes of books, took some out.'

'I see.' He scribbled some more in his notebook then shot me a thoughtful gaze. 'Most women would be afraid, alone with a dead body.'

'I'm not like most women,' I said loftily.

He tapped at his notebook with his index finger. 'No, I don't think you are,' he said, so softly I had to strain to catch the words. In a louder tone he barked out, 'What about the man who was in the basement with you – Jeffrey Connors? Did he touch anything that you noticed?'

I shook my head immediately. 'No. He started to touch the body, but I pulled him away. I told him that the cellar would most likely be a crime scene and it would be best if we left things untouched.'

His lips twitched. 'And all you touched besides the chest was the box of books?'

I shifted my weight from one foot to the other. 'Not exactly,' I admitted. 'My fingerprints are probably all over that floor. I lost my phone when I slipped and I crawled all over hunting for it.'

He scribbled again in the notebook, then set down his pen, steepled his fingers beneath his chin. 'You said your friend, Zane Adams, is opening a store in the other half?'

'Yes, a bakery.'

'The stores have separate entrances, and separate basements.' It sounded like a statement, not a question, so I didn't respond. 'Would you know if your friend ever had any occasion to be in your basement?'

'She might have. I would imagine that they looked the property over before they agreed to rent it. They most likely went into each other's basements.'

'I see. And that chest – do you know if your friend ever touched that?'

I tapped my foot impatiently. 'No, I do not. I don't understand this line of questioning, Detective. Don't tell me you suspect Zane killed Sheila and stuffed her body in that trunk.' When he looked away from me, I let out a sharp gasp. 'Oh my God,' I cried. 'You do think that! Why? What gave you that idea?'

'Calm down. You're getting a bit ahead of yourself. The lab boys reported there were a few sets of fingerprints found on the trunk, is all. I'm just trying to narrow them down.' Grant fingered his notebook and met my gaze. 'Right now I don't think anything. I'm just gathering evidence. When it's all in, the facts will speak for themselves.' He paused. 'We really should take that trunk in as evidence, but our evidence room is pretty small and we really don't have the room right now . . .'

I held up my hand. 'Say no more. Just cover it with your crime scene tape. No one will touch it, I promise.'

Grant scraped his chair back, got to his feet, and came around the table to stand in front of me. For a moment we just stood there letting an awkward silence stretch between us. Then he reached into his jacket pocket, whipped out a card, and laid it on the counter. 'My card. If you should think of anything else you feel significant, call.' He paused. 'Day or night.'

I took the card and jammed it into my pants pocket without

looking at it. 'Someone killed that poor girl and stuffed her in that trunk like so much trash. I didn't know her, but I doubt that she deserved to die that way. No one deserves to die that way.'

'True, but I see it all the time.' He inclined his head toward the counter. 'It looks like you're getting supper ready.'

I shrugged. 'It's nothing fancy. Just something simple.'

Those lips twitched again and he sniffed at the air. 'Garlic, parsley, Parmesan. And you've got a package of fettuccine there. Looks like the beginnings of one-pot Parmesan garlic pasta.' At my surprised look, he actually grinned. 'I'm a pretty good cook,' he said. 'No gourmet, but I've taken a few classes. I find a good dinner relaxing after a hard day's work.'

'So that was why you were so critical of the food at Jumpin' Beans,' I blurted out.

'I believe I said it was adequate.' His gaze strayed back toward the kitchen counter. 'Looks like you have the makings of a more than adequate dinner there,' he said softly.

I found myself struggling not to frown back at him. Was this his subtle way of angling for a dinner invitation? And did I even want to have dinner with him? Zane would, no doubt, be mortified. Plus, I had a hair appointment. I was just about to mention that when Grant reached into his pocket, pulled out his cell, glanced at the screen, then shoved the phone back in his pocket. 'I've got to go,' he said. 'Remember, if you think of anything else . . .'

'Yes, I know.' I patted my pants pocket. 'Day or night.' I paused. 'There was a reporter outside the store when I left. Officer Donaldson told him that an official statement would be issued.'

'A statement was issued,' Grant replied. 'Oh, and I'd appreciate it if—'

I held up my hand. 'I know. Don't mention details to anyone. Don't worry, Detective. I'm not particularly anxious to advertise the fact someone was murdered in my store.'

He pulled his car keys out of his pocket and with another curt nod, opened the door and was gone. I walked over, leaned against it. Austin was a small town and, as Barbie had pointed out earlier, the last murder had occurred three years ago. Tongues would be wagging, no doubt. I knew police sometimes withheld certain details during an investigation to help them determine the guilt or innocence of their suspects. I couldn't help but wonder if Grant was doing the same thing.

My thoughts took another turn. Grant hadn't really answered my question when I'd asked him if he suspected Zane of the crime. He'd merely said he was gathering evidence. Evidence that pointed to Zane? What could that possibly be?

I grabbed my tote bag and removed my jacket from the peg on the wall. It was almost time for my hair appointment. Maybe my visit to the Clip N Curl would shed some light on the mysterious Sheila.

NINE

The Clip N Curl was only about ten minutes from Zane's house, on the corner of Wells Place and Fifth. As I pushed through the door, my nostrils were immediately assailed with a double whammy: the odor of perm solution and hairspray. In addition to the assault on my nostrils, I felt almost blinded – the walls were painted a stark white, and the linoleum floor was a white and gray marbled design. A black and white lacquered counter was off to the left next to a coatrack that held a few jackets and sweaters. The woman sitting behind the counter had her head down, and as I drew closer I saw that she was reading a newspaper that vaguely resembled the *Inquirer*. She glanced up as I approached, and snapped the gum in her mouth loudly. 'Welcome to the Clip N Curl,' she said in a nasal tone. 'I'm Josie. Do you have an appointment?'

'Yes, for a trim with Mara.' I glanced at the clock. 'I'm a few minutes early.'

'Oh, OK. You're Charley James.' She snapped her gum as she looked down at the register, then twisted her neck to look at the room beyond. 'Mara must still be in the back, but you can follow me to her station. She'll be glad you're a little early.' She leaned in closer to me and said in a loud whisper, 'I think she has a big date tonight.'

Josie motioned for me to follow her. There were six stations in all, and three of them were occupied. All the customers appeared to be women in their late fifties or early sixties getting haircuts. One woman had foil in her hair suggesting highlighting. The three hairdressers were all thin and blonde, wearing skintight leggings and low-cut tank tops under stark white smocks. Josie led me to the station farthest from the front entrance and motioned for me to sit down. 'Mara'll be right out,' she said.

She disappeared through a door in the back and I settled into the vinyl chair. I tugged at a stray curl. I knew that this trim wouldn't take more than a few minutes, and I tried to plan out in my head just how to approach Mara about Sheila. I wanted to make the most of this visit and get what information I could in a short period of time.

The door opened and a chubby woman, also wearing black leggings, her dark hair caught up in a ponytail, emerged. The name stitched on the front of her white smock read Marilyn. She walked over and stood behind me and looked at my reflection in the mirror. 'So you want a trim?' she asked. She ran her hand through my hair. 'It looks pretty good to me.'

I looked up into her face, which was heavily made up. Bright blue eyes were almost concealed by a heavy layer of eyeshadow and her eyes were ringed with black, reminding me of a raccoon. 'I'm assuming you're Mara?'

She inverted her index finger and pointed at her chest. 'That's me,' she said. 'So you want a trim?' she repeated.

'Yes. I know it doesn't look as if I need it but trust me, I do. When my hair gets past a certain length I just can't do a thing with it.'

'Oh, I hear ya.' Her hand shot out, and she fingered my auburn curls. 'How much you want taken off?'

'Just an inch or so,' I said. 'All the split ends.'

Mara let out a throaty chuckle. 'Miss, you don't have any split ends.' She fingered my curls again. 'You've got gorgeous hair. So, you want the trim wet or dry?'

'Dry's fine.' I shifted in my chair. 'I know that you only work till five tonight. I'm sorry to come in so late, but . . .'

Mara picked up a pair of scissors and a comb and started running it through my hair. 'No problem. It just so happens my date punked out on me, so I've got plenty of time.'

'Oh, I'm sorry.'

She shrugged. 'It happens. I wasn't that crazy about him anyway, but it was a free dinner.'

Mara combed my hair, then pulled a stool over and started to snip at my ends. We sat in silence for several minutes, while my brain tried to formulate the best plan of attack. 'Your hair color's pretty,' Mara remarked. 'Natural too.' She puffed out her chest a bit. 'Hair color's the first thing I notice about a client. It's my specialty.'

'I could see where that would be a special skill,' I said. 'I saw plenty of girls in high school trying to become blondes and ending up with green hair.'

Mara let out a laugh. 'Hair color can be challenging. It can really be a major transformation for the client, depending on the color. I mean, if you're a blonde and you're going lighter or darker that's one thing. But if you're a brunette or a redhead and you want to be a blonde, well, you've got to have a hairdresser that knows what they're doing, or the hair could suffer a lot of damage.'

'I didn't realize it was such an involved process.'

'Oh, it is.' Mara seemed to warm to her subject. 'The most common way to go from brown to blonde is to do a double process. That's stripping the base or natural color before toning it to the shade you want. A natural brunette always has to do the double process because the color has to be lifted first.' She paused to take a breath. 'I had one customer who had really dark brown hair. She wanted it dyed blonde – frosted, no less. That was a real trip, took a couple hours, but she tipped well, so . . .' Mara shrugged. 'I gritted my teeth and did it for her.'

Ah, there was my opening. 'I've always thought frosted hair was pretty. A friend of mine was thinking about frosting her hair. Sheila Blackwell.'

'Isn't that funny. My customer's name was Sheila too.' She resumed cutting as she continued, 'Said she needed a change, wanted an entirely new look. Well, I gave it to her all right. Brightened her face right up. I saw her in town a few times after that. She'd changed her makeup – 'n went on the lighter side – and her clothes were different too. It was like she was a whole other person.' Mara snipped some more off my ends and went on, 'I saw her in the superstore up on the highway about a week ago, told her that she was due for a color touch-up. She said she'd call to make an appointment, but she never did.' Mara leaned in closer and said in a conspiratorial tone, 'Ya know, it wouldn't surprise me if she blew this town.'

I craned my neck around to look at her. 'What makes you say that?'

'Well . . .' She gave a quick glance around and then said in a low tone, 'The last time she came in here for a trim, she was all wound up. Nervous. I asked her what was wrong and she said, "What do you think, Mara? It's a man." Then she looks me straight in the eyes and she says, "Mara, take it from me – sometimes guys aren't worth all the trouble we woman go to. I'd be much better off if I never laid eyes on him again." I agreed with her one hundred and twenty percent. I mean, I'd only just had my own little set-to with my own boyfriend – well now ex-boyfriend – the night before.' Mara snorted. 'He thought he was God's gift to women, he did, and I should be just thrilled he deigns to go out with me, so I should kiss his feet, or somethin'.'

I cleared my throat. I had to get Mara back on track before she launched into a lengthy description of her ex's faults. 'Yes, men can be difficult,' I said. 'So, you think Sheila had a bad experience with this man?'

'It sounded that way. She sounded kind of . . . oh, I don't know how to describe it.'

'Scared?' I ventured.

Mara shook her head. 'Nope, not scared. She wasn't the type to get scared. It was more aggravated. Now mind you, she didn't come right out and say it, but . . .' Mara glanced around the salon once again, then leaned in a bit closer to me. 'If you ask me, I think she was whoopin' it up with some married guy.'

I had to grab the sides of the chair to keep from falling off. I hadn't expected to hear anything like that. 'What makes you think she was going with a married man?'

Mara pulled a stool over and plopped down on it. She hitched it close to my chair and said, 'Just a feeling I got. She talked about meeting this guy in out-of-the-way places. One restaurant she named is miles from here. It seemed like they didn't want to be seen together. Oh, that girl had secrets. Mark my words.' Mara picked up a mirror from the counter and held it up so I could see the back of my head. 'So what do you think? Is that OK, or do you want more taken off?'

I left the Clip N Curl at exactly five o'clock. Mara had managed to give me a nice trim, not to mention information, and I rewarded her with a tip that was twice the price of the trim. She gave me her card, told me to give her a call when I needed another trim, or anything really. Personally, I had the feeling she was itching to try her hand at changing my hair color. She'd mentioned how nice I'd look with my hair a more vibrant shade of red at least a half-dozen times.

I thought about Mara's assertion that Sheila's boyfriend had been married. Maybe she'd wanted to break it off and the man hadn't taken her rejection well. Or, there was another possibility as well. Perhaps the man's wife had found out, confronted Sheila, and they'd argued. A knife wasn't usually a woman's weapon of choice, but it was possible. After all, hadn't I written two books in which a woman had stabbed her victim to death? I was so wrapped up in my thoughts that I didn't see the man loom up in front of me until I almost stepped on his foot. 'Oh, I'm so sorry,' I began, and then stopped as I recognized him as the reporter, Derek Proust.

Proust smiled at me. 'You're Charlotte James, right? I understand you're the one who found the body? It was in the basement of your store, correct?'

I narrowed my eyes and took a step backward. 'I'm sorry, but I'm not at liberty to discuss details,' I murmured.

I started to turn away, but Proust was at my side in an instant. 'The police statement didn't say much, just that there would be an investigation. I'm thinking it could be more along the lines of a suspicious death. You found the body. Would you agree?'

I blew out a breath. 'I'm sorry, what part of I'm not at liberty to discuss details didn't you understand,' I snapped. 'Now if you'll kindly excuse me.'

He stepped to one side. 'Fine, Ms James. Just know I think there's a bigger story here somewhere, and I intend to find it.'

I tossed him a wave over one shoulder. 'Good luck.'

Zane's Chevy was in the driveway when I arrived back at the house. I parked behind her and hurried inside. Zane wasn't at the kitchen table, so I went over to the stairway and shouted, 'Zane, I'm home. I found out something interesting.'

I heard a door slam and then Zane came rushing down the

stairs. She launched herself into my arms before I could say another word.

'You've got to help me Charley,' she cried into my shoulder. 'I think the police believe I had something to do with Sheila's death.'

TEN

I slipped my arm around Zane's waist and led her over to the kitchen table. Poe was snoozing on one of the chairs. I gave him a gentle nudge and he jumped down, giving me a baleful glare over his shoulder. I squeezed Zane's arm. 'Sit here,' I directed. 'Take a deep breath.'

Zane did as I directed, then looked at me. 'Thanks. I feel a little better now.' She let out a sigh. 'I had to accompany Barbie – oh, excuse me, *Officer Donaldson* – to the morgue,' Zane said. She dropped her head into her hands. 'It was Sheila, all right. No doubt about it.'

I eased into the chair beside Zane and rubbed my hand up and down her back. 'I'm sorry, honey,' I said.

Zane raised her gaze to meet mine, and I saw the rims of her eyes were red. Apparently she'd had herself a good cry. 'Thanks. There was a small part of me that hoped it wasn't so, but . . .' She moaned and waved her hands helplessly.

'I'm so sorry,' I said again. We sat silently for a few moments and then I reached out and covered Zane's hand with my own. 'When you came down you said you thought the police suspected you had something to do with Sheila's death. What made you say that?'

Zane averted her gaze slightly and waved her hand in a lazy circle. 'Nothing specific. I mean, Barbie didn't come out and accuse me, it was just something in her manner, the way she spoke to me. She surely likes to throw her police power muscle around.'

'Yeah, she told me to call her *Officer Donaldson* too. I honestly wouldn't worry about what Barbie thinks, Zane. After all, there's no reason for the police to suspect you, right?'

Zane stared down at the floor as if she'd never seen gray and black checked linoleum before. She mumbled, 'Of course not. I didn't kill Sheila. But after I ID'd the body, Barbie took me into a little room and asked me a ton of questions about Sheila.' Zane leaned back in the chair, dabbed at her eyes with the edge of her sweater. 'I answered what I could, but she kept asking me about Sheila's past, where she'd come from, her relationships. I told her that those topics never came up in conversation and I never thought to ask her about it, but I don't think she believed me.' Zane paused and then added, 'She wanted to know if Sheila ever wanted out of our partnership.'

'Did she?' I asked as Zane fell silent.

'Of course not.' Zane dropped her head into her hands. 'Why would they suspect me,' she wailed. 'I had no reason to want to kill her. If anything, her death caused a big problem. If you hadn't come along and made that offer to take over the business, I don't know where I'd be.' She lifted her head up and looked at me. 'You said you found out something interesting?'

'Yeah. Remember the name on the note I found underneath the hot plate? It turns out Mara's short for Marilyn. She works at the Clip N Curl, and she was Sheila's hairstylist. She said that she thought Sheila had a married lover.'

Zane pushed hair out of her eyes with the heel of her hand. 'I know Marilyn,' she said. 'She likes to gossip just as much as Phyllis, or any of the other old biddies in this town. Sheila was pretty private, but Marilyn has a gift, a way of drawing information out. If she thought Sheila had a married lover, then chances are good she did. But don't ask me who it could be, because I have no clue.'

I got up, walked over to the island and brought my laptop back to the table. 'I want to show you something,' I said. I opened it up and showed Zane the screen I'd been looking at prior to Grant's visit. 'This photograph most closely resembled the body I saw in the trunk,' I said. 'What do you think?'

Zane leaned forward to peer at the photograph. 'It's hard to say,' she said at last. 'I can't picture Sheila with brown hair, but . . . this photo does resemble her a bit.' She frowned and pointed to the words on the side of the screen. 'The name's Sheila Blackwell, though, not Crowder.'

'Well . . . it could be the same Sheila. I'm thinking she might have changed her name as well as hair color.' I pulled out the sliver of lilac stationery and laid it on the table in front of Zane. 'I found that on the cellar floor – or rather Poe did.'

As Zane looked at it I explained my theory and added what Phyllis and Mara had said about Sheila possibly hiding from an ex. Zane listened and when I was finished said, 'I guess it's possible. But won't the police be able to find out who she is?'

'Yes, but it could take a while. There are three ways to identify a body I know of. One is through fingerprints, the second is dental records, and the third is DNA. DNA is the most accurate, but it takes quite a while, at least six to eight weeks. Fingerprints are usually the fastest method. They can run them through IAFIS for fingerprint identification to see if she might have had a criminal record.'

'A criminal record!' Zane cried, aghast. 'Oh gee, I doubt that.'

'We have to stay open to all possibilities,' I replied. 'I'm sure Grant will do an internet search too.'

'I take it you're not going to show him this little sliver of paper? If he finds out, won't he accuse you of withholding evidence in a police investigation?'

'I have no proof that this is any sort of evidence,' I said. 'That paper could have been down there for years. That the first name is the same as the victim's could just be a coincidence.'

Zane looked at the photo on my laptop screen. 'You've just proven it's not a coincidence, though.'

I took the paper and shoved it back into my pocket. 'Grant seems a very thorough sort of person. I'm sure he'll leave no stone unturned trying to find out about Sheila, but I can't help but wish that we could get one jump ahead of them.'

'It seems to me you already are,' Zane said dryly. 'You always wanted to be the first to solve a puzzle, Charley. You haven't changed one bit.'

'Funny, Jeff said pretty much the same thing.'

'Oh, I almost forgot about him!' Zane slapped her forehead with her palm. 'How'd it go today? Did you two hit it off – before you found the body, that is?'

'Sort of. He actually asked if I wanted to meet him for lunch later, but my appetite had already taken a nosedive.'

'Too bad. But I bet there'll be more opportunities for you two to get together. He's got to come back to finish looking at the wiring, right?'

'Right.' I moved my finger around in a lazy circle. 'So I take it Jeff isn't going with anyone? That's kind of hard to believe. He was always so popular in high school.'

'He's still popular. I heard talk that he was seeing someone until recently . . . Rumor has it she broke it off with him, and he was pretty devastated over it. I guess he really liked her.' Zane paused. 'Maybe the two of you shouldn't get together. You don't want to be his rebound person.'

I chuckled. 'For that matter, he'd be mine too, after Henry.'

'Oh yeah. Almost forgot about good old Henry. Seriously, though, Charley, I always liked Jeff. Ladies like him, and vice versa, but he's one of the good guys, not a jerk like my exes – oh jeez!'

I looked at my friend. Her cheeks were red, and her eyes had started to bug out of her head. 'What's the matter?' I asked.

'Bobby Proctor,' she said. 'Thinking about him made me remember that Sheila came over here one night with some wine. She was trying to cheer me up. I'd been complaining to her earlier about him.'

I pulled a face. 'This would be the same Bobby Proctor who ate a tadpole in biology class?'

'Yeah, that one. And he didn't really eat the tadpole, he just pretended to. Anyway, we went out for a while, but Bobby being Bobby, and a colossal jerk to boot, well, it didn't last long. So I was complaining to Sheila and she said she understood how I felt because she had an ex, too. I remember how her expression changed when she said it, like she'd just sucked on a lemon.' Zane's forehead crinkled in thought. 'She said "I know the feeling. I've got a doozy of an ex as well." She clammed up after that, and I didn't press for details. I could see she didn't want to talk about him.'

'Do you think it's possible she had some contact with him since she came here to Austin?'

'Not from the way she talked about him,' replied Zane. 'If she did, it sure wasn't her idea.'

I bit back my sigh of frustration and said, 'OK, let's table that area for now. You said Sheila handled the paperwork for the stores?'

At Zane's nod I went on, 'I looked on the Chamber of Commerce website, but I didn't see any listing for Mainly

Mysteries – that was what she was going to call the bookstore, right?'

Zane nodded. 'Yes. I remember because she said she was going to spell it like the state.'

'Spell it like the state?'

'Yeah. M-A-I-N-E-L-Y Mysteries.'

'That's interesting,' I murmured. 'That she would think of that. Maybe it's possible she came from Maine?'

Zane shrugged. 'Maybe. She said the different spelling would make an impression, make the store stand out in people's minds. Anyway, I don't know why it wasn't on there. Most likely they haven't updated the C of C website yet. They are pretty slow.'

'That's possible. By the way, what is the name of your bakery?'

Zane's face split in a wide smile. 'Zaney's Sweet Treats. And before you ask, yes, that was Sheila's idea too.'

'Seems as if Sheila was pretty good at making up things,' I murmured. Just how well remained to be seen. I called up the Chamber of Commerce website again and typed in M-A-I-N-E-L-Y Mysteries. Still nothing.

Zane's voice wobbled a little as she said, 'I know I filled out a form. I gave her a copy of my driver's license to take with it.' She grabbed my arm. 'Oh gosh, Charley, what if Sheila never did get around to registering the businesses! For sure we won't be able to open on time.' She dropped her head into her hands. 'I trusted her with all these details, and now . . .'

I reached out to pat her hand. 'Don't fret. I'll look into everything tomorrow,' I assured her.

Zane shot me a grateful look. 'Thanks, Charley. I just never gave all these details any consideration, because Sheila seemed to have it so well under control – or so I thought.'

'Well, how about you go get changed, and I'll put dinner on. I don't know about you, but I've always found a good meal helps me put things in perspective.'

'I wasn't hungry when I came home, but now . . . I could definitely go for a bite.' Zane pushed back her chair and stood. 'I'll just grab a quick shower and wash the stench of that morgue away.'

Zane hurried upstairs and I moved over to the stove. I melted butter in the skillet and tossed the garlic in. After about two minutes,

I added chicken broth, milk, and fettuccine, well-seasoned with salt and pepper. As I stood stirring my concoction, I let my thoughts wander. Sheila was certainly a person of mystery, that was for sure. Finding out information about her wasn't going to be easy, considering all the possible suspects were vague: an ex from somewhere that she might have feared, and a possible married lover and his jealous wife. There could be other possible scenarios as well. Might she have been involved in some sort of illegal activity? And, if I really wanted to stretch it, maybe she'd been witness to a major crime and was in the Witness Protection Program. Perhaps the perpetrator had found out where she was hiding and . . .

I gave myself a whack on the side of the head. Those scenarios were worthy of C.J. Barrett, mystery writer, but did they play in real life? It was hard to say. It was possible if not probable. One thing was apparent – the key to the whole thing was in finding out more about Sheila's past. How to do that, though, was an even bigger mystery.

Zane returned just as I stirred in the Parmesan. I gave it a few more turns, then sprinkled parsley on top of it and divided everything on to two plates which I brought to the table. I set them down, then went to the refrigerator and pulled out a bottle of white wine. Zane eyed it as I set it down.

'Riesling, that's my favorite,' she cried. She twirled some fettuccine around her fork, popped it into her mouth, and then made a little sound, deep in her throat. 'Ooh, so good. You should have been a chef, Charley.'

'Yeah, don't get carried away. I'm not that great a cook, but there are a few things I can do well.' I raised my glass. 'Let's just relax and enjoy the meal.'

We clinked glasses and for a few minutes neither of us spoke, just hunkered down over the meal. I watched her as I twirled more pasta around my fork. I'd seen Zane in this sort of mood before, usually when she was trying to keep a secret from me. I had the uncomfortable feeling that was the case now. Zane knew a bit more than she was letting on, and she was holding something back. But just what that something might be, I had no idea. I couldn't get what Grant had said earlier out of my mind, and I hoped that whatever it was Zane was keeping from me wouldn't end up getting her in trouble.

ELEVEN

The Austin Chamber of Commerce had their offices on the second floor of City Hall, an imposing brick structure located right in the center of town. The website said the office opened at nine a.m., so precisely at two minutes past the hour I pushed through the double glass doors and walked up to the wide counter. The counter was bare save for a holder that contained several brochures. A computer and monitor sat at a small desk just behind the counter. There was no one in the office, but there was a bell next to the brochures with a little placard beside it which read, RING FOR SERVICE. I slapped my hand down on the bell, which let out a sharp *br-ring*! About a minute later a door at the rear of the room opened and a woman stepped out. She was average height, and dressed in a simple black skirt, matching jacket, and a pale blue V-necked blouse. Her hair was caught up in a chignon at the nape of her neck and as she drew closer I saw a few strands of gray peeping out at her temples. Sharp blue eyes peered at me from behind a pair of horn-rimmed glasses perched on the bridge of her nose. She shot me a smile that seemed a bit forced as she said, 'Good morning. I'm Miss Ames. How may I help you?'

I stretched my lips in as wide a smile as I could muster. 'Good morning. My name is Charlotte James. I'm taking over a business here in Austin from someone else and I'd like to make sure everything is in order. I tried looking up the business last night on your database, but I couldn't find it.'

Miss Ames gave a soft grunt. 'Most likely our admin hasn't updated our database yet,' she said, 'but I'll check.' She moved over to the computer, adjusted her glasses, and started tapping at the keyboard. In a brisk, businesslike tone she asked, 'What's the name of the business?'

'Mainely Mysteries. It's spelled like the state.' I spelled Mainely out. 'By the way, it's a double storefront and my partner's paperwork should also have been filed. Zaney's Sweet Treats.'

Miss Ames looked up from the computer screen. 'Those names are very familiar. Oh, yes, here they are. Yes, paperwork was filed two weeks ago by a Ms Sheila Blackwell.'

My head jerked up. 'You said Sheila Blackwell? Not Crowder?'

She looked back at the screen. 'Actually, she signed the paperwork Sheila Crowder Blackwell. You're taking over the business from her?'

'Yes, she . . . ah . . . had a family emergency and had to abandon the project. I'm assuming I'll need to fill out new paperwork?'

Miss Ames shook her head. 'In this case, a notice of principal name change will suffice. Ms Blackwell registered both businesses as sole proprietorships. It's often easier that way, especially with two separate storefronts. But you probably should cancel the existing DBA and file for a new one if you want a name change. And of course you'll have to contact the IRS to see if you need a new EIN. As for the permits . . .' She tapped at the keyboard again. 'The business license can be updated for the bookstore. Oh, and the health department will have to inspect the bakery premises. I'll arrange that for you. Ordinarily this would have been done already but the check she gave us bounced. We sent her a letter but to date have not received a reply.'

I sighed. There was a lot more to opening a business than I'd realized. Sheila, on the other hand, had apparently known just what needed to be done. How had she gained that knowledge? Had she operated a similar business wherever she'd come from? I needed to check that out too. Aloud I said to Miss Ames, 'I didn't realize there was so much involved. Perhaps I should consult a lawyer?'

'You could, but it really isn't necessary. Everything pretty much can be done online. If you want to change your store's name, you just need to file a new fictitious name registration. You can reserve an available name for a hundred twenty days by filing a Name Reservation/Transfer of Reservation form with the Pennsylvania DOS. I can give you the name of some websites which can walk you through the process.'

'Thanks, I'd appreciate that,' I said. 'If you tell me what's owed, I'll write you a check right now.'

Miss Ames told me the fee, then took paper and pen and jotted down a few names for me while I finished writing out the check. She handed me the paper and I stuck it in my tote bag. She took the check, tapped on the keyboard again, and then said to me, 'The health department will be in touch for a good time to come out for an inspection of the bakery. Should they contact you or Ms Adams?'

'Either of us.' I gave Miss Ames both cell numbers. She took them down, then printed out a paper and rose. 'I'll see if I can get hold of the health inspector now, if you don't mind waiting a few minutes?'

'No problem.'

Miss Ames vanished into the back room, leaving me alone in the office – but not for long. A few minutes later the front door opened and a plump, gray-haired woman wearing a denim skirt and embroidered denim blouse came in. I recognized her instantly. Betty Stubing owned the Frozen Spoon, Austin's only ice cream parlor. It had been in her family for generations. The ice cream was home churned and delicious, and the shop was well known for unique flavor not found anywhere else, like trail mix or curry and lime. They didn't sound very appetizing but trust me . . . they were. Betty stepped up to the counter and glanced over at me. Her head inclined slightly. 'Hello,' she said.

'Hello, Ms Stubing,' I said. 'You may not remember me, but I surely remember your delicious ice cream.' I held out my hand. 'I'm Charley – Charlotte James.'

Betty gave me a warm smile as she took my outstretched hand. 'Charlotte James! I heard you'd come back to town! And after all this time, too. You've been living and working in Chicago?'

'New York. I worked for a magazine there.'

'Right, right. And your parents moved to Orlando?'

'Mesa, Arizona. And they're doing fine. They both love the hundred-degree-plus weather and the low humidity.'

Betty wrinkled her nose. 'On a below-zero day out here I wouldn't mind a hundred degrees myself,' she said. She inclined her head toward the counter. 'Anybody working here today?'

'Yes, Miss Ames. She's in the back, getting something for me. I've decided to go into business with my friend Zane. You remember Zane Adams?'

'Indeed I do.' Betty paused and then said, 'What a shame about her friend.'

Ah, so the news was out. I figured as much. I nodded. 'Yes, it's a shame. I don't believe a definite cause of death has been established yet, though.'

'I saw the yellow tape. I hope it doesn't hold up your opening. It's nice of you to help your friend out. I imagine this means you'll be sticking around Austin for a while?'

'I'm planning on it.'

'That's good.' Betty hesitated and then said, 'I don't like to speak ill of the dead, but I truly think your friend is better off going into business with you.'

'Why do you say that?'

'Just the impression I got.' The corners of Betty's thin lips drooped. 'Mind you, I didn't know her but she did come in the ice cream parlor a few times.' She paused and then added, 'She met a *friend* there once or twice.'

I caught the inflection in Betty's tone when she said the word friend. I decided to bite the bullet. 'A boyfriend? I'd heard she might have been seeing someone.'

Betty sniffed. 'I guess you could call him her boyfriend. I'd say lover was a better word.' She inched closer to me. 'They used to meet at least once a week in my shop. They both wore dark glasses and sat in the back, as if that would fool anyone. I mean, they were two people I'd never have put together, not in a million years.' She gave a derisive snort. 'The last time they were in was about a week and a half ago. Apparently, they had some sort of argument and she stormed out. I didn't see it myself – I was in the back – but my cashier gave me a blow by blow.' She leaned closer to me and whispered, 'She was with Gino Galante!'

'Gino Galante?' I couldn't help it. My jaw dropped. I remembered Gino. He and his wife Connie had owned the Leaning Tower, which was a pizzeria done up to look like the Leaning Tower of Pisa, for years. I remembered their food from high school. The pizza had been superb, and they also served sandwiches and salads. I had to agree with Betty. Talk about an odd coupling!

Betty was nodding, her gray curls swinging to and fro. She warmed to her subject and continued, 'Oh yeah. And according to my cashier, they had more than a lover's spat. Sheila hurled some insults at him, and he threatened to wring her neck.'

That coupling just didn't seem right to me. 'Are you certain that they were dating? Maybe they met for some other reason.'

Betty shot me a stupefied look. She might as well have said, *Are you nuts*? 'What other reason would the two of them have for getting together?'

'Well, Sheila was starting up a business. Maybe she needed capital.'

'If she needed money she should have gone to the bank. Besides, everyone knows Gino's tight with a buck. Although, maybe for her he'd have made an exception.' She shook her head. 'I bet they were fighting because Gloria found out about them.'

'Gloria? I thought his wife's name was Connie?'

'Oh, that's right, you've been away. Connie was his first wife. Gloria is his second. She's a trophy wife, and believe you me she's not one to abdicate her throne so easily.' Betty nodded her head in satisfaction. 'Sheila's taking off like that makes perfect sense, now. Gloria probably confronted her, maybe even threatened her.'

Or worse. 'What does Gloria look like?'

'Like every other forty-something ex-beauty queen. Very well preserved.'

Miss Ames chose that moment to return from the other room, and Betty stepped quickly aside, our conversation ended. Miss Ames informed me that the health department was a trifle backed up, but someone would be calling later in the week to set up an appointment. I bid her and Betty goodbye and headed on to my next stop.

After spending an hour at the First Mercantile Bank I decided to grab a cup of coffee and something light to eat at Jumpin' Beans. I'd been fortunate enough to have the same woman who'd assisted Sheila wait on me at the bank. It had been the same deal – Sheila had opened the account under the name Sheila Crowder Blackwell. I signed a new account card listing myself as the principal, and she gave me another set to return when I decided on a new business name. She too didn't seem too surprised to learn that Sheila had abandoned the business, and also mentioned that Sheila had seemed to be unduly nervous when she'd come in to open the business account. She'd chalked it up to nerves, and echoed Miss Ames' sentiments about being able to handle the pressure of running her own business. Neither one seemed to have heard about Sheila's body being found, and I wondered how those women might react when the truth finally came out.

Phyllis was behind the counter when I entered the coffee shop, and she waved me over. 'Charlotte James! You've been holding out on me! Why didn't you tell me that Sheila died in your store?' she cried out.

I gave a quick look around, but the other patrons seemed more interested in their own conversation and coffee than in Phyllis's outburst. 'It's not exactly a hot conversation topic,' I said. 'Besides, Detective Grant and Bar— Officer Donaldson both swore me to secrecy.'

'I knew it!' Phyllis's eyes gleamed and she snapped her fingers in the air. She leaned across the counter and lowered her voice to a stage whisper. 'She was murdered, wasn't she?'

I gave my head a brisk shake. 'I can't say,' I replied. 'No offense, but it's the whole sworn to secrecy thing. I don't need Grant's wrath coming down on me.'

Phyllis's eyes twinkled. 'What about Barbara Jeanne Donaldson's?'

I waved my hand in a dismissive gesture. 'Hers I can handle.'

'Well, you know the old saying. Hell hath no fury and all that. Rumor has it that Barbara Jeanne feels you're cutting in on her territory.'

Now I did laugh. 'You mean Detective Grant?'

Phyllis laughed. 'Of course Detective Grant. It's no secret Barbara Jeanne has it bad for the guy. He's been here a lot over the past year, attending various lectures at Swarthmore, and she wasted no time honing in on him.' She slid me a look. 'I don't think he feels the same about her, though. At least not that I've noticed.'

Oddly enough, that made me feel pretty good. Aloud I said, 'Yeah, well, I'm sorry to disappoint you, but there's definitely nothing romantic between the good detective and myself.'

'Well, not yet anyway. But I saw the way the two of you looked at each other the other day.'

I goggled at her. 'Oh, you mean when he was chastising me for bumping his briefcase? Shooting dagger looks at me?'

'There's a fine line between love and hate. Not that the two of you hate each other. You don't, do you?'

'Hate's a strong word. I reserve that for Brussels sprouts. Intensely dislike would be a better description.'

'OK, you don't want to talk about it. I get it. Let's talk about something else.' Phyllis cocked her head at me. 'Your hair looks different. Did you do something to it?'

I fussed with my ends self-consciously. 'I got a trim last night.'

She studied me again. 'It looks nice, but you look all worn out, dearie, and so early in the day.'

'Well, I've had a busy morning, taking care of odds and ends for the stores. I never realized just what went into setting up a small business.'

Phyllis nodded. 'It can be stressful. Are you sorry you told your friend you'd do it?'

I shook my head. 'No, not at all. But I could use a nice mocha latte to help me keep up my strength.' My stomach let out a loud growl as I said that, and I glanced at the blackboard behind the counter. 'It seems like forever since I've eaten. All I had this morning was a cup of coffee and a slice of dry toast.'

Phyllis clucked her tongue at me. 'Well now, you need to keep up your energy. How about a ham and egg breakfast sandwich? I'll even throw in an extra slice of ham.' She made a shooing motion with her hand. 'Have a seat and I'll bring that coffee right over.'

'Thanks.'

There was a small stand off to the side with newspapers and magazines on it. I picked up a copy of the *Austin Bugle* and settled myself in at the table near the kitchen door. I found the story about Sheila on page three. It was sketchy at best. Proust merely said that Ms Crowder's body had been found in her store, and police were treating the circumstances of death as 'suspicious.'

I set the newspaper off to one side and let my gaze wander around the room, settling on a woman seated a few tables over. She had what I'd describe as a kind face, framed by an iron-gray pixie cut. Her clothes weren't shabby, but they appeared to be well worn. What really attracted my attention, though, was the large yellow dog seated beside her. He looked like a golden retriever, and he wore a blue vest. The patch on its side identified him as a service animal. I wondered if the animal was the woman's, and if so, why she needed him.

Phyllis arrived a few minutes later and set my latte down. She noticed me eyeing the dog and remarked, 'Beautiful animal, isn't he? That's Finn. He's a service dog. That's his owner, Nancy Marker.'

'He is a beautiful dog,' I agreed. 'Why does that woman need a service dog?'

'Poor thing. She suffers from PTSD and sometimes gets disoriented. Finn helps keep her grounded.'

Well, there was my answer. Phyllis, as usual, came through. I glanced over at Nancy, who had set down her coffee and was now bent over, patting the dog on his head. 'PTSD you say? That's a shame.' I'd done research for a character in one of my books and I knew that PTSD, or post-traumatic stress disorder, can develop after a very stressful, frightening, or distressing event. The character in my book had suffered a physical assault. I wondered briefly what Nancy might have suffered to have contracted the malady.

'She used to be in the army,' said Phyllis. 'I never asked her but it's probably something that happened during her term of service. I know she's retired now, lives over in that retirement community on the highway – Brookvale Senior Community.'

Nancy got up and so did Finn. The two of them headed for the door. 'Her illness doesn't stop her from leading a full life,' observed Phyllis. 'She works over at Kitchen on the Fry on Elm Street part time. Sells small appliances and cookbooks.' Phyllis shook her head. 'She had a hard time getting a job because of Finn. A lot of the shop owners couldn't be bothered with having a dog, even a service dog, on the premises. Come to think of it, she might not even have that job if not for Sheila.'

I paused, coffee midway to my lips. 'What did Sheila have to do with it?'

'Sheila saw Nancy in here a few times and the two of them got to talking, about the dog I think. Nancy had just put in for a job at Kitchen on the Fry and had gotten turned down. The owner just happened to come in the same day and Sheila wasted no time in ripping right into him about it. Called him inhuman and threatened to go to the Better Business Bureau and register a complaint.' She let out a chuckle. 'Two days later, Nancy had a job. That's probably where she's headed now. Works three days a week, from noon to five.'

'Interesting.' I made a mental note to look up Nancy later. I turned to Phyllis and said, 'I met Betty Stubing down at the Chamber offices this morning. She told me Sheila used to meet a man at her shop.'

Phyllis let out a chuckle. 'Oh yes. Gino Galante.'

I raised an eyebrow. 'You knew?'

'Lots of people knew. I'm sure they thought they were being discreet, but . . .' Phyllis spread her hands.

'You think they were dating?'

'A friend of mine saw them together one evening at the Iron Griddle out on Highway 101. They were tucked in a dark corner, all cozy like. I'm sure they weren't discussing the weather,' she added with a sly grin. 'And I know they met a few times at Betty's ice cream parlor. Tried to act all casual, but . . .' she shrugged.

I took a sip of my coffee. 'Do you think his wife knew?'

'Gloria? I'm sure she did. Whether she cared or not is something else again. Anyway, I'm sure Gloria had nothing to worry about. Like I said, Sheila liked to flirt. And Gino wouldn't have wanted a divorce.' She wiggled her fingers. 'That would have cost him plenty, trust me.'

'You said Sheila liked to flirt,' I said. 'Did she have another boyfriend?'

Phyllis shrugged. 'She could have. There were lots of rumors.' A bell rang in the back and Phyllis rose. 'Your sandwich must be almost ready. You want ketchup with that?'

'Yes, please.' I picked up my cup, gulped down the remainder of my latte. Judging from the line that had started to form, I figured I'd missed my opportunity to get any more information out of Phyllis today. I glanced out the window and saw Nancy and Finn turn the corner, and inspiration struck. 'Oh, Phyllis,' I called after her. 'Would you mind making my sandwich to go?'

I looked up where Kitchen on the Fry was located while I waited for my sandwich, but as it happened, I didn't need to. As I passed the town square, I caught sight of Nancy seated on one of the benches by the gazebo, Finn at her feet. Finn's head lifted immediately as I drew near, and he gave me a curious look before rising to his feet. I stood a few steps back and cleared my throat. 'Good morning,' I said.

Nancy fixed her sharp brown eyes on me, then glanced at the watch on her wrist. 'It's eleven fifteen so yes, it's still morning.' Her head cocked to one side and she paused, studying me for a minute. 'Do I know you?' she asked at last.

I shook my head. 'No, we've never met. I'm Charlotte James, but my friends call me Charley.'

'Nancy Marker.' Nancy nodded toward the dog. 'And this is Finn.'

I leaned toward the dog. 'Hello, Finn,' I said softly. I looked at Nancy. 'Can I pet him?'

Nancy nodded, and I extended my hand. Finn raised his head and stepped up to me. He gave my hand a curious sniff and studied me for a moment with his limpid brown eyes. Then, apparently deciding I posed no threat to his human, he returned to Nancy and lay down at her feet. He placed his head on his paws and after giving me one more look, closed his eyes.

Nancy laughed. 'Well, you've passed inspection,' she said. She looked at the dog with a fond expression. 'And Finn is pretty fussy.'

I grinned and gestured toward the bench. 'Mind if I join you?' I asked.

Nancy nodded. 'Please do. I'd enjoy the company. I usually work in the afternoon, but I took the day off today. Finn has a vet appointment.'

I eased into the space beside her and inclined my head toward the dog. 'I see Finn wears a service vest,' I ventured.

'Yes, he does.' Nancy gave the dog a fond look. 'I suffer from a mental disorder, and Finn is my rock. I've gotten disoriented quite a few times – didn't know just where I was – and he always leads me back home.' She reached down and gave the dog another pat on the head. 'He's a good dog.'

I smiled. 'He certainly seems to be. He's very protective of you.'

'He's trained to be that way, but yes. He's very smart.' She returned her hand to her lap and gave me another sharp look. 'You're new in town,' she said.

'Actually, I grew up here. I've only recently moved back a few days ago.'

'Moved back, eh?' Nancy let out a chuckle. 'What's that old

saying? You can't go home again? Personally, I never put much stock in it. I hear lots of young people complaining about life around here, but for my money there's nothing wrong with Austin. It's a nice town.' Her gaze raked me up and down. 'Where did you move back from?'

'New York City.'

Nancy let out a low whistle. 'Austin's quite a change from that, I'm sure. What did you do in New York, if you don't mind my asking?'

'Not at all. I was a researcher for a magazine.'

Nancy wrinkled her nose. 'That sounds boring. So, what sort of work are you looking for here? You're way too young to be retired.'

'A friend of mine was supposed to go into business with another woman, but she backed out of the venture rather suddenly, so I decided to take it over.' I paused. 'Maybe you've seen it. The vacant storefront on Elm and Water?'

'Elm and Water, you said?' Nancy's eyes widened, and she let out a little gasp and raised her hands to the sides of her face. 'Oh my goodness! That's Sheila's store,' she cried.

TWELVE

'Yes, Sheila Crowder,' I said. 'Did you know her?'

'Crowder. Was that her last name? She never said. I haven't spoken to her in a while.' Nancy shook her head. 'You said she backed out?'

Apparently, Nancy hadn't read the morning paper. I thought about breaking the news, but then I saw Grant in my mind's eye telling me not to discuss what had happened. So I just swallowed and said, 'She . . . ah . . . told my friend she had to leave town. I assume it was some sort of family emergency,' I answered. 'It all happened quite suddenly.'

Nancy scratched at her ear. 'I guess it did. We chatted a few times in the coffee shop. I wouldn't call her a friend. She was more of an acquaintance. But we had something in common.' Nancy hesitated and then said, 'Did I mention I suffer from a mental disorder? It's PTSD. Sheila suffered from that too.'

'Did she? I'm sorry to hear that,' I said, my mind racing. If Sheila had PTSD that might explain why people thought she'd seemed nervous the past few days. PTSD victims often suffered feelings of intense fear, helplessness, and stress. If that was so, however, then something had to have triggered it. A call or a visit from this ex, perhaps?

Nancy shifted on the bench. 'I don't talk about my disorder much. Most people don't understand. They hear PTSD and right away they put you in the mentally ill category. PTSD doesn't mean that at all. We just have to learn how to best manage our symptoms, and avoid what causes them.' She gave Finn's leash a tug. The dog lifted his head, then scooted over and placed it in Nancy's lap. Nancy started to stroke the dog's head. 'First time I saw her in Jumpin' Beans she admired Finn. Said that she had a dog like him once, but she had to give him up. Seems the guy she was livin' with at the time wasn't a fan of animals of any sort.' She gave a heartfelt sigh. 'You can't trust people who don't like animals. Unconditional love, that's what they give.

Anyway, I don't think she wanted to give up the dog, but I think she did it because she was afraid this guy might harm the animal. She never came out and said that, mind you. It was just the impression I got.'

'That's terrible,' I said. 'If that's the case she was better off without him.'

Nancy's head bobbed up and down. 'That's exactly what I said. She never came right out and said it, but I got the feeling that her PTSD stemmed from that guy.'

'What made you think that?'

'Little things she said. For instance, one day when we met for coffee she showed me her paperwork on the store. "If only Gary could see me now," she said, "he'd have a cow. He never thought I was capable of running my life let alone a business. But I tell you, the best thing I ever did was leave that loser."' She sighed again. 'It's such a shame. She sounded really upbeat about opening that store. Said it was the beginning of a whole new chapter in her life.'

I stretched my legs out in front of me. 'It sounds as if the breakup wasn't an amicable one.'

'I'm not sure about that. She never went into detail, but . . .' Nancy leaned in closer to me and lowered her voice to just above a whisper. 'I don't think they formally broke up. I think she just up and left him.'

I let my eyes widen a bit. 'You think she ran away from him?'

'She might have.' Nancy shifted a bit on the bench. 'It's just a gut feeling I got. Like I said, she never went into detail. Sheila was very close-mouthed. She only told people what she wanted them to know.'

Nancy's hand, poised over Finn's head, stilled for a moment, then she continued petting the dog. 'I know that Sheila liked attention from men.'

'I'd heard she was a bit of a flirt.'

'A bit?' Nancy let out a guffaw. 'That's putting it mildly. Anyway, she was seeing someone pretty steadily, that I know. And as was typical of Sheila, she didn't talk about it very much. She did mention at one point that he was younger than her, and it could be a problem. Apparently, he was more interested in her than she in him.'

I frowned. 'You're certain she said he was younger? Not older?'

Nancy shook her head. 'No, I'm positive she said younger. Why?'

'Well, I'd heard that she'd been seen around with Gino Galante.'

'Gino Galante!' Nancy's lips formed an O of surprise. 'The guy who owns the Leaning Tower. Oh, gosh no. I doubt that's true. If she was seen with Galante, there was some other reason. They weren't dating, I'd bet my life on it. But . . .' Nancy stopped petting Finn and jabbed at the air with her finger. 'We met up last week, and she wasn't herself at all. Seemed real nervous, kept looking out the window. Nearly jumped out of her seat a few times. I thought maybe her PTSD was acting up. Finally, I asked her what was wrong and she looked at me – I tell you, it was a look that chilled me to the bone – and she said, "Nancy, life is a game that one plays according to the rules, and I've never been one for rules." Then she shook her head and laughed. "Nancy, just ignore me," she said, "I'm probably making too much out of nothing and my PTSD is rearing its ugly head. Forget I said anything."' Nancy looked me straight in the eye. 'I kept hoping after that night I'd run into her, but no dice.' She tapped at her stomach. 'I've had a bad feeling about her, ever since.'

'You had no way to contact her? No phone number to call?'

Nancy shook her head. 'I had to give up my cell – it cost too much money. I remember Sheila had a nice big phone – one of those new Android models – and she had it in a shiny pink case. We just ran into each other around the same time. Like I said, we were just acquaintances. To be honest, if it weren't for the fact we both suffered from PTSD I doubt we'd have spoken as often as we did.' She let out a sigh. 'I suppose I could have gone over to Mrs Dinwiddie's. Now I'm kicking myself that I didn't.'

'Mrs Dinwiddie's?'

'It's a rooming house over on Seventh Street and South. Actually, calling it a rooming house is being kind. It's a dive,' Nancy said bluntly.

'Sheila was living there?'

'Well, she never came right out and said so, but she mentioned a few times how noisy it was there. If she weren't staying there, how would she know that?' Nancy stared off into space for a few moments, and I wondered if her PTSD was acting up. After a few moments she swung her gaze back to me. 'So, when are you planning on opening the bookstore?'

I paused, a bit off-put by the rapid change in subject. 'We're shooting for the first week in October.' I held up my hand. 'Fingers crossed.'

'That's good. Just in time for holiday shopping. I'll be sure to drop in. I like mystery novels. You're still going to stock them, right?'

'Absolutely. I plan on stocking other types of books as well, but the concentration will be mainly mysteries and thrillers, just as Sheila intended.'

'Mainely Mysteries,' murmured Nancy. 'That is a catchy name. Sheila struggled with finding just the right name. Then one day she says to me, "I've got it, Nancy. What am I going to stock? Mainly mysteries, right? Isn't that just the perfect name?"' She let out a sigh. 'She was so proud about changing the spelling to be like the state. Said it would stand out, make people remember the name.'

'You've got a point there,' I conceded. 'Funny how she zeroed in on Maine, though.'

Nancy's lips screwed into a pensive expression. 'Sheila knew a lot about that state, trivial stuff. For instance, we were walking down Center Street one time and she saw a billboard and told me that would never fly in Maine. Some sort of law prohibited outdoor advertising on billboards. Who would know something like that unless you want to be a contestant on *Jeopardy!* right? And there were lots of other little things,' Nancy went on before I could reply. 'Like Maine was the only state that didn't have any venomous spiders. And one other time she told me actors couldn't drink onstage, not even water.' She glanced at her watch again and jumped up. 'Oh, goodness, how the time flies. Finn has a vet appointment in twenty minutes, so we'll have to get going.' She gave a sharp tug on the leash and Finn rose to his feet.

I rose. 'It was very nice talking to you, Nancy,' I said. 'Maybe we'll run into each other again.'

'Oh, count on it,' the woman said with a wide smile. 'I plan on being a regular at your store, once it's open.'

'I look forward to seeing you there.' I bent over and patted the dog on the head. 'It was very nice to meet you, Finn. Come to the bookstore with Nancy and I'll make sure I have a treat handy for you.'

Finn looked at me and let out a soft woof.

Nancy smiled. 'He says thank you. Well, it's been nice making your acquaintance, Charley. Stop by my retirement complex and visit, won't you? Finn and I would love to have you.' Suddenly she reached out and grasped my hand. 'Think about keeping that name, won't you? Mainely Mysteries. It really is a good name.'

With another wave Nancy and Finn ambled off. I watched them go, then sat back down. Something about my conversation with Nancy niggled at me, but I couldn't pinpoint exactly what it was. I pushed the thought to the back of my mind and decided to concentrate on what I did know, that today had certainly been a banner day for information. Sheila, apparently, had craved male attention and I'd learned of not one more, but three more possible suspects and where Sheila'd been living. I whipped out my smartphone. A quick search revealed that Mrs Dinwiddie's rooming house was a good distance away from here, all the way over on the outskirts of town. It was definitely out of the way. Could that be why Sheila had chosen it? From what I'd learned so far, Sheila seemed to like to keep a low profile.

I said a silent prayer that Grant and Barbie hadn't discovered this yet and dialed Zane's number. She answered on the second ring. 'I found out where Sheila's been living,' I blurted out after Zane said hello. 'Someplace called Mrs Dinwiddie's. Ever heard of it?'

'Oh yeah, I've heard of it. That place is a dump,' said Zane. 'I can't picture Sheila there.'

'Exactly what Nancy said.'

'Who?'

'It's a long story. I'll fill you in later. I'm going to check it out now. Say a prayer that the police haven't beaten me to it.'

'Whoa, Charley, slow down. That's not a place you should go to by yourself,' said Zane. 'The neighborhood isn't the greatest.'

'Zane, are you forgetting I lived in New York City for years? I've seen more than my share of undesirable neighborhoods.'

There was a moment of silence and then, 'Give me a half hour to finish up here and I'll go with you. Please, Charley – I'd feel a lot better if we went together.'

I frowned. I hated to waste more time, but I knew that tone of Zane's. 'Are you sure you can get away?'

'Oh, I'm sure.' Zane barked out a nervous laugh. 'Sit tight and I'll see you in a few.' Then she hung up before I could say another word. I shoved my phone back in my tote bag and turned toward where I'd parked my SUV. As I did so, I caught a flash of blue out of the corner of my eye. I turned just in time to see a man wearing blue jeans and a faded denim jacket disappear around the corner of the gazebo. I was too far away to see his face clearly, but from the height and build he'd seemed to resemble the man I'd caught looking in the storefront window. If it were him, then this was the second time I'd caught him lurking around nearby.

Could he be following me? And if so, why? I paused, as one possibility flitted through my mind.

Could this be Sheila's mysterious ex? More importantly, could he be her killer?

I let out a gasp as something else came to mind. The pink phone case I'd noticed in his pocket that day. Now I knew what it was about my conversation with Nancy that had struck a chord. It was her mentioning that Sheila kept her phone in a shiny pink case – just like the one I'd seen in his pocket. I wrapped my jacket more tightly around myself to ward off the sudden chill that coursed through my body and headed for home.

THIRTEEN

Poe wound around my feet the moment I stepped in the door. I bent over to give him a pat on the head, and then I noticed that his food bowl was empty. I placed my hands on my hips and gave the cat a hard stare. 'Really, Poe? I filled that with dry food before I left this morning.'

Poe let out a sharp meow that probably meant, 'Hey human, I'm a growing boy.' I shrugged out of my jacket and tossed it across the kitchen island, then went to the cupboard and got out more dry food for Poe. While he hunkered down for his afternoon snack, I got my laptop and settled down at the kitchen table. The first thing I did was type into the search engine, 'obscure facts about the state of Maine.' A ton of them came up, including the three that Nancy had mentioned.

Poe, his meal finished, lofted on to the chair beside me and regarded me with wide eyes, his head cocked. 'Looks as if Sheila might have been from Maine, buddy,' I told the cat. 'Or at the very least, spent some time there.'

The kitchen door creaked open before I could pull up the page on Sheila I'd bookmarked. I looked up and saw Zane, and the expression on her face made a chill run down my spine. 'Something's wrong,' I said. 'What's the matter?'

Zane shrugged out of her jacket and tossed it on the kitchen island on top of mine. She crossed over to the kitchen table, pulled out the chair opposite mine, and sat down heavily. 'I didn't want to go into it over the phone, but I wasn't at work when you called.' She paused. 'I was at the police station.'

'Oh no,' I moaned. 'What did Barbie want now?'

Zane leaned back in the chair and stretched her legs out in front of her. 'It wasn't Barbie who wanted to see me. It was Mr Personality. Detective Grant.'

I felt a chill nicker down my spine. 'What did he want? Not more questions about Sheila's past?'

Zane averted her gaze. 'No, it was something else.'

As my friend lapsed into silence, I felt my temper start to rise. I pushed the laptop off to one side, leaned across the table and grasped my friend's hand. 'Look, Zane, I want to help you but I can't if you're not honest with me. I have the feeling that you've been keeping something from me, and I'd like to know what it is.'

After a few moments Zane raised her gaze to meet mine. 'I guess there's no fooling the expert, C.J. Barrett,' she said. She let out an enormous sigh. 'There is one little detail I sort of omitted.'

'I certainly don't feel like an expert,' I said. 'I just know you and your moods. So, what have you been holding back?'

'I kind of lied about something. Well, not lied. Just not told the whole truth.' Zane pulled her hand away, clasped hers together. 'Sheila did sort of say she might want out of the partnership. And, well, I might have threatened to kill her over it in public.'

I bit down hard on my lower lip to keep from crying out, *'What in hell is wrong with you?'* I counted to ten, then let out a breath. 'OK, start from the beginning. Tell me everything and don't leave anything out.'

'Well, I'd been sensing for a few weeks that something was up with her but every time I asked, she just brushed it off. Anyway, that day she called me at work and said that she had to talk to me. We decided to meet at the Egg Platter for dinner. You know, the diner over on Fourth street? Anyway, she was already there when I arrived. I'd no sooner sat down than she said, "Zane, don't get me wrong, I want to open that store, but I don't know if it's going to be possible right now." I asked her what she meant by that, and she started getting all defensive, said real snotty like, "Just what I said. I don't think I can open up the bookstore." Well, I'd had a bad day at the bakery already, and that was just the icing on the cake, so to speak. I started to yell at her, told her that if she backed out now, I'd be in a real bind. Finally, she said, "Look, I just said it might not be possible. I want this to happen as much as you. I only wanted to let you know it was a possibility." She said she was sorry about that, and that made me madder. Finally, she said, "Look – I'm not sure. It might be all right, but I just wanted to let you know my backing out is a possibility."'

'Then what?' I prompted as Zane grew silent. 'What did you say?'

Zane's tongue darted out, licked at her lower lip. 'I may have said something like, "If you put me in this position, Sheila Crowder, I'll kill you. I'll see you dead before you ruin my life."'

My face fell and I slapped my forehead with my palm. 'Oh, Zane. You didn't!'

'I did. You know how I get when I'm upset, Charley. I talk without thinking. And, of course, two days later she sent me that note – or someone did. Anyway, that's what Grant wanted to question me about.'

My eyes narrowed. 'I wonder how he found out about it?'

Her lips screwed into a pout. 'Seems someone there called it in. They overheard us arguing and when they read about Sheila . . .' Zane's head dropped back and she let out a low moan. 'I guess the good news is Grant didn't arrest me. Just told me to be available in case he had more questions.'

'He'd need more evidence than just someone's account of your argument with Sheila to arrest you, although it doesn't put you in a good light,' I said. I thought about Grant's earlier questions to me and asked abruptly, 'Did you ever touch that trunk in the bookstore basement?'

Zane's brows drew together. 'He asked me that too. I told him yes, I did. We both did. It was that first day, when we went to look over the storefronts. We both touched it. Sheila went really crazy over it, though. I could tell she really liked it. She even made a remark about it being magical.' Her voice broke a little as she added, 'And to think it ended up being a sort of coffin for her . . . oh God.'

I didn't want to upset Zane any more than she already was, so I kept my tone light. 'Well, I had a productive day,' I said. I repeated my conversations with Betty, Phyllis, and Nancy. 'So, we may have four suspects. Sheila's ex who might be named Gary, Gino Galante and his wife Gloria, and this other younger man Nancy said Sheila was seeing.'

Zane picked up a napkin, started to fiddle with the ends. 'I'd be more inclined to think two – the ex and the younger guy. I'm sorry but I just can't wrap my head around the possibility of Sheila having an affair with Gino Galante, of all people. He's always had a reputation for being a womanizer, but I just don't think he would have been Sheila's type. From the little she said, it seemed she went for looks. And you can cross Gloria Galante off your list. She's been away the past two weeks, visiting her mother in California.'

'I found it hard to believe Sheila and Gino were a couple too,' I said, 'but I'm still going to follow up on it. We can't afford to discount any possibility, no matter how remote it might seem.' I slapped my hand down on the table and stood up. 'Let's go check out Sheila's room and see if we can find out anything that will shed some light on this situation. Afterward we'll go out to dinner. My treat.'

'OK,' said Zane. She cut me an eyeroll. 'Just not the Egg Platter. Please.'

As I parked my SUV on the corner, I noticed that Zane had been right. The neighborhood certainly looked shabby and rundown. The houses that lined the street all looked in need of a great deal of repair, and garbage was strewn across several of the lawns. In comparison, Mrs Dinwiddie's rooming house seemed a veritable mansion. It actually reminded me of the house in the old *Addams Family* cartoons. It was large, Victorian style, with a wraparound porch that had ivy growing all over it. The windows were round and most of them looked as if they hadn't been washed in years. The stairs leading up to the porch creaked with every step we took, and I noticed that the few chairs scattered on the porch were wicker and pretty well worn. One had a broken arm. The place was less than inviting, to say the least. Even the doorbell had a hollow, echoing sound. I shifted my weight to the other foot, half expecting Lurch, the Addams Family butler, to shuffle out and greet us.

'Creepy,' muttered Zane. 'Sheila had to be pretty desperate to be living here. Maybe she *was* hiding from someone.'

'Let's hope Mrs Dinwiddie hasn't read today's paper,' I said as the door suddenly swung open and a tall, thin woman stood framed in the doorway. She had pitch-black hair that she wore in a sloppy bun on the top of her head. Her rail-thin figure was encased in a plain housedress of mousy brown, and she wore slippers on her feet of the same color that had definitely seen better days. A vision of the witch in the *Wizard of Oz* flashed through my mind, and I tamped the image down as I said, 'Mrs Dinwiddie?'

The woman's lips thinned. 'Who wants to know?'

'I'm Charlotte James and this is Zane Adams. We're friends of Sheila Crowder's.'

Her brown eyes widened. 'Sheila, eh? Well, if you're lookin' for her, she ain't been around much this past week. I can't remember the last time I saw her, and she owes me this month's rent and half of last. Promised me I'd have it before the end of the month, but . . .' she let her voice trail off as she fixed us with a piercing stare. 'I don't suppose either of you know what's up with her?'

'She's gone,' Zane blurted out before I could answer.

Mrs Dinwiddie's eyes narrowed to almost slits. 'Gone? What do you mean, gone?'

'She left town. Some sort of family emergency,' I said quickly. 'She told my friend here she had to go away for a while.'

'She did, did she?' Mrs Dinwiddie sniffed. 'You'd think she'd have let me know.'

'It all came up rather suddenly,' I said.

'I'll say.' Mrs Dinwiddie trained her gaze on Zane. 'How come she told you her business and didn't say a word to me, her landlady?'

'We–we were supposed to go in business together,' stammered Zane. 'We rented a double storefront on Elm and Water. Sheila was going to open a bookstore. And I–I'm opening a bakery.'

Mrs Dinwiddie's eyebrows angled upward, rivaling Spock's in proportion. 'A bookstore? If that don't beat all. The fact that she'd open any sort of store shocks me. If you ask me, that girl was antisocial. I can't see her waiting on customers.'

'She didn't have friends over?' I asked casually. 'No girlfriends? Or boyfriends?'

Mrs Dinwiddie let out a snort. 'Not that I saw, and I try and see plenty. So, what do the two of you want, seeing as she's not here?'

'She has my bank paperwork,' Zane piped up. 'She was going to take it in for me, but she didn't have time, and I need to get it. We–we wondered if we might take a quick look around her room.'

Mrs Dinwiddie frowned. 'I'm not sure I should do that,' she said stiffly. 'After all, even though the girl's not here, and she didn't have the courtesy to tell me she was leaving and didn't pay her rent, it's still her room and I suppose I should respect her privacy.'

I stepped forward. 'Of course, and we understand completely. We wouldn't even ask if it weren't for the fact that Sheila has Zane's business certification and it's the only copy.' I saw the woman hesitate and my hand dipped inside my tote bag, and I pulled out my checkbook. 'Just how much back rent does Sheila owe?'

A crafty light entered her eyes, and she put a finger to her lips. 'Let me think. Half of this month, all of last. It comes to four hundred seventy-five dollars. Even.'

I swallowed. That sum seemed enormous for just a room on the outskirts of town and there was no doubt in my mind that Mrs Dinwiddie was inflating it. However, I was in no position to argue the point right now. I quickly wrote out a check and handed it to the woman. 'This should cover it,' I said.

Mrs Dinwiddie looked at the check, then folded it and slipped it into the pocket of her dress. Without a word of thanks, she crooked her finger at us. 'Follow me.'

We followed Mrs Dinwiddie to a room that was just as dingy as the rest of the building. It was located at the far end of the third-floor hall. I noticed a door leading to a back stairwell only a few feet away. *Four hundred dollars, my ass*, I thought. Mrs Dinwiddie had surely gotten a windfall out of me. I wouldn't have paid four hundred cents to live here. The front door opened directly into a small living area with a dirty hardwood floor, covered by a threadbare woven rug. A small, tattered divan sat off to one side, next to it a small wooden desk. There was a hardback chair in the other corner, in front of which sat a small table with a small flat-screen TV on top. A cot with what appeared to be a lumpy mattress was positioned near the window, which looked dirty and grimy and not washed in probably a decade. The kitchen area was barely the size of a postage stamp, and I noticed a teakettle on the stove and a hot plate on the dingy white counter. My first impression of the room was that it didn't look at all lived in. There were no personal touches around, like photographs or the like, that I could see. I was dying to look in the closets, but Mrs Dinwiddie stood in the doorway and watched us with her beady eyes, arms folded across her chest.

She gestured toward the desk as Zane and I hesitated. 'What you're lookin' for is probably in there,' she suggested.

Mrs Dinwiddie turned away and I shot Zane a pointed look, and mouthed *Get her talking. Distract her.* My friend immediately turned toward the woman. She wrapped her arms around her torso and hunched her shoulders in a shiver. 'It's kind of cold in here. Do you allow electric heaters?'

'Lord, no. And I'll tell you why.' Mrs Dinwiddie launched into a diatribe about the evils of electric heaters in a rooming house. Zane stepped in front of the woman, shielding me from her gaze as I bent over the desk and started pulling out drawers. Every single one was empty.

Mrs Dinwiddie had warmed to her subject, and with Zane as her captive audience was really getting into it. I took that opportunity to walk over to the divan, run my hand underneath the cushion. Nothing but dust bunnies. Likewise, the chair. I walked over to the window, knelt beside the bed, felt underneath. My fingers touched something rough, and I drew out a piece of paper. I glanced at it quickly. It appeared to be a receipt of some sort. I shoved that into my pocket and walked over to the closet. I inched the door open and took a quick peek inside, saw one pair of black slacks and a bright red tunic top hanging there. There was no suitcase that I noticed. I was about to shut the door when I saw something way back on the floor. I went over and picked it up. It was a small notebook. I thumbed through it quickly. Most of the pages had been torn out, but there were a few left with cramped writing on them. I slid it into my pocket along with the receipt, then shut the door and moved swiftly over to where the other two stood.

Mrs Dinwiddie was just finishing her speech. 'And that's why I don't allow them,' she said. She glanced up and saw me. 'Find what you were looking for?' she asked.

I caught Zane's eye and inclined my head ever so slightly. I turned to Mrs Dinwiddie. 'The papers don't appear to be here,' I said. 'She must have packed them. We'll have to send her a text, ask her to mail them.' I gave Zane a slight push toward the door and turned to smile at Mrs Dinwiddie. 'We've bothered you enough. Thank you for your time.'

Mrs Dinwiddie let out a grunt. 'If you talk to Sheila, let her know I'm only gonna hold this room for her until the end of the month. I got a long wait list for rooms. Ask her – no, tell her – to call me.'

I practically dragged Zane out of the room. Mrs Dinwiddie locked the door and we followed her back down the stairs. 'Whew,' said Zane when we were back on the street again. 'What a place! I still can't imagine Sheila living there.'

'Neither can I,' I responded. 'That room didn't look as if someone lived in it at all. It was devoid of any personal touches. I peeked inside the closet and there was only one pair of pants and a top hanging there. No suitcase. Either she didn't really live there, or whoever killed her went in and cleared everything out.'

Zane frowned. 'How could they do that? Mrs Dinwiddie said she never saw anyone visiting Sheila?'

'Her room wasn't far from the backstairs. Anyone could have snuck up them and into Sheila's place. Her killer probably took her key.'

Zane frowned. 'But why would they clear the place out?'

'Probably to perpetuate the notion that Sheila had left town. And they might also have been looking for something. But they missed some stuff.' I pulled the notebook and paper out of my pocket. I held up the notebook. 'I found this on the closet floor. The paper I found under the bed.'

Zane reached for them, but I drew back. 'Not here,' I cautioned. I slid them back into my pocket and we hurried to my SUV and jumped in. As I started the engine, I caught a glimpse of a police cruiser turning the corner. I was positive Grant was behind the wheel. 'Duck,' I said, and pushed Zane down in her seat. I slunk down in mine, angling my head so I could see through the side mirror. The cruiser had parked in front of the rooming house and a few minutes later Barbie and Grant exited the car and started up the short walkway. Once they were out of view, I straightened in my seat and motioned for Zane to do the same.

'What was that all about?' my friend grumbled.

I inclined my head toward the police cruiser. 'It looks as if we got out of there just in time,' I remarked. 'With any luck, they didn't notice us.' I patted my pocket. 'Let's find somewhere quiet where we can get a bite to eat and study these.'

FOURTEEN

Ten minutes later I guided the SUV into the parking lot of the Bite Me Diner. 'Catchy name,' I observed as I cut the motor.

'Isn't it, though? It's pretty new,' said Zane. 'Opened about a month ago, and they've gotten stellar reviews on Yelp. I hear their Reuben is to die for.'

I glanced around the half-empty lot. 'Seems like business is slow tonight. Let's go in and get a table, preferably in the back, away from potential prying eyes.'

We entered the diner, and I immediately felt as if I'd been transported back into the 1950s. The vinyl flooring was done in big black and white checks. The tables scattered throughout were a mixture of black and silver chrome, and there were red and white checked tablecloths on every table. The booths were likewise done in black vinyl, and I noticed there was an old-time mini jukebox at every booth. A girl of not more than nineteen emerged from behind the counter. Her blonde hair was done up in an elaborate beehive hairdo, and she wore a flowing pink poodle skirt with a matching pink sweater. She plucked two plastic menus from a holder attached to the side of the counter and her heavily made-up red lips parted in a wide smile, revealing pearl-white teeth. 'Welcome to the Bite Me Diner,' she said. 'Table or booth?'

'A booth,' I said quickly. 'How about that one?' The back section appeared pretty empty, and I pointed to a booth all the way in the back, near the sign that said Restrooms.

'Sure. Follow me.'

We followed her and I noticed there were only two other occupants in that section, a middle-aged couple eating what looked to be a cherry pie with ice cream on top, and a man in a plaid flannel shirt seated near the window scoffing down a hamburger. Neither party was seated close to the booth I'd chosen. We slid in, and the girl plopped the menus down on the table. 'Mandy will be your server. She'll be right with you.' With another wide smile, she turned on her heel and flounced off.

I passed Zane one of the menus and gave mine a quick look. It appeared to be standard diner fare: lots of breakfast dishes, hamburgers, and sandwiches. There were several appetizing photographs scattered on the menu, and I noticed one was of the aforementioned Reuben. A notation at the bottom of the menu read, *Check the board for our daily specials, or ask your server.* I looked up and saw a blackboard on the wall opposite our booth. The specials today were Cream of Mushroom soup, a Broccoli Quiche, and a Turkey Dinner 'with all the fixin's' – I wondered if it were real turkey, or the pressed kind they sold at delis. I hated that pressed turkey.

A pretty, dark-haired girl dressed in black slacks and a white blouse appeared at our booth with two glasses of water. She set them down in front of us and then said with a bright smile, 'Hello there! I'm Mandy, and I'm your server tonight.' She flourished pad and pen in front of her. 'Do you ladies need another minute, or do you need me to explain anything on our menu?'

I handed Mandy my menu. 'That Turkey Dinner – is that real turkey, or the pressed deli kind?'

Mandy's brows drew together. 'Why, I have no idea. I can ask, if you want.'

'That's OK. It's probably too much food anyway. I think I'll just have the Reuben.'

'Excellent choice,' Mandy looked relieved as she scribbled on her pad. She looked at Zane. 'And for you?'

'I'll have the Reuben also,' she said, handing Mandy her menu. 'And I'll have a sweet tea with that, too.'

Mandy slid me a glance and I raised my water glass. 'This'll do fine for me, thanks.'

She hurried off toward the kitchen and I pulled out the notebook and paper from my pocket and laid them on the table. 'May as well take a look at these before she brings our food,' I said. I unfolded the receipt and spread it out before us. 'Ellison's' was printed at the top of the paper in a bold script. Below that were the words, 'Hand carved jewelry chest' and next to that, an amount that made both our eyes pop.

'Six hundred for a jewelry box? Was she out of her mind?!' Zane cried.

'Not necessarily,' I said. 'If it's anything like the chest in the store basement, I've seen ones in the city that went for far more.' I tapped at the name on the receipt. 'I'm not familiar with Ellison's. Is it an antique store?'

'No, it's owned by some guy from North Carolina. He does woodworking and repairs, and some handmade furniture. It's only been in business a little over a year, but I understand they have pretty nice stuff in there. I always wanted to have a look inside, but if that's a sampling of the prices – I'll pass.'

I pulled out my phone and called up the website. 'They're open till nine tonight,' I said. 'Let's stop on the way home. With any luck they might remember the transaction.'

'At that price, I should hope so,' sniffed Zane. She tapped at the receipt. 'I bet Sheila never picked it up. If not, I'd sure like to see it.'

I slid the receipt into my pocket, then turned my attention to the notebook. I opened it and flipped through the few remaining pages. Sheila's handwriting was pretty bad – very small and cramped – but I could make out enough to tell that what I was looking at wasn't very significant. One page had what appeared to be a grocery list: bananas, cereal, milk, coffee. Another was a list of names: The BookWorm, Booked UP, Lotta Books, Mystery Corner. Apparently, Sheila had been trying out several names for her store. Mainely Mysteries was a prize compared to what was listed here.

On the next-to-last page, I found something interesting. 'Look at this,' I said to Zane. I pointed to what was scrawled across the top of the page. HOLICRSGRCOL45225K.

Zane frowned as she looked at the notebook. 'Maybe it's some sort of password – or maybe a code,' she suggested. She snapped her fingers in the air. 'Say, isn't your character Steve Sheppard an ace code cracker? Which would also make you one too?'

'He unraveled codes in three books. Unfortunately, I can't take the credit for them. Max put me in touch with this guy he knows who's an expert on codes. He made them all up for me. I did thank him for his assistance on my acknowledgement page.'

'Well, that's good, right? Maybe you can get in touch with him, see if he can figure this out,' suggested Zane.

'Not a bad idea, except I don't remember the guy's name.'

'You can look him up on one of the acknowledgement pages, can't you?'

'I could, but he wanted to be kept anonymous, so I just used his middle name.'

'Well, then, can't you just call Max?' Zane said. 'He'll probably know right away.'

'Ordinarily that would be a splendid idea, but as it happens Max and I aren't on the best of terms right now.'

'Oh, for pity's sake!' Zane clucked her tongue. 'Don't tell me you're going to let some stupid argument over *Green Acres* ruin your relationship with your agent?'

'It wasn't over *Green Acres* per se, it was over Hooterville. And that was just a metaphor for our real argument. Max can't seem to get it through his head why I need this time off.'

'Well, number one he's a man, and number two, he's an agent. He's just a little shortsighted, that's all. I'm sure if you explained your reasoning, he'd listen.'

'I've already tried that.'

'You should try again. Max got you your start, guided you in the writing business. Didn't you once tell me he was like the brother you never had?'

'I guess I did say that, didn't I?' I sighed. 'I'll think about it.' I turned my attention back to the notebook and flipped to the last page. 'Oh, great.'

'What?'

I pointed to the cramped notation, scrawled on the last page of the notebook. ESS36650

Zane let out a groan. 'Another code? Charley that settles it. You've got to get in touch with that code guy, even if you have to call Max— uh-oh.'

My friend was facing the entryway to the diner, and suddenly I saw her face pale. She shrank down lower in the booth. I turned my head slightly to see what had upset her. Ian Grant stood at the entry counter, talking to the girl who seated us in our booth. Beside him was Barbie. The beatific expression on her face was enough to make me want to puke. 'Oh swell,' I muttered. 'What are the two of them doing here?'

'Eat, I suppose. Unless they're following me,' whispered Zane as the girl picked up menus and motioned for Grant and Barbie to follow her. Fortunately, she led them to a booth on the other side of the diner. Barbie slid into the booth with her back to us, leaving Grant to take the opposite side, facing our section. Both Zane and I slouched lower in our seats.

'Maybe he won't see us all the way back here,' whispered Zane. She was so far down on the bench that if she slid down another inch she'd be on the floor. 'Looking at him once today was quite enough for me, thanks.'

I raised my head slightly and peered around the corner of the booth. Grant appeared to be studying the same plastic menu as we had. Only the top of Barbie's head was visible. 'I think we're safe,' I whispered. 'Maybe they'll eat fast and leave.'

'When have you ever known a cop to eat fast,' hissed Zane. She started craning her neck to and fro. 'Do you see Mandy? Maybe we'd better get those Reubens to go.'

Out of the corner of my eye I saw our server emerge from the kitchen, balancing a large tray that held two platters and a large glass of iced tea. 'Too late,' I said. 'Here she comes now.'

Mandy sidled up to our table. 'Here you go ladies. Two Reubens.'

I reached out and grabbed her arm. 'Would it be a lot of trouble to have these wrapped?' I asked. I pointed to Zane. 'My friend isn't feeling too well. Stomach issues.'

Mandy let out a yelp and turned to Zane. 'Oh no! I'm so sorry! Can I get you something to settle your stomach? Bicarb of soda usually works pretty good for me when my tummy aches. I know there's some in the kitchen.'

Zane let out a low moan and rubbed at her stomach. 'Whenever this happens the best thing is for me to go home and lie down,' she said. 'We'll just take our dinners to go.'

Mandy frowned. 'If you're having tummy problems a Reuben probably isn't the best choice to eat. Would you like a container of nice, hot chicken soup instead?'

'The chicken soup is very good here. I can recommend it.'

Ian Grant had come up behind Mandy and now stood staring down at us. He lifted his hand, touched two fingers to his forehead. 'Good evening, Ms James. Ms Adams. Fancy running into you here.'

'Yes, it is a small world,' I said. Zane said nothing, merely nodded.

Mandy looked at Grant, then me. 'Y'all know each other?' she asked.

Grant immediately responded 'Yes', while I said, 'Not really.' Zane looked over at Mandy and said, 'Never mind about wrapping these. My stomach's feeling better, so we'll just eat here.'

'Yeah? Well, OK, if you say so.' Mandy looked at Grant and her face brightened. 'Your order should be out shortly.'

Grant smiled right back at her. 'Thanks.'

She shot Grant another shy glance before moving off in the direction of the kitchen. Grant edged closer to our booth and angled a glance at Zane. 'Tummy problems?' he asked.

'Just hunger pains,' replied Zane. She cut off a slice of Reuben and popped it in her mouth.

Grant looked at her for a long moment, then switched his gaze to me. 'If I didn't know better, I'd think you two were trying to avoid me.'

I picked up the container of ketchup that was on the table and squirted it over my fries, then picked one up, popped it in my mouth, and mumbled around it, 'Whatever gave you that idea?'

He placed his hands on his hips. 'Oh, I don't know. Maybe it was the note of desperation in your voice when you asked Mandy to have your dinners wrapped to go.'

I raised an eyebrow. 'On a first-name basis with the server, are we?'

Now he did smile. 'I've been eating in here a lot since I've been attending classes. I like to be on a first-name basis with the staff. You get better service that way.'

'Hm, well, from what I see your theory appears to be working.'

'Mandy's a nice kid. Too smart to be a server, if you ask me.'

I shot him a saccharine smile. 'I didn't.'

There was a brief moment of silence and then Grant looked from me to Zane and then back to me. 'So,' he said. 'What are the two of you up to?'

I waved my arm to encompass the table. 'At the moment, having dinner. Isn't that what you're here for? Unless you're following the two of us?'

'Officer Donaldson and I decided to discuss the case over a quick bite to eat. As for me following you, maybe keeping a closer eye on you is a good idea.' His gaze bored into mine and he crossed his arms over his broad chest. 'Want to tell me what the two of you were doing at Mrs Dinwiddie's rooming house earlier? Oh, and don't bother trying to deny it. I caught a glimpse of you slouched down in your SUV when I parked the car. Mrs Dinwiddie confirmed the fact that Sheila's former business partner and her friend came there looking for bank paperwork.'

So he had seen us. So much for a low profile. I picked up my knife and fork and cut off a large hunk of the Reuben before raising my gaze to Grant's. 'Why would we deny it? We did go there looking for bank paperwork for the stores.'

'Uh-huh,' he said. His gaze shifted to Zane. 'I thought you said you didn't know where Sheila lived?'

'I didn't,' Zane said.

'She didn't,' I chimed in. 'I'm the one who found out. And before you say anything, I stumbled upon the information purely by accident. I wasn't out questioning people, if that's what you think.'

He arched a brow. 'Uh-huh. And did you find what you were looking for?'

'The bank paperwork?' I asked carefully. I shook my head. 'Nope. Didn't find a thing.'

'That's not surprising. That apartment was barer than Old Mother Hubbard's cupboard. Someone cleaned it out good.' He fixed me with a stern gaze. 'Mrs Dinwiddie seemed to be under the impression that you two were in contact with Sheila. Which, under the circumstances, is impossible, unless one of your talents is communicating with the dead,' Grant barked out. 'But no worries. We set her straight.'

I sliced off a large piece of my Reuben, put it in my mouth and chewed. I swallowed and then looked at Grant. 'For the record, we didn't break any laws,' I said.

'No, not unless you count interfering in a police investigation.'

'We weren't interfering,' I said. 'We were just looking for something that we need for our business, and Sheila was the last one to have it.'

Zane tossed down her napkin and pushed her plate over to the side. 'I need to visit the ladies' room,' she said. She slid out of the booth and vanished through the doorway without a backward glance. Grant slid into the seat she'd occupied without waiting for an invitation from me – not that he'd have gotten one.

'Look,' he said, 'I imagine that your friend has already informed you that I questioned her earlier today. I'm sure you know I'd be remiss and not doing my job if I didn't follow up once I learned about that argument,' he said.

'I see.' I set down my fork and folded my arms on the table in front of me. 'Zane didn't kill Sheila. She might have said those things in the heat of an argument, but I've known her all my life, and that girl hasn't got a murderous bone in her body.'

Grant leaned back a bit. 'Honestly? I don't think so either. But like I said, I had to follow up.' Suddenly he let out a chuckle. 'Officer Donaldson, on the other hand, wouldn't put it past either of you to commit a murder. Apparently, you didn't get on too well in high school.'

I bit back a cry of annoyance. Barbie sure hadn't wasted much time bad-mouthing us to Grant. 'Surely you don't put any stock in what Officer Donaldson says. Zane isn't the murdering kind, and I never even knew Sheila.'

He held up his hand. 'Whoa, hold on. I didn't say she was accusing either of you of killing Sheila. I just said that she thought either one of you might be capable of the deed.'

'Hers, maybe,' I muttered. 'Back in high school Barbara Jeanne might have been capable of killing some people herself. It was a shock to me when I found out she was on the police force here.'

'Barbara can be a bit hotheaded at times, but she's a good officer. I've worked with her before, even taken some classes with her. She's very dedicated.'

'I'm sure she is,' I said. I refrained from adding, *dedicated man-chaser*. The fact that he'd now switched to referring to her as Barbara rather than Officer Donaldson irked me for some reason. I picked up my water glass and took a long swig. Grant looked past me into the other dining area, then rose.

'Well, I'd best get back to my table. I see Mandy has arrived with our dinners.' He paused and then added in a softer tone, 'I expect that you'll be able to go back into your store within a day or two. Just a few more things the crime scene boys have to finish up. Someone will let you know definitely.'

I looked up at him. 'Thank you. I appreciate that.'

He stared at me so intently I wanted to scream. 'Please, stay out of police business from now on,' he said finally. 'I gave you my card. If you should run across anything you think is connected to the case, please call me. Don't go off on your own.'

For a minute I was nonplussed. Grant actually sounded concerned, although whether it was over my safety or his investigation I had no clue. I thought about what I'd learned, the other possible suspects, the receipt and notebook in my pocket. The right thing – the smart thing – to do would be to whip all that out and confide in him. Possibly if he'd lose that know-it-all attitude I would have done so. Instead, I inclined my head and said: 'You'd better get back to your table, before Barbara Jeanne comes looking for you.'

He didn't answer, just stood staring at me for a moment. Then he turned on his heel and walked off. I leaned my head back against the back of the booth and closed my eyes. What on earth was the matter with me? Just that brief encounter with him had my pulse racing. The man was annoying, no doubt about it. And my reaction to his nearness even more so. But I was sure I'd done the right thing. After all, I had nothing concrete to substantiate the rumors about the younger man or the married lover, let alone the ex. With a guy like Grant, I needed something more definite. As for the notebook and receipt, well . . . that was just me being stubborn.

Zane emerged from the restrooms and slid back into the booth. 'I waited until I was sure he was gone,' she said. 'I didn't mean to duck out on you, but I just couldn't sit there with him next to me.'

'I completely understand, believe me,' I said. I smiled at my friend. 'For what it's worth, he doesn't think you killed Sheila.'

Zane's jaw dropped. 'He doesn't? Then what was with the third degree earlier?'

'He said he was just doing his job in following up.' I picked up my fork, tapped it against the side of my plate. 'The two of them are apparently on a first-name basis now. And he thinks Barbie is a dedicated officer.'

Zane paused, her glass halfway to her lips. 'No! Really? He said that!'

'Yep. Said she could be a bit hotheaded, but she was dedicated.' I turned my head, saw Grant laughing at something Barbie must have said. I frowned. 'Men and their egos,' I muttered. 'She's probably feeding it, and he's loving every minute of it.'

Zane cocked her head and shot me a maddening smile. 'You know, you sound a wee bit jealous.'

'Jealous? Of him? Not on your life. I just hope he's not unduly influenced by her.' I took another sip of water, set the glass down. 'He told me Barbie thinks the two of us are capable of murder.'

'I am capable of murder. Hers,' said Zane. Then she started to giggle. 'Honest, Charley, I'm not kidding. I could see me bashing in that bleached blonde head with a two by four. No problem.'

'Want to know something? I could too.'

The two of us looked at each other and then burst out laughing so hard tears started to run down our cheeks. It was a good thing no one else was seated in our section or they would have thought we were nuts. When I came up for air I said, 'In addition to telling me that I should be able to get back in the store in a few days, he cautioned us against interfering in his investigation. He and Barbie can handle it.'

'Yeah, but can he handle Barbie?'

That brought on a fresh wave of giggles. I caught sight of Mandy coming out of the kitchen again and signaled for the check. I took a deep breath and said, 'Let's get going. We still have time to make a stop at Ellison's.'

Zane's lips twisted into a half-smile. 'Wouldn't that be considered interfering in Grant's investigation?'

I waited until Mandy dropped off the check holder before I replied. 'Probably, if he knew what we were up to,' I said. I whipped a twenty and a five out of my wallet, placed it inside the holder and then slid out of the booth. 'But he's not going to. Come on, let's get out of here.'

FIFTEEN

Ellison's Fine Furnishings was located on the outskirts of Austin, in a building that resembled a reconditioned barn. I pulled into the dirt parking lot and parked in a spot a few feet from the entrance. Zane stared at the building as we made our way to the entrance. 'This looks like a dump too,' she whispered. 'For the prices you'd think he could afford prime real estate in the center of town.'

We pushed through the front door and were immediately hit by a blast of cold air. The interior was dimly lit by hanging lamps that seemed to be miles away. I gave a swift glance around. Jumbled furniture filled the first floor and the lofts on both sides.

'For a place called Fine Furnishings, it sure is messy. Looks like they have a lot of inventory,' remarked Zane.

'Hello out there,' bellowed a voice from the back of the shop. 'I'll be out in a little bit. Just finishing up a repair. Feel free to look around.'

'Thanks, we will,' I called back, then I nodded to Zane. 'You take the left side, I'll take the right. Shout if you see anything resembling a jewelry box.'

Zane gave me a quick salute. 'Yes, ma'am.'

I gave her a playful punch on her arm, and we separated. I walked slowly through my section, pausing every now and then to admire a piece of furniture. I had to admit, what I saw did indeed seem to be well crafted. The wood furniture – cherry, dark walnut, and pine – shone with a glossy finish. I passed pedestal tables, armoires, chests, and highboys, each more beautiful than the last. I paused before one piece, a cabinet that used an old casement window for a door. A tag dangled from it. I walked over, held my breath, and looked at it. One hundred seventy dollars. Not exorbitant at all.

Next, I paused before a repurposed bookcase that had two louvered shutters for doors. That too had a price tag of under two hundred dollars. I checked out a few more pieces. The most expensive was a five-shelf barrister's bookcase with glass doors that came in at just under three hundred. I'd seen them in New York, not as nice, for over nine hundred. The prices here seemed very reasonable to me. I wondered what might be so unique about the chest Sheila had purchased that caused it to be priced so high.

Zane met me back in the middle of the showroom. 'They have some really nice stuff,' she said. 'I saw a whole forest of bookcases that would work well in your new shop, all priced under three hundred. No jewelry boxes, though.'

'Neither did I. Maybe it was some sort of special order.'

'Ladies?'

We turned to see a man in his late thirties, wiping his hands on a rag, approaching us. He was tall, ruggedly built, with a shock of curly blond hair and ice-blue eyes behind the wire-framed glasses perched on his nose. A handlebar moustache the same color as his hair obscured his upper lip. He finished wiping his hands and shoved the rag into the back pocket of his well-worn jeans. 'I'm Hans Ellison,' he said. He rubbed his hands together. 'Is there any piece in particular you're interested in? The prices on the tags aren't cut in stone. I'm always willing to make a deal.'

'Right now, I'm interested in one particular piece.' I pulled the receipt out of my pocket and handed it to him. 'Do you recall this transaction?'

Hans took the receipt and looked at it. He handed it back to me, then stuck his thumbs in the loopholes of his jeans. 'I recall this because I had to shop it out to a friend of mine in North Carolina. She wanted alterations done to the piece, and I've been pretty backed up with orders. My brother took care of it. He could probably tell you more.' He turned his head slightly and yelled out, 'George! Can you come out here a minute?'

'Brother?' Zane hissed in my ear. 'I didn't know he had a brother.'

'Be right there,' called a gruff voice. A few minutes later a tall man built like a Philadelphia Eagles linebacker emerged from the back of the store. He was taller than his brother, over six feet I was guessing, and had dark hair and eyes. The faint stubble of a five o'clock shadow graced a prominent chin with a deep cleft in the center. He stepped forward, his gaze sweeping over Zane and me.

'This is my brother George,' said Hans.

I smiled at him. 'We've met, but not formally.' As George looked at me quizzically, I added, 'You were in the Jumpin' Beans the other day. Two tables away from me.'

'Was I?' George let out a grunt. 'It's possible. I go in there when I'm in town. Coffee's good.'

Hans turned to his brother. 'These ladies are inquiring about that woman and her special order.'

George frowned. 'Special order?'

'Yeah. Don't you remember? It was that pretty, blonde woman who bought the jewelry chest. You've got to remember. She asked specifically that you wait on her.'

'Oh, yeah, her. She was in the Jumpin' Beans one day when I was putting business cards on the counter. She took one, said she might stop by. I think she was trying to do me a favor. Probably thought asking for me would get me a commission, or something.' George crossed his arms over his chest and shot us a belligerent look. 'What about it?'

I shot George my brightest smile. 'Ms Crowder had to leave town suddenly and she . . . ah . . . wanted us to make sure that all her business here was taken care of. We found this receipt and just wanted to pay what was owed and pick up the merchandise.'

George held out his hand, and I gave him the receipt. He looked at it, then shook his head. 'There's nothing that needs to be done with this,' he said. 'She paid for everything, and the chest was delivered to her last week.'

'It was?' Now I was really puzzled. 'Do you know where? Was it to a rooming house, or maybe to the shop on Elm and Water?'

George shook his head. 'I couldn't say. She made the arrangements directly with Hans's friend. The driver just called to tell us it had been delivered. It was more of a courtesy call.'

'We should have a copy of the receipt on our computer,' Hans offered. He looked at his brother. 'Why don't you show them, George?'

George shot his brother a black look, then turned on his heel.

'Follow me,' he said over his shoulder. We all trooped after him into a small cubbyhole that I figured was the office. A small desk bearing a state-of-the-art computer, two chairs, and a filing cabinet was crammed into the small space. I noticed a few books on top of the filing cabinet – the latest James Patterson thriller, and an old mystery by Mary Higgins Clark. George saw me looking at them and I said, 'I see you read thrillers. I'm a Patterson fan myself.'

He grunted. 'I used to read a lot more. Kind of lost my zest for it.' He plopped behind the computer and started tapping at the keyboard. A few seconds later a duplicate of the receipt I had appeared on the screen. George pointed to it. 'See – it says PAID IN FULL. And there's no address. Sorry.'

'I see,' I said. 'I don't suppose you could describe the piece? It might aid us in finding it.'

'Sorry,' George muttered. 'I don't pay much attention to that sort of thing. That's his specialty.' He jerked his thumb at Hans.

'It was a beautiful piece,' said Hans, 'and it was pretty large, but not so large that it wouldn't fit on a good-sized dresser. It was made of oak. The top lifted open to reveal a mirror and a felt-lined jewelry compartment with dividers. It has seven felt-lined drawers and there are two doors on the sides that open to reveal more compartments with hooks to hold necklaces, bracelets, little scarves and the like.'

'So, it was more like a tabletop armoire,' I said. That made a bit more sense. 'I don't suppose you have a record of the alterations she wanted made?'

'Nope,' said George. 'That was between her and Hans' friend. We collected the money, he got his cut, and we got ours. And that's that.' He rose from the chair. 'If that's all, I have got some work in the storeroom I need to finish up.' Without waiting for an answer, he turned and strode from the room, slamming the door behind him.

Hans shot me an apologetic look. 'I apologize for my brother's rudeness,' he said. 'Had I handled the transaction, I would have been sure to get a list of what she wanted done, just to double-check – but like I said, she asked for George.'

Zane gave me a nudge with her elbow, then turned to Hans. 'I wasn't aware you had a brother,' she said. 'Or that he was in business with you.'

'He's not in the business with me – at least, not yet. It's kind of a trial period. He's only relocated here from up north a few weeks ago.' Hans paused and then added, 'He does have a bit of a chip on his shoulder. Always did. But . . . family is family, right?' He blew out a long sigh. 'No matter what.'

'It's no problem,' I assured Hans. 'If you have a few minutes, I would like to order some of your bookcases for my store,' I said.

Hans' eyes lit up at making a potential sale. 'Why certainly. What ones were you interested in?'

'I think two of the barristers for now, and I also like that one with the two louvered shutters. I think that would be perfect for shelving the children's mysteries in. I can give you a deposit now, but I won't need them delivered for at least a week, maybe two. There are still some finishing touches that need to be completed before I can move furniture in.' *Like having a crime scene released,* I silently added.

'That'll be fine,' he said. He opened one of the desk drawers and removed some yellow placards. 'Just show me which ones you want, and I'll put a sold sign on them.'

'Thanks.' I shot Zane a look over my shoulder. 'Why don't you wait here? I'll only be a few minutes.' To Hans I said, 'My friend has a bad ankle. I don't like to make her walk around if she doesn't have to.'

'No problem,' said Hans. 'She can wait here. Let's go.'

I followed Hans out of the office and back into the showroom. I pointed out the pieces so he could put the 'Sold' signs on them, and then we returned to the office so he could write up the receipt and I could give him a check. Zane was sitting in the chair in front of the desk, an innocent expression on her face.

Hans pulled a pad out of the drawer and wrote up a receipt. I pulled out my checkbook and wrote out a hefty check for the second time tonight, for a deposit of 20 percent of the total. When I handed it to him, he didn't even look at it, just folded it and shoved it into his shirt pocket. Then he reached into the desk drawer and pulled out a business card, which he handed to me. 'Cell number's on the back. When you're ready to have the bookcases delivered, just give me a holler and we'll arrange a date. You can pay the balance upon delivery.'

I took the card and shoved it into my tote bag. 'Thank you so much. It was a pleasure meeting you, Mr Ellison.'

'Call me Hans,' he said. 'A pleasure meeting you ladies as well. Sorry we couldn't be more helpful, but . . .' His shoulders lifted in a careless shrug.

'No problem,' I assured him. 'I'll be in touch.'

Zane and I didn't speak until we were back out in the parking lot and seated in the SUV. Then she looked at me. 'You wanted me to go back into that file and make a copy of the receipt, right? At least that's what I hope that look you gave me meant.'

'That's exactly what I wanted,' I said. 'I assume you were successful?'

Zane's hand dipped into her purse and she removed a folded piece of paper. 'Of course. But I'm still puzzled as to why you wanted it. It's the same as the one you found in Sheila's room, only it's marked Paid.'

'No, there's more to it than that,' I said. I whipped out the original receipt and laid the two on the dashboard. 'Look closely at the two of them. What's different?'

Zane leaned over, peered at the receipts. Suddenly her eyes popped. 'There's a phone number on the second one,' she cried. 'And a name. Tucker Custom Designs.'

I smiled triumphantly. 'Exactly. I'm thinking that's the friend of Hans's who did the alterations for Sheila. Let's give him a call and see if he can tell us just what those custom changes were.'

SIXTEEN

Unfortunately, it seemed as if my lucky streak for gleaning information was at an end. The woman who answered the phone wasted no time informing me that the owner, Chad Tucker, was on a much-needed vacation. She did recall the order for Sheila and told me that Chad had handled it personally; however all his files regarding his custom orders were on his personal computer, which was, also unfortunately for me, with him. The woman took my number and said she'd try to reach him, but if she was unsuccessful, she promised to have him call when he returned on Saturday.

'Think he'll call when he gets back?' asked Zane.

'I hope so – if she remembers to give him the message.' I hadn't been too impressed with Tucker's assistant. She'd reminded me of one of Max's early admins. She had been a sweet girl who embodied the stigma of the air-headed blonde. 'If I don't hear from him, I'll call again.' I pressed the ignition button. 'Come on, let's go home and see what other information we can dig up on Sheila.'

Poe greeted us at the door when we entered, twining his portly body around our ankles. I saw the food and water dishes needed refilling, so I took care of that and then got out my laptop. Zane and I settled in at the kitchen table and I called up the page on Sheila Crowder I'd previously bookmarked. I hit the information tab, and another page popped up. I scanned it quickly. There was no mention of a Crowder or Blackwell anywhere on the page, but under Associates it listed a Gary M. Hollis and a Jaime Sparks. I nudged Zane. 'This might be something,' I said. 'You said she mentioned a Gary, right?'

'Right,' said Zane. She peered over my shoulder. 'It also lists an Evan R. Richardson. And here's a phone number. Oh my gosh!' Zane's nails dug into my shoulder blade. 'That's her cell number,' she cried. 'That's the one I have.'

I typed Gary M. Hollis in the search engine and then added Calais, Maine, as that was the town listed on Sheila's page. Five records popped up. I immediately discarded two because their ages were over sixty. One was nineteen and I discarded him as well. That left two remaining. One was forty-four, the other forty-six. I did an eeny-meeny-miney-moe and clicked on the forty-six-year-old's info. Gary Marvin Hollis. Lives in Calais, Maine. Under Associates were two names: Sheila Blackwell and Evan R. Richardson.

'What are the odds that they would both know this Evan R. Richardson?' I said. I called up a fresh page, typed in Evan R. Richardson, Calais, Maine and hit enter. When the page popped up, I scrolled down slowly. Near the bottom I found a listing for Evan R. Richardson, Richardson Antiquarian Books. The address and phone number were for Robbinston, Maine. I looked that up. Robbinston was only about six miles away from Calais. 'This might be their connection,' I said excitedly. 'Antique books.'

I held my breath and called up the website for Richardson Antiquarian Books. It popped up and beneath that: Rare and Worthwhile Books, Periodicals, and Autographs. I skimmed it quickly. The shop specialized in rare first editions, but also carried other books as well. It seemed their inventory was mostly used books, although there were a few new titles as well. I plugged C.J. Barrett into the search bar and noticed that several of my books popped up, including my latest release. Next, I clicked on the About page. A brief history of how the store came to be popped up. At the bottom Richardson mentioned his knowledgeable staff, Gary, Burton, Maggie, and Sheila. No last names, no photos of the staff.

Zane had been watching intently. Now she said, 'Well, if Sheila had anything to do with this bookstore it would explain why she was so gung-ho to open one of her own. At least I was right about her having retail experience.'

'Provided she's the Sheila mentioned here. There's one way to find out.' I clicked on the page marked Contact. There was a spot for an email inquiry, as well as an address and phone number. I checked the store hours. They were open until ten p.m. tonight, and it was a little after nine. I whipped out my phone and dialed the number, hoping that Richardson would be working tonight.

A male voice answered on the fourth ring. 'Richardson Antiquarian Books. How may I help you?'

'Good evening,' I said. I clicked on the speaker icon, so Zane could hear the conversation too. 'I was wondering if I might speak with the owner? Mr Richardson?'

'He's not here now. This is Burton Farrell. I'm the assistant manager. Might I be of service?'

I had to think fast. 'I'm looking for a signed first edition of *Carrie*,' I said, using the first title that came to mind.

'Ah, Stephen King's first novel. I believe we have some copies of it in stock, and a few are firsts, but none are signed,' he added, and I could hear the tinge of regret in his tone. 'I can, however, put out some feelers and try to locate one for you.'

'Would you? I'd really appreciate that.'

'OK.' A cautious note crept into his voice as he continued, 'Well then, how much were you looking to spend? Because a signed first edition of King's first novel can get a bit pricey.'

I understood the underlying message: *If you don't have the funds, let's not waste each other's time*. 'I'm willing to pay top dollar,' I said. 'Maybe more depending on the condition of the book.'

'Yes, that is another consideration. Do you want one in pristine condition? With or without dustjacket? Those are considerably higher priced. Let me do this,' he rambled on before I could say anything more. 'Let me take down your information, and exactly what you're looking for, and I'll see what I can come up with.'

I gave Burton my contact information, told him I wanted as clean a copy as possible, with or without dust jacket, preferably with. When I finished listing my preferences he said, 'I'll put out some feelers and see what I can come up with. I'll try to get back to you by this weekend.'

Fearing he was about to end the call I said quickly, 'You certainly live up to your reputation. A woman I met recently recommended your store. She said that you could put your hands on practically any rare book.'

I could hear the swell of pride in Burton's voice as he responded. 'We try to accommodate our customers in every way possible.'

'Yes, that's exactly what Sheila said. She raved on and on so much, I got the impression she might have worked there at one time.' I waited for a response and when there was none I continued, 'Her name is Sheila Crowder. Do you know her?'

A slight pause, and then, 'I'm sorry. I don't know anyone by the name of Sheila Crowder.'

I decided to press on. 'What about Sheila Blackwell? She worked there, didn't she?'

Dead silence, so thick you could cut it with a knife. Then Burton said, 'I'm sorry, I'm not at liberty to discuss former employees. So, if there's nothing else . . .'

'Wait,' I cried. 'Look, I admit the book wasn't the only reason for my call. I . . . ah . . . have something that belongs to Sheila, and she left town rather abruptly before I could return it. I actually was wondering if you might have some recent contact information for her. Or if not her, then maybe Gary Hollis?'

Burton cleared his throat loudly before he said, 'I'm sorry, Ms James, but if you want information on either or both of those two individuals, you'll have to speak with Mr Richardson directly.'

'OK, fine. When will he be in?'

'He's out of town until the weekend but I'll see he gets the message.' He paused. 'I'm safe in assuming you're not looking for a first edition of *Carrie,* are you, Ms James?'

'No, I'm sorry. I'm not. But—'

Then all I heard was a disconnect tone. Burton Farrell had hung up.

SEVENTEEN

Zane looked at me as I set down my phone. 'What do you make out of that?' she asked.

'What I make is, something happened at that bookstore,' I said. 'Something that involved both Sheila and Gary, and from Burton's tone and his reluctance to talk, I'm thinking it wasn't anything good.'

'Charley!' Zane gripped my arm. 'Maybe it's not Gary that Sheila was running from. The ex might be an ex-boss, not an ex-boyfriend. It could be this Evan Richardson.'

I typed in the name of the bookstore and after that, recent news articles. A few things popped up, but nothing that suggested anything remotely sinister. A few notices about upcoming sales, one article from three years ago about the store being named 'Shop of the Year.' Finally, I hit on one from *Maine Today* magazine. It was about used bookstores in Maine, and *Richardson Antiquarian Books* got a half-page spread in the article. What interested me most, though, was the accompanying photograph. Taken in front of the bookstore, which looked to be a charming red-brick building with a large picture window in which books were prominently displayed, Richardson, a tall bearish-looking man, stood front and center, surrounded by his 'loyal and competent staff.'

On his right was Burton Farrell, who reminded me of an owl. He was short, compact, with a beak nose on which a similar-looking pair of wire-rimmed glasses rested. On Burton's right was a tall, thin woman who was listed as Maggie Pace. Standing just behind Maggie was Sheila. Her face was turned to the side, but I recognized what I could see of her from the photograph on the search engine. She was listed as Sheila Blackwell. Off to her right was a sturdily built man with dark hair. His head was turned toward Sheila, and there was an adoring look on his face that I was fairly certain wasn't aimed at Richardson. The name under that photo was Gary Hollis. I leaned forward and studied the photo. It was hard to tell if the Gary pictured here was the same man who I thought might be following me. This Gary was clean-shaven, and not half-bad looking. I tried to visualize him with a beard. He could be the guy, but I just wasn't one hundred percent certain. There was something else about his picture that bothered me, but I couldn't put my finger on it. I mentioned as much to Zane, who regarded me with a worried expression.

'Maybe you should tell Grant all this,' she said.

'It's not that I haven't considered doing just that,' I responded. 'But I have no proof that the guy is Hollis, or for that matter, if he had anything to do with Sheila's death.'

'But what if he did? Grant will be royally pissed you didn't say anything, especially if something should happen to you.' She came over and put her arms around my shoulders. 'I don't want to see anything happen to you, and not just because you're my partner. We're BFFs, Charley. Always have been and always will. And if you don't tell Grant about this, I guess I'll have to. And you know how I love talking to him'

'Fine,' I mumbled into her elbow. 'I'll call him.'

Zane studied my face. 'Promise? You're not just saying that?'

I sighed and made a crossing motion over my heart. 'I promise. Cross my heart and hope to die. Oops.' I covered my mouth with my hand. 'Poor choice of words.'

Zane wiggled her pinky in the air. 'Pinky swear, and I'll believe you.'

I twined my pinky around hers. 'I swear. Are you satisfied?'

'For now.' She stifled a yawn. 'Well, I think that's enough detecting for me for one night. I still have more than two weeks left at the bakery, so tomorrow is another early day for me. Good night, Charley.'

Zane went upstairs, and Poe immediately rubbed up against my ankle. I picked up the cat and gave him a big hug. His tongue swiped across my chin, and he inclined his head toward his empty bowl. 'More food? You're going to eat me out of house and home,' I admonished the cat. I set him down and then refilled his bowl with more of the tuna I'd found in the fridge earlier. Poe settled down and started slurping, and I hunkered back down at the kitchen table and pulled out Grant's business card. I hesitated. Doing this would most likely earn me another lecture about interfering in police business, but Zane was right. Grant should know. I dialed his number, and after three rings went into voicemail.

Hello, you've reached Detective Ian Grant of Philadelphia Homicide. Please leave your name and number and I'll get back to you as soon as I can. If this is an emergency, please dial my beeper at 555-6785.

I figured that while I thought it important, Grant most likely would not, so I just left him a brief message: *Detective Grant, this is Charley James. I've found out something that could be considered important. Please call me at your earliest convenience.* I left my number and disconnected, then walked over to the kitchen island and my tote bag that I'd carelessly tossed there. I pulled out the notebook and returned to the kitchen table. I turned to the first odd set of letters and numbers and looked at it. HOLICRSGRCOL45225K.

What in the heck could that mean?

I wracked my brain, trying to remember just what I'd learned about codes when I'd written those Steve Sheppard novels. I knew that there were different types of codes and ciphers, some simple, some not so simple. One example of a simple code was writing the words in reverse, but I didn't see that applying to what Sheila had written here.

I remembered there was another cipher with numbers in it. Since I hadn't actually done the code in any of those novels, I was unfamiliar with how it actually worked. Thank goodness for Google. I typed the number cipher into the search engine, and a few minutes later I was reading about the date-shift cipher. I wasn't certain how it might apply to what Sheila had written, though, because it was a mix of numbers and letters. I found a pad and pen in the kitchen drawer and tried a few different combinations that ended up making less sense than the code before I threw the pen across the room.

I sighed. I wasn't even going to bother to attempt cracking the other one. It looked as if I were going to have to contact Max and get that code expert's contact info.

I reached for my phone but before I could punch in Max's contact number, it rang. A name popped up on the screen: Ian Grant. Wow, he hadn't wasted any time. Should I be flattered? I hit the answer icon. 'Charley James.'

'Ms James,' Grant's deep voice rumbled out. 'You left me a message about finding out important information?'

'I'm not certain how important you'll think it is,' I blurted. 'I think it could be significant.'

I could hear the smile in his voice as he replied, 'Well, I'm all ears. What have you found out?'

I paused. There was no easy way to spin this that it wouldn't appear I'd been investigating on my own, so I decided the truth was probably the best way to go. 'I've been doing a little digging into Sheila's past,' I began.

A giant sigh erupted from the other end of the phone. 'Even after I asked you not to interfere in a police investigation?'

'I wouldn't call looking up information on the internet interfering in your investigation,' I shot back. 'I was just satisfying my own curiosity as to Sheila, that's all.'

'Very well. And did you? Satisfy your curiosity?'

'To some extent. For instance, I learned that she might have also gone by the name of Sheila Blackwell.' I paused, waiting for some sort of reaction. When there was none, I continued, 'I also found out that she previously worked at a bookstore in Maine, up near the Canadian border. Richardson Antiquarian Books, to be precise.'

I heard a quick intake of breath. 'Anything else?'

It seemed to me Grant wasn't unduly surprised by any of this. 'You already know all this,' I accused.

'Sorry, I can't confirm or deny,' he said. 'I believe I have mentioned to you that I can't share details of ongoing investigations with civilians.'

'Yet you want the civilians to share details with you,' I bit out.

'Unfortunately, Charlotte, that's the way law enforcement works. So, if there's nothing else . . .'

'Sheila had an ex,' I blurted out.

'Pardon?'

'Sheila had an ex-boyfriend. Gary Hollis.'

Once again, the silence was so thick you could cut it with a knife. Finally, Grant ground out, 'And you know this how?'

'I stumbled on to that information quite by accident,' I said. 'But trust me, it's legit. Sheila's ex-boyfriend is named Gary

Hollis, and he's from Maine. As far as I can tell, they worked together at this Richardson bookstore.' I paused. 'And I think I might have seen him here, in Austin.'

'*What*?!'

I explained about the strange man I'd caught looking in the yet-to-be-opened bookstore window, and that I thought I'd seen him following me on two separate occasions. 'I'm not one hundred percent sure,' I finished. 'The man I saw had a heavy beard that obscured the bottom half of his face. The Gary in the photo I saw was clean-shaven, but they looked to be the same height, the same build.'

'I don't suppose you remember where you saw that article?'

'I bookmarked it on my laptop. I can send it to you.'

'Good. Do that. Please.' He paused and then added in a softer tone, 'This actually might be pretty helpful information, Charlotte. Thanks.'

'You're welcome,' I said. And then, because I've never been good at letting things go, I asked 'What's with the Charlotte? You called me that twice. And the pleasantries? Please? Thanks?'

The smile was back in his voice again. 'Sorry. I just can't call you Charley. As for the pleasantries, well, my momma taught me not to be rude. Unless it's necessary.'

'Or unless girls who like boy's names better than their own keep sticking their noses in your investigation?' I couldn't resist adding.

'Pretty much.'

There was another awkward pause and then, 'I don't suppose you'd be willing to come down to the station tomorrow, see one of the sketch artists? It would be helpful to have a likeness of this man who you say might be following you.'

'Or he might not,' I said quickly. 'Like I said, I could be off entirely. He just might be an overzealous mystery enthusiast.'

'Best not to take chances in a murder investigation. So, how's nine o'clock?'

'I'll be there.'

'Good. And Charlotte? Thanks for calling.'

He hung up, leaving me staring open-mouthed at my phone. Poe leapt into the chair next to mine, cocked his head at me quizzically.

I looked at the cat. 'Poe, I feel like Alice gone down the rabbit hole. Detective Grant actually thanked me for something!'

Poe butted his head against my arm. *Meow.*

'Yes, maybe I should buy a lottery ticket,' I said with a laugh. I picked up my phone again and hit Max's number on speed dial. My lucky streak was apparently continuing, because he hadn't changed his number. However, it went right to voicemail.

'Hello, Max,' I said. 'It's Charley. If you're still speaking to me, I need a favor . . .'

EIGHTEEN

The next morning when I checked my email I found one from Max. It consisted of two words: Freddie Mason, and an email address. Nothing else. I considered myself fortunate Max had answered me at all, even though he obviously wasn't ready to forgive me for what he considered a major betrayal on my part. I took a picture of the coded pages and sent off an email to Freddie Mason, refreshing his memory on who I was and asking if he could possibly decipher what I'd sent him.

The Austin Police Station was tucked into a skinny, two-story brown building on the other side of town. I pulled into the parking lot of said police station at precisely one minute before nine. I exited my SUV, walked up the short flight of steps to the entrance, and pushed through the double glass doors and into a wide reception area. The station area seemed to be swarming with activity. A police officer stood off to one side, taking down a report from an elderly woman. As I passed, I heard the police officer say, 'So the cat has a blue collar?' The woman nodded, tears in her eyes. 'Yes, and a medallion that has her name on it,' she answered. 'Bootsie.'

I made my way over to the reception desk, where a woman wearing a denim shirt, her long hair pulled back from her face, sat staring at a computer. The nameplate on the desk read Officer Gibbons. She eyed me warily as I approached.

'Charlotte James,' I said. 'Detective Grant wanted me to come in and speak with a sketch artist this morning?'

Gibbons didn't say a word, just picked up the phone and dialed a number. After a few seconds she said, 'There's a Charlotte James out here for you.' She listened a minute, then replaced the receiver and looked at me. 'Detective Grant will be right out,' she said. She motioned toward the far wall and a bank of highly uncomfortable-looking chairs. 'You can have a seat over there.'

I went over and eased myself into one of the chairs. And yes, they were twice as uncomfortable as they looked. I was only sitting there a few moments when the glass doors opened and in walked Derek Proust. He spotted me almost at once and made a beeline for where I sat. He walked right up to me and said 'Hello, Ms James. Remember me?'

'Yes, hello Mr Proust,' I said.

Proust flopped into the chair next to mine. 'This is rather an odd place to find you,' he said. 'Are you here for more questioning?'

I arched a brow. 'I don't believe that's any of your business.'

He held up both hands. 'Right you are. Sorry. Me, I'm here following up on my story. I want to speak to Detective Grant, see if he has any further news on what caused Ms Crowder's death.'

'What are you doing here, Derek?' came a voice off to our left. We both looked up to see Barbie glaring at the two of us. She marched right over and leaned over so that her nose was level with the reporter's. 'I told you, when we have more news we'll call you and make a statement. Did I call you?'

Derek frowned. 'No, but . . .'

'Well, then, there's nothing further to add right now. Sheila Crowder's death is still under investigation. So run along and dig up some real news.'

'Fine.' With a curt nod to me, Proust rose and stalked out of the station. Barbie watched until he was out the door, then shook her head. 'He's such a pest,' she muttered. 'Thinks he still works on that big Boston paper.'

'Oh, he's from Boston? What did he report on there? Crime?'

Barbie looked at me as if she'd just realized I was there. 'Not sure. What are you doing here, Charley?' she asked, in none too friendly a tone.

I gave her my sunniest smile. 'Good morning to you, too, Ba— Officer Donaldson,' I amended quickly. I slid my gaze over to the far end of the seating area, where Bootsie's owner had settled. The devil on my shoulder whispered in my ear and I said innocently, 'Are you here to help locate Bootsie?'

Barbie shot me a confused look. 'What? What's a Bootsie?'

'Nothing.' I waved my hand to make the devil vanish. 'Detective Grant wanted to see me this morning.'

Barbie's eyebrows drew together, cutting a deep V in the center of her forehead and making those pesky crow's feet lines around the corners of her eyes stand out. 'He did? What for? More follow-up questioning?'

It was on the tip of my tongue to tell her that he called to ask me for a date, but before I could act upon it a voice off to my left said gruffly, 'I've got this, Officer.' I turned my head and saw Grant standing there. The rims of his eyes were a bit red, indicating that he probably hadn't had much sleep. Otherwise, he looked fit and ready for anything in a blue shirt, dark blue jacket, and straight-leg dark denim jeans.

'Of course, Detective,' Barbie murmured, all sweetness and light now. 'Will you be needing my assistance?'

'Not necessary. If so, I'll let you know.'

'Thank you, Detective.' Barbie's gaze on Grant bordered on worshipful. Then it shifted to me, and now it was practically poisonous. I could almost swear those baby blues were tinged with green. She turned and flounced off into the back room, and Grant turned toward me. 'Thanks for coming in, Charlotte,' he said, his tone soft. 'The sketch artist is running a few minutes late, so how about I get you a cup of coffee?'

I rose. 'Coffee is always appreciated.'

He motioned for me to follow him, so follow him I did, through that back door and down a long, narrow corridor to a small room almost at the end. It held a small desk, a scarred file cabinet tucked into a corner, and two leather chairs that had seen better days. A new-looking Keurig coffee machine was on top of one of the file cabinets, and there were some paper cups beside it. Grant walked over to the filing cabinet, opened the top drawer. He looked over his shoulder at me. 'Pumpkin spice or mocha madness?' he asked.

'Oh, definitely pumpkin spice,' I said.

The coffee took less than a minute to brew. He pulled out a can of powdered milk, some packets of sugar. 'How do you take it?' he asked.

'Two sugars. Hold the powdered milk. I can drink it black.'

He put two sugars in the cup, then added a wooden stirrer and handed it to me. 'A woman after my own heart,' he remarked. He turned back to the Keurig and fixed himself a cup of coffee, then walked around the desk and sat down. He motioned for me to take a seat, and I slid into one of the other two chairs. Definitely an improvement from the ones in the lobby – but not by much.

'I probably should have called you,' he said, 'but I only just found out the sketch artist is running late. Austin only has one – in Philly we have three.'

'Yeah, well, I guess there's a lot more crime there.' I took a sip of the coffee, which was quite good. 'Do you miss it?'

He shrugged. 'Crime is crime, wherever the location. I miss the extra staff,' he added.

I leaned back a bit in the chair. 'So how's the investigation coming? Oh, sorry – I forgot. Taboo subject with outsiders, right?'

Grant wagged his finger. 'We're working on all leads, Charlotte. That I can tell you.'

'That reporter was here, looking for more information on the cause of death. Officer Donaldson chased him away.'

Grant sighed. 'Proust is a bit overeager, to say the least. I suppose I'll have to give him something to keep him happy – and out of my hair.'

'That might be wise. He seems . . . persistent.'

Grant chuckled. 'That's being kind.'

I slumped a bit in the chair. 'My friend Zane is under the impression that she's under serious consideration as a suspect in Sheila's death.'

He stared at his coffee cup for a few seconds before he spoke. 'I can see how she might have gotten that impression. We found several sets of fingerprints on that chest, and one of them was hers. And that argument with Ms Crowder in the diner didn't help. However, in my estimation, your friend stood to lose more from Ms Crowder's death than she'd gain. Our biggest problem, right now, is finding any suspects. Apparently Ms Crowder was a bit of a loner.' He took a sip of his coffee. 'By the way, I plan on releasing your store later on today. The lab's finished with what they need there.'

'Great. Thanks.'

'You're welcome.' He leaned back in his chair and let his gaze sweep over me again. 'So, let's talk about you.'

My head snapped up. 'Me?' I squeaked.

'Yes. I understand you've been living in New York. It's such an exciting city. Makes one wonder why you'd want to give all that up and come back to the old homestead.'

I shifted in the chair. 'I was getting bored with my work,' I said. 'I felt as if I needed a change.'

He leaned back, laced his fingers behind his neck. 'Austin surely is quite a change from New York. What did you do there, anyway?'

Why did I have the feeling that was a loaded question? I hesitated. If Grant were so inclined, he could no doubt find out that I hadn't worked on *New York Today* magazine as a researcher for the past fifteen years. Fortunately, I'd written contributing articles to several magazines under my own name over the years, as a sort of cover for inquisitive people. 'I started out as a researcher,' I said. 'I found that work boring, so I left and started freelancing articles.'

'Freelance, eh? You made enough from that to afford to live in Manhattan?'

'Believe it or not, New York magazines pay very well. What's with the third degree? Since when am I under investigation,' I said, indignantly.

'You're not under investigation. I'm merely curious. I find you a very interesting person, Charlotte James.'

'Really? I don't consider myself so,' I said. 'And wouldn't your time be better spent trying to track down Sheila's killer?'

'I'm working on it,' Grant began, then stopped as a light tap sounded on his door. He turned his head and called, 'Come in.'

The door opened and a young officer holding a manila file folder walked in. 'Officer Donaldson said you'd want to see this right away, Detective,' he said. 'It's the au—'

Grant reached out and plucked the folder from the officer's hand. 'Thank you, Officer Stevens,' he said, cutting off the rest of his sentence.

Stevens looked a bit confused, but he backed up. 'You're welcome, Detective. Oh, and Captain Reynolds would like to see you as soon as possible.'

'Tell him I'll be right there.'

Stevens turned on his heel and practically ran out the door. Grant opened the bottom desk drawer, shoved the file into it, and then stood up. 'Sorry, I have to go,' he said. 'Graves – that's the sketch artist – shouldn't be too much longer. Unfortunately, you can't wait here alone. You'll have to go back in the lobby.'

I raised my cup. 'As long as I have this, no problem.'

I'd slid my bag off my shoulder when I sat down and it was resting at my feet. As I rose, I gave it a swift kick so it landed underneath the desk. Clutching my coffee cup, I followed Grant out of the office and back down the corridor. Once back in the reception area, Grant made a left turn in the direction of what I assumed was the Captain's office. As soon as he was out of sight, I gave a little cry. 'Oh dear,' I said to Gibbons, 'I left my handbag in Detective Grant's office. Can I run back and grab it? It will only take a minute.'

She frowned. 'An officer should really accompany you,' she said. 'I shouldn't let you go into Detective Grant's office without an escort.'

'I understand your concerns,' I said. 'But I really need to get my purse. It'll only take a few minutes.'

Gibbons hesitated, obviously uncertain of protocol. I had the feeling she was leaning toward letting me go, but unfortunately for me Officer Stevens chose that moment to walk past, and she waved him over, a relieved expression on her face. 'Take this woman back to Detective Grant's office,' she said. 'She forgot her purse in there.'

Stevens gave me a quick once-over and then, obviously satisfied that I wasn't carrying a handbag, gave me a brief nod. 'Sure. Follow me.'

Stevens was a pretty fast walker and I had to hurry to keep up with him. I wanted to get a look at that report Grant had stuffed into his bottom drawer, because I was pretty certain Stevens had started to say autopsy, and I was pretty certain it was Sheila's. If Stevens was going to bodyguard me, though, I had no idea just how I might manage that. Luck was with me. As we approached Grant's office, a perky blonde in a tight skirt and even tighter sweater emerged from an office down the hall. 'Oh, Stevens, good,' she said. 'I need your help. That cabinet door is stuck again.'

Stevens paused uncertainly, clearly torn between keeping an eye on me and going to the blonde's aid. I flashed him a wide smile. 'You can go help her,' I said. 'I'll just duck in here and grab my bag. It'll only take a second.'

He hesitated, obviously torn. 'I really shouldn't,' he began.

'Stevens,' the blonde said again, with just the merest touch of aggravation in her tone. 'Are you gonna help me or not?'

Seeing the indecision on his face I stepped forward and said in a low tone, 'Go on. I'll be quick. And I won't say a word,' I made a crossing motion over my heart. 'As far as I'm concerned you were with me in Grant's office the whole time.'

Stevens hesitated, then nodded. 'OK.' He moved off toward the blonde and I pushed open the door to Grant's office. I retrieved my bag and then jerked open the desk's bottom drawer. I picked up the manila folder and glanced at the label on the tab.

SHEILA CROWDER PRELIMINARY AUTOPSY REPORT.

I opened the folder and riffled through the pages. The autopsy report wasn't very long – three pages. But there was a fourth page that wasn't part of the autopsy – the letterhead indicated that it came from the FBI-Identification Division.

I wanted to read it more thoroughly to be certain, but I knew I couldn't take the time now. I photographed all the pages with my phone camera, closed the file, and slid it back into the bottom drawer. Then I slung my bag over my shoulder and exited the office. I could hear Stevens and the blonde talking in the other room, so I walked swiftly back up the corridor and out into the reception area. Gibbons eyed me as I passed. 'Where's Stevens?' she barked.

'He . . . ah . . . stopped to help another young lady. She seemed to be having trouble with a cabinet,' I said.

'Aha,' Gibbons muttered. 'He turns to jelly whenever he sees her.' She shot another suspicious glance my way. I smiled again, then held up my bag. 'Thanks,' I said. 'I got my bag.' I didn't wait for her reply, but made my way over to the bank of chairs. Once seated, I whipped out my cell phone and called up the photos I'd taken. I skimmed through the autopsy stuff, pausing at the manner of death.

Victim died of blood loss caused by extreme injuries caused by knife blade, most likely spear-point.

So I'd been right about the cause of death. A spear-point blade could indicate the murder weapon was a Swiss Army knife. I'd used that in a few of my books as well. I skipped the rest, since I'd read autopsies before and went right to the FBI information. And there, right in the first paragraph, I found important information.

Fingerprints sent of murder victim have been identified as those of Sheila Blackwell, forty-three, of Calais, Maine.

And right below that:

Open Item: Sheila Blackwell wanted for informal questioning by Robbinston Maine PD.

Informal questioning? What could that mean? Before I could read anything else, a shadow fell across my lap. 'Ms James?'

I looked up into the bright blue eyes of a tall, leggy blonde woman. She extended her hand. 'So sorry to keep you waiting. I'm Cecily Graves. Detective Grant wanted me to work with you on a sketch?'

An hour later I was back in my SUV. In addition to being drop-dead gorgeous, Cecily Graves was an excellent artist, and the sketch she'd made from my description was so lifelike he could have jumped off the page and started talking. I'd taken a photo of it with my phone when Cecily wasn't looking. I intended to show it around a bit on my own, and I was fairly certain Grant would not approve. I hit the ignition button and pulled out of the police station. I was anxious to get home so I could print out and read the rest of the FBI report in peace. I made the turn to get on to Main Street, then noticed that one lane was closed for some type of repair. I frowned. There was a back road that would take me to Zane's house. It was a longer, more secluded route, but I was anxious to get home and didn't feel like sitting in traffic. I hesitated, then made the turn. As I drove, I mulled over my conversation with Grant, and what I'd seen so far in the report. I couldn't wait to read the rest, and find out why Sheila was wanted for questioning.

I was so involved with my thoughts that the sound of something behind me didn't register right away. As the vrooming sound became louder, I glanced in my rearview mirror. A black van was approaching fast. I frowned. It was a narrow road, but there was ample room to pass. Why didn't the van surge ahead if the driver thought I was driving too slowly?

The next second I knew why. The van surged forward and hit the back of my SUV.

I gripped the wheel and fought to keep my vehicle on the road. The van geared up and rammed the SUV's rear fender again. Then it dropped back and sped forward. It slid up on my left side, and before I knew what was happening, it had plunged into the left fender.

The steering wheel slid through my fingers like butter. In the next instant, my vehicle plunged into a muddy ditch on the side of the road . . .

NINETEEN

I slumped behind the wheel, my groggy brain struggling to recover from the shock of what had just transpired. I heard the van gun its engine as it sped away, disappearing over the rise of a hill.

My left shoulder had hit the car door when it slid into the ditch. I felt woozy – whether it was from shock or the accident itself, I wasn't sure. I took several deep breaths to calm my racing heart and took stock of my situation. I carefully unhooked my seat belt and moved my arms. I winced as a shooting pain shot through my left shoulder. Next, I moved my hands and fingers. All good there. I leaned forward, moved each leg. I knew there was always an adrenaline rush after an accident and sometimes people didn't realize how badly they were injured. Fortunately, I seemed to be OK. I wished I could say the same for my vehicle.

I pried my door open and peered out. The SUV leaned to the right, and it took a huge step to reach the ground. I sank into mud well over the instep of my tooled leather boots. One of my favorite pairs, too. I frowned as I realized they might not survive the accident. I took a quick glance around at the SUV and it was obvious that it would need to be towed. Swell. I went back into the car, grabbed my tote bag, and fished out my cell phone. I dialed Zane's number. Fortunately, she answered on the second ring. 'Don't panic,' I said. 'I've been in an accident.'

'What!' she cried into the phone. 'Charley, what happened? Are you hurt?'

'Not too badly. My shoulder is pretty banged up. Some person in a black van ran me into a ditch. My SUV will need to be towed.'

'Oh my gosh,' Zane said. She lowered her voice and hissed into the phone, 'Did you see who did it? Was it that guy who's been following you, the one who might be Gary?'

'No, I didn't see the driver,' I said. 'But I had the same thought. I'd better hang up now and call the auto club and then Grant.'

'If I were you, I'd reverse that order,' said Zane. 'But try and relax, OK?'

I disconnected and called Triple A, who promised to send a truck out as quickly as possible. Then I dialed Grant's number. Voicemail. I left a terse message describing the incident, then slid my phone back into my pocket and leaned against the back of my vehicle. Zane had suggested I relax, but that wasn't too easy right now. Someone had deliberately run me off the road. My first thought was, of course, the mysterious stranger. Although it could have been someone else, one of my other suspects possibly. Sheila's younger suitor? Gino Galante? Somehow the thought of Gino running me off the road didn't quite gel.

Ten minutes later I spotted a vehicle coming at me from the opposite direction. As it drew closer, I recognized the driver – Ian Grant. He drew abreast of me and rolled down his window. 'I was on the road not far from here when I got your message,' he said. 'Are you OK?'

'Just dandy,' I replied. 'A black van ran me off the road.'

Grant exited the vehicle and walked over to me. He whipped out his notebook and pen, then looked at me. 'Can you describe the vehicle?'

'I just did. A black van.'

He paused, pen poised over the notebook. 'That's it? Your powers of observation are far better than that.'

'OK. It was a big black van. I didn't see who was driving it, although I can make an educated guess.'

'The man who's been following you,' Grant said. 'The one you think might be Gary Hollis.'

'He's my first choice.'

'There are others?' A muscle in Grant's lower jaw twitched. 'I don't suppose you'd care to share them with me?'

'Well, gee, since you asked me so nicely.' I shifted my weight from one foot to the other, then eased my hip back against the SUV. 'One might be Gino Galante.'

Grant's eyes widened. 'Gino Galante? How did you settle on him?'

'I've heard rumors about him and Sheila possibly having an affair.'

One eyebrow rose. 'So you think he might be the killer?'

'It's possible, I suppose. A lover's quarrel gone bad – it happens. Or it might have been Sheila's other suitor. There was a younger man she was supposed to have been seeing. She remarked to someone that he could be a problem. Apparently he was more invested in the relationship than she.' I thought about mentioning Richardson but discarded that idea. After all, I had no evidence that he was the man Sheila had been avoiding, or even in the area.

Grant slid the pen and notebook back into his pocket. 'In other words, speculation. Rumor. No fact on either of those . . . suspects.'

'No. For all I know maybe it was just some drunk, or maybe some kid cowboying around. Maybe whoever did this never intended to run me off the road.'

Now both eyebrows rose. 'You don't believe that, though, do you?'

'No. I don't,' I admitted. We were both silent for a few minutes and then I said, 'Now that I think about it, the van had tinted windows. No lettering on it that I noticed.'

Grant whipped out his notebook again, scribbled my meager description down. 'Well, at least that's something,' he said. He reached out and touched my arm. 'Now do you understand why I don't want you interfering in police business? I can't concentrate on my investigation if I have to worry about you putting yourself in danger.'

My heart skipped a beat. 'Why, Detective Grant – you worry about me?' I asked softly.

He rubbed lightly at his forehead. 'My job is to protect civilians. You're a civilian. And it would appear you are in desperate need of protection.'

A slight twinge of disappointment arrowed through me. 'Well thanks, but I can take care of myself,' I grumbled. I moved my shoulder forward and winced. Grant noticed and gave me a sharp look.

'You're not dandy, are you? You're hurt,' he said.

I touched my shoulder gingerly. 'It's just bruised. I'll live.'

'You are one stubborn woman, do you know that,' he growled.

I allowed myself to smile. 'Indeed I do. It's one of my best qualities.'

The corners of his lips twitched upward, ever so slightly. He cleared his throat. 'You're sure that's it? You're not keeping anything else from me?'

I shot him a look of mock innocence and pushed thoughts of Richardson Antiquarian Books from my mind. I turned a finger inward and pointed at myself. 'Moi? Keep something from you?'

He looked as if he wanted to say something more, but then he just motioned toward his car. 'Get in. I'll take you to the ER. They can examine that shoulder and give you something for the pain.'

I shook my head. 'I really should wait for the tow truck,' I said. No sooner were the words out of my mouth than the auto service truck appeared at the crest of the hill. Grant wagged his finger.

'No excuses,' he said. 'Get in the car. I'll speak to the driver.'

His tone clearly indicated arguing the point would do no good. He escorted me over to his car, held the door open for me to slide inside. After giving me another searching look head to toe – maybe to reassure himself that I wasn't going to pass out on him – he shut the door and went over to speak to the driver. I leaned my head back against the seat cushion.

The words 'white knight' ran through my brain. I gave my head a shake. Maybe I did have a concussion after all. One good thing: at least Grant hadn't noticed that I failed to respond when he'd asked if I were keeping anything else from him.

Grant dropped me off at the ER. He couldn't stay – he'd gotten a call that I was fairly certain was from Barbie on the way down – but he'd called Zane and told her to meet us there. Zane was all concern over me, even after the doctor had said all I'd suffered was a sprain to my shoulder. She took me back home, got me an ice pack for my shoulder, and made sure that I took the naproxen the doctor had given me for the pain. I leaned back against the pillows she'd plumped for me on the sofa. 'You really don't have to fuss,' I said. 'It's not like I'm dying, or anything.'

'No, but your shoulder got a pretty good whack. You should just lie here and rest.'

I shifted my position on the couch, fighting back a moan. 'One thing's for sure,' I said. 'Someone thinks I'm getting close to something. I just wish I knew what it was they think I'm getting close to.'

Zane perched herself on the arm of the couch. 'Who do you think it was? The guy who might be Gary Hollis?'

'Like I told Grant, he's my first choice. But let's not discount the other possibilities. Sheila's younger suitor and Gino Galante.'

Zane wrinkled her nose. 'Sheila's younger guy could be anybody. As for Gino – sorry, I just can't see it.'

'The right answer isn't always real obvious. Someone said that once, but I can't remember who,' I said.

'Well Gino isn't real obvious. And I bet Sheila wasn't having an affair with him,' said Zane. 'If they were meeting up, there was some other reason. What it might be, though, is beyond me.'

'There's only one way to find out,' I said. 'Maybe that reason is why she was killed.'

Zane eyed me. 'What are you gonna do? Go over there and ask him? If he was involved with her, which I seriously doubt, he's not gonna admit it.'

'Of course he's not. That's why I have to think of another way to get the truth out of him. What I need is proof that they were having an affair.'

Zane rose. 'Yeah, good luck with that. I have to get back to the bakery. Will you be all right here?'

'Just put my phone there on the coffee table where I can reach it, and yes, I'll be fine.' I yawned. 'Those pills are starting to get to me. I probably will take a nap.'

'Good. I'll bring home dinner. How's Chinese?'

'Make it General Tso's Chicken and you've got a deal.'

Zane put my phone on the coffee table and left. I snuggled under the down blanket she'd draped over me and let my thoughts wander. I closed my eyes and tried to visualize what had happened with the black van earlier. I remembered looking at it in the rearview mirror, thinking it was awfully close – and then, like a flash, I saw two numbers in my mind's eye – 5–0. The last two numbers on that license plate had been 5 and 0!

I reached for my phone to call Grant with what I'd remembered, and just as my hand closed over it, the phone rang. I looked at the screen. Jeff Connors. I pressed the answer icon and said, 'Hi, Jeff.'

'Hi yourself,' he said. 'Say, I just drove past your store, and I see they're taking the crime scene tape down. Does that mean you'll want me back there to finish up?'

'Wow, that was fast,' I said. 'Detective Grant did mention he'd be releasing the store today.'

'I've got some free time now,' said Jeff. 'Want to meet over there?'

I shifted my position, winced at the twinge of pain in my shoulder. 'I can't today,' I said. 'How's Friday morning? Does that fit into your schedule?'

'I think that should be OK. Just give me a sec.' After a minute he said, 'Yep, actually my mornings are clear for the rest of this week. Friday, you said? How's nine thirty?'

'Works for me'

'Great. So . . . since you're unavailable today, how about lunch tomorrow? We could go to the Egg Platter. Tomorrow's their meatloaf special.'

It crossed my mind that here might be an excellent opportunity to kill two birds with one stone, so to speak. 'So I've heard, but I really would like to go to the Leaning Tower. I haven't had Italian in a while, and I always liked their food.'

'Yeah, Gino might change wives, but I still think he's got the same chef he had when we were in high school. The thin crust pizza hasn't changed one bit. OK, then, the Leaning Tower it is. I'll meet you there at noon?'

'Perfect,' I said. After I hung up, I looked up a local car rental agency and made arrangements to pick up a car the following morning. I disconnected and leaned back against the pillows. I could feel the drugs kicking in, and I closed my eyes – just for a moment . . .

The next thing I knew, Zane was beside me, waving a cardboard carton in the air.

'Hey, sleepyhead. Your dinner has arrived.'

'Oh my God,' I struggled to a sitting position. 'I slept the whole afternoon.'

'And you probably needed it.' She shot me a critical look. 'You look better. You've got color back in your cheeks.'

'Thanks.'

'Do you think you can make it to the kitchen, or shall I serve milady on the couch?'

'I can make it,' I said. 'The shoulder's feeling a lot better.' I swung my feet off the couch and reached for my phone. I punched in Grant's number. Voicemail again. I left a message about remembering the last two digits of the van's license plate, and said if he had any questions to call me. Then I opened up the FBI's report on Sheila and turned eagerly to the last entry. All it said, however, was that the Robbinston PD was interested in questioning Sheila Blackwell in connection with a recent complaint. The name of the complainant was withheld at their request. The questioning was strictly informal, no warrant for arrest had been issued. I shut my phone off then went into the kitchen for dinner, feeling disappointed.

The Galante's restaurant was about a fifteen-minute ride from Zane's house. I could see the edifice from down the road – who could miss that gigantic leaning tower? Galante had certainly done an excellent job of reproducing it. Even though they'd only just opened at eleven, the parking lot was pretty full. I found a spot not far from the entrance, parked my rented Chevy sedan, and then turned to look at Poe, curled up in a ball on the back seat. I'd originally intended to leave him home, but the little bugger had followed me and jumped into the car, giving me a move-me-if-you-dare look when I started to reach for him. 'OK, Poe,' I said. 'You wait here. This time I promise, I'll bring you back something.'

Poe winked one eye open, gave me a big yawn, then closed his eyes and tucked his head between his paws. I had the feeling he didn't believe me. I locked the car, leaving the windows open a crack for ventilation for the cat, then started up the short walkway to the front entrance. I checked my watch. It was eleven fifteen. I had plenty of time before I was to meet Jeff.

The first thing I noticed upon pushing through the double-doored entrance was that Jeff was correct – the inside hadn't changed. Not at all. The color wash on the walls emulated that of aged stucco. All the tables in the good-sized dining room were covered with red and white checkered tablecloths, and empty Chianti bottles covered with candle wax from a drip candle served as centerpieces. The cabinets that lined one corner of the room had faux grapevines atop them, and bottles and cans of imported olive oil sat on the shelves, with labels written in Italian. The large bar that took up the entire left wall had the Italian flag as well as the American flag draped behind it, and the shelves were stocked with fine Italian wines.

A man dressed in white pants and shirt with a red and white checked apron tied loosely around his waist came toward me. 'Table for one, signora?' he asked. I noted he had a slight Italian accent, but I couldn't detect whether it was real or put on. I raised two fingers. 'I'm meeting a friend,' I said.

The waiter led me to a table near a far window, and handed me a large, laminated menu. I glanced at it quickly. The menu size had changed. This one was large and dotted with photos of many Italian favorites: pizza, manicotti, lasagna, chicken and veal parmigiana, both platters and sandwiches. Standard Italian fare. My mouth watered at the thought of a chicken parm hero, but first things first. When the waiter returned with water and a basket of bread, I asked, 'Which way to the ladies' room?'

He pointed to a little alcove on the opposite end of the restaurant. 'Through there and to your right.'

'Thanks.' I paused. 'Oh, would Mr Galante be working today?'

The waiter nodded. 'Yes, but I believe he's out at the moment. Did you wish to speak with him?'

'It's not important. I'll catch him some other time.' I thanked him and moved off. I'd found out what I wanted to know. I didn't really have to go to the bathroom, I just wanted to do a little exploring – OK, snooping – and it was far better for my purposes if Gino wasn't around. If I remembered correctly, the offices were down the hall from the restrooms. I got up, hurried over to the alcove, and hung a left rather than a right. I went down a short hallway and then made another quick right.

Sure enough, there was a closed door at the end of the hall with a plaque that read 'Office' hanging on it. I glanced over my shoulder to make sure that no one was around, and then I went over to the door, knocked softly. 'Hello,' I called. 'Is anyone in there? Mr Galante?'

No answer.

I gripped the knob, twisted it. The door swung inward. I stepped inside and took a quick look around. The office was small and very messy. Papers were scattered everywhere, across the wide oak desk that stood in the middle of the room, and across the top of the large file cabinet that sat beside the small window. The middle file cabinet drawer hung open, and a file folder peeked out, as if it had been hastily shoved back inside. Curious, I crossed over to the cabinet and plucked the folder out. I looked at the label. One name was on it. SHEILA. My heart started to race. Why would he have a folder on her? I held my breath and opened it. Inside lay a receipt for . . . I gasped as I saw the item listed there.

It was for a first edition of *Mission at Victory Square*, a novel I knew well. It was my first Steve Sheppard novel. Why did Galante have a receipt for this book in Sheila's folder?

Suddenly all the hairs on the back of my neck tingled. It was as if I could feel eyes on me, watching my every move. Folder still clutched in my hand, I turned slowly around. I hadn't closed the door behind me and now I saw a figure standing there – and a flash of blue steel. I let the folder slide to the floor and instinctively raised my arms above my head.

'Don't shoot!' I cried.

TWENTY

Gino Galante lowered the gun and came all the way into the room. His beady eyes bulged as he barked, 'Who the heck are you and what are you doing in my private office?'

I lowered my hands to my sides. 'My name is Charley James. You don't know me, Mr Galante, but I used to eat here when I was in high school. I recently relocated back here to Austin and I wanted to know if you might have a few minutes to speak with me?'

One shaggy eyebrow winged upward. 'You want to speak with me? About what? You want to tell me how much you still like our cooking?'

'Well, that's a given,' I said. I glanced down at the folder on the floor. 'What I wanted to talk to you about was Sheila Crowder.'

'Sheila?' The other eyebrow went up. 'What about her?' he barked.

I walked around to stand in front of the desk. 'She was supposed to open up a bookstore here in Austin. I've decided to take it over.'

Galante's eyes narrowed. 'So? What's that got to do with me? You think I should offer you congratulations?'

'I've heard rumors that you knew Sheila well. Quite well, as a matter of fact.'

One corner of his mouth turned down derisively. 'See, this is what I hate about small towns. That's how rumors get started, and people's reputations get sullied. Yeah, I knew Sheila. But not the way you're thinking.'

'So you weren't having an affair with her?'

His eyebrows rose, and then he let out a soft chuckle. 'Pretty blunt, aren't you? Truth? If she'd been willing, I would have. But she wasn't. That's not what she wanted from me.' The corners of his lips turned down. 'She thought I was a sucker.'

'I'm sorry?'

'You heard me.' Galante crossed the room, stooped to pick up the folder I'd dropped. He walked around to the other side of the desk, pulled back the chair, and sat down heavily. He opened the desk's middle drawer and shoved the gun inside, then placed the folder in front of him and folded his hands on top of it. 'She thought I was a sucker. A patsy. And no one plays me for a fool. No one.'

I stepped forward, leaned over and splayed my palms across his desk. I leaned over so my nose was only a few inches from his. 'Is that what the two of you argued about at the Frozen Spoon? Is that why you threatened to wring her neck?'

Gino stared at me, and then he burst out laughing. 'See, what did I tell you,' he finally gasped out. 'See how rumors start.'

'So you're saying that didn't happen?'

'Oh, it happened. We quarreled, yes. But all my dealings with Sheila were strictly of a business nature.'

'What sort of business? Were you investing in her store?'

His eyes widened. 'Nah. That's not the type of thing I'd invest in. But our business did have to do with books.' He picked up a framed photograph from his desk, and I saw it was of a good-looking woman in a low-cut blouse. He tapped at the photo with his index finger. 'This is my wife. Gloria. It's on account of her I got involved with Sheila in the first place.'

Galante leaned back and laced his hands behind his neck. 'My wife, Gloria, is what you call a voracious reader. She loves mysteries and thrillers, and she's especially fond of James Patterson and that C.J. Barrett fellow. Well, Sheila promised to get a signed first edition of Barrett's first novel for her. She said she had connections. Charged me two thousand dollars for it. I thought it was overpriced, but I figured, what the heck. Gloria would love it, and I've been a bit in the doghouse lately.' The corner of his lip pulled downward. 'My wife listens to gossip – and sometimes actually believes it, you see. Anyway, she's been giving me the cold shoulder for a few weeks, if you get my drift. She went to visit her mother, who just had a hip operation, and I figured if I gave her that book when she got back, well, maybe she'd get over her snit. Sheila got me the book, all right, but as it turns out, it wasn't a true first edition, and it wasn't autographed by that C.J. Barrett. I had a handwriting expert look it over. I guess Sheila never figured on my doing that. When I met her at the ice cream parlor, I told her I wanted my money back and she refused. Said she'd been sold a bill of goods on the book too, and she didn't have my money. So I threatened to take her to small claims court. She just laughed at me, said I could threaten all I wanted, but if I did that, she'd make darn sure that my wife knew we were having an affair, even though we weren't. That's when I told her I'd wring her scrawny neck.'

I straightened. 'So that's why the receipt was in the folder,' I murmured. 'She must have taken one of the copies she'd ordered for the store and forged my— I mean, C.J. Barrett's signature, figuring you wouldn't notice.'

Fortunately, Gino didn't catch my little slip of the tongue. 'Yeah, that's just what she did. Played me for a fool,' he muttered.

'I can see why that might have made you angry,' I said. 'Very angry.'

His head snapped up. 'Yeah, I was plenty mad at her. I do take some consolation, though, that I wasn't the only one she was scamming.'

I frowned. 'How do you know that?'

'I overheard her on the phone that night when I went over to the table. She had her head turned so she didn't see me approach. She was telling some guy that she didn't have that periodical anymore and he'd better not keep bothering her about it. Then she said something about life being a game and playing by the rules, and then she laughed and hung up.' He swiped his hand across his chin. 'She wasn't too happy to see me, either. Accused me of eavesdropping on her private conversation.'

My mind was whirling. 'You're certain that's what she said?'

He looked hurt. 'Hey, my hearing is excellent. Like a bat's.'

'How do you know she was talking to a guy? It could have been a woman.'

'Trust me. I know when a woman's talking to a guy, and she was talking to a guy.' He motioned toward the door. 'Now, if there's nothing else you'd like to accuse me of, I have paperwork to finish.'

'Of course,' I murmured. 'I am so sorry for the misunderstanding. Tell you what, once my bookstore is open, stop in. I can guarantee you that I'll locate a signed copy of that C.J.

Barrett novel for your wife, and the signature will be authentic. I won't charge you two thousand dollars, either.'

'Promises, promises,' Gino said. 'Thanks, but no thanks. I think I'll stick to buying Gloria jewelry. After all, diamonds are a girl's best friend, right? Not James Patterson. And definitely not that C.J. Barrett.' His hand dipped into the middle drawer, and he pulled out a Swiss Army knife. He flicked it open, revealing a metal toothpick, and raised it to his lips. 'Now get out of here,' he growled.

I hurried out of Gino's office, back into the restaurant area and over to my table. The vision of Gino picking his teeth with the toothpick blade of his Swiss Army knife was stuck in my head, especially after reading that autopsy report. Gino himself admitted he'd been furious with her, but had he been furious enough to kill her? Well, he had the weapon, he had a temper, and he possibly had a motive. I wasn't ready to cross him off my suspect list just yet.

It was a few minutes past twelve, and Jeff was nowhere to be seen. I reached into my pocket and pulled out my phone after I sat back at my table. I turned it on and saw that I had two messages: one from Zane and the other from Jeff. Zane just said that she'd probably be home late tonight. Jeff's was an apology. A rush job had come up – could I give him a raincheck on the lunch?

I sighed. It was probably for the best. My appetite had diminished anyway. I stopped at the counter and ordered two small meatballs to go. Ten minutes later I got in the Chevy and looked over my shoulder at Poe in the back seat. He'd obviously smelled the meatballs, because he lifted his head, and I could see his little black nose twitch as he sniffed the aroma. I opened the container and set it in front of him, sniffing the air myself at the delicious smell. 'I had them hold the garlic,' I said. 'That's not good for cats. And they went light on the sauce. But I'm sure you'll still enjoy them.'

Poe's tongue snaked out, and he licked at the meatballs, then let out a rumbling purr. I leaned back against the headrest and replayed my conversation with Gino. Something had bothered me – what? Suddenly it hit me, and I whipped out my phone and called up Google. A few minutes later, my hunch confirmed,

I hit the ignition button, then gripped the wheel of the car and put it in reverse. There was someone I had to see.

As I started to back out, I saw a yellow convertible come into the lot. It slid into a spot near the side entrance of the restaurant and a moment later Derek Proust emerged. I watched him as he hurried up the steps and into the restaurant. Was he here for lunch, or had he too gotten a line on Gino Galante?

I looked at Poe. 'If he confronts Gino, he'd better be careful,' I said as I drove out of the lot. 'I've got a feeling Gino's pretty good with that gun, and he wouldn't hesitate to use it.'

TWENTY-ONE

The Brookvale Senior Community was a large sprawling complex located just off the main highway. I'd looked up Nancy's phone number and called her after I'd left the Leaning Tower. She remembered me and told me that she and Finn would love to see me again. She gave me her unit number, and I drove up the long, winding driveway, stopping at the entrance gate where I gave my name and destination to the guard. He disappeared inside and a few minutes later raised the gate and waved me through. The complex consisted of twelve buildings, all alike – red brick with white trim. I found the building where Nancy's apartment was located without too much difficulty and parked in one of the two remaining spaces marked 'Visitor.'

I looked at Poe in the back seat. He was still slurping away at his treat. 'Sorry, pal, I'm going to have to leave you here,' I said. 'Nancy has a service dog, and I'm not sure how he'll behave around you, or vice versa.'

All I heard was more slurping. I figured Poe would finish the meatballs then settle in for a catnap. Once again, I locked him in the car, then proceeded to the building entrance.

Inside the lobby was wide and spacious, with love seats and chairs scattered around near a wide fireplace. There was a reception desk off to the right, and a girl who looked to be no more than nineteen or twenty sat behind it, her nose in a book that she hastily shoved off to the side as I approached. I gave her Nancy's name, and she picked up the phone, dialed a number. 'There's a Ms James here to see you,' she said. After a moment she replaced the receiver and gave me a smile. 'You can go right on up,' she said. She pointed to a bank of elevators at the far end of the room. 'Fifth floor, apartment 506. Or you can take the stairs.'

'Thanks.'

I opted for the elevator. It was quicker. A good thing too because when the elevator doors slid open on floor number five,

Nancy and Finn were right there, waiting for me. I stepped out and immediately bent over to give Finn a pat on the head. He responded with a soft *woof*.

'It's so nice of you to come visit us,' said Nancy.

'Oh, no problem. I actually have my cat with me, but I left him in the car.' I angled my head toward Finn. 'I wasn't sure how they'd get along.'

'Oh, Finn loves cats,' said Nancy. 'It's better you left him, though. Sometimes the cats aren't too fond of him.' She pointed to the dog's nose, and I noticed a long scratch on the side. 'One of the women here has a calico, and they met in the hall one day. That scar is his little souvenir.' She chuckled. 'That's what he gets for being a little gentleman.'

I followed her and Finn down the long hallway to a door at the end. Nancy opened it and we stepped into the apartment. I noted that it was fairly good-sized, although it might have been the lack of furniture that made it appear that way. A small galley kitchen was off to the right, a small table with two chairs tucked into one corner. The living room boasted a large picture window, with an excellent view of the back parking lot. There was a small sofa, a beat-up recliner, and a wooden stand on which a thirty-two-inch flat-screen TV rested. Under the window was a large crate and a soft Sherpa-lined bed which I assumed were Finn's. A medium-sized bookcase adorned the far wall, and I noted that it seemed overloaded with books, mainly paperbacks. An open door off to the left revealed a glimpse of a full-sized bed and a dresser.

I turned and smiled at Nancy. 'This is nice,' I said.

Nancy shrugged. 'It's a roof over my head. Nothing fancy. Now, can I offer you something? I've got some delicious lemon raspberry pound cake that one of my neighbors here baked fresh this morning, and I can offer you tea or coffee?'

My stomach let out a soft growl, reminding me I'd skipped lunch. 'I'll take a slice of that pound cake,' I said. 'And tea sounds lovely.'

'Wonderful. I have Darjeeling and Earl Grey.' She paused. 'They were gifts from Sheila. She did love her tea.'

'Darjeeling, please.'

Nancy padded into the kitchen and both Finn and I followed.

Finn lay down near the doorway, head on paws. I eased into one of the two chairs at the table. Nancy went to the cupboard, pulled out two mugs and two plates, and set them on the counter. She took the top off of a footed cake plate and I saw a delicious golden loaf cake resting there. She removed a knife from the drawer, cut off two large slices, and put them on the plates. There was a steel teakettle on the stove. She filled it with water, put it on, and then delivered the cake to the table along with two forks. She set my plate in front of me, then pulled out the other chair and sat down. I dug right into the cake, slicing off a good hunk and popping it in my mouth. 'Oh, this is very good,' I said. 'It's very moist, and you can really taste the lemon and raspberries.'

'I'll tell Maxine you liked it. She so loves it when people praise her baking.' She broke off a smaller piece of the cake, put it in her mouth, chewed, and then raised her gaze to meet mine. 'So, Sheila died in the store?' she asked.

I started, and then my eyes fell on the newspaper sitting at the far end of the kitchen counter. 'Yes,' I replied. I didn't know what else to say.

Nancy shook her head. 'The news report didn't say very much. Just that her body was found in the storefront, and the police were investigating.'

It was on the tip of my tongue to tell Nancy the entire story, but then I heard both Grant and Barbie's voices in my head, cautioning me about revealing any details. I looked down at my plate. 'I'm really not at liberty to say,' I said. 'Detective Grant specifically told me I couldn't discuss any details.'

Nancy let out a sigh. 'Oh dear. That poor girl. I knew something was up.' She tapped at her midsection. 'My gut's hardly ever wrong. I just hope whatever happened, she didn't suffer too much.'

I pushed the image of Sheila's bloody body out of my mind as I said, 'I hope not either.'

The teakettle let out a loud whistle. Nancy pushed her chair back, went over, and poured water into two mugs with teabags. She set the kettle back on the stove and brought the mugs to the table, set one in front of me before resuming her seat. 'She so wanted to open that bookstore. Said it would be a new lease on life for her.' She fixed me with a stare. 'The article said Officer

Donaldson was in charge of the investigation, but you mentioned a Detective Grant?'

Oops. I gave myself a mental slap upside the head. 'Yes, Ian Grant. Officer Donaldson asked for his assistance. I believe he's serving in a consultant capacity.'

Nancy's eyes narrowed. 'That wouldn't be the same Ian Grant who's on the Philly Homicide Squad? He's been coming into Phyllis's café quite a bit lately.' At my nod she added, 'It can't be a clear-cut case, then,' she said. 'If Officer Donaldson feels she needs help. Actually, I think the term used in the article was "suspicious death".'

'That's not unusual. In instances where the manner of death isn't crystal clear, they always treat it as a suspicious death.'

Nancy let out a long sigh. 'Well, I'm glad this Detective Grant is on the case. Half the time I don't think Officer Donaldson knows what she's doing.'

I fought the urge to smile as I responded, 'I'm sure she's doing her best. She took great pains to assure me that she knows how to do her job.'

'Hmph,' muttered Nancy. 'That's not saying much.' She glanced at the table and then said, 'Where are my manners? Do you take cream and sugar? I usually just drink flavored tea straight.'

'This is fine, thanks.' I set the mug down, ran my finger around its rim. 'I was hoping that perhaps you might be able to tell me something more about Sheila,' I said.

Nancy looked at me over the rim of her mug. 'If I can, but as I think I told you, Sheila was a pretty private person.'

I pushed the mug off to the side and leaned across the table. 'I've done a little digging,' I said. 'Crowder wasn't Sheila's real name. It was Blackwell. I think she was using Crowder because she was trying to avoid someone.'

Nancy's eyes widened. 'You think it was that ex she talked about?'

'Perhaps, but . . . do you think it's possible she didn't mean an ex-lover, but someone else? An ex-boss, perhaps?'

Nancy's lips screwed up into a pensive expression as she digested that. Then she gave her head a brisk shake. 'No. She remarked on how he hated her dog, and how he thought she wasn't capable of managing her own life. I'm positive it was that guy she lived with. She never mentioned an ex-boss.'

I leaned back a bit in the chair. 'You mentioned the last time she seemed very knowledgeable about the state of Maine. I located a Sheila Blackwell who came from Calais, Maine, up near the Canadian border. She worked in a bookstore up there, Richardson Antiquarian Books.'

'Really? Well, that would explain her love of books and why she wanted to open a bookstore,' said Nancy. 'So I'm guessing this ex-boss is from that bookstore?'

'I believe so,' I said. I leaned forward again. 'Nancy, you said that Sheila said something to you about life being a game, correct?'

Nancy nodded. 'Yes. I remember distinctly because it was so odd. She said, "Life is a game that one plays according to the rules." It sounded to me like a quote from somewhere.'

'It is. That quote bothered me,' I said. 'And then someone else told me that he overheard her on the phone, repeating that same quote to someone else. That piqued my curiosity, so I looked it up. That quote is from *Catcher in the Rye.* That quote was important to her for some reason. I guess I'm trying to figure out why.'

'Maybe she just liked it,' suggested Nancy. 'People often repeat quotes they like. I know there's a woman I work with who's always spouting quotes from *Gone with the Wind.* Not a day passes that she doesn't manage to work in "Tomorrow is another day" somehow.'

'Maybe you're right.' I looked at Nancy. 'What about this younger man she'd been seeing. You said that Sheila mentioned he might be a problem?'

Nancy nodded. 'Yes. She said he seemed more interested in her than she was in him, and he didn't take hints well. Apparently, he wrote her little notes and left her some gifts.'

'And she never mentioned him by name?'

'No, wait.' Nancy passed a hand over her eyes. 'She did say something once. She was muttering to herself. She said "Men! They're all alike. Darn that J—" and then she saw me and stopped.'

'So you think she started to say his name,' I said.

'I think so. Something with a "juh" sound. Joe? Jim?'

I frowned. 'Could it have been Gino?'

Nancy paused, considering this, then said, 'Maybe, but I doubt it was Gino. I just don't think she was involved with him that way.'

'And it was definitely a "juh" sound? Not a "guh"?'

'I'm positive.' Suddenly she scraped back her chair and stood up, her hands gripping the sides of the table. Finn rose to his feet, looked at his mistress, and let out a sharp bark.

'No worries, Finn,' Nancy said to the dog. 'I just remembered something.' She shot me an apologetic smile. 'Sometimes with my PTSD it takes me awhile. She came by a week ago with something that she said she wanted me to look after for her.' Nancy motioned with her hand for me to follow her. 'It's in my bedroom.'

I scraped back my own chair and followed Nancy into her bedroom. She snapped on the light and pointed to a small dresser in the far corner, near the window. 'There it is,' she said. 'On top of the dresser. She called it a jewelry armoire. It's a bit large, but isn't it beautiful?'

For a moment all I could do was stare at the armoire. I had to agree, it was a beautiful piece of workmanship. It was a good-sized piece, and took up nearly the entire left side of the dresser. I stepped up to it and ran my hand across the wood. The finish was smooth to the touch. I noted the intricate workmanship along the edges, the tiny rosette carvings. They were similar to the ones I'd noticed on the chest in the bookstore's basement.

I looked over my shoulder at Nancy. 'It is beautiful,' I agreed. 'You said that she wanted you to look after it for her?'

Nancy nodded. 'Yep. She said that it held all her secrets, and it wasn't safe with her. And then I opened the box and looked all through it and what do you know? It was empty! So I said, "Sheila, you're crazy. There's nothing in here. How can it hold all your secrets?" And she just looked at me, and gave me this little half-smile and said, "Nancy, you'd be surprised. Just please keep it for me. At least I know it'll be safe here with you."' Nancy reached up to brush a sudden tear from her cheek. 'That was the last time I saw her.'

I motioned toward the armoire. 'Would you mind if I took a closer look at it?'

Nancy shook her head. 'No, not at all. It's not a heavy piece, just a bit awkward.' She moved over to the nightstand next to the bed, picked up the lamp and clock and set them on the floor. 'You can put it here and sit on the edge of the bed.'

I lifted up the chest. Nancy was right – it wasn't too heavy, but the size of it made it a bit unwieldy. I carried it over to the nightstand and set it down, then perched myself on the edge of the bed and slowly lifted the lid. It was exactly as Hans had described. The base was wide, made of sturdy oak. The top lifted up to reveal a mirror and a good-sized jewelry compartment with dividers. There were places for rings and earrings, and some hooks for necklaces. The interior was lined in a rich red velvet material. I ran my hand along the lining, but I couldn't feel any lumps or bumps indicative of something hidden beneath. I went and methodically opened each of the seven drawers as well as the two doors on the sides. All were lined in the same red velvet, and all the linings appeared to be smooth. I pulled on the hooks. None wiggled or were loose. I sat back and stared at the chest. I was stumped.

Nancy had been watching me intently. 'See, nothing,' she said. 'Just what did you think you might find?'

'I'm not sure,' I said slowly. 'Did you know that Sheila had special alterations made to this chest?'

'She did? She never mentioned anything,' said Nancy. She ran her hand along the side of the chest. 'It's hard to believe she'd have wanted to do anything to it. I mean, it's so beautiful.'

'That it is. Nancy, would you mind if I borrowed it for a little while? I'd like to examine it more closely.'

Nancy hesitated. 'Well, she did entrust it to me,' she said slowly. 'And it's the only thing I have to remind me of her.'

I reached out and covered her hand with mine. 'I know. I wouldn't ask, but I think it's important.'

She gave me a sharp look. 'You think there might be some clue in this chest as to why she died, don't you?'

I looked her right in the eyes. 'Yes, I do.'

'Well, I'm for anything that will bring closure to that poor girl's death.' She made a shooing motion toward the armoire. 'OK, then. You can borrow it. Take as long as you need.'

I reached out and gripped her hand. 'Thank you, Nancy.'

'Sure.' Her face brightened. 'Now, how about another cup of tea before you leave?'

Twenty minutes later I was back in my rental car. The jewelry armoire was in the trunk, bundled in a large black garbage bag. Before I pulled out, I looked around carefully. I didn't want a repeat of the van incident, not with the precious cargo I was carrying. Poe, who'd been napping after his meal, glanced up when I put the bag in the trunk. His eyes widened a bit, and then he jumped into the passenger seat next to me.

I debated where to take the chest. I didn't want to bring it to Zane's house, lest the van driver decide to pay a personal visit. My only other option was the store. I hadn't seen the mysterious stranger for a few days, although I wasn't discounting him as the driver of the van. I pulled into the driveway beside the side entrance of the store and looked around carefully before I unlocked the door and, followed closely by Poe, carried the chest inside. I carried it into the curtained storeroom, removed it from the bag, and set it on the small wooden desk. Poe followed me as I walked around the chest, inspecting it from all sides. What possible addition could she have made to it, I wondered. Poe had lofted on to the desk and sat beside the chest, his head cocked. His paw snaked out and he swiped at one of the carved rosettes.

'Of course,' I murmured. 'Those rosettes are similar to the ones on the chest in the basement.' I pulled out my phone, dialed the number for Ellison's. Hans answered. 'Hello, Mr Ellison. It's Charlotte James.'

Hans's voice brightened immediately. 'Ah, Ms James. Are you ready for us to deliver your bookcases?'

I'd almost forgotten about that order. 'Not quite yet,' I said. 'Soon. I had a question about the chest Sheila purchased. Do you remember if there was any carving on it? Maybe rosettes on its sides?'

'That I can tell you,' said Hans. 'There was nothing carved on the sides of that jewelry chest. It was just plain, polished wood.'

'Thank you, Mr Ellison,' I said. 'I'll be in touch soon about a definite delivery date for those bookcases.' I disconnected and looked at Poe. 'Why don't we have a look at that other chest?'

Poe cocked his head. *Ow— orr*?

'I said a look. We're not going to touch.'

Poe leapt down from the desk, and together we went over to the basement door, and cautiously descended the steps. This was the first time I was back in the basement since finding Sheila's body, and I had to admit it gave me a weird sensation. I shrugged and tried to ignore the chill that crept up my spine.

I walked over to the chest and studied it. It was a beautiful piece of workmanship, too, and I took particular note of the rosettes carved along its side. As far as I could tell, they were identical to the ones in the jewelry armoire. I grinned at Poe. 'I think I know what Sheila had done,' I said. 'She duplicated the rosette design from the large chest, and I bet she added some sort of secret drawer somewhere too. Let's check it out.'

Back upstairs, I went immediately over to the armoire and ran my fingers along each of the rosettes. Then I tugged at each one. None wiggled or seemed loose.

My phone vibrated in my pocket, and I pulled it out. The number wasn't familiar, but I decided to answer anyway. 'Charlotte James.'

'Ms James.' The voice on the other end was deep, very masculine, and sounded very far away and faint. 'This is Chad Tucker. My assistant said that you were most anxious to speak with me, and since I decided to extend my vacation another week, I thought I'd best call you. How can I help you?'

His voice had become very faint. 'Can you speak up, Mr Tucker?' I asked. 'I can hardly hear you.'

'Sorry!' He shouted so loud I had to hold the phone away from my ear. 'I can't vouch for how long this connection will last, though. I'm in the Canadian mountains and the reception here is spotty.'

'I'm inquiring about the order you did for Sheila Crowder? You made some alterations to a jewelry armoire for her?'

'Oh yes. That was quite a challenge, but I welcomed it. I used to be an engineer, so any time I get to utilize that talent I appreciate.'

'I was wondering if you could share just what those alterations were. You see, she gave that box to a friend of hers and told her that something was inside, but as far as we can see, it's empty.'

Tucker let out a chuckle. 'Ever heard of puzzle boxes, Ms James?'

'I'm familiar with the concept,' I said. 'She asked you to transform the armoire into a puzzle box? That means . . .'

'Yes. She wanted to put in secret compartments.' A loud blast of static sounded in my ear. 'Ros . . . sliding . . . mir . . .'

And then the line went dead.

TWENTY-TWO

'Oh no! Mr Tucker!'

I tapped at the phone and shook it, but it was no use. The connection had been severed. I tried dialing the number back, but all I got was empty air. I sighed. Great. Still, the conversation hadn't been a total bust. I'd learned what alteration Sheila had wanted made to the armoire.

I'd used the concept of a puzzle box in two of my novels. Some could be fairly simple, others complicated. Originally developed in Japan to keep children safe from needles, it had evolved into an item with many and varied uses. Some were used by workers to keep tools safe, by samurai or warlords to send secret messages, or for travelers to protect their belongings during journeys. They could only be opened if one knew the correct sequence of moves. Simple boxes had as few as four moves, while more elaborate designs could require sixty or more. I was hoping that Sheila might have opted for a simple sequence. But where to start?

I'd originally thought it might have had something to do with the rosettes, but none of them had moved an inch. I tried to remember what Tucker had said before we'd been cut off. His words had been pretty garbled, but I remembered one had definitely been 'sliding.' And right after that I was positive he'd started to say 'mir.' Mirror?

I went over to the jewelry chest and opened the lid. I looked at the good-sized mirror on the inside. 'OK, so maybe it wasn't the rosettes,' I murmured. I put my finger around the edge of the mirror and gave a sharp tug. Nothing. OK, not that easy. I tried sliding the mirror to the sides. Still nothing. Then I ran my index finger all around the edges of the mirror. On the bottom left side I touched a small ridge. I pressed on it with my nail, and I heard a sharp *click*! The end of the mirror popped open. I slid the mirror forward and saw a small cavity beyond. I wiggled my finger in as far as it would go, and touched a piece of paper. I pulled it out. It was the same lilac stationery that I'd found in the storeroom before, that had Mara's name on it. This one said simply 'Jaime.' But this time it included a phone number: 602-555-8962.

My heart started to hammer in my chest. Jaime. That was a name that started with a 'juh' sound. Sheila's mysterious boyfriend? Something else niggled at me, though, and then it came to me. When Zane and I had been poking around on Sheila Blackwell's information on the internet, two names had come up: Gary Hollis and Jaime Sparks. The same Jaime?

'Only one way to find out,' I murmured. I whipped out my phone and dialed the number. After three rings a female voice answered. 'Hello.'

'Hello. I'm trying to get hold of Jaime Sparks?'

'Speaking. Who is this?'

For a minute I didn't know what to say. I hadn't anticipated Jaime would be a woman, but it was one of those names that could be either male or female. *Like a nickname of Charley*, I thought. 'My name is Charley James,' I said. 'I'm calling about Sheila.'

'Sheila, huh?' Jaime let out a snort. 'I figured it was about time for my luck to run out. What's she done now?'

I wasn't quite sure just what sort of reaction I'd been expecting, but it definitely wasn't that. 'I'm sorry?'

'You said you were calling about Sheila. You do mean Sheila Blackwell, right?'

I licked my lips. 'Ah, actually she goes by the name of Sheila Crowder.'

Another snort. 'Oh, so she's using her mother's maiden name now? Please don't tell me she's been arrested.'

'Arrested? Oh, no,' I said. 'She was supposed to go into business with a friend of mine, and backed out at the last minute.'

Jaime let out a long sigh. 'Well, that doesn't surprise me. When she got that job at that bookstore, we all thought she'd finally gotten her act together, but I guess she's up to her old tricks again.'

'You were listed as one of her contact persons,' I went on. 'You and a Gary Hollis?'

She let out a loud snort. 'Of course I'd be on it. I'm the only cousin who ever had anything to do with her, and I tell you, that was a mistake. We kept in touch for a good while. She'd call me every other week, let me know what she was doing. She promised me that she was going to straighten out her life, but then the next thing I heard she left that bookstore and took off. As for Gary, well . . . that was a volatile relationship. One I guess she could never quite shake.'

'I'd heard that Sheila suffered from PTSD,' I said. 'I thought that perhaps that might have been a result of her relationship with Gary.'

'Sheila got PTSD because she was in a terrible car wreck when she was twenty-one. The driver of the car that hit her died, and Sheila was hospitalized for weeks. She was a wreck after that. Had to see a shrink. Why did you think Gary had anything to do with that?'

'Well, sometimes PTSD can be caused by violent personal relationships.'

'No,' Jaime said firmly. 'You mean if he beat her up, or something like that?' Jaime barked out a laugh. 'Trust me. If anyone did the beating in that relationship, it would have been Sheila.'

'So this Gary was on the wimpy side?'

'I wouldn't call him a wimp. They could both give as good as they got, it's just Sheila was better at it. I know they argued a lot. It was one of those relationships that was usually more off than on.'

Jaime was quite talkative, considering she didn't know me from Adam. I'm not ashamed to admit I took full advantage of it. 'She mentioned something about having a dog, but had to get rid of it on account of Gary?'

'Oh yeah. They did have a huge fight over that poor dog. In Gary's defense, he was allergic. She wanted him to get shots, and he wouldn't. She kept saying she couldn't get rid of the dog because he helped her with her PTSD, kept her grounded. Gary said that was a load of bull. This went on for months, and finally she agreed to get rid of the dog after Gary had a real bad asthma attack.' She paused and then added, 'Actually I ended up with the dog. He's a cute spaniel mix. No offense to either of them, but Ollie's better off with me.' She paused and then said, 'It's funny you should bring Gary up. He called me a couple of days ago, wanted to know if Sheila had left anything with me. I told him if she'd left anything with me I sure as heck wouldn't give it to him.'

'Ms Sparks, when I first mentioned Sheila's name, your reaction was that you thought she might have been arrested. Had she been arrested before? I couldn't find any criminal record for her online.'

'It happened years ago, when she was a teenager. The case got thrown out, not enough evidence, and I think the records were sealed because she was underage. She was running scams even then.'

'Running scams?'

'Yes. It started when she was real young. She got it from that father of hers. He spent more time in jail for fraud than he did supporting his family. Sheila's mother tried to be a good influence, but all for naught. The kid was a little con artist, and she was real good at it too. The only thing that changed as she got older was she was more careful not to get caught, only that one time and even then she got lucky. She kept out of trouble for a while . . . and then she met Gary.'

'So Gary was a con artist too?'

'He thought he was. I'd call him more of a two-bit hustler. She never said if they pulled off any scams together and I didn't ask. I didn't want to know. She was insistent that she was going to turn over a new leaf.'

'You didn't believe her?'

'I wanted to, but you know that old saying . . . a leopard never changes its spots. I was happy as long as she wasn't calling me to bail her out of jail.' Jaime coughed lightly and then continued, 'The last time I spoke with her was quite a while ago. "Jaime," she says to me, "it's happened. My ship has finally come in. I'm finally going to be able to get my act together. No more scams." So, I said, "Good for you, Sheila. I hope you mean it." Then she told me that she was through with Gary. I said I hoped she meant it, and she laughed and said that she didn't much care, but he was going to be really, really mad at her.' She paused for a breath and then continued, 'Then I get a phone call from her boss. Seems she abruptly left that bookstore job, no explanation or anything. She just vanished. Gary too. I figured what she'd told me had been a bunch of bull, that they must have pulled some sort of scam together and were getting the heck out of Dodge. If you say she started going under the name of Crowder, well, that aces it for me.'

'A few people mentioned that she seemed afraid her ex would find her. I was thinking it might be this Gary, but perhaps it could be her ex-boss.'

'It could be either,' Jaime agreed. 'I know Richardson wasn't too happy about how she left his employ. Or it could be someone else she scammed.'

'Oh, one last thing. Did Sheila happen to have a boyfriend other than Gary? Maybe one who had the initial J or whose name started with a "juh" sound?'

'You think she was two-timing him? Well, it's possible. That girl did like to flirt with anything that wore pants. Initial J you said? The only male she raved about with the initial J wasn't a boyfriend. It was that author. J.D. Salinger? She absolutely adored him. As a matter of fact, that's what she said to me the last time we spoke. That thanks to J.D., her ship had finally come in.'

Hm, that was interesting. So she had a fixation on J.D. Salinger. That could explain the quote from *Catcher in the Rye*. 'Thank you very much for taking the time to speak with me,' I said. 'I'm very sorry to have bothered you.'

'It's fine,' Jaime said. 'At least you've given me a heads-up. I suppose I'll be hearing from Sheila any day now.' She sighed. 'And I thought my days of bailing her out of a jam were finally over.'

I thought it best that I not be the one to tell her what had happened to her cousin. I was pretty sure Grant would eventually find her, he or Barbie could deliver the sad news. I was just about to say goodbye when a thought occurred to me. 'One last question, if you don't mind,' I said. 'Did Sheila have any hobbies? Woodworking, or maybe magic?'

'Funny you should ask that,' murmured Jaime. 'She was always fascinated by magic. Used to always watch those David Copperfield shows, and I really think she would have liked to go to Las Vegas and try to get hired as one of those magician's assistants. She was always looking through furniture magazines for chests, the kind magicians used. She used to try and figure out if they had secret compartments or not. Odd hobby, right? But that was Sheila.'

I thanked Jaime again and hung up. The conversation had been profitable. So Sheila had been good at running scams. Had she run one at the bookstore? Something that made it necessary for her to flee and change her name? And was she hiding from Richardson, or Gary Hollis? Or both?

I ran my hand through my hair. Could Evan Richardson have possibly tracked Sheila here? Had they argued, and had he killed her? There had been no sign of forced entry, so it was a likely assumption Sheila had known her killer. I kept going back to the fact that whoever had done it had stuffed her body in that trunk. It had to be someone who knew the store was vacant, who planned on returning and disposing of the body. But they hadn't. Why?

I was also pretty certain Sheila had been excited over the chest because she'd probably recognized it as one of those 'magician chests.' She'd passed a remark to Zane that the chest seemed magical. No doubt it had inspired her to make the adjustments in the armoire. 'It holds all of my secrets,' she'd told Nancy. But where, exactly?

'More questions, not enough answers,' I muttered.

Poe's paw swiped out again and his claw found one of the rosettes. As he started to pull it free, I thought I saw it move, ever so slightly. 'What's going on there, buddy?' I asked the cat.

Poe blinked at me. *Meow*.

'You think I should keep trying the rosettes? OK.'

My fingers gravitated toward the one Poe had touched. It was at the very end of the carved sequence on the chest's right side. 'This one moved. I'm certain of it,' I said. I placed my index finger on the rosette and moved it in a back-and-forth motion. Sure enough, I felt it wiggle underneath my finger. I moved it first to the right, then to the left. I tried to remember some of the basic puzzle box movements that I'd looked up when I'd been writing *Appointment in Sudan.* Steve Sheppard had moved the button icon first left, then right, then up slightly, and the secret drawer clicked open. I placed my finger on the rosette and repeated those movements. When I pushed the rosette up, I held my breath, and then . . . the rosette moved inward. I pressed on it again and then jumped back as a drawer shot out from the side of the box, directly underneath that rosette.

'Bingo!' I yelled the word out, startling Poe. The drawer had what looked like several sheets of stationery in it, neatly tied with a blue ribbon. I pulled the packet out and pushed the drawer shut, then undid the ribbon. There were four sheets of paper in total, and I could see there was writing on both sides of the papers. I looked at Poe. 'Looks like we might have finally found one of Sheila's secrets, Poe.' I picked up the top one. It was dated about a month ago, and the salutation was simply: My Darling 'S.' Below that was written what I imagined the author thought was a love poem:

Eyes like stars
Hair like the sun
You walk like a dream
More than I ever could have imagined
You are Poetry in motion to me
I will love you all the days of my life.

It was signed 'J.'

I turned the paper over. Written in a bold scrawl was: *Words cannot adequately express how I feel about you. I never did well in English in school, but I put all my feelings into this.*

Once again it was signed simply 'J.'

I looked at the other three letters. They had been written over the course of a few weeks. Each one contained a small poem on the front, and on the reverse a declaration that got more intense with each entry. The last one indicated that Sheila had initiated a breakup:

You sever ties
Breaking my heart
This cannot last
You have to see
How good I am for you
And you are for me.

The note on the reverse side read:

My Darling S,

I cannot believe that you no longer want to see me. You have to know my feelings for you are genuine. I would never hurt you like G.

Please, please, reconsider.

J

I frowned. 'G' no doubt meant Gary. There was also a small card from Ziwicki's Florist in the next town: *Love you always. J.* The card had been tucked into the second letter which had been dated two weeks ago. I grabbed my phone, looked up the number of Ziwicki's, and dialed. A bored-sounding girl answered 'Ziwicki's Florist. How can we help you?'

'Good afternoon,' I said. 'I was wondering if I could get some information on an order that was placed two weeks ago?'

'Sure. Do you have the slip with the order number?'

'Ah, no. I'm getting the information for a friend, who received the order. She'd like to reciprocate, but she's not sure who sent the . . . arrangement.'

'OK, well, it's easier to look up with the number,' the girl said. 'But if you have the recipient's name, I'll see what we have on file.'

'Thank you. It's Ms Sheila Crowder, and it would have been delivered . . .' I paused. 'It would have been delivered to Mrs Dinwiddie's Rooming House,' I said at last. I somehow doubted that flowers would have been sent to the storefront, and I didn't have any other address for Sheila.

'Just a sec.' The girl put me on hold, and I found myself listening to Muzak for what seemed an eternity but was in actuality only about five minutes. 'OK,' she said when she came back on the line. 'I think I have it here. Actually, there were three orders for Sheila Crowder. One was yellow roses, then pink roses, and the last one red roses. All delivered to that rooming house.'

Hm, three orders of roses? The guy must have had it bad. I could count the time Henry had bought me roses on one hand, and not the whole hand either. 'Yes, do you have a record of who sent them?'

'Unfortunately, no. They were all paid for in cash, and the guy came in and wrote out the cards himself.' She giggled. 'I do remember now. I waited on him for the pink roses. He seemed real nervous.'

'You waited on him? Do you remember what he looked like?' I said.

'Hm. Well . . . he was tall. Not real tall, but taller than me. I'm five eight so . . . maybe five ten, five eleven? I don't think he was six feet. Good-looking.'

'How about his build? Was he fat, skinny? Well-built? Did he look as if he exercised?'

'Gee, I dunno. I didn't pay that much attention to him. I kinda focused on his face.'

'Any outstanding characteristics? How about his features?'

'He was good-looking, you know, like a Ryan Phillippe type maybe. Oh wait. More like a young Brad Pitt. He had dirty blond hair that kept falling over his forehead.'

I figured that was the best I was going to get out of her, description wise anyway. 'Could you tell me the dates of those orders?' I asked.

'Sure.' She rattled off the dates. I noted that the red roses had been delivered last week, right around the time Sheila had been murdered. I thanked her for her help and was about to hang up when she said, 'Oh, wait. I remember something else. He wore black coveralls, kind of a uniform. I remembered thinking what a shame it was to cover up that body, because he looked like he was well built.'

'Coveralls? So he was a workman of some sort?'

'I guess so.'

'Think. Was there a name stitched on those coveralls?'

There was silence for a moment, and then she let out an excited squeal. 'Oh, right, I remember now. There was a name. Jeff. Does that help you?'

'I— yes, yes it does. Thank you.' I disconnected, then leaned against the counter. I tapped my phone against my chin. Well built, dirty blond hair, reminded her of a younger Brad Pitt. That could surely describe a lot of young men, but the name gave it away for sure. Jeff Connors.

Jeff was a name that started with a 'juh' sound. I remembered the day he'd come into the store. He'd worn black coveralls, and his name – Jeff – had been on the right chest pocket in bright yellow. I recalled something else too, something that Zane had said. Jeff had recently broken up with someone, and reportedly had taken it pretty hard.

Could Jeff Connors, my high school crush, be the mysterious 'J'? Was he Sheila's younger suitor? Was it possible my old high school flame could be her killer?

Poe looked at me. He raised one paw. *Meow.*

I grabbed my tote bag. What I had in mind was probably not the smartest idea, but I had to find out, and I had to find out *now*.

TWENTY-THREE

Connors Electrical was located in the center of town, on the corner of Twelfth and Main, in a plain, whitewashed storefront. A bell tinkled overhead as I let myself and Poe in the front door. I paused to look around. There was a wide counter in the center of the store, and a glass case that displayed all sorts of electrical equipment. I could hear the sounds of banging coming from the rear of the store. I walked up to the counter and rapped my knuckles against the wood. 'Hello,' I called. 'Anybody here?'

A moment later Jeff himself peeked around the corner from the back room. His face brightened when he saw me. 'Charley,' he said. 'What a nice surprise. What are you doing here? I thought we were meeting at your store Friday morning?'

I swallowed. 'We were . . . we are supposed to, but I had to see you now,' I blurted.

His eyes widened just a tad. 'Oh? Well needless to say, I'm flattered,' he said. He glanced at the clock. 'I just have to finish something up, and then I'm free the rest of the evening. Do you want to grab an early supper?'

'Actually, I'm not very hungry. I just need to talk to you.'

He came around the counter to stand in front of me, and his smile faded a bit when he saw Poe curled in a ball at my feet. 'You brought your cat,' he said.

'Yes. You don't mind, do you? He was at the store with me, and I didn't want to waste time bringing him home.'

Jeff gave Poe a wary look, then shook his head. 'No, it's fine.' The smile was back. 'You sound very serious,' he said. 'Is something wrong?'

'I hope not.' I glanced around. 'Are we alone here?'

'Yep. It's just me.' He shot me a wide grin. 'Why, what did you have in mind?'

'I thought you might be able to give me some information.'

The grin faded, replaced with a puzzled expression. 'You

mean about the light fixtures? Why sure. I've got a catalog in the back you can look at. Pick out what you want, and I'll order 'em. If we place the order by the end of the week, I should be able to pick them up and install them next week, week after at the latest.'

'I don't want information about light fixtures. I mean, yes, I do need to order them, but there's something else I need to ask you about. Something far more important.'

His brows knit together. 'OK, well, ask away. What is it?'

I cleared my throat. 'I found Sheila's jewelry armoire.'

'Sheila had a jewelry armoire?' His frown deepened. 'O–K. So why would I care?'

I eased a hip against the counter and crossed my arms over my chest. Poe took up a protective stance at my side. 'I'm not quite certain. Yet.'

Jeff made an impatient gesture with his hand. 'Get to the point, Charley. I'm not as fond of puzzles as you are. What does a jewelry box have to do with me?'

'Sheila had this box altered. She turned it into a puzzle box.'

Now he stared at me as if I'd grown another head. 'A puzzle box? What's that?'

'Short version, it's a box or a chest that can only be opened by solving a puzzle. Just like its name. It's usually boxes or pieces of furniture with secret compartments and hidden openings.'

Jeff let out a hollow laugh. 'So this chest has a secret compartment?'

'I've found one so far. There could be more.' I paused. 'I found something very interesting inside. Care to make a guess what it was?'

He shifted his weight from one foot to the other and clasped his hands in front of him. 'Well, you said it's a jewelry box so . . . some sort of jewelry?'

'No. Something far more interesting.' I reached into my jacket pocket and pulled out the bundle of letters. 'Recognize these?'

Jeff swallowed, and his cheeks paled. He made no move to take the letters from my outstretched hand. 'Should I?'

'I think so.' I waved the letters in front of him. 'You wrote these to Sheila, didn't you? You're "J", the "younger man" she was seeing.'

Jeff looked down at the ground. 'I hate that phrase, younger man,' he mumbled. 'I'm not that much younger. What, nine, ten years the most?'

I felt my stomach sink. There had been a part of me that hoped I'd been wrong. 'So you are "J". You were in love with Sheila.' I phrased it as a statement, not a question, and waited for the response.

Now he raised his head and his gaze bored into mine. 'Yeah, OK. We went out for a while. So what?'

I set the letters on the counter. Poe leapt up, settled beside them and placed his paws over them. 'Zane mentioned that you'd recently broken up with someone and that you'd taken it pretty hard.'

He emitted a hollow laugh. 'Yeah. Some joke, right? The playboy of Austin High going all gaga over a woman. But I did. Honest, Charley, I never thought I could fall as hard for someone than I did for Sheila.'

'I can tell that from these poems,' I said. 'You had deep feelings for her.'

'I sure did.' He sighed and eased one hip against the counter. 'I met her at a bar out on the highway – Leon's. She was sitting at a stool all the way over in the corner. Said that she was trying to avoid some guy who'd been pestering her. We got to talking, and we went out a few times. Nowhere fancy. Dinner a few times, the movies. She had a grand sense of humor, and she really knew a lot about books. She said that she'd worked at a bookstore for a couple years, and she learned the business and now was going to open one of her own.' He paused for a breath. 'Anyway, I started sending her those poems and flowers. She called me after I sent the pink ones, told me that I should stop, that she liked me but she didn't feel the same way about me. She said that she'd had a boyfriend that left a bad taste in her mouth about relationships and she really just needed a friend.'

'But you didn't stop trying, did you?' I prompted as Jeff lapsed into silence.

He shook his head. 'No. I really couldn't.'

'What about this guy who you said was pestering her,' I asked. 'Is it possible that it could have been her ex?'

Jeff stared off into space for a few minutes, then looked back at me and shrugged. 'I guess it could have been. I don't know for sure. All I know is she seemed to be real annoyed with him. Why do you think it could have been her ex?'

'In your last note you said you would never hurt her like "G"? I thought perhaps that might be him because his name is Gary.'

'Oh. Well, she never called him by a name. She just said, "G doesn't know how to take no for an answer."' He paused a moment and then said, 'You know, now that I think about it, she might have said, "*He* doesn't know how to take no for an answer." She was talking very low, so I'm not sure.'

My face fell. 'So his name might not have started with a G after all?'

'Like I said, I'm not sure.' He blew out a breath. 'Anyway, I made a last-ditch attempt with those red roses. I thought for sure she'd at least call, but nothing. Then, when we found her . . .' His voice cracked and he bowed his head.

'You surprised me, Jeff,' I said. 'You're a better actor than I ever gave you credit for. You stank in drama club in high school, yet that day you acted as if you barely knew Sheila, when all the time . . .'

He cut me off with a slicing motion. 'I wasn't acting. I was in shock. That was the last place I ever expected to see her. And I sure as heck didn't expect to see her dead.'

'Didn't you?'

His head snapped up and his jaw went slack. 'Charley! You don't think . . . you can't think that I . . . that I could possibly do something like that?' he floundered.

'I don't want to think it Jeff,' I said. 'I've known you practically all my life. You were my first crush, my first boyfriend. We went to the prom together. But I've heard several people say how Sheila was worried that this "younger man" she'd been seeing could be a real problem.'

Jeff's chin went up. 'Yeah well, it wasn't me.' He stepped forward and lightly touched my arm, an earnest expression on his face. 'I know it seems bad, what with the love letters and all, but you have to believe me, Charley. I didn't kill Sheila. I couldn't kill her or anyone else for that matter.' He laughed hollowly. 'Heck, I can't even swat at a fly. And I threw up when we had to dissect that frog in biology class, remember?'

'I do.' I looked right into his eyes. 'I believe you,' I said softly. 'And I'm sorry for bringing it up this way, but . . . I had to know. I had to be sure.'

He nodded. 'Of course. I understand.' We were both silent for a moment and then he cleared his throat and said tentatively, 'So, are we still on for Friday morning? At your shop? You still want me to do your fixtures, right?'

I nodded. 'Sure.' I picked up the letters and shoved them back in my pocket. 'Nine, right?'

'Right.' He pointed at the packet in my hand. 'Those letters . . . what are you going to do with them?'

I motioned to Poe and together we walked to the front door. 'At the moment . . . nothing,' I said. I slid the letters into my jacket pocket, and then I left.

Back in my rental car, I settled Poe in the back seat, then pulled the letters out of my pocket and looked at them. If Jeff hadn't killed Sheila, then there was really no point in showing them to Grant. I didn't want to put Jeff on his radar if it wasn't necessary, and I was pretty convinced that Jeff hadn't killed her.

Right now, my money was on Gary Hollis. It seemed more likely to me, after my conversation with Jaime, that the two of them had been involved in some scheme connected with the bookstore, and that Sheila had most likely pulled a fast one on Gary. She'd told her cousin that Gary was going to be really, really mad at her. Scamming him would surely account for that, but was it enough of a scam to warrant murder? I sighed. I hadn't seen hide or hair of the mystery man I suspected was Gary for a few days now. Had he finally decided to take off?

My phone buzzed in my pocket, signaling I had an incoming text. I pulled it out and saw that it was from Freddie Mason, Max's code expert. I opened it and read the message:

Reviewed both sets of letters and numbers. They don't

resemble any code that I've ever seen. I'd be more likely to think that first string is shorthand for something. The other set looks more like a license plate number. Hope this helps. Freddie.

I sighed. 'Not really, Freddie.' I got my tote bag and opened the zipper compartment where I'd put Sheila's notebook for safekeeping, and turned to the last page. I looked at the string of numbers, and almost fell over.

ESS36650. The last two numbers were the same as the black van's. Coincidence? I frowned as I studied the number. I grabbed my phone and called Grant again. This time he answered. 'Charlotte. To what do I owe the pleasure?'

'I think I've got the whole number of that license plate. The one on the black van,' I blurted out.

'Really? And just how did you manage to accomplish that? If I remember correctly, you said that the plate was obscured so all you could see was the last two figures.'

'Well, to be quite honest I'm not entirely certain that this is the correct plate number, but the last two digits match so I figure it's worth a shot. You can run this and find out who it belongs to, right?'

'I have the contacts to do so,' he replied. 'Give me the plate number.'

I rattled it off. 'Almost sounds as if it's a commercial number,' Grant said. 'OK, I'll see what I can find out.'

'Great. Oh, and you might want to check different states.'

The frown was back in the voice. 'You think it was an out-of-state plate?'

'It could be. I'd check Maine first.'

Silence. Then, 'You want to tell me what prompted all this?'

'It's just a hunch,' I said quickly. 'I could be wrong.'

Silence and then, 'OK, I'll get on it. Thank you, Charlotte,' he added in a softer tone.

'You know, it's getting to be quite a habit.'

'What is?'

'You thanking me.'

Grant chuckled. 'Yes, you're right. We're going to have to do something about that.'

I wanted to ask what, but I was half-afraid to hear the answer.

Instead, I just said goodbye and hung up. No sooner had I done that than my phone rang again. I looked at the screen and my heart skipped a beat. Richardson Antiquarian Books. I hit the answer icon. 'Hello. Charlotte James speaking.'

'Ms James, this is Evan Richardson,' said a deep baritone voice. 'I understand from my assistant manager that you were inquiring about Sheila Blackwell?'

'Yes, Mr Richardson, thank you so much for returning my call.'

'No problem. I'm rather interested in why you wish to learn about her. Have you had contact with her?' His tone had turned almost eager.

'In a way.' I had no intention of disclosing the information that Sheila was deceased. 'She . . . ah . . . was planning on going into business with a friend of mine, but she backed out at the last minute. We've been trying to locate her, and I thought perhaps you might have a forwarding address.'

'Ah,' he said, and I caught a note of disappointment in his tone. 'Sorry, I have no address of any sort for her. Furthermore, I can tell you from experience that if Sheila doesn't want to be found, no one's going to find her. The woman has a definite talent for vanishing off the face of the earth.'

'She worked for you, correct?'

'Yes, she did, and I can tell you she was an exemplary employee. Came in on time, was great with the customers, and knew her books. If it weren't for the . . . incident, why, I might have promoted her.'

'I understand that she's wanted by the Robbinston police department for some questioning. Would that have anything to do with this . . . incident you mention?'

When Richardson spoke again, there was a slight hint of suspicion in his tone. 'Why do you want to know? Are you a private eye, Ms James? Is that why you wanted to speak with me?'

'No, I'm not a private investigator, Mr Richardson. I'm just trying to get to the bottom of a matter for my friend.'

'I see.' There was a moment of silence, and then Richardson spoke again. 'Well, I guess there's no harm in telling you. Sheila left my employment rather abruptly, as did her . . . friend, Gary

Hollis. A few days after their departure, I discovered a valuable magazine was missing.'

'A magazine?'

'Yes. A pristine copy of *Collier's* magazine, published in December 1945.'

'I'm familiar with *Collier's*,' I said. That was no lie. Max collected vintage magazines, and I always scoured eBay every year to find him one to add to his collection. 'From what I've seen they aren't that pricey.'

'Quite true. But this magazine was special. Are you familiar with the author J.D. Salinger?'

I swallowed. Butterflies had started to flutter in my stomach. 'Yes.'

'Well, this magazine has the first story narrated by Holden Caulfield himself. Many consider it to be the real beginning of *Catcher in the Rye*. It was called "I'm Crazy".'

'So it was the December 22nd issue? I've seen copies of that magazine for sale, Mr Richardson. One in excellent condition went for a thousand dollars.'

'True. But then again, it wasn't autographed by J.D. Salinger himself.'

I knew Salinger was noted for his reclusive lifestyle. Anything signed by him would no doubt bring big bucks from an avid collector. 'I see. And was Salinger's signature authenticated?'

'Of course.' Richardson's tone indicated that anything else would be unacceptable. 'It's the genuine article.'

'I see. How much was the magazine worth?'

'With the signature, it would be priceless to a true Salinger fan. I have several clients who are willing to pay a great deal of money for it,' said Richardson. 'One offered over two hundred thousand dollars.'

I forced myself to exhale the breath I'd been holding. 'And Sheila knew this?'

'Of course she did. I'm convinced that she took it, but I have no proof with which to accuse her directly, or Hollis either. I anticipated her trying to contact one of the interested parties, but so far that hasn't happened. I think she's lying low, biding her time. I'm convinced she and Hollis plotted this together. He left right after she did. It was too much of a coincidence for me.'

Richardson sighed. 'I couldn't convince the police to issue a warrant due to lack of evidence, but I did manage to get them to agree to bring them in for questioning the moment either of them showed their faces around Robbinston. I have a feeling, though, that's not going to happen, and that magazine is lost to me forever.' He paused. 'I'm sorry about what she did to your friend. If I might ask a favor? If you should, by any chance, hear from or about her, if you would . . .'

'Notify you? Certainly.'

I hung up and then just sat for a few moments, digesting what I'd learned. Then I reached across for my tote bag, pulled the notebook out again and flipped to the page with the string of numbers. I stared at it.

HOLICRSGRCOL45225K.

Freddie Mason had been correct. This wasn't a coded message, it was shorthand. My tote bag was on the seat next to me. I fumbled in it for a pen and a slip of paper. I found an old Walmart receipt and started to scribble. A few minutes later I surveyed my handiwork.

HOL became 'Holden'; ICR could stand for 'I'm Crazy'; SGR, Salinger. COL45 was undoubtedly *Collier's* 1945 and 225K – probably the most recent asking price. I frowned as another thought occurred to me. Richardson had mentioned several clients would be interested. He'd said none so far had been contacted, but what if Sheila had sworn them to secrecy? She might have been playing two potential buyers off against one another? If so, and one had found out, that could have resulted in a violent argument, and Sheila's demise. Hell hath no fury like a potential buyer scorned. I remembered the look on Gino's face when he talked about Sheila playing him for a patsy, and I gave a small shudder. It was possible.

I shoved the notebook into my tote bag. I had no choice. I had to go to Grant with this, and the sooner the better. And just as I was about to press the ignition button, my phone buzzed with an incoming call. I fished it out of my pocket and looked at the number. It seemed oddly familiar and for the life of me, I couldn't think why.

And then suddenly it hit me. That was Sheila's cell number! But she couldn't be calling me! An image of a pink phone stuffed into a pocket came into my mind's eye, and my fingers trembled as I pressed the answer icon. 'Hello,' I said.

'Charley James,' said a gruff voice. 'You'll want to talk to me. This is Gary Hollis. I know you have it, and I'm willing to strike a deal.'

TWENTY-FOUR

My heart was beating so loudly I feared it could be heard miles away. I struggled to keep my tone neutral as I responded, 'I'm sorry. I have no idea what you're talking about.'

A note of exasperation crept into Hollis's tone. 'You're Charley James, aren't you?' Without waiting for my answer he went on, 'I've been keeping tabs on you. I know you have it.'

My fear dissipated, replaced by anger. 'You've been following me? You're the man I caught peering in my shop window, aren't you?'

'Guilty,' Hollis sneered. 'I saw you haul that garbage bag out of that old lady's complex. And since you seem to be such a big snoop, I'm pretty sure that you've found it.'

'It might help,' I said evenly, 'If you'd tell me just what *it* is.'

He laughed mirthlessly. 'Oh, I think you know.'

I swallowed. 'I presume you mean the *Collier's* magazine signed by Salinger? The one that you and Sheila stole from Richardson.'

'Correction. The one *Sheila* stole from Richardson. She knew there were several collectors eager to pay big bucks for it. She said we would be partners, though, and then she went and disappeared on me. We'd been together three years. After all we'd meant to each other, she betrayed me,' he snarled.

'So that's why you killed her? Because you thought she betrayed you?'

'You think I killed her?' Hollis sounded genuinely amazed. 'Oh, heck no. I might have wanted to, but I'd never actually do it. I'm not a killer, lady. I just want what's mine, now that she's gone.'

'If you didn't kill her, how do you explain having her phone,' I said. 'I know this is Sheila's cell number. Admit it, you took it from her after you killed her. You wrote that note to my friend Zane to make it appear Sheila had deserted her, and then you snuck into her room at Mrs Dinwiddie's and cleaned it out.'

He made an exasperated sound deep in his throat. 'Look, lady. You're giving me way too much credit. I'm telling you, I never did any of that.'

'So you deny you killed her, then stuffed her body in a trunk in the store basement?'

He sounded genuinely shocked when he replied, 'Oh my gosh! Is that what they did to her?'

'You know it was. You were hanging around the shop looking to get back in and dispose of her body. Why didn't you do it the night you killed her? Did something scare you off?'

'Oh, jeez. You've got some imagination, you know that? Look, I admit I took her phone, but *I* didn't go into that store, and *I* didn't kill her.'

Was I nuts, or did he actually sound sincere? 'You didn't?'

'No. Look, Sheila and I were supposed to go fifty-fifty on the sale of that magazine. We'd . . . ah . . . been having a few disagreements, and she decided to teach me a lesson. She lifted it a day early and took off. I went after her. It never occurred to me that she might use her mother's maiden name until a few weeks ago. I tracked her down here, demanded that she cut me in. She said no, she'd taken all the risk herself and I didn't deserve any part of it. She was planning on using those funds to start a new life that didn't include me. So I decided to follow her, wait for the right moment to confront her and demand my share of the sale of that magazine. I'd taken plenty of risks for her in the past. She owed me. But it never got that far.' He paused and then added dramatically, 'You see, I was outside the store that night. I saw the man who killed her. Or at least I assume he did.'

'Did you recognize this man?'

Gary paused. 'No, but I've got a pretty good idea who the guy might be. She was getting pretty tight with some guy who used to come into the bookstore in Maine, always when I wasn't around. I called her on it, and she just laughed and said, "JoJo and I are just friends. I'm helping him complete his collection," but I knew she was lying. They were more than just friends, I'm sure of it,' he added, and I could hear the bitterness in his tone.

'She called him JoJo?' I asked. 'That's a rather odd name, to say the least.'

'Most likely a nickname. Sheila liked to give them to people. Anyway, the day before she cut out they had a little set-to in the back of the store. I didn't see it, but Maggie, another woman who works there, mentioned it to me. She said he stormed out.'

'Do you think they were arguing over this magazine?'

'Who knows? Maybe. Maggie said he looked pretty angry. Sheila was trying to calm him down.'

'Why do you think this JoJo killed her?'

'Who knows? She probably tried to hustle him or maybe he thought she was stringing him along. Maybe he's the unstable kind and just snapped. It happens. I'm not sure he's the guy I saw, but rest assured I can give a flawless description. Your detective friend should have no problem finding him. But . . . I'll only do that if you come across with what I want. So, do we have a deal?'

'I don't make deals with killers,' I said. 'Besides, I couldn't even if I wanted to. I told you, I don't have the magazine.'

'I'm not a killer,' he said it so loudly, I had to hold the phone away from my ear. 'As for the magazine, you have to have it. She didn't put those secret drawers in that jewelry chest to hide jewelry. She had none. The only thing of value she had was that magazine.'

'How do you know she put drawers in that chest?' I demanded.

'Same way I know about you. I told you, I was keeping tabs on her.'

'How do I know you're telling the truth? How do I know you didn't kill her?'

'Now how would I benefit from her death without that magazine?' snarled Hollis. 'For the millionth time, I'm not a killer. I was planning on stealing that magazine, just as soon as I located where she'd hidden that chest. I never figured on her giving it to that old lady.'

'You're bluffing,' I said. 'I don't believe you.'

'This is getting old,' he snarled. 'For one thing, I have no idea how she was killed. You said her body was stuffed in a trunk, but how did he kill her? Strangle her? Shoot her? I have no idea, and if I'd killed her, I certainly would, wouldn't I?'

'Yes, and I'm pretty sure you'd also be smart enough to lie about it.'

He blew out a long breath, and I could visualize him rolling his eyes in exasperation. 'Look,' he said finally, 'I was outside the shop that night. I saw her inside, fixing things up, getting ready to start this "new life" she was bragging about, and I debated confronting her right there and then. Before I could make up my mind, this other guy comes over and knocks on the door. She let him in. I waited a bit and when the guy didn't come out, I went over and looked in the window. I saw the guy wielding a broom, and it looked like he was sweeping up some debris. I didn't see any sign of Sheila. I tried the door, but it was locked tight. I debated breaking in, but then some cars came, so I just got the heck out of there. The next day, when I saw the cops and then the yellow tape . . . well, you don't have to be a genius to put two and two together. I figured the worst.'

I had to admit the guy sounded sincere. But I still wasn't entirely convinced. 'You still haven't told me how you got her phone.'

'That was a stroke of dumb luck. I found it out back, near the trash. I figured when that guy cleaned up, he must have dropped it. So I grabbed it. I thought maybe there might be something on it that might tell me who she planned on selling the magazine to, or where she might have hidden it. But there were no contacts, no messages . . . nothing. I figured that guy must have deleted everything. And that's the truth. I'd swear to it on a stack of Bibles. So? What's it gonna be?'

My palms were sweating and I gripped my phone more tightly. 'Even if I wanted to agree to this, I don't have that magazine, and I have no idea where it could be.'

'Well, then, find it,' he growled. 'Unless you want this killer to walk around free? There's an abandoned shack out on the old River Road, about two miles south of town. I'll meet you there tonight, at midnight. Oh, and no cops. Or else.'

'Or else what? You'll try to run me down again?'

'Run you down? What are you talking about?'

Once again, the guy sounded genuinely puzzled. He was either a fabulous actor or he had no clue. 'I was nearly killed the other day. A black van tried to run me off the road. That was you, correct?'

'I did own a black van,' he admitted, 'but I traded it in when I got here. I've been driving a rented Ford Focus.' He paused. 'Maybe it was the guy I saw. Maybe he thinks you're getting close to exposing him.'

'Yeah, well, then he's better informed than I am,' I said. 'To be perfectly honest, Gary, you're my number one suspect.'

'Gee, thanks. Look, I gotta get goin'. Do we have a deal or not?'

I hesitated. If Gary Hollis was serious, this was my chance to find out who had killed Sheila. On the other hand, there was an excellent possibility he was lying, that if I did bring him the magazine, he'd simply kill me and take off.

I had to take a chance.

'I can't promise I can find the magazine,' I said.

'You will,' he said. 'No magazine, no killer description. And I know you want to see justice done. You're that do-goody type. See you tonight.' And then he hung up.

I put my phone down and realized my hands were shaking. I leaned forward, against the steering wheel. The smart thing to do would be to contact Grant, explain what had just happened. He'd know how to handle it.

I heard a *thunk*, and out of the corner of my eye saw Poe land on the passenger seat. He leaned over, touched my arm with his paw. His tongue snaked out, licked my hand. I reached down to give him a pat on the head. 'I can always count on you for support,' I said. 'Come on, boy. We've got another stop to make.'

For the second time in two days, I found myself pulling into the Austin PD parking lot. Poe let out a soft *purr* of protest when I locked him in the car again, but I figured he wouldn't exactly be welcome inside the station. There was a heavyset woman behind the reception counter this time, and she eyed me warily as I approached.

'Good afternoon,' I said. 'I'm looking for Detective Grant?'

The wary expression deepened. 'He's not in,' she said.

'He's not? But I talked to him not an hour ago?'

'He had to leave. I think he said he had a lead on something. Can someone else help you?'

I was going to ask if she knew if the lead was in the Crowder case, but before I could open my mouth a shadow fell across the counter. I whirled around and met Barbie's unfriendly gaze.

'Well, well, Charley James. What are you doing here? If you're looking for Detective Grant, he's not here. He got a hot lead on another case of his.'

That surprised me. 'Another case?'

Barbie leaned against the counter and angled me a sour look. 'Yes. Believe it or not, his only focus isn't on Sheila Crowder's murder. He does work for Philly, not us. A colleague of his called with a tip on something they've been working on, so he had to rush out.' She put her fingers in the loopholes of the pressed blue jeans she had on. 'Does your little visit here have something to do with the Crowder case? If so, I can help you.' She puffed out her chest a bit. 'After all, I am the officer of record,' she added, a note of pride evident in her tone.

I hesitated. That was true, she was. But I knew darn well if I told Barbie what had just transpired, she'd either laugh me out of the station or arrest me for interfering in their investigation. No way was I going to put myself through that torture.

'Yes, so I understand,' I said, trying to make my tone as saccharine sweet as possible. 'However, since I've already spoken to Detective Grant on this matter, I'll just wait until he becomes available.'

Barbie's smile faltered a bit. 'I couldn't tell you just when that will be,' she responded. 'He might not be back for several days.'

I gave an exaggerated sigh. 'Gee, I guess our recipe exchange will just have to wait, then.'

Barbie tried hard to keep her jaw from dropping, but was not successful. 'Recipe exchange?'

'Yes. He wanted my recipe for one-pot garlic Parmesan pasta, and he was going to give me one of his. Since the two of you appear to be so close, I'm sure you know he's quite the amateur chef.'

'I–I didn't know that,' Barbie sputtered, her cheeks red.

'Oh. Well, he is.' I wiggled my fingers at her. 'See ya.'

I turned on my heel and hurried out of the station, aware of Barbie glaring daggers into my back. One thing was certain: With Grant MIA, tonight I was on my own.

* * *

'You can't be serious!'

It was after eleven p.m. Zane stood at the kitchen counter, cup of coffee halfway to her lips. She stared at me as if I'd lost my mind.

I'd spent the entire afternoon after leaving the police station examining and tapping every inch of the jewelry armoire, and I couldn't find any more secret drawers other than the two I'd found. I couldn't show up for my meeting with Hollis empty-handed, though, so now I was busy wrapping an issue of *Glamour* magazine in tissue paper and bubble wrap. 'I realize how this looks,' I said, 'but right now it's the best shot I have to get to the bottom of Sheila's murder.'

'There has to be another way,' cried Zane. 'Charley, this guy is a psycho. He made up all that just to lure you out there. He probably doesn't really expect you to have that magazine. He missed killing you with the van, and now he just wants to get you out of the way.'

'I did think about that,' I admitted. 'But what if he is telling the truth? What if he did see the man who killed Sheila? I can't let this opportunity slide by.' I leaned back to survey my handiwork. I had the magazine so thickly wrapped you couldn't tell what it was.

Zane plopped down in the chair next to me. 'Think about what you are doing,' she said. She pointed to the bundle in front of me. 'Charley, he'll probably want to look at the magazine before he tells you anything. And once he sees it's not the right one, why he'll probably kill you on the spot.' She reached out, covered my hand with hers. 'Please, please call Detective Grant. He'll know what to do.'

'I wanted to tell him, but Barbie said that he's following up a lead on a Philly case. And I sure as heck am not telling Barbie this.'

Zane sighed. 'I can't believe I'm actually saying this, but why not tell Barbie? She's the officer of record, isn't she?'

I arched my brow at my friend. 'Do you really think she'd believe me?'

'Whether she believes you or not she'd have to follow up. Don't they take an oath to serve and protect when they're sworn in? That includes you, no matter how she may feel about you personally.'

'Well, Gary Hollis said no cops. Grant might know how to be subtle in all this, but Barbie's a novice. She'd go barreling in there and that would be the end of it.'

Zane shook her head. 'I still think it's a foolish move.'

'I do too, but right now I haven't any other option. If Hollis is telling the truth, and he really did see a man go into the store that night, well, it needs to be followed up on.'

Zane sighed. 'And I can't talk you out of this?'

'Nope.' I glanced at the clock. 'I'd better get going. It's at least a half-hour drive to that abandoned cabin.' I shot her a small smile. 'Wish me luck.'

'Luck heck,' said Zane. She made a grab for her jacket. 'I'm coming with you. If you ever needed a backup person, it's now.'

Poe insisted on coming along too, running out the door before I could stop him, so the three of us got in my rental car and drove out the deserted back road to the cabin that Gary had designated. I was slightly familiar with the area. That cabin had been deserted for as long as I could remember. It was an old, silver-gray structure with a weathered and tarnished metal roof. Hunters sometimes used it for shelter in the winter, when the snow was four feet deep. I parked a few feet away and cut the lights.

Zane pulled the collar of her coat more tightly around her. 'So what now? Do we go into the cabin, or do we wait for this Hollis guy to come to us?'

'Good point. He didn't say,' I replied.

Zane peered out the window into the darkness. Out of the corner of my eye I saw Poe, in the back seat, do the same. 'I don't see any sign of anyone else,' Zane remarked. 'No car, no nothing.'

'He could have hidden his car in that thicket over there,' I said, inclining my head. I glanced at my watch. 'It's just midnight. Let's give it a few minutes.'

We huddled down and waited. Outside we heard the mournful wail of an owl, and crickets chirping. After five minutes had passed, I reached underneath my seat and pulled out my bubble-wrapped package. 'Showtime,' I said. 'I'm going in.'

'Correction,' said Zane, gripping the door handle. 'We're going in.'

In the back seat, Poe let out a loud meow of assent.

I waved my hand back and forth. 'That's not a good idea. He may bolt if he sees I've brought reinforcements.'

'Fine. Poe and I will stay back, but you're not going in there alone,' Zane said firmly.

I shrugged, and we all exited the car and made our way down the short path to the cabin. We stepped up on to the rickety porch and I walked over to one of the windows, peered inside. It was pitch black within. 'Gary,' I hissed. 'Are you here?'

Silence.

Zane plucked at my sleeve. 'He's not here,' she whispered. 'Let's go. This place is giving me the creeps.'

'Let me try something,' I said. I moved over to the door, rapped sharply on it. 'Gary? Are you here?'

No answer.

I reached down and touched the door handle. The door swung inward, its hinges making a loud creaking sound.

Behind me, Zane moaned. 'I really don't like this, Charley. This is the part in all the slasher movies where the ingénue gets trapped by the serial killer. Let's go back to the car.'

I was going to agree, when Poe, who'd been walking beside me, suddenly cocked his head. His ears flicked forward, then flattened against his skull. He let out a low growl.

I leaned toward the cat. 'What is it?' I cried. 'What do you hear, Poe?'

With another low growl, he wiggled his bottom and then launched himself forward into the cabin.

'Oh, swell,' I cried. I started into the cabin after him, but Zane grabbed my arm. 'Charley,' she said. 'Don't go in there. Let's go back to the car and call the police. So what if Barbara Jeanne shows up?'

I gritted my teeth. 'Fine, but first I've got to get Poe.' I whipped out my phone, called up my flashlight app and shone the light in front of me. I saw Poe up ahead, a black blur. He was standing in the middle of the room, staring at something. I fought against the rising butterflies in my stomach and stepped over the threshold. The moment I did so, my foot stumbled as it came into contact with something slick. I instinctively reached out to grasp the wall to steady myself and looked down. I saw what appeared to be a splotch of red.

Poe threw back his head and let out a mournful wail. Behind me Zane moaned.

I advanced forward slowly. I had a feeling of what might lie ahead, and as the circle of light cut through the darkness, I saw my worst fears confirmed.

Poe was crouched next to an inert figure. A figure that wasn't moving. I held my breath and shone my light full on the face. Then I called over my shoulder, 'Zane. Call 911.

'I've found Gary Hollis.'

TWENTY-FIVE

Blue and red strobes from the police cruiser played across the cabin's porch. The police had wasted no time in responding to Zane's 911 call. The police cruiser pulled in front of the cabin, followed by a black sedan. I stifled a groan as Barbie and another officer who looked about twelve hopped out of the cruiser and made their way purposefully toward us. At the door to the cabin Barbie paused and looked at the young officer. 'Higgens, go inside and secure the crime scene,' she barked.

'Yes, Officer Donaldson.' Higgens gave a curt nod and then disappeared inside the cabin. I'd almost thought he was going to salute Barbie. Poor kid. This was, no doubt, his very first experience with a murder scene. Too bad it had to be with Barbie. She glanced over at where Zane and Poe stood, then turned and made her way over to me. She stopped before me and stood, feet planted apart, her hands on her hips. 'Well, well, we meet again,' she said. 'Another dead body, Charley?'

I gritted my teeth and tried to smile sweetly. 'Unfortunately, yes. There was a bullet hole right in the center of his forehead, and he looked pretty dead to me.'

'Thank you for your observations,' Barbie said dryly. She pulled her notebook and pen out of her pocket. 'Any chance you knew the victim?'

'We hadn't been formally introduced, but I believe it's Gary Hollis.'

Barbie nearly dropped her pen. Her head snapped up. 'Gary Hollis? The same Gary Hollis who's a suspect in Sheila Crowder's death?'

'Yes, the same one. Of course I can't make a positive identification, but it's a natural assumption,' I said.

'A natural assumption?' Barbie frowned. 'And why is that?'

I swallowed. 'Because I was supposed to meet him here.'

'You WHAT?!'

I whirled around and found myself meeting Ian Grant's stormy gaze. I gave him a quick once-over. His blue-black hair was combed straight off his high forehead and his muscled body was encased in tight blue jeans and a tan windbreaker. He looked sexy – and angry. Very angry. I drew myself up to my full height and said, 'Detective Grant – what are you doing here? I heard you were out of town, following up a lead.'

'I was, but it turned out to be a dead end. I had just gotten back when this call came through on the police radio. I came straight here.' He placed his hands on his hips and glared at me. 'Did I hear right? You were supposed to meet Gary Hollis here? The same Gary Hollis that you believed was following you?'

'You heard correctly,' I said. The words came out sounding like a squeak. I lowered my gaze, but Grant reached out and grabbed my chin. He tilted my face up so that his gaze bored into mine.

'Care to elaborate?' he said, his tone soft. 'Why on earth would you be meeting a murder suspect alone at a deserted cabin?'

'I wasn't exactly alone.' I inclined my head over to where Zane stood, Poe curled around her feet. 'I had backup.'

His brow arched. 'Nice. Great backup, especially the cat.' He crossed his arms over his chest. 'Well? I'm waiting. Why were you meeting Gary Hollis here?'

Barbie had walked over to stand beside Grant. She too folded her arms over her chest and fixed me with a stare. 'Yes, Charley, do tell us. Why would anyone in their right mind meet a murder suspect at a deserted cabin?'

I took a deep breath, exhaled, then said 'Because he said that he could identify Sheila's killer.'

Both Grant and Barbie's eyes widened. They looked at me, then at each other, then back to me. 'Say that again,' said Grant.

'He called me earlier today. He said that he could identify Sheila's killer.'

'He called you?' Barbie asked. Her lips twisted into a condescending smile. 'On the phone?'

'Of course on the phone,' I snapped. 'He didn't send me a smoke signal.' I ran my hand through my tangle of curls. 'He thought that I had something that he wanted, something that

Sheila had been keeping from him. He offered to trade. That, in exchange for a description of the man who killed Sheila.'

Barbie turned her head and motioned toward Zane, who held my bubble-wrapped *Glamour* magazine in her hands. 'Is that package Zane's clutching for dear life what you were going to trade?'

'Yes, but it's not what he wanted. I–I thought I could trick him with it, get the information and get out of here before he realized it wasn't the right article.'

Barbie and Grant exchanged a look and then Grant took a step closer to me. His brows drew together, giving his face a thundercloud effect. 'What on earth ever possessed you to think that was a smart idea,' he ground out. 'Didn't it occur to you that Hollis would have examined what you brought him before he gave out any information? And that once he realized you were scamming him, he could have killed you?'

'Of course I thought about that,' I bit out. 'I thought that maybe I could do some fast talking, tell him I wasn't handing over the magazine until he came across with the description of the killer first.'

Grant reached up, rubbed at the side of his face. 'I credited you with more intelligence than that, Charlotte,' he said. 'What I want to know is, why in blazes didn't you call me or Officer Donaldson immediately!'

'Well, for one thing he said no cops.' Behind me Barbie gave a loud snort. I turned, glared at her over my shoulder, and then looked back at Grant. 'For another, he insisted that he didn't kill Sheila.' I paused. 'And I have to say, I believed him.'

'Oh my God,' cried Barbie. 'You've got to be kidding. And if he'd told you he could make you a great deal on the Walt Whitman Bridge, would you have believed that too?'

I started to utter a sharp retort, but Grant held up his hand in a gesture of silence. I swallowed and crossed my arms over my chest. Barbie frowned, then clamped her lips together. Grant gave a satisfied nod, then looked at me. In a softer tone he said, 'OK, Charlotte. Explain to me why you suddenly believed what this guy told you, *after* you told me you suspected he might be Sheila's killer and was possibly stalking you.'

'It was just something in the tone of his voice,' I replied. I pressed my fingers against my stomach. 'I know it sounds bizarre, but I just felt it . . . in here. That he wasn't lying. And I think he really did see Sheila's killer. As a matter of fact, I bet that's who killed him. The killer saw him that night, and has probably been following him, waiting for the right moment to do him in.'

'Oh, for the love of Pete,' muttered Barbie. 'Of all the ridiculous . . .'

Grant once again held up his hand, and Barbie lapsed into silence. At that moment a car pulled up behind Grant's black sedan, and Derek Proust hopped out. 'Oh, great. Just what we need right now,' he muttered.

Barbie squared her shoulders. 'I'll take care of him,' she said. She started off purposefully to cut Derek off before he could approach us. Grant took me by the arm and led me over to the far corner of the porch, away from everyone. 'We're alone now. Nice and slow,' he said. 'From the beginning. Tell me everything Gary Hollis said to you.'

Fifteen minutes later and twice as many questions, I'd told Grant the entire story – well not the entire story. I'd left out the part about Sheila turning the armoire into a puzzle box. I merely said that he believed Sheila had hidden the magazine somewhere in the store. Grant took notes as I talked, and when I finished, he shut his notebook, slid it back into his pocket, and just stood for a few minutes, hands on hips, staring out into space. Finally, he looked at me. 'You took some chance,' he said. 'You couldn't be certain Hollis was telling the truth about any of it.'

'I know, but I told you . . .'

'Yes. You felt he was sincere. In here.' He patted his stomach, then reached up and rubbed at the back of his neck. 'Charlotte, I don't know how to convince you that real-life murders are vastly different from fictional ones. You and your friend might have been killed.' He paused. 'You've already had one close call.'

'Yes, and I confronted Hollis about that. He said that he did own a black van at one time, but he traded it in. He denied running me off the road, and I believed him. And speaking of that, did you have any luck with that number I gave you?'

'We're still running it. However, we did find out that a black van was registered to a Gary M. Hollis in Maine. The last two numbers ended in 50, but the rest of the plate differed from the number you gave me.' He paused. 'I don't suppose you want to tell me where you got that plate number?'

I shrugged. 'It was on a piece of paper in the store. I thought maybe Sheila might have written it down.'

'I see.' Grant reached out and put his hands on my shoulders. 'Did you ever stop to think that if your theory about Hollis is correct, you might have just missed running into the real killer?'

'Actually, that did cross my mind,' I admitted. 'I thought about touching the body to see if it was still warm, but . . .' I slid him a look. 'I didn't want to be accused of interfering with a crime scene.'

The edges of Grant's lips quirked a bit, almost as if he might be amused by what I'd said. When he spoke, though, his tone was stern. 'How good of you. Glad to see you learned something, at least.'

We returned to the front porch, and I noticed that Proust's car was gone. Barbie hurried over to us. 'I got rid of Proust,' she said to Grant. 'He wanted to know if all this activity was in any way related to Sheila's death. I told him the investigation was still ongoing, but we'd give him an exclusive statement after we got the coroner's report.'

Grant frowned. 'And that satisfied him?'

She shrugged. 'He left. Oh, and we found the victim's wallet. The driver's license identifies him as Gary M. Hollis of Calais, Maine.' She handed the wallet to Grant. 'Photo resembles the sketch that was made of the suspect,' she added, casting a disparaging look over her shoulder at me. 'So now our best suspect – our only suspect, really – in the Crowder case is gone. We're back to square one.'

'Maybe not,' I said. They both turned to look at me and I added, 'Hollis mentioned some guy that Sheila was friendly with back when they worked at the bookstore. He thought maybe Sheila might have tried to hustle him, or something.'

Grant and Barbie exchanged a look and then Grant asked, 'Did Hollis give you a name?'

'All he knew was that she called him JoJo.'

'JoJo? Really, Charley? Sounds more like a name for a French poodle,' snickered Barbie.

Grant cut his gaze from me to Barbie. 'Don't you have a report to finish writing, Officer?'

'Yes, sir,' Barbie said meekly. She shuffled off toward the other end of the porch, but not before she caught my eye and shot me another black look. I figured if looks could kill I'd have been six feet under about a dozen times by now.

Grant turned back to me. 'I think that will be all for now, Charlotte. But—'

I held up my hand. 'I know, I know. If I think of anything significant, I should call you. Day or night.'

I started to turn away, but he caught my arm. 'Yes, and next time make sure you do just that. It doesn't matter if I'm in the area or not. I always pick up my messages – especially yours.'

His gaze bored into mine with an intensity that sent a shiver up my spine – and not necessarily a bad one. 'I'll remember that,' I said softly.

We stared at each other for a long moment, then Grant turned away and walked back over to Barbie. I hurried over to where Zane and Poe were still huddled on the porch. 'Come on,' I said. 'Let's get out of here.'

'Finally.' Zane and Poe fell into step beside me. 'Looked like you and Grant were having a moment there,' she ventured.

'Yeah, we were having a moment. Quite a few tense ones, actually. I got the requisite lecture from him, and Barbie threw in her two cents too.'

'Thank goodness the other officer took my statement. I was shocked that Barbie didn't want to butt in, seeing as how she's been having such fun torturing me.' She let out a soft chuckle. 'She sure did a number on Proust. I almost felt sorry for him. I think he really wanted to argue with her, but she wasn't having any of it.'

I sighed. 'Well, that's one good thing she did tonight, anyway.'

Zane touched my arm. 'So? Was it Gary Hollis?'

'According to his driver's license, yes. Grant thought we might have just missed the real murderer.'

Zane stopped dead in her tracks. 'Oh, Charley! That thought never entered my mind!'

'It did mine, but I didn't touch the body so I had no idea how long Gary was dead before we walked in. I'm thinking not long.'

I paused. 'Apparently, he's switched from knives to guns now too. Hollis was shot in the head. I bet he saw Gary outside the store that night and knew he could describe him. He's probably been following him, waiting for an opportunity to silence him.'

'Swell.' Zane shuddered. 'So we almost had a tête-à-tête with a killer.'

'Looks that way.' I was silent for a few moments and then I said 'Sheila's secrets are what killed her, and the biggest one of all is that magazine. Finding that could be the key to figuring out who killed both her and Gary.

'The million-dollar question is, where could it be?'

TWENTY-SIX

I didn't think I could get a wink of sleep after the night's events, but I had no sooner closed my eyes than I felt a heavy weight on my chest, and a rough tongue against my cheek. I winked one eye open and saw a pair of golden ones about an inch away from my nose, staring back at me. I turned my head toward the end table and let out a sharp cry when I saw it was eight o'clock! I threw back the covers so fast, Poe slid down the comforter and landed – *plunk* – on the floor next to my slippers.

'Sorry, boy,' I said as I slid my feet into the slippers. 'But we've got a lot to do today.'

Poe cocked his head at me. *Meow*?

I leaned over and rubbed his head. 'The key to all this is that magazine. Somehow, I've got to find where Sheila might have stashed it. So, first order of business . . . let's see if I can find out anything about this mysterious JoJo.'

Poe let out a sharp meow and flopped over on to his belly. I gave him a quick rub, then headed off to the shower. Twenty minutes later, attired in jeans and a soft Sherpa sweatshirt, I padded down to the kitchen in my bedroom slippers, Poe right behind me. He wound his body expectantly around my ankles as I stood at the kitchen counter. Zane had made a pot of coffee before she'd left for work, knowing I preferred fresh-ground to the pods. I put it on to heat, then filled Poe's bowls with water and some leftover tuna. I left him happily slurping while I filled my mug to the brim with coffee. I added milk and sugar, then carried the mug and my cell phone over to the kitchen table. I took a long sip of coffee and thought about how to broach the subject of 'JoJo' to Mr Richardson without revealing that either Gary or Sheila were dead. What excuse could I offer for wanting information on him. As I debated this, I heard a sharp knock on the kitchen door. I frowned. It was ten minutes to nine. Who might it be at this hour? A vision of Ian Grant filled my head, and I gave it a brisk shake. That was all I needed right now. I pushed my coffee off to the side and walked over to the door. 'Who is it?' I called.

'Otto Krebs.'

I paused, then realized who it was. Our landlord! What was he doing here? I opened the door and took a minute to study the man who stood on the stoop. Krebs was about average height, no more than five foot seven, and he was definitely carrying around more than a few extra pounds. His face was long and thin, his features sharp. His best feature was undoubtedly his hair, which was thick and streaked with gray. He reminded me of a drawing of Ebenezer Scrooge I'd seen once in an old volume of *A Christmas Carol.* I held out my hand. 'Good morning, Mr Krebs. I'm Charlotte James.'

Krebs made no move to take my proffered hand. Instead, he placed both hands on his wide hips and his thick brows drew together, giving him a thundercloud effect. 'Where's Zane?' he barked.

'She's still working at the bakery for another week,' I said. 'Can I help you?'

'That depends. Do you know when she planned to tell me she found Sheila's body in my storefront?' he barked.

I held up my hand. 'Actually, I'm the one who found Sheila,' I said. 'You can blame the police for us not mentioning anything to you. They told me to keep everything quiet, so naturally I assumed they'd take care of the necessary notifications.'

He whipped a handkerchief from his jacket pocket, mopped at his brow with it. 'Oh. Sorry. It's just that a heads-up would have been nice, but I guess if the police told you not to say anything . . .' He stuffed the handkerchief back in his pocket. 'I darn near fell over when that Officer Donaldson told me. The paper intimates it might have been a suspicious death?'

'I don't know if the exact cause of death has been determined yet,' I said carefully.

Krebs shook his head. 'She always seemed to be so . . . so vibrant. That reporter who wrote up the story came by, asking questions about Sheila. That girl was really looking forward to making a go of her store. Heck, I was looking forward to it too. Steady rental income.'

'Well, you won't lose anything there,' I said. 'I'm going to be taking over Sheila's lease.'

His eyes widened. 'You want to take over the lease?'

I nodded. 'You were on my list to contact. I was going to see you tomorrow. I expect I'll have to sign a new one?'

He nodded. 'Yes. Well, I don't have to tell you this is a load off my mind. I thought for sure Zane was going to try and get out of the lease – although I suppose I couldn't blame her for wanting to do that,' he added quickly. 'So, what sort of store are you planning on opening?'

'A bookstore, the same as Sheila,' I replied. 'I'm looking forward to it. We hope to have the grand opening first week in October.'

'That's not far away,' said Krebs. He backed up a step. 'Well, if you want to stop by my office tomorrow, I'll have the new papers drawn up for you to sign. The first three months' rent has been paid, so there's nothing you have to give me.'

He turned to leave when a thought occurred to me. 'Mr Krebs,' I said. He stopped and turned back to look at me. 'There's a beautiful oak chest in the basement of my storefront. I was just wondering if you knew anything about it.'

Krebs' thick brows drew together. 'Oh, that old thing. The tenant before Mamie Fitch left it there. The store he opened wasn't doing well, and he cleared out in the dead of night owing me two months' rent. The only thing he left behind was that chest. Probably too much for him to sneak off with. I kept it since he'd stiffed me. I thought maybe I might sell it, but then Mamie Fitch and her sister came around and to tell you the truth, I forgot until just now that it's been down there.'

'I see,' I said. 'If you still want to sell that chest, Mr Krebs, I'd like to buy it. I think I could find a place for it in my store.'

'Yeah?' His eyes took on a gleam. My mother would have characterized it as dollar signs. 'I'll think about a price and get back to you,' he said.

'Out of curiosity, what sort of store did that tenant have?'

'He had a magic shop.'

'A magic shop!'

'Yeah. I heard he used to do a magic act in Vegas before he

retired and decided to open up a store.' He shook his head. 'Takes all kinds.'

Once Krebs left, I resumed my seat at the kitchen table and punched in the number for Richardson's. It rang four times before a feminine voice answered. 'Richardson Antiquarian Books. How may I help you?'

'I'm looking for Mr Richardson. Would he be in?'

'Mr Richardson is away for a few days visiting a sick relative. I'm Maggie Pace, one of the associate managers. What can I help you with?'

'Possibly a little information. I'd been speaking with Mr Richardson about a former employee, Sheila Blackwell.'

'Oh?' Maggie's tone turned guarded. 'What about her?'

'I recently received a tip that she might have last been seen by someone here in Pennsylvania who is possibly a customer of your store.'

'Really?!' The tone turned from guarded to eager. 'Mr Richardson will be very interested to hear that! Do you have the customer's name?'

'That's the reason I'm calling,' I said. 'The only name I have sounds more like a nickname. JoJo.'

'JoJo? That is an odd name.' Maggie was silent for a few seconds and then said, 'I'm not positive, mind you, but there was a man who came in a few times. He only dealt with her.'

'I see. Could you describe him?'

'Honestly, I never paid him much attention. The last time I saw him in here he and Sheila were arguing in the back of the store. I only caught the tail end of the conversation. Sheila said he had to have faith in her, that of course she planned to share. Then he turned and just stalked out of the store.'

'I see. And there's nothing else you could tell me about him?'

'Well, this guy always bought thrillers. Cussler, Patterson, Barrett. He especially liked the ones that had serial killers in them.' She made a disgusted sound. 'Not my cup of tea. I prefer a historical romance, myself.'

'That's interesting, but I was hoping you might be able to describe him.'

'Oh. As I said, I really never paid him much attention, except

. . . he was very similar in looks and build to another employee, Gary Hollis.' Maggie let out a nervous giggle. 'It figured, I guess. Sheila always did go for the same type. Dark, brooding. They were both built like, well, like big teddy bears.'

'Thank you for your time, Maggie. If you should remember anything else, please call or text me,' I said. I gave her my number, then hung up. I sat at the table for a few minutes, tapping my phone against my chin. Poe launched himself into the chair beside me and stared at me with his wide golden eyes. I looked at the cat. 'There's something I'm missing,' I said. 'But I just can't think what.' I pushed back my chair and stood up. 'Busy hands make busy minds, or something like that, right? Maybe if I go over to the storefront and start getting it in shape, inspiration will hit. What do you think?'

Poe let out a loud meow.

'And yes, I agree. We can give that jewelry armoire another once-over too. I have a feeling that it hasn't given up all its secrets quite yet.'

Jeff called. I thought at first he wanted to cancel, but he'd gotten in some new fixtures that he thought might go nicely in the store and he wanted to show them to me and get my blessing before he installed them. The health inspector called as well, wanting to know if today was a good day to inspect the bakery. I made arrangements for him to come at three o'clock.

By four o'clock I was pretty tired, but satisfied with the day's accomplishments. The bakery had passed inspection, and I approved the fixtures Jeff brought over – recessed domes that would give off a soft, inviting glow. He promised to have them installed by the end of next week. He didn't mention anything about our previous conversation, and I didn't either. I felt that the past was the past, and we should just put it behind us and move on. No sooner had the door shut behind the health inspector than Poe hurled himself on to the glass counter and fixed me with a golden stare.

'Yes, I know. We didn't have time to look over the jewelry armoire, but look at what we got accomplished!' I spread my arms wide. 'I think I'll call Hans Ellison and tell him that he can deliver that furniture Saturday. It's time to start making this place look like a store.'

I called Ellison's and Hans was thrilled when I told him that he could deliver my bookcases on Saturday. 'I'm not sure if my brother will be around to help me,' said Hans. 'We had a bit of a disagreement and he decided to take off. I'm not sure if he'll be back, but I have another guy I can call to help if he doesn't show. What time would you like everything delivered?'

'The earlier the better, so I can get started filling them. How's nine thirty?'

'You got it.'

I hung up and let out a satisfied sigh. The next order of business would be hauling the boxes of stock up from the basement so I could start loading up the bookcases when they arrived Saturday. I looked at my watch. I'd promised Zane I'd cook dinner tonight, so I didn't have time right now. I looked at Poe. 'We could come back later,' I suggested. 'After all, we never did get a chance to go over that armoire again. What do you think?'

Poe let out a meow of assent, and I laughed. 'OK, later it is. Let's get home and start cooking.'

I'd decided to make macaroni and cheese, which was one of Zane's favorite dishes. It was a simple dish, easy to make, and I could serve it with a salad. I boiled the macaroni, then layered it in a greased pan with three different kinds of cheeses. I set the oven at three seventy-five, then slid the pan in. That would take an hour, plenty of time for me to make the accompanying salad and have a glass of wine.

I poured myself a glass of Merlot and sipped it while I chopped up lettuce, tomatoes, cucumber, and onion for a simple salad. As I worked, I let my mind wander. That magazine was connected to Sheila's death, whether it was the immediate reason or not. I had a feeling that the mysterious JoJo figured into this equation somewhere, but just where I didn't know. I finished chopping and put the ingredients into the salad bowl, then took another sip of wine.

I thought about what Krebs had told me, that a former tenant had a magic shop, and also that the man had been a magician. I looked at Poe. 'A magician usually uses chests with secret compartments in their acts, right? Maybe that chest had been part of that guy's act.'

Poe let out a soft meow.

I set the wine down and moved over to my laptop on the kitchen island. I searched through YouTube and finally found a video an amateur magician had made. He had a chest similar to the one in the basement, and he demonstrated several secret compartments and a false bottom. I took special note of one compartment, a drawer that slid out from the side of the chest, underneath the molding.

'Hm, I didn't try that,' I said. Poe, who'd been sitting next to the laptop and watching with great interest (or at least it seemed that way) looked up at me and let out a loud yowl. 'OK,' I said. 'We'll try that when we go back to the shop later.'

Poe butted his head against my arm. I took that for a yes.

The kitchen door opened, and Zane came in. She stopped and sniffed the air. 'What smells so good?' she asked. 'Is that macaroni and cheese?'

'Sure is,' I answered. 'It'll be ready in a few minutes.' I gestured toward the table. 'You can set the table, and then if you're a good girl, I'll tell you about all the progress I made today.'

Over dinner I filled Zane in on the day's activities. She listened in-between shoveling forkfuls of macaroni and cheese into her mouth. When I finished, she picked up her napkin, wiped her lips and then said, 'Well, you certainly were busy. I bet the store looks great.'

'It does. I'm going to go back later and start bringing up those books. I don't suppose you'd like to come along and help?'

'I would, but tomorrow is going to be a killer day. A client ordered a selection of pies for a seminar they're having in the afternoon, so tonight's an early night for me.' She paused. 'Are you sure you want to go back to the store at night? After all, the killer hasn't been caught yet. What if he's watching the store?'

'Good point. I'll call Grant, tell him what I plan on doing. Anyway, I shouldn't be that long. If Poe and I start now, I should be back here by eleven.'

Zane chuckled. 'Don't forget and tell me how many boxes of books Poe carts up from the basement.'

Poe let out a sharp meow. I laughed. 'I think you've insulted him,' I said.

Zane headed upstairs. I put the dishes in the dishwasher, then pulled out my phone. I dialed Grant's number, and as per usual it went to voicemail. 'You said you always check messages from me, so I'm leaving you one,' I said. 'I'm going to go over to the store and bring up some of those books from the basement. I'm just letting you know, just in case the killer decides to return to the scene of the crime. Just kidding,' I added hastily. 'Anyway, I just thought I'd let you know. I told Zane I'd most likely be home by eleven.'

I hung up. Something about my earlier conversation with Maggie niggled at me, but I couldn't pinpoint what. I shrugged. Maybe I'd figure it out after I got started on those books. There was nothing like a little hard work to clear out the cobwebs from one's brain.

Once inside the store, I switched on the lights and then headed directly for the jewelry armoire in the back room. 'First things first,' I said to Poe, who'd followed me. 'We didn't get a chance to look at this earlier, so we're going to do it now.'

I ran my fingers along the side of the chest again. I poked at the half-rosette that was on the edge of the molding. I pressed down hard with the edge of my thumb, as the man had in the video, and heard a soft click! The next moment a drawer shot out from underneath the rosette.

'I knew it,' I cried. I looked inside the drawer. Lying there was a folded piece of paper. I pulled it out and opened it. My eyes widened as I saw what it was. It was a drawing of a chest that looked almost exactly like the one in the basement. What grabbed my attention, though, was the drawer sliding out from the middle of the chest. 'Well, what do you know,' I said. 'Looks as if that chest downstairs might really be a very big puzzle box.' I rose and looked at Poe. 'Come on, let's check it out.'

Poe slit his eyes and glared at me.

'I know, I know. This will involve touching but . . . if it cracks the case wide open, won't it be worth it?'

Poe gave me another dirty look, but followed me.

I decided to take my tote bag with me. If, as I suspected, the magazine might be hidden in that drawer, then I'd put it right into it and take it straight home. I'd turn it over to Grant in the morning. Poe and I descended the stairs quickly, and I went straight over to the chest. I wrapped a tissue around my fingers, lifted the lid, and peered inside, suppressing a shudder when I saw the red drops dotted across its bottom – Sheila's blood, no doubt. If I ever wanted to use the chest, I'd definitely have to have it professionally cleaned. But that wasn't my objective now.

I pulled the drawing out of my tote bag and set the bag on the floor. I looked at the picture. There were little arrows drawn around the rosettes, perhaps to indicate movement? I tapped at the rosettes that dotted the center portion. I noticed that on the left side, one rosette seemed to be a bit larger than the others. I tapped at it. Nothing happened. Then I pressed my finger against it. Still nothing.

I reached up to scratch at my head. Maybe I was wrong? But why else would Sheila have hidden that drawing in the jewelry box? She'd told Nancy it held all her secrets, and I couldn't shake the feeling this large puzzle box held her biggest secret of all.

I put my nail underneath the edge of the rosette and wiggled it to the left. Suddenly I heard a soft whirring sound and then a drawer shot out from the middle of the chest, narrowly avoiding hitting me right in the stomach. A bubble-wrapped package, very similar to the one I'd made with the *Glamour* issue, lay nestled inside the drawer. I lifted it out slowly, then carried it over to where I'd set the tote bag. I'd tucked a pair of scissors inside it too, and now I carefully started cutting around the outer edge of the package. The bubble wrap fell away, revealing a magazine whose cover depicted a mother juggling an armload of Christmas presents while a boy and a girl grabbed at her arms. I removed the magazine and held it reverently. It was definitely in what a collector would refer to as pristine condition. My fingers trembled as I opened the magazine. I turned to the table of contents, saw the listing for the Salinger story, and turned to that page. Sure enough, written there in black marker was the phrase, 'Happy reading.' And Salinger's signature.

I exhaled the breath I'd been holding. 'So this is what all the fuss was about, eh, Poe? Poe?' I glanced down and saw my cat's upper torso buried in my tote bag. 'Poe, what are you doing?' I cried.

Poe wiggled out of the tote bag, and I saw a piece of paper stuck to one claw. I reached over and gently disengaged it. It was the paper I'd found previously in the store, the one with Mara's name on it. I turned it over and saw the erasure that had claimed my attention. The lighting down here was pretty poor, but I held the paper up and squinted at it. Sheila had done a good job with the erasure, but I could make out something – letters? I went back to the tote bag and found the pencil I always carried, then put the paper on top of one of the boxes of books and started to shade the erased area with the tip of the lead. After a few seconds, some letters started to appear. I stopped shading, and squinted down at them.

GELL.

'Gel's only spelled with one L,' I said, frowning. I stared at the letters, and something went *click* in my brain. Suddenly all the little clues just seemed to fall into place. I needed to call Grant, but first I had to check one last thing. I whipped my phone out of my pocket and typed 'names that JoJo could be a nickname for' into the search engine. A few seconds later a listing appeared. About halfway down I found what I was looking for.

'JoJo' was listed . . . as a nickname for George.

My heart started to hammer in my chest. All the little clues made sense, now that I thought about it. Hans had said that his brother had relocated from up north, had hinted that he might have been in some trouble, that he was giving him a second chance. There was something else too, something significant, although I'd glossed over it at the time. Hans had said Sheila had specifically wanted George to wait on her. Yet George himself said he knew little about furniture. She would have wanted him to wait on her, though, if they'd known each other. Maggie had said Sheila went for a specific type, and George and Gary both had the same build. That was why George had seemed so familiar to me. I picked up the paper and squinted at it, and I noticed something I hadn't before. There was a small dot in-between the G and the E, making it read: G.ELL

'For George Ellison,' I said aloud. 'I'm right. George Ellison is JoJo. He knew Sheila from the bookstore in Maine, and he's her killer. I bet that Grant will confirm this license plate number is George's, and it's registered to a black van – the van that ran me off the road.'

Beside me, Poe let out a loud hiss, then turned and vanished into a dark corner. I started after him, but paused as out of the corner of my eye I saw movement in the shadows near the service entrance. A moment later a figure stepped out of the shadows into the dim light.

It was none other than George Ellison, and the gun he held was pointed right at my heart.

TWENTY-SEVEN

Ellison made a little clucking sound in his throat. The gun he held didn't waver once as he said, 'I had you pegged as a snoop, and I was right.' He wiggled his fingers at the magazine I held in my hands. 'I'll take that, thanks.'

My throat felt dry, constricted. Even as the last piece of the puzzle clicked into place, I could hardly get the words out. 'You were Sheila's lover,' I rasped. 'You're the customer from Richardson's. JoJo.'

His lips twisted in an expression of distaste. 'Yeah. I hated that stupid nickname, but that was Sheila.' He gestured again with his hand. 'I'll take that magazine. It's mine, you know. I'm the one who brought it to her.'

My knees were so wobbly, I thought for sure I'd fall down. I eased my hip against one of the boxes of books. Still clutching the magazine I said, 'I don't understand. You say you brought this to Sheila?'

He made a sound deep in his throat. 'Yes. I'd bought a box of books and magazines at an estate sale. I kept the ones I liked – I only read thrillers – and I brought the rest over to the store, figuring I'd get some money, or at the least, a store credit. Sheila wasted no time taking 'em off my hands. I saw her eyes light up, though, when she saw that magazine, so I researched it. I remembered seeing Salinger's signature and I figured it might be worth a lot more than the forty bucks she gave me for the box. So I went back, told her I'd changed my mind and wanted the magazine back. I was straight with her, told her I'd looked it up, and I figured a collector would pay plenty for it. So then she took me on the side, said that I was right. She said Richardson had some folks who would pay lots for it, and she'd found one who would pay upward of two hundred twenty thousand for it. She said that she was going to sell it, take the money and start a new life. She was tired of pulling scams. She told me that of course she'd planned to share whatever she got with me . . . after all, we were lovers, right? Partners. We could start this new life she planned on together.' He made a sound like a wounded animal, deep in his throat. 'Fool me, I fell for it.'

His other hand came up, swiped at his jaw. 'She said that her old boyfriend thought he should be cut in too, but she was going to take care of him.'

'This old boyfriend was Gary Hollis, I take it.'

'Yep. Well, she double-crossed both of us. Took off with the magazine without a word.'

'So you tracked her down here?'

'It took a while,' he admitted. 'I had no idea she'd use her mother's maiden name, or change her hair and makeup. But I finally found her. She apologized. Said that she was really running from Gary and Richardson and not me, and she intended to get in touch with me once she'd gotten her act together. I told her that I'd hooked back up with my brother and was working with him now.'

'That's how she found Ellison's,' I said. 'You never ran into her at the Jumpin' Beans, did you?'

'No. I'd told her about my brother and his shop, so she came there. She wanted to deal with me for the sale of the chest, but then she got very cagey, wouldn't tell me what sort of alterations she wanted made. She said it was a custom order for a friend, but I didn't believe her.' His fists clenched and unclenched at his sides. 'I started tailing her. I saw her with that young guy – that electrician. I saw them kissing, saw the way he was touching her. Then I knew. She had no intention of sharing anything with me, money or a life together. She wanted it all – the money from the magazine sale, and him.'

I shook my head. 'You're wrong,' I said. 'Jeff was in love with her, but she didn't feel the same way about him. She ended it with him. It devastated him.'

Ellison's eyes narrowed. 'That's what she said when I confronted her the first time outside her rooming house, but I didn't believe her. I saw them together afterward, and she was in his arms.'

'He made a last-ditch effort to win her back, but it didn't work.'

Ellison's eyes glazed over, and I wondered if he'd heard what

I said. 'I went to the store. She seemed happy to see me. Said she knew I couldn't stay mad at her. She sounded sincere, and for a minute I almost reconsidered. But then I saw the two of them in my mind, in each other's arms, and . . . she had to pay. She betrayed me and not only with the magazine. She broke my heart.'

I looked at the gun in his hand. 'You didn't shoot her, though,' I said. 'You stabbed her.'

'Yeah. With my Swiss Army knife. I'd had it since grammar school, and I hated to get rid of it, but . . . it was covered in her blood. I pitched it in the Fords River afterward and got this for future use.' His hand tightened on the gun handle. 'She was so surprised when she saw the knife in my hand. She knew what I was going to do . . . what I had to do.'

I licked my lips. Maybe if I could keep him talking, I'd think of a way out of this mess. I inclined my head toward the chest. 'Why did you stuff her body in the trunk? Why didn't you just get rid of it?'

'I planned to. I cleaned upstairs, wiped up the blood, all the stuff she knocked over when she fought me. I heard sounds outside and I panicked. I was afraid maybe the police were making rounds or something, so I brought her body down here. The trunk seemed a good place. I intended to come back, get rid of the body. I actually came along with the delivery guy that day, so I knew there was a problem with the lock and I knew how to get around it. But then you came and had the darn lock changed.' His face twisted into a dark scowl. 'I didn't count on that, or on you discovering the body so fast. I knew after that I had to keep an eye on you.' He sniffed. 'I was right to do that, too. I'd only just finished cleaning out her room when you and your friend showed up.'

'And what about Gary Hollis? He said he saw you that night.'

'And I saw him,' George sneered. 'I saw him sneak away from the dumpster with Sheila's phone. I'd forgotten to take it with me, and now he had it. Fortunately, I'd erased all her texts and phone numbers. So I kept tabs on him too. I saw him following you, and I was hiding in the bushes when he called you from behind the park gazebo and said he'd trade a description of Sheila's killer for the magazine. So, you see, he had to be eliminated.' He raised the arm holding the gun again. 'As, I'm sorry to say, do you.'

My eyes darted around, looking for some possible avenue of escape, but the only other way out was through the service entrance, and he was standing right in front of it. I had to keep him talking. 'You'll never get away with this,' I said. 'If I figured out that you were responsible, it's a sure bet Detective Grant will too.'

'By the time he does, I'll be long gone. My van is gassed up and ready to go.'

I stared at him. 'It was you, wasn't it? You own the black van that ran me off the road.'

'Guilty. I was trying to scare you. It's a shame you didn't take the hint. Now you're going to have to pay with your life.' He gestured with his free hand. 'No more stalling now, Charlotte. The cavalry isn't going to rush here to save you. Now, slide that magazine over here, nice and easy.'

I hesitated, then put the magazine on the floor and gave it a shove. It slid across the floor, landed at George's feet. He reached down and picked it up, then waved the gun in the air again. 'Now your phone.'

My hand dipped into the pocket that contained my phone. I whipped it out, held it up, and waved it in the air. 'You want it,' I said. 'Go get it.' And with that, I pulled my arm back and threw my phone into the far corner of the basement.

'Tut-tut, bad move,' George growled. He set the magazine on top of one of the boxes, then crossed over to where I stood. As he reached for my arm, I brought my knee up and hit him hard in the groin.

'*Yow-owww*,' he cried. He doubled over, and the gun fell from his hand and skidded across the floor. I started to make a run for the stairs but before I'd taken two steps his hand shot out and he grasped my ankle, causing me to lose my balance. As I teetered my gaze fell upon the boxes stacked off to my left. I regained my balance and twisted my body to give the boxes a mighty shove, knocking them in front of George, who had straightened and was headed for me. As he stumbled, I turned back toward the stairs, but my foot skidded on one of the books and I fell down, banging my arm against the chest as I did so.

George lunged for me, his fingers digging into the edge of my sweatshirt, and he pulled me toward him. 'You foolish, foolish girl,' he muttered. 'Well, instead of one clean shot to the heart, you'll now have to choke slowly to death.' His other hand came up and tried to close around my throat.

I kicked out again, this time connecting with his knee. He let out a growl and loosened his grip enough for me to twist away. I banged into another box, and I saw this one had some Stephen King novels inside. He lunged for me again, and his fingers gripped my elbow.

And then Poe appeared out of nowhere. With a loud hiss he launched himself on George, his claws digging into the man's shoulder. '*What the—*' George cried. He let out a loud yowl of pain. 'Get off me, you mangy thing!' he yelled.

George tried to pull him off, but Poe held on, hissing and spitting. It gave me the time I needed to dip my hand into the box of books. My fingers closed around a copy of *The Stand* and I gripped it, then swung my arm up and out as hard as I could, making very satisfying contact with the top of George's head as Poe leapt off him. His eyes rolled back and his arms dropped to his sides and he dropped to the floor like a stone.

And just then the cellar door burst open, and Grant and Barbie stood in the doorway, guns drawn. Grant's eyes widened as he took in my disheveled appearance and George lying prostrate on the floor.

I pointed at George. 'There's your killer. He made a full confession to me. I'm pretty sure I got it all on my recording app. I flicked it on when I first caught sight of him. My phone's somewhere over there.'

TWENTY-EIGHT

Six weeks later . . .

'Goodness, Charlotte, what a turnout. And your store is lovely.'

I smiled at Phyllis as I rang up her copy of the latest Sandra Brown romance. Our grand opening was today, and both the bookstore and bakery had been packed since we'd opened at ten a.m. 'Thanks,' I said. I slid the book into the bright pink bag that had 'MAINELY MYSTERIES' emblazoned in bright gold letters. 'So you're a romance fan?'

'I like books in general, and anything by Nora Roberts of course,' said Phyllis. 'But I'm planning on expanding my horizons, maybe trying a mystery next time.' She glanced at her watch. 'I'm stopping by Zane's store next. I want to give her a standing order for Danish and bear claws.'

'She'll appreciate that,' I said.

Phyllis leaned in a bit closer to me. 'You were so brave, dear. That must have been a harrowing experience.'

'It definitely wasn't fun,' I said. 'I can tell you this it's one I don't care to repeat.'

'It certainly was fortunate for you that reporter called the police,' remarked Phyllis.

'Yes, very,' I agreed. It was true. I probably owed my life to both Poe and, of all people, Derek Proust. He'd decided to tail me after seeing me at the scene of Hollis's murder, convinced that I'd lead him to a big story, and he'd been right. He had seen George slip in through the service entrance and had wasted no time in calling 911. Grant, who'd made the license plate connection, had gone to Ellison's only to learn George had vanished. He'd wasted no time in jumping on Derek's tip. As a result, Derek had gotten a honey of a scoop, and the story had been picked up nationally. As a result, he'd been offered a job on the *Philadelphia Inquirer*. His last day on the *Austin Bugle* had been yesterday.

'Well, I for one hope they throw the book at Ellison,' said Phyllis. 'Apparently he's always been a bad seed – nothing like his poor brother. I understand he had several citations against him in New York State for stalking.'

I nodded. Apparently, George had been somewhat of a serial stalker of women he'd imagined had wronged him. George had relocated to Maine to try and make a new life for himself, but then the incident with Sheila had set him off again. Hans had taken him into the business, hopeful that his brother might turn over a new leaf, but it was not to be. He'd been going to mortgage his business to put up bail for George, but the judge had denied bail at the arraignment – something I thought a wise move.

Phyllis glanced around the store. 'I thought maybe Ian Grant would be here,' she said.

'I haven't seen much of Grant since that night,' I confessed. 'Of course, with George in custody and the murder solved, there's really no reason for us to see each other.'

'Uh-huh,' said Phyllis. 'I still say, he's got a bit of a thing for you.' She waved her hand. 'He's probably just been busy. I know he's been back and forth a lot to Philly. Some case he'd been working on. Anyway, absence makes the heart grow fonder, right?'

I let out a soft chuckle. 'If you say so.'

'I do.' She glanced at her watch. 'Goodness, I've got to get going and relieve my backup Lois. She wants to come over here too. You've got the latest C.J. Barrett in stock, I hope.'

'Oh yes. Plenty of those.'

'Good. He's Lois's favorite. Well, tootles for now.'

Phyllis left and I leaned against the counter. My thoughts turned to Grant. I'd known he'd been busy the past few weeks, what with George's arrest and the other case in Philly he'd been working on, but I'd thought he'd at least have stopped by the shop to see how I'd been doing. I sniffed. There was no reason for me to feel upset. After all, in spite of what Phyllis thought, there was nothing between Grant and myself, nor did I want there to be.

Right?

I noticed a customer looking at her phone and it reminded me of the text I'd gotten from Max that morning, congratulating me on the opening of my store:

If you're not going to write them, at least you can sell them. But remember, Charley, I'm here when things start to get dull out in Hoo— sorry, I mean Austin.

I'd smiled. That was so Max. He'd never give up trying to get me back to New York.

I took a minute to look around my store. In spite of everything going on with George, Hans had made time to deliver my furniture. The bookcases fitted in perfectly with the shelving that Sheila had put up, and the two reader's nooks with their overstuffed club chairs, ottomans, and tables with soft reading lamps were particularly inviting.

'Hey, Ms James.'

I smiled at the pretty brunette. 'Hey, Mandy. Ready to go to work?'

She beamed at me. 'Sure thing. Thanks for hiring me. I just love books!' She giggled. 'I'll have to watch it, or I'll be spending most of my salary on them.'

Mandy from the diner had been the first applicant when I'd put the ad in the paper two weeks before. I'd actually taken Grant's advice and interviewed her. He'd been right. She was very smart and very knowledgeable about books and authors, particularly the mystery/thriller genres.

The bell above the door tinkled again. I looked up, thinking it might be Grant, but it was Nancy who entered, Finn at her side. The dog came right over to the counter, lifted his head, and let out a soft woof.

Poe, who'd been lounging on the windowsill, rose. His lips drew back and he let out a soft hiss.

'Poe, watch your manners,' I said. 'Finn is a nice dog. He's a service dog.'

Poe leapt from the windowsill to the counter, leaned across to give Finn a sniff. Then, apparently satisfied that I was telling the truth, he let out a yawn and returned to his supine position on the windowsill.

I chuckled as I dug a doggie treat out from beneath the counter and placed it on the floor in front of Finn. I smiled at Nancy. 'I'm glad you could make it.'

'I told you I'd be here. I would have been the first one in if I hadn't had to work the early shift at the store.' She looked around. 'You certainly seem to have a nice selection. If you'll just point me toward the cozy mystery section, Finn and I will be on our way.'

'Yes. Aisle three.'

Nancy and Finn ambled off, and a woman sidled up to the counter with an armload of books. I'd just finished ringing her up and sent her off when a shadow fell across the counter. I turned, ready to ring up another purchase, and then paused as I saw who stood there.

'Nice opening.' Ian Grant actually smiled at me as he eased one elbow on my counter. 'You've got quite a little crowd here, and so does the bakery. Congratulations.'

'Thanks.' I felt myself warm at his words of praise. We looked at each other awkwardly for a few moments and then I cleared my throat. 'Any more news on George?'

'I understand the district attorney is really looking forward to this trial. He intends to see him put away for a long, long time.'

Oddly, that news didn't thrill me as much as I thought it would. 'What he really needs is good psychiatric help,' I said.

'His lawyer is pushing for an insanity defense, but it's doubtful he could make it stick. George went there intending to kill her, and he had presence of mind enough to write Zane a note and clean out Sheila's room. My guess he'll definitely do prison time.' Grant shook his head. 'And all over a magazine.'

'Not just any magazine,' I said, wiggling my finger in the air. 'One signed by J.D. Salinger. What happened to it, anyway?'

'Well, it will be held as evidence until after the trial, and then returned to the rightful owner, which would probably be Evan Richardson, since George had officially sold that box of books to the store.'

'That's a shame,' I said. 'Sheila hid the clue where to find it in the armoire, which she gave to Nancy.' I glanced over at aisle three, where Nancy and Finn stood. Nancy had a book in her hands and was leafing through it. 'I think she wanted Nancy to benefit from it, in case anything happened to her. She felt they were kindred spirits.'

Grant gave me a stern look. 'You do realize that magazine

really wasn't Sheila's to give to anyone. She didn't own it.'

I sighed. 'I know, but . . . it just seems a shame.'

'Well, maybe there is a way Nancy could benefit.' Grant's lips edged upward. 'Richardson mentioned a reward for finding the magazine, and quite a nice one. I could put a little bug in his ear, say that it was on account of Nancy that the magazine was found, so . . .'

'Why Detective Grant,' I said. 'What a nice thing to do. You have a heart after all.'

He let out a chuckle. 'Just don't spread that around. You'll ruin my reputation.'

He stared at me intently for a moment, then shifted his gaze around the store. 'I'm on duty, or I'd stay a bit longer and browse around. Believe it or not, I do read mysteries – when I have the time.' He sighed. 'Between doing the paperwork on George, and my other case, I've had very little free time these past weeks. But, that's going to change.' He looked straight into my eyes. 'I've been asked to stick around Austin, at least for a while.'

I felt a little flip-flop in my chest. 'You're not going back to Philadelphia?'

He shook his head. 'I've actually been asked to give a series of lectures at Swarthmore over the next two semesters, in their criminal justice program. Two nights a week.'

'Really? That's wonderful . . . but you could commute from Philly for that.'

'True, but . . . the chief and the mayor are considering replacing Rodney Bratt's position. Until they make a final decision, they decided to promote Donaldson to detective and put her in the slot temporarily. They asked if I could stick around, on a consulting basis of course, and . . . ah . . . help her out a bit if needed. So I agreed. Besides, I could use a break from Philly.'

Barbie, a homicide detective? That certainly qualified as one of the wonders of the world. 'Well,' I said, 'it certainly sounds as if you'll be kept busy.'

'Not too busy, I hope,' he said, fixing me with an intent gaze. 'There are some, ah, matters I'd like to pursue here in Austin. Matters I find quite interesting.'

There went my cheeks again! 'Oh? And what would those matters be? Or aren't you at liberty to say?'

'Well . . .' He cleared his throat. 'I suppose I could give you a hint . . .'

The rest of Grant's sentence was drowned out as a loud yelp came from behind me. I turned to see Zane, pink apron around her waist, grinning at me.

'What a nice crowd you've got here,' she said. 'Almost as big as the one in the bakery.' She glanced over at Grant and nodded. 'Hello, Detective Grant.'

He nodded. 'Ms Adams.'

Zane turned back to me, and I noticed she had both hands behind her back. 'What have you got there?' I asked.

Zane brought her hands forward and I saw a platter of tempting-looking pastries. 'I thought since you don't seem to want to take a break, I'd bring you some treats,' she said, setting the platter on the counter.

'Thanks. They look delicious. I'm just surprised you came up for air, as well.'

Zane waved her hand. 'Masie can handle it.' Zane had hired Masie Hanson away from Frederick's. The girl had been thrilled, since now she'd get a chance to utilize her baking skills and not just stock shelves. 'Smartest move I ever made,' Zane crowed. 'She was wasted at Frederick's. Masie bakes almost as good a pie as I do. And wait till you see what she's got planned for Halloween.'

Grant cleared his throat. 'I should get going,' he said.

Zane frowned. 'I'm sorry. Did I interrupt something?'

'No,' I said quickly. 'Detective Grant was just telling me he's going to be sticking around Austin for a bit. He's going to train Barbie as a homicide detective.'

'Oh,' Zane made a face. 'Good luck with that. I should be getting back. I'll see you at five, Charley. We've got that leftover shepherd's pie for dinner.'

Zane hurried off and Grant stood by the counter awkwardly for a moment, then turned and started for the door. He paused, hand on the knob. 'I guess I'll see you around, Charlotte,' he said.

Before I could answer the bell jangled again as the door opened, and Grant stepped backward as none other than Barbie walked in. She wasn't in uniform, though. Now she had on a bright red tank-dress with matching jacket and red and white high heels. Her makeup was flawless, right down to the bright red lipstick. It reminded me of prom night, when she'd made her grand entrance in a sparkling, low-cut gown. Her eyes lit up at the sight of Grant, and I thought that she looked like a hunter with its prey in its sights. She gave him a big smile which faded as she turned her gaze to me.

'Hey, Charley. I heard some people raving about your store, so I thought I'd just check it out.'

I was tempted to say I hadn't been aware she knew how to read, but thought better of it. 'Well, you certainly dressed for the occasion,' I said, and waved my arm. 'Have a look around. True crime and police procedurals are in aisle five.'

'Oh, I'd much rather read romance,' she said, with another side glance Grant's way. 'You do stock them as well, don't you?'

'Aisle seven,' I said.

'Thanks.' She looked over at Grant, and batted her heavily mascaraed eyelashes. 'Are you looking for a book, Detective?'

He shook his head and glanced quickly at the watch on his wrist. 'No, I was just leaving. I'm on duty in about ten minutes.'

'Oh.' Barbie's face fell.

He started to open the door then paused and looked back at me. 'You know we didn't finish our conversation, Charlotte, about those unresolved matters?'

My head jerked up. Out of the corner of my eye I saw Barbie stop and select a book from one of the bookcases, start to thumb through it. Since she was in the thriller aisle, it was plain to me she was stalling to hear what Grant had to say.

Grant went on, 'We never did have our recipe exchange. We'll definitely have to set up another. And may I say, I'm looking forward to it. Very much so. Oh, and it will be your turn to bring the cookware.'

He turned his head so Barbie couldn't see him close one eye in a broad wink, and then he was out the door. Out of the corner of my eye I saw Barbie's cheeks turn redder than her dress. She slammed the book she held back on the shelf, and then she too flounced out the door without a backward glance.

I leaned against the counter. 'It looks like Max was wrong,' I said. 'I think things might just be getting interesting around here. What do you think, Poe?'

Behind me in the window, Poe rose and stretched, then let out a very loud, very satisfied purr.